THE ADVENTURES OF TOM SAWYER

THE ADVENTURES OF HUCKLEBERRY FINN

THE PRINCE AND THE PAUPER

Mark Twain

THE ADVENTURES OF
TOM SAWYER

THE ADVENTURES OF
HUCKLEBERRY FINN

THE PRINCE AND
THE PAUPER

Mark Twain

OCTOPUS

Mark Twain was the pseudonym adopted by Samuel Clemens, who was born in 1835 in Missouri, and was taken from the leadsman's call which had become familiar to him while he worked as a pilot on the Mississippi. He became a journalist and popular lecturer and was well known by the 1870's for his humorous and satirical writings inspired by his travels in Europe and by English history (*The Prince and the Pauper* was published in 1882). But his own childhood on the banks of the Mississippi provided him with the material for his greatest books – *The Adventures of Tom Sawyer* (published in 1876) and *The Adventures of Huckleberry Finn* (published in 1884). He died in 1910, having dictated a large part of his autobiography and written numerous other tales.

This edition first published in Great Britain in 1978 by
Octopus Books Limited
59 Grosvenor Street, London W.1.

Reprinted 1978

© 1978 Illustrations Octopus Books Limited

ISBN 0 7064 0783 0

Printed in Czechoslovakia

Illustrated by Dan Pearce
50368/2

THE ADVENTURES OF
TOM SAWYER

THE ADVENTURES OF
TOM SAWYER

Mark Twain

Preface

Most of the adventures recorded in this book really occurred; one or two were experiences of my own, the rest those of boys who were schoolmates of mine. Huck Finn is drawn from life; Tom Sawyer also, but not from an individual – he is a combination of the characteristics of three boys whom I knew, and therefore belongs to the composite order of architecture.

The odd superstitions touched upon were all prevalent among children and slaves in the West at the period of this story – that is to say, thirty or forty years ago.

Although my book is intended mainly for the entertainment of boys and girls, I hope it will not be shunned by men and women on that account, for part of my plan has been to try pleasantly to remind adults of what they once were themselves, and of how they felt and thought and talked, and what queer enterprises they sometimes engaged in.

THE AUTHOR.

Hartsford: 1876.

List of Illustrations

Chapter 1

'Tom!'

No answer.

'Tom!'

No answer.

'What's gone with that boy, I wonder? You Tom!'

The old lady pulled her spectacles down and looked over them, about the room; then she put them up and looked out under them. She seldom or never looked *through* them for so small a thing as a boy, for they were her state pair, the pride of her heart, and were built for 'style' not service; she could have seen through a pair of stove lids as well. She looked perplexed a moment and said, not fiercely, but still loud enough for the furniture to hear, 'Well, I lay if I get hold of you, I'll——'

She did not finish, for by this time she was bending down and punching under the bed with the broom – and so she needed breath to punctuate the punches with. She resurrected nothing but the cat.

'I never did see the beat of that boy!'

She went to the open door and stood in it, and looked out among the tomato vines and 'jimpson' weeds that constituted the garden. No Tom. So she lifted up her voice, at an angle calculated for distance, and shouted:

'Y-o-u-u Tom!'

There was a slight noise behind her, and she turned just in time to seize a small boy by the slack of his roundabout and arrest his flight. 'There! I might 'a thought of that closet. What you been doing in there?'

'Nothing.'

'Nothing! Look at your hands, and look at your mouth. What *is* that truck?'

'*I* don't know, Aunt.'

'Well, *I* know. It's jam, that's what it is. Forty times I've said if you didn't let that jam alone I'd skin you. Hand me that switch.'

The switch hovered in the air. The peril was desperate.

'My! Look behind you, Aunt!'

The old lady whirled around and snatched her skirts out of danger, and the lad fled, on the instant, scrambled up the high board fence, and disappeared over it. His Aunt Polly stood surprised a moment, and then broke into a gentle laugh.

'Hang the boy, can't I never learn anything? Ain't he played me tricks enough like that for me to be looking out for him by this time? But old fools is the biggest fools there is. Can't learn any old dog new tricks, as the saying is. But, my goodness, he never plays them alike two days, and how is a body to know what's coming? He 'pears to know just how long he can torment me before I get my dander up, and he knows if he can make out to put me off for a minute, or make me laugh, it's all down again, and I can't hit him a lick. I ain't doing my duty by that boy, and that's the Lord's truth, goodness knows. Spare the rod and spile the child, as the good book says. I'm a-laying up sin and suffering for us both, *I* know. He's full of the old scratch, but laws-a-me! he's my own dead sister's boy, poor thing, and I ain't got the heart to lash him somehow. Every time I let him off my conscience does hurt me so; and every time I hit him my old heart 'most breaks. Well-a-well, man that is born of a woman is of few days and full of trouble, as the Scripture says, and I reckon it's so. He'll play hookey this evening,[1] and I'll just be obliged to make him work tomorrow, to punish him. It's mighty hard to make him work Saturdays, when all the boys is having a holiday, but he hates work more than he hates anything else, and I've got to do some of my duty by him, or I'll be the ruination of the child.'

Tom did play hookey, and he had a very good time. He got back home barely in season to help Jim, the small coloured boy, saw next day's wood, and split the kindlings before supper – at least he was there in time to tell his adventures to Jim while Jim did three-fourths of the work. Tom's younger brother (or rather half-brother) Sid was already through with his part of the work (picking up chips), for he was a quiet boy, and had no adventurous, troublesome ways. While Tom was eating his supper and stealing sugar as opportunity offered, Aunt Polly asked him questions that were full of guile, and very deep – for she wanted to trap him into damaging revealments. Like many other simple-hearted souls, it was her pet vanity to believe she was endowed with a talent for dark and mysterious diplomacy, and she loved to contemplate her most transparent devices as marvels of low cunning. Said she, 'Tom, it was middling warm in school, warn't it?'

'Yes'm.'

'Powerful warm, warn't it?'

'Yes'm.'

'Didn't you want to go in a swimming, Tom?'

A bit of a scare shot through Tom – a touch of uncomfortable suspicion. He searched Aunt Polly's face, but it told him nothing. So he said:

'No'm – well, not very much.'

The old lady reached out her hand and felt Tom's shirt, and said:

'But you ain't too warm now, though.'

And it flattered her to reflect that she had discovered that the shirt was dry without anybody knowing that that was what she had in her mind. But in spite of her Tom knew where the wind lay now. So he forestalled what might be the next move.

'Some of us pumped on our heads – mine's damp yet. See?'

Aunt Polly was vexed to think she had overlooked that bit of circumstantial evidence and missed a trick. Then she had a new inspiration:

'Tom, you didn't have to undo your shirt collar where I sewed it to pump on your head, did you? Unbutton your jacket!'

The trouble vanished out of Tom's face. He opened his jacket. His shirt collar was securely sewed.

'Bother! Well, go 'long with you. I made sure you'd played hookey and been a swimming. But I forgive ye, Tom, I reckon you're a kind of a singed cat, as the saying is – better'n you look, *this* time.'

She was half sorry her sagacity had miscarried, and half glad that Tom had stumbled into obedient conduct for once.

But Sidney said:

'Well, now, if I didn't think you sewed his collar with white thread, but it's black.'

'Why, I did sew it with white! Tom!'

But Tom did not wait for the rest. As he went out of the door, he said:

'Siddy, I'll lick you for that.'

In a safe place Tom examined two large needles which were thrust into the lapels of his jacket – and had thread bound about them – one needle carried white thread and the other black. He said:

'She'd never noticed if it hadn't been for Sid. Confound it, sometimes she sews it with white and sometimes she sews it with black. I wish to geeminy she'd stick to one or t'other – *I* can't keep the run of 'em. But I bet you I'll lam Sid for that. If I don't, blame my cats.'

He was not the model boy of the village. He knew the model boy very well, though, and loathed him.

Within two minutes, or even less, he had forgotten all his troubles. Not because his troubles were one whit less heavy and bitter to him than a man's are to a man, but because a new and powerful interest bore them down and drove them out of his mind for the time; just as men's misfortunes are forgotten in the excitement of new enterprises. This new interest was a valued novelty in whistling, which he had just acquired from a Negro, and he was suffering to practise it undisturbed. It consisted in a peculiar bird-like turn, a sort of liquid warble, produced by touching the tongue to the roof of the mouth at short intervals in the midst of the music. The reader probably remembers how to do it if he has ever been a boy. Diligence and attention soon gave him the knack of it, and he strode down the street with his mouth full of harmony and his soul full of gratitude. He felt much as an astronomer feels who has discovered a new planet. No doubt as far as strong, deep, unalloyed pleasure is concerned, the advantage was with the boy, not the astronomer.

The summer evenings were long. It was not dark yet. Presently Tom checked his whistle. A stranger was before him; a boy a shade larger than himself. A new-comer of any age or either sex was an impressive curiosity in the poor little village of St Petersburg. This boy was well dressed, too – well dressed on a week-day. This was simply astounding. His cap was a dainty thing, his close-buttoned blue cloth roundabout was new and natty, and so were his pantaloons. He had shoes on, and yet it was only Friday. He even wore a neck-tie, a bright bit of ribbon. He had a citified air about him that ate into Tom's vitals. The more Tom stared at the splendid marvel, the higher he turned up his nose at his finery, and the shabbier and shabbier his own outfit seemed to him to grow. Neither boy spoke, If one moved the other moved – but only sidewise, in a circle. They kept face to face and eye to eye all the time. Finally, Tom said:

'I can lick you!'

'I'd like to see you try it.'

'Well, I can do it.'

'No you can't, either.'

'Yes I can.'

'No you can't.'

'I can.'

'You can't.'

'Can.'

'Can't.'

An uncomfortable pause. Then Tom said:

'What's your name?'

''Tisn't any of your business, maybe.'

'Well, I 'low I'll *make* it my business.'

'Well, why don't you?'

'If you say much I will.'

'Much – much – much! There, now.'

'Oh, you think you're mighty smart, *don't* you? I could lick you with one hand tied behind me, if I wanted to.'

'Well, why don't you *do* it? You *say* you can do it.'

'Well, *I will*, if you fool with me.'

'Oh, yes – I've seen whole families in the same fix.'

'Smarty! you think you're *some* now, *don't* you?'

'Oh, what a hat!'

'You can lump that hat if you don't like it. I dare you to knock it off; and anybody that'll take a dare will suck eggs.'

'You're a liar!'

'You're another.'

'You're a fighting liar, and darn't take it up.'

'Aw – take a walk!'

'Say – if you give me much more of your sass, I'll take and bounce a rock off 'n your head.'

'Oh, of *course* you will.'

'Well, I *will*.'

'Well, why don't you *do* it, then? What do you keep *saying* you will for? Why don't you *do* it? It's because you're afraid.'

'I *ain't* afraid.'

'You are.'

'I ain't.'

'You are.'

Another pause, and more eyeing and sidling around each other. Presently they were shoulder to shoulder. Tom said:

'Get away from here!'

'Get away yourself!'

'I won't.'

'*I* won't, either.'

So they stood, each with a foot placed at an angle as a brace, and both shoving with might and main, and glowering at each other with hate. But neither could get an advantage. After struggling till both were hot and flushed, each relaxed his strain with watchful caution, and Tom said:

'You're a coward and a pup. I'll tell my big-brother on you, and he can lam you with his little finger, and I'll make him do it, too.'

'What do I care for your big brother? I've got a brother that's bigger than he is; and, what's more, he can throw him over that fence, too.' (Both brothers were imaginary.)

'That's a lie.'

'*Your* saying so don't make it so.'

Tom drew a line in the dust with his big toe, and said:

'I dare you to step over that, and I'll lick you till you can't stand up. Anybody that'll take a dare will steal a sheep.'

The new boy stepped over promptly, and said:

'Now you said you'd do it, now let's see you do it.'

'Don't you crowd me, now; you'd better look out.'

'Well, you *said* you'd do it – why don't you do it?'

'By jingoes, for two cents I *will* do it.'

The new boy took two broad coppers out of his pocket and held them out with derision.

Tom struck them to the ground.

In an instant both boys were rolling and tumbling in the dirt, gripped together like cats; and for the space of a minute they tugged and tore at each other's hair and clothes, punched and scratched each other's noses, and covered themselves with dust and glory. Presently the confusion took form, and through the fog of battle Tom appeared, seated astride the new boy, and pounding him with his fists.

'Holler 'nuff!' said he.

The boy only struggled to free himself. He was crying, mainly from rage.

'Holler 'nuff!' and the pounding went on.

At last the stranger got out a smothered ' 'nuff!' and Tom let him up, and said, 'Now that'll learn you. Better look out who you're fooling with next time.'

The new boy went off brushing the dust from his clothes, sobbing, snuffling, and occasionally looking back and shaking his head, and threatening what he would do to Tom the 'next time he caught him out'. To which Tom responded with jeers, and started off in high feather; and as soon as his back was turned the new boy snatched up a stone, threw it, and hit him between the shoulders, and then turned tail and ran like an antelope. Tom chased the traitor home, and thus found out where he lived. He then held a position at the gate for some time, daring the enemy to come outside; but the enemy only made faces at him through the window, and declined. At last the enemy's mother appeared, and called Tom a bad, vicious, vulgar child, and ordered him away. So he went away, but he said he ' 'lowed' to 'lag' for that boy.

He got home pretty late that night, and when he climbed cautiously in at the window he uncovered an ambuscade in the person of his aunt; and when she saw the state his clothes were in, her resolution to turn his Saturday holiday into captivity at hard labour became adamantine in its firmness.

1   South-western for 'afternoon'.

Chapter 2

Saturday morning was come, and all the summer world was bright and fresh, and brimming with life. There was a song in every heart; and if the heart was young the music issued at the lips. There was cheer in every face, and a spring in every step. The locust trees were in bloom, and the fragrance of the blossoms filled the air.

Cardiff Hill, beyond the village and above it, was green with vegetation, and it lay just far enough away to seem a Delectable Land, dreamy, reposeful, and inviting.

Tom appeared on the side-walk with a bucket of whitewash and a long-handled brush. He surveyed the fence, and the gladness went out of nature, and a deep melancholy settled down upon his spirit. Thirty yards of board fence nine feet high! It seemed to him that life was hollow, and existence but a burden. Sighing he dipped his brush and passed it along the topmost plank; repeated the operation; did it again; compared the insignificant whitewashed streak with the far-reaching continent of unwhitewashed fence, and sat down on a tree-box discouraged. Jim came skipping out at the gate with a tin pail, and singing *Buffalo Gals*. Bringing water from the town pump had always been hateful work in Tom's eyes before, but now it did not strike him so. He remembered that there was company at the pump. White, mulatto, and Negro boys and girls were always there waiting their turns, resting, trading playthings, quarrelling, fighting, skylarking. And he remembered that although the pump was only a hundred and fifty yards off Jim never got back with a bucket of water under an hour; and even then somebody generally had to go after him. Tom said:

'Say, Jim; I'll fetch the water if you'll whitewash some.'

Jim shook his head, and said:

'Can't, Mar's Tom. Ole missis she tole me I got to go an' git dis water an' not stop foolin' 'roun' wid anybody. She say she spec' Ma'rs Tom gwyne to ax me to whitewash, an' so she tole me go 'long an' 'tend to my own business – she 'lowed *she'd* 'tend to de whitewashin'.'

'Oh, never you mind what she said, Jim. That's the way she always talks. Gimme the bucket – I won't be gone only a minute. *She* won't ever know.'

'Oh, I dasn't, Ma'rs Tom. Ole missis she'd take an' tar de head off'n me.

'Deed she would.'

'*She*! she never licks anybody – whacks 'em over the head with her thimble, and who cares for that, I'd like to know? She talks awful, but talk don't hurt – anyways, it don't if she don't cry. Jim, I'll give you a marble. I'll give you a white alley!'

Jim began to waver.

'White alley, Jim; and it's a bully taw.'

'My; dat's a mighty gay marvel, *I* tell you. But, Ma'rs Tom, I's powerful 'fraid ole missis.'

'And besides, if you will, I'll show you my sore toe.'

But Jim was only human – this attraction was too much for him. He put down his pail, took the white alley. In another minute he was flying down the street with his pail and a tingling rear. Tom was whitewashing with vigour, and Aunt Polly was retiring from the field with a slipper in her hand and triumph in her eye.

But Tom's energy did not last. He began to think of the fun he had planned for this day, and his sorrows multiplied. Soon the free boys would come tripping along on all sorts of delicious expeditions, and they would make a world of fun of him for having to work – the very thought of it burnt him like fire. He got out his wordly wealth and examined it – bits of toys, marbles, and trash; enough to buy an exchange of work maybe, but not enough to buy so much as half an hour of pure freedom. So he returned his straitened means to his pocket, and gave up the idea of trying to buy the boys. At this dark and hopeless moment an inspiration burst upon him. Nothing less than a great, magnificent inspiration.

He took up his brush and went tranquilly to work. Ben Rogers hove in sight presently; the very boy of all boys whose ridicule he had been dreading. Ben's gait was the hop, skip, and jump – proof enough that his heart was light and his anticipations high. He was eating an apple, and giving a long melodious whoop at intervals, followed by a deep-toned ding dong dong, ding dong dong, for he was personating a steamboat! As he drew near he slackened speed, took the middle of the street, leaned far over to starboard, and rounded-to ponderously, and with laborious pomp and circumstance, for he was personating the *Big Missouri*, and considered himself to be drawing nine feet of water. He was boat, and captain, and engine-bells combined, so he had to imagine himself standing on his own hurricane-deck giving the orders and executing them.

'Stop her, sir! Ling-a-ling-ling.' The headway ran almost out, and he drew up slowly towards the side-walk. 'Ship up to back! Ling-a-ling-ling!' His arms straightened and stiffened down his sides. 'Set her back on the stabboard! Ling-a-ling-ling! Chow! ch-chow-wow-chow!' his right hand meantime describing stately circles, for it was representing a forty-foot wheel.

'Let her go back on the labboard! Ling-a-ling-ling! Chow-ch-chow-chow!'
The left hand began to describe circles.

'Stop the stabboard! Ling-a-ling-ling! Stop the labboard! Come ahead
on the stabboard! Stop her! Let your outside turn over slow! Ling-a-ling-ling!
Chow-ow-ow! Get out that head-line! Lively, now! Come – out with your
spring-line – what're you about there? Take a turn round that stump with the
bight of it! Stand by that stage now – let her go! Done with the engines, sir!
Ling-a-ling-ling!'

'Sht! s'sht! sht!' (Trying the gauge-cocks.)

Tom went on whitewashing – paid no attention to the steamer. Ben
stared a moment, and then said:

'Hi-yi! You're up a stump, ain't you?'

No answer. Tom surveyed his last touch with the eye of an artist; then he
gave his brush another gentle sweep, and surveyed the result as before. Ben
ranged up alongside of him. Tom's mouth watered for the apple, but he stuck
to his work. Ben said:

'Hello, old chap; you got to work, hey?'

'Why, it's you, Ben! I warn't noticing.'

'Say, I'm going in a swimming, I am. Don't you wish you could? But of
course, you'd druther work, wouldn't you 'Course you would!'

Tom contemplated the boy a bit, and said:

'What do you call work?'

'Why, ain't that work?'

Tom resumed his whitewashing, and answered carelessly:

'Well, maybe it is, and maybe it ain't. All I know is, it suits Tom Sawyer.'

'Oh, come now, you don't mean to let on that you like it?'

The brush continued to move.

'Like it? Well, I don't see why I oughtn't to like it. Does a boy get a
chance to whitewash a fence every day?'

That put the thing in a new light. Ben stopped nibbling his apple. Tom
swept his brush daintily back and forth – stepped back to note the effect –
added a touch here and there – criticized the effect again, Ben watching every
move, and getting more and more interested, more and more absorbed.
Presently he said:

'Say, Tom, let me whitewash a little.'

Tom considered; was about to consent; but he altered his mind: 'No, no;
I reckon it wouldn't hardly do, Ben. You see, Aunt Polly's awful particular
about this fence – right here on the street, you know – but if it was the back
fence I wouldn't mind, and she wouldn't. Yes, she's awful particular about
this fence; it's got to be done very careful; I reckon there ain't one boy in a
thousand, maybe two thousand, that can do it the way it's got to be done.'

'No – is that so? Oh, come now; lemme just try, only just a little. I'd let

'*Tom surveyed his last touch with the eye of an artist*'

you, if you was me, Tom.'

'Ben, I'd like to, honest injun; but Aunt Polly – well, Jim wanted to do it, but she wouldn't let him. Sid wanted to do it, but she wouldn't let Sid. Now, don't you see how I am fixed? If you was to tackle this fence, and anything was to happen to it——'

'Oh, shucks; I'll be just as careful. Now lemme try. Say – I'll give you the core of my apple.'

'Well, here. No, Ben; now don't; I'm afeard——'

'I'll give you all of it!'

Tom gave up the brush with reluctance in his face, but alacrity in his heart. And while the late steamer *Big Missouri* worked and sweated in the sun, the retired artist sat on a barrel in the shade close by, dangled his legs, munched his apple, and planned the slaughter of more innocents. There was no lack of material; boys happened along every little while; they came to jeer, but remained to whitewash. By the time Ben was fagged out, Tom had traded the next chance to Billy Fisher for a kite in good repair; and when he played out, Johnny Miller bought in for a dead rat and a string to swing it with; and so on, and so on, hour after hour. And when the middle of the afternoon came, from being a poor poverty-stricken boy in the morning Tom was literally rolling in wealth. He had besides the things I have mentioned, twelve marbles, part of a jew's harp, a piece of blue bottle-glass to look through, a spool-cannon, a key that wouldn't unlock anything, a fragment of chalk, a glass stopper of a decanter, a tin soldier, a couple of tadpoles, six fire-crackers, a kitten with only one eye, a brass door-knob, a dog-collar – but no dog – the handle of a knife, four pieces of orange-peel, and a dilapidated old window-sash. He had had a nice, good, idle time all the while – plenty of company – and the fence had three coats of whitewash on it! If he hadn't run out of whitewash he would have bankrupted every boy in the village.

Tom said to himself that it was not such a hollow world after all. He had discovered a great law of human action, without knowing it, namely, that, in order to make a man or a boy covet a thing, it is only necessary to make the thing difficult to attain. If he had been a great and wise philosopher, like the writer of this book, he would now have comprehended that work consists of whatever a body is obliged to do, and that play consists of whatever a body is not obliged to do. And this would help him to understand why constructing artificial flowers, or performing on a tread-mill, is work, whilst rolling nine-pins or climbing Mont Blanc is only amusement. There are wealthy gentlemen in England who drive four-horse passenger-coaches twenty or thirty miles on a daily line, in the summer, because the privilege costs them considerable money; but if they were offered wages for the service that would turn it into work, then they would resign.

Chapter 3

Tom presented himself before Aunt Polly, who was sitting by an open window in a pleasant rearward apartment which was bed-room, breakfast-room, dining-room, and library combined. The balmy summer air, the restful quiet, the odour of the flowers, and the drowsing murmur of the bees had had their effect, and she was nodding over her knitting – for she had no company but the cat, and it was asleep in her lap. Her spectacles were propped up on her grey head for safety. She had thought that of course Tom had deserted long ago, and she wondered to see him place himself in her power again in this intrepid way. He said:

'Mayn't I go and play now, Aunt?'

'What, a'ready? How much have you done?'

'It's all done, Aunt.'

'Tom, don't lie to me. I can't bear it.'

'I ain't, Aunt; it *is* all done.'

Aunt Polly placed small trust in such evidence. She went out to see for herself; and she would have been content to find twenty per cent of Tom's statement true. When she found the entire fence whitewashed, and not only whitewashed but elaborately coated and recoated, and even a streak added to the ground, her astonishment was almost unspeakable. She said:

'Well, I never! There's no getting around it; you *can* work when you're a mind to, Tom.' And then she diluted the compliment by adding, 'But it's powerful seldom you're a mind to, I'm bound to say. Well, go 'long and play; but mind you get back some time in a week, or I'll tan you.'

She was so overcome by the splendour of his achievement that she took him into the closet and selected a choice apple, and delivered it to him, along with an improving lecture upon the added value and flavour a treat took to itself when it came without sin through virtuous effort. And while she closed with a happy Scriptural flourish, he 'hooked' a doughnut.

Then he skipped out, and saw Sid just starting up the outside stairway that led to the back rooms on the second floor. Clods were handy, and the air was full of them in a twinkling. They raged around Sid like a hailstorm; and before Aunt Polly could collect her surprised faculties and rally to the rescue, six or seven clods had taken personal effect, and Tom was over the fence and gone. There was a gate, but as a general thing he was too crowded for time to make use of it. His soul was at peace now that he had settled with Sid for calling attention to his black thread and getting him into trouble.

Tom skirted the block and came around into a muddy alley that led by the back of his aunt's cow-stable. He presently got safely beyond the reach of capture and punishment, and wended towards the public square of the village, where two 'military' companies of boys had met for conflict, according to previous appointment. Tom was general of one of these armies, Joe Harper (a bosom friend) general of the other. These two great commanders did not condescend to fight in person – that being better suited to the smaller fry – but sat together on an eminence and conducted the field operations by orders delivered through aides-de-camp. Tom's army won a great victory, after a long and hard-fought battle. Then the dead were counted, prisoners exchanged, the terms of the next disagreement agreed upon, and the day for the necessary battle appointed; after which the armies fell into line and marched away, and Tom turned homeward alone.

As he was passing by the house where Jeff Thatcher lived, he saw a new girl in the garden – a lovely little blue-eyed creature with yellow hair plaited into two long tails, white summer frock, and embroidered pantalettes. The fresh-crowned hero fell without firing a shot. A certain Amy Lawrence vanished out of his heart, and left not even a memory of herself behind. He had thought he loved her to distraction; he had regarded his passion as adoration; and behold it was only a poor little evanescent partiality. He had been months winning her, she had confessed hardly a week ago; he had been the happiest and the proudest boy in the world only seven short days, and here, in one instant of time, she had gone out of his heart like a casual stranger whose visit is done.

He worshipped this new angel with furtive eye, till he saw that she had discovered him; then he pretended he did not know she was present, and began to 'show off' in all sorts of absurd boyish ways in order to win her admiration. He kept up this grotesque foolishness for some little time; but by-and-by, while he was in the midst of some dangerous gymnastic perfor-mances, he glanced aside, and saw that the little girl was wending towards the house. Tom came up to the fence, and leaned on it, grieving, and hoping she would tarry yet a while longer. She halted a moment on the steps, and then moved towards the door. Tom heaved a great sigh as she put her foot on the threshold, but his face lit up, right away, for she tossed a pansy over the fence a moment before she disappeared. The boy ran around and stopped within a foot or two of the flower, and then shaded his eyes with his hand, and began to look down street as if he had discovered something of interest going on in that direction. Presently he picked up a straw and began trying to balance it on his nose, with his head tilted far back; and as he moved from side to side in his efforts he edged nearer and nearer towards the pansy; finally his bare foot rested upon it, his pliant toes closed upon it, and he hopped away with his treasure, and disappeared around the corner. But only for a minute – only while he could button the flower inside his jacket, next his heart, or next his stomach possibly, for he was not much posted in anatomy and not hypercritical anyway.

He returned now and hung about the fence till night-fall, 'showing off' as before; but the girl never exhibited herself again, though Tom comforted himself a little with the hope that she had been near some window meantime, and been aware of his attentions. Finally, he went home reluctantly with his poor head full of visions.

All through supper his spirits were so high that his aunt wondered 'what had got into the child'. He took a good scolding about clodding Sid, and did not seem to mind it in the least. He tried to steal sugar under his aunt's very nose, and got his knuckles rapped for it. He said:

'Aunt, you don't whack Sid when he takes it.'

'Well, Sid don't torment a body the way you do. You'd be always into that sugar if I warn't watching you.'

Presently she stepped into the kitchen, and Sid, happy in his immunity, reached for the sugar-bowl, a sort of glorying over Tom which was well-nigh unbearable. But Sid's fingers slipped, and the bowl dropped and broke. Tom was in ecstasies – in such ecstasies that he even controlled his tongue and was silent. He said to himself that he would not speak a word, even when his aunt came in, but would sit perfectly still till she asked who did the mischief; and then he would tell, and there would be nothing so good in the world as to see that pet model 'catch it'. He was so brim-full of exultation that he could hardly hold himself when the old lady came back and stood above the wreck discharging lightnings of wrath from over her spectacles. He said to himself, 'Now it's coming!' And the next instant he was sprawling on the floor! The potent palm was uplifted to strike again, when Tom cried out:

'Hold on, now, what're you belting *me* for? Sid broke it!'

Aunt Polly paused perplexed, and Tom looked for healing pity. But when she got her tongue again she only said:

'Umph! Well, you didn't get a lick amiss, I reckon. You'd been into some other owdacious mischief when I wasn't around, like enough.'

Then her conscience reproached her, and she yearned to say something kind and loving; but she judged that this would be construed into a confession that she had been in the wrong, and discipline forbade that. So she kept silence, and went about her affairs with a troubled heart. Tom sulked in a corner, and exalted his woes. He knew that in her heart his aunt was on her knees to him, and he was morosely gratified by the consciousness of it. He would hang out no signals, he would take notice of none. He knew that a yearning glance fell upon him, now and then, through a film of tears, but he refused recognition of it. He pictured himself lying sick unto death and his aunt bending over him, beseeching one little forgiving word, but he would turn his face to the wall, and die with that word unsaid. Ah, how would she feel then? And he pictured himself brought home from the river, dead, with his curls all wet, and his poor hands still for ever, and his sore heart at rest. How she would throw herself upon him, and how her tears would fall like rain, and her lips pray God to give her back her boy, and she would never, never, abuse him any more! But he would lie there cold and white and make no sign – a poor little sufferer whose griefs were at an end. He so worked upon his feelings with the pathos of these dreams that he had to keep swallowing – he was so like to choke; and his eyes swam in a blur of water, which overflowed when he winked, and ran down and trickled from the end of his nose. And such a luxury to him was this petting of his sorrows that he could not bear to have any worldly cheeriness or any grating delight intrude upon it; it was too sacred for such contact; and so presently, when his cousin Mary danced in, all alive with the joy of seeing home again after an age-long visit of one week to the country, he got up and moved in clouds and darkness out at one door as she brought song and sunshine in at the other. He wandered far away from the accustomed haunts of boys, and sought desolate places that were in harmony with his spirit. A log raft in the river invited him, and he seated himself on its outer edge, and contemplated the dreary vastness of the stream, wishing the while that he could only be drowned all at once and unconsciously, without undergoing the uncomfortable routine devised by nature. Then he thought of his flower. He got it out, rumpled and wilted, and it mightily increased his dismal felicity. He wondered if *she* would pity him if she knew! Would she cry, and wish that she had a right to put her arms around his neck and comfort him? Or would she turn coldly away like all the hollow world? This picture brought such an agony of pleasurable suffering that he worked it over and over again in his mind and set it up in new and varied lights till he wore it threadbare. At last he rose up sighing and departed in the darkness. About half past nine or ten o'clock he came along the deserted street to where the adored unknown lived; he paused a moment, no sound fell upon his listening ear; a candle was casting a dull glow upon the curtain of a second-story window. Was the sacred presence there? He climbed the fence, threaded his stealthy way through the plants, till he stood under that window; he looked up at it long, and with emotion; then he laid him down on the ground under it, disposing himself upon his back, with his hands clasped upon his breast, and holding his poor wilted flower. And thus he would die – out in the cold world with no shelter over his homeless head, no friendly hand to wipe the death-damps from his brow, no loving face to bend pityingly over him when the great agony came. And thus *she* would see him when she looked out upon the glad morning – and oh, would she drop one tear upon his poor lifeless form, would she heave one little sigh to see a bright young life so rudely blighted, so untimely cut down?

The window went up; a maid-servant's discordant voice profaned the holy calm, and a deluge of water drenched the prone martyr's remains!

The strangling hero sprang up with a relieving snort; there was a whizz as of a missile in the air, mingled with the murmur of a curse, a sound as of shivering glass followed, and a small vague form went over the fence and shot away in the gloom.

Not long after, as Tom, all undressed for bed, was surveying his drenched garments by the light of a tallow dip, Sid woke up; but if he had any dim idea of making 'references to allusions', he thought better of it, and held his peace – for there was danger in Tom's eye. Tom turned in without the added vexation of prayers, and Sid made mental note of the omission.

Chapter 4

The sun rose upon a tranquil world, and beamed down upon the peaceful village like a benediction. Breakfast over, Aunt Polly had family worship; it began with a prayer built from the ground up of solid courses of scriptural quotations wedded together with a thin mortar of originality; and from the summit of this she delivered a grim chapter of the Mosaic Law, as from Sinai.

Then Tom girded up his loins, so to speak, and went to work to 'get his verses'. Sid had learned his lesson days before. Tom bent all his energies to the memorizing of five verses; and he chose part of the Sermon on the Mount, because he could find no verses that were shorter.

At the end of half an hour Tom had a vague general idea of his lesson, but no more, for his mind was traversing the whole field of human thought, and his hands were busy with distracting recreations. Mary took his book to hear him recite, and he tried to find his way through the fog.

'Blessed are the – a – a——'

'Poor——'

'Yes – poor; blessed are the poor – a – a——'

'In spirit——'

'In spirit; blessed are the poor in spirit, for they – they——'

'Theirs——'

'For theirs. Blessed are the poor in spirit, for theirs – is the kingdom of Heaven. Blessed are they that mourn, for they – they——'

'Sh——'

'For they – a——'

'S-H-A——'

'For they S-H – Oh, I don't know what it is!'

'Shall!'

'Oh, shall! for they shall – for they shall – a – a – shall mourn – a – a – blessed are they that shall – they that – a – they that shall mourn, for they shall – a – shall what? Why don't you tell me, Mary? What do you want to be so mean for?'

'Oh, Tom, you poor thick-headed thing, I'm not teasing you. I wouldn't do that. You must go and learn it again. Don't you be discouraged, Tom, you'll manage it – and if you do, I'll give you something ever so nice! There, now, that's a good boy.'

'All right! What is it, Mary? Tell me what it is.'

'Never you mind, Tom. You know if I say it's nice, it is nice.'

'You bet you that's so, Mary. All right, I'll tackle it again.'

And he did 'tackle it again'; and under the double pressure of curiosity and prospective gain, he did it with such spirit that he accomplished a shining success.

Mary gave him a brand-new 'Barlow' knife, worth twelve and a half cents; and the convulsion of delight that swept his system shook him to his foundations. True, the knife would not cut anything, but it was a 'sure-enough' Barlow, and there was inconceivable grandeur in that – though where the western boys ever got the idea that such a weapon could possibly be counterfeited to its injury is an imposing mystery, and will always remain so, perhaps. Tom contrived to scarify the cupboard with it and was arranging to begin on the bureau, when he was called off to dress for Sunday-school.

Mary gave him a tin basin of water and a piece of soap, and went outside the door and set the basin on a little bench there; then he dipped the soap in the water and laid it down; turned up his sleeves; poured out the water on the ground gently, and then entered the kitchen, and began to wipe his face diligently on the towel behind the door. But Mary removed the towel and said:

'Now ain't you ashamed, Tom? You mustn't be so bad. Water won't hurt you.'

Tom was a trifle disconcerted. The basin was refilled, and this time he stood over it a little while, gathering resolution; took in a big breath and began. When he entered the kitchen presently, with both eyes shut, and groping for the towel with his hands, an honourable testimony of suds and water was dripping from his face. But when he emerged from the towel, he was not yet satisfactory; for the clean territory stopped short at his chin and his jaws like a mask; below and beyond this line there was a dark expanse of unirrigated soil that spread downward in front and backward around his neck. Mary took him in hand, and when she was done with him he was a man and a brother, without distinction of colour, and his saturated hair was neatly brushed, and its short curls wrought into a dainty and symmetrical general effect. (He privately smoothed out the curls, with labour and difficulty, and plastered his hair close down to his head; for he held curls to be effeminate, and his own filled his life with bitterness.) Then Mary got out a suit of his clothing that had been used only on Sundays during two years – they were simply called his 'other clothes' – and so by that we know the size of his wardrobe. The girl 'put him to rights' after he had dressed himself; she buttoned his neat round-about up to his chin, turned his vast shirt-collar down over his shoulders, brushed him off and crowned him with his speckled straw hat. He now looked exceedingly improved and uncomfortable; and he was fully as uncomfortable as he looked; for there was a restraint about whole clothes and cleanliness that galled him. He hoped that Mary would forget his shoes, but the hope was blighted; she coated them thoroughly with tallow, as was the custom, and brought them out. He lost his temper, and said he was always being made to do everything he didn't want to do. But Mary said persuasively:

'Please, Tom – that's a good boy.'

So he got into his shoes, snarling. Mary was soon ready, and the three children set out for Sunday-school, a place that Tom hated with his whole heart; but Sid and Mary were fond of it.

Sabbath-school hours were from nine to half past ten; and then church service. Two of the children always remained for the sermon voluntarily; and the other always remained too, for stronger reasons. The church's high-backed uncushioned pews would seat about three hundred persons; the edifice was but a small, plain affair, with a sort of pine-board tree-box on top of it for a steeple. At the door Tom dropped back a step and accosted a Sunday-dressed comrade:

'Say, Bill, got a yaller ticket?'

'Yes.'

'What'll you take for her?'

'What'll you give?'

'Piece of lickrish and a fish-hook.'

'Less see 'em.'

Tom exhibited. They were satisfactory, and the property changed hands. Then Tom traded a couple of white alleys for three red tickets, and some small trifle or other for a couple of blue ones. He waylaid other boys as they came, and went on buying tickets of various colours ten or fifteen minutes longer. He entered the church, now, with a swarm of clean and noisy boys and girls, proceeded to his seat and started a quarrel with the first boy that came handy. The teacher, a grave, elderly man, interfered; then turned his back a moment, and Tom pulled a boy's hair in the next bench, and was absorbed in his book when the boy turned around; stuck a pin in another boy, presently, in order to hear him say 'Ouch!' and got a new reprimand from his teacher. Tom's whole class were of a pattern – restless, noisy, and troublesome. When they came to recite their lessons, not one of them knew his verses perfectly, but had to be prompted all along. However, they worried through, and each got his reward in small blue tickets, each with a passage of Scripture on it; each blue ticket was pay for two verses of the recitation. Ten blue tickets equalled a red one, and could be exchanged for it; ten red tickets equalled a yellow one; for ten yellow tickets the Superintendent gave a very plainly bound Bible (worth forty cents in those easy times) to the pupil. How many of my readers would have the industry and the application to memorize two thousand verses, even for a Doré Bible? And yet Mary had acquired two Bibles in this way; it was the patient work of two years: and a boy of German parentage had won four or five. He once recited three thousand verses without stopping; but the strain upon his mental faculties was too great, and he was little better than an idiot from that day forth – a grievous misfortune for the school, for on great occasions before company the Superintendent (as Tom expressed it) had always made this boy come out and 'spread himself'. Only the older pupils managed to keep their tickets and stick to their tedious work long enough to get a Bible, and so the delivery of one of these prizes was a rare and noteworthy circumstance; the successful pupil was so great and conspicuous for that day that on the spot every scholar's breast was fired with a fresh ambition that often lasted a couple of weeks. It is possible that Tom's mental stomach had never really hungered for one of those prizes, but unquestionably his entire being had for many a day longed for the glory and the *éclat* that came with it.

In due course the Superintendent stood up in front of the pulpit, with a closed hymn-book in his hand and his forefinger inserted between its leaves, and commanded attention. When a Sunday-school superintendent makes his customary little speech, a hymn-book in the hand is as necessary as is the inevitable sheet of music in the hand of a singer who stands forward on the platform and sings a solo at a concert – though why is a mystery; for neither the hymn-book nor the sheet of music is ever referred to by the sufferer. This Superintendent was a slim creature of thirty-five, with a sandy goatee, and short sandy hair; he wore a stiff standing-collar whose upper edge almost reached his ears, and whose sharp points curved forward abreast the corners of his mouth – a fence that compelled a straight look-out ahead, and a turning of the whole body when a side view was required. His chin was propped on a spreading cravat, which was as broad and as long as a bank-note, and had fringed ends; his boot toes were turned sharply up, in the fashion of the day, like sleigh-runners – an effect patiently and laboriously produced by the young men by sitting with their toes pressed against a wall for hours together. Mr. Walters was very earnest of mien, and very sincere and honest at heart; and he held sacred things and places in such reverence, and so separated them from worldly matters, that unconsciously to himself his Sunday-school voice had acquired a peculiar intonation which was wholly absent on weekdays. He began after this fashion:

'Now, children, I want you all to sit up just as straight and pretty as you can, and give me all your attention for a minute or two. There, that is it. That is the way good little boys and girls should do. I see one little girl who is looking out of the window – I am afraid she thinks I am out there somewhere – perhaps up in one of the trees making a speech to the little birds.

[Applausive titter.] I want to tell you how good it makes me feel to see so many bright, clean little faces assembled in a place like this, learning to do right and be good.'

And so forth, and so on. It is not necessary to set down the rest of the oration. It was of a pattern which does not vary, and so it is familiar to us all.

The latter third of the speech was marred by the resumption of fights and other recreations among certain of the bad boys, and by fidgetings and whisperings that extended far and wide, washing even to the bases of isolated and incorruptible rocks like Sid and Mary. But now every sound ceased suddenly with the subsidence of Mr. Walter's voice, and the conclusion of the speech was received with a burst of silent gratitude.'

A good part of the whispering had been occasioned by an event which was more or less rare – the entrance of visitors; Lawyer Thatcher, accompanied by a very feeble and aged man, a fine, portly, middle-aged gentleman with iron-grey hair, and a dignified lady who was doubtless the latter's wife. The lady was leading a child. Tom had been restless and full of chafings and repinings, conscience-smitten, too – he could not meet Amy Lawrence's eye, he could not brook her loving gaze. But when he saw this small new-comer his soul was all ablaze with bliss in a moment. The next moment he was 'showing off' with all his might – cuffing boys, pulling hair, making faces, in a word, using every art that seemed likely to fascinate a girl, and win her applause. His exultation had but one alloy – the memory of his humiliation in this angel's garden; and that record in sand was fast washing out under the waves of happiness that were sweeping over it now. The visitors were given the highest seat of honour, and as soon as Mr. Walter's speech was finished he introduced them to the school. The middle-aged man turned out to be a prodigious personage; no less a one than the county judge – altogether the most august creation these children had ever looked upon; and they wondered what kind of material he was made of; and they half wanted to hear him roar, and were half afraid he might, too. He was from Constantinople, twelve miles away – so he had travelled and seen the world – these very eyes had looked upon the County Court House, which was said to have a tin roof. The awe which these reflections inspired was attested by the impressive silence and the ranks of staring eyes. This was the great Judge Thatcher, brother of their own lawyer. Jeff Thatcher immediately went forward to be familiar with the great man and be envied by the school. It would have been music to his soul to hear the whisperings.

'Look at him, Jim! he's a going up there. Say, look! he's a going to shake hands with him; he *is* a shaking hands with him. By jinks, don't you wish you was Jeff?'

Mr. Walters fell to 'showing off' with all sorts of official bustlings and activities, giving orders, delivering judgements, discharging directions here, there, and everywhere that he could find a target. The librarian 'showed off', running hither and thither with his arms full of books and making a deal of the splutter and fuss that insect authority delights in. The young lady teachers 'showed off' – bending sweetly over pupils that were lately being boxed, lifting pretty warning fingers at bad little boys and patting good ones lovingly. The young gentleman teachers 'showed off' with small scoldings and other little displays of authority and fine attention to discipline; and most of the teachers, of both sexes, found business up at the library by the pulpit; and it was business that frequently had to be done over again two or three times (with much seeming vexation). The little girls 'showed off' in various ways, and the little boys 'showed off' with such diligence that the air was thick with paper wads and the murmur of scufflings. And above it all the great man sat and beamed a majestic judicial smile upon all the house, and warmed himself in the sun of his own grandeur, for he was 'showing off' too. There was only one thing wanting to make Mr. Walters's ecstasy complete, and that was a chance to deliver a Bible-prize and exhibit a prodigy. Several pupils had a few yellow tickets, but none had enough – he had been around among the star pupils inquiring. He would have given worlds, now, to have that German lad back again with a sound mind.

And now at this moment, when hope was dead, Tom Sawyer came forward with nine yellow tickets, nine red tickets, and ten blue ones, and demanded a Bible! This was a thunderbolt out of a clear sky. Walters was not expecting an application from this source for the next ten years. But there was no getting around it – here were the certified checks, and they were good for their face. Tom was therefore elevated to a place with the Judge and the other elect, and the great news was announced from headquarters. It was the most stunning surprise of the decade; and so profound was the sensation that it lifted the new hero up to the judicial one's altitude, and the school had two marvels to gaze upon in place of one. The boys were all eaten up with envy; but those that suffered the bitterest pangs were those who perceived too late that they themselves had contributed to his hated splendour by trading tickets to Tom for the wealth he had amassed in selling whitewashing privileges. These despised themselves, as being the dupes of a wily fraud, a guileful snake in the grass.

The prize was delivered to Tom with as much effusion as the Superintendent could pump up under the circumstances; but it lacked somewhat of the true gush, for the poor fellow's instinct taught him that there was a mystery here that could not well bear the light, perhaps; it was simply preposterous that *this* boy had warehoused two thousand sheaves of Scriptural wisdom on his premises – a dozen would strain his capacity, without a doubt. Amy Lawrence was proud and glad, and she tried to make Tom see it in her face; but he wouldn't look. She wondered; then she was just a grain troubled; next a dim suspicion came and went – came again; she watched; a furtive glance told her worlds – and then her heart broke, and she was jealous, and angry, and the tears came and she hated everybody; Tom most of all, she thought.

Tom was introduced to the Judge; but his tongue was tied, his breath would hardly come, his heart quaked – partly because of the awful greatness of the man, but mainly because he was *her* parent. He would have liked to fall down and worship him, if it were in the dark. The Judge put his hand on Tom's head and called him a fine little man, and asked him what his name was. The boy stammered, gasped, and got it out.

'Tom.'

'Oh, no, not Tom – it is——'

'Thomas.'

'Ah, that's it. I thought there was more to it, maybe. That's very well. But you've another one, I dare say, and you'll tell it to me, won't you?'

'Tell the gentleman your other name, Thomas,' said Walters, 'and say *sir*. You mustn't forget your manners.'

'Thomas Sawyer – sir.'

'That's it! that's a good boy. Fine boy. Fine, manly little fellow. Two thousand verses is a great many – very, very great many. And you never can be sorry for the trouble you took to learn them; for knowledge is worth more than anything there is in the world; it's what makes great men and good men; you'll be a great man and a good man yourself some day, Thomas, and then you'll look back and say, It's all owing to the precious Sunday-school privileges of my boyhood; it's all owing to my dear teachers that taught me to learn; it's all owing to the good Superintendent, who encouraged me and watched over me, and gave me a beautiful Bible, a splendid, elegant Bible, to keep and have it all for my own, always; it's all owing to right bringing up! That is what you will say, Thomas; and you wouldn't take any money for those two thousand verses, then – no, indeed you wouldn't. And now you wouldn't mind telling me and this lady some of the things you've learned – no, I know you wouldn't – for we are proud of little boys that learn. Now no doubt you know the names of all the twelve disciples. Won't you tell us the names of the first two that were appointed?'

Tom was tugging at a button and looking sheepish. He blushed, now, and his eyes fell. Mr. Walters's heart sank within him. He said to himself, It is not possible that the boy can answer the simplest question – why *did* the Judge ask him? Yet he felt obliged to speak up and say:

'Answer the gentleman, Thomas – don't be afraid.'

Tom still hung fire.

'Now I know you'll tell *me*,' said the lady. 'The names of the first two disciples were——'

'DAVID AND GOLIATH!'

Let us draw the curtain of charity over the rest of the scene.

Chapter 5

About half past ten the cracked bell of the small church began to ring, and presently the people began to gather for the morning sermon. The Sunday-school children distributed themselves about the house, and occupied pews with their parents, so as to be under supervision. Aunt Polly came, and Tom, and Sid and Mary sat with her, Tom being placed next the aisle, in order that he might be as far away from the open window and the seductive outside summer scenes as possible. The crowd filed up the aisle; the aged and needy postmaster, who had seen better days; the mayor and his wife – for they had a mayor there, among other unnecessaries; the justice of the peace; the widow Douglas, fair, smart, and forty, a generous, good-hearted soul and well-to-do, her hill mansion the only palace in the town, and the most hospitable and much the most lavish in the matter of festivities that St Petersburg could boast; the bent and venerable mayor and Mrs. Ward; Lawyer Riverson, the new notable from a distance; next the belle of the village, followed by a troop of lawn-clad and ribbon-decked young heart-breakers; then all the young clerks in town in a body – for they had stood in the vestibule sucking their cane-heads, a circling wall of oiled and simpering admirers, till the last girl had run their gauntlet; and last of all came the model boy, Willie Mufferson, taking as heedful care of his mother as if she were cut glass. He always brought his mother to church, and was the pride of all the matrons. The boys all hated him, he was so good; and besides, he had been 'thrown up to them' so much. His white handkerchief was hanging out of his pocket behind, as usual on Sundays – accidentally. Tom had no handkerchief and he looked upon boys who had as snobs. The congregation being fully assembled now, the bell rang once more, to warn laggards and stragglers, and then a solemn hush fell upon the church, which was only broken by the tittering and whispering of the choir in the gallery. The choir always tittered and whispered all through service. There was once a church choir that was not ill-bred, but I have forgotten where it was, now. It was a great many years ago, and I can scarcely remember anything about it, but I think it was in some foreign country.

The minister gave out of the hymn, and read it through with a relish, in a peculiar style which was much admired in that part of the country. His voice began on a medium key, and climbed steadily up till it reached a certain point, where it bore with strong emphasis upon the topmost word, and then plunged down as if from a spring-board.

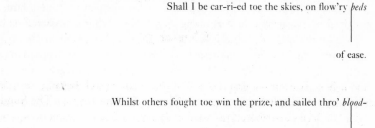

Shall I be car-ri-ed toe the skies, on flow'ry beds

of ease.

Whilst others fought toe win the prize, and sailed thro' blood-

y seas?

He was regarded as a wonderful reader. At church 'sociables' he was always called upon to read poetry; and when he was through, the ladies would lift up their hands and let them fall helplessly in their laps, and 'wall' their eyes, and shake their heads, as much as to say, 'Words cannot express it; it is too beautiful, *too* beautiful for this mortal earth.'

After the hymn had been sung, the Rev. Mr. Sprague turned himself into a bulletin board and read off 'notices' of meetings and societies and things till it seemed that the list would stretch out to the crack of doom – a queer custom which is still kept up in America, even in cities, away here in this age of abundant newspapers. Often the less there is to justify a traditional custom, the harder it is to get rid of it.

And now the minister prayed. A good, generous prayer it was, and went into details; it pleaded for the Church, and the little children of the Church; for the other churches of the village; for the village itself; for the county; for the State; for the State officers; for the United States; for the churches of the United States; for Congress; for the President; for the officers of the Government; for poor sailors, tossed by stormy seas; for the oppressed millions groaning under the heel of European monarchies and Oriental despotisms; for such as have the light and the good tidings, and yet have no eyes to see nor ears to hear withal; for the heathen in the far islands of the sea; and closed with a supplication that the words he was about to speak might find grace and favour, and be as seed sown in fertile ground, yielding in time a grateful harvest of good. Amen.

There was a rustling of dresses, and the standing congregation sat down. The boy whose history this book relates did not enjoy the prayer, he only endured it – if he even did that much. He was restive all through it; he kept tally of the details of the prayer, unconsciously – for he was not listening, but he knew the ground of old and the clergyman's regular route over it – and when a little trifle of new matter was interlarded, his ear detected it and his whole nature resented it; he considered additions unfair, and scoundrelly. In the midst of the prayer a fly had lit on the back of the pew in front of him, and tortured his spirit by calmly rubbing its hands together; embracing its head with its arms and polishing it so vigorously that it seemed to almost part company with the body, and the slender thread of a neck was exposed to view; scraping its wings with its hind legs and smoothing them to its body as if they had been coat-tails; going through its whole toilet as tranquilly as if it knew it was perfectly safe. As indeed it was; for as sorely as Tom's hands itched to grab for it they did not dare – he believed his soul would be instantly destroyed if he did such a thing while the prayer was going on. But with the closing sentence his hand began to curve and steal forward; and the instant the 'Amen' was out, the fly was a prisoner of war. His aunt detected the act, and made him let it go.

The minister gave out his text and droned along monotonously through an argument that was so prosy that many a head by-and-by began to nod – and yet it was an argument that dealt in limitless fire and brimstone, and thinned the predestined elect down to a company so small as to be hardly worth the saving. Tom counted the pages of the sermon; after church he always knew how many pages there had been, but he seldom knew anything else about the discourse. However, this time he was really interested for a little while. The minister made a grand and moving picture of the assembling together of the world's hosts at the millennium when the lion and the lamb should lie down together and a little child should lead them. But the pathos, the lesson, the moral of the great spectacle were lost upon the boy; he only thought of the conspicuousness of the principal character before the onlooking nations; his face lit up with the thought, and he said to himself that he wished he could be that child, if it was a tame lion.

Now he lapsed into suffering again as the dry argument was resumed. Presently he bethought himself of a treasure he had, and got it out. It was a large black beetle with formidable jaws – a 'pinch-bug', he called it. It was in a percussion-cap box. The first thing the beetle did was to take him by the finger. A natural fillip followed, the beetle went floundering into the aisle, and lit on its back, and the hurt finger went into the boy's mouth. The beetle lay there working its helpless legs, unable to turn over. Tom eyed it, and longed for it, but it was safe out of his reach. Other people, uninterested in the sermon, found relief in the beetle, and they eyed it too.

Presently a vagrant poodle dog came idling along, sad at heart, lazy with the summer softness and the quiet, weary of captivity, sighing for change. He spied the beetle; the drooping tail lifted and wagged. He surveyed the prize;

walked around it; smelt of it from a safe distance; walked around it again; grew bolder, and took a closer smell; then lifted his lips, and made a gingerly snatch at it, just missing it; made another, and another; began to enjoy the diversion; subsided to his stomach with the beetle between his paws, and continued his experiments; grew weary at last, and then indifferent and absent-minded. His head nodded, and little by little his chin descended and touched the enemy, who seized it. There was a sharp yelp, a flirt of the poodle's head and the beetle fell a couple of yards away, and lit on its back once more. The neighbouring spectators shook with a gentle inward joy, several faces went behind fans and handkerchiefs, and Tom was entirely happy. The dog looked foolish, and probably felt so; but there was resentment in his heart, too, and a craving for revenge. So he went to the beetle and began a wary attack on it again; jumping at it from every point of a circle, lighting with his forepaws within an inch of the creature, making even closer snatches at it with his teeth, and jerking his head till his ears flapped again. But he drew tired once more, after a while; tried to amuse himself with a fly, but found no relief; followed an ant around, with his nose close to the floor, and quickly wearied of that; yawned, sighed, forgot the beetle entirely, and sat down on it! Then there was a wild yelp of agony, and the poodle went sailing up the aisle; the yelps continued, and so did the dog; he crossed the house in front of the altar, he flew down the other aisle; he crossed before the doors; he clamoured up the home-stretch; his anguish grew with his progress, till presently he was but a woolly comet moving in its orbit with the gleam and the speed of light. At last the frantic sufferer sheered from its course and sprang into its master's lap; he flung it out of the window, and the voice of distress quickly thinned away and died in the distance.

By this time the whole church was red-faced and suffocating with suppressed laughter, and the sermon had come to a dead standstill. The discourse was resumed presently, but it went lame and halting, all possibility of impressiveness being at an end; for even the gravest sentiments were constantly being received with a smothered burst of unholy mirth, under cover of some remote pew-back, as if the poor parson had said a rarely facetious thing. It was a genuine relief to the whole congregation when the ordeal was over and the benediction pronounced.

Tom Sawyer went home quite cheerful, thinking to himself that there was some satisfaction about divine service when there was a bit of variety in it. He had but one marring thought; he was willing that the dog should play with his pinch-bug, but he did not think it was upright in him to carry it off.

Chapter 6

Monday morning found Tom Sawyer miserable. Monday morning always found him so, because it began another week's slow suffering in school. He generally began that day with wishing he had had no intervening holiday, it made the going into captivity and fetters again so much more odious.

Tom lay thinking. Presently it occurred to him that he wished he was sick; then he could stay home from school. Here was a vague possibility. He canvassed his system. No ailment was found, and he investigated again. This time he thought he could detect colicky symptoms, and he began to encourage them with considerable hope. But they soon grew feeble and presently died wholly away. He reflected further. Suddenly he discovered something. One of his upper teeth was loose. This was lucky; he was about to begin to groan, as a 'starter', as he called it, when it occurred to him that if he came into court with that argument his aunt would pull it out, and that would hurt. So he thought he would hold the tooth in reserve for the present, and seek further. Nothing offered for some little time, and then he remembered hearing the doctor tell about a certain thing that laid up a patient for two or three weeks and threatened to make him lose a finger. So the boy eagerly drew his sore toe from under the sheet and held it up for inspection. But now he did not knnw the necessary symptoms. However, it seemed well worth while to chance it, so he fell to groaning with considerable spirit.

But Sid slept on, unconscious.

Tom groaned louder, and fancied that he began to feel pain in the toe. No result from Sid.

Tom was panting with his exertions by this time. He took a rest and then swelled himself up and fetched a succession of admirable groans.

Sid snored on.

Tom was aggravated. He said, 'Sid, Sid!' and shook him. This course worked well, and Tom began to groan again. Sid yawned, stretched, then brought himself up on his elbow with a snort, and began to stare at Tom. Tom went on groaning. Sid said:

'Tom! say, Tom!'

No response.

'Here, Tom! Tom! What is the matter, Tom?' And he shook him, and looked in his face anxiously.

Tom moaned out:

'Oh, don't, Sid. Don't joggle me.'

'Why, what's the matter, Tom? I must call Auntie.'

'No, never mind. It'll be over by and by, maybe. Don't call anybody.'

'But I must! Don't groan so, Tom, it's awful. How long you been this way?'

'Hours. Ouch! Oh, don't stir so, Sid. You'll kill me.'

'Tom, why didn't you wake me sooner? Oh, Tom, don't! It makes my flesh crawl to hear you. Tom, what *is* the matter?'

'I forgive you everything, Sid. [Groan.] Everything you've ever done to me. When I'm gone——'

'Oh, Tom, you ain't dying, are you? Don't, Tom. Oh, don't. Maybe——'

'I forgive everybody, Sid. [Groan.] Tell 'em so, Sid. And, Sid, you give my window-sash, and my cat with one eye to that new girl that's come to town, and tell her——'

But Sid had snatched his clothes and gone. Tom was suffering in reality now, so handsomely was his imagination working, and so his groans had gathered quite a genuine tone.

Sid flew downstairs and said:

'Oh, Aunt Polly, come! Tom's dying!'

'Dying!'

'Yes'm. Don't wait, come quick!'

'Rubbage! I don't believe it!'

But she fled upstairs nevertheless, with Sid and Mary at her heels. And her face grew white, too, and her lips trembled. When she reached the bedside she gasped out:

'You Tom! Tom, what's the matter with you?'

'Oh, Auntie, I'm——'

'What's the matter with you – what *is* the matter with you, child?' ·

'Oh, Auntie, My sore toe's mortified!'

The old lady sank down into a chair and laughed a little, then cried a little, then did both together. This restored her, and she said:

'Tom, what a turn you did give me. Now you shut up that nonsense and climb out of this.'

The groans ceased, and the pain vanished from the toe. The boy felt a little foolish, and he said:

'Aunt Polly, it *seemed* mortified, and it hurt so I never minded my tooth at all.'

'Your tooth, indeed! What's the matter with your tooth?'

'One of them's loose, and it aches perfectly awful.'

'There, there now, don't begin that groaning again. Open your mouth. Well, your tooth *is* loose, but you're not going to die about that. Mary, get me a silk thread, and a chunk of fire out of the kitchen.'

Tom said:

'Oh, please, Auntie, don't pull it out, it don't hurt any more. I wish. I may never stir if it does. Please don't, Auntie, *I* don't want to stay home from school.'

'Oh, you don't, don't you? So all this row was because you thought you'd get to stay home from school and go a fishing? Tom, Tom, I love you so, and you seem to try every way you can to break my old heart with your outrageousness.'

By this time the dental instruments were ready. The old lady made one end of the silk thread fast to Tom's tooth with a loop and tied the other to the bed-post. Then she seized the chunk of fire and suddenly thrust it almost into the boy's face. The tooth hung dangling by the bed-post, now.

But all trials bring their compensations. As Tom wended to school after breakfast, he was the envy of every boy he met because the gap in his upper row of teeth enabled him to expectorate in a new and admirable way. He gathered quite a following of lads interested in the exhibition; and one that had cut his finger and had been a centre of fascination and homage up to this time, now found himself suddenly without an adherent, and shorn of his glory. His heart was heavy, and he said with a disdain which he did not feel, that it wasn't anything to spit like Tom Sawyer; but another boy said 'Sour grapes!' and he wandered away a dismantled hero.

Shortly Tom came upon the juvenile pariah of the village, Huckleberry Finn, son of the town drunkard. Huckleberry was cordially hated and dreaded by all the mothers of the town because he was idle, and lawless, and vulgar, and bad – and because all their children admired him so, and delighted in his forbidden society, and wished they dared to be like him. Tom was like the rest of the respectable boys in that he envied Huckleberry his gaudy outcast condition, and was under strict orders not to play with him. So he played with him every time he got a chance. Huckleberry was always dressed in the cast-off clothes of full-grown men, and they were in perennial bloom and fluttering with rags. His hat was a vast ruin with a wide crescent lopped out of its brim; his coat, when he wore one, hung nearly to his heels, and had the rearward buttons far down the back; but one suspender supported his trousers; the seat of the trousers bagged low and contained nothing; the fringed legs dragged in the dirt when not rolled up. Huckleberry came and went at his own free will. He slept on door-steps in fine weather, and in empty hogsheads in wet; he did not have to go to school or to church, or call any being master, or obey anybody; he could go fishing or swimming when and where he chose, and stay as long as it suited him; nobody forbade him to fight; he could sit up as late as he pleased; he was always the first boy that went barefoot in the spring and the last to resume leather in the fall; he never had to wash, nor put on clean clothes; he could swear wonderfully. In a word, everything that goes to make life precious, that boy had. So thought every harassed, hampered, respectable boy in St Petersburg. Tom hailed the romantic outcast:

'Hello, Huckleberry!'

'Hello yourself, and see how you like it.'

'What's that you got?'

'Dead cat.'

'Lemme see him, Huck. My, he's pretty stiff. Where'd you get him?'

'Bought him off'n a boy.'

'What did you give?'

'I give a blue ticket and a bladder that I got at the slaughter-house.'

'Where'd you get the blue ticket?'

'Bought if off'n Ben Rogers two weeks ago for a hoop-stick.'

'Say – what is dead cats good for, Huck?'

'Good for? Cure warts with.'

'No? Is that so? I know something that's better.'

'I bet you don't. What is it?'

'Why, spunk-water.'

'Spunk-water! I wouldn't give a dern for spunk-water.'

'You wouldn't, wouldn't you? D'you ever try it?'

'No, I hain't. But Bob Tanner did.'

'Who told you so?'

'Why, he told Jeff Thatcher, and Jeff told Johnny Baker, and Johnny told Jim Hollis, and Jim told Ben Rogers, and Ben told a nigger, and the nigger told me. There now!'

'Well, what of it? They'll all lie. Leastaways all but the nigger, I don't know *him*. But I never see a nigger that *wouldn't* lie. Shucks! Now you tell me how Bob Tanner done it, Huck.'

'Why, he took and dipped his hand in a rotten stump where the rain-water was.'

'In the daytime?'

'Certainly.'

'With his face to the stump?'

'Yes. Least I reckon so.'

'Did he *say* anything?'

'I don't reckon he did, I don't know.'

'Aha! Talk about trying to cure warts with spunk-water such a blame fool way as that! Why, that ain't a going to do any good. You got to go by yourself to the middle of the woods, where you know there's a spunk-water stump, and just as it's midnight you back up against the stump and jam your hand in and say:

> Barley-corn, barley-corn, injun-meal shorts,
> Spunk-water, spunk-water, swaller these warts,

and then walk away quick, eleven steps, with your eyes shut, and then turn around three times and walk home without speaking to anybody. Because if you speak the charm's busted.'

'Well, that sounds like a good way; but that ain't the way Bob Tanner done.'

'No, sir, you can bet he didn't; becuz he's the wartiest boy in this town; and he wouldn't have a wart on him if he'd knowed how to work spunk-water. I've took off thousands of warts off of my hands that way, Huck. I play with frogs so much that I've always got considerable many warts. Sometimes I take 'em off with a bean.'

'Yes, bean's good. I've done that.'

'Have you? What's your way?'

'You take and split the bean, and cut the wart so as to get some blood, and then you put the blood on one piece of the bean, and take and dig a hole and bury it 'bout midnight at the cross-roads in the dark of the moon, and then you burn up the rest of the bean. You see that piece that's got the blood on it will keep drawing and drawing, trying to fitch the other piece to it, and so that helps the blood to draw the wart, and pretty soon off she comes.'

'Yes, that's it, Huck – that's it; though, when you're burying it, if you say, "Down bean, off wart; come no more to bother me!" it's better. That's the way Joe Harper does, and he's ben nearly to Coonville, and most everywhere. But say – how do you cure 'em with dead cats?'

'Why, you take your cat and go and get in the graveyard, long about midnight, where somebody that was wicked has been buried; and when it's midnight a devil will come, or maybe two or three, but you can't see 'em, you can only hear something like the wind, or maybe hear 'em talk; and when they're taking that feller away, you heave your cat after 'em and say, "Devil follow corpse, cat follow devil, warts follow cat. *I'm* done with ye!" That'll fetch *any* wart.'

'Sounds right. D'you every try it, Huck?'

'No, but old Mother Hopkins told me.'

'Well, I reckon it's so, then, becuz they say she's a witch.'

'*Say*! Why, Tom, I *know* she is. She witched pap. Pap says so his own self. He came along one day, and he see she was a witching him, so he took up a rock, and if she hadn't dodged he'd a got her. Well, that very night he rolled off'n a shed wher' he was a layin' drunk, and broke his arm.'

'Why, that's awful. How did he know she was a witching him?'

'Lord, Pap can tell, easy. Pap says when they keep looking at you right stiddy, they're a witching you, specially if they mumble. Becuz when they mumble they're a saying the Lords' Prayer backards.'

'Say, Hucky, when you going to try the cat?'

'Tonight. I reckon they'll come after old Hoss Williams tonight.'

'But they buried him Saturday, Huck. Didn't they get him Saturday night?'

'Why, how you talk! How could their charms work till midnight? and then it's Sunday. Devils don't slosh around much of a Sunday, I don't reckon.'

'I never thought of that. That's so. Lemme go with you?'

'Of course – if you ain't afeard.'

'Afeard! 'Tain't likely. Will you meow?'

'Yes, and you meow back if you get a chance. Last time you kep' me a meowing around till old Hays went to throwing rocks at me, and says, "Dern that cat!" So I hove a brick through his window – but don't you tell.'

'I won't. I couldn't meow that night becuz Auntie was watching me; but I'll meow this time. Say, Huck, what's that?'

'Nothing but a tick.'

'Where'd you get him?'

'Out in the woods.'

'What'll you take for him?'

'I don't know. I don't want to sell him.'

'All right. It's a mighty small tick, anyway.'

'Oh, anybody can run a tick down that don't belong to them. I'm satisfied with it. It's a good enough tick for me.'

'Sho, there's ticks a plenty. I could have a thousand of 'em if I wanted to.'

'Well, why don't you? Becuz you know mighty well you can't. This is a pretty early tick, I reckon. It's the first one I've seen this year.'

'Say, Huck, I'll give you my tooth for him.'

'Less see it.'

Tom got out a bit of paper and carefully unrolled it. Huckleberry viewed it wistfully. The temptation was very strong. At last he said:

'Is it genuwyne?'

Tom lifted his lip and showed the vacancy.

'Well, all right,' said Huckleberry; 'it's a trade.'

Tom enclosed the tick in the percussion-cap box that had lately been the pinch-bug's prison, and the boys separated, each feeling wealthier than before.

When Tom reached the little isolated frame school-house, he strode in briskly, with the manner of one who had come with all honest speed. He hung his hat on a peg, and flung himself into his seat with businesslike alacrity. The master, throned on high in his great splint-bottom armchair, was dozing, lulled by the frowsy hum of study. The interruption roused him:

'Thomas Sawyer!'

Tom knew that when his name was pronounced in full, it meant trouble.

'Sir!'

'Come up here. Now, sir, why are you late again, as usual?'

Tom was about to take refuge in a lie, when he saw two long tails of yellow hair hanging down a back that he recognized by the electric sympathy of love; and by that form was *the only vacant place* on the girls' side of the school-house. He instantly said:

'I STOPPED TO TALK WITH HUCKLEBERRY FINN!'

The master's pulse stood still, and he stared helplessly. The buzz of study ceased; the pupils wondered if this foolhardy boy had lost his mind. The master said:

'You – you did what?'

'Stopped to talk with Huckleberry Finn.'

There was no mistaking the words.

'Thomas Sawyer, this is the most astounding confession I have ever listened to; no mere ferule will answer for this offence. Take off your jacket.'

The master's arm performed until it was tired, and the stock of switches notably diminished. Then the order followed:

'Now, sir, go and sit with the *girls*! And let this be a warning to you.'

The titter that rippled around the room appeared to abash the boy, but in reality that result was caused rather more by his worshipful awe of his unknown idol and the dread pleasure that lay in his high good fortune. He sat down upon the end of the pine bench, and the girl hitched herself away from him with a toss of the head. Nudges and winks and whispers traversed the room, but Tom sat still, with his arms upon the long, low desk before him, and seemed to study his book. By and by attention ceased from him, and the accustomed school murmur rose upon the dull air once more. Presently the boy began to steal furtive glances at the girl. She observed it, 'made a mouth' at him, and gave him the back of her head for the space of a minute. When she cautiously faced around again, a peach lay before her. She thrust it away; Tom gently put it back; she thrust it away again, but with less animosity. Tom patiently returned it to its place; then she let it remain. Tom scrawled on his slate, 'Please take it – I got more.' The girl glanced at the words, but made no sign. Now the boy began to draw something on the slate, hiding his work with his left hand. For a time the girl refused to notice; but her human curiosity presently began to manifest itself by hardly perceptible signs. The boy

'Now the boy began to draw something on the slate'

worked on, apparently unconscious. The girl made a sort of non-committal attempt to see, but the boy did not betray that he was aware of it. At last she gave in, and hesitatingly whispered:

'Let me see it.'

Tom partly uncovered a dismal caricature of a house with two gable ends to it and a cork-screw of smoke issuing from the chimney. Then the girl's interest began to fasten itself upon the work, and she forgot everything else. When it was finished, she gazed a moment, then whispered:

'It's nice – make a man.'

The artist erected a man in the front yard, that resembled a derrick. He could have stepped over the house; but the girl was not hypercritical; she was satisfied with the monster, and whispered:

'It's a beautiful man – now make me coming along.'

Tom drew an hourglass, with a full moon and straw limbs to it, and armed the spreading fingers with a portentous fan. The girl said:

'It's ever so nice – I wish I could draw.'

'It's easy,' whispered Tom. 'I'll learn you.'

'Oh, will you? When?'

'At noon. Do you go home to dinner?'

'I'll stay if you will.'

'Good – that's a go.'

'What's your name?'

'Becky Thatcher.'

'What's yours? Oh, I know. It's Thomas Sawyer.'

'That's the name they lick me by. I'm Tom when I'm good. You call me Tom, will you?'

'Yes.'

Now Tom began to scrawl something on the slate, hiding the words from the girl. But she was not backward this time. She begged to see. Tom said:

'Oh, it ain't anything.'

'Yes it is.'

'No it ain't; you don't want to see.'

'Yes I do, indeed I do. Please let me.'

'You'll tell.'

'No I won't – deed and deed and double deed I won't.'

'You won't tell anybody at all? Ever as long as you live?'

'No, I won't ever tell anybody. Now let me.'

'Oh, *you* don't want to see!'

'Now that you treat me so I *will* see, Tom' – and she put her small hand on his, and a little scuffle ensued. Tom pretending to resist in earnest, but letting his hand slip by degrees till these words were revealed: '*I love you.*'

'Oh, you bad thing!' And she hit his hand a smart rap, but reddened and looked pleased nevertheless.

Just at this juncture the boy felt a slow fateful grip closing on his ear, and a steady lifting impulse. In that vice he was borne across the house and deposited in his own seat, under a peppering fire of giggles from the whole school. Then the master stood over him during a few awful moments, and finally moved away to his throne without saying a word. But although Tom's ear tingled, his heart was jubilant.

As the school quieted down, Tom made an honest effort to study, but the turmoil within him was too great. In turn he took his place in the reading class and made a botch of it, then in the geography class and turned lakes into mountains, mountains into rivers, and rivers into continents, till chaos was come again; then in the spelling class, and got 'turned down' by a succession of mere baby words till he brought up at the foot and yielded up the pewter medal which he had worn with ostentation for months.

Chapter 7

The harder Tom tried to fasten his mind on his book, the more his ideas wandered. So at last, with a sigh and a yawn, he gave it up. It seemed to him that the noon recess would never come. The air was utterly dead. There was not a breath stirring. It was the sleepiest of sleepy days. The drowsing murmur of the five-and-twenty studying scholars soothed the soul like the spell that is in the murmur of bees. Away off in the flaming sunshine Cardiff Hill lifted its soft green sides through a shimmering veil of heat tinted with the purple of distance; a few birds floated on lazy wing high in the air; no other living thing was visible but some cows, and they were asleep.

Tom's heart ached to be free, or else to have something of interest to do to pass the dreary time. His hand wandered into his pocket, and his face lit up with a glow of gratitude that was prayer, though he did not know it. Then furtively the percussion-cap box came out. He released the tick, and put him on the long flat desk. The creature probably glowed with a gratitude that amounted to prayer, too, at this moment, but it was premature; for when he started thankfully to travel off, Tom turned him aside with a pin, and made him take a new direction.

Tom's bosom friend sat next him, suffering just as Tom had been, and now he was deeply and gratefully interested in this entertainment in an instant. This bosom friend was Joe Jarper. The two boys were sworn friends all the week, and embattled enemies on Saturdays. Joe took a pin out of his lapel, and began to assist in exercising the prisoner. The sport grew in interest momently. Soon Tom said that they were interfering with each other, and neither getting the fullest benefit of the tick. So he put Joe's slate on the desk and drew a line down the middle of it from top to bottom.

'Now,' said he, 'as long as he is on your side you can stir him up and I'll let him alone: but if you let him get away and get on my side, you're to leave him alone as long as I can keep him from crossing over.'

'All right, go ahead – start him up.'

The tick escaped from Tom, presently, and crossed the equator. Joe harassed him awhile, and then he got away and crossed back again. This change of base occurred often. While one boy was worrying the tick with absorbing interest, the other would look on with interest as strong, the two heads bowed together over the slate and the two souls dead to all things else. At last luck seemed to settle and abide with Joe. The tick tried this, that, and the other course, and got as excited and as anxious as the boys themselves, but time and again, just as he would have victory in his very grasp, so to speak, and Tom's fingers would be twitching to begin, Joe's pin would deftly head him off and keep possession. At last Tom could stand it no longer. The temptation was too strong. So he reached out and lent a hand with his pin. Joe was angry in a moment. Said he:

'Tom, you let him alone.'

'I only just want to stir him up a little, Joe.'

'No, sir, it ain't fair; you just let him alone.'

'Blame it, I ain't going to stir him much.'

'Let him alone, I tell you!'

'I won't!'

'You shall – he's on my side of the line.'

'Look here, Joe Harper, whose is that tick?'

'*I* don't care whose tick he is – he's on my side of the line, and you shan't touch him.'

'Well, I'll just bet I will, though. He's my tick, and I'll do what I blame please with him, or die!'

A tremendous whack came down on Tom's shoulders, and its duplicate on Joe's; and for the space of two minutes the dust continued to fly from the two jackets and the whole school to enjoy it. The boys had been too absorbed to notice the hush that had stolen upon the school a while before when the master came tiptoeing down the room and stood over them. He had contemplated a good part of the performance before he contributed his bit of variety to it. When school broke up at noon, Tom flew to Becky Thatcher, and whispered in her ear.

'Put on your bonnet and let on you're going home; and when you get to the corner, give the rest of 'em the slip, and turn down through the lane and come back. I'll go the other way, and come it over 'em the same way.'

So the one went off with one group of scholars, and the other with another. In a little while the two met at the bottom of the lane, and when they reached the school they had it all to themselves. Then they sat together, with a slate before them, and Tom gave Becky the pencil and held her hand in his, guiding it, and so created another surprising house. When the interest in art began to wane, the two fell to talking. Tom was swimming in bliss. He said:

'Do you love rats?'

'No, I hate them!'

'Well, I do too – live ones. But I mean dead ones, to swing around your head with a string.'

'No, I don't care for rats much, anyway. What *I* like is chewing gum!'

'Oh, I should say so! I wish I had some now!'

'Do you? I've got some. I'll let you chew it awhile, but you must give it back to me.'

That was agreeable, so they chewed it turn about, and dangled their legs against the bench in excess of contentment.

'Was you ever at a circus?' said Tom.

'Yes, and my pa's going to take me again sometime, if I'm good.'

'I been to the circus three or four times – lots of times. Church ain't shucks to a circus. There's things going on at a circus all the time. I'm going to be a clown in a circus when I grow up.'

'Oh, are you? That will be nice. They're so lovely all spotted up.'

'Yes, that's so. And they get slathers of money – most a dollar a day, Ben Rogers says. Say, Becky, was you ever engaged?'

'What's that?'

'Why, engaged to be married.'

'No.'

'Would you like to?'

'I reckon so. I don't know. What is it like?'

'Like? Why it ain't like anything. You only just tell a boy you won't ever have anybody but him, ever ever *ever*, and then you kiss, and that's all. Anybody can do it.'

'Kiss? What do you kiss for?'

'Why that, you know, is to – well, they always do that.'

'Everybody?'

'Why, yes, everybody that's in love with each other. Do you remember what I wrote on the slate?'

'Ye – yes.'

'What was it?'

'I shan't tell you.'

'Shall I tell *you*?'

'Ye – yes – but some other time.'

'No, now.'

'No, not now – tomorrow.'

'Oh, no, *now*, please, Becky. I'll whisper it, I'll whisper it ever so easy.'

Becky hesitating, Tom took silence for consent, and passed his arm about her waist and whispered the tale ever so softly, with his mouth close to her ear. And then he added:

'Now you whisper it to me – just the same.'

She resisted for a while, and then said:

'You turn your face away, so you can't see, and then I will. But you mustn't ever tell anybody – *will* you, Tom? Now you won't – *will* you?'

'No, indeed, indeed I won't. Now, Becky.'

He turned his face away. She bent timidly around till her breath stirred his curls, and whispered, 'I love you!'

Then she sprang away and ran around and around the desks and benches, with Tom after her, and took refuge in a corner at last, with her little white apron to her face. Tom clasped her about her neck and pleaded.

'Now, Becky, it's all over – all over but the kiss. Don't you be afraid of that – it ain't anything at all. Please, Becky.'

And he tugged at the apron and the hands.

By-and-by she gave up and let her hands drop; her face, all glowing with the struggle, came up and submitted. Tom kissed the red lips and said:

'Now it's all done, Becky. And always after this, you know, you ain't ever to love anybody but me, and you ain't ever to marry anybody but me, never never and for ever. Will you?'

'No, I'll never love anybody but you, Tom, and I'll never marry anybody but you, and you ain't to ever marry anybody but me, either.'

'Certainly. Of course. That's *part* of it. And always, coming to school, or when we're going home, you're to walk with me, when there ain't anybody looking – and you choose me and I choose you at parties, because that's the way you do when you're engaged.'

'It's so nice. I never heard of it before.'

'Oh, it's ever so jolly! Why me and Amy Lawrence——'

The big eyes told Tom his blunder, and he stopped, confused.

'Oh, Tom! Then I ain't the first you've ever been engaged to!'

The child began to cry. Tom said:

'Oh, don't cry, Becky. I don't care for her any more.'

'Yes you do, Tom – you know you do.'

Tom tried to put his arm about her neck, but she pushed him away and turned her face to the wall, and went on crying. Tom tried again, with soothing words in his mouth, and was repulsed again. Then his pride was up, and he strode away and went outside. He stood about, restless and uneasy, for a while, glancing at the door every now and then, hoping she would repent and come to find him. But she did not. Then he began to feel badly, and fear that he was in the wrong. It was a hard struggle with him to make new advances now, but he nerved himself to it and entered; She was still standing back there in the corner, sobbing with her face to the wall. Tom's heart smote him. He went to her and stood a moment, not knowing exactly how to proceed. Then he said, hesitatingly:

'Becky, I – I don't care for anybody but you.'

No reply – but sobs.

'Becky,' pleadingly.

'Becky, won't you say something?'

More sobs.

Tom got out his chiefest jewel, a brass knob from the top of an andiron, and passed it around her so that she could see it, and said:

'Please, Becky, won't you take it?'

She struck it to the floor. Then Tom marched out of the house and over the hills and far away, to return to school no more that day. Presently Becky began to suspect. She ran to the door; he was not in sight; she flew around to the play-yard; he was not there. Then she called:

'Tom! Come back, Tom!'

She listened intently, but there was no answer. She had no companions but silence and loneliness. So she sat down to cry again and upbraid herself, and by this time the scholars began to gather again, and she had to hide her grief and still her broken heart, and take up the cross of a long dreary aching afternoon with none among the strangers about her to exchange sorrows with.

Chapter 8

Tom dodged hither and thither through lanes until he was well out of the track of returning scholars, and then fell into a moody jog. He crossed a small 'branch' two or three times, because of a prevailing juvenile superstition that to cross water baffled pursuit. Half an hour later he was disappearing behind the Douglas mansion on the summit of Cardiff Hill, and the school-house was hardly distinguishable away off in the valley behind him. He entered a dense wood, picked his pathless way to the centre of it, and sat down on a mossy spot under a spreading oak. There was not even a zephyr stirring; the dead noonday heat had even still the songs of the birds; nature lay in a trance that was broken by no sound but the occasional far-off hammering of a woodpecker, and this seemed to render the pervading silence and sense of loneliness the more profound. The boy's soul was steeped in melancholy; his feelings were in happy accord with his surroundings. He sat long with his elbows on his knees and his chin in his hands, meditating. It seemed to him that life was but a trouble at best, and he more than half envied Jimmy Hodges, so lately released. It must be very peaceful, he thought, to lie and slumber and dream for ever and ever, with the wind whispering through the trees and caressing the grass and the flowers of the grave, and nothing to bother and grieve about, ever any more. If he only had a clean Sunday-school record he could be willing to go, and be done with it all. Now as to this girl. What had he done? Nothing. He had meant the best in the world and been treated like a dog – like a very dog. She would be sorry some day – maybe when it was too late. Ah, if he could only die *temporarily*!

But the elastic heart of youth cannot be kept compressed into one constrained shape long at a time. Tom presently began to drift insensibly back into the concerns of this life again. What if he turned his back, now, and disappeared mysteriously? What if he went away – ever so far away, into unknown countries beyond the seas – and never came back any more! How would she feel then? The idea of being a clown recurred to him now, only to fill him with disgust. For frivolity and jokes, and spotted tights, were an offence when they intruded themselves upon a spirit that was exalted into the vague, august realm of the romantic. No, he would be a soldier, and return after long years, all war-worn and illustrious. No, better still, he would join the Indians and hunt buffaloes, and go on the war-path in the mountain ranges and the trackless great plains of the Far West, and away in the future come back a great chief, bristling with feathers, hideous with paint, and prance into Sunday-school, some drowsy summer morning, with a blood-curdling war-whoop, and sear the eyeballs of all his companions with unappeasable envy. But no, there was something grander even than this. He would be a pirate! That was it! *Now* his future lay plain before him, and glowing with unimaginable splendour. How his name would fill the world, and make people shudder! How gloriously he would go ploughing the dancing seas, in his long, low, black racer, the *Spirit of the Storm*, with his grisly flag flying at the fore! And at the zenith of his fame, how he would suddenly appear at the old village and stalk into church all brown and weather-beaten, in his black velvet doublet and trunks, his great jack-boots, his crimson sash, his belt bristling with horse-pistols, his crime-rusted cutlass at his side, his slouch hat with waving plumes, his black flag unfurled with the skull and crossbones on it, and hear with swelling ecstasy the whisperings: 'It's Tom Sawyer the Pirate! the Black Avenger of the Spanish Main!'

Yes, it was settled; his career was determined. He would run away from home and enter upon it. He would start the very next morning. Therefore he must now begin to get ready. He would collect his resources together. He went to a rotten log near at hand, and began to dig under one end of it with his Barlow knife. He soon struck wood that sounded hollow. He put his hand there, and uttered this incantation impressively:

'What hasn't come here, *come*! What's here, *stay* here!'

Then he scraped away the dirt, and exposed a pine shingle. He took it up and disclosed a shapely little treasure-house whose bottom and sides were of shingles. In it lay a marble. Tom's astonishment was boundless! He scratched his head with a perplexed air, and said:

'Well, that beats anything!'

Then he tossed the marble away pettishly, and stood cogitating. The truth was that a superstition of his had failed here, which he and all his comrades had always looked upon as infallible. If you buried a marble with certain necessary incantations, and left it alone a fortnight, and then opened the place with the incantation he had just used, you would find that all the marbles you had ever lost had gathered themselves together there, meantime, no matter how widely they had been separated. But now this thing had actually and unquestionably failed. Tom's whole structure of faith was shaken to its foundations. He had many a time heard of this thing succeeding, but never of its failing before. It did not occur to him that he had tried it several times before, himself, but could never find the hiding-place afterwards. He puzzled over the matter some time, and finally decided that some witch had interfered and broken the charm. He thought he would satisfy himself on that point, so he searched around till he found a small sandy spot with a little funnel-shaped depression in it. He laid himself down and put his mouth close to this depression and called:

Doodle-bug, doodle-bug, tell me what I want to know!
Doodle-bug, doodle-bug, tell me what I want to know!

The sand began to work, and presently a small black bug appeared for a second, and then darted under again in a fright.

'He dasn't tell! So it *was* a witch that done it. I just knowed it.'

He well knew the futility of trying to contend against witches, so he gave up, discouraged. But it occurred to him that he might as well have the marble he had just thrown away, and therefore he went and made a patient search for it. But he could not find it. Now he went back to his treasure-house, and carefully placed himself just as he had been standing when he tossed the marble away; then he took another marble from his pocket, and tossed it in the same way, saying:

'Brother, go find your brother!'

He watched where it stopped, and went there and looked. But it must have fallen short or gone too far, so he tried twice more. The last repetition was successful. The two marbles lay within a foot of each other.

Just here the blast of a toy tin trumpet came faintly down the green aisles of the forest. Tom flung off his jacket and trousers, turned a suspender into a belt, raked away some brush behind the rotten log, disclosing a rude bow and arrow, a lath sword, and a tin trumpet, and in a moment had seized these things, and bounded away, barelegged, with fluttering shirt. He presently halted under a great elm, blew an answering blast, and then began to tip-toe and look warily out, this way and that. He said cautiously – to an imaginary company:

'Hold, my merry men! Keep hid till I blow.'

Now appeared Joe Harper, as airily clad and elaborately armed as Tom. Tom called:

'Hold! Who comes here into Sherwood Forest without my pass?'

'Guy of Guisborne wants no man's pass! Who art thou that – that——'

'Dares to hold such language,' said Tom, prompting, for they talked 'by the book', from memory.

'Who art thou that dares to hold such language?'

'I, indeed! I am Robin Hood, as thy caitiff carcase soon shall know.'

'Then art thou indeed that famous outlaw? Right gladly will I dispute with thee the passes of the merry wood. Have at thee!'

They took their lath swords, dumped their other traps on the ground, struck a fencing attitude, foot to foot, and began a grave, careful combat, 'two up and two down'. Presently Tom said:

'Now if you've got the hang, go it lively!'

So they 'went it lively', panting and perspiring with the work. By-and-by Tom shouted:

'Fall! fall! Why don't you fall?'

'I shan't! Why don't you fall yourself? You're getting the worst of it.'

'Why, that ain't anything. *I* can't fall. That ain't the way it is in the book. The book says, "Then with one back-handed stroke he slew poor Guy of Guisborne!" You're to turn around and let me hit you in the back.'

There was no getting around the authorities, so Joe turned, received the whack, and fell.

'Now,' said Joe, getting up, 'you got to let me kill you. That's fair.'

'Why, I can't do that. It ain't in the book.'

'Well, it's blamed mean. That's all.'

'Well, say, Joe, you can be Friar Tuck, or Much the Miller's son, and lam me with a quarter-staff; or I'll be the Sheriff of Nottingham, and you be Robin Hood a little while, and kill me.'

This was satisfactory, and so these adventures were carried out. Then Tom became Robin Hood again, and was allowed by the treacherous nun to bleed his strength away through his neglected wound. And at last Joe, representing a whole tribe of weeping outlaws, dragged him sadly forth, gave his bow into his feeble hands, and Tom said, 'Where this arrow falls, there bury poor Robin Hood under the greenwood tree.' Then he shot the arrow, and fell back, and would have died; but he lit on a nettle, and sprang up too gaily for a corpse.

The boys dressed themselves, hid their accoutrements, and went off grieving that there were no outlaws any more, and wondering what modern civilization could claim to have done to compensate for their loss. They said they would rather be outlaws a year in Sherwood Forest than President of the United States for ever.

Chapter 9

At half past nine that night, Tom and Sid were sent to bed as usual. They said their prayers, and Sid was soon asleep. Tom lay awake and waited in restless impatience. When it seemed to him that it must be nearly daylight, he heard the clock strike ten! This was despair. He would have tossed and fidgeted, as his nerves demanded, but he was afraid he might wake Sid. So he lay still and stared up into the dark. Everything was dismally still. By-and-by, out of the stillness little scarcely perceptible noises began to emphasize themselves. The ticking of the clock began to bring itself into notice. Old beams began to crack mysteriously. The stairs creaked faintly. Evidently spirits were abroad. A measured, muffled snore issued from Aunt Polly's chamber. And now the tiresome chirping of a cricket that no human ingenuity could locate began. Next the ghastly ticking of a death-watch in the wall at the bed's head made Tom shudder – it meant that somebody's days were numbered. Then the howl of a far-off dog rose on the night air and was answered by a fainter howl from a remoter distance. Tom was in an agony. At last he was satisfied that time had ceased and eternity begun; he began to doze in spite of himself; the clock chimed eleven, but he did not hear it. And then there came, mingling with his half-formed dreams, a most melancholy caterwauling. The raising of a neighbouring window disturbed him. A cry of 'Scat! you devil!' and the crash of an empty bottle against the back of his aunt's wood-shed brought him wide awake, and a single minute later he was dressed and out of the window and creeping along the roof of the 'ell' on all fours. He 'meow'd' with caution once or twice as he went; then jumped to the roof of the wood-shed, and thence to the ground. Huckleberry Finn was there, with his dead cat. The boys moved off and disappeared in the gloom. At the end of half an hour they were wading through the tall grass of the graveyard.

It was a graveyard of the old-fashioned western kind. It was on a hill, about a mile and a half from the village. It had a crazy board fence around it, which leaned inward in places, and outward the rest of the time, but stood upright nowhere. Grass and weeds grew rank over the whole cemetery. All the old graves were sunken in. There was not a tombstone on the place; round-topped, worm-eaten boards staggered over the graves, leaning for support and finding none. 'Sacred to the memory of' so-and-so had been painted on them once, but it could no longer have been read, on the most of them, now, even if there had been light.

A faint wind moaned through the trees, and Tom feared it might be the spirits of the dead complaining at being disturbed. The boys talked little, and only under their breath, for the time and the place and the pervading solemnity and silence oppressed their spirits. They found the sharp new heap they were seeking, and ensconced themselves within the protection of three great elms that grew in a bunch within a few feet of the grave.

Then they waited in silence for what seemed a long time. The hooting of a distant owl was all the sound that troubled the dead stillness. Tom's reflection grew oppressive. He must force some talk. So he said in a whisper:

'Hucky, do you believe the dead people like it for us to be here?'

Huckleberry whispered:

'I wisht I knowed. It's awful solemn like, ain't it?'

'I bet it is.'

There was a considerable pause, while the boys canvassed this matter inwardly. Then Tom whispered:

'Say, Hucky – do you reckon Hoss Williams hears us talking?'

'O' course he does. Least his spirit does.'

Tom, after a pause:

'I wish I'd said *Mister* Williams. But I never meant any harm. Everybody calls him Hoss.'

'A body can't be too particular how they talk 'bout these yer dead people, Tom.'

This was a damper, and conversation died again. Presently Tom seized his comrade's arm and said:

'*Sh!*'

'What is it, Tom?' And the two clung together with beating hearts.

'Sh! There 'tis again! Didn't you hear it?'

'I——'

'There! Now you hear it!'

'Lord, Tom, they're coming! They're coming, sure. What'll we do?'

'I dono. Think they'll see us?'

'Oh, Tom, they can see in the dark same as cats. I wish I hadn't come.'

'Oh, don't be afeard. I don't believe they'll bother us. We ain't doing any harm. If we keep perfectly still, maybe they won't notice us at all.'

'I'll try to, Tom, but Lord, I'm all of a shiver.'

'Listen!'

The boys bent their heads together and scarcely breathed. A muffled sound of voices floated up from the far end of the graveyard.

'Look! see there!' whispered Tom. 'What is it?'

'It's devil-fire. Oh, Tom, this is awful.'

Some vague figures approached through the gloom, swinging an old-fashioned tin lantern that freckled the ground with innumerable little spangles of light. Presently Huckleberry whispered with a shudder:

'It's the devils, sure enough. Three of 'em! Lordy, Tom, we're goners! Can you pray?'

'I'll try, but don't you be afeard. They ain't going to hurt us. "Now I lay me down to sleep, I——"'

'*Sh!*'

'What is it, Huck?'

'They're *humans*! One of 'em is, anyway. One of 'em's old Muff Potter's voice.'

'No – 'tain't so, is it?'

'I bet I know it. Don't you stir nor budge. He ain't sharp enough to notice us. Drunk, same as usual, likely – blamed old rip!'

'All right, I'll keep still. Now they're stuck. Can't find it. Here they come again. Now they're hot. Cold again. Hot again. Red-hot! They're pinted right, this time. Say, Huck, I know another o' them voices; it's Injun Joe.'

'That's so – that murderin' half-breed! I'd druther they was devils a dern sight. What kin they be up to?'

The whispers died wholly out now, for the three men had reached the grave, and stood within a few feet of the boys' hiding-place.

'Here it is,' said the third voice; and the owner of it held the lantern up and revealed the face of young Dr. Robinson.

Potter and Injun Joe were carrying a hand-barrow with a rope and a couple of shovels on it. They cast down their load and began to open the grave. The doctor put the lantern at the head of the grave, and came and sat down with his back against one of the elm-trees. He was so close the boys could have touched him.

'Hurry, men!' he said in a low voice. 'The moon might come out at any moment.'

They growled a response and went on digging. For some time there was no noise but the grating sound of the spades discharging their freight of mould and gravel. It was very monotonous. Finally a spade struck upon the coffin with a dull, woody accent, and within another minute or two the men had hoisted it out on the ground. They prised off the lid with their shovels, got out the body and dumped it rudely on the ground. The moon drifted from behind the clouds and exposed the pallid face. The barrow was got ready and the corpse placed on it, covered with a blanket, and bound to its place with the rope. Potter took out a large spring-knife and cut off the dangling end of the rope, and then said:

'Now the cussed thing's ready, Sawbones, and you'll just out with another five, or here she stays.'

'Injun Jo sprang to his feet . . . and snatched up Potter's knife'

'That's the talk!' said Injun Joe.

'Look here; what does this mean?' said the doctor. 'You required your pay in advance and I've paid you.'

'Yes, and you done more than that,' said Injun Joe, approaching the doctor, who was now standing. 'Five years ago you drove me away from your father's kitchen one night when I come to ask for something to eat, and you said I warn't there for any good; and when I swore I'd get even with you if it took a hundred years, your father had me jailed for a vagrant. Did you think I'd forget? The Injun blood ain't in me for nothing. And now I've got you, and you got to *settle*, you know!'

He was threatening the doctor with his fist in his face by this time. The doctor struck out suddenly, and stretched the ruffian on the ground. Potter dropped his knife, and exclaimed:

'Here, now, don't you strike my pard!' and the next moment he had grappled with the doctor, and the two were struggling with might and main, trampling the grass, and tearing the ground with their heels. Injun Joe sprang to his feet, his eyes flaming with passion, snatched up Potter's knife, and went creeping, catlike, and stooping round and round about the combatants, seeking an opportunity. All at once the doctor flung himself free, seized the heavy headboard of Williams's grave and felled Potter to the earth with it; and in the same instant the half-breed saw his chance, and drove the knife to the hilt in the young man's breast. He reeled and fell partly upon Potter, flooding him with his blood, and in the same moment the clouds blotted out the dreadful spectacle, and the two frightened boys went speeding away in the dark.

Presently, when the moon emerged again Injun Joe was standing over the two forms, contemplating them. The doctor murmured inarticulately, gave a long gasp or two, and was still. The half-breed muttered:

'That score is settled, damn you.'

Then he robbed the body. After which he put the fatal knife in Potter's open right hand, and sat down on the dismantled coffin. Three – four – five minutes passed, and then Potter began to stir and moan. His hand closed upon the knife, he raised it, glanced at it, and let it fall with a shudder. Then he sat up, pushing the body from him, and gazed at it and then around him confusedly. His eyes met Joe's.

'Lord, how is this, Joe?' he said.

'It's a dirty business,' said Joe, without moving. 'What did you do it for?'

'I! I never done it!'

'Look here! that kind of talk won't wash.'

Potter trembled and grew white.

'I thought I'd got sober. I'd no business to drink tonight. But it's in my head yet – worsen' when we started here. I'm all in a muddle; can't recollect anything of it hardly. Tell me, Joe – *honest*, now, old feller – did I do it, Joe? I never meant to; 'pon my soul and honour I never meant to, Joe. Tell me how it was, Joe. Oh, it's awful – and him so young and promising.'

'Why, you two was scuffling and he fetched you one with the headboard, and you fell flat; and then up you come, all reeling and staggering like, and snatched the knife and jammed it into him just as he fetched you another awful clip, and here you've laid dead as a wedge till now.'

'Oh, I didn't know what I was a doing. I wish I may die this minute if I did. It was all on accounts of the whisky and the excitement, I reckon. I never used a weapon in my life before, Joe. I've fought, but never with weapons. They'll all say that, Joe, don't tell! Say you won't tell, Joe; that's a good feller. I always liked you, Joe, and stood up for you too. Don't you remember? You won't tell, will you, Joe?' And the poor creature dropped on his knees before the stolid murderer, and clasped his appealing hands.

'No, you've always been fair and square with me, Muff Potter, and I won't go back on you. There, now, that's as fair as a man can say.'

'Oh, Joe, you're an angel! I'll bless you for this the longest day I live.' And Potter began to cry.

'Come, now, that's enough of that. This ain't any time for blubbering. You be off yonder way, and I'll go this. Move, now, and don't leave any tracks behind you.'

Potter started on a trot that quickly increased to a run. The half-breed stood looking after him. He muttered:

'If he's as much stunned with the lick and fuddled with the rum as he had the look of being, he won't think of the knife till he's gone so far he'll be afraid to come back after it to such a place by himself – chicken-heart!'

Two or three minutes later the murdered man, the blanketed corpse, the lidless coffin, and the open grave, were under no inspection but the moon's. The stillness was complete again, too.

Chapter 10

The two boys flew on and on towards the village, speechless with horror. They glanced backward over their shoulders from time to time apprehensively, as if they feared they might be followed. Every stump that started up in their path seemed a man and an enemy, and made them catch their breath; and as they sped by some outlying cottages that lay near the village, the barking of the aroused watch-dogs seemed to give wings to their feet.

'If we can only get to the old tannery before we break down!' whispered Tom, in short catches between breaths. 'I can't stand it much longer.'

Huckleberry's hard pantings were his only reply, and the boys fixed their eyes on the goal of their hopes, and bent to their work to win it. They gained steadily on it, and at last, breast to breast, they burst through the open door, and fell, grateful and exhausted, in the sheltering shadows beyond. By and by their pulses slowed down, and Tom whispered:

'Huckleberry, what do you reckon'll come of this?'

'If Dr. Robinson dies, I reckon hanging'll come of it.'

'Do you, though?'

'Why, I know it, Tom.'

Tom thought awhile; then he said:

'Who'll tell? We?'

'What are you talking about? S'pose something happened and Injun Joe didn't hang, why he'd kill us some time or other, just as dead sure as we're a lying here.'

'That's just what I was thinking to myself, Huck.'

'If anybody tells, let Muff Potter do it, if he's fool enough. He's generally drunk enough.'

Tom said nothing – went on thinking. Presently he whispered:

'Huck, Muff Potter don't know it. How can he tell?'

'What's the reason he don't know it?'

'Because he'd just got that whack when Injun Joe done it. D'you reckon he could see anything? D'you reckon he knowed anything?'

'By hokey, that's so, Tom!'

'And besides, look-a-here – maybe that whack done for him!'

'No, 'tain't likely, Tom. He had liquor in him; I could see that; and besides, he always has. Well, when Pap's full, you might take and belt him over the head with a church and you couldn't phase him. He says so his own self. So it's the same with Muff Potter, of course. But if a man was dead sober, I reckon, maybe that whack might fetch him; I dono.'

After another reflective silence, Tom said:

'Hucky, you sure you can keep mum?'

'Tom, we got to keep mum. You know that. That Injun devil wouldn't make any more of drownding us than a couple of cats, if we was to squeak 'bout this and they didn't hang him. Now look-a-here, Tom, less take and swear to one another – that's what we got to do – swear to keep mum.'

'I'm agreed, Huck. It's the best thing. Would you just hold hands and swear that we——'

'Oh, no, that wouldn't do for this. That's good enough for little rubbishy common things – specially with gals, cuz they go back on you any way, and blab if they get into a huff – but there orter be writing 'bout a big thing like this. And blood.'

Tom's whole being applauded this idea. It was deep, and dark, and awful; the hour, the circumstances, the surroundings, were in keeping with it. He picked up a clean pine shingle that lay in the moonlight, took a little fragment of 'red keel' out of his pocket, got the moon on his work, and painfully scrawled these lines, emphasizing each slow down-stroke by clamping his tongue between his teeth, and letting up the pressure on the up-strokes:

> "Huck Finn and
> Tom Sawyer swears
> they will keep mum
> about this and they
> wish they may drop
> down dead in their
> tracks if they ever
> tell and Rot."

Huckleberry was filled with admiration of Tom's facility in writing and the sublimity of his language. He at once took a pin from his lapel and was going to prick his flesh, but Tom said:

'Hold on! Don't do that. A pin's brass. It might have verdigrease on it.'

'What's verdigrease?'

'It's p'ison. That's what it is. You just swaller some of it once – you'll see.'

So Tom unwound the thread from one of his needles, and each boy pricked the ball of his thumb and squeezed out a drop of blood.

In time, after many squeezes, Tom managed to sign his initials, using the ball of his little finger for a pen. Then he showed Huckleberry how to make an H and an F, and the oath was complete. They buried the shingle close to the wall, with some dismal ceremonies and incantations, and the fetters that bound their tongues were considered to be locked and the key thrown away.

A figure crept stealthily through a break in the other end of the ruined building now, but they did not notice it.

'Tom,' whispered Huckleberry, 'does this keep us from ever telling – always?'

'Of course it does. It don't make any difference what happens, we got to keep mum. We'd drop down dead – don't you know that?'

'Yes, I reckon that's so.'

They continued to whisper for some little time. Presently a dog set up a long, lugubrious howl just outside – within ten feet of them. The boys clasped each other suddenly, in an agony of fright.

'Which of us does he mean?' gasped Huckleberry.

'I dono – peep through the crack. Quick!'

'No, you, Tom!'

'I can't – I can't do it, Huck!'

'Please, Tom. There 'tis again!'

'Oh, Lordy, I'm thankful!' whispered Tom. 'I know his voice. It's Bull Harbison.'[1]

'Oh, that's good – I tell you, Tom, I was most scared to death: I'd a bet anything it was a stray dog.'

The dog howled again. The boys' hearts sank once more.

'Oh, my! that ain't no Bull Harbison!' whispered Huckleberry. 'Do, Tom!'

Tom quaking with fear, yielded, and put his eye to the crack. His whisper was hardly audible when he said:

'Oh, Huck, it's A STRAY DOG!'

'Quick, Tom, quick! Who does he mean?'

'Huck, he must mean us both – we're right together.'

'Oh, Tom, I reckon we're goners. I reckon there ain't no mistake 'bout where I'll go to. I been so wicked.'

'Dad fetch it! This comes of playing hookey and doing everything a feller's told not to do. I might a been good, like Sid, if I'd tried – but no, I wouldn't, of course. But if ever I get off this time, I lay I'll just *waller* in Sunday-schools!'

And Tom began to snuffle a little.

'*You* bad!' And Huckleberry began to snuffle, too. 'Confound it, Tom Sawyer, you're just old pie 'longside o' what *I am*. Oh, *Lordy*, Lordy, Lordy, I wisht I only had half your chance.'

Tom choked off and whispered:

'Look, Hucky, look! He's got his *back* to us!'

Hucky looked with joy in his heart.

'Well he has, by jingoes! Did he before?'

'Yes, he did. But I, like a fool, never thought. Oh, this is bully, you know. *Now*, who can he mean?'

The howling stopped. Tom pricked up his ears.

'*Sh*! What's that?' he whispered.

'Sounds like – like hogs grunting. No – it's somebody snoring, Tom.'

'That *is* it? Where'bouts is it, Huck?'

'I b'leeve it's down at t'other end. Sounds so, anyway. Pap used to sleep there sometimes, 'long with the hogs, but, laws bless you, he just lifts things when he snores. Besides, I reckon he ain't ever coming back to this town any more.'

The spirit of adventure rose in the boys' souls once more.

'Hucky, do you das't to go if I lead?'

'I don't like to, much, Tom. S'pose it's Injun Joe!'

Tom quailed. But presently the temptation rose up strong again and the boys agreed to try, with the understanding that they would take to their heels if the snoring stopped. So they went tip-toeing stealthily down, the one behind the other. When they had got to within five steps of the snorer, Tom stepped on a stick, and it broke with a sharp snap. The man moaned, writhed a little, and his face came into the moonlight. It was Muff Potter. The boys' hearts had stood still, and their bodies too, when the man moved, but their fears passed away now. They tip-toed out, through the broken weatherboarding, and stopped at a little distance to exchange a parting word. That long, lugubrious howl rose on the night air again! They turned and saw the strange dog standing within a few feet of where Potter was lying, and facing Potter with his nose pointing heavenward.

'Oh, geeminy, it's *him*!' exclaimed both boys in a breath.

'Say, Tom, they say a stray dog came howling around Johnny Miller's house, 'bout midnight, as much as two weeks ago; and a whippowill come in and lit on the banisters and sung, the very same evening; and there ain't anybody dead there yet.'

'Well, I know that. And suppose there ain't. Didn't Gracie Miller fall in the kitchen fire and burn herself terrible the very next Saturday?'

'Yes, but she ain't *dead*. And what's more, she's getting better too.'

'All right; you wait and see. She's a goner, just as dead sure as Muff Potter's a goner. That's what the niggers say, and they know all about these kind of things, Huck.'

Then they separated, cogitating.

When Tom crept in at his bedroom window, the night was almost spent. He undressed with excessive caution, and fell asleep congratulating himself that nobody knew of his escapade. He was not aware that the gently snoring Sid was awake, and had been so for an hour.

When Tom awoke, Sid was dressed and gone. There was a late look in the light, a late atmosphere. He was startled. Why had he not been called – persecuted till he was up as usual? The thought filled him with bodings. Within five minutes he was dressed and downstairs, feeling sore and drowsy. The family were still at table, but they had finished breakfast. There was no voice of rebuke; but there were averted eyes; there was a silence and an air of solemnity that struck a chill to the culprit's heart. He sat down and tried to seem gay, but it was up-hill work; it roused no smile, no response, and he lapsed into silence and let his heart sink down to the depths.

After breakfast his aunt took him aside, and Tom almost brightened in the hope that he was going to be flogged; but it was not so. His aunt wept over him and asked him how he could go and break her old heart so; and finally told him to go on, and ruin himself, and bring her grey hairs with sorrow to the grave, for it was no use for her to try any more. This was worse than a thousand whippings, and Tom's heart was sorer now than his body. He cried, he pleaded for forgiveness, promised reform over and over again, and then received his dismissal, feeling that he had won but an imperfect forgiveness and established but a feeble confidence.

He left the presence too miserable to even feel vengeful towards Sid; and so the latter's prompt retreat through the back gate was unnecessary. He moped to school gloomy and sad, and took his flogging along with Joe Harper for playing hookey the day before, with the air of one whose heart was busy with heavier woes and wholly dead to trifles. Then he betook himself to his seat, rested his elbows on his desk and his jaws in his hands, and stared at the wall with the stony stare of suffering that has reached the limit and can no further go. His elbow was pressing against some hard substance. After a long time he slowly and sadly changed his position, and took up this object with a sigh. It was in a paper. He unrolled it. A long, lingering, colossal sigh followed, and his heart broke. It was his brass andiron knob! This final feather broke the camel's back.

1   If Mr. Harbison had owned a slave named Bull, Tom would have spoken of him as 'Harbison's Bull'; but a son or a dog of that name was 'Bull Harbison'.

Chapter 11

Close upon the hour of noon the whole village was suddenly electrified with the ghastly news. No need of the as yet undreamed-of telegraph; the tale flew from man to man, from group to group, from house to house with little less than telegraphic speed. Of course the schoolmaster gave holiday for that afternoon; the town would have thought strangely of him if he had not. A gory knife had been found close to the murdered man, and it had been recognized by somebody as belonging to Muff Potter – so the story ran. And it was said that a belated citizen had come upon Potter washing himself in the 'branch' about one or two o'clock in the morning, and that Potter had at once sneaked off – suspicious circumstances, especially the washing, which was not a habit with Potter. It was also said that the town had been ransacked for this 'murderer' (the public are not slow in the matter of sifting evidence and arriving at a verdict), but that he could not be found. Horsemen had departed down all the roads in every direction, and the Sheriff was confident that he would be captured before night.

All the town was drifting towards the graveyard. Tom's heartbreak vanished, and he joined the procession, not because he would not a thousand times rather go anywhere else, but because an awful, unaccountable fascination drew him on. Arrived at the dreadful place, he wormed his small body through the crowd and saw the dismal spectacle. It seemed to him an age since he was there before. Somebody pinched his arm. He turned, and his eyes met Huckleberry's. Then both looked elsewhere at once, and wondered if anybody had noticed anything in their mutual glance. But everybody was talking, and intent upon the grisly spectacle before them.

'Poor fellow!' 'Poor young fellow!' 'This ought to be a lesson to grave-robbers!' 'Muff Potter'll hang for this if they catch him!' This was the drift of remark, and the minister said, 'It was a judgement; His hand is here.'

Now Tom shivered from head to heel; for his eye fell upon the stolid face of Injun Joe. At this moment the crowd began to sway and struggle, and voices shouted, 'It's him! it's him! he's coming himself!'

'Who? who?' from twenty voices.

'Muff Potter!'

'Hallo, he's stopped! Look out, he's turning! Don't let him get away!'

People in the branches of the trees over Tom's head said he wasn't trying to get away – he only looked doubtful and perplexed.

'Infernal impudence!' said a bystander; 'wanted to come and take a quiet look at his work – didn't expect any company.'

The crowd fell apart now, and the Sheriff came through ostentatiously, leading Potter by the arm. The poor fellow's face was haggard, and his eyes showed the fear that was upon him. When he stood before the murdered man, he shook as with a palsy, and he put his face in his hands and burst into tears.

'I didn't do it, friends,' he sobbed; ''pon my word and honour I never done it.'

'Who's accused you?' shouted a voice.

This shot seemed to carry home. Potter lifted his face and looked around him with a pathetic hopelessness in his eyes. He saw Injun Joe, and exclaimed:

'Oh, Injun Joe, you promised me you'd never——'

'Is that your knife?' and it was thrust before him by the Sheriff.

Potter would have fallen if they had not caught him and eased him to the ground. Then he said:

'Something told me 't if I didn't come back and get——' He shuddered; then waved his nerveless hand with a vanquished gesture and said, 'Tell 'em, Joe' tell 'em – it ain't no use any more.'

Then Huckleberry and Tom stood dumb and staring, and heard the stony-hearted liar reel off his serene statement, they expecting every moment that the clear sky would deliver God's lightnings upon his head, and wondering to see how long the stroke was delayed. And when he had finished and still stood alive and whole, their wavering impulse to break their oath and save the poor betrayed prisoner's life faded and vanished away, for plainly this miscreant had sold himself to Satan, and it would be fatal to meddle with the property of such a power as that.

'Why didn't you leave? What did you want to come here for?' somebody said.

'I couldn't help it – I couldn't help it.' Potter moaned. 'I wanted to run away, but I couldn't seem to come anywhere but here.' And he fell to sobbing again.

Injun Joe repeated his statement, just as calmly, a few minutes afterwards on the inquest, under oath; and the boys, seeing that the lightnings were still withheld, were confirmed in their belief that Joe had sold himself to the devil. He was now become, to them, the most balefully interesting object they had ever looked upon, and they could not take their fascinated eyes from his face. They inwardly resolved to watch him, nights, when opportunity should offer, in the hope of getting a glimpse of his dread master.

Injun Joe helped to raise the body of the murdered man, and put it in a wagon for removal; and it was whispered through the shuddering crowd that the wound bled a little! The boys thought that this happy circumstance would turn suspicion in the right direction; but they were disappointed, for more than one villager remarked:

'It was within three feet of Muff Potter when it done it.'

Tom's fearful secret and gnawing conscience disturbed his sleep for as much as a week after this; and at breakfast one morning Sid said:

'Tom, you pitch around and talk in your sleep so much that you keep me awake about half the time.'

Tom blanched and dropped his eyes.

'It's a bad sign,' said Aunt Polly, gravely. 'What you got on your mind, Tom?'

'Nothing. Nothing 't I know of.' But the boy's hand shook so that he spilled his coffee.

'And you do talk such stuff,' Sid said. 'Last night you said, "It's blood, it's blood, that's what it is!" You said that over and over. And you said, "Don't torment me so – I'll tell." Tell what? What is it you'll tell?'

Everything was swimming before Tom. There is no telling what might have happened now, but luckily the concern passed out of Aunt Polly's face, and she came to Tom's relief without knowing it. She said:

'Sho! It's that dreadful murder. I dream about it most every night myself. Sometimes I dream it's me that done it.'

Mary said she had been affected much the same way. Sid seemed satisfied. Tom got out of the presence as quickly as he plausibly could, and after that he complained of toothache for a week, and tied up his jaws every night. He never knew that Sid lay nightly watching, and frequently slipped the bandage free, and then leaned on his elbow listening a good while at a time, and afterwards slipped the bandage back to its place again. Tom's distress of mind wore off gradually, and the toothache grew irksome and was discarded. If Sid really managed to make anything out of Tom's disjointed mutterings, he kept it to himself.

It seemed to Tom that his schoolmates never would get done holding inquests on dead cats, and thus keeping his trouble present to his mind. Sid noticed that Tom never was coroner at one of these inquiries, though it had been his habit to take the lead in all new enterprises; he noticed, too, that Tom never acted as a witness – and that was strange; and Sid did not overlook the fact that Tom even showed a marked aversion to the inquests, and always avoided them when he could. Sid marvelled, but said nothing. However, even inquests went out of vogue at last, and ceased to torture Tom's conscience.

Every day or two during this time of sorrow, Tom watched his opportunity and went to the little grated jail window and smuggled such small comforts through to the 'murderer' as he could get hold of. The jail was a trifling little brick den that stood in a marsh at the edge of the village, and no guards were afforded for it; indeed, it was seldom occupied. These offerings greatly helped to ease Tom's conscience.

The villagers had a strong desire to tar-and-feather Injun Joe and ride him on a rail for body-snatching, but so formidable was his character that nobody could be found who was willing to take the lead in the matter, so it was dropped. He had been careful to begin both of his inquest-statements with the fight, without confessing the grave-robbery that preceded it; therefore it was deemed wisest not to try the case in the court at present.

Chapter 12

One of the reasons why Tom's mind had drifted away from its secret troubles was that it had found a new and weighty matter to interest itself about. Becky Thatcher had stopped coming to school. Tom had struggled with his pride a few days, and tried to 'whistle her down the wind', but failed. He began to find himself hanging around her father's house, nights, and feeling very miserable. She was sick. What if she should die! There was distraction in the thought. He no longer took an interest in war, nor even in piracy. The charm of life was gone, there was nothing but dreariness left. He put his hoop away, and his bat; there was no joy in them any more. His aunt was concerned; she began to try all manner of medicines on him. She was one of those people who are infatuated with patent medicines and all new-fangled methods of producing health or mending it. She was an inveterate experimenter in these things. When something fresh in this line came out she was in a fever right away to try it; not on herself, for she was never ailing; but on anybody else that came handy. She was a subscriber for all the 'Health' periodicals and phrenological frauds; and the solemn ignorance they were inflated with was breath to her nostrils. All the rot they contained about ventilation, and how to go to bed, and how to get up, and what to eat, and what to drink, and how much exercise to take, and what frame of mind to keep oneself in, and what sort of clothing to wear, was all gospel to her, and she never observed that her health journals of the current month customarily upset everything they had recommended the month before. She was as simple-hearted and honest as the day was long, and so she was an easy victim. She gathered together her quack periodicals and her quack medicines, and, thus armed with death, went about on her pale horse, metaphorically speaking, with 'hell following after'. But she never suspected that she was not an angel of healing and the balm of Gilead in disguise to the suffering neighbours.

The water treatment was new, now, and Tom's low condition was a windfall to her. She had him out at daylight every morning, stood him up in the wood-shed and drowned him with a deluge of cold water; then she scrubbed him down with a towel like a file, and so brought him to; then she rolled him up in a wet sheet and put him away under blankets till she sweated his soul clean and 'the yellow stains of it came through his pores', as Tom said.

Yet notwithstanding all this the boy grew more and more melancholy and pale and dejected. She added hot baths, sitz baths, and plunges. The boy remained as dismal as a hearse. She began to assist the water with a slim oatmeal diet and blister plasters. She calculated his capacity as she would a jug's, and filled him up every day with quack cure-alls.

Tom had become indifferent to persecution by this time. This phase filled the old lady's heart with consternation. This indifference must be broken up at any cost. Now she heard of Pain-killer for the first time. She ordered a lot at once. She tasted it and was filled with gratitude. It was simply fire in a liquid form. She dropped the water treatment and everything else, and pinned her faith to Pain-killer. She gave Tom a teaspoonful and watched with the deepest anxiety for the result. Her troubles were instantly at rest, her soul at peace again; for the 'indifference' was broken up. The boy could not have shown a wilder, heartier interest if she had built a fire under him.

Tom felt that it was time to wake up; this sort of life might be romantic enough in his blighted condition, but it was getting to have too little sentiment and too much distracting variety about it. So he thought over various plans for relief, and finally hit upon that of professing to be fond of Pain-killer. He asked for it so often that he became a nuisance, and his aunt ended by telling him to help himself and quit bothering her. If it had been Sid she would have had no misgivings to alloy her delight; but since it was Tom she watched the bottle clandestinely. She found that the medicine did really diminish, but it did not occur to her that the boy was mending the health of a crack in the sitting room floor with it.

One day Tom was in the act of dosing the crack when his aunt's yellow cat came along, purring, eyeing the tea-spoon avariciously, and begging for a taste, Tom said:

'Don't ask for it unless you want it, Peter.'

But Peter signified that he did want it.

'You better make sure.'

Peter was sure.

'Now you've asked for it, and I'll give it to you, because there ain't anything mean about *me*; but if you find you don't like it you mustn't blame anybody but your own self.'

Peter was agreeable, so Tom pried his mouth open and poured down the Pain-killer. Peter sprang a couple of yards into the air, and then delivered a war-whoop and set off round and round the room, banging against furniture, upsetting flower-pots, and making general havoc. Next he rose on his hind feet and pranced around, in a frenzy of enjoyment, with his head over his shoulder and his voice proclaiming his unappeasable happiness. Then he went tearing around the house again, spreading chaos and destruction in his path. Aunt Polly entered in time to see him throw a few double summersets, deliver a final mighty hurrah, and sail through the open window, carrying the rest of the flower-pots with him. The old lady stood petrified with astonishment, peering over her glasses; Tom lay on the floor, expiring with laughter.

'Tom, what on earth ails that cat?'

'*I* don't know, Aunt,' gasped the boy.

'Why, I never seen anything like it. What *did* make him act so?'

''Deed I don't know, Aunt Polly; cats always act so when they're having a good time.'

'They do, do they?' There was something in the tone that made Tom apprehensive.

'Yes'm. That is, I believe they do.'

'You *do*?'

'Yes'm.'

The old lady was bending down, Tom watching with interest emphasized by anxiety. Too late he divined her 'drift'. The handle of the tell-tale teaspoon was visible under the bed-valance. Aunt Polly took it, held it up. Tom winced, and dropped his eyes. Aunt Polly raised him by the usual handle – his ear – and cracked his head soundly with her thimble.

'Now, sir, what did you want to treat that poor dumb beast so for?'

'I done it out of pity for him – because he hadn't any aunt.'

'Hadn't any aunt! – you numskull. What has that got to do with it?'

'Heaps. Because if he'd a had one she'd a burnt him out herself! She'd a roasted his bowels out of him 'thout any more feeling than if he was a human!'

Aunt Polly felt a sudden pang of remorse. This was putting the thing in a new light; what was cruelty to a cat *might* be cruelty to a boy too. She began to soften: she felt sorry. Her eyes watered a little, and she put her hand on Tom's head and said gently:

'I was meaning for the best, Tom. And, Tom, it *did* do you good.'

Tom looked up in her face with just a perceptible twinkle peeping through his gravity:

'I know you was meaning for the best, Aunty, and so was I with Peter. It done *him* good, too. I never see him get around so nice——'

'Oh, go 'long with you, Tom, before you aggravate me again. And you try and see if you can't be a good boy for once, and you needn't take any more medicine.'

Tom reached school ahead of time. It was noticed that this strange thing had been occurring every day latterly. And now, as usual of late, he hung about the gate of the school-yard instead of playing with his comrades. He was sick, he said; and he looked it. He tried to seem to be looking everywhere but whither he was really looking – down the road. Presently Jeff Thatcher hove in sight, and Tom's face lighted; he gazed a moment, and then turned sorrowfully away. When Jeff Thatcher arrived, Tom accosted him, and 'led up' warily to opportunities for remark about Becky, but the giddy lad never could see the bait. Tom watched and watched, hoping whenever a frisking frock came in sight, and hating the owner of it as soon as he saw she was not the right one. At last frocks ceased to appear, and he dropped hopelessly into the dumps; he entered the empty school-house and sat down to suffer. Then one more frock passed in at the gate, and Tom's heart gave a great bound. The next instant he was out, and 'going on' like an Indian; yelling, laughing, chasing boys, jumping over the fence at risk of life and limb, throwing handsprings, standing on his head – doing all the heroic things he could conceive of, and keeping a furtive eye out, all the while, to see if Becky · Thatcher was noticing. But she seemed to be unconscious of it all; she never looked. Could it be possible that she was not aware that he was there? He carried his exploits to her immediate vicinity; came war-whooping around, snatched a boy's cap, hurled it to the roof of the school-house, broke through a group of boys, tumbling them in every direction, and fell sprawling himself under Becky's nose, almost upsetting her – and she turned, with her nose in the air, and he heard her say, 'Mf! some people think they're mighty smart – always showing off!'

Tom's cheeks burned. He gathered himself up and sneaked off, crushed and crestfallen.

Chapter 13

Tom's mind was made up now. He was gloomy and desperate. He was a forsaken, friendless boy, he said; nobody loved him; when they found out what they had driven him to, perhaps they would be sorry; he had tried to do right and get along, but they would not let him; since nothing would do them but to be rid of him, let it be so; and let them blame him for the consequences – why shouldn't they? what right had the friendless to complain? Yes, they had forced him to it at last: he would lead a life of crime. There was no choice. By this time he was far down Meadow Lane, and the bell for school to 'take up' tinkled faintly upon his ear. He sobbed, now, to think he should never, never hear that old familiar sound any more – it was very hard, but it was forced on him; since he was driven out into the cold world, he must submit – but he forgave them. Then the sobs came thick and fast.

Just at this point he met his soul's sworn comrade, Joe Harper – hard-eyed, and with evidently a great and dismal purpose in his heart. Plainly here were 'two souls with but a single thought'. Tom, wiping his eyes with his sleeve, began to blubber out something about a resolution to escape from hard usage and lack of sympathy at home by roaming abroad into the great world, never to return; and ended by hoping that Joe would not forget him.

But it transpired that this was a request which Joe had just been going to make of Tom, and had come to hunt him up for that purpose. His mother had whipped him for drinking some cream which he had never tasted and knew nothing about; it was plain that she was tired of him and wished him to go; if she felt that way, there was nothing for him to do but to succumb; he hoped she would be happy, and never regret having driven her poor boy out into the unfeeling world to suffer and die.

As the two boys walked sorrowing along, they made a new compact to stand by each other and be brothers, and never separate till death relieved them of their troubles. Then they began to lay their plans. Joe was for being a hermit, and living on crusts in a remote cave, and dying, sometime, of cold, and want, and grief; but, after listening to Tom, he conceded that there were some conspicuous advantages about a life of crime, and so he consented to be a pirate.

Three miles below St Petersburg, at a point where the Mississippi river was a trifle over a mile wide, there was a long, narrow, wooded island, with a shallow bar at the head of it, and this offered well as a rendezvous. It was not inhabited; it lay far over towards the farther shore, abreast a dense and almost wholly unpeopled forest. So Jackson's Island was chosen. Who were to be the subjects of their piracies was a matter that did not occur to them. Then they hunted up Huckleberry Finn, and he joined them promptly, for all careers were one to him; he was indifferent. They presently separated, to meet at a lonely spot on the river bank two miles above the village, at the favourite hour, which was midnight. There was a small log raft there which they meant to capture. Each would bring hooks and lines, and such provisions as he could steal in the most dark and mysterious way – as became outlaws; and before the afternoon was done, they had all managed to enjoy the sweet glory of spreading the fact that pretty soon the town would 'hear something'. All who got this vague hint were cautioned to 'be mum and wait'.

About midnight Tom arrived with a boiled ham and a few trifles, and stopped in a dense undergrowth on a small bluff overlooking the meeting-place. It was starlight, and very still. The mighty river lay like an ocean at rest. Tom listened a moment, but no sound disturbed the quiet. Then he gave a low, distinct whistle. It was answered from under the bluff. Tom whistled twice more; these signals were answered in the same way. Then a guarded voice said:

'Who goes there?'

'Tom Sawyer, the Black Avenger of the Spanish Main. Name your names.'

'Huck Finn the Red-handed, and Joe Harper the Terror of the Seas.' Tom had furnished these titles from his favourite literature.

''Tis well. Give the countersign.'

Two hoarse whispers delivered the same awful word simultaneously to the brooding night:

'BLOOD!'

Then Tom tumbled his ham over the bluff and let himself down after it, tearing both skin and clothes to some extent in the effort. There was an easy, comfortable path along the shore under the bluff, but it lacked the advantages of difficulty and danger so valued by a pirate.

The Terror of the Seas had brought a side of bacon, and had about worn himself out with getting it there. Finn the Red-handed had stolen a skillet, and a quantity of half-cured leaf-tobacco, and had also brought a few corn-cobs to make pipes with. But none of the pirates smoked or 'chewed' but himself. The Black Avenger of the Spanish Main said it would never do to start without some fire. That was a wise thought; matches were hardly known there in that day. They saw a fire smouldering upon a great raft a hundred yards above, and they went stealthily thither and helped themselves to a chunk. They made an imposing adventure of it, saying 'hist' every now and then and suddenly halting with finger on lip; moving with hands on imaginary dagger-hilts; and giving orders in dismal whispers that if 'the foe' stirred to 'let him have it to the hilt', because 'dead men tell no tales'. They knew well enough that the raftmen were all down at the village laying in stores or having a spree, but still that was no excuse for their conducting this thing in an unpiratical way.

They shoved off presently, Tom in command, Huck at the left oar and Joe at the forward. Tom stood amidships, gloomy-browed and with folded arms, and gave his orders in a low, stern whisper.

'Luff, and bring her to the wind!'

'Aye, aye, sir!'

'Steady, stead-y-y-y!'

'Steady it is, sir!'

'Let her go off a point!'

'Point it is, sir!'

As the boys steadily and monotonously drove the raft towards mid-stream, it was no doubt understood that these orders were given only for 'style', and were not intended to mean anything in particular.

'What sail's she carrying?'

'Courses, tops'ls, and flying-jib, sir!'

'Send the r'yals up! Lay out aloft there, half a dozen of ye, foretomast-stuns'l! Lively, now!'

'Aye, aye, sir!'

'Shake out that mainto-galans'l! Sheets and braces! *Now*, my hearties!'

'Aye, aye, sir!'

'Hellum-a-lee – hard a-port! Stand by to meet her when she comes! Port, port! *Now*, men! With a will! Stead-y-y!'

'Steady it is, sir!'

The raft drew beyond the middle of the river; the boys pointed her head right and then lay on their oars. The river was not high, so there was not more than a two or three mile current. Hardly a word was said during the next three-quarters of an hour. Now the raft was passing before the distant town. Two or three glimmering lights showed where it lay, peacefully sleeping, beyond the vague vast sweep of star-gemmed water, unconscious of the tremendous event that was happening. The Black Avenger stood still with folded arms, 'looking his last' upon the scene of his former joys and his later sufferings, and wishing 'she' could see him, now abroad on the wild sea, facing peril and death with dauntless heart, going to his doom with a grim smile on his lips. It was but a small strain on his imagination to remove Jackson's Island beyond eye-shot of the village, and so he 'looked his last' with a broken and satisfied heart. The other pirates were looking their last, too; and they all looked so long that they came near letting the current drift them out of the range of the island. But they discovered the danger in time, and made shift to avert it. About two o'clock in the morning the raft grounded on the bar two hundred yards above the head of the island, and they waded back and forth until they had landed their freight. Part of the little raft's belongings consisted of an old sail, and this they spread over a nook in the bushes for a tent to shelter their provisions; but they themselves would sleep in the open air in good weather, as became outlaws.

They built a fire against the side of a great log twenty or thirty steps within the sombre depths of the forest, and then cooked some bacon in the frying-pan for supper, and used up half of the corn 'pone' stock they had brought. It seemed glorious sport to be feasting in that wild free way in the virgin forest of an unexplored and uninhabited island, far from the haunts of men, and they said they would never return to civilization. The climbing fire lit up their faces and threw its ruddy glare upon the pillared tree-trunks of their forest temple, and upon the varnished foliage and festooning vines. When the last crisp slice of bacon was gone, and the last allowance of corn pone devoured, the boys stretched themselves out on the grass, filled with contentment. They could have found a cooler place, but they would not deny themselves such a romantic feature as the roasting campfire.

'*Ain't* it jolly?' said Joe.

'It's *nuts*,' said Tom.

'What would the boys say if they could see us?'

'Say? Well, they'd just die to be here – hey, Hucky?'

'I reckon so,' said Huckleberry; 'anyways *I'm* suited. I don't want nothing better'n this. I don't ever get enough to eat gen'ally – and here they can't come and kick at a feller and bullyrag him so.'

'It's just the life for me,' said Tom. 'You don't have to get up, mornings, and you don't have to go to school, and wash, and all that blame foolishness.'

'You see a pirate don't have to do *anything*, Joe, when he's ashore, but a hermit *he* has to be praying considerable, and then he don't have any fun, any way, all by himself that way.'

'Oh yes, that's so,' said Joe, 'but I hadn't thought much about it, you know. I'd a good deal ruther be a pirate now that I've tried it.'

'You see,' said Tom, 'people don't go much on hermits, now-a-days, like they used to in old times, but a pirate's always respected. And a hermit's got to sleep on the hardest place he can find, and put sackcloth and ashes on his head, and stand out in the rain, and——'

'What does he put sackcloth and ashes on his head for?' inquired Huck.

'*I* dunno. But they've *got* to do it. Hermits always do. You'd have to do that if you was a hermit.'

'Dern'd if I would,' said Huck.

'Well, what would you do?'

'I dunno. But I wouldn't do that.'

'Why, Huck, you'd *have* to. How'd you get around it?'

'Why, I just wouldn't stand it. I'd run away.'

'Run away! Well, you *would* be a nice old slouch of a hermit. You'd be a disgrace.'

The Red-handed made no response, being better employed. He had finished gouging out a cob, and now he fitted a weed stem to it, Loaded it with tobacco, and was pressing a coal to the charge and blowing a cloud of fragrant smoke; he was in the full bloom of luxurious contentment. The other pirates envied him this majestic vice, and secretly resolved to acquire it shortly. Presently Huck said:

'What does pirates have to do?'

Tom said:

'Oh, they have just a bully time – take ships, and burn them, and get the money and bury it in awful places in their island where there's ghosts and things to watch it, and kill everybody in the ships – make 'em walk a plank.'

'And they carry the women to the island,' said Joe; 'they don't kill the women.'

'No,' assented Tom, 'they don't kill the women – they're too noble. And the women's always beautiful, too.'

'And don't they wear the bulliest clothes! Oh, no! All gold and silver and di'monds,' said Joe with enthusiasm.

'Who?' said Huck.

'Why, the pirates.'

Huck scanned his own clothing forlornly.

'I reckon I ain't dressed fitten for a pirate,' said he, with a regretful pathos in his voice; 'but I ain't got none but these.'

But the other boys told him the fine clothes would come fast enough after they should have begun their adventures. They made him understand that his poor rags would do to begin with, though it was customary for wealthy pirates to start with a proper wardrobe.

Gradually their talk died out and drowsiness began to steal upon the eyelids of the little waifs. The pipe dropped from the fingers of the Red-handed, and he slept the sleep of the conscience-free and the weary. The Terror of the Seas and the Black Avenger of the Spanish Main had more difficulty in getting to sleep. They said their prayers inwardly, and lying down, since there was nobody there with authority to make them kneel and recite aloud; in truth they had a mind not to say them at all, but they were afraid to proceed to such lengths as that, lest they might call down a sudden and special thunder-bolt from heaven. Then at once they reached and hovered upon the imminent verge of sleep – but an intruder came now that would not 'down'. It was conscience. They began to feel a vague fear that they had been doing wrong to run away; and next they thought of the stolen meat, and then the real torture came. They tried to argue it away by reminding conscience that they had purloined sweetmeats and apples scores of times; but conscience was not to be appeased by such thin plausibilities. It seemed to them, in the end, that there was no getting around the stubborn fact that taking sweetmeats was only 'hooking' while taking bacon and ham and such valuables was plain, simple stealing – and there was a command against that in the Bible. So they inwardly resolved that so long as they remained in the business, their piracies should not again be sullied with the crime of stealing. Then conscience granted a truce, and these curiously inconsistent pirates fell peacefully to sleep.

Chapter 14

When Tom awoke in the morning, he wondered where he was. He sat up and rubbed his eyes and looked around; then he comprehended. It was the cool grey dawn, and there was a delicious sense of repose and peace in the deep pervading calm and silence of the woods. Not a leaf stirred; not a sound obtruded upon great Nature's meditation. Beaded dewdrops stood upon the leaves and grasses. A white layer of ashes covered the fire, and a thin blue wreath of smoke rose straight into the air. Joe and Huck still slept. Now, far away in the woods, a bird called; another answered; presently the hammering of a woodpecker was heard. Gradually the cool dim grey of the morning whitened, and as gradually sounds multiplied and life manifested itself. The marvel of Nature shaking off sleep and going to work unfolded itself to the musing boy. A little green worm came crawling over a dewy leaf, lifting two- . thirds of his body into the air from time to time, 'sniffling around', then proceeding again, for he was measuring, Tom said; and when the worm approached him of his own accord, he sat as still as a stone, with his hopes rising and falling by turns as the creature still came towards him or seemed inclined to go elsewhere; and when at last it considered a painful moment with its curved body in the air and then came decisively down upon Tom's leg and began a journey over him, his whole heart was glad – for that meant that he was going to have a new suit of clothes – without the shadow of a doubt, a gaudy piratical uniform. Now a procession of ants appeared, from nowhere in particular, and went about their labours; one struggled manfully by with a dead spider five times as big as itself in its arms, and lugged it straight up a tree-trunk. A brown spotted lady-bug climbed the dizzy heights of a grass-blade, and Tom bent down close to it and said:

> Lady-bug, lady-bug, fly away home,
> Your house is on fire, your children's alone;

and she took wing and went off to see about it – which did not surprise the boy, for he knew of old that this insect was credulous about conflagrations, and he had practised upon its simplicity more than once. A tumble-bug came next, heaving sturdily at its ball, and Tom touched the creature, to see it shut its legs against its body and pretend to be dead. The birds were fairly rioting by this time. A cat-bird, the northern mocker, lit in a tree over Tom's head, and trilled out her imitations of her neighbours in a rapture of enjoyment; then a shrill jay swept down, a flash of blue flame, and stopped on a twig almost within the boy's reach, cocked his head to one side, and eyed the strangers with a consuming curiosity; a grey squirrel and a big fellow of the 'fox' kind came scurrying along, sitting up at intervals to inspect and chatter at the boys, for the wild things had probably never seen a human being before, and scarcely knew whether to be afraid or not. All Nature was wide awake and stirring now, long lances of sunlight pierced down through the dense foliage far and near, and a few butterflies came fluttering upon the scene.

Tom stirred up the other pirates and they all clattered away with a shout, and in a minute or two were stripped and chasing after and tumbling over each other in the shallow limpid water of the white sand-bar. They felt no longing for the little village sleeping in the distance beyond the majestic waste of water. A vagrant current or a slight rise in the river had carried off their raft, but this only gratified them, since its going was something like burning the bridge between them and civilization.

They came back to camp wonderfully refreshed, glad-hearted, and ravenous; and they soon had the campfire blazing up again. Huck found a spring of clear cold water close by, and the boys made cups of broad oak or hickory leaves, and felt that water, sweetened with such a wild-wood charm as that, would be a good enough substitute for coffee. While Joe was slicing bacon for breakfast, Tom and Huck asked him to hold on a minute; they stepped to a promising nook in the river bank and threw in their lines; almost immediately they had reward. Joe had not had time to get impatient before they were back again with some handsome bass, a couple of sun-perch, and a small catfish – provision enough for quite a family. They fried the fish with the bacon and were astonished; for no fish had ever seemed so delicious before. They did not know that the quicker a freshwater fish is on the fire after he is caught the better he is; and they reflected little upon what a sauce open-air sleeping, open-air exercise, bathing, and a large ingredient of hunger make, too.

They lay around in the shade after breakfast, while Huck had a smoke, and then went off through the woods on an exploring expedition. They tramped gaily along, over decaying logs, through tangled underbrush, among solemn monarchs of the forest, hung from their crowns to the ground with a drooping regalia of grape-vines. Now and then they came upon snug nooks carpeted with grass and jewelled with flowers.

They found plenty of things to be delighted with, but nothing to be astonished at. They discovered that the island was about three miles long and a quarter of a mile wide, and that the shore it lay closest to was only separated from it by a narrow channel hardly two hundred yards wide. They took a swim about every hour, so it was close upon the middle of the afternoon when they got back to camp. They were too hungry to stop to fish, but they fared sumptuously upon cold ham, and then threw themselves down in the shade to talk. But the talk soon began to drag, and then died. The stillness, the solemnity, that brooded in the woods, and the sense of loneliness, began to tell upon the spirits of the boys. They fell to thinking. A sort of undefined longing crept upon them. This took dim shape presently – it was budding homesickness. Even Finn the Red-handed was dreaming of his door-steps and empty hogsheads. But they were all ashamed of their weakness, and none was brave enough to speak his thought.

For some time, now, the boys had been dully conscious of a peculiar sound in the distance, just as one sometimes is of the ticking of a clock which he takes no distinct note of. But now this mysterious sound became more pronounced, and forced a recognition. The boys started, glanced at each other, and then each assumed a listening attitude. There was a long silence, profound and unbroken; then a deep, sullen boom came floating down out of the distance.

'What is it?' exclaimed Joe, under his breath.

'I wonder,' said Tom in a whisper.

'''Tain't thunder,' said Huckleberry, in an awed tone, 'becuz thunder——'

'Hark!' said Tom; 'listen – don't talk.'

They waited a time that seemed an age, and then the same muffled boom troubled the solemn hush.

'Let's go and see.'

They sprang to their feet and hurried to the shore towards the town. They parted the bushes on the bank and peered out over the water. The little steam ferry-boat was about a mile below the village, drifting with the current. Her broad deck seemed crowded with people. There were a great many skiffs rowing about or floating with the stream in the neighbourhood of the ferry-boat, but the boys could not determine what the men in them were doing. Presently a great jet of white smoke burst from the ferry-boat's side, and as it expanded and rose in a lazy cloud, that same dull throb of sound was borne to the listeners again.

'I know now!' exclaimed Tom; 'somebody's drownded!'

'That's it,' said Huck; 'they done that last summer when Bill Turner got drownded; they shoot a cannon over the water, and that makes him come up to the top. Yes, and they take loaves of bread and put quicksilver in 'em and set 'em afloat, and wherever there's anybody that's drownded, they'll float right there and stop.'

'Yes, I've heard about that,' said Joe. 'I wonder what makes the bread do that.'

'Oh, it ain't the bread so much,' said Tom; 'I reckon it's mostly what they *say* over it before they start it out.'

'But they don't say anything over it,' said Huck. 'I've seen 'em, and they don't.'

'Well, that's funny,' said Tom. 'But maybe they say it to themselves. Of *course* they do. Anybody might know that.'

The others agreed that there was reason in what Tom said, because an ignorant lump of bread, uninstructed by an incantation, could not be expected to act very intelligently when sent upon an errand of such gravity.

'By jings, I wish I was over there now,' said Joe.

'I do too,' said Huck. 'I'd give heaps to know who it is.'

The boys still listened and watched. Presently a revealing thought flashed through Tom's mind, and he exclaimed:

'Boys, I know who's drownded; it's us!'

They felt like heroes in an instant. Here was a gorgeous triumph; they were missed; they were mourned; hearts were breaking on their account; tears were being shed; accusing memories of unkindnesses to these poor lost lads were rising up, and unavailing regrets and remorse were being indulged; and best of all, the departed were the talk of the whole town, and the envy of all the boys, as far as this dazzling notoriety was concerned. This was fine. It was worth while to be a pirate, after all.

As twilight drew on, the ferry-boat went back to her accustomed business and the skiffs disappeared. The pirates returned to camp. They were jubilant with vanity over their new grandeur and the illustrious trouble they were making. They caught fish, cooked supper, and ate it, and then fell to guessing at what the village was thinking and saying about them; and the pictures they drew of the public distress on their account were gratifying to look upon from their point of view. But when the shadows of night closed them in, they gradually ceased to talk, and sat gazing into the fire, with their minds evidently wandering elsewhere. The excitement was gone, now, and Tom and Joe could not keep back thoughts of certain persons at home who were not enjoying this fine frolic as much as they were. Misgivings came; they grew troubled and unhappy; a sigh or two escaped unawares. By-and-by Joe timidly ventured upon a roundabout 'feeler' as to how the others might look upon a return to civilization – not right now, but——

Tom withered him with derision. Huck, being uncommitted as yet, joined in with Tom, and the waverer quickly 'explained', and was glad to get out of the scrape with as little taint of chickenhearted homesickness clinging to his garments as he could. Mutiny was effectually laid to rest for the moment.

As the night deepened, Huck began to nod, and presently to snore; Joe followed next. Tom lay upon his elbow motionless for some time, watching

'*The pirates returned to camp*'

the two intently. At last he got up cautiously on his knees, and went searching among the grass and the flickering reflections flung by the campfire. He picked up and inspected several large semi-cylinders of the thin white bark of a sycamore, and finally chose two which seemed to suit him. Then he knelt by the fire and painfully wrote something upon each of these with his 'red keel'; one he rolled up and put in his jacket-pocket, and the other he put in Joe's hat and removed it to a little distance from the owner. And he also put into the hat certain schoolboy treasures of almost inestimable value, among them a lump of chalk, an indiarubber ball, three fish-hooks, and one of that kind of marbles known as a 'sure' 'nough crystal'. Then he tip-toed his way cautiously among the trees till he felt that he was out of hearing, and straightway broke into a keen run in the direction of the sand-bar.

Chapter 15

A few minutes later Tom was in the shoal water of the bar, wading towards the Illinois shore. Before the depth reached his middle he was half-way over: the current would permit no more wading now, so he struck out confidently to swim the remaining hundred yards. He swam quartering up stream, but still was swept downward rather faster than he had expected. However, he reached the shore finally, and drifted along till he found a low place and drew himself out. He put his hand on his jacket pocket, found his piece of bark safe, and then struck through the woods, following the shore with streaming garments. Shortly before ten o'clock he came out into an open place opposite the village, and saw the ferry-boat lying in the shadow of the trees and the high bank. Everything was quiet under the blinking stars. He crept down the bank, watching with all his eyes, slipped into the water, swam three or four strokes, and climbed into the skiff that did 'yawl' duty at the boat's stern. He laid himself down under the thwarts and waited, panting.

Presently the cracked bell tapped, and a voice gave the order to 'cast off'. A minute or two later the skiff's head was standing high up against the boat's swell, and the voyage was begun. Tom felt happy in his success, for he knew it was the boat's last trip for the night. At the end of a long twelve or fifteen minutes the wheels stopped, and Tom slipped overboard and swam ashore in the dusk, landing fifty yards down stream, out of danger of possible stragglers. He flew along unfrequented alleys, and shortly found himself at his aunt's back fence. He climbed over, approached the 'ell' and looked in at the sitting-room window, for a light was burning there. There sat Aunt Polly, Sid, Mary, and Joe Harper's mother, grouped together, talking. They were by the bed, and the bed was between them and the door. Tom went to the door and began to softly lift the latch; then he pressed gently and the door yielded a crack; he continued pushing cautiously, and quaking every time it creaked, till he judged he might squeeze through on his knees; and so he put his head through and began, warily.

'What makes the candle blow so?' said Aunt Polly. Tom hurried up. 'Why, that door's open, I believe. Why, of course it is. No end of strange things now. Go along and shut it, Sid.'

Tom disappeared under the bed just in time. He lay and 'breathed' himself for a time, and then crept to where he could almost touch his aunt's foot.

'But as I was saying,' said Aunt Polly, 'he warn't *bad*, so to say – only misch*ee*vous. Only just giddy, and harum-scarum, you know. He warn't any more responsible than a cold. *He* never meant any harm, and he was the best-hearted boy that ever was' – and she began to cry.

'It was just so with my Joe – always full of his devilment, and up to every kind of mischief, but he was just as unselfish and kind as he could be – and, laws bless me, to think I went and whipped him for taking that cream, never, once recollecting that I throwed it out myself because it was sour, and I never to see him again in this world, never, never, never, poor abused boy!' And Mrs. Harper sobbed as if her heart would break.

'I hope Tom's better off where he is,' said Sid; 'but if he'd been better in some ways——'

'*Sid*!' Tom felt the glare of the old lady's eye, though he could not see it. 'Not a word against my Tom, now that he's gone! God'll take care of *him* – never you trouble *your*self, sir. Oh, Mrs. Harper, I don't know how to give him up, I don't know how to give him up! He was such a comfort to me, although he tormented my old heart out of me, 'most.'

'The Lord giveth, and the Lord taketh away. Blessed be the name of the Lord! But it's *so* hard – oh, it's so hard! Only last Saturday my Joe bursted a shooting-cracker right under my nose, and I knocked him sprawling. Little did I know then, how soon – oh, if it was to do over again I'd hug him and bless him for it.'

'Yes, yes, yes, I know just how you feel, Mrs. Harper, I know just exactly how you feel. No longer ago than yesterday noon, my Tom took and filled the cat full of Pain-killer, and I did think the cretur would tear the house down. And, God forgive me, I cracked Tom's head with my thimble, poor boy, poor dead boy. But he's out of all his troubles now. And the last words I ever heard him say was to reproach——'

But this memory was too much for the old lady, and she broke entirely down. Tom was snuffling now himself – and more in pity of himself than anybody else. He could hear Mary crying, and putting in a kindly word for him from time to time. He began to have a nobler opinion of himself than ever before. Still he was sufficiently touched by his aunt's grief to long to rush out from under the bed and overwhelm her with joy – and the theatrical gorgeousness of the thing appealed strongly to his nature, too, but he resisted and lay still. He went on listening, and gathered by odds and ends that it was conjectured at first that the boys had got drowned while taking a swim; then the small raft had been missed; next, certain boys said the missing lads had promised that the village should 'hear something' soon; and wise heads had 'put this and that together', and decided that the lads had gone off on that raft, and would turn up at the next town below presently; but towards noon the raft had been found, lodged against the Missouri shore some five or six miles below the village, and then hope perished; they must be drowned, else hunger would have driven them home by nightfall if not sooner. It was believed that the search for the bodies had been a fruitless effort merely because the drowning must have occurred in mid-channel, since the boys, being good swimmers, would otherwise have escaped to shore. This was Wednesday night. If the bodies continued missing until Sunday, all hope would be given over, and the funerals would be preached on that morning. Tom shuddered.

Mrs. Harper gave a sobbing good night and turned to go. Then with a mutual impulse the two bereaved women flung themselves into each other's arms and had a good consoling cry, and then parted. Aunt Polly was tender far beyond her wont in her good night to Sid and Mary. Sid snuffled a bit, and Mary went off crying with all her heart.

Aunt Polly knelt down and prayed for Tom so touchingly, so appealingly, and with such measureless love in her words and her old trembling voice, that he was weltering in tears again long before she was through.

He had to keep still long after she went to bed, for she kept making broken-hearted ejaculations from time to time, tossing unrestfully, and turning over. But at last she was still, only moaning a little in her sleep. Now the boy stole out, rose gradually by the bedside, shaded the candle-light with his hand, and stood regarding her. His heart was full of pity for her. He took out his sycamore scroll and placed it by the candle. But something occurred to him, and he lingered considering. His face lighted with a happy solution of his thought; he put the bark hastily in his pocket, then he bent over and kissed the faded lips, and straightway made his stealthy exit, latching the door behind him.

He threaded his way back to the ferry landing, found nobody at large there, and walked boldly on board the boat, for he knew she was tenantless except that there was a watchman, who always turned in and slept like a graven image. He untied the skiff at the stern, slipped into it, and was soon rowing cautiously up stream. When he had pulled a mile above the village, he started quartering across, and bent himself stoutly to his work. He hit the landing on the other side neatly, for this was a familiar bit of work to him. He was moved to capture the skiff, arguing that it might be considered a ship and therefore legitimate prey for a pirate; but he knew a thorough search would be made for it, and that might end in revelations. So he stepped ashore and entered the wood. He sat down and took a long rest, torturing himself meantime to keep awake, and then started wearily down the home stretch. The night was far spent. It was broad daylight before he found himself fairly abreast the island bar. He rested again until the sun was well up and gilding the great river with its splendour, and then he plunged into the stream. A little later he paused, dripping, upon the threshold of the camp, and heard Joe say:

'No, Tom's true-blue, Huck, and he'll come back. He won't desert. He knows that would be a disgrace to a pirate, and Tom's too proud for that sort of thing. He's up to something or other. Now, I wonder what?'

'Well, the things is ours anyway, ain't they?'

'Pretty near, but not yet, Huck. The writing says they are if he ain't back to breakfast.'

'Which he is!' exclaimed Tom, with fine dramatic effect, stepping grandly into camp.

A sumptuous breakfast of bacon and fish was shortly provided, and as the boys set to work upon it Tom recounted (and adorned) his adventures. They were a vain and boastful company of heroes when the tale was done. Then Tom hid himself away in a shady nook to sleep till noon, and the other pirates got ready to fish and explore.

Chapter 16

After dinner all the gang turned out to hunt for turtle eggs on the bar. They went about poking sticks into the sand, and when they found a soft place they went down on their knees and dug with their hands. Sometimes they would take fifty or sixty eggs out of one hole. They were perfectly round, white things, a trifle smaller than an English walnut. They had a famous fried-egg feast that night, and another on Friday morning. After breakfast they went whooping and prancing out on the bar, and chased each other round and round, shedding clothes as they went, until they were naked, and then continued the frolic far away up the shoal water of the bar, against the stiff current, which latter tripped their legs from under them from time to time, and greatly increased the fun. And now and then they stood in a group and splashed water in each other's faces with their palms, gradually approaching each other with averted faces, to avoid the straggling sprays, and finally gripping and struggling till the best man ducked his neighbour, and then they all went under in a tangle of white legs and arms, and came up blowing, spluttering, laughing, and gasping for breath at one and the same time.

When they were well exhausted, they would run out and sprawl on the dry, hot sand, and lie there and cover themselves up with it, and by-and-by break for the water again and go through the original performance once more. Finally it occurred to them that their naked skin represented flesh-coloured 'tights' very fairly; so they drew a ring in the sand and had a circus – with three clowns in it, for none would yield this proudest post to his neighbour.

Next they got their marbles, and played 'knucks' and 'ring-taw' and 'keeps', till that amusement grew stale. Then Joe and Huck had another swim, but Tom would not venture, because he found that in kicking off his trousers he had kicked his string of rattlesnake rattles off his ankle, and he wondered how he had escaped cramp so long without the protection of this mysterious charm. He did not venture again until he had found it, and by that time the other boys were tired and ready to rest. They gradually wandered apart, dropped into the 'dumps', and fell to gazing longingly across the wide river to where the village lay drowsing in the sun. Tom found himself writing '*Becky*' in the sand with his big toe; he scratched it out and was angry with himself for his weakness. But he wrote it again, nevertheless; he could not help it. He erased it once more, and then took himself out of temptation by driving the other boys together, and then joining them.

But Joe's spirits had gone down almost beyond resurrection. He was so homesick that he could hardly endure the misery of it. The tears lay very near the surface. Huck was melancholy too. Tom was downhearted, but tried hard not to show it. He had a secret which he was not ready to tell yet, but if this mutinous depression was not broken up soon, he would have to bring it out. He said with a great show of cheerfulness:

'I bet there's been pirates on this island before, boys. We'll explore it again. They've hid treasures here somewhere. How'd you feel to light on a rotten chest full of gold and silver – hey?'

But it roused only a faint enthusiasm, which faded out with no reply. Tom tried one or two other seductions; but they failed too. It was discouraging work. Joe sat poking up the sand with a stick, and looking very gloomy. Finally he said:

'Oh boys, let's give it up. I want to go home. It's so lonesome.'

'Oh, no, Joe, you'll feel better by-and-by,' said Tom. 'Just think of the fishing that's here.'

'I don't care for the fishing. I want to go home.'

'But, Joe, there ain't such another swimming-place anywhere.'

'Swimming's no good; I don't seem to care for it, somehow, when there ain't anybody to say I shan't go in. I mean to go home.'

'Oh, shucks! baby! You want to see your mother, I reckon.'

'Yes, I *do* want to see my mother, and you would too, if you had one. I ain't any more baby than you are.' And Joe snuffled a little.

'Well, we'll let the cry-baby go home to his mother, won't we, Huck? Poor thing – does it want to see its mother? And so it shall. *You* like it here, don't you, Huck? We'll stay, won't we?'

Huck said 'Y-e-s——' without any heart in it.

'I'll never speak to you again as long as I live,' said Joe, rising. 'There now!' And he moved moodily away and began to dress himself.

'Who cares?' said Tom. 'Nobody wants you to. Go 'long home and get laughed at. Oh, you're a nice pirate. Huck and me ain't cry-babies. We'll stay, won't we, Huck? Let him go if he wants to. I reckon we can get along without him, per'aps.'

But Tom was uneasy nevertheless, and was alarmed to see Joe go sullenly on with his dressing. And then it was discomforting to see Huck eyeing Joe's preparations so wistfully, and keeping up such an ominous silence. Presently, without a parting word, Joe began to wade off towards the Illinois shore. Tom's heart began to sink. He glanced at Huck. Huck could not bear the look, and dropped his eyes. Then he said:

'I want to go too, Tom; it was getting so lonesome anyway, and now it'll be worse. Let's go too, Tom.'

'I won't; you can all go if you want to. I mean to stay.'

'Tom, I better go.'

'Well, go 'long – who's hindering you?'

Huck began to pick up his scattered clothes. He said:

'Tom, I wisht you'd come too. Now, you think it over. We'll wait for you when we get to shore.'

'Well, you'll wait a blame long time, that's all.'

Huck started sorrowfully away, and Tom stood looking after him, with a strong desire tugging at his heart to yield his pride and go along too. He hoped the boys would stop, but they still waded slowly on. It suddenly dawned on Tom that it was become very lonely and still. He made one final struggle with his pride, and then he darted after his comrades, yelling:

'Wait! wait! I want to tell you something!'

They presently stopped and turned round. When he got to where they were, he began unfolding his secret, and they listened moodily till at last they saw the 'point' he was driving at, and then they set up a war-whoop of applause and said it was 'splendid!' and said if he had told them that at first, they wouldn't have started away. He made a plausible excuse; but his real reason had been the fear that not even the secret would keep them with him any very great length of time, and so he had meant to hold it in reserve as a last seduction.

The lads came gaily back and went at their sports again with a will, chatting all the time about Tom's stupendous plan and admiring the genius of it. After a dainty egg and fish dinner, Tom said he wanted to learn to smoke now. Joe caught at the idea, and said he would like to try too. So Huck made pipes and filled them. These novices had never smoked anything before but cigars made of grape-vine, and they 'bit' the tongue, and were not considered manly, anyway.

Now they stretched themselves out on their elbows and began to puff charily, and with slender confidence. The smoke had an unpleasant taste, and they gagged a little, but Tom said:

'Why, it's just as easy! If I'd a knowed *this* was all, I'd a learnt long ago.'

'So would I,' said Joe. 'It's just nothing.'

'Why, many a time I've looked at people smoking and thought, Well, I wish I could do that; but I never thought I could,' said Tom. 'That's just the way with me, ain't it, Huck? You've heard me talk just that way, haven't you, Huck? I'll leave it to Huck if I haven't.'

'Yes, heaps of times,' said Huck.

'Well, I have too,' said Tom; 'oh, hundreds of times. Once down there by the slaughter-house. Don't you remember, Huck? Bob Tanner was there, and Johnny Miller, and Jeff Thatcher, when I said it. Don't you remember,

Huck, 'bout me saying that?'

'Yes, that's so,' said Huck. 'That was the day after I lost a white alley – no, 'twas the day before!'

'There, I told you so,' said Tom. 'Huck recollects it.'

'I believe I could smoke this pipe all day,' said Joe. '*I* don't feel sick.'

'Neither do I,' said Tom. '*I* could smoke it all day, but I bet you Jeff Thatcher couldn't.'

'Jeff Thatcher! Why, he'd keel over just with two draws. Just let him try it once; *he'd* see!'

'I bet he would, and Johnny Miller – I wish I could see Johnny Miller tackle it once.'

'Oh, don't *I*?' said Joe. 'Why, I bet you Johnny Miller couldn't any more do this than nothing. Just one little snifter would fetch *him*.'

''Deed it would, Joe. Say – I wish the boys could see us now.'

'So do I!'

'Say, boys, don't say anything about it, and some time when they're around I'll come up to you and say, "Joe, got a pipe? I want a smoke!" And you'll say, kind of careless like, as if it warn't anything, you'll say. "Yes. I got my *old* pipe, and another one, but my tobacker ain't very good." And I'll say, "Oh, that's all right, if it's *strong* enough." And then you'll out with the pipes, and we'll light up just as ca'm, and then just see 'em look!'

'By jings, that'll be gay, Tom; I wish it was *now*!'

'So do I! And when we tell 'em we learned when we was off pirating, won't they wish they'd been along!'

'Oh, I reckon not! I'll just *bet* they will!'

So the talk ran on; but presently it began to flag a trifle, and grow disjointed. The silences widened; the expectoration marvellously increased. Every pore inside the boys' cheeks became a spouting fountain; they could scarcely bale out the cellars under their tongues fast enough to prevent an inundation; little overflowings down their throats occurred in spite of all they could do, and sudden retchings followed every time. Both boys were looking very pale and miserable now. Joe's pipe dropped from his nerveless fingers. Tom's followed. Both fountains were going furiously, and both pumps baling with might and main. Joe said feebly:

'I've lost my knife. I reckon I better go and find it.'

Tom said, with quivering lips and halting utterance:

'I'll help you. You go over that way, and I'll hunt around by the spring. No, you needn't come, Huck – we can find it.'

So Huck sat down again, and waited an hour. Then he found it lonesome, and went to find his comrades. They were wide apart in the woods, both very pale, both fast asleep. But something informed him that if they had had any trouble they had got rid of it.

They were not talkative at supper that night; they had a humble look; and when Huck prepared his pipe after the meal, and was going to prepare theirs, they said no, they were not feeling very well – something they ate at dinner had disagreed with them.

Chapter 17

About midnight Joe awoke, and called the boys. There was a brooding oppressiveness in the air that seemed to bode something. The boys huddled themselves together, and sought the friendly companionship of the fire, though the dull dead heat of the breathless atmosphere was stifling. They sat still, intent and waiting. Beyond the light of the fire, everything was swallowed up in the blackness of darkness. Presently there came a quivering glow that vaguely revealed the foliage for a moment and then vanished. By-and-by another came, a little stronger. Then another. Then a faint moan came sighing through the branches of the forest, and the boys felt a fleeting breath upon their cheeks, and shuddered with the fancy that the Spirit of the Night had gone by. There was a pause. Now a weird flash turned night into day, and showed every little grass-blade separate and distinct, that grew about their feet. And it showed three white startled faces, too. A deep peal of thunder went rolling and tumbling down the heavens, and lost itself in sullen rumblings in the distance. A sweep of chilly air passed by, rustling all the leaves and snowing the flaky ashes broadcast about the fire. Another fierce glare lit up the forest, and an instant crash followed that seemed to rend the tree-tops right over the boys' heads. They clung together in terror, in the quick gloom that followed. A few big rain-drops fell pattering upon the leaves.

'Quick, boys, go for the tent!' exclaimed Tom.

They sprang away, stumbling over roots and among vines in the dark, no two plunging in the same direction. A furious blast roared through the trees, making everything sing as it went. One blinding flash after another came, and peal on peal of deafening thunder. And now a drenching rain poured down, and the rising hurricane drove it in sheets along the ground. The boys cried out to each other, but the roaring wind and the booming thunder-blasts drowned their voices utterly. However, one by one they straggled in at last, and took shelter under the tent, cold, scared, and streaming with water; but to have company in misery seemed something to be grateful for. They could not talk, the old sail flapped so furiously, even if the other noises would have allowed them. The tempest rose higher and higher, and presently the sail tore loose from its fastenings, and went winging away on the blast. The boys seized each others' hands, and fled, with many tumblings and bruises, to the shelter of a great oak that stood upon the river bank. Now the battle was at its highest. Under the ceaseless conflagrations of lightnings that flamed in the skies, everything below stood out in clean-cut and shadowless distinctness; the bending trees, the billowy river white with foam, the driving spray of spume-flakes, the dim outlines of the high bluffs on the other side, glimpsed through the drifting cloud-rack and the slanting veil of rain. Every little while some giant tree yielded the fight and fell crashing through the younger growth; and the unflagging thunder-peals came now in ear-splitting explosive bursts, keen and sharp, and unspeakably appalling. The storm culminated in one matchless effort that seemed likely to tear the island to pieces, burn it up, drown it to the tree-tops, blow it away and deafen every creature in it, all at one and the same moment. It was a wild night for homeless young heads to be out in.

But at last the battle was done, and the forces retired, with weaker and weaker threatenings and grumblings, and peace resumed her sway. The boys went back to camp a good deal awed; but they found there was still something to be thankful for, because the great sycamore, the shelter of their beds, was a ruin, now, blasted by the lightnings, and they were not under it when the catastrophe happened.

Everything in camp was drenched, the campfire as well; for they were but heedless lads, like their generation, and had made no provision against rain. Here was matter for dismay, for they were soaked through and chilled. They were eloquent in their distress: but they presently discovered that the fire had eaten so far up under the great log it had been built against (where it curved upward and separated itself from the ground), that a hand-breadth or so of it had escaped wetting; so they patiently wrought until, with shreds and bark gathered from under sides of sheltered logs, they coaxed the fire to burn again. Then they piled on great dead boughs till they had a roaring furnace and were glad-hearted once more. They dried their boiled ham and had a feast, and after that they sat by the fire and expanded and glorified their midnight adventure until morning, for there was not a dry spot to sleep on anywhere around.

As the sun began to steal in upon the boys, drowsiness came over them and they went out on the sand-bar and lay down to sleep. They got scorched out by-and-by, and drearily set about getting breakfast. After the meal they felt rusty, and stiff-jointed, and a little homesick once more. Tom saw the signs, and fell to cheering up the pirates as well as he could. But they cared nothing for marbles, or circus, or swimming, or anything. He reminded them of the imposing secret, and raised a ray of cheer. While it lasted he got them interested in a new device. This was to knock off being pirates for a while, and be Indians for a change. They were attracted by this idea; so it was not long before they were stripped, and striped from head to heel with black mud, like so many zebras, all of them chiefs, of course, and then they went tearing through the woods to attack an English settlement.

By-and-by they separated into three hostile tribes, and darted upon each other from ambush with dreadful war-whoops, and killed and scalped each other by thousands. It was a gory day. Consequently it was a satisfactory one.

They assembled in camp towards supper-time, hungry and happy. But now a difficulty arose – hostile Indians could not break the bread of hospitality together without first making peace, and this was a simple impossibility without smoking a pipe of peace. There was no other process that ever they had heard of. Two of the savages almost wished they had remained pirates. However, there was no other way, so with such show of cheerfulness as they could muster they called for the pipe and took their whiff, as it passed, in due form.

And behold they were glad they had gone into savagery, for they had gained something; they found that they could now smoke a little without having to go and hunt for a lost knife; they did not get sick enough to be seriously uncomfortable. They were not likely to fool away this high promise for lack of effort. No, they practised cautiously after supper with right fair success, and so they spent a jubilant evening. They were prouder and happier in their new acquirement than they would have been in the scalping and skinning of the Six Nations. We will leave them to smoke and chatter and brag, since we have no further use for them at present.

Chapter 18

But there was no hilarity in the little town that tranquil Saturday afternoon. The Harpers and Aunt Polly's family were being put into mourning with great grief and many tears. An unusual quiet possessed the village, although it was ordinarily quiet enough in all conscience. The villagers conducted their concerns with an abstracted air, and talked little; but they sighed often. The Saturday holiday seemed a burden to the children. They had no heart in their sports, and gradually gave them up.

In the afternoon Becky Thatcher found herself moping about the deserted school-house yard, and feeling very melancholy. But she found nothing there to comfort her. She soliloquized:

'Oh, if I only had his brass andiron knob again! But I haven't got anything now to remember him by,' and she choked back a little sob.

Presently she stopped, and said to herself:

'It was right here. Oh, if it was to do over again, I wouldn't say that – I wouldn't say it for the whole world. But he's gone now; I'll never, never, never see him any more.'

This thought broke her down, and she wandered away with the tears rolling down her cheeks. Then quite a group of boys and girls – playmates of Tom's and Joe's – came by, and stood looking over the paling fence and talking in reverent tones of how Tom did so-and-so the last time they saw him, and how Joe said this and that small trifle (pregnant with awful prophecy, as they could easily see now!) – and each speaker pointed out the exact spot where the lost lads stood at the time, and then added something like, 'and I was a standing just so – just as I am now, and as if you was him – I was as close as that – and he smiled, just this way – and then something seemed to go all over me, like – awful, you know – and I never thought what it meant, of course, but I can see now!'

Then there was a dispute about who saw the dead boys last in life, and many claimed that dismal distinction, and offered evidences more or less tampered with by the witness; and when it was ultimately decided who did see the departed last, and exchanged the last words with them, the lucky parties took upon themselves a sort of sacred importance, and were gaped at and envied by all the rest. One poor chap who had no other grandeur to offer, said, with tolerably manifest pride in the remembrance:

'Well, Tom Sawyer he licked me once.'

But that bid for glory was a failure. Most of the boys could say that, and so that cheapened the distinction too much. The group loitered away, still recalling memories of the lost heroes in awed voices.

When the Sunday-school hour was finished the next morning, the bell began to toll, instead of ringing in the usual way. It was a very still Sabbath, and the mournful sound seemed in keeping with the musing hush that lay upon nature. The villagers began to gather, loitering a moment in the vestibule to converse in whispers about the sad event. But there was no whispering in the house; only the funeral rustling of dresses, as the women gathered to their seats, disturbed the silence there. None could remember when the little church had been so full before. There was finally a waiting pause, an expectant dumbness, and then Aunt Polly entered, followed by Sid and Mary, and then by the Harper family, all in deep black, and the whole congregation, the old minister as well, rose reverently and stood, until the mourners were seated in the front pew. There was another communing silence, broken at intervals by muffled sobs, and then the minister spread his hands abroad and prayed. A moving hymn was sung, and the text followed: 'I am the resurrection and the life.'

As the service proceeded, the clergyman drew such pictures of the graces, the winning ways, and the rare promise of the lost lads, that every soul there, thinking he recognized these pictures, felt a pang in remembering that he had persistently blinded himself to them always before, and had as persistently seen only faults and flaws in the poor boys. The minister related many a touching incident in the lives of the departed, too, which illustrated their sweet, generous natures, and the people could easily see, now, how noble and beautiful those episodes were, and remembered with grief that at the time they occurred they had seemed rank rascalities, well deserving the cowhide. The congregation became more and more moved as the pathetic tale went on, till at last the whole company broke down and joined the weeping mourners in a chorus of anguished sobs, the preacher himself giving way to his feelings, and crying in the pulpit.

There was a rustle in the gallery which nobody noticed; a moment later the church door creaked; the minister raised his streaming eyes above his handkerchief, and stood transfixed! First one and then another pair of eyes followed the minister's, and then, almost with one impulse, the congregation rose and stared while the three dead boys came marching up the aisle, Tom in the lead, Joe next, and Huck, a ruin of drooping rags, sneaking sheepishly in the rear. They had been hid in the unused gallery, listening to their own funeral sermon!

Aunt Polly, Mary, and the Harpers threw themselves upon their restored ones, smothered them with kisses and poured out thanksgivings, while poor Huck stood abashed and uncomfortable, not knowing exactly what to do or where to hide from so many unwelcoming eyes. He wavered, and started to slink away, but Tom seized him and said:

'Aunt Polly, it ain't fair. Somebody's got to be glad to see Huck.'

'And so they shall! I'm glad to see him, poor motherless thing!' And the loving attentions Aunt Polly lavished upon him were the one thing capable of making him more uncomfortable than he was before.

Suddenly the minister shouted at the top of his voice:

'"Praise God from whom all blessings flow" – SING! – and put your hearts in it!'

And they did. Old Hundred swelled up with a triumphant burst, and while it shook the rafters Tom Sawyer the Pirate looked around upon the envying juveniles about him, and confessed in his heart that this was the proudest moment of his life.

As the 'sold' congregation trooped out, they said they would almost be willing to be made ridiculous again to hear Old Hundred sung like that once more.

Tom got more cuffs and kisses that day – according to Aunt Polly's varying moods – than he had earned before in a year; and he hardly knew which expressed the most gratefulness to God and affection for himself.

Chapter 19

That was Tom's great secret – the scheme to return home with his brother pirates and attend their own funerals. They had paddled over to the Missouri shore on a log, at dusk on Saturday, landing five or six miles below the village; they had slept in the woods at the edge of the town till nearly day-light, and had then crept through back lanes and alleys and finished their sleep in the gallery of the church among a chaos of invalid benches.

At breakfast, Monday morning, Aunt Polly and Mary were very loving to Tom, and very attentive to his wants. There was an unusual amount of talk. In the course of it Aunt Polly said:

'Well, I don't say it wasn't a fine joke, Tom, to keep everybody suffering 'most a week so you boys had a good time, but it is a pity you could be so hard-hearted as to let me suffer so. If you could come over on a log to get to your funeral, you could have come over and give me a hint some way that you warn't dead, but only run off.'

'Yes, you could have done that, Tom,' said Mary; 'and I believe you would if you had thought of it.'

'Would you, Tom?' said Aunt Polly, her face lighting wistfully. 'Say, now, would you, if you'd thought of it?'

'I – well, I don't know. 'Twould a spoiled everything.'

'Tom, I hoped you loved me that much,' said Aunt Polly, with a grieved tone that discomforted the boy. 'It would been something if you'd cared enough to think of it, even if you didn't do it.'

'Now, Auntie, that ain't any harm,' pleaded Mary; 'it's only Tom's giddy way – he is always in such a rush that he never thinks of anything.'

'More's the pity. Sid would have thought. And Sid would have come and done it, too. Tom, you'll look back, some day, when it's too late, and wish you'd cared a little more for me when it would have cost you so little.'

'Now, Auntie, you know I do care for you,' said Tom.

'I'd know it better if you acted more like it.'

'I wish now I'd thought,' said Tom, with a repentant tone; 'but I dreamed about you, anyway. That's something, ain't it?'

'It ain't much – a cat does that much – but it's better than nothing. What did you dream?'

'Why, Wednesday night I dreamt that you was sitting over there by the bed, and Sid was sitting by the wood-box, and Mary next to him.'

'Well, so we did. So we always do. I'm glad your dreams could take even that much trouble about us.'

'And I dreamt that Joe Harper's mother was here.'

'Why, she was here! Did you dream any more?'

'Oh, lots. But it's so dim now.'

'Well, try to recollect – can't you?'

'Somehow it seems to me that the wind – the wind blowed the – the——'

'Try harder, Tom! The wind did blow something, come!'

Tom pressed his fingers on his forehead an anxious minute, and then said:

'I've got it now! I've got it now! It blowed the candle!'

'Mercy on us! Go on, Tom, go on!'

'And it seems to me that you said, "Why, I believe that that door——"'

'Go on, Tom!'

'Just let me study a moment – just a moment. Oh, yes – you said you believed the door was open.'

'As I'm a sitting here, I did! Didn't I, Mary? Go on!'

'And then – and then – well, I won't be certain, but it seems like as if you made Sid go and – and——'

'Well? Well? What did I make him do, Tom? What did I make him do?'

'You made him – you – Oh, you made him shut it!'

'Well, for the land's sake! I never heard the beat of that in all my days! Don't tell me there ain't anything in dreams any more. Sereny Harper shall know of this before I'm an hour older. I'd like to see her get around this with her rubbage about superstition. Go on, Tom!'

'Oh, it's all getting just as bright as day, now. Next you said I warn't bad, only mischeevous and harum-scarum, and not any more responsible than – than – I think it was a colt, or something.'

'And so it was! Well! Goodness gracious! Go on, Tom!'

'And then you began to cry.'

'So I did. So I did. Not the first time, neither. And then——'

'Then Mrs. Harper she began to cry, and said Joe was just the same, and she wished she hadn't whipped him for taking cream when she'd throwed it out her ownself——'

'Tom! The sperrit was upon you! You was a prophesying – that's what you was doing! Land alive! – go on, Tom!'

'Then Sid he said – he said——'

'I don't think I said anything,' said Sid.

'Yes, you did, Sid,' said Mary.

'Shut your heads and let Tom go on! What did he say, Tom?'

'He said – I think he said he hoped I was better off where I was gone to, but if I'd been better sometimes——'

'There, d'you hear that? It was his very words!'

'And you shut him up sharp.'

'I lay I did! There must a been an angel there. There was an angel there, somewheres!'

'And Mrs. Harper told about Joe scaring her with a fire-cracker, and you told about Peter and the Pain-killer——'

'Just as true as I live!'

'And then there was a whole lot of talk 'bout dragging the river for us, and 'bout having the funeral Sunday, and then you and old Mrs. Harper hugged and cried, and she went.'

'It happened just so! It happened just so, as sure as I'm a sitting in these very tracks. Tom, you couldn't told it more like if you'd a seen it! And then what? Go on, Tom.'

'Then I thought you prayed for me – and I could see you and hear every word you said. And you went to bed, and I was so sorry that I took and wrote on a piece of sycamore bark, "We ain't dead – we are only off being pirates", and put it on the table by the candle; and then you looked so good, laying there asleep, that I thought I went and leaned over and kissed you on the lips.'

'Did you, Tom, did you? I just forgive you everything for that!' And she seized the boy in a crushing embrace that made him feel like the guiltiest of villains.

'It was very kind, even though it was only a – dream,' Sid soliloquized just audibly.

'Shut up, Sid! A body does just the same in a dream as he'd do if he was awake. Here's a big Milum apple I've been saving for you. Tom, if you was ever found again – now go 'long to school. I'm thankful to the good God and Father of us all I've got you back, that's long-suffering and merciful to them that believe on Him and keep His word, though goodness knows I'm unworthy of it, but if only the worthy ones got His blessings and had His hand to help them over the rough places, there's a few enough would smile here or ever enter into His rest when the long night comes. Go 'long, Sid, Mary, Tom – take yourselves off – you've hendered me long enough.'

The children left for school, and the old lady to call on Mrs. Harper, and vanquish her realism with Tom's marvellous dream. Sid had better judgement than to utter the thought that was in his mind as he left the house. It was this:

'Pretty thin – as long a dream as that, without any mistakes in it!'

What a hero Tom was become now! He did not go skipping and prancing, but moved with a dignified swagger, as became a pirate who felt that the public eye was on him. And indeed it was; he tried not to seem to see the looks or hear the remarks as he passed along, but they were food and drink to him. Smaller boys than himself flocked at his heels, as proud to be seen with him and tolerated by him as if he had been the drummer at the head of a procession, or the elephant leading a menagerie into town. Boys of his own size pretended not to know he had been away at all, but they were consuming with envy, nevertheless. They would have given anything to have that swarthy, sun-tanned skin of his, and his glittering notoriety; and Tom would not have parted with either for a circus.

At school the children made so much of him and Joe, and delivered such eloquent admiration from their eyes, that the two heroes were not long in becoming insufferably 'stuck-up'. They began to tell their adventures to hungry listeners – but they only began; it was not a thing likely to have an end, with imaginations like theirs to furnish material. And finally, when they got out their pipes and went serenely puffing around, the very summit of glory was reached.

Tom decided that he could be independent of Becky Thatcher now. Glory was sufficient. He would live for glory. Now that he was distinguished, maybe she would be wanting to 'make up'. Well, let her – she should see that he could be as indifferent as some other people. Presently she arrived. Tom pretended not to see her. He moved away and joined a group of boys and girls, and began to talk. Soon he observed that she was tripping gaily back and forth with flushed face and dancing eyes, pretending to be busy chasing schoolmates, and screaming with laughter when she made a capture, but he noticed that she always made her captures in his vicinity, and that she seemed to cast a conscious eye in his direction at such times, too. It gratified all the vicious vanity that was in him; and so, instead of winning him, it only 'set him up' the more and made him the more diligent to avoid betraying that he knew she was about. Presently, she gave over skylarking, and moved irresolutely about, sighing once or twice and glancing furtively and wistfully towards Tom. Then she observed that now Tom was talking more particularly to Amy Lawrence than to anyone else. She felt a sharp pang and grew disturbed and uneasy at once. She tried to go away, but her feet were treacherous, and carried her to the group instead. She said to a girl almost at Tom's elbow – with sham vivacity:

'Why, Mary Austin! you bad girl, why didn't you come to Sunday-school?'

'I did come – didn't you see me?'

'Why, no! Did you? Where did you sit?'

'I was in Miss Peters's class, where I always go. I saw you.'

'Did you? Why, it's funny I didn't see you. I wanted to tell you about the picnic.'

'Oh, that's jolly. Who's going to give it?'

'My ma's going to let me have one.'

'Oh, goody; I hope she'll let me come.'

'Well, she will. The picnic's for me. She'll let anybody come that I want, and I want you.'

'That's ever so nice. When is it going to be?'

'By-and-by. Maybe about vacation.'

'Oh, won't it be fun! You going to have all the girls and boys?'

'Yes, everyone that's friends to me – or wants to be,' and she glanced ever so furtively at Tom, but he talked right along to Amy Lawrence about the terrible storm on the island, and how the lightning tore the great sycamore tree 'all to flinders' while he was 'standing within three feet of it'.

'Oh, may I come?' said Gracie Miller.

'Yes.'

'And me?' said Sally Rogers.

'Yes.'

'And me too?' said Susy Harper. 'And Joe?'

'Yes.'

And so on, with clapping of joyful hands, till all the group had begged for invitations but Tom and Amy. Then Tom turned coolly away, still talking, and took Amy with him. Becky's lips trembled and the tears came to her eyes; she hid these signs with a forced gaiety and went on chattering, but the life had gone out of the picnic, now, and out of everything else; she got away as soon as she could and hid herself, and had what her sex call 'a good cry'. Then she sat moody, with wounded pride, till the bell rang. She roused up, now, with a vindictive cast in her eye, and gave her plaited tails a shake, and said she knew what she'd do.

At recess Tom continued his flirtation with Amy with jubilant self-satisfaction. And he kept drifting about to find Becky and lacerate her with the performance. At last he spied her, but there was a sudden falling of his mercury. She was sitting cosily on a little bench behind the school-house, looking at a picture-book with Alfred Temple; and so absorbed were they, and their heads so close together over the book, that they did not seem to be conscious of anything in the world beside. Jealousy ran red-hot through Tom's veins. He began to hate himself for throwing away the chance Becky had offered for a reconciliation. He called himself a fool, and all the hard names he could think of. He wanted to cry with vexation. Amy chatted happily along, as they walked, for her heart was singing, but Tom's tongue had lost its function. He did not hear what Amy was saying, and whenever she paused expectantly, he could only stammer an awkward assent, which was as often misplaced as otherwise. He kept drifting to the rear of the school-house again and again, to sear his eyeballs with the hateful spectacle there. He could not help it. And it maddened him to see, as he thought he saw, that Becky

Thatcher never once suspected that he was even in the land of the living. But she did see, nevertheless; and she knew she was winning her fight, too, and was glad to see him suffer as she had suffered.

Amy's happy prattle became intolerable. Tom hinted at things he had to attend to; things that must be done; and time was fleeting. But in vain – the girl chirped on. Tom thought, 'Oh, hang her, ain't I ever going to get rid of her?' At last he must be attending to those things; she said artlessly that she would be 'around' when school let out. And he hastened away, hating her for it.

'Any other boy!' Tom thought, grating his teeth. 'Any boy in the whole town but that Saint Louis smarty, that thinks he dresses so fine and is aristocracy! Oh, all right. I licked you the first time you ever saw this town, mister, and I'll lick you again! You just wait till I catch you out! I'll just take and——'

And he went through the motions of thrashing an imaginary boy – pummelling the air, and kicking and gouging.

'Oh, you do, do you? you holler 'nough, do you? Now, then, let that learn you!'

And so the imaginary flogging was finished to his satisfaction.

Tom fled home at noon. His conscience could not endure any more of Amy's grateful happiness, and his jealousy could bear no more of the other distress. Becky resumed her picture-inspections with Alfred, but as the minutes dragged along and no Tom came to suffer, her triumph began to cloud and she lost interest; gravity and absent-mindedness followed, and then melancholy; two or three times she pricked up her ear at a footstep, but it was a false hope; no Tom came. At last she grew entirely miserable, and wished she hadn't carried it so far. When poor Alfred, seeing that he was losing her he did not know how, kept exclaiming: 'Oh, here's a jolly one! look at this!' she lost patience at last and said, 'Oh, don't bother me! I don't care for them!' and burst into tears, and got up and walked away.

Alfred dropped alongside and was going to try and comfort her, but she said:

'Go away and leave me alone, can't you. I hate you!'

So the boy halted, wondering what he could have done – for she had said she would look at pictures all through the nooning – and she walked on, crying. Then Alfred went musing into the deserted school-house. He was humiliated and angry. He easily guessed his way to the truth – the girl had simply made a convenience of him to vent her spite on Tom Sawyer. He was far from hating Tom the less when this thought occurred to him. He wished there was some way to get that boy into trouble without much risk to himself. Tom's spelling-book fell under his eye. Here was his opportunity. He gratefully opened to the lesson for the afternoon, and poured ink upon the page. Becky, glancing in at a window behind him at the moment, saw the act and moved on without discovering herself. She started homeward, now, intending to find Tom and tell him: Tom would be thankful, and their troubles would be healed. Before she was half-way home, however, she had changed her mind. The thought of Tom's treatment of her when she was talking about her picnic came scorching back, and filled her with shame. She resolved to let him get whipped on the damaged spelling-book's account, and to hate him for ever into the bargain.

Chapter 20

Tom arrived at home in a dreary mood, and the first thing his aunt said to him showed him that he had brought his sorrows to an unpromising market:

'Tom, I've a notion to skin you alive.'

'Auntie, what have I done?'

'Well, you've done enough. Here I go over to Sereny Harper like an old softy, expecting I'm going to make her believe all that rubbage about that dream, when, lo and behold you, she'd found out from Joe that you was over here and heard all the talk we had that night. Tom, I don't know what is to become of a boy that will act like that. It makes me feel so bad to think you could let me go to Sereny Harper, and make such a fool of myself, and never say a word.'

This was a new aspect of the thing. His smartness of the morning had seemed to Tom a good joke before, and very ingenious. It merely looked mean and shabby now. He hung his head and could not think of anything to say for a moment; then he said:

'Auntie, I wish I hadn't done it – but I didn't think.'

'Oh, child, you never think. You never think of anything but your own selfishness. You could think to come all the way over here from Jackson's Island in the night to laugh at our troubles, and you could think to fool me with a lie about a dream: but you couldn't ever think to pity us and save us from sorrow.'

'Auntie, I know now it was mean, but I didn't mean to be mean; I didn't honest. And besides, I didn't come over here to laugh at you that night.'

'What did you come for, then?'

'It was to tell you not to be uneasy about us, because we hadn't got drownded.'

'Tom, Tom, I would be the thankfullest soul in this world if I could believe you ever had as good a thought as that, but you know you never did – and I know it, Tom.'

'Indeed and 'deed I did, Auntie – I wish I may never stir if I didn't.'

'Oh, Tom, don't lie – don't do it. It only makes things a hundred times worse.'

'It ain't a lie, Auntie; it's the truth. I wanted to keep you from grieving –

'"Oh, Tom, don't lie – don't do it"'

that was all that made me come.'

'I'd give the whole world to believe that – it would cover up a power of sins, Tom. I'd 'most be glad you'd run off and acted so bad. But it ain't reasonable; because why didn't you tell me, child?'

'Why, you see, Auntie, when you got to talking about the funeral, I just got all full of the idea of our coming and hiding in the church, and I couldn't, somehow, bear to spoil it. So I just put the bark back in my pocket and kept mum.'

'What bark?'

'The bark I had wrote on to tell you we'd gone pirating. I wish now, you'd waked up when I kissed you – I do, honest.'

The hard lines in his aunt's face relaxed, and sudden tenderness dawned in her eyes.

'*Did* you kiss me, Tom?'

'Why, yes, I did.'

'Are you sure you did, Tom?'

'Why, yes, I did, Auntie – certain sure.'

'What did you kiss me for, Tom?'

'Because I loved you so, and you laid there moaning, and I was so sorry.'

The words sounded like truth. The old lady could not hide a tremor in her voice when she said:

'Kiss me again, Tom! – and be off with you to school, now, and don't bother me any more.'

The moment he was gone, she ran to a closet and got out the ruin of a jacket which Tom had gone pirating in. Then she stopped with it in her hand, and said to herself:

'No, I don't dare. Poor boy, I reckon he's lied about it – but it's a blessed, blessed lie, there's such comfort in it. I hope the Lord – I *know* the Lord will forgive him because it was such good-heartedness in him to tell it. But I don't want to find out it's a lie. I won't look.'

She put the jacket away, and stood by musing a minute. Twice she put out her hand to take the garment again, and twice she refrained. Once more she ventured, and this time she fortified herself with the thought: 'It's a good lie – it's a good lie – I won't let it grieve me.' So she sought the jacket pocket. A moment later she was reading Tom's piece of bark through flowing tears, and saying:

'I could forgive the boy, now, if he'd committed a million sins!'

Chapter 21

There was something about Aunt Polly's manner when she kissed Tom, that swept away his low spirits and made him light-hearted and happy again. He started to school, and had the luck of coming upon Becky Thatcher at the head of Meadow Lane. His mood always determined his manner. Without a moment's hesitation he ran to her and said:

'I acted mighty mean today, Becky, and I'm so sorry. I won't ever, ever do it that way again as long as ever I live – please make up, won't you?'

The girl stopped and looked him scornfully in the face:

'I'll thank you to keep yourself *to* yourself, Mr. Thomas Sawyer. I'll never speak to you again.'

She tossed her head and passed on. Tom was so stunned that he had not even presence of mind enough to say 'Who cares, Miss Smarty?' until the right time to say it had gone by. So he said nothing. But he was in a fine rage, nevertheless. He moped into the school-yard wishing she were a boy, and imagining how he would trounce her if she were. He presently encountered her and delivered a stinging remark as he passed. She hurled one in return, and the angry breach was complete. It seemed to Becky, in her hot resentment, that she could hardly wait for school to 'take in', she was so impatient to see Tom flogged for the injured spelling-book. If she had had any lingering notion of exposing Alfred Temple, Tom's offensive fling had driven it entirely away.

Poor girl, she did not know how fast she was nearing trouble herself. The master, Mr. Dobbins, had reached middle age with an unsatisfied ambition. The darling of his desires was to be a doctor, but poverty had decreed that he should be nothing higher than a village schoolmaster. Every day he took a mysterious book out of his desk, and absorbed himself in it at times when no classes were reciting. He kept that book under lock and key. There was not an urchin in school but was perishing to have a glimpse of it, but the chance never came. Every boy and girl had a theory about the nature of that book; but no two theories were alike, and there was no way of getting at the facts in the case. Now as Becky was passing by the desk, which stood near the door, she noticed that the key was in the lock! It was a precious moment. She glanced around; found herself alone, and the next instant she had the book in her hands. The title-page – Professor somebody's *Anatomy* – carried no information to her mind; so she began to turn the leaves. She came at once upon a handsomely engraved and coloured frontispiece – a human figure. At that moment a shadow fell on the page, and Tom Sawyer stepped in at the door and caught a glimpse of the picture. Becky snatched at the book to close it, and had the hard luck to tear the pictured page half down the middle. She thrust the volume into the desk, turned the key, and burst out crying with shame and vexation:

'Tom Sawyer, you are just as mean as you can be, to sneak up on a person and look at what they're looking at.'

'How could *I* know you was looking at anything?'

'You ought to be ashamed of yourself, Tom Sawyer; you know you're going to tell on me; and, oh, what shall I do, what shall I do? I'll be whipped, and I never was whipped in school.'

Then she stamped her little foot and said:

'*Be* so mean if you want to! *I* know something that's going to happen. You just wait, and you'll see! Hateful, hateful, hateful!' – and she flung out of the house with a new explosion of crying.

Tom stood still, rather flustered by this onslaught. Presently he said to himself:

'What a curious kind of a fool a girl is. Never been licked in school! Shucks, what's a licking! That's just like a girl – they're so thin-skinned and chicken-hearted. Well, of course *I* ain't going to tell old Dobbins on this little fool, because there's other ways of getting even on her that ain't so mean; but what of it? Old Dobbins will ask who it was tore his book. Nobody'll answer. Then he'll do just the way he always does – ask first one and then t'other, and when he comes to the right girl he'll know it, without any telling. Girls' faces always tell on them. They ain't got any backbone. She'll get licked. Well, it's a kind of a tight place for Becky Thatcher, because there ain't any way out of it.' Tom conned the thing a moment longer, and then added: 'All right, though; she'd like to see me in just such a fix – let her sweat it out!'

Tom joined the mob of skylarking scholars outside. In a few moments the master arrived and school 'took in'. Tom did not feel a strong interest in his studies. Every time he stole a glance at the girls' side of the room, Becky's face troubled him. Considering all things, he did not want to pity her, and yet it was all he could do to help it. He could get up no exultation that was really worth the name. Presently the spelling-book discovery was made, and Tom's mind was entirely full of his own matters for a while after that. Becky roused up from her lethargy of distress, and showed good interest in the proceedings. She did not expect that Tom could get out of his trouble by denying that he spilt the ink on the book himself; and she was right. The denial only seemed to make the thing worse for Tom. Becky supposed she would be glad of that, and she tried to believe she was glad of it, but she found she was not certain. When the worst came to the worst, she had an impulse to get up and tell on Alfred Temple, but she made an effort and forced herself to keep still, because, said she to herself, 'he'll tell about me tearing the picture, sure. I wouldn't say a word, not to save his life!'

Tom took his whipping and went back to his seat not at all broken-hearted, for he thought it was possible that he had unknowingly upset the ink on the spelling-book himself, in some skylarking bout – he had denied it for form's sake and because it was custom, and had stuck to the denial from principle.

A whole hour drifted by; the master sat nodding in his throne, the air was drowsy with the hum of study. By-and-by Mr. Dobbins straightened himself up, yawned, then unlocked his desk, and reached for his book, but seemed undecided whether to take it out or leave it. Most of the pupils glanced up languidly, but there were two among them that watched his movements with intent eyes. Mr. Dobbins fingered his book absently for a while, then took it out, and settled himself in his chair to read.

Tom shot a glance at Becky. He had seen a hunted and helpless rabbit look as she did, with a gun levelled at its head. Instantly he forgot his quarrel with her. Quick, something must be done! done in a flash, too! But the very imminence of the emergency paralysed his invention. Good! he had an inspiration! He would run and snatch the book, spring through the door and fly! but his resolution shook for one little instant, and the chance was lost – the master opened the volume. If Tom only had the wasted opportunity back again! Too late; there was no help for Becky now, he said. The next moment the master faced the school. Every eye sank under his gaze; there was that in it which smote even the innocent with fear. There was silence while one might count ten; the master was gathering his wrath. Then he spoke:

'Who tore this book?'

There was not a sound. One could have heard a pin drop. The stillness continued; the master searched face after face for signs of guilt.

'Benjamin Rogers, did you tear this book?'

A denial. Another pause.

'Joseph Harper, did you?'

Another denial. Tom's uneasiness grew more and more intense under the slow torture of these proceedings. The master scanned the ranks of boys, considered a while, then turned to the girls:

'Amy Lawrence?'

A shake of the head.

'Gracie Miller?'

The same sign.

'Susan Harper, did you do this?'

Another negative. The next girl was Becky Thatcher. Tom was trembling from head to foot with excitement, and a sense of the hopelessness of the situation.

'Rebecca Thatcher' – (Tom glanced at her face; it was white with terror) – 'did you tear – no, look me in the face' – (her hands rose in appeal) – 'did you tear this book?'

A thought shot like lightning through Tom's brain. He sprang to his feet and shouted:

'*I* done it!'

The school stared in perplexity at this incredible folly. Tom stood a moment to gather his dismembered faculties; and when he stepped forward to go to his punishment, the surprise, the gratitude, the adoration that shone upon him out of poor Becky's eyes seemed pay enough for a hundred floggings. Inspired by the splendour of his own act, he took without an outcry the most merciless flogging that even Mr. Dobbins had ever administered; and also received with indifference the added cruelty of a command to remain two hours after school should be dismissed – for he knew who would wait for him outside till his captivity was done, and not count the tedious time as loss either.

Tom went to bed that night planning vengeance against Alfred Temple; for with shame and repentance Becky had told him all, not forgetting her own treachery; but even the longing for vengeance had to give way soon to pleasanter musings, and he fell asleep at last with Becky's latest words lingering dreamily in his ear:

'Tom, how *could* you be so noble!'

Chapter 22

Vacation was approaching. The schoolmaster, always severe, grew severer and more exacting than ever, for he wanted the school to make a good showing on 'Examination' day. His rod and his ferule were seldom idle now – at least among the smaller pupils. Only the biggest boys, and young ladies of eighteen and twenty, escaped lashing. Mr. Dobbins's lashings were very vigorous ones too; for although he carried, under his wig, a perfectly bald and shiny head, he had only reached middle age and there was no sign of feebleness in his muscle. As the great day approached, all the tyranny that was in him came to the surface; he seemed to take a vindictive pleasure in punishing the least short-comings. The consequence was that the smallest boys spent their days in terror and suffering and their nights in plotting revenge. They threw away no opportunity to do the master a mischief. But he kept ahead all the time. The retribution that followed every vengeful success was so sweeping and majestic that the boys always retired from the field badly worsted. At last they conspired together and hit upon a plan that promised a dazzling victory. They swore in the sign-painter's boy, told him the scheme, and asked his help. He had his own reasons for being delighted, for the master boarded in his father's family and had given the boy ample cause to hate him. The master's wife would go on a visit to the country in a few days, and there would be nothing to interfere with the plan; the master always prepared himself for great occasions by getting pretty well fuddled, and the sign-painter's boy said that when the dominie had reached the proper condition on 'Examination' evening he could 'manage the thing' while he napped on his chair; then he would have him awakened at the right time and hurried away to school.

In the fullness of time the interesting occasion arrived. At eight in the evening the school-house was brilliantly lighted and adorned with wreaths and festoons of foliage and flowers. The master sat throned in his great chair upon a raised platform, with his blackboard behind him. He was looking tolerably mellow. Three rows of benches on each side and six rows in front of him were occupied by the dignitaries of the town and by the parents of the pupils. To his left, back of the rows of citizens, was a spacious temporary platform upon which were seated the scholars who were to take part in the exercises of the evening; rows of small boys, washed and dressed to an intolerable state of discomfort; rows of gawky big boys; snow-banks of girls and young ladies clad in lawn and muslin, and conspicuously conscious of their bare arms, their grandmothers' ancient trinkets, their bits of pink and blue ribbon, and the flowers in their hair. All the rest of the house was filled with non-participating scholars.

The exercises began. A very little boy stood up and sheepishly recited 'You'd scarce expect one of my age, to speak in public on the stage,' etc., accompanying himself with the painfully exact and spasmodic gestures which a machine might have used – supposing the machine to be a trifle out of order. But he got through safely, though cruelly scared, and got a fine round of applause when he made his manufactured bow and retired.

A little shamefaced girl lisped 'Mary had a little lamb,' etc., performed a compassion-inspiring curtsey, got her meed of applause, and sat down flushed and happy.

Tom Sawyer stepped forward with conceited confidence, and soared into the unquenchable and indestructible 'Give me liberty or give me death' speech, with fine fury and frantic gesticulation, and broke down in the middle of it. A ghastly stage-fright seized him, his legs quaked under him and he was like to choke. True, he had the manifest sympathy of the house – but he had the house's silence too, which was even worse than its sympathy. The master frowned, and this completed the disaster. Tom struggled a while and then retired, utterly defeated. There was a weak attempt at applause, but it died early.

'The Boy Stood on the Burning Deck' followed; also 'The Assyrian Came Down', and other declamatory gems. Then there were reading exercises, and a spelling fight. The meagre Latin class recited with honour. The prime feature of the evening was in order, now – original 'compositions' by the young ladies. Each in her turn stepped forward to the edge of the platform, cleared her throat, held up her manuscript (tied with dainty ribbon), and proceeded to read, with laboured attention to 'expression' and punctuation. The themes were the same that had been illuminated upon similar occasions by their mothers before them, their grandmothers, and doubtless all their ancestors in the female line clear back to the Crusades. 'Friendship' was one; 'Memories of other Days'; 'Religion in History'; 'Dream Land'; 'The Adventures of Culture'; 'Forms of Political Government Compared and Contrasted'; 'Melancholy'; 'Filial Love'; 'Heart Longings', etc., etc.

A prevalent feature in these compositions was a nursed and petted melancholy; another was a wasteful and opulent gush of 'fine language'; another was a tendency to lug in by the ears particularly prized words and phrases until they were worn entirely out; and a peculiarity that conspicuously marked and marred them was the inveterate and intolerable sermon that wagged its crippled tail at the end of each and every one of them. No matter what the subject might be, a brainracking effort was made to squirm it into some aspect or other that the moral and religious mind could contemplate with edification. The glaring insincerity of these sermons was not sufficient to compass banishment of the fashion from the schools, and it is not sufficient today; it never will be sufficient while the world stands, perhaps. There is no school in all our land where the young ladies do not feel obliged to close their compositions with a sermon; and you will find that the sermon of the most frivolous and least religious girl in the school is always the longest and the most relentlessly pious. But enough of this. Homely truth is unpalatable. Let us return to the 'Examination'. The first composition that was read was one entitled 'Is this, then, Life?' Perhaps the reader can endure an extract from it:

'In the common walks of life, with what delightful emotions does the youthful mind look forward to some anticipated scene of festivity! Imagination is busy sketching rose-tinted pictures of joy. In fancy, the voluptuous votary of fashion sees herself amid the festive throng, "the observed of all observers". Her graceful form, arrayed in snowy robes, is whirling through the mazes of the joyous dance; her eye is brightest, her step is lightest in the gay assembly. In such delicious fancies time quickly glides by, and the welcome hour arrives for her entrance into the Elysian world, of which she has had such bright dreams. How fairylike does everything appear to her enchanted vision! Each new scene is more charming than the last. But after a while she finds that beneath this goodly exterior, all is vanity; the flattery which once charmed her soul, now grates harshly upon her ear; the ballroom has lost its charms; and with wasted health and embittered heart, she turns away with the conviction that earthly pleasures cannot satisfy the longings of the soul!'

And so forth and so on. There was a buzz of gratification from time to time during the reading, accompanied by whispered ejaculations of 'How sweet!' 'How eloquent!' 'So true!' etc., and after the thing had closed with a peculiarly afflicting sermon, the applause was enthusiastic.

Then arose a slim, melancholy girl, whose face had the 'interesting' paleness that comes of pills and indigestion, and read a 'poem'. Two stanzas of it will do.

> A MISSOURI MAIDEN'S FAREWELL TO ALABAMA
> Alabama, good-bye! I love thee well!
> But yet for a while do I leave thee now!
> Sad, yes, sad thoughts of thee my heart doth swell,
> And burning recollections throng my brow!
> For I have wandered through thy flowery woods;
> Have roamed and read near Tallapoosa's stream;
> Have listened to Talassee's warring floods,
> And wooed on Coosa's side Aurora's beam.

Yet shame I not to bear an o'er-full heart,
Nor blush to turn behind my tearful eyes;
'Tis from no stranger land I now must part,
'Tis to no strangers left I yield these sighs.
Welcome and home were mine within this State
Whose vales I leave, whose spires fade fast from me;
And cold must be mine eyes, and heart, and *tête*,
When, clear Alabama! they turn cold on thee!

There were very few there who knew what '*tête*' meant but the poem was very satisfactory nevertheless.

Next appeared a dark-complexioned, black-eyed, black-haired young lady, who paused an impressive moment, assumed a tragic expression, and began to read in a measured tone:

A Vision

Dark and tempestuous was the night. Around the throne on high not a single star quivered; but the deep intonations of the heavy thunder constantly vibrated upon the ear; whilst the terrific lightning revelled in angry mood through the cloudy chambers of heaven, seeming to scorn the power exerted over its terrors by the illustrious Franklin! Even the boisterous winds unanimously came forth from their mystic homes, and blustered about as if to enhance by their aid the wildness of the scene. At such a time, so dark, so dreary, for human sympathy my very spirit sighed; but instead thereof,

My dearest friend, my counsellor, my comforter and guide,
My joy is grief, my second bliss in joy, came to my side.

She moved like one of those bright beings pictured in the sunny walks of fancy's Eden by the romantic and young, a queen of beauty unadorned save by her own transcendent loveliness. So soft was her step, it failed to make even a sound, and but for the magical thrill imparted by her genial touch, as other unobtrusive beauties she would have glided away unperceived – unsought. A strange sadness rested upon her features, like icy tears upon the robe of December, as she pointed to the contending elements without, and bade me contemplate the two beings presented.

This nightmare occupied some ten pages of manuscript, and wound up with a sermon so destructive of all hope to non-Presbyterians that it took the first prize. This composition was considered to be the very finest effort of the evening. The mayor of the village, in delivering the prize to the author of it, made a warm speech, in which he said that it was by far the most 'eloquent thing he had ever listened to, and that Daniel Webster himself might well be proud of it.'

It may be remarked in passing, that the number of compositions in which the word 'beauteous' was over-fondled, and human experience referred to as 'life's page', was up to the usual average.

Now the master, mellow almost to the verge of geniality, put his chair aside, turned his back to the audience, and began to draw a map of America on the blackboard, to exercise the geography class upon. But he made a sad business of it with his unsteady hand, and a smothered titter rippled over the house. He knew what the matter was, and set himself to right it. He sponged out lines and remade them; but he only distorted them more than ever, and the tittering was more pronounced. He threw his entire attention upon his work, now, as if determined not to be put down by the mirth. He felt that all eyes were fastened upon him; he imagined he was succeeding, and yet the tittering continued; it even manifestly increased. And well it might. There was a garret above, pierced with a scuttle over his head; down through this scuttle came a cat suspended around the haunches by a string; she had a rag tied about her head and jaws to keep her from mewing; she slowly descended, she curved upward and clawed at the string, she swung downward and clawed at the intangible air. The tittering rose higher and higher, the cat was within six inches of the absorbed teacher's head; down, down, a little lower, and she grabbed his wig with her desperate claws, clung to it, and was snatched up into the garret in an instant with her trophy still in her possession! And how the light did blaze abroad from the master's bald pate, for the sign-painter's boy had *gilded* it!

That broke up the meeting. The boys were avenged. Vacation was come.

NOTE.—The pretended 'compositions' quoted above are taken without alteration from a volume entitled *Prose and Poetry by a Western Lady*, but they are exactly and precisely after the school-girl pattern, and hence are much happier than any mere imitations could be.

Chapter 23

Tom joined the new order of Cadets of Temperance, being attracted by the showy character of their 'regalia'. He promised to abstain from smoking, chewing, and profanity as long as he remained a member. Now he found out a new thing – namely, that to promise not to do a thing is the surest way in the world to make a body want to go and do that very thing. Tom soon found himself tormented with a desire to drink, and swear; the desire grew to be so intense that nothing but the hope of a chance to display himself in his red sash kept him from withdrawing from the order. Fourth of July was coming: but he soon gave that up – gave it up before he had worn his shackles over forty-eight hours, and fixed his hopes upon old Judge Frazer, justice of the peace, who was apparently on his deathbed, and would have a big public funeral, since he was so high an official. During three days Tom was deeply concerned about the Judge's condition, and hungry for news of it. Sometimes his hopes ran high, so high that he would venture to get out his regalia and practise before the looking-glass. But the Judge had a most discouraging way of fluctuating. At last he was pronounced upon the mend, and then convalescent. Tom was disgusted; and felt a sense of injury, too. He handed in his resignation at once, and that night the Judge suffered a relapse and died. Tom resolved that he would never trust a man like that again. The funeral was a fine thing. The Cadets paraded in a style calculated to kill the late member with envy.

Tom was a free boy again, however; there was something in that. He could drink and swear now, but found to his surprise that he did not want to. The simple fact that he could took the desire away, and the charm of it.

Tom presently wondered to find his coveted vacation was beginning to hang a little heavily on his hands.

He attempted a diary, but nothing happened during three days, and so he abandoned it.

The first of all the Negro minstrel shows came to town, and made a sensation. Tom and Joe Harper got up a band of performers, and were happy for two days.

Even the Glorious Fourth was in some sense a failure, for it rained hard; there was no procession in consequence, and the greatest man in the world (as

Tom supposed), Mr. Benton, an actual United States Senator, proved an overwhelming disappointment, for he was not twenty-five feet high, nor even anywhere in the neighbourhood of it.

A circus came. The boys played circus for three days afterwards in tents made of rag carpeting – admission, three pins for boys, two for girls – and then circusing was abandoned.

A phrenologist and a mesmerizer came – and went again and left the village duller and drearier than ever.

There were some boys' and girls' parties, but they were so few and so delightful that they only made the aching voids between ache the harder.

Becky Thatcher was gone to her Constantinople home to stay with her parents during vacation – so there was no bright side to life anywhere.

The dreadful secret of the murder was a chronic misery. It was a very cancer for permanency and pain.

Then came the measles.

During two long weeks Tom lay a prisoner, dead to the world and its happenings. He was very ill, he was interested in nothing. When he got upon his feet at last and moved feebly down town, a melancholy change had come over everything and every creature. There had been a 'revival', and everybody had 'got religion'; not only the adults, but even the boys and girls. Tom went about, hoping against hope for the sight of one blessed sinful face, but disappointment crossed him everywhere. He found Joe Harper studying a Testament, and turned sadly away from the depressing spectacle. He sought Ben Rogers, and found him visiting the poor with a basket of tracts. He hunted up Jim Hollis, who called his attention to the precious blessing of his late measles as a warning. Every boy he encountered added another ton to his depression; and when, in desperation, he flew for refuge at last to the bosom of Huckleberry Finn and was received with a scriptural quotation, his heart broke, and he crept home and to bed, realizing that he alone of all the town was lost, for ever and for ever.

And that night there came on a terrific storm, with driving rain, awful claps of thunder and blinding sheets of lightning. He covered his head with the bedclothes and waited in a horror of suspense for his doom; for he had not the shadow of a doubt that all this hubbub was about him. He believed he had taxed the forbearance of the powers above to the extremity of endurance, and that this was the result. It might have seemed to him a waste of pomp and ammunition to kill a bug with a battery of artillery, but there seemed nothing incongruous about the getting up of such an expensive thunderstorm as this to knock the turf from under an insect like himself.

By-and-by the tempest spent itself and died without accomplishing its object. The boy's first impulse was to be grateful and reform. His second was to wait – for there might not be any more storms.

The next day the doctors were back; Tom had relapsed. The three weeks he spent on his back this time seemed an entire age. When he got abroad at last he was hardly grateful that he had been spared, remembering how lonely was his estate, how companionless and forlorn he was. He drifted listlessly down the street and found Jim Hollis acting as judge in a juvenile court that was trying a cat for murder, in the presence of her victim, a bird. He found Joe Harper and Huck Finn up an alley eating a stolen melon. Poor fellows, they, like Tom, had suffered a relapse.

Chapter 24

At last the sleepy atmosphere was stirred, and vigorously. The murder trial came on in the court. It became the absorbing topic of village talk immediately. Tom could not get away from it. Every reference to the murder sent a shudder to his heart, for his troubled conscience and his fears almost persuaded him that these remarks were put forth in his hearing as 'feelers'; he did not see how he could be suspected of knowing anything about the murder, but still he could not be comfortable in the midst of this gossip. It kept him in a cold shiver all the time. He took Huck to a lonely place to have a talk with him. It would be some relief to unseal his tongue for a little while, to divide his burden of distress with another sufferer. Moreover, he wanted to assure himself that Huck had remained discreet.

'Huck, have you ever told anybody about that?'

''Bout what?'

'You know what.'

'*Oh*, 'course I haven't.'

'Never a word?'

'Never a solitary word, so help me. What makes you ask?'

'Well, I was afeard.'

'Why, Tom Sawyer, we wouldn't be alive two days if that got found out. *You* know that.'

Tom felt more comfortable. After a pause:

'Huck, they couldn't anybody get you to tell, could they?'

'Get me to tell? Why, if I wanted that half-breed devil to drownd me they could get me to tell. They ain't no different way.'

'Well, that's all right then. I reckon we're safe as long as we keep mum. But let's swear again, anyway. It's more surer!'

'I'm agreed.'

So they swore again with dread solemnities.

'What is the talk around, Huck? I've heard a power of it.'

'Talk? Well, it's just Muff Potter, Muff Potter, Muff Potter all the time. It keeps me in a sweat, constant, so's I want to hide som'ers.'

'That's just the same way they go on round me. I reckon he's a goner. Don't you feel sorry for him sometimes?'

''Most always – 'most always. He ain't no account; but then he ain't ever done anything to hurt anybody. Just fishes a little to get money to get drunk on – and loafs around considerable; but, Lord, we all do that – leastways most of us – preachers and such like. But he's kind of good – he give me half a fish, once, when there wasn't enough for two; and lots of times he's kind of stood by me when I was out of luck.'

'Well, he's mended kites for me, Huck, and knitted hooks on to my line. I wish we could get him out of there.'

'My! we couldn't get him out, Tom. And besides, 'twouldn't do any good; they'd ketch him again.'

'Yes – so they would. But I hate to hear 'em abuse him so like the dickens when he never done – that.'

'I do too, Tom. Lord, I hear 'em say he's the bloodiest-looking villain in this country, and they wonder he wasn't ever hung before.'

'Yes; they talk like that all the time. I've heard 'em say that if he was to get free they'd lynch him.'

'And they'd do it, too.'

The boys had a long talk, but it brought them little comfort. As the twilight drew on, they found themselves hanging about the neighbourhood of the little isolated jail, perhaps with an undefined hope that something would happen that might clear away their difficulties. But nothing happened; there seemed to be no angels or fairies interested in this luckless captive.

The boys did as they had often done before – went to the cell grating and gave Potter some tobacco and matches. He was on the ground floor, and there were no guards.

His gratitude for their gifts had always smote their consciences before – it cut deeper than ever, this time. They felt cowardly and treacherous to the last degree when Potter said:

'You've ben mighty good to me, boys – better'n anybody else in this town. And I don't forget it, I don't. Often I says to myself, says I, "I used to mend all the boys' kites and things, and show 'em where the good fishin' places was, and befriend 'em when I could, and now they've all forgot old Muff when he's in trouble, but Tom don't, and Huck don't – *they* don't forget him," says I, "and I don't forget *them*!" Well, boys, I done an awful thing – drunk and crazy at the time, that's the only way I account for it, and now I got to swing for it, and it's right. Right, and *best*, too, I reckon; hope so, anyway. Well, we won't talk about that. I don't want to make *you* feel bad; you've befriended me. But what I want to say is, don't *you* ever get drunk, then you won't ever get here. Stand a little furder west; so, that's it; it's a prime comfort to see faces that's friendly when a body's in such a muck of trouble, and there don't none come here but yourn. Good friendly faces – good friendly faces. Get up on one another's backs, and let me touch 'em. That's it. Shake hands –

yourn'll come through the bars, but mine's too big. Little hands, and weak –
but they've helped Muff Potter a power, and they'd help him more if they
could.'

Tom went home miserable, and his dreams that night were full of
horrors. The next day and the day after, he hung about the court-room,
drawn by an almost irresistible impulse to go in, but forcing himself to stay
out. Huck was having the same experience. They studiously avoided each
other. Each wandered away from time to time, but the same dismal
fascination always brought them back presently. Tom kept his ears open
when idlers sauntered out of the court-room, but invariably heard distressing
news; the toils were closing more and more relentlessly around poor Potter.
At the end of the second day the village talk was to the effect that Injun Joe's
evidence stood firm and unshaken, and that there was not the slightest
question as to what the jury's verdict would be.

Tom was out late that night, and came to bed through the window. He
was in a tremendous state of excitement. It was hours before he got to sleep.
All the village flocked to the court-house the next morning, for this was to be
the great day. Both sexes were about equally represented in the packed
audience. After a long wait the jury filed in and took their places; shortly
afterwards, Potter, pale and haggard, timid and hopeless, was brought in with
chains upon him, and seated where all the curious eyes could stare at him; no
less conspicuous was Injun Joe, stolid as ever. There was another pause, and
then the judge arrived, and the sheriff proclaimed the opening of the court.
The usual whisperings among the lawyers and gathering together of papers
followed. These details and accompanying delays worked up an atmosphere
of preparation that was as impressive as it was fascinating.

Now a witness was called who testified that he found Muff Potter
washing in the brook at an early hour of the morning that the murder was
discovered, and that he immediately sneaked away. After some further
questioning, counsel for the prosecution said.

'Take the witness.'

The prisoner raised his eyes for a moment, but dropped them again when
his own counsel said:

'I have no questions to ask him.'

The next witness proved the finding of the knife near the corpse. Counsel
for the prosecution said:

'Take the witness.'

'I have no questions to ask him,' Potter's lawyer replied.

A third witness swore he had often seen the knife in Potter's possession.

'Take the witness.'

Counsel for Potter declined to question him.

The faces of the audience began to betray annoyance. Did this attorney mean to throw away his client's life without an effort?

Several witnesses deposed concerning Potter's guilty behaviour when brought to the scene of the murder. They were allowed to leave the stand without being cross-questioned.

Every detail of the damaging circumstances that occurred in the graveyard upon that morning which all present remembered so well was brought out by credible witnesses, but none of them were cross-examined by Potter's lawyer. The perplexity and dissatisfaction of the house expressed itself in murmurs and provoked a reproof from the bench. Counsel for the prosecution now said:

'By the oaths of citizens whose simple word is above suspicion, we have fastened this awful crime beyond all possibility of question upon the unhappy prisoner at the bar. We rest our case here.'

A groan escaped from poor Potter, and he put his face in his hands, and rocked his body softly to and fro, while a painful silence reigned in the court-room. Many men were moved, and many women's compassion testified itself in tears. Counsel for the defence rose and said:

'Your Honour, in our remarks at the opening of this trial, we foreshadowed our purpose to prove that our client did this fearful deed while under the influence of a blind and irresponsible delirium produced by drink. We have changed our mind; we shall not offer that plea. [Then to the clerk.] Call Thomas Sawyer.'

A puzzled amazement awoke in every face in the house, not even excepting Potter's. Every eye fastened itself with wondering interest upon Tom as he rose and took his place upon the stand. The boy looked wild enough, for he was badly scared. The oath was administered.

'Thomas Sawyer, where were you on the seventeenth of June, about the hour of midnight?'

Tom glanced at Injun Joe's face, and his tongue failed him. The audience listened breathless, but the words refused to come. After a few moments, however, the boy got a little of his strength back, and managed to put enough of it into his voice to make part of the house hear:

'In the graveyard!'

'A little bit louder, please. Don't be afraid. You were——'

'In the graveyard.'

A contemptuous smile flitted across Injun Joe's face.

'Were you anywhere near Horse Williams's grave?'

'Yes, sir.'

'Speak up a trifle louder. How near were you?'

'Near as I am to you.'

'Were you hidden or not?'

'I was hid.'

'Where?'

'Behind the elms that's on the edge of the grave.'

Injun Jo gave a barely perceptible start.

'Anyone with you?'

'Yes, sir. I went there with——'

'Wait – wait a moment. Never mind mentioning your companion's name. We will produce him at the proper time. Did you carry anything there with you?'

Tom hesitated and looked confused.

'Speak out, my boy – don't be diffident. The truth is always respectable. What did you take there?'

'Only a – a – dead cat.'

There was a ripple of mirth, which the court checked.

'We will produce the skeleton of that cat. Now my boy, tell us everything that occurred – tell it in your own way – don't skip anything, and don't be afraid.'

Tom began – hesitatingly at first, but, as he warmed to his subject, his words flowed more and more easily; in a little while every sound ceased but his own voice; every eye fixed itself upon him; with parted lips and bated breath the audience hung upon his words, taking no note of time, rapt in the ghastly fascinations of the tale. The strain upon pent emotions reached its climax when the boy said, 'And as the doctor fetched the board around and Muff Potter fell, Injun Joe jumped with his knife and——'

Crash! Quick as lightning, the half-breed sprang for a window, tore his way through all opposers, and was gone!

Chapter 25

Tom was a glittering hero once more – the pet of the old, the envy of the young. His name even went into immortal print, for the village paper magnified him. There were some that believed he would be President yet, if he escaped hanging.

As usual, the fickle unreasoning world took Muff Potter to its bosom, and fondled him as lavishly as it had abused him before. But that sort of conduct is to the world's credit; therefore it is not well to find fault with it.

Tom's days were days of splendour and exultation to him, but his nights were seasons of horror. Injun Joe infested all his dreams, and always with doom in his eye. Hardly any temptation could persuade the boy to stir abroad after nightfall. Poor Huck was in the same state of wretchedness and terror, for Tom had told the whole story to the lawyer the night before the great day of the trial, and Huck was sore afraid of his share in the business might leak out yet, notwithstanding Injun Joe's flight had saved him the suffering of testifying in court. The poor fellow had got the attorney to promise secrecy, but what of that? Since Tom's harassed conscience had managed to drive him to the lawyer's house by night and wring a dread tale from lips that had been sealed with the dismalest and most formidable of oaths, Huck's confidence in the human race was well-nigh obliterated. Daily Muff Potter's gratitude made Tom glad he had spoken; but nightly he wished he had sealed up his tongue. Half the time Tom was afraid Injun Joe would never be captured; the other half he was afraid he would be. He felt sure he never could draw a safe breath again until that man was dead and he had seen the corpse.

Rewards had been offered, the country had been scoured, but no Injun Joe was found. One of those omniscient and awe-inspiring marvels, a detective, came up from St Louis, moused around, shook his head, looked wise, and made that sort of astounding success which members of that craft usually achieve. That is to say, 'he found a clue'. But you can't hang a 'clue' for murder, and so after that detective had got through and gone home, Tom felt just as insecure as he was before.

The slow days drifted on, and each left behind it a slightly lightened weight of apprehension.

Chapter 26

There comes a time in every rightly constructed boy's life when he has a raging desire to go somewhere and dig for hidden treasure. This desire suddenly came upon Tom one day. He sallied out to find Joe Harper, but failed of success. Next he sought Ben Rogers; he had gone fishing. Presently he stumbled upon Huck Finn the Red-handed. Huck would answer. Tom took him to a private place, and opened the matter to him confidentially. Huck was willing. Huck was always willing to take a hand in any enterprise that offered entertainment and required no capital, for he had a troublesome superabundance of that sort of time which is *not* money.

'Where'll we dig?' said Huck.

'Oh, 'most anywhere.'

'Why, is it hid all around?'

'No indeed it ain't. It's hid in mighty particular places, Huck – sometimes on islands, sometimes in rotten chests under the end of a limb of an old dead tree, just where the shadow falls at midnight; but mostly under the floor in ha'nted houses.'

'Who hides it?'

'Why, robbers, of course – who'd you reckon? Sunday-school sup'rintendents?'

'I don't know. If it was mine I wouldn't hide it; I'd spend it and have a good time.'

'So would I; but robbers don't do that way, they always hide it and leave it there.'

'Don't they come after it any more?'

'No, they think they will, but they generally forget the marks, or else they die. Anyway it lays there a long time and gets rusty; and by-and-by somebody finds an old yellow paper that tells how to find the marks – a paper that's got to be ciphered over about a week because its mostly signs and hy'roglyphics.'

'Hyro – which?'

'Hy'roglyphics – pictures and things, you know, that don't seem to mean anything.'

'Have you got one of them papers, Tom?'

'No.'

'Well, then, how you going to find out the marks?'

'I don't want any marks. They always bury it under a ha'nted house, or on an island, or under a dead tree that's got one limb sticking out. Well, we've tried Jackson's Island a little, and we can try it again sometime; and there's the old ha'nted house up the Still-House branch, and there's lots of dead-limb trees – dead loads of 'em.'

'Is it under all of them?'

'How you talk! No!'

'Then how you going to know which one to go for?'

'Go for all of 'em.'

'Why, Tom, it'll take all summer.'

'Well, what of that? Suppose you find a brass pot with a hundred dollars in it, all rusty and gay, or a rotten chest full of di'monds. How's that?'

Huck's eyes glowed.

'That's bully, plenty bully enough for me. Just you gimme the hundred dollars, and I don't want no di'monds.'

'All right. But I bet you *I* ain't going to throw off on di'monds. Some of 'em's worth twenty dollars apiece. There ain't any, hardly, but's worth six bits or a dollar.'

'No! Is that so?'

'Cert'nly – anybody'll tell you so. Hain't you ever seen one, Huck?'

'Not as I remember.'

'Oh, kings have slathers of them.'

'Well, I don't know no kings, Tom.'

'I reckon you don't. But if you was to go to Europe you'd see a raft of 'em hopping around.'

'Do they hop?'

'Hop? – your granny! No!'

'Well, what did you say they did for?'

'Shucks! I only meant you'd *see* 'em – not hopping, of course – what do they want to hop for? But I mean you'd just see 'em – scattered around, you know, in a kind of a general way. Like that old hump-backed Richard.'

'Richard! What's his other name?'

'He didn't have any other name. Kings don't have any but a given name.'

'No?'

'But they don't.'

'Well, if they like it, Tom, all right; but I don't want to be a king and have only just a given name, like a nigger. But say – where you going to dig first?'

'Well, I don't know. S'pose we tackle that old dead limb tree on the hill t'other side of Still-House branch?'

'I'm agreed.'

So they got a crippled pick and a shovel, and set out on their three-mile tramp. They arrived hot and panting, and threw themselves down in the shade of a neighbouring elm to rest and have a smoke.

'I like this,' said Tom.

'So do I.'

'Say, Huck, if we find a treasure here, what you going to do with your share?'

'Well, I'll have a pie and a glass of soda every day, and I'll go to every circus that comes along. I'll bet I'll have a gay time.'

'Well, ain't you going to save any of it?'

'Save it? What for?'

'Why, so as to have something to live on by-and-by.'

'Oh, that ain't any use. Pap would come back to thish yer town some day and get his claws on it if I didn't hurry up, and I tell you he'd clean it out pretty quick. What you going to do with yourn, Tom?'

'I'm going to buy a new drum, and a sure-'nough sword, and a red necktie, and a bull-pup, and get married.'

'Married!'

'That's it.'

'Tom, you – why, you ain't in your right mind.'

'Wait – you'll see.'

'Well, that's the foolishest thing you could do, Tom. Look at Pap and my mother. Fight! why they used to fight all the time. I remember, mighty well.'

'That ain't anything. The girl I'm going to marry won't fight.'

'Tom, I reckon they're all alike. They'll all comb a body. Now you better think about this a while. I tell you you better. What's the name of the gal?'

'It ain't a gal at all – it's a girl.'

'It's all the same, I reckon; some says gal, some says girl – both's right, like enough. Anyway, what's her name, Tom?'

'I'll tell you some time – not now.'

'All right – that'll do. Only if you get married I'll be more lonesomer than ever.'

'No, you won't, you'll come and live with me. Now stir out of this, and we'll go to digging.'

They worked and sweated for half an hour. No result. They toiled another half hour. Still no result. Huck said:

'Do they always bury it as deep as this?'

'Sometimes – not always. Not generally. I reckon we haven't got the right place.'

So they chose a new spot and began again. The labour dragged a little, but still they made progress. They pegged away in silence for some time. Finally Huck leaned on his shovel, swabbed the beaded drops from his brow with his sleeve, and said:

'Where you going to dig next, after we get this one?'

'I reckon maybe we'll tackle the old tree that's over yonder on Cardiff Hill, back on the widows.'

'I reckon that'll be a good one. But won't the widow take it away from us, Tom? It's on her land.'

'She take it away! Maybe she'd like to try it once. Whoever finds one of these hid treasures, it belongs to him. It don't make any difference whose land it's on.'

That was satisfactory. The work went on. By-and-by Huck said:

'Blame it, we must be in the wrong place again. What do you think?'

'It is mighty curious, Huck. I don't understand it. Sometimes witches interfere. I reckon maybe that's what's the trouble now.'

'Shucks! witches ain't got no power in the daytime.'

'Well, that's so. I didn't think of that. Oh, I know what the matter is! What a blamed lot of fools we are! You got to find out where the shadow of the limb falls at midnight, and that's where you dig!'

'Then confound it, we've fooled away all this work for nothing. Now hang it all, we got to come back in the night. It's an awful long way. Can you get out?'

'I bet I will. We've got to do it tonight, too, because if somebody sees these holes they'll know in a minute what's here and they'll go for it.'

'Well, I'll come around and meow tonight.'

'All right. Let's hide the tools in the bushes.'

The boys were there that night about the appointed time. They sat in the shadow waiting. It was a lonely place, and an hour made solemn by old traditions. Spirits whispered in the rustling leaves, ghosts lurked in the murky nooks, the deep baying of a hound floated up out of the distance, an owl answered with his sepulchral note. The boys were subdued by these solemnities, and talked little. By-and-by they judged that twelve had come; they marked where the shadow fell and began to dig. Their hopes commenced to rise. Their interest grew stronger, and their industry kept pace with it. The hole deepened and still deepened, but every time their hearts jumped to hear the pick strike upon something, they only suffered a new disappointment. It was only a stone or a chunk. At last Tom said:

'It ain't any use, Huck, we're wrong again.'

'Well, but we can't be wrong. We spotted the shadder to a dot.'

'I know it, but then there's another thing.'

'What's that?'

'Why, we only guessed at the time. Like enough it was too late or too early.'

Huck dropped his shovel.

'That's it,' said he. 'That's the very trouble. We got to give this one up.

'By and by they judged that twelve had come . . . and began to dig'

We can't ever tell the right time, and besides, this kind of thing's too awful, here this time of night with witches and ghosts a fluttering around so. I feel as if something's behind me all the time; and I'm afeard to turn around, becuz maybe there's others in front a waiting for a chance. I been creeping all over ever since I got here.'

'Well, I've been pretty much so too, Huck. They 'most always put in a dead man when they bury a treasure under a tree, to look out for it.'

'Lordy!'

'Yes, they do. I've always heard that.'

'Tom, I don't like to fool around much where there's dead people. A boy's bound to get into trouble with 'em, sure.'

'I don't like to stir 'em up, either, Huck. S'pose this one here was to stick his skull out and say something!'

'Don't, Tom! It's awful.'

'Well, it just is, Huck. I don't feel comfortable a bit.'

'Say, Tom, let's give this place up, and try somewheres else.'

'All right, I reckon we better.'

'What'll it be?'

Tom considered awhile, and then said:

'The ha'nted house. That's it.'

'Blame it. I don't like ha'nted houses, Tom. Why, they're a dern sight worse'n dead people. Dead people might talk maybe, but they don't come sliding around in a shroud when you ain't noticing, and peep over your shoulder all of a sudden and grit their teeth the way a ghost does. I couldn't stand such a thing as that, Tom – nobody could.'

'Yes; but, Huck, ghosts don't travel around only at night – they won't hinder us from digging there in the daytime.'

'Well, that's so. But you know mighty well people don't go about that ha'nted house in the day nor the night.'

'Well, that's mostly because they don't like to go where a man's been murdered, anyway. But nothing's ever been seen around that house in the night – just some blue light slipping by the window – no regular ghosts.'

'Well, where you see one of them blue lights flickering around, Tom, you can bet there's a ghost mighty close behind it. It stands to reason. Becuz you know that they don't anybody but ghosts use 'em.'

'Yes, that's so. But anyway they don't come around in the daytime, so what's the use of our being afeard?'

'Well, all right. We'll tackle the ha'nted house if you say so; but I reckon it's taking chances.'

They had started down the hill by this time. There in the middle of the moonlit valley below them stood the 'haunted' house, utterly isolated, its fences gone long ago, rank weeds smothering the very door-step, the chimney crumbled to ruin, the window-sashes vacant, a corner of the roof caved in. The boys gazed awhile, half expecting to see a blue light flit past a window; then talking in a low tone, as befitted the time and the circumstances, they struck far off to the right, to give the haunted house a wide berth, and took their way homeward through the woods that adorned the rearward side of Cardiff Hill.

Chapter 27

About noon the next day the boys arrived at the dead tree; they had come for their tools. Tom was impatient to go to the haunted house; Huck was measurably so, also, but suddenly said:

'Looky here, Tom, do you know what day it is?'

Tom mentally ran over the days of the week and then quickly lifted his eyes with a startled look in them:

'My! I never once thought of it, Huck!'

'Well, I didn't, neither, but all at once it popped on to me that it was Friday.'

'Blame it; a body can't be too careful, Huck. We might a got into an awful scrape, tackling such a thing on a Friday.'

'Might! Better say we would! There's some lucky days, maybe, but Friday ain't.'

'Any fool knows that. I don't reckon you was the first that found it out, Huck.'

'Well, I never said I was, did I?' And Friday ain't all, neither. I had a rotten bad dream last night – dreamt about rats.'

'No! Sure sign of trouble. Did they fight?'

'No.'

'Well, that's good, Huck. When they don't fight, it's only a sign that there's trouble around, you know. All we got to do is to look mighty sharp and keep out of it. We'll drop this thing for today, and play. Do you know Robin Hood, Huck?'

'No. Who's Robin Hood?'

'Why, he was one of the greatest men that was ever in England – and the best. He was a robber.'

'Cracky, I wisht I was. Who did he rob?'

'Only sheriffs and bishops and rich people and kings, and such like. But he never bothered the poor. He loved 'em. He always divided up with 'em perfectly square.'

'Well, he must a ben a brick.'

'I bet you he was, Huck. Oh, he was the noblest man that ever was. They ain't any such men now, I can tell you. He could lick any man in England with one hand tied behind him; and he could take his yew bow and plug a ten cent piece every time, a mile and a half.'

'What's a *yew* bow?'

'I don't know. It's some kind of a bow, of course. And if he hit that dime only on the edge he could set down and cry – and curse. But we'll play Robin Hood – it's noble fun. I'll learn you.'

'I'm agreed.'

So they played Robin Hood all the afternoon, now and then casting a yearning eye down upon the haunted house and passing a remark about the morrow's prospects and possibilities there. As the sun began to sink into the west, they took their way homeward athwart the long shadows of the trees and soon were buried from sight in the forests of Cardiff Hill.

On Saturday, shortly after noon, the boys were at the dead tree again. They had a smoke and a chat in the shade, and then dug a little in their last hole, not with great hope, but merely because Tom said there were so many cases where people had given up a treasure after getting down within six inches of it, and then somebody else had come along and turned it up with a single thrust of a shovel. The thing failed this time, however, so the boys shouldered their tools and went away, feeling that they had not trifled with fortune, but had fulfilled all the requirements that belong to the business of treasure-hunting.

When they reached the haunted house, there was something so weird and grisly about the dead silence that reigned there under the baking sun, and something so depressing about the loneliness and desolation of the place, that they were afraid, for a moment, to venture in. Then they crept to the door and took a trembling peep. They saw a weed-grown, floorless room, unplastered, an ancient fire-place, vacant windows, a ruinous staircase; and here, there, and everywhere, hung ragged and abandoned cobwebs. They presently entered softly, with quickened pulses, talking in whispers, ears alert to catch the slightest sound, and muscles tense and ready for instant retreat.

In a little while familiarity modified their fears, and they gave the place a critical and interested examination, rather admiring their own boldness, and wondering at it, too. Next they wanted to look upstairs. This was something like cutting off retreat, but they got to daring each other, and of course there could be but one result – they threw their tools into a corner and made the ascent. Up there were the same signs of decay. In one corner they found a closet that promised mystery, but the promise was a fraud – there was nothing in it. Their courage was up now, and well in hand. They were about to go down and begin work when——

'*Sht*!' said Tom.

'What is it?' whispered Huck, blanching with fright.

'*Sh*! There! Hear it?'

'Yes! Oh, my! Let's run!'

'Keep still! Don't you budge! They're coming right towards the door.'

The boys stretched themselves upon the floor with their eyes to knot-holes in the planking, and lay waiting in a misery of fear.

'They've stopped – No – coming – Here they are. Don't whisper another word, Huck. My goodness, I wish I was out of this!'

Two men entered. Each boy said to himself:

'There's the old deaf and dumb Spaniard that's been about town once or twice lately – never saw t'other man before.'

'T'other' was a ragged, unkempt creature, with nothing very pleasant in his face. The Spaniard was wrapped in a *serape*; he had bushy white whiskers, long white hair flowed from under his sombrero, and he wore green goggles. When they came in, 't'other' was talking in a low voice; they sat down on the ground, facing the door, with their backs to the wall, and the speaker continued his remarks. His manner became less guarded and his words more distinct as he proceeded.

'No,' said he, 'I've thought it all over, and I don't like it. It's dangerous.'

'Dangerous!' grunted the 'deaf and dumb' Spaniard, to the vast surprise of the boys. 'Milksop!'

This voice made the boys gasp and quake. It was Injun Joe's! There was silence for some time. Then Joe said:

'What's any more dangerous than the job up yonder – but nothing's come of it.'

'That's different. Away up the river so, and not another house about. 'Twon't ever be known that we tried, anyway, long as we didn't succeed.'

'Well, what's more dangerous than coming here in the daytime? – anybody would suspicion us that saw us.'

'I know that. But there wasn't any other place as handy after that fool of a job. I want to quit this shanty. I wanted to yesterday, only it wasn't any use trying to stir out of here with those infernal boys playing over there on the hill right in full view.'

'Those infernal boys' quaked again under the inspiration of this remark, and thought how lucky it was that they had remembered it was Friday and concluded to wait a day. They wished in their hearts they had waited a year. The two men got out some food and made a luncheon. After a long and thoughtful silence Injun Joe said:

'Look here, lad, you go back up the river where you belong. Wait there till you hear from me. I'll take the chances on dropping into this town just once more, for a look. We'll do that "dangerous" job after I've spied around a little and think things look well for it. Then for Texas! We'll leg it together!'

This was satisfactory. Both men presently fell to yawning, and Injun Joe said:

'I'm dead for sleep! It's your turn to watch.'

He curled down in the weeds and soon began to snore. His comrade stirred him once or twice, and he became quiet. Presently the watcher began to nod; his head drooped lower and lower; both men began to snore now.

The boys drew a long grateful breath. Tom whispered:

'Now's our chance – come!'

Huck said: 'I can't – I'd die if they was to wake.'

Tom urged – Huck held back. At last Tom rose slowly and softly, and started alone. But the first step he made wrung such a hideous creak from the crazy floor that he sank down almost dead with fright. He never made a second attempt. The boys lay there counting the dragging moments till it seemed to them that time must be done and eternity growing grey; and then they were grateful to note that at last the sun was setting.

Now one snore ceased. Injun Joe sat up, stared around – smiled grimly upon his comrade, whose head was drooping upon his knees – stirred him up with his foot and said:

'Here! You're a watchman, ain't you!'

'All right, though – nothing's happened.'

'My! Have I been asleep?'

'Oh, partly, partly. Nearly time for us to be moving, pard. What'll we do with that little swag we've got left?'

'I don't know – leave it here as we've always done, I reckon. No use to take it away till we start south. Six hundred and fifty in silver's something to carry.'

'Well – all right – it won't matter to come here again.'

'No – but I'd say come in the night as we used to do – it's better.'

'Yes, but look here; it may be a good while before I get the right chance at that job; accidents might happen, 'tain't in such a very good place; we'll just regularly bury it – and bury it deep.'

'Good idea,' said the comrade, who walked across the room, knelt down, raised one of the rearward hearth-stones and took out a bag that jingled pleasantly. He subtracted from it twenty or thirty dollars for himself and as much for Injun Joe, and passed the bag to the latter, who was on his knees in the corner, now, digging with his bowie-knife.

The boys forgot all their fears, all their miseries in an instant. With gloating eyes they watched every movement. Luck! – the splendour of it was beyond all imagination! Six hundred dollars was money enough to make half a dozen boys rich! Here was treasure-hunting under the happiest auspices – there would not be any bothersome uncertainty as to where to dig. They nudged each other every moment – eloquent nudges and easily understood, for they simply meant, 'Oh, but ain't you glad now we're here!'

Joe's knife struck upon something.

'Hello!' said he.

'What is it?' said his comrade.

'Half-rotten plank – no, it's a box, I believe. Here bear a hand, and we'll see what it's here for. Never mind, I've broke a hole.'

He reached his hand in and drew it out.

'Man, it's money!'

The two men examined the handful of coins. They were gold. The boys above were as excited as themselves, and as delighted.

Joe's comrade said:

'We'll make quick work of this. There's an old rusty pick over amongst the weeds in the corner, the other side of the fire-place – I saw it a minute ago.'

He ran and brought the boys' pick and shovel. Injun Joe took the pick, looked it over critically, shook his head, muttered something to himself, and then began to use it.

The box was soon unearthed. It was not very large; it was iron-bound and had been very strong before the slow years had injured it. The men contemplated the treasure awhile in blissful silence.

'Pard, there's thousands of dollars here,' said Injun Joe.

''Twas always said that Murrel's gang used around here one summer,' the stranger observed.

'I know it,' said Injun Joe; 'and this looks like it, I should say.'

'Now you won't need to do that job.'

The half-breed frowned. Said he:

'You don't know me. Least you don't know all about that thing. 'Tain't robbery altogether – it's revenge!' and a wicked light flamed in his eyes. 'I'll need your help in it. When it's finished – then Texas. Go home to your Nance and your kids, and stand by till you hear from me.'

'Well, if you say so. What'll we do with this – bury it again?'

'Yes. [Ravishing delight overhead.] No! by the great Sacham, no! [Profound distress overhead.] I'd nearly forgot. That pick had fresh earth on it! [The boys were sick with terror in a moment.] What business has a pick and a shovel here? What business with fresh earth on them? Who brought them here – and where are they gone? Have you heard anybody? – seen anybody? What! bury it again and leave them to come and see the ground disturbed? Not exactly – not exactly. We'll take it to my den.'

'Why, of course! Might have thought of that before. You mean number one?'

'No – number two – under the cross. The other place is bad – too common.'

'All right. It's nearly dark enough to start.'

Injun Joe got up and went about from window to window, cautiously peeping out. Presently he said:

'Who could have brought those tools here? Do you reckon they can be upstairs?'

The boys' breath forsook them. Injun Joe put his hand on his knife, halted a moment, undecided, and then turned towards the stairway. The boys thought of the closet, but their strength was gone. The steps came creaking up the stairs – the intolerable distress of the situation woke the stricken resolution of the lads – they were about to spring for the closet, when there was a crash of rotten timbers, and Injun Joe landed on the ground amid the débris of the ruined stairway. He gathered himself up cursing, and his comrade said:

'Now what's the use of all that? If it's anybody, and they're up there, let them stay there – who cares? If they want to jump down, now, and get into trouble, who objects? It will be dark in fifteen minutes – and then let them follow us if they want to; I'm willing. In my opinion, whoever hove those things in here caught a sight of us, and took us for ghosts or devils or something. I'll bet they're running yet.'

Joe grumbled awhile; then he agreed with his friend that what daylight was left ought to be economized in getting things ready for leaving. Shortly afterwards they slipped out of the house in the deepening twilight, and moved towards the river with their precious box.

Tom and Huck rose up, weak but vastly relieved, and stared after them through the chinks between the logs of the house. Follow? Not they – they were content to reach the ground again without broken necks, and take the townward track over the hill. They did not talk much, they were too much absorbed in hating themselves – hating the ill-luck that made them take the spade and the pick there. But for that, Injun Joe never would have suspected. He would have hidden the silver with the gold to wait there till his 'revenge' was satisfied, and then he would have had the misfortune to find that money turn up missing. Bitter, bitter luck that the tools were ever brought there! They resolved to keep a lookout for that Spaniard when he should come to town spying out for chances to do his revengeful job, and follow him to 'number two', wherever that might be. Then a ghastly thought occurred to Tom:

'Revenge? What if he means us, Huck!'

'Oh, don't,' said Huck, nearly fainting.

They talked it all over, and as they entered town they agreed to believe that he might possibly mean somebody else – at least that he might at least mean nobody but Tom, since only Tom had testified.

Very, very small comfort it was to Tom to be alone in danger! Company would be a palpable improvement, he thought.

Chapter 28

The adventure of the day mightily tormented Tom's dreams that night. Four times he had his hands on that rich treasure, and four times it wasted to nothingness in his fingers as sleep forsook him, and wakefulness brought back the hard reality of his misfortune. As he lay in the early morning recalling the incidents of his great adventure he noticed that they seemed curiously subdued and far away, somewhat as if they had happened in another world, or in a time long gone by. Then it occurred to him that the great adventure itself must be a dream! There was one very strong argument in favour of this idea, namely, that the quantity of coin he had seen was too vast to be real. He had never seen as much as fifty dollars in one mass before, and he was like all boys of his age and station in life, in that he imagined that all references to 'hundreds' and 'thousands' were mere fanciful forms of speech, and that no such sums existed in the world. He never had supposed for a moment that so large a sum as a hundred dollars was to be found in actual money in anybody's possession. If his notions of hidden treasure had been analysed, they would have been found to consist of a handful of real dimes, and a bushel of vague, splendid, ungraspable ones.

But the incidents of his adventure grew sensibly sharper and clearer under the attrition of thinking them over, and so he presently found himself leaning to the impression that the thing might not have been a dream after all. This uncertainty must be swept away. He would snatch a hurried breakfast, and go and find Huck.

Huck was sitting on the gunwale of a flat-boat, listlessly dangling his feet in the water, and looking very melancholy. Tom concluded to let Huck lead up to the subject. If he did not do it, then the adventure would be proved to have been only a dream.

'Hello, Huck!'

'Hello, yourself.'

Silence for a minute.

'Tom, if we'd a left the blame tools at the dead tree we'd a got the money. Oh, ain't it awful!'

''Tain't a dream, then, 'tain't a dream! Somehow I 'most wish it was. Dog'd if I don't.'

'What ain't a dream?'

'Oh, that thing yesterday. I ben half thinking it was.'

'Dream! If them stairs hadn't broke down you'd a seen how much dream it was! I've had dreams enough all night, with that patch-eyed Spanish devil going for me all through 'em, rot him!'

'No, not rot him. Find him! Track the money!'

'Tom, we'll never find him. A feller don't only have one chance for such a pile, and that one's lost. I'd feel mighty shaky if I was to see him, anyway.'

'Well, so'd I; but I'd like to see him anyway, and track him out – to his number two.'

'Number two; yes, that's it. I ben thinking 'bout that. But I can't make nothing out of it. What do you reckon it is?'

'I dono. It's too deep. Say, Huck – maybe it's the number of a house!'

'Goody! – No, Tom, that ain't it. If it is, it ain't in this one-horse town. They ain't no numbers here.'

'Well, that's so. Lemme think a minute. Here – it's the number of a room – in a tavern, you know!'

'Oh, that's the trick! They ain't only two taverns. We can find out quick.'

'You stay here, Huck, till I come.'

Tom was off at once. He did not care to have Huck's company in public places. He was gone half an hour. He found that in the best tavern number two had long been occupied by a young lawyer, and was still so occupied. In the less ostentatious house number two was a mystery. The tavern-keeper's young son said it was kept locked all the time, and he never saw anybody go into it or come out of it except at night; he did not know any particular reason for this state of things; had had some little curiosity, but it was rather feeble; had made the most of the mystery by entertaining himself with the idea that that room was 'ha'nted'; had noticed that there was a light in there the night before.

'That's what I've found out, Huck. I reckon that's the very number two we're after.

'I reckon it is, Tom. Now what you going to do?'

'Lemme think.'

Tom thought a long time. Then he said:

'I'll tell you. The back door of that number two is the door that comes out into that little close alley between the tavern and the old rattle-trap of a brick-store. Now you get hold of all the door keys you can find and I'll nip all of Auntie's, and the first dark night we'll go there and try 'em. And mind you keep a look out for Injun Joe, because he said he was going to drop into town and spy around once more for a chance to get his revenge. If you see him, you just follow him; and if he don't go to that number two, that ain't the place.'

'Lordy, I don't want to foller him by myself!'

'Why, it'll be night, sure. He mightn't ever see you – and if he did, maybe he'd never think anything.'

'Well, if it's pretty dark I reckon I'll track him. I dono – I dono. I'll try.'

'You bet I'll follow him if it's dark, Huck! Why, he might a found out he couldn't get his revenge, and be going right after that money.'

'It's so, Tom, it's so. I'll foller him; I will, by jingoes.'

'Now you're talking! Don't you ever weaken. Huck, and I won't.'

Chapter 29

That night Tom and Huck were ready for their adventure. They hung about the neighbourhood of the tavern until after nine, one watching the alley at a distance and the other the tavern door. Nobody entered the alley or left it; nobody resembling the Spaniard entered or left the tavern door. The night promised to be a fair one; so Tom went home with the understanding that if a considerable degree of darkness came on, Huck was to come and 'meow', whereupon he would slip out and try the keys. But the night remained clear, and Huck closed his watch and retired to bed in an empty sugar hogshead about twelve.

Tuesday the boys had the same ill-luck. Also Wednesday. But Thursday night promised better. Tom slipped out in good season with his aunt's old tin lantern, and a large towel to blindfold it with. He hid the lantern in Huck's sugar hogshead and the watch began. An hour before midnight the tavern closed up, and its lights (the only one thereabouts) were put out. No Spaniard had been seen. Nobody had entered or left the alley. Everything was auspicious. The blackness of darkness reigned, the perfect stillness was interrupted only by occasional mutterings of distant thunder.

Tom got his lantern, lit it in the hogshead, wrapped it closely in the towel, and the two adventurers crept in the gloom towards the tavern. Huck stood sentry and Tom felt his way into the alley. Then there was a season of waiting anxiety that weighed upon Huck's spirits like a mountain. He began to wish he could see a flash from the lantern – it would frighten him, but it would at least tell him that Tom was alive yet.

It seemed hours since Tom had disappeared. Surely he must have fainted; maybe he was dead; maybe his heart had burst under terror and excitement. In his uneasiness Huck found himself drawing closer and closer to the alley, fearing all sorts of dreadful things, and momentarily expecting some catastrophe to happen that would take away his breath. There was not much to take away, for he seemed only able to inhale it by thimblefuls, and his heart would soon wear itself out, the way it was beating. Suddenly there was a flash of light, and Tom came tearing by him:

'Run!' said he; 'run for your life!'

He needn't have repeated it; once was enough; Huck was making thirty

"'Run!" said he; "run for your life!"'

or forty miles an hour before the repetition was uttered. The boys never stopped till they reached the shed of a deserted slaughter-house at the lower end of the village. Just as they got within its shelter the storm burst and the rain poured down. As soon as Tom got his breath he said:

'Huck, it was awful! I tried two of the keys just as soft as I could; but they seemed to make such a power of racket that I couldn't hardly get my breath, I was so scared. They wouldn't turn in the lock either. Well, without noticing what I was doing, I took hold of the knob, and open comes the door! It wasn't locked! I hopped in and shook off the towel, and, *great Caesar's ghost*!'

'What! – what'd you see, Tom?,

'Huck, I 'most stepped on to Injun Joe's hand!'

'No!'

'Yes. He was laying there, sound asleep on the floor, with his old patch on his eye and his arms spread out.'

'Lordy, what did you do? Did he wake up?'

'No, never budged. Drunk, I reckon. I just grabbed that towel and started!'

'I'd never a thought of the towel, I bet!'

'Well, I would. My aunt would make me mighty sick if I lost it.'

'Say, Tom, did you see that box?'

'Huck, I didn't wait to look around. I didn't see the box, I didn't see the cross. I didn't see anything but a bottle and a tin cup on the floor by Injun Joe! Yes, and I saw two barrels and lots more bottles in the room. Don't you see, now, what's the matter with that ha'nted room?'

'How?'

'Why, it's ha'nted with whisky! Maybe all the Temperance Taverns have got a ha'nted room, hey, Huck?'

'Well, I reckon maybe that's so. Who'd a thought such a thing? But say, Tom, now's a mighty good time to get that box, if Injun Joe's drunk.'

'It is that! You try it!'

Huck shuddered.

'Well, no – I reckon not.'

'And I reckon not, Huck. Only one bottle alongside of Injun Joe ain't enough. If there'd been three he'd be drunk enough and I'd do it.'

There was a long pause for reflection, and then Tom said:

'Looky here, Huck, less not try that thing any more till we know Injun Joe's not in there. It's too scary. Now if we watch every night, we'll be dead sure to see him go out some time or other, then we'll snatch that box quicker'n lightning.'

'Well, I'm agreed. I'll watch the whole night long, and I'll do it every night, too, if you'll do the other part of the job.'

'All right, I will. All you got to do is to trot up Hooper Street a block and meow – and if I'm asleep, you throw some gravel at the window and that'll fetch me.'

'Agreed, and good as wheat!'

'Now, Huck, the storm's over, and I'll go home. It'll begin to be daylight in a couple of hours. You go back and watch that long, will you?'

'I said I would, Tom, and I will. I'll ha'nt that tavern every night for a year. I'll sleep all day and I'll stand watch all night.'

'That's all right. Now where are you going to sleep?'

'In Ben Rogers's hay-loft. He lets me, and so does his pap's nigger man, Uncle Jake. I tote water for Uncle Jake whenever he wants me to, and any time I ask him he gives me a little something to eat if he can spare it. That's a mighty good nigger, Tom. He likes me, becuz I don't ever act as if I was above him. Sometimes I've set right down and eat with him. But you needn't tell that. A body's got to do things when he's awful hungry he wouldn't want to do as a steady thing.'

'Well, if I don't want you in the daytime, Huck, I'll let you sleep. I won't come bothering around. Any time you see something's up in the night, just skip right around and meow.'

Chapter 30

The first thing Tom heard on Friday morning was a glad piece of news –
Judge Thatcher's family had come back to town the night before. Both Injun
Joe and the treasure sank into secondary importance for a moment, and Becky
took the chief place in the boy's interest. He saw her, and they had an
exhausting good time playing 'hi-spy' and 'gully-keeper' with a crowd of their
schoolmates. The day was completed and crowned in a peculiarly satisfactory
way: Becky teased her mother to appoint the next day for the long-promised
and long-delayed picnic, and she consented. The child's delight was
boundless, and Tom's not more moderate. The invitations were sent out
before sunset, and straightway the young folks of the village were thrown into
a fever of preparation and pleasurable anticipation. Tom's excitement
enabled him to keep awake until a pretty late hour, and he had good hopes of
hearing Huck's 'meow' and of having his treasure to astonish Becky and the
picnickers with, next day; but he was disappointed. No signal came that
night.

   Morning came eventually, and by ten or eleven o'clock a giddy and
rollicking company were gathered at Judge Thatcher's, and everything was
ready for a start. It was not the custom for elderly people to mar picnics with
their presence. The children were considered safe enough under the wings of
a few young ladies of eighteen and a few young gentlemen of twenty-three or
thereabouts. The old steam ferry-boat was chartered for the occasion:
presently the gay throng filed up the main street laden with provision baskets.
Sid was sick and had to miss the fun; Mary remained at home to entertain
him. The last thing Mrs. Thatcher said to Becky was:

   'You'll not get back till late. Perhaps you'd better stay all night with some
of the girls that live near the ferry landing, child!'

   'Then I'll stay with Susy Harper, mamma.'

   'Very well. And mind and behave yourself, and don't be any trouble.'

   Presently, as they tripped along, Tom said to Becky:

   'Say – I'll tell you what we'll do. 'Stead of going to Joe Harper's, we'll
climb right up the hill and stop at Widow Douglas's. She'll have ice-cream!
She has it 'most every day – dead loads of it. And she'll be awful glad to have
us.'

'Oh, that will be fun!'

Then Becky reflected a moment, and said:

'But what will mamma say?'

'How'll she ever know?'

The girl turned the idea over in her mind, and said reluctantly:

'I reckon it's wrong – but——'

'But – shucks! Your mother won't know, and so what's the harm? All she wants is that you'll be safe; and I bet you she'd a said go there if she'd a thought of it. I know she would!'

The Widow Douglas's splendid hospitality was a tempting bait. It and Tom's persuasions presently carried the day. So it was decided to say nothing to anybody about the night's programme.

Presently it occurred to Tom that maybe Huck might come this very night and give the signal. The thought took a deal of the spirit out of his anticipations. Still he could not bear to give up the fun at Widow Douglas's. And why should he give it up, he reasoned – the signal did not come the night before, so why should it be any more likely to come tonight? The sure fun of the evening outweighed the uncertain treasure; and, boy-like, he determined to yield to the stronger inclination and not allow himself to think of the box of money another time that day.

Three miles below town the ferry-boat stopped at the mouth of a woody hollow and tied up. The crowd swarmed ashore, and soon the forest distances and craggy heights echoed far and near with shoutings and laughter. All the different ways of getting hot and tired were gone through with, and by-and-by the rovers straggled back to camp fortified with responsible appetites, and then the destruction of the good things began. After the feast there was a refreshing season of rest and chat in the shade of spreading oaks. By-and-by somebody shouted:

'Who's ready for the cave?'

Everybody was. Bundles of candles were produced, and straightway there was a general scamper up the hill. The mouth of the cave was high up the hill-side, an opening shaped like the letter A. It's massive oaken door stood unbarred. Within was a small chamber, chilly as an ice-house, and walled by Nature with solid lime-stone that was dewy with a cold sweat. It was romantic and mysterious to stand here in the deep gloom and look out upon the green valley shining in the sun. But the impressiveness of the situation quickly wore off, and the romping began again. The moment a candle was lighted, there was a general rush upon the owner of it; a struggle and a gallant defence followed, but the candle was soon knocked down or blown out, and then there was a glad clamour of laughter and a new chase. But all things have an end. By-and-by the procession went filing down the steep descent of the main avenue, the flickering rank of lights dimly revealing the lofty walls of rock almost to their point of junction sixty feet overhead. This main avenue was not more than eight or ten feet wide. Every few steps other lofty and still narrower crevices branched from it on either hand, for McDougal's cave was but a vast labyrinth of crooked aisles that ran into each other and out again and led nowhere. It was said that one might wander days and nights together through its intricate tangle of rifts and chasms, and never find the end of the cave; and that he might go down and down, and still down into the earth, and it was just the same – labyrinth underneath labyrinth, and no end to any of them. No man 'knew' the cave. That was an impossible thing. Most of the young men knew a portion of it, and it was not customary to venture much beyond this known portion. Tom Sawyer knew as much of the cave as anyone.

The procession moved along the main avenue some three-quarters of a mile, and then groups and couples began to slip aside into branch avenues, fly along the dismal corridors, and take each other by surprise at points where the corridors joined again. Parties were able to elude each other for the space of half an hour without going beyond the 'known' ground.

By-and-by, one group after another came straggling back to the mouth of the cave, panting, hilarious, smeared from head to foot with tallow drippings, daubed with clay, and entirely delighted with the success of the day. Then they were astonished to find that they had been taking no note of time, and that night was about at hand. The clanging bell had been calling for half an hour. However, this sort of close to the day's adventures was romantic and therefore satisfactory. When the ferry-boat with her wild freight pushed into the stream, nobody cared sixpence for the wasted time but the captain of the craft.

Huck was already upon his watch when the ferry-boat's lights went glinting past the wharf. He heard no noise on board, for the young people were as subdued and still as people usually are who are nearly tired to death. He wondered what boat it was, and why she did not stop at the wharf – and then he dropped her out of his mind and put his attention upon his business. The night was growing cloudy and dark. Ten o'clock came, and the noise of vehicles ceased, scattered lights began to wink out, all straggling foot-passengers disappeared, the village betook itself to its slumbers and left the small watcher alone with the silence and the ghosts. Eleven o'clock came, and the tavern lights were put out; darkness everywhere, now. Huck waited what seemed a weary long time, but nothing happened. His faith was weakening. Was there any use? Was there really any use? Why not give it up and turn in?

A noise fell upon his ear. He was all attention in an instant. The alley door closed softly. He sprang to the corner of the brick-store. The next moment two men brushed by him, and one seemed to have something under his arm. It must be that box! So they were going to remove the treasure. Why call Tom now? It would be absurd – the men would get away with the box and never be found again. No, he would stick to their wake and follow them; he would trust to the darkness for security from discovery. So communing with himself, Huck stepped out and glided along behind the men, cat-like, with bare feet, allowing them to keep just far enough ahead not to be invisible.

They moved up the river street three blocks, then turned to the left up a cross street. They went straight ahead, then, until they came to the path that led up Cardiff Hill; this they took. They passed by the old Welshman's house, half way up the hill, without hesitating, and still climbed upward. Good, thought Huck, they will bury it in the old quarry. But they never stopped at the quarry. They passed on, up the summit. They plunged into the narrow path between the tall sumach bushes, and were at once hidden in the gloom. Huck closed up and shortened his distance, now, for they would never be able to see him. He trotted along a while; then slackened his pace, fearing he was gaining too fast; moved on a piece, then stopped altogether; listened; no sound; none, save that he seemed to hear the beating of his own heart. The hooting of an owl came from over the hill – ominous sound! But no footsteps. Heavens, was everything lost? He was about to spring with winged feet, when a man cleared his throat not four feet from him! Huck's heart shot into his throat, but he swallowed it again; and then he stood there shaking as if a dozen agues had taken charge of him at once, and so weak that he thought he must surely fall to the ground. He knew where he was. He knew he was within five steps of the stile leading into Widow Douglas's grounds. 'Very well,' he thought, 'let them bury it there; it won't be hard to find.'

Now there was a low voice – a very low voice – Injun Joe's:

'Damn her, maybe she's got company – there's lights, late as it is.'

'I can't see any.'

This was that stranger's voice – the stranger of the haunted house. A deadly chill went to Huck's heart – this, then, was the 'revenge' job! His thought was to fly. Then he remembered that the Widow Douglas had been kind to him more than once, and maybe these men were going to murder her. He wished he dared venture to warn her; but he knew he didn't dare – they might come and catch him. He thought all this and more in the moment that elapsed between the stranger's remark and Injun Joe's next – which was:

'Because the bush is in your way. Now – this way – now you see, don't you?'

'Yes. Well, there is company there, I reckon. Better give it up.'

'Give it up, and I just leaving this country for ever! Give it up, and maybe never have another chance. I tell you again, as I've told you before, I don't care for her swag – you may have it. But her husband was rough on me – many times he was rough on me – and mainly he was the justice of the peace that jugged me for a vagrant. And that ain't all! It ain't the millionth part of it! He had me horsewhipped! – horsewhipped in front of the jail, like a nigger! – with all the town looking on! Horsewhipped! – do you understand? He took advantage of me and died. But I'll take it out of her!'

'Oh, don't kill her! Don't do that!'

'Kill? Who said anything about killing? I would kill him if he was here; but not her. When you want to get revenge on a woman you don't kill her – bosh! you go for her looks. You slit her nostrils – you notch her ears like a sow's!'

'By God, that's———'

'Keep your opinion to yourself! It will be safest for you. I'll tie her to the bed. If she bleeds to death, is that my fault? I'll not cry if she does. My friend, you'll help me in this thing – for my sake – that's why you're here – I mightn't be able alone. If you flinch, I'll kill you! Do you understand that? And if I have to kill you, I'll kill her – and then I reckon nobody'll ever know much about who done this business.'

'Well, if it's got to be done, let's get at it. The quicker the better – I'm all in a shiver.'

'Do it now? – and company there? Look here – I'll get suspicious of you, first thing, you know. No – we'll wait till the lights are out – there's no hurry.'

Huck felt that a silence was going to ensue – a thing still more awful than any amount of murderous talk; so he held his breath and stepped gingerly back; planted his foot carefully and firmly, after balancing, one-legged, in a precarious way and almost toppling over, first on one side and then on the other. He took another step back with the same elaboration and the same risks; then another and another, and a twig snapped under his foot! His breath stopped and he listened. There was no sound – the stillness was perfect. His gratitude was measureless. Now he turned in his tracks between the walls of sumach bushes – turned himself as carefully as if he were a ship – and then stepped quickly but cautiously along. When he emerged at the quarry he felt secure, so he picked up his nimble heels and flew. Down, down he sped till he reached the Welshman's. He banged at the door, and presently the heads of the old man and his two stalwart sons were thrust from windows.

'What's the row there? Who's banging? What do you want?'

'Let me in – quick! I'll tell everything.'

'Why, who are you?'

'Huckleberry Finn – quick, let me in!'

'Huckleberry Finn, indeed! It ain't a name to open many doors, I judge! But let him in, lads, and let's see what's the trouble?'

'Please don't ever tell I told you,' were Huck's first words when he got in. 'Please don't – I'd be killed sure – but the widow's been good friend to me sometimes, and I want to tell – I will tell if you'll promise you won't ever say it was me.'

'By George, he has got something to tell, or he wouldn't, act so!' exclaimed the old man. 'Out with it, and nobody here'll ever tell, lad.'

Three minutes later the old man and his sons, well armed, were up the hill, and just entering the sumach path on tip-toe, their weapons in their hands. Huck accompanied them no farther. He hid behind a great boulder and fell to listening. There was a lagging, anxious silence, and then all of a sudden there was an explosion of firearms and a cry. Huck waited for no particulars. He sprang away and sped down the hill as fast as his legs could carry him.

Chapter 31

As the earliest suspicion of dawn appeared on Sunday morning, Huck came groping up the hill and rapped gently at the old Welshman's door. The inmates were asleep, but it was a sleep that was set on a hair-trigger, on account of the exciting episode of the night. A call came from a window:

'Who's there?'

Huck's scared voice answered in a low tone:

'Do please let me in! It's only Huck Finn!'

'It's a name that can open this door night or day, lad! – and welcome!'

These were strange words to the vagabond boy's ears, and the pleasantest he had ever heard. He could not recollect that the closing word had ever been applied in his case before.

The door was quickly unlocked and he entered. Huck was given a seat, and the old man and his brace of tall sons speedily dressed themselves.

'Now, my boy, I hope you're good and hungry, because breakfast will be ready as soon as the sun's up, and we'll have a piping hot one, too – make yourself easy about that. I and the boys hoped you'd turn up and stop here last night.'

'I was awful scared,' said Huck, 'and I run. I took out when the pistols went off, and I didn't stop for three mile. I've come now becuz I wanted to know about it, you know; and I come before daylight becuz I didn't want to run across them devils, even if they was dead.'

'Well, poor chap, you do look as if you'd had a hard night of it – but there's a bed here for you when you've had your breakfast. No, they ain't dead, lad – we are sorry enough for that. You see, we knew right where to put our hands on them, by your description; so we crept along on tip-toe till we got within fifteen feet of them – dark as a cellar that sumach path was – and just then I found I was going to sneeze. It was the meanest kind of luck! I tried to keep it back, but no use – 'twas bound to come, and it did come! I was in the lead, with my pistol raised, and when the sneeze started those scoundrels a rustling to get out of the path, I sang out "Fire, boys!" and blazed away at the place where the rustling was. So did the boys. But they were off in a jiffy, those villains, and we after them, down through the woods. I judge we never touched them. They fired a shot apiece as they started, but their bullets whizzed by and didn't do us any harm. As soon as we lost the sound of their feet we quit chasing, and went down and stirred up the constables. They got a posse together, and went off to guard the river bank and as soon as it is light the sheriff and a gang are going to beat up the woods. My boys will be with them presently. I wish we had some sort of a description of those rascals – 'twould help a good deal. But you couldn't see what they were like in the dark, lad, I suppose?'

'Oh, yes, I saw them down town, and follered them.'

'Splendid! Describe them – describe them, my boy!'

'One's the old deaf and dumb Spaniard that's been around here once or twice, and t'other's a mean-looking, ragged——'

'That's enough, lad, we know the men! Happened on them in the woods back of the widow's one day, and they slunk away. Off with you, boys, and tell the sheriff – get your breakfast tomorrow morning!'

The Welshman's sons departed at once. As they were leaving the room Huck sprang up and exclaimed:

'Oh, please don't tell anybody it was me that blowed on them! Oh, please!'

'All right if you say it, Huck, but you ought to have the credit of what you did.'

'Oh, no, no! Please don't tell!'

When the young men were gone, the old Welshman said:

'They won't tell – and I won't. But why don't you want it known?'

Huck would not explain further than to say that he already knew too much about one of those men, and would not have the man know that he knew anything against him for the whole world – he would be killed for knowing it, sure.

The old man promised secrecy once more, and said:

'How did you come to follow these fellows, lad? Were they looking suspicious?'

Huck was silent, while he framed a duly cautious reply. Then he said:

'Well, you see, I'm a kind of a hard lot – least everybody says so, and I don't see nothing agin it – and sometimes I can't sleep much, on accounts of thinking about it; and sort of trying to strike out a new way of doing. That was the way of it last night. I couldn't sleep, and so I came along up street 'bout midnight a turning it all over, and when I got to that old shackly brick-store by the Temperance Tavern, I backed up agin the wall to have another think. Well, just then along comes these two chaps slipping along close by me, with something under their arm, and I reckoned they'd stole it. One was a smoking, and t'other one wanted a light; so they stopped right before me, and the cigars lit up their faces, and I see that the big one was the deaf and dumb Spaniard, by his white whiskers and the patch on his eye, and t'other one was a rusty, ragged-looking devil.'

'Could you see the rags by the light of the cigars?'

This staggered Huck for a moment. Then he said:

'Well, I don't know, but somehow it seems as if I did.'

'Then they went on, and you——'

'Followed 'em – yes. That was it. I wanted to see what was up – they sneaked along so. I dogged 'em to the widder's stile, and stood in the dark, and heard the ragged one beg for the widder, and the Spaniard swear he'd spile her looks, just as I told you and your two——'

'What! the deaf and dumb man said all that?'

Huck had made another terrible mistake! He was trying his best to keep the old man from getting the faintest hint of who the Spaniard might be, and yet his tongue seemed determined to get him into trouble in spite of all he could do. He made several efforts to creep out of his scrape, but the old man's eye was upon him, and he made blunder after blunder. Presently the Welshman said:

'My boy, don't be afraid of me, I wouldn't hurt a hair of your head for all the world. No – I'd protect you – I'd protect you. This Spaniard is not deaf and dumb; you've let that slip without intending it; you can't cover that up now. You know something about that Spaniard that you want to keep dark. Now trust me – tell me what it is, and trust me – I won't betray you.'

Huck looked into the old man's honest eyes a moment, then bent over and whispered in his ear:

''Tain't a Spaniard – it's Injun Joe!'

The Welshman almost jumped out of his chair. In a moment he said:

'It's all plain enough now. When you talked about notching ears and slitting noses, I judged that that was your own embellishment, because white men don't take that sort of revenge. But an Injun! That's a different matter, altogether.'

During breakfast the talk went on, and in the course of it the old man said that the last thing which he and his sons had done, before going to bed, was to get a lantern and examine the stile and its vicinity for marks of blood. They found none, but captured a bulky bundle of——

'Of WHAT?'

If the words had been lightning, they could not have leaped with a more stunning suddenness from Huck's blanched lips. His eyes were staring wide, now, and his breath suspended – waiting for the answer. The Welshman started – started in return – three seconds – five seconds – ten – then replied:

'Of burglar's tools.'

'Why, what's the matter with you?'

Huck sank back, panting gently, but deeply, unutterably grateful. The Welshman eyed him gravely, curiously – and presently said:

'Yes, burglar's tools. That appears to relieve you a good deal. But what did give you that turn? What were you expecting we'd found?'

Huck was in a close place; the inquiring eye was upon him – he would have given anything for material for a plausible answer. Nothing suggesting itself; the inquiring eye was boring deeper and deeper – a senseless reply offered – there was no time to weigh it, so at a venture he uttered it, feebly:

'Sunday-school books, maybe.'

Poor Huck was too distressed to smile, but the old man laughed loud and joyously, shook up the details of his anatomy from head to foot, and ended by saying that such a laugh was money in a man's pocket, because it cut down the doctor's bills like everything. Then he added:

'Poor old chap, you're white and jaded; you ain't well a bit. No wonder you're a little flighty and off your balance. But you'll come out of it. Rest and sleep will fetch you all right, I hope.'

Huck was irritated to think he had·been such a goose and betrayed such a suspicious excitement, for he had dropped the idea that the parcel brought from the tavern was the treasure as soon as he had heard the talk at the widow's stile. He had only thought it was not the treasure, however; he had not known that it wasn't; and so the suggestion of a captured bundle was too much for his self-possession. But on the whole he felt glad the little episode had happened, for now he knew beyond all question that the bundle was not *the* bundle, and so his mind was at rest and exceedingly comfortable. In fact everything seemed to be drifting just in the right direction, now; the treasure must be still in number two, the men would be captured and jailed that day, and he and Tom could seize the gold that night without any trouble or any fear of interruption.

Just as breakfast was completed there was a knock at the door. Huck jumped for a hiding-place, for he had no mind to be connected even remotely with the late event. The Welshman admitted several ladies and gentlemen, among them the Widow Douglas, and noticed the groups of citizens were climbing the hill to stare at the stile. So the news had spread.

The Welshman had to tell the story of the night to the visitors. The widow's gratitude for her preservation was outspoken.

'Don't say a word about it, madam. There's another that you're more beholden to than you are to me and my boys maybe, but he don't allow me to tell his name. We wouldn't ever have been there but for him.'

Of course this excited a curiosity so vast that it almost belittled the main matter; but the Welshman allowed it to eat into the vitals of his visitors, and through them he transmitted it to the whole town, for he refused to part with his secret. When all else had been learned the widow said:

'I went to sleep reading in bed, and slept straight through all that noise. Why didn't you come and wake me?'

'We judged it wasn't worth while. Those fellows weren't likely to come again; they hadn't any tools left to work with, and what was the use of waking you up and scaring you to death? My three Negro men stood guard at your house all the rest of the night. They've just come back.'

More visitors came, and the story had to be told and retold for a couple of hours more.

There was no Sabbath-school during day-school vacation, but everybody was early at church. The stirring event was well canvassed. News came that not a sign of the villains had been yet discovered. When the sermon was finished Judge Thatcher's wife dropped alongside of Mrs. Harper as she moved down the aisle with the crowd, and said:

'Is my Becky going to sleep all day? I just expected she would be tired to death.'

'Your Becky?'

'Yes,' with a startled look. 'Didn't she stay with you last night?'

'Why, no.'

Mrs. Thatcher turned pale, and sank into a pew just as Aunt Polly, talking briskly with a friend, passed by. Aunt Polly said:

'Good morning, Mrs. Thatcher. Good morning, Mrs. Harper. I've got a boy that's turned up missing. I reckon my Tom stayed at your house last night – one of you. And now he's afraid to come to church. I've got to settle with him.'

Mrs. Thatcher shook her head feebly and turned paler than ever.

'He didn't stay with us,' said Mrs. Harper, beginning to look uneasy. A marked anxiety came into Aunt Polly's face.

'Joe Harper, have you seen my Tom this morning?'

'No'm.'

'When did you see him last?'

Joe tried to remember, but was not sure he could say. The people had stopped moving out of church. Whispers passed along, and a brooding uneasiness took possession of every countenance. Children were anxiously questioned, and young teachers. They all said they had not noticed whether Tom and Becky were on board the ferry-boat on the homeward trip; it was dark; no one thought of inquiring if anyone was missing. One young man finally blurted out his fear that they were still in the cave! Mrs. Thatcher swooned away; Aunt Polly fell to crying and wringing her hands.

The alarm swept from lip to lip, from group to group, from street to street; and within five minutes the bells were wildly clanging, and the whole town was up! The Cardiff Hill episode sank into instant insignificance, the burglars were forgotten, horses were saddled, skiffs were manned, the ferry-boat ordered out, and before the horror was half an hour old two hundred men were pouring down high-road and river towards the cave.

All the long afternoon the village seemed empty and dead. Many women visited Aunt Polly and Mrs. Thatcher, and tried to comfort them. They cried with them, too, and that was still better than words.

All the tedious night the town waited for news; but when the morning dawned at last, all the word that came was 'Send more candles, and send food.' Mrs. Thatcher was almost crazed, and Aunt Polly also. Judge Thatcher sent messages of hope and encouragement from the cave, but they conveyed no real cheer.

The old Welshman came home towards daylight, spattered with candle-grease, smeared with clay, and almost worn out. He found Huck still in the bed that had been provided for him, and delirious with fever. The physicians were all at the cave, so the Widow Douglas came and took charge of the patient. She said she would do her best by him, because, whether he was good, bad, or indifferent, he was the Lord's and nothing that was the Lord's · was a thing to be neglected. The Welshman said Huck had good spots in him, and the widow said:

'You can depend on it. That's the Lord's mark. He don't leave it off. He never does. Puts it somewhere on every creature that comes from His hands.'

Early in the forenoon parties of jaded men began to straggle into the village, but the strongest of the citizens continued searching. All the news that could be gained was that remotenesses of the cavern were being ransacked that had never been visited before; that every corner and crevice was going to be thoroughly searched; that wherever one wandered through the maze of passages, lights were to be seen flitting hither and thither in the distance, and shoutings and pistol-shots sent their hollow reverberations to the ear down the sombre aisles. In one place, far from the section usually traversed by tourists, the names 'BECKY' and 'TOM' had been found traced upon the rocky wall with candle smoke, and near at hand a grease-soiled bit of ribbon. Mrs. Thatcher recognized the ribbon and cried over it. She said it was the last relic she should ever have of her child; and that no other memorial of her could ever be so precious, because this one parted latest from the living body before the awful death came. Some said that now and then in the cave a far-away speck of light would glimmer, and then a glorious shout would burst forth and a score of men go trooping down the echoing aisle – and then a sickening disappointment always followed; the children were not there; it was only a searcher's light.

Three dreadful days and nights dragged their tedious hours along, and the village sank into a hopeless stupor. No one had heart for anything. The accidental discovery, just made, that the proprietor of the Temperance Tavern kept liquor on his premises, scarcely fluttered the public pulse, tremendous as the fact was. In a lucid interval, Huck feebly led up to the subject of taverns and finally asked, dimly dreading the worst, if anything had been discovered at the Temperance Tavern since he had been ill.

'Yes,' said the widow.

Huck started up in bed, wild-eyed:

'What! What was it?'

'Liquor! – and the place has been shut up. Lie down, child – what a turn you did give me!'

'Only tell me one thing – only just one – please! Was it Tom Sawyer that found it?'

The widow burst into tears.

'Hush, hush, child, hush! I've told you before, you must *not* talk. You are very, very sick!'

Then nothing but liquor had been found; there would have been a great pow-pow if it had been the gold. So the treasure was gone for ever – gone for ever. But what could she be crying about? Curious that she should cry.

These thoughts worked their dim way through Huck's mind, and under the weariness they gave him he fell asleep. The widow said to herself:

'There – he's asleep, poor wreck. Tom Sawyer find it! Pity but somebody could find Tom Sawyer! Ah, there ain't many left, now, that's got hope enough, or strength enough either, to go on searching.'

Chapter 32

Now to return to Tom and Becky's share in the picnic. They tripped along the murky aisles with the rest of the company, visiting the familiar wonders of the cave – wonders dubbed with rather over-descriptive names, such as 'The Drawing-room', 'The Cathedral', 'Aladdin's Palace', and so on. Presently the hide-and-seek frolicking began, and Tom and Becky engaged in it with zeal until the exertion began to grow a trifle wearisome; then they wandered down a sinuous avenue, holding their candles aloft and reading the tangled web-work of names, dates, post-office addresses, and mottoes with which the rocky walls had been frescoed (in candle smoke). Still drifting along and talking, they scarcely noticed that they were now in a part of the cave whose walls were not frescoed. They smoked their own names under an overhanging shelf and moved on. Presently they came to a place where a little stream of water, trickling over a ledge and carrying a limestone sediment with it, had, in the slow-dragging ages, formed a laced and ruffled Niagara in gleaming and imperishable stone. Tom squeezed his small body behind it in order to illuminate it for Becky's gratification. He found that it curtained a sort of steep natural stairway which was enclosed between narrow walls, and at once the ambition to be a discoverer seized him. Becky responded to his call, and they made a smoke mark for future guidance and started upon their quest. They wound this way and that, far down into the secret depths of the cave, made another mark, and branched off in search of novelties to tell the upper world about. In one place they found a spacious cavern, from whose ceiling depended a multitude of shining stalactites of the length and circumference of a man's leg; they walked all about it, wondering and admiring, and presently left it by one of the numerous passages that opened into it. This shortly brought them to a bewitching spring, whose basin was encrusted with a frost-work of glittering crystals; it was in the midst of a cavern whose walls were supported by many fantastic pillars which had been formed by the joining of great stalactites and stalagmites together, the result of the ceaseless water-drip of centuries. Under the roof vast knots of bats had packed themselves together, thousands in a bunch; the lights disturbed the creatures, and they came flocking down by hundreds, squeaking and darting furiously at the candles. Tom knew their ways, and the danger of this sort of conduct. He seized Becky's hand and hurried her into the first corridor that offered; and none too soon, for a bat struck Becky's light out with its wing while she was passing out of the cavern. The bats chased the children a good distance; but the fugitives plunged into every new passage that offered, and at last got rid of the perilous things. Tom found a subterranean lake, shortly, which stretched its dim length away until its shape was lost in the shadows. He wanted to explore its borders, but concluded that it would be best to sit down and rest a while first. Now for the first time the deep stillness of the place laid a clammy hand upon the spirits of the children. Becky said:

'Why, I didn't notice, but it seems ever so long since I heard any of the others.'

'Come to think, Becky, we are away down below them, and I don't know how far away north, or south, or east, or whichever it is. We couldn't hear them here.'

Becky grew apprehensive.

'I wonder how long we've been down here, Tom. We better start back.'

'Yes, I reckon we better. P'raps we better.'

'Can you find the way, Tom? It's all a mixed-up crookedness to me.'

'I reckon I could find it, but then the bats. If they put both our candles out it will be an awful fix. Let's try some other way, so as not to go through there.'

'Well, but I hope we won't get lost. It would be so awful!' and the child shuddered at the thought of the dreadful possibilities.

They started through a corridor, and traversed it in silence a long way, glancing at each new opening, to see if there was anything familiar about the look of it; but they were all strange. Every time Tom made an examination, Becky would watch his face for an encouraging sign, and he would say cheerily:

'Oh, it's all right. This ain't the one, but we'll come to it right away!' But he felt less and less hopeful with each failure, and presently began to turn off into diverging avenues at sheer random, in the desperate hope of finding the one that was wanted. He still said it was 'All right', but there was such a leaden dread at his heart, that the words had lost their ring, and sounded as if he had said, 'All is lost!' Becky clung to his side in an anguish of fear, and tried hard to keep back the tears, but they would come. At last she said:

'Oh, Tom, never mind the bats; let's go back that way! We seem to get worse and worse off all the time.'

Tom stopped.

'Listen!' said he.

Profound silence; silence so deep that even their breathings were conspicuous in the hush. Tom shouted. The call went echoing down the empty aisles, and died out in the distance in a faint sound that resembled a

"'*Tom, Tom, we're lost! we're lost!*'"

ripple of mocking laughter.

'Oh, don't do it again, Tom, it is too horrid,' said Becky.

'It is horrid, but I better, Becky; they *might* hear us, you know,' and he shouted again.

The 'might' was even a chillier horror than the ghostly laughter, it so confessed a perishing hope. The children stood still and listened; but there was no result. Tom turned upon the back track at once, and hurried his steps. It was but a little while before a certain indecision in his manner revealed another fearful fact to Becky; he could not find his way back!

'Oh, Tom, you didn't make any marks!'

'Becky, I was such a fool! such a fool! I never thought we might want to come back! No, I can't find the way. It's all mixed up.'

'Tom, Tom, we're lost! we're lost! We never, never can get out of this awful place! Oh, why did we ever leave the others?'

She sank to the ground, and burst into such a frenzy of crying that Tom was appalled with the idea that she might die, or lose her reason. He sat down by her and put his arms around her; she buried her face in his bosom, she clung to him, she poured out her terrors, her unavailing regrets and the far echoes turned them all to jeering laughter. Tom begged her to pluck up hope again, and she said she could not. He fell to blaming and abusing himself for getting her into this miserable situation; this had a better effect. She said she would try to hope again, she would get up and follow wherever he might lead, if only he would not talk like that any more. For he was no more to blame than she, she said.

So they moved on again – aimlessly – simply at random – all they could do was to move, keep moving. For a little while hope made a show of reviving – not with any reason to back it, but only because it is its nature to revive when the spring has not been taken out of it by age and familiarity with failure.

By-and-by Tom took Becky's candle and blew it out. This economy meant so much. Words were not needed. Becky understood, and her hope died again. She knew that Tom had a whole candle and three or four pieces in his pocket – yet he must economize.

By-and-by fatigue began to assert its claims; the children tried to pay no attention, for it was dreadful to think of sitting down when time was grown to be so precious; moving, in some direction, in any direction, was at least progress and might bear fruit; but to sit down was to invite death and shorten its pursuit.

At last Becky's frail limbs refused to carry her farther. She sat down. Tom rested with her, and they talked of home, and the friends there, and the comfortable beds, and above all, the light! Becky cried, and Tom tried to think of some way of comforting her, but all his encouragements were grown threadbare with use, and sounded like sarcasms. Fatigue bore so heavily upon

Becky that she drowsed off to sleep. Tom was grateful. He sat looking into her drawn face and saw it grow smooth and natural under the influence of pleasant dreams; and by-and-by a smile dawned and rested there. The peaceful face reflected somewhat of peace and healing into his own spirit, and his thoughts wandered away to bygone times and dreamy memories. While he was deep in his musings, Becky woke up with a breezy little laugh: but it was stricken dead upon her lips, and a groan followed it.

'Oh, how *could* I sleep! I wish I never, never had waked! No, no, I don't, Tom! Don't look so! I won't say it again.'

'I'm glad you slept, Becky; you'll feel rested, now, and we'll find the way out.'

'We can try, Tom; but I've seen such a beautiful country in my dream. I reckon we are going there.'

'Maybe not, maybe not. Cheer up, Becky, and let's go on trying.'

They rose up and wandered along, hand in hand and hopeless. They tried to estimate how long they had been in the cave, but all they knew was that it seemed days and weeks, and yet it was plain that this could not be, for their candles were not gone yet.

A long time after this – they could not tell how long – Tom said they must go softly and listen for dripping water – they must find a spring. They found one presently, and Tom said it was time to rest again. Both were cruelly tired, yet Becky said she thought she could go a little farther. She was surprised to hear Tom dissent. She could not understand it. They sat down, and Tom fastened his candle to the wall in front of them with some clay. Thought was soon busy; nothing was said for some time. Then Becky broke the silence:

'Tom, I am so hungry!'

Tom took something out of his pocket.

'Do you remember this?' said he.

Becky almost smiled.

'It's our wedding-cake, Tom.'

'Yes – I wish it was as big as a barrel, for it's all we've got.'

'I saved it from the picnic for us to dream on, Tom, the way grown-up people do with wedding-cake – but it'll be our——'

She dropped the sentence where it was. Tom divided the cake, and Becky ate with good appetite, while Tom nibbled at his moiety. There was abundance of cold water to finish the feast with. By-and-by Becky suggested that they move on again. Tom was silent a moment. Then he said:

'Becky, can you bear it if I tell you something?'

Becky's face paled, but she said she thought she could.

'Well, then, Becky, we must stay here, where there's water to drink. That little piece is our last candle!'

Becky gave loose to tears and wailings. Tom did what he could to comfort her, but with little effect. At length Becky said:

'Tom!'

'Well, Becky?'

'They'll miss us and hunt for us!'

'Yes, they will! Certainly they will!'

'Maybe they're hunting for us now, Tom?'

'Why, I reckon maybe they are! I hope they are.'

'When would they miss us, Tom?'

'When they get back to the boat, I reckon.'

'Tom, it might be dark, then – would they notice we hadn't come?'

'I don't know. But anyway, your mother would miss you as soon as they got home.'

A frightened look in Becky's face brought Tom to his senses, and he saw that he had made a blunder. Becky was not to have gone home that night! The children became silent and thoughtful. In a moment a new burst of grief from Becky showed Tom that the thing in his mind had struck hers also – that the Sabbath morning might be half spent before Mrs. Thatcher discovered that Becky was not at Mrs. Harper's. The children fastened their eyes upon their bit of candle and watched it melt slowly and pitilessly away; saw the half inch of wick stand alone at last: saw the feeble flame rise and fall, rise and fall, climb the thin column of smoke, linger at its top a moment, and then – the horror of utter darkness reigned.

How long afterwards it was that Becky came to a slow consciousness that she was crying in Tom's arms, neither could tell. All that they knew was that after what seemed a mighty stretch of time, both awoke out of a dead stupor of sleep, and resumed their miseries once more. Tom said it might be Sunday now – maybe Monday. He tried to get Becky to talk, but her sorrows were too oppressive, all her hopes were gone. Tom said that they must have been missed long ago, and no doubt the search was going on. He would shout, and maybe someone would come. He tried it; but in the darkness the distant echoes sounded so hideously that he tried it no more.

The hours wasted away, and hunger came to torment the captives again. A portion of Tom's half of the cake was left; they divided and ate it. But they seemed hungrier than before. The poor morsel of food only whetted desire.

By-and-by Tom said:

'*Sh*! Did you hear that?'

Both held their breath and listened. There was a sound like the faintest far-off shout. Instantly Tom answered it, and leading Becky by the hand, started groping down the corridor in its direction. Presently he listened again; again the sound was heard, and apparently a little nearer.

'It's them!' said Tom; 'they're coming! Come along, Becky – we're all right now!'

The joy of the prisoners was almost overwhelming. Their speed was slow, however, because pitfalls were somewhat common, and had to be guarded against. They shortly came to one, and had to stop. It might be three feet deep, it might be a hundred – there was no passing it, at any rate. Tom got down on his breast, and reached as far down as he could. No bottom. They must stay there and wait until the searchers came. They listened; evidently the distant shoutings were growing more distant! A moment or two more, and they had gone altogether. The heart-sinking misery of it! Tom whooped until he was hoarse, but it was of no use. He talked hopefully to Becky; but an age of anxious waiting passed and no sound came again.

The children groped their way back to the spring. The weary time dragged on; they slept again, and awoke famished and woe-stricken. Tom believed it must be Tuesday by this time.

Now an idea struck him. There were some side-passages near at hand. It would be better to explore some of these than bear the weight of the heavy time in idleness. He took a kite-line from his pocket, tied it to a projection, and he and Becky started, Tom in the lead, unwinding the line as he groped along. At the end of twenty steps the corridor ended in a 'jumping-off place'. Tom got down on his knees and felt below, and then as far around the corner as he could reach with his hands conveniently; he made an effort to stretch yet a little further to the right, and at that moment, not twenty yards away, a human hand, holding a candle, appeared from behind a rock! Tom lifted up a glorious shout, and instantly that hand was followed by the body it belonged to – Injun Joe's! Tom was paralysed; he could not move. He was vastly gratified the next moment to see the 'Spaniard' take to his heels and get himself out of sight. Tom wondered that Joe had not recognized his voice and come over and killed him for testifying in court. But the echoes must have disguised the voice. Without doubt that was it, he reasoned. Tom's fright weakened every muscle in his body. He said to himself that if he had strength enough to get back to the spring he would stay there, and nothing should tempt him to run the risk of meeting Injun Joe again. He was careful to keep from Becky what it was he had seen. He told her he had only shouted 'for luck'.

But hunger and wretchedness rise superior to fears in the long run. Another tedious wait at the spring, and another long sleep brought changes. The children awoke, tortured with a raging hunger. Tom believed it must be Wednesday or Thursday, or even Friday or Saturday, now, and that the search had been given over. He proposed to explore another passage. He felt willing to risk Injun Joe and all other terrors. But Becky was very weak. She had sunk into a dreary apathy, and would not be roused. She said she would wait, now, where she was, and die – it would not be long. She told Tom to go with the kite-line and explore if he chose; but she implored him to come back every little while and speak to her; and she made him promise that when the awful time came, he would stay by her and hold her hand until all was over. Tom kissed her, with a choking sensation in his throat, and made a show of being confident of finding the searchers or an escape from the cave; then he took the kite-line in his hand and went groping down one of the passages on his hands and knees, distressed with hunger and sick with bodings of coming doom.

Chapter 33

Tuesday afternoon came, and waned to the twilight. The village of St Petersburg still mourned. The lost children had not been found. Public prayers had been offered up for them, and many and many a private prayer that had the petitioner's whole heart in it; but still no good news came from the cave. The majority of the searchers had given up the quest and gone back to their daily avocations, saying that it was plain the children could never be found. Mrs. Thatcher was very ill, and a great part of the time delirious. People said it was heart-breaking to hear her call her child, and raise her head and listen a whole minute at a time, then lay it wearily down again with a moan. Aunt Polly had drooped into a settled melancholy, and her grey hair had grown almost white. The village went to its rest on Tuesday night, sad and forlorn.

Away in the middle of the night a wild peal burst from the village bells, and in a moment the streets were swarming with frantic half-clad people, who shouted, 'Turn out! turn out! they're found! they're found!' Tin pans and horns were added to the din, the population massed itself and moved towards the river, met the children coming in an open carriage drawn by shouting citizens, thronged around it, joined its homeward march, and swept magnificently up the main street roaring huzza after huzza!

The village was illuminated; nobody went to bed again; it was the greatest night the little town had ever seen. During the first half-hour a procession of villagers filed through Judge Thatcher's house, seized the saved ones and kissed them, squeezed Mrs. Thatcher's hand, tried to speak but couldn't, and drifted out raining tears all over the place.

Aunt Polly's happiness was complete, and Mrs. Thatcher's nearly so. It would be complete, however, as soon as the messenger despatched with the great news to the cave should get the word to her husband.

Tom lay upon a sofa with an eager auditory about him, and told the history of the wonderful adventure, putting in many striking additions to adorn it withal; and closed with a description of how he left Becky and went on an exploring expedition; how he followed two avenues as far as his kite-line would reach; how he followed a third to the fullest stretch of the kite-line, and was about to turn back when he glimpsed a far-off speck that looked like daylight; dropped the line and groped towards it, pushed his head and shoulders through a small hole and saw the broad Mississippi rolling by! And if it had only happened to be night he would not have seen that speck of daylight, and would not have explored that passage any more! He told how he went back for Becky and broke the good news, and she told him not to fret her with such stuff, for she was tired, and knew she was going to die, and wanted to. He described how he laboured with her and convinced her, and how she almost died for joy when she had groped to where she actually saw the blue speck of daylight; how he pushed his way out of the hole and then helped her out; how they sat there and cried for gladness; how some men came along in a skiff, and Tom hailed them and told them their situation and their famished condition; how the men didn't believe the wild tale at first, 'because', said they, 'you are five miles down the river below the valley the cave is in'; then took them aboard, rowed to a house, gave them supper, made them rest till two or three hours after dark, and then brought them home.

Before day-dawn Judge Thatcher and the handful of searchers with him were tracked out in the cave by the twine clues they had strung behind them, and informed of the great news.

Three days and nights of toil and hunger in the cave were not to be shaken off at once, as Tom and Becky soon discovered. They were bedridden all of Wednesday and Thursday, and seemed to grow more and more tired and worn all the time. Tom got about a little on Thursday, was down town Friday, and nearly as whole as ever Saturday; but Becky did not leave her room until Sunday, and then she looked as if she had passed through a wasting illness.

Tom learned of Huck's sickness, and went to see him on Friday, but could not be admitted to the bedroom; neither could he on Saturday or Sunday. He was admitted daily after that, but was warned to keep still about his adventure and introduce no exciting topic. The Widow Douglas stayed by to see that he obeyed. At home Tom learned of the Cardiff Hill event; also that the ragged man's body had eventually been found in the river near the ferry landing; he had been drowned while trying to escape perhaps.

About a fortnight after Tom's rescue from the cave he started off to visit Huck, who had grown plenty strong enough, now, to hear exciting talk, and Tom had some that would interest him, he thought. Judge Thatcher's house was on Tom's way, and he stopped to see Becky. The judge and some friends set Tom to talking, and someone asked him ironically if he wouldn't like to go to the cave again. Tom said yes, he thought he wouldn't mind it.

The Judge said:

'Well, there are others just like you, Tom, I've not the least doubt. But we have taken care of that. Nobody will get lost in that cave any more.'

'Why?'

'Because I had its big door sheathed with boiler iron two weeks ago, and triple locked; and I've got the keys.'

Tom turned as white as a sheet.

'What's the matter, boy? Here, run, somebody! Fetch a glass of water!'

The water was brought and thrown into Tom's face.

'Ah, now you're all right. What was the matter with you, Tom?'

'Oh, Judge, Injun Joe's in the cave!'

Chapter 34

Within a few minutes the news had spread, and a dozen skiff-loads of men were on their way to McDougal's cave, and the ferry-boat well filled with passengers, soon followed. Tom Sawyer was in the skiff that bore Judge Thatcher. When the cave door was unlocked, a sorrowful sight presented itself in the dim twilight of the place. Injun Joe lay stretched upon the ground, dead, with his face close to the crack of the door, as if his longing eyes had been fixed to the latest moment upon the light and cheer of the free world outside. Tom was touched, for he knew by his own experience how this wretch had suffered. His pity was moved, but nevertheless he felt an abounding sense of relief and security, now, which revealed to him in a degree which he had not fully appreciated before, how vast a weight of dread had been lying upon him since the day he lifted his voice against this bloody-minded outcast.

Injun Joe's bowie-knife lay close by, its blade broken in two. The great foundation-beam of the door had been chipped and hacked through with tedious labour; useless labour, too, it was, for the native rock formed a sill outside it, and upon that stubborn material the knife had wrought no effect; the only damage done was to the knife itself. But if there had been no stony obstruction there, labour would have been useless still, for if the beam had been wholly cut away Injun Joe could not have squeezed his body under the door, and he knew it. So he had only hacked that place in order to be doing something – in order to pass the weary time – in order to employ his tortured faculties. Ordinarily one could find half a dozen bits of candle stuck around in the crevices of this vestibule, left by tourists; but there were none, now. The prisoner had searched them out and eaten them. He had also contrived to catch a few bats, and these, also, he had eaten, leaving only their claws. The poor unfortunate had starved to death. In one place near at hand, a stalagmite had been slowly growing up from the ground for ages, builded by the water-drip from a stalactite overhead. The captive had broken off the stalagmite, and upon the stump had placed a stone wherein he had scooped a shallow hollow to catch the precious drop that fell once in every twenty minutes with the dreary regularity of a clock-tick – a dessert-spoonful once in four-and-twenty hours. That drop was falling when the Pyramids were new; when

Troy fell; when the foundations of Rome were laid; when Christ was crucified; when the Conqueror created the British Empire; when Columbus sailed; when the massacre at Lexington was 'news'. It is falling now; it will still be falling when all these things shall have sunk down the afternoon of history and the twilight of tradition, and been swallowed up in the thick night of oblivion. Has everything a purpose and a mission? Did this drop fall patiently during five thousand years to be ready for this flitting human insect's need, and had it another important object to accomplish ten thousand years to come? No matter. It is many and many a year since the hapless half-breed scooped out the stone to catch the priceless drops, but to this day the tourist stares longest at that pathetic stone and that slow-dropping water when he comes to see the wonders of McDougal's cave. Injun Joe's cup stands first in the list of the cavern's marvels; even 'Aladdin's Palace' cannot rival it.

Injun Joe was buried near the mouth of the cave; and people flocked there in boats and wagons from the town and from all the farms and hamlets for seven miles around; they brought their children, and all sorts of provisions, and confessed that they had had almost as satisfactory a time at the funeral as they could have had at the hanging.

This funeral stopped the further growth of one thing – the petition to the Governor for Injun Joe's pardon. The petition had been largely signed; many tearful and eloquent meetings had been held, and a committee of sappy women appointed to go in deep mourning and wail around the Governor, and implore him to be a merciful ass, and trample his duty underfoot. Injun Joe was believed to have killed five citizens of the village, but what of that? If he had been Satan himself, there would have been plenty of weaklings ready to scribble their names to a pardon-petition, and drip a tear on it from their permanently impaired and leaky waterworks.

The morning after the funeral Tom took Huck to a private place to have an important talk. Huck had learned all about Tom's adventure from the Welshman and the Widow Douglas by this time, but Tom said he reckoned there was one thing they had not told him; that thing was what he wanted to talk about now. Huck's face saddened. He said:

'I know what it is. You got into number two, and never found anything but whisky. Nobody told me it was you, but I just knowed it must a ben you, soon as I heard 'bout that whisky business; and I knowed you hadn't got the money becuz you'd a got at me some way or other, and told me, even if you was mum to everybody else. Tom, something's always told me we'd never get hold of that sag.'

'Why, Huck, I never told on that tavern-keeper. You know his tavern was all right the Saturday I went to the picnic. Don't you remember you was to watch there that night?'

'Oh, yes! Why, it seems 'bout a year ago. It was that very night that I follered Injun Joe to the widder's.'

'You followed him?'

'Yes – but you keep mum. I reckon Injun Joe's left friends behind him. I don't want 'em souring on me, and doing me mean tricks. If it hadn't been for me he'd be down in Texas now, all right.'

Then Huck told his entire adventure in confidence to Tom, who had only heard of the Welshman's part of it before.

'Well,' said Huck, presently, coming back to the main question, 'whoever nipped the whisky in number two nipped the money too, I reckon – anyways it's a goner for us, Tom.'

'Huck, that money wasn't ever in number two!'

'What!' Huck searched his comrade's face keenly. 'Tom, have you got on the track of that money again?'

'Huck, it's in the cave!'

Huck's eyes blazed.

'Say it again, Tom!'

'The money's in the cave!'

'Tom – honest injun, now – is it fun or earnest?'

'Earnest, Huck – just as earnest as ever I was in my life. Will you go in there with me and help get it out?'

'I bet I will! I will if it's where we can blaze our way to it and not get lost.'

'Huck, we can do that without the least little bit of trouble in the world.'

'Good as wheat! What makes you think the money's——'

'Huck, you just wait till we get in there. If we don't find it, I'll agree to give you my drum and everything I've got in the world. I will, by jings.'

'All right – it's a whizz. When do you say?'

'Right now, if you say it. Are you strong enough?'

'Is it far in the cave? I ben on my pins a little three or four days, now, but I can't walk more'n a mile, Tom – least I don't think I could.'

'It's about five miles into there the way anybody but me would go, Huck, but there's a mighty short cut that they don't anybody but me know about. Huck, I'll take you right to it in a skiff. I'll float the skiff down there, and I'll pull it back again, all by myself. You needn't ever turn your hand over.'

'Less start right off, Tom.'

'All right. We want some bread and meat, and our pipes, and a little bag or two, and two or three kite-strings, and some of those new-fangled things they call lucifer-matches. I tell you many's the time I wished I had some when I was in there before.'

A trifle after noon the boys borrowed a small skiff from a citizen who was absent, and got under way at once. When they were several miles below 'Cave Hollow', Tom said:

'Now you see this bluff here looks all alike all the way down from the cave hollow – no houses, no woodyards, bushes all alike. But do you see that white place up yonder where there's been a land-slide? Well, that's one of my marks. We'll get ashore now.'

They landed.

'Now, Huck, where we're a standing you could touch that hole I got out of with a fishing-pole. See if you can find it.'

Huck searched all the place about, and found nothing. Tom proudly marched into a thick clump of sumach bushes and said:

'Here you are! Look at it, Huck; it's the snuggest hole in this country. You just keep mum about it. All along I've been wanting to be a robber, but I knew I'd got to have a thing like this, and where to run across it was the bother. We've got it now, and we'll keep it quiet, only we'll let Joe Harper and Ben Rogers in – because of course there's got to be a gang, or else there wouldn't be any style about it. Tom Sawyer's Gang – it sounds splendid, don't it, Huck?'

'Well, it just does, Tom. And who'll we rob?'

'Oh, 'most anybody. Waylay people – that's mostly the way.'

'And kill them.'

'No – not always. Hive them in the cave till they raise a ransom!'

'What's a ransom?'

'Money. You make them raise all they can off'n their friends, and after you've kept them a year, if it ain't raised then you kill them. That's the general way. Only you don't kill the women. You shut up the women, but you don't kill them. They're always beautiful and rich, and awfully scared. You take their watches and things, but you always take your hat off and talk polite. They ain't anybody as polite as robbers – you'll see that in any book. Well, the women get to loving you, and after they've been in the cave a week or two weeks they stop crying, and after that you couldn't get them to leave. If you drove them out, they'd turn right around and come back. It's so in all the books.'

'Why, it's real bully, Tom. I b'lieve it's better'n to be a pirate.'

'Yes, it's better in some ways, because it's close to home, and circuses, and all that.'

By this time everything was ready and the boys entered the hole, Tom in the lead. They toiled their way to the farther end of the tunnel, then made their spliced kite-strings fast and moved on. A few steps brought them to the spring, and Tom felt a shudder quiver all through him He showed Huck the fragment of candle-wick perched on a lump of clay against the wall, and described how he and Becky had watched the flame struggle and expire.

The boys began to quiet down to whispers, now, for the stillness and gloom of the place oppressed their spirits. They went on, and presently entered and followed Tom's other corridor until they reached the 'jumping-off place'. The candles revealed the fact that it was not really a precipice, but only a steep clay hill, twenty or thirty feet high. Tom whispered:

'Now I'll show you something, Huck.'

He held his candle aloft and said:

'Look as far around the corner as you can. Do you see that? There – on the big rock over yonder – done with candle smoke.'

'Tom, it's a *cross*!'

'Now where's your number two? "*Under the cross*", hey? Right yonder's where I saw Injun Joe poke up his candle, Huck!'

Huck stared at the mystic sign a while, and then said with a shaky voice:

'Tom, less git out of here!'

'What! and leave the treasure?'

'Yes – leave it. Injun Joe's ghost is round about there, certain.'

'No it ain't, Huck, no it ain't. It would ha'nt the place where he died – away out at the mouth of the cave – five mile from here.'

'No, Tom, it wouldn't. It would hang round the money. I know the ways of ghosts, and so do you.'

Tom began to fear that Huck was right. Misgivings gathered in his mind. But presently an idea occurred to him.

'Looky here, Huck, what fools we're making of ourselves! Injun Joe's ghost ain't a going to come around where there's a cross!'

The point was well taken. It had its effect.

'Tom, I didn't think of that. But that's so. It's luck for us, that cross is. I reckon we'll climb down there and have a hunt for that box.'

Tom went first, cutting rude steps in the clay hill as he descended. Huck followed. Four avenues opened out of the small cavern which the great rock stood in. The boys examined three of them with no result. They found a small recess in the one nearest the base of the rock, with a pallet of blankets spread down in it; also an old suspender, some bacon rind, and the well-gnawed bones of two or three fowls. But there was no money-box. The lads searched and re-searched this place, but in vain. Tom said:

'He said *under* the cross. Well, this comes nearest to being under the cross. It can't be under the rock itself, because that sets solid on the ground.'

They searched everywhere once more, and then sat down discouraged. Huck could suggest nothing. By-and-by Tom said:

'Looky here, Huck; there's foot-prints and some candle-grease on the clay about one side of this rock, but not on the other sides. Now what's that for? I bet you the money *is* under the rock. I'm going to dig in the clay.'

'That ain't no bad notion, Tom!' said Huck, with animation.

Tom's 'real Barlow' was out at once, and he had not dug four inches before he struck wood.

'Hey, Huck! you hear that?'

Huck began to dig and scratch now. Some boards were soon uncovered and removed. They had concealed a natural chasm which led under the rock. Tom got into this and held his candle as far under the rock as he could, but said he could not see to the end of the rift. He proposed to explore. He stooped and passed under; the narrow way descended gradually. He followed its winding course, first to the right, then to the left, Huck at his heels. Tom turned a short curve by-and-by, and exclaimed:

'My goodness, Huck, looky here!'

It was the treasure-box, sure enough, occupying a snug little cavern, along with an empty powder-keg, a couple of guns in leather cases, two or three pairs of old moccasins, a leather belt, and some other rubbish well soaked with the water drip.

'Got it at last!' said Huck, ploughing among the tarnished coins with his hands. 'My, but we're rich, Tom!'

'Huck, I always reckoned we'd get it. It's just too good to believe, but we *have* got it, sure! Say, let's not fool around here, let's snake it out. Lemme see if I can lift the box.'

It weighed about fifty pounds. Tom could lift it after an awkward fashion, but could not carry it conveniently.

'I thought so,' he said; 'they carried it like it was heavy that day at the ha'nted house – I noticed that. I reckon I was right to think of fetching the little bags along.'

The money was soon in the bags, and the boys took it up to the cross rock.

'Now let's fetch the guns and things,' said Huck.

'No, Huck, leave them there. They're just the tricks to have when we go to robbing. We'll keep them there all the time, and we'll hold our orgies there, too. It's an awful snug place for orgies.'

'What's orgies?'

'I dunno. But robbers always have orgies, and of course we've got to have them too. Come along, Huck, we've been in here a long time. It's getting late, I reckon. I'm hungry, too. We'll eat and smoke when we get to the skiff.'

They presently emerged into the clump of sumach bushes, looked warily out, found the coast clear, and were soon lunching and smoking in the skiff. As the sun dipped towards the horizon they pushed out and got under way. Tom skimmed up the shore through the long twilight, chatting cheerily with Huck, and landed shortly after dark.

'Now, Huck,' said Tom, 'We'll hide the money in the loft of the widow's wood-shed, and I'll come up in the morning and we'll count and divide, and then we'll hunt up a place out in the woods for it where it will be safe. Just you lay quiet here and watch the stuff till I run and hook Benny Taylor's little wagon. I won't be gone a minute.'

He disappeared, and presently returned with the wagon, put the two small sacks into it, threw some old rags on top of them, and started off, dragging his cargo behind him. When the boys reached the Welshman's house they stopped to rest. Just as they were about to move on the Welshman stepped out and said:

'Hallo, who's that?'

'Huck and Tom Sawyer.'

'Good! Come along with me, boys, you are keeping everybody waiting. Here, hurry up, trot ahead; I'll haul the wagon for you. Why, it's not as light as it might be. Got bricks in it, or old metal?'

'Old metal,' said Tom.

'I judged so; the boys in this town will take more trouble and fool away more time hunting up six bits' worth of old iron to sell to the foundry, than they would to make twice the money at regular work. But that's human nature. Hurry along, hurry along!'

The boys wanted to know what the hurry was about.

'Never mind; you'll see when we get to the Widow Douglas's.'

Huck said with some apprehension, for he was long used to being falsely accused:

'Mr. Jones, we haven't been doing nothing.'

The Welshman laughed.

'Well, I don't know, Huck, my boy. I don't know about that. Ain't you and the widow good friends?'

'Yes. Well, she's ben a good friend to me, anyways.'

'All right, then. What do you want to be afraid for?'

This question was not entirely answered in Huck's slow mind before he found himself pushed, along with Tom, into Mrs. Douglas's drawing-room. Mr. Jones left the wagon near the door and followed.

The place was grandly lighted, and everybody that was of any conse-quence in the village was there. The Thatchers were there, the Harpers, the Rogerses, Aunt Polly, Sid, Mary, the minister, the editor, and a great many more, and all dressed in their best. The widow received the boys as heartily as anyone could well receive two such looking beings. They were covered with clay and candle-grease. Aunt Polly blushed crimson with humiliation, and frowned and shook her head at Tom. Nobody suffered half as much as the two boys did, however. Mr. Jones said:

'Tom wasn't at home, yet, so I gave him up; but I stumbled on him and Huck right at my door, and so I just brought them along in a hurry.'

'And you did just right,' said the widow. 'Come with me, boys.'

She took them to a bedchamber and said:

'Now wash and dress yourselves. Here are two new suits of clothes – shirts, socks, everything complete. They're Huck's – no, no thanks, Huck –

Mr. Jones bought one and I the other. But they'll fit both of you. Get into them. We'll wait – come down when you are slicked up enough.'

Then she left.

Chapter 35

Huck said:

'Tom, we can slope if we find a rope. The window ain't high from the ground.'

'Shucks! what do you want to slope for?'

'Well, I ain't used to that kind of a crowd. I can't stand it. I ain't going down there, Tom.'

'Oh, bother! It ain't anything. I don't mind it a bit. I'll take care of you.'

Sid appeared.

'Tom,' said he, 'Auntie has been waiting for you all the afternoon. Mary got your Sunday clothes ready, and everybody's been fretting about you. Say, ain't this grease and clay on your clothes?'

'Now, Mr. Siddy, you just 'tend to your own business. What's all this blow-out about, anyway?'

'It's one of the widow's parties that she's always having. This time it's for the Welshman and his sons, on account of that scrape they helped her out of the other night. And say – I can tell you something, if you want to know.'

'Well, what?'

'Why, old Mr. Jones is going to try to spring something on the people here tonight, but I overheard him tell Auntie today about it, as a secret, but I reckon it's not much of a secret now. Everybody knows – the widow, too, for all she tries to let on she don't. Oh, Mr. Jones was bound Huck should be here – couldn't get along with his grand secret without Huck, you know!'

'Secret about what Sid?'

'About Huck tracking the robbers to the widow's. I reckon Mr. Jones was going to make a grand time over his surprise, but I bet you it will drop pretty flat.'

Sid chuckled in a very contented and satisfied way.

'Sid, was it you that told?'

'Oh, never mind who it was. Somebody told, that's enough.'

'Sid, there's only one person in this town mean enough to do that, and that's you. If you had been in Huck's place you'd a sneaked down the hill and never told anybody on the robbers. You can't do any but mean things, and you can't bear to see anybody praised for doing good ones. There – no thanks, as the widow says.' And Tom cuffed Sid's ears and helped him to the door with several kicks. 'Now go and tell Auntie if you dare, and tomorrow you'll catch it!'

Some minutes later the widow's guests were at the supper table, and a dozen children were propped up at little side tables in the same room, after the fashion of that country and day. At the proper time Mr. Jones made his little speech, in which he thanked the widow for the honour she was doing himself and his sons, but said that there was another person whose modesty——

And so forth and so on. He sprang his secret about Huck's share in the adventure in the finest dramatic manner he was master of, but the surprise it occasioned was largely counterfeit, and not as clamorous and effusive as it might have been under happier circumstances. However, the widow made a pretty fair show of astonishment, and heaped so many compliments and so much gratitude upon Huck, that he almost forgot the nearly intolerable discomfort of his new clothes in the entirely intolerable discomfort of being set up as a target for everybody's gaze and everybody's laudations.

The widow said she meant to give Huck a home under her roof and have him educated; and that when she could spare the money she would start him in business in a modest way. Tom's chance was come. He said:

'Huck don't need it. Huck's rich!'

Nothing but a heavy strain upon the good manners of the company kept back the due and proper complimentary laugh at this pleasant joke. But the silence was a little awkward. Tom broke it.

'Huck's got money. Maybe you don't believe it, but he's got lots of it. Oh, you needn't smile; I reckon I can show you. You just wait a minute.'

Tom ran out of doors. The company looked at each other with a perplexed interest, and inquiringly at Huck, who was tongue-tied.

'Sid, what ails Tom?' said Aunt Polly. 'He – well, there ain't ever any making of that boy out. I never——'

Tom entered, struggling with the weight of his sacks, and Aunt Polly did not finish her sentence. Tom poured the mass of yellow coin upon the table and said:

'There – what did I tell you? Half of it's Huck's, and half of it's mine!'

The spectacle took the general breath away. All gazed, nobody spoke for a moment. Then there was a unanimous call for the explanation. Tom said he could furnish it, and he did. The tale was long, but brimful of interest. There was scarcely an interruption from anyone to break the charm of its flow. When he had finished, Mr. Jones said:

'I thought I had fixed up a little surprise for this occasion, but it don't amount to anything now. This one makes it sing mighty small, I'm willing to allow.'

The money was counted. The sum amounted to a little over twelve thousand dollars. It was more than anyone present had ever seen at one time before, though several persons were there who were worth considerably more than that in property.

Chapter 36

The reader may rest satisfied that Tom's and Huck's windfall made a mighty stir in the poor little village of St Petersburg. So vast a sum, all in actual cash, seemed next to incredible. It was talked about, gloated over, glorified, until the reason of many of the citizens tottered under the strain of the unhealthy excitement. Every 'haunted' house in St Petersburg and the neighbouring villages was dissected, plank by plank, and its foundations dug up and ransacked for hidden treasures – and not by boys, but men – pretty grave, unromantic men, too, some of them. Wherever Tom and Huck appeared they were courted, admired, stared at. The boys were not able to remember that their remarks had possessed weight before; but now their sayings were treasured and repeated; everything they did seemed somehow to be regarded as remarkable; they had evidently lost the power of doing and saying commonplace things; moreover, their past history was raked up and discovered to bear marks of conspicuous originality. The village paper published biographical sketches of the boys.

The Widow Douglas put Huck's money out at six per cent and Judge Thatcher did the same with Tom's at Aunt Polly's request. Each lad had an income now that was simply prodigious – a dollar for every weekday in the year and half of the Sundays. It was just what the minister got – no, it was what he was promised – he generally couldn't collect it. A dollar and a quarter a week would board, lodge, and school a boy in those old simple days – and clothe him and wash him, too, for that matter.

Judge Thatcher had conceived a great opinion of Tom. He said that no commonplace boy would ever have got his daughter out of the cave. When Becky told her father, in strict confidence, how Tom had taken her whipping at school, the Judge was visibly moved; and when she pleaded grace for the mighty lie which Tom had told in order to shift that whipping from her shoulders to his own, the Judge said with a fine outburst that it was a noble, a generous, a magnanimous lie – a lie that was worthy to hold up its head and march down through history breast to breast with George Washington's lauded Truth about the hatchet! Becky thought her father had never looked so tall and so superb as when he walked the floor and stamped his foot and said that. She went straight off and told Tom about it.

Judge Thatcher hoped to see Tom a great lawyer or a great soldier some day. He said he meant to look to it that Tom should be admitted to the National Military Academy, and afterwards trained in the best law-school in the country, in order that he might be ready for either career, or both.

Huck Finn's wealth, and the fact that he was under the Widow Douglas's protection, introduced him into society – no, dragged him into it, hurled him into it – and his sufferings were almost more than he could bear. The widow's servants kept him clean and neat, combed and brushed, and they bedded him nightly in unsympathetic sheets that had not one little spot or stain which he could press to his heart and know for a friend. He had to eat with knife and fork; he had to use napkin, cup, and plate; he had to learn his book; he had to go to church; he had to talk so properly that speech was become insipid in his mouth; whithersoever he turned, the bars and shackles of civilization shut him in and bound him hand and foot.

He bravely bore his miseries three weeks, and then one day turned up missing. For forty-eight hours the widow hunted for him everywhere in great distress. The public were profoundly concerned; they searched high and low, they dragged the river for his body. Early the third morning Tom Sawyer wisely went poking among some old empty hogsheads down behind the abandoned slaughterhouse, and in one of them he found the refugee. Huck had slept there; he had just breakfasted upon some stolen odds and ends of food, and was lying off, now, in comfort with his pipe. He was unkempt, uncombed, and clad in the same old ruin of rags that had made him picturesque in the days when he was free and happy. Tom routed him out, told him the trouble he had been causing, and urged him to go home. Huck's face lost its tranquil content and took a melancholy cast. He said:

'Don't talk about it, Tom. I've tried it, and it don't work; it don't work, Tom. It ain't for me; I ain't used to it. The widder's good to me, and friendly; but I can't stand them ways. She makes me git up just at the same time every morning; she makes me wash, they comb me all to thunder; she won't let me sleep in the woodshed; I got to wear them blamed clothes that just smothers me, Tom; they don't seem to any air git through 'em, somehow; and they're so rotten nice that I can't set down, or lay down, nor roll around anywheres; I ain't slid on a cellar door for – well, it 'pears to be years; I got to go to church, and sweat and sweat – I hate them ornery sermons! I can't ketch a fly in there, I can't chaw, I got to wear shoes all Sunday. The widder eats by a bell; she goes to bed by a bell; she gits up by a bell – everything's so awful reg'lar a body can't stand it.'

'Well, everybody does that way, Huck.'

'Tom, it don't make no difference. I ain't everybody and I can't stand it. It's awful to be tied up so. And grub comes too easy – I don't take no interest in vittles that way. I got to ask to go a fishing; I got to ask to go in a swimming dern'd if I hain't got to ask to do everything. Well, I'd got to talk so nice it wasn't no comfort; I'd got to go up in the attic and rip out a while every day to git a taste in my mouth, or I'd a died, Tom. The widder wouldn't let me smoke, she wouldn't let me yell, she wouldn't let me gape, nor stretch, nor scratch before folks.' Then with a spasm of special irritation and injury: 'And dad fetch it, she prayed all the time! I never see such a woman! I had to shove, Tom, I just had to. And besides, that school's going to open, and I'd a had to go to it; well, I wouldn't stand that, Tom. Looky here, Tom, being rich ain't what it's cracked up to be. It's just worry and worry, and sweat and sweat, and a wishing you was dead all the time. Now these clothes suits me and this bar'l suits me, and I ain't ever going to shake 'em any more. Tom, I wouldn't ever got into all this trouble if it hadn't a ben for that money; now you just take my sheer of it along with yourn, and gimme a ten-center sometimes – not many times, becuz I don't give a dern for a thing 'thout it's tollable hard to git – and you go and beg off for me with the widder.'

'Oh, Huck, you know I can't do that. 'Tain't fair; and besides, if you'll try this thing just a while longer you'll come to like it.'

'Like it! Yes – the way I'd like a hot stove if I was to set on it long enough. No Tom, I won't be rich, and I won't live in them cussed smothery houses. I like the woods, and the river, and hogsheads, and I'll stick to 'em too. Blame it all! just as we'd got guns, and a cave, and all just fixed to rob, here this dern foolishness had got to come up and spile it all!'

Tom saw his opportunity:

'Looky here, Huck, being rich ain't going to keep me back from turning robber.'

'No! Oh, good licks, are you in real dead-wood earnest, Tom?'

'Just as dead earnest as I'm a sitting here. But, Huck, we can't let you into the gang if you ain't respectable, you know.'

Huck's joy was quenched.

'Can't let me in, Tom? Didn't you let me go for a pirate?'

'Yes, but that's different. A robber is more high-toned than what a pirate is – as a general thing. In most countries they're awful high up in the nobility – dukes and such.'

'Now, Tom, hain't you always ben friendly to me? You wouldn't shet me out, would you, Tom? You wouldn't do that, now, would you, Tom?'

'Huck, I wouldn't want to and I don't want to, but what would people say? Why, they'd say, "Mph! Tom Sawyer's Gang! pretty low characters in it!" They'd mean you, Huck. You wouldn't like that, and I wouldn't.'

Huck was silent for some time, engaged in a mental struggle. Finally he said:

'Well, I'll go back to the widder for a month and tackle it and see if I come to stand it, if you'll let me b'long to the gang, Tom.'

'All right, Huck, it's a whizz! Come along, old chap, and I'll ask the widow to let up on you a little, Huck.'

'Will you, Tom, now will you? That's good. If she'll let up on some of the roughest things, I'll smoke private and cuss private, and crowd through or bust. When you going to start the gang and turn robbers?'

'Oh, right off. We'll get the boys together and have the initiation tonight, maybe.'

'Have the which?'

'Have the initiation.'

'What's that?'

'It's to swear to stand by one another, and never tell the gang's secrets, even if you're chopped all to flinders, and kill anybody and all his family that hurts one of the gang.'

'That's gay – that's mighty gay, Tom, I tell you.'

'Well, I bet it is. And all that swearing's got to be done at midnight, in the lonesomest, awfullest place you can find – a ha'nted house is the best, but they're all ripped up, now.'

'Well, midnight's good, anyway, Tom.'

'Yes, so it is. And you've got to swear on a coffin, and sign it with blood.'

'Now that's something like! Why, it's a million times bullier than pirating. I'll stick to the widder till I rot, Tom; and if I git to be a reg'lar ripper of a robber, and everybody talking 'bout it, I reckon she'll be proud she snaked me in out of the wet.'

CONCLUSION

So endeth this chronicle. It being strictly a history of a boy, it must stop here; the story could not go much further without becoming the history of a man. When one writes a novel about grown people, he knows exactly where to stop – that is, with a marriage; but when he writes of juveniles, he must stop where he best can.

Most of the characters that perform in this book still live, and are prosperous and happy. Some day it may seem worth while to take up the story of the younger ones again, and see what sort of men and women they turned out to be; therefore it will be wisest not to reveal any of that part of their lives at present.

THE ADVENTURES OF
HUCKLEBERRY FINN

THE ADVENTURES OF
HUCKLEBERRY FINN

Mark Twain

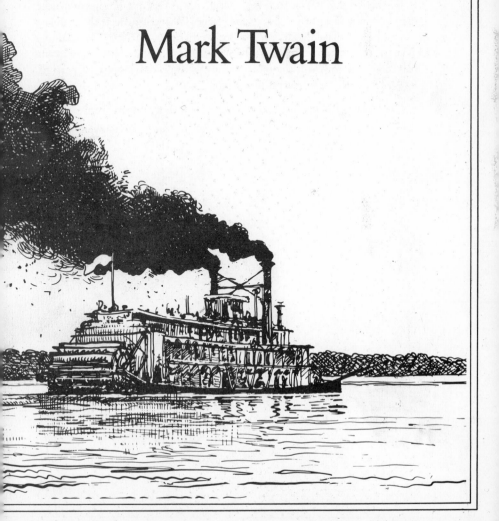

Notice

Persons attempting to find a motive in this narrative will be prosecuted; persons attempting to find a moral in it will be banished; persons attempting to find a plot in it will be shot.

BY ORDER OF THE AUTHOR

per G. G., CHIEF OF ORDNANCE.

Explanatory

In this book a number of dialects are used, to wit: the Missouri negro dialect; the extremest form of the backwoods South-Western dialect; the ordinary 'Pike-County' dialect; and four modified varieties of this last. The shadings have not been done in a haphazard fashion, or by guess-work; but painstakingly, and with the trustworthy guidance and support of personal familiarity with these several forms of speech

I make this explanation for the reason that without it many readers would suppose that all these characters were trying to talk alike and not succeeding.

THE AUTHOR

List of Illustrations

Chapter 1

You don't know about me, without you have read a book by the name of *The Adventures of Tom Sawyer*, but that ain't no matter. That book was made by Mr. Mark Twain, and he told the truth, mainly. There was things which he stretched, but mainly he told the truth. That is nothing. I never seen anybody but lied, one time or another, without it was Aunt Polly, or the widow, or maybe Mary. Aunt Polly – Tom's Aunt Polly, she is – and Mary, and the Widow Douglas, is all told about in that book – which is mostly a true book; with some stretchers, as I said before.

Now the way that the book winds up, is this: Tom and me found the money that the robbers hid in the cave, and it made us rich. We got six thousand dollars apiece – all gold. It was an awful sight of money when it was piled up. Well, Judge Thatcher, he took it and put it out at interest, and it fetched us a dollar a day apiece, all the year round – more than a body could tell what to do with. The Widow Douglas, she took me for her son, and allowed she would civilize me; but it was rough living in the house all the time, considering how dismal regular and decent the widow was in all her ways; and so when I couldn't stand it no longer, I lit out. I got into my old rags and my sugar-hogshead again, and was free and satisfied. But Tom Sawyer he hunted me up and said he was going to start a band of robbers, and I might join if I would go back to the widow and be respectable. So I went back.

The widow she cried over me, and called me a poor lost lamb, and she called me a lot of other names, too, but she never meant no harm by it. She put me in them new clothes again, and I couldn't do nothing but sweat and sweat, and feel all cramped up. Well, then, the old thing commenced again. The widow rung a bell for supper, and you had to come to time. When you got to the table you couldn't go right to eating, but you had to wait for the widow to tuck down her head and grumble a little over the victuals, though there warn't really anything the matter with them. That is, nothing only everything was cooked by itself. In a barrel of odds and ends it is different; things get mixed up, and the juice kind of swaps around, and the things go better.

After supper she got out her book and learned me about Moses and the 'Bulrushers'; and I was in a sweat to find out all about him; but by and by she let it out that Moses had been dead a considerable long time; so then I didn't care no more about him; because I don't take no stock in dead people.

Pretty soon I wanted to smoke, and asked the widow to let me. But she wouldn't. She said it was a mean practice and wasn't clean, and I must try to not do it any more. That is just the way with some people. They get down on a thing when they don't know nothing about it. Here she was a-bothering about Moses, which was no kin to her, and no use to anybody, being gone, you see, yet finding a power of fault with me for doing a thing that had some good in it. And she took snuff too; of course that was all right, because she done it herself.

Her sister, Miss Watson, a tolerable slim old maid, with goggles on, had just come to live with her, and took a set at me now, with a spelling book. She worked me middling hard for about an hour, and then the widow made her ease up. I couldn't stood it much longer. Then for an hour it was deadly dull, and I was fidgety. Miss Watson would say, 'Don't put your feet up there, Huckleberry'; and 'don't scrunch up like that, Huckleberry – set up straight'; and pretty soon she would say, 'Don't gap and stretch like that, Huckleberry – why don't you try to behave?' Then she told me all about the bad place, and I said I wished I was there. She got mad, then, but I didn't mean no harm. All I wanted was to go somewheres; all I wanted was a change, I warn't particular. She said it was wicked to say what I said; said she wouldn't say it for the whole world; *she* was going to live so as to go to the good place. Well, I couldn't see no advantage in going where she was going, so I made up my mind I wouldn't try for it. But I never said so, because it would only make trouble, and wouldn't do no good.

Now she had got a start, and she went on and told me all about the good place. She said all a body would have to do there was to go around all day long with a harp and sing for ever and ever. So I didn't think much of it. But I never said so. I asked her if she reckoned Tom Sawyer would go there, and she said, not by a considerable sight. I was glad about that, because I wanted him and me to be together.

Miss Watson she kept pecking at me, and it got tiresome and lonesome. By and by they fetched the niggers in and had prayers, and then everybody was off to bed. I went up to my room with a piece of candle and put it on the table. Then I set down in a chair by the window and tried to think of something cheerful, but it warn't no use. I felt so lonesome I most wished I was dead. The stars was shining, and the leaves rustled in the woods ever so mournful; and I heard an owl, away off, who-whooing about somebody that was dead, and a whippowill and a dog crying about somebody that was going to die; and the wind was trying to whisper something to me and I couldn't make out what it was, and so it made the cold shivers run over me. Then away out in the woods I heard that kind of a sound that a ghost makes when it wants to tell about something that's on its mind and can't make itself understood, and so can't rest easy in its grave and has to go about that way every night grieving. I got so downhearted and scared, I did wish I had some company. Pretty soon a spider went crawling up my shoulder, and I flipped it off and it lit in the candle; and before I could budge it was all shrivelled up. I didn't need anybody to tell me that that was an awful bad sign and would fetch me some bad luck, so I was scared and most shook the clothes off of me. I got up and turned around in my tracks three times and crossed my breast every time; and then I tied up a little lock of my hair with a thread to keep witches away. But I hadn't no confidence. You do that when you've lost a horse-shoe that you've found, instead of nailing it up over the door, but I hadn't ever heard anybody say it was any way to keep off bad luck when you'd killed a spider.

I set down again, a-shaking all over, and got out my pipe for a smoke; for the house was all as still as death, now, and so the widow wouldn't know. Well, after a long time I heard the clock away off in the town go boom – boom – boom – twelve licks – and all still again – stiller than ever. Pretty soon I heard a twig snap, down in the dark amongst the trees – something was a-stirring. I set still and listened. Directly I could just barely hear a 'me-yow! me-yow!' down there. That was good! Says I, 'me-yow! me-yow!' as soft as I could, and then I put out the light and scrambled out of the window on to the shed. Then I slipped down to the ground and crawled in amongst the trees, and sure enough there was Tom Sawyer waiting for me.

Chapter 2

We went tiptoeing along a path amongst the trees back towards the end of
widow's garden, stooping down so as the branches wouldn't scrape our heads.
When we was passing by the kitchen I fell over a root and made a noise. We
scrouched down and laid still. Miss Watson's big nigger, named Jim, was
setting in the kitchen door; we could see him pretty clear, because there was a
light behind him. He got up and stretched his neck out about a minute,
listening. Then he says:

'Who dah?'

He listened some more; then he come tiptoeing down and stood right
between us; we could a touched him, nearly. Well, likely it was minutes and
minutes that there warn't a sound, and we all there so close together. There
was a place on my ankle that got to itching; but I dasn't scratch it; and then my
ear begun to itch; and next my back, right between my shoulders. Seemed like
I'd die if I couldn't scratch. Well, I've noticed that thing plenty of times since.
If you are with the quality, or at a funeral, or trying to go to sleep when you
ain't sleepy – if you are anywheres where it won't do for you to scratch, why
you will itch all over in upwards of a thousand places. Pretty soon Jim says:

'Say – who is you? Whar is you? Dog my cats ef I didn' hear sumf'n.
Well, I knows what I's gwyne to do. I's gwyne to set down here and listen tell
I hears it agin.'

So he sat down on the ground betwixt me and Tom. He leaned his back
up against a tree, and stretched his legs out till one of them most touched one
of mine. My nose begun to itch. It itched till the tears come into my eyes. But
I dasn't scratch. Then it begun to itch on the inside. Next I got to itching
underneath. I didn't know how I was going to set still. This miserableness
went on as much as six or seven minutes; but it seemed a sight longer than
that. I was itching in eleven different places now. I reckoned I couldn't stand
it more'n a minute longer, but I set my teeth hard and got ready to try. Just
then Jim begun to breathe heavy; next he begun to snore – and then I was
pretty soon comfortable again.

Tom he made a sign to me – kind of a little noise with his mouth – and we
went creeping away on our hands and knees. When we was ten foot off, Tom
whispered to me and wanted to tie Jim to the tree for fun; but I said no; he

might wake and make a disturbance, and then they'd find out I warn't in. Then Tom said he hadn't got candles enough, and he would slip in the kitchen and get some more. I didn't want him to try. I said Jim might wake up and come. But Tom wanted to resk it; so we slid in there and got three candles, and Tom laid five cents on the table for pay. Then we got out, and I was in a sweat to get away; but nothing would do Tom but he must crawl to where Jim was, on his hands and knees, and play something on him. I waited, and it seemed a good while, everything was so still and lonesome.

As soon as Tom was back, we cut along the path, around the garden fence, and by and by fetched up on the steep top of the hill the other side of the house. Tom said he slipped Jim's hat off of his head and hung it on a limb right over him, and Jim stirred a little, but he didn't wake. Afterwards Jim said the witches betwitched him and put him in a trance, and rode him all over the State, and then set him under the trees again and hung his hat on a limb to show who done it. And next time Jim told it he said they rode him down to New Orleans; and after that, every time he told it he spread it more and more, till by and by he said they rode him all over the world, and tired him most to death, and his back was all over saddle-boils. Jim was monstrous proud about it, and he got so he wouldn't hardly notice the other niggers. Niggers would come miles to hear Jim tell about it, and he was more looked up to than any nigger in that country. Strange niggers would stand with their mouths open and look him all over, same as if he was a wonder. Niggers is always talking about witches in the dark by the kitchen fire; but whenever one was talking and letting on to know all about such things, Jim would happen in and say, 'Hm! What you know 'bout witches?' and that nigger was corked up and had to take a back seat. Jim always kept that five-center piece around his neck with a string, and said it was a charm the devil give to him with his own hands and told him he could cure anybody with it and fetch witches whenever he wanted to, just by saying something to it; but he never told what it was he said to it. Niggers would come from all around there and give Jim anything they had, just for a sight of that five-center piece; but they wouldn't touch it, because the devil had had his hands on it. Jim was most ruined, for a servant, because he got so stuck up on account of having seen the devil and been rode by witches.

Well, when Tom and me got to the edge of the hill-top, we looked away down into the village and could see three or four lights twinkling, where there was sick folks, maybe; and the stars over us was sparkling ever so fine; and down by the village was the river, a whole mile broad, and awful still and grand. We went down the hill and found Jo Harper, and Ben Rogers, and two or three more of the boys, hid in the old tanyard. So we unhitched a skiff and pulled down the river two miles and a half, to the big scar on the hillside, and went ashore.

We went to a clump of bushes, and Tom made everybody swear to keep the secret, and then showed them a hole in the hill, right in the thickest part of the bushes. Then we lit the candles and crawled in on our hands and knees. We went about two hundred yards, and then the cave opened up. Tom poked about amongst the passages and pretty soon ducked under a wall where you wouldn't a noticed that there was a hole. We went along a narrow place and got into a kind of room, all damp and sweaty and cold, and there we stopped. Tom says:

'Now we'll start this band of robbers and call it Tom Sawyer's Gang. Everybody that wants to join has got to take an oath, and write his name in blood.'

Everybody was willing. So Tom got out a sheet of paper that he had wrote the oath on, and read it. It swore every boy to stick to the band, and never tell any of the secrets; and if anybody done anything to any boy in the band, whichever boy was ordered to kill that person and his family must do it, and he mustn't sleep till he had killed them and hacked a cross in their breasts, which was the sign of the band. And nobody that didn't belong to the band could use that mark, and if he did he must be sued; and if he done it again he must be killed. And if anybody that belonged to the band told the secrets, he must have his throat cut, and then have his carcass burnt up and the ashes scattered all around, and his name blotted off of the list with blood and never mentioned again by the gang, but have a curse put on it and be forgot, for ever.

Everybody said it was a real beautiful oath, and asked Tom if he got it out of his own head. He said, some of it, but the rest was out of pirate books, and robber books, and every gang that was high-toned had it.

Some thought it would be good to kill the *families* of boys that told the secrets. Tom said it was a good idea, so he took a pencil and wrote it in. Then Ben Rogers says:

'Here's Huck Finn, he hain't got no family – what you going to do 'bout him?'

'Well, hain't he got a father?' says Tom Sawyer.

'Yes, he's got a father, but you can't never find him, these days. He used to lay drunk with the hogs in the tanyard, but he hain't been seen in these parts for a year or more.'

They talked it over, and they was going to rule me out, because they said every boy must have a family or somebody to kill, or else it wouldn't be fair and square for the others. Well, nobody could think of anything to do – everybody was stumped, and set still. I was most ready to cry; but all at once I thought of a way, and so I offered them Miss Watson – they could kill her. Everybody said:

'Oh, she'll do, she'll do. That's all right. Huck can come in.'

Then they all stuck a pin in their fingers to get blood to sign with, and I made my mark on the paper.

'Now,' says Ben Rogers, 'what's the line of business of this Gang?'

'Nothing only robbery and murder,' Tom said.

'But who are we going to rob? houses – or cattle – or——' ·

'Stuff! stealing cattle and such things ain't robbery, it's burglary,' says Tom Sawyer. 'We ain't burglars. That ain't no sort of style. We are highwaymen. We stop stages and carriages on the road, with masks on, and kill the people and take their watches and money.'

'Must we always kill the people?'

'Oh, certainly. It's best. Some authorities think different, but mostly it's considered best to kill them. Except some that you bring to the cave here and keep them till they're ransomed.'

'Ransomed? What's that?'

'I don't know. But that's what they do. I've seen it in books; and so of course that's what we've got to do.'

'But how can we do it if we don't know what it is?'

'Why blame it all, we've *got* to do it. Don't I tell you it's in the books? Do you want to go to doing different from what's in the books, and get things all muddled up?'

'Oh, that's all very fine to *say*, Tom Sawyer, but how in the nation are these fellows going to be ransomed if we don't know how to do it to them? that's the thing *I* want to get at. Now what do you *reckon* it is?'

'Well, I don't know. But per'aps if we keep them till they're ransomed, it means that we keep them till they're dead.'

'Now, that's something *like*. That'll answer. Why couldn't you said that before? We'll keep them till they're ransomed to death – and a bothersome lot they'll be, too, eating up everything and always trying to get loose.'

'How you talk, Ben Rogers. How can they get loose when there's a guard over them, ready to shoot them down if they move a peg?'

'A guard. Well, that *is* good. So somebody's got to set up all night and never get any sleep, just so as to watch them. I think that's foolishness. Why can't a body take a club and ransom them as soon as they get here?'

'Because it ain't in the books so – that's why. Now, Ben Rogers, do you want to do things regular, or don't you? – that's the idea. Don't you reckon that the people that made the books knows what's the correct thing to do? Do you reckon *you* can learn 'em anything? Not by a good deal. No, sir, we'll just go on and ransom them in the regular way.'

'All right. I don't mind; but I say it's a fool way, anyhow. Say – do we kill the women, too?'

'Well, Ben Rogers, if I was as ignorant as you I wouldn't let on. Kill the women? No – nobody ever saw anything in the books like that. You fetch them to the cave, and you're always as polite as pie to them; and by and by they fall in love with you and never want to go home any more.'

'Well, if that's the way. I'm agreed, but I don't take no stock in it. Mighty soon we'll have the cave so cluttered up with women, and fellows waiting to be ransomed, that there won't be no place for the robbers. But go ahead, I ain't got nothing to say.'

Little Tommy Barnes was asleep, now, and when they waked him up he was scared, and cried, and said he wanted to go home to his ma, and didn't want to be a robber any more.

So they all made fun of him, and called him cry-baby, and that made him mad, and he said he would go straight and tell all the secrets. But Tom give him five cents to keep quiet, and said we would all go home and meet next week and rob somebody and kill some people.

Ben Rogers said he couldn't get out much, only Sundays, and so he wanted to begin next Sunday, but all the boys said it would be wicked to do it on Sunday, and that settled the thing. They agreed to get together and fix a day as soon as they could, and then we elected Tom Sawyer first captain and Jo Harper second captain of the Gang, and so started home.

I clumb up the shed and crept into my window just before day was breaking. My new clothes was all greased up and clayey, and I was dog-tired.

Chapter 3

Well, I got a good going-over in the morning, from old Miss Watson, on account of my clothes; but the widow she didn't scold, but only cleaned off the grease and clay, and looked so sorry that I thought I would behave a while if I could. Then Miss Watson she took me in the closet and prayed, but nothing come of it. She told me to pray every day, and whatever I asked for I would get it. But it warn't so. I tried it. Once I got a fish-line, but no hooks. It warn't any good to me without hooks. I tried for the hooks three or four times, but somehow I couldn't make it work. By and by, one day, I asked Miss Watson to try for me, but she said I was a fool. She never told me why, and I couldn't make it out no way.

I set down, one time, back in the woods, and had a long think about it. I says to myself, if a body can get anything they pray for, why don't Deacon Winn get back the money he lost on pork? Why can't the widow get back her silver snuffbox that was stole? Why can't Miss Watson fat up? No, says I to myself, there ain't nothing in it. I went and told the widow about it, and she said the thing a body could get by praying for it was 'spiritual gifts'. This was too many for me, but she told me what she meant – I must help other people, and do everything I could for other people, and look out for them all the time, and never think about myself. This was including Miss Watson, as I took it. I went out in the woods and turned it over in my mind a long time, but I couldn't see no advantage about it – except for the other people – so at last I reckoned I wouldn't worry about it any more, but just let it go. Sometimes the widow would take me one side and talk about Providence in a way to make a body's mouth water; but maybe next day Miss Watson would take hold and knock it all down again. I judged I could see that there was two Providences, and a poor chap would stand considerable show with the widow's Providence, but if Miss Watson's got him there warn't no help for him any more. I thought it all out, and reckoned I would belong to the widow's, if he wanted me, though I couldn't make out how he was a-going to be any better off then than what he was before, seeing I was so ignorant and so kind of low-down and ornery.

Pap he hadn't been seen for more than a year, and that was comfortable for me; I didn't want to see him no more. He used to always whale me when he was sober and could get his hands on me; though I used to take to the woods most of the time when he was around. Well, about this time he was found in the river drowned, about twelve mile above town, so people said. They judged it was him, anyway; said this drowned man was just his size, and was ragged, and had uncommon long hair – which was all like pap – but they couldn't make nothing out of the face, because it had been in the water so long it warn't much like a face at all. They said he was floating on his back in the water. They took him and buried him on the bank. But I warn't comfortable long, because I happened to think of something. I knowed mighty well that a drownded man don't float on his back, but on his face. So I knowed, then, that this warn't pap, but a woman dressed up in a man's clothes. So I was uncomfortable again. I judged the old man would turn up again by and by, though I wished he wouldn't.

We played robbers now and then about a month, and then I resigned. All the boys did. We hadn't robbed nobody, we hadn't killed any people, but only just pretended. We used to hop out of the woods and go charging down on hog-drovers and women in carts taking garden stuff to market, but we never hived any of them. Tom Sawyer called the hogs 'ingots', and he called the turnips and stuff 'julery', and we would go to the cave and pow-wow over what we had done and how many people we had killed and marked. But I couldn't see no profit in it. One time Tom sent a boy to run about town with a blazing stick, which he called a slogan (which was the sign for the Gang to get together), and then he said he had got secret news by his spies that next day a whole parcel of Spanish merchants and rich A-rabs was going to camp in Cave Hollow with two hundred elephants, and six hundred camels, and over a thousand 'sumter' mules, all loaded down with di'monds, and they didn't have only a guard of four hundred soldiers, and so we would lay in ambuscade, as he called it, and kill the lot and scoop the things. He said we must slick up our swords and guns, and get ready. He never could go after even a turnip-cart but he must have the swords and guns all scoured up for it; though they was only lath and broom-sticks, and you might scour at them till you rotted, and then they warn't worth a mouthful of ashes more than what they was before. I didn't believe we could lick such a crowd of Spaniards and A-rabs, but I wanted to see the camels and elephants, so I was on hand next day, Saturday, in the ambuscade; and when we got the word, we rushed out of the woods and down the hill. But there warn't no Spaniards and A-rabs, and there warn't no camels nor no elephants. It warn't anything but a Sunday-school picnic, and only a primer-class at that. We busted it up, and chased the children up the hollow; but we never got anything but some doughnuts and jam, though Ben Rogers got a rag doll, and Jo Harper got a hymn-book and a tract; and then the teacher charged in and made us drop everything and cut. I didn't see no di'monds, and I told Tom Sawyer so.

He said there was loads of them there, anyway; and he said there was A-rabs there, too, and elephants and things. I said, why couldn't we see them, then? He said if I warn't so ignorant, but had read a book called *Don Quixote*, I would know without asking. He said it was all done by enchantment. He said there was hundreds of soldiers there, and elephants and treasure, and so on, but we had enemies which he called magicians, and they had turned the whole thing into an infant Sunday school, just out of spite. I said all right, then the thing for us to do was to go for the magicians. Tom Sawyer said I was a numskull.

'Why,' says he, 'a magician could call up a lot of genies, and they would hash you up like nothing before you could say Jack Robinson. They are as tall as a tree and as big around as a church.'

'Well,' I says, 's'pose we got some genies to help *us* – can't we lick the other crowd then?'

'How you going to get them?'

'I don't know. How do *they* get them?'

'Why, they rub an old tin lamp or an iron ring, and then the genies come tearing in, with the thunder and lightning a-ripping around and the smoke a-rolling, and everything they're told to do they up and do it. They don't think nothing of pulling a shot tower up by the roots, and belting a Sunday school superintendent over the head with it – or any other man.'

'Who makes them tear around so?'

'Why, whoever rubs the lamp or the ring. They belong to whoever rubs the lamp or the ring, and they've got to do whatever he says. If he tells them to build a palace forty miles long, out of di'monds, and fill it full of chewing gum, or whatever you want, and fetch an emperor's daughter from China for you to marry, they've got to do it – and they've got to do it before sun-up next morning, too. And more – they've got to waltz that palace around over the country wherever you want it, you understand.'

'Well,' says I, 'I think they are a pack of flatheads for not keeping the palaces themselves 'stead of fooling them away like that. And what's more – if I was one of them I would see a man in Jericho before I would drop my business and come to him for the rubbing of an old tin lamp.'

'How you talk, Huck Finn. Why, you'd *have* to come when he rubbed it, whether you wanted to or not.'

'What, and I as high as a tree and as big as a church? All right, then; I *would* come; but I lay I'd make that man climb the highest tree there was in the country.'

'Shucks, it ain't no use to talk to you, Huck Finn. You don't seem to know anything, somehow – perfect sap-head.'

I thought all this over for two or three days, and then I reckoned I would see if there was anything in it. I got an old tin lamp and an iron ring and went out in the woods and rubbed and rubbed till I sweat like an Injun, calculating to build a palace and sell it; but it warn't no use, none of the genies come. So then I judged that all that stuff was only just one of Tom Sawyer's lies. I reckoned he believed in the A-rabs and the elephants, but as for me I think different. It had all the marks of a Sunday school.

Chapter 4

Well, three or four months run along, and it was well into the winter, now. I had been to school most all the time, and could spell, and read, and write just a little, and could say the multiplication table up to six times seven is thirty-five, and I don't reckon I could ever get any further than that if I was to live for ever. I don't take no stock in mathematics, anyway.

At first I hated the school, but by and by I got so I could stand it. Whenever I got uncommon tired I played hookey, and the hiding I got next day done me good and cheered me up. So the longer I went to school the easier it got to be. I was getting sort of used to the widow's ways, too, and they warn't so raspy on me. Living in a house, and sleeping in a bed, pulled on me pretty tight, mostly, but before the cold weather I used to slide out and sleep in the woods, sometimes, and so that was a rest to me. I liked the old ways best, but I was getting so I liked the new ones, too, a little bit. The widow said I was coming along slow but sure, and doing very satisfactory. She said she warn't ashamed of me.

One morning I happened to turn over the salt-cellar at breakfast. I reached for some of it as quick as I could, to throw over my left shoulder and keep off the bad luck, but Miss Watson was in ahead of me, and crossed me off. She says, 'Take your hands away, Huckleberry – what a mess you are always making!' The widow put in a good word for me, but that warn't going to keep off the bad luck, I knowed that well enough. I started out, after breakfast, feeling worried and shaky, and wondering where it was going to fall on me, and what it was going to be. There is ways to keep off some kinds of bad luck, but this wasn't one of them kind; so I never tried to do anything, but just poked along low-spirited and on the watch-out.

I went down the front garden and clumb over the stile, where you go through the high board fence. There was an inch of new snow on the ground, and I seen somebody's tracks. They had come up from the quarry and stood around the stile a while, and then went on around the garden fence. It was funny they hadn't come in, after standing around so. I couldn't make it out. It was very curious, somehow. I was going to follow around, but I stooped down to look at the tracks first. I didn't notice anything at first, but next I did. There was a cross in the left boot-heel made with big nails, to keep off the devil.

I was up in a second and shinning down the hill. I looked over my shoulder every now and then, but I didn't see nobody. I was at Judge Thatcher's as quick as I could get there. He said:

'Why, my boy, you are all out of breath. Did you come for your interest?'

'No, sir,' I says; 'is there some for me?'

'Oh, yes, a half-yearly is in, last night. Over a hundred and fifty dollars. Quite a fortune for you. You better let me invest it along with your six thousand, because if you take it you'll spend it.'

'No, sir,' I says, 'I don't want to spend it. I don't want it at all – nor the six thousand, nuther. I want you to take it; I want to give it to you – the six thousand and all.'

He looked surprised. He couldn't seem to make it out. He says:

'Why, what can you mean, my boy?'

I says, 'Don't you ask me no questions about it, please. You'll take it – won't you?'

He says:

'Well, I'm puzzled. Is something the matter?'

'Please take it,' says I, 'and don't ask me nothing – then I won't have to tell no lies.'

He studied a while, and then he says:

'Oho-o. I think I see. You want to *sell* all your property to me – not give it. That's the correct idea.'

Then he wrote something on a paper and read it over, and says:

'There – you see it says "for a consideration." That means I have bought it of you and paid you for it. Here's a dollar for you, Now you sign it.'

So I signed it, and left.

Miss Watson's nigger, Jim, had a hair-ball as big as your fist, which had been took out of the fourth stomach of an ox, and he used to do magic with it. He said there was a spirit inside of it, and it knowed everything. So I went to him that night and told him pap was here again, for I found his tracks in the snow. What I wanted to know, was, what he was going to do, and was he going to stay? Jim got out his hair-ball, and said something over it, and then he held it up and dropped it on the floor. It fell pretty solid, and only rolled about an inch. Jim tried it again, and then another time, and it acted just the same. Jim got down on his knees and put his ear against it and listened. But it warn't no use; he said it wouldn't talk. He said sometimes it wouldn't talk without money. I told him I had an old slick counterfeit quarter that warn't no good because the brass showed through the silver a little, and it wouldn't pass nohow, even if the brass didn't show, because it was so slick it felt greasy, and so that would tell on it every time. (I reckoned I wouldn't say nothing about the dollar I got from the judge.) I said it was pretty bad money, but maybe the hair-ball would take it, because maybe it wouldn't know the difference. Jim smelt it, and bit it, and rubbed it, and said he would manage so the hair-ball would think it was good. He said he would split open a raw Irish potato and stick the quarter in between and keep it there all night, and next morning you couldn't see no brass, and it wouldn't feel greasy no more, and so anybody in town would take it in a minute, let alone a hair-ball. Well, I knowed a potato would do that, before, but I had forgot it.

Jim put the quarter under the hair-ball and got down and listened again. This time he said the hair-ball was all right. He said it would tell my whole fortune if I wanted it to. I says, go on. So the hair-ball talked to Jim, and Jim told it to me. He says:

'Yo' ole father doan' know, yit, what he's a-gwyne to do. Sometimes he spec he'll go 'way, en den agin he spec he'll stay. De bes' way is to res' easy en let de ole man take his own way. Dey's two angels hoverin' roun' 'bout him. One uv 'em is white en shiny, en t'other one is black. De white one gits him to go right, a little while, den de black one sail in en bust it all up. A body can't tell, yit, which one gwyne to fetch him at de las'. But you is all right. You gwyne to have considable trouble in yo' life, en considable joy. Sometimes you gwyne to git hurt, en sometimes you gwyne to git sick; but every time you's gwyne to git well agin. Dey's two gals flyin' 'bout you in yo' life. One uv 'em's light en t'other one is dark. One is rich en t'other is po'. You's gwyne to marry de po' one fust en de rich one by en by. You want to keep 'way fum de water as much as you kin, en don't run no resk, 'kase it's down in de bills dat you's gwyne to git hung.'

When I lit my candle and went up to my room that night, there set pap, his own self!

Chapter 5

I had shut the door to. Then I turned around, and there he was. I used to be scared of him all the time, he tanned me so much. I reckoned I was scared now, too; but in a minute I see I was mistaken. That is, after the first jolt, as you may say, when my breath sort of hitched – he being so unexpected; but right away after, I see I warn't scared of him worth bothering about.

He was most fifty, and he looked it. His hair was long and tangled and greasy, and hung down, and you could see his eyes shining through like he was behind vines. It was all black, no grey; so was his long, mixed-up whiskers. There warn't no colour in his face, where his faced showed; it was white; not like another man's white, but a white to make a body sick, a white to make a body's flesh crawl – a tree-toad white, a fish-belly white. As for his clothes – just rags, that was all. He had one ankle resting on t'other knee; the boot on that foot was busted, and two of his toes stuck through, and he worked them now and then. His hat was laying on the floor; an old black slouch with the top caved in, like a lid.

I stood a-looking at him; he set there a-looking at me, with his chair tilted back a little. I set the candle down. I noticed the window was up; so he had clumb in by the shed. He kept a-looking me all over. By and by he says:

'Starchy clothes – very. You think you're a good deal of a big-bug, *don't* you?'

'Maybe I am, maybe I ain't,' I says.

'Don't you give me none o' your lip,' says he. 'You've put on considerable many frills since I been away. I'll take you down a peg before I get done with you. You're educated, too, they say; can read and write. You think you're better'n your father, now, don't you, because he can't? *I'll* take it out of you. Who told you you might meddle with such hifalut'n foolishness, hey? – who told you you could?'

'The widow. She told me.'

'The widow, hey? – who told the widow she could put in her shovel about a thing that ain't none of her business?'

'Nobody never told her.'

'Well, I'll learn her how to meddle. And looky here – you drop that school, you hear? I'll learn people to bring up a boy to put on airs over his own

'"You git me that money to-morrow – I want it"'

father and let on to be better'n what *he* is. You lemme catch you fooling around that school again, you hear? Your mother couldn't read, and she couldn't write, nuther, before she died. None of the family couldn't, before *they* died. *I* can't; and here you're a-swelling yourself up like this. I ain't the man to stand it – you hear? Say – lemme hear you read.'

I took up a book and begun something about General Washington and the wars. When I'd read about a half minute, he fetched the book a whack with his hand and knocked it across the house. He says:

'It's so. You can do it. I had my doubts when you told me. Now looky here; you stop that putting on frills. I won't have it. I'll lay for you, my smarty; and if I catch you about that school I'll tan you good. First you know you'll get religion, too. I never see such a son.'

He took up a little blue and yaller picture of some cows and a boy, and says:

'What's this?'

'It's something they give me for learning my lessons good.'

He tore it up, and says:

'I'll give you something better – I'll give you a cowhide.'

He set there a-mumbling and a-growling a minute, and then he says:

'*Ain't* you a sweet-scented dandy, though? A bed; and bedclothes; and a look'n-glass; and a piece of carpet on the floor – and your own father got to sleep with the hogs in the tanyard. I never see such a son. I bet I'll take some o' these frills out o' you before I'm done with you. Why, there ain't no end to your airs – they say you're rich. Hey? – how's that?'

'They lie – that's how.'

'Looky here – mind how you talk to me; I'm a-standing about all I can stand, now – so don't gimme no sass. I've been in town two days, and I hain't heard nothing but about you bein' rich. I heard about it away down the river, too. That's why I come. You git me that money to-morrow – I want it.'

'I hain't got no money.'

'It's a lie. Judge Thatcher's got it. You git it. I want it.'

'I hain't got no money, I tell you. You ask Judge Thatcher; he'll tell you the same.'

'All right. I'll ask him; and I'll make him pungle, too, or I'll know the reason why. Say – how much you got in your pocket? I want it.'

'I hain't got only a dollar, and I want that to——'

'It don't make no difference what you want it for – you just shell it out.'

He took it and bit it to see if it was good, and then he said he was going down town to get some whisky; said he hadn't had a drink all day. When he had got out on the shed, he put his head in again, and cussed me for putting on frills and trying to be better than him; and when I reckoned he was gone, he came back and put his head in again, and told me to mind about that school, because he was going to lay for me and lick me if I didn't drop that.

Next day he was drunk and he went to Judge Thatcher's and bullyragged him and tried to make him give up the money, but he couldn't, and then he swore he'd make the law force him.

The judge and the widow went to law to get the court to take me away from him and let one of them be my guardian; but it was a new judge that had just come, and he didn't know the old man; so he said courts mustn't interfere and separate families if they could help it; said he'd druther not take a child away from its father. So Judge Thatcher and the widow had to quit on the business.

That pleased the old man till he couldn't rest. He said he'd cowhide me till I was black and blue if I didn't raise some money for him. I borrowed three dollars from Judge Thatcher, and pap took it and got drunk and went a-blowing around and cussing and whooping and carrying on; and he kept it up all over town, with a tin pan, till most midnight; then they jailed him, and next day they had him before court, and jailed him again for a week. But he said *he* was satisfied; said he was boss of his son, and he'd make it warm for *him*.

When he got out the new judge said he was a-going to make a man of him. So he took him to his own house, and dressed him up clean and nice, and had him to breakfast and dinner and supper with the family, and was just old pie to him, so to speak. And after supper he talked to him about temperance and such things till the old man cried, and said he'd been a fool, and fooled away his life; but now he was a-going to turn over a new leaf and be a man nobody wouldn't be ashamed of, and he hoped the judge would help him and not look down on him. The judge said he could hug him for them words; so *he* cried, and his wife she cried again; pap said he'd been a man that had always been misunderstood before, and the judge said he believed it. The old man said that what a man wanted that was down, was sympathy; and the judge said it was so; so they cried again. And when it was bedtime, the old man rose up and held out his hand, and says:

'Look at it, gentlemen, and ladies all; take ahold of it; shake it. There's a hand that was the hand of a hog; but it ain't so no more; it's the hand of a man that's started in on a new life, and'll die before he'll go back. You mark them words – don't forget I said them. It's a clean hand now; shake it – don't be afeard.'

So they shook it, one after the other, all around, and cried. The judge's wife she kissed it. Then the old man he signed a pledge – made his mark. The judge said it was the holiest time on record, or something like that. Then they tucked the old man into a beautiful room, which was the spare room, and in the night some time he got powerful thirsty and clumb out on to the porch-roof and slid down a stanchion and traded his new coat for a jug of forty-rod, and clumb back again and had a good old time; and towards daylight he crawled out again, drunk as a fiddler, and rolled off the porch and broke his left arm in two places and was most froze to death when somebody found him after sun-up. And when they come to look at that spare room, they had to take soundings before they could navigate it.

The judge he felt kind of sore. He said he reckoned a body could reform the ole man with a shot-gun, maybe, but he didn't know no other way.

Chapter 6

Well, pretty soon the old man was up and around again, and then he went for Judge Thatcher in the courts to make him give up that money, and he went for me, too, for not stopping school. He catched me a couple of times and thrashed me, but I went to school just the same, and dodged him or out-run him most of the time. I didn't want to go to school much, before, but I reckoned I'd go now to spite pap. That law trial was a slow business; appeared like they warn't ever going to get started on it; so every now and then I'd borrow two or three dollars off of the judge for him, to keep from getting a cowhiding. Every time he got money he got drunk; and every time he got drunk he raised Cain around town; and every time he raised Cain he got jailed. He was just suited – this kind of thing was right in his line.

He got to hanging around the widow's too much, and so she told him at last, that if he didn't quit using around there she would make trouble for him. Well, *wasn't* he mad? He said he would show who was Huck Finn's boss. So he watched out for me one day in the spring, and catched me, and took me up the river about three mile, in a skiff, and crossed over to the Illinois shore where it was woody and there warn't no houses but an old log hut in a place where the timber was so thick you couldn't find it if you didn't know where it was.

He kept me with him all the time, and I never got a chance to run off. We lived in that old cabin, and he always locked the door and put the key under his head, nights. He had a gun which he had stole, I reckon, and we fished and hunted, and that was what we lived on. Every little while he locked me in and went down to the store, three miles to the ferry, and traded fish and game for whisky and fetched it home and got drunk and had a good time, and licked me. The widow she found out where I was by and by, and she sent a man over to try to get hold of me, but pap drove him off with the gun, and it warn't long after that till I was used to being where I was, and liked it, all but the cowhide part.

It was kind of lazy and jolly, laying off comfortable all day, smoking and fishing, and no books nor study. Two months or more run along, and my clothes got to be all rags and dirt, and I didn't see how I'd ever got to like it so well at the widow's, where you had to wash, and eat on a plate, and comb up,

and go to bed and get up regular, and be for ever bothering over a book and
have old Miss Watson pecking at you all the time. I didn't want to go back no
more. I had stopped cussing, because the widow didn't like it; but now I took
to it again because pap hadn't no objections. It was pretty good times up in the
woods there, take it all around.

But by and by pap got too handy with his hick'ry, and I couldn't stand it.
I was all over welts. He got to going away so much, too, and locking me in.
Once he locked me in and was gone three days. It was dreadful lonesome. I
judged he had got drowned and I wasn't ever going to get out any more. I was
scared. I made up my mind I would fix up some way to leave there. I had tried
to get out of that cabin many a time, but I couldn't find no way. There warn't
a window to it big enough for a dog to get through. I couldn't get up the
chimbly, it was too narrow. The door was thick solid oak slabs. Pap was pretty
careful not to leave a knife or anything in the cabin when he was away; I
reckon I had hunted the place over as much as a hundred times; well, I was
most all the time at it, because it was about the only way to put in the time. But
this time I found something at last; I found an old rusty wood-saw without
any handle; it was laid in between a rafter and the clapboards of the roof. I
greased it up and went to work. There was an old horse-blanket nailed against
the logs at the far end of the cabin behind the table, to keep the wind from
blowing through the chinks and putting the candle out. I got under the table
and raised the blanket and went to work to saw a section of the big bottom log
out, big enough to let me through. Well, it was a good long job, but I was
getting towards the end of it when I heard pap's gun in the woods. I got rid of
the signs of my work, and dropped the blanket and hid my saw, and pretty
soon pap come in.

Pap warn't in a good humour – so he was his natural self. He said he was
down to town, and everything was going wrong. His lawyer said he reckoned
he would win his lawsuit and get the money, if they ever got started on the
trial; but then there was ways to put if off a long time, and Judge Thatcher
knowed how to do it. And he said people allowed there'd be another trial to
get me away from him and give me to the widow for my guardian, and they
guessed it would win, this time. This shook me up considerable, because I
didn't want to go back to the widow's any more and be so cramped up, and
civilized, as they called it. Then the old man got to cussing, and cussed
everything and everybody he could think of, and then cussed them all over
again to make sure he hadn't skipped any, and after that he polished off with a
kind of a general cuss all round, including a considerable parcel of people
which he didn't know the names of, and so called them what's-his-name,
when he got to them, and went right along with his cussing.

He said he would like to see the widow get me. He said he would watch
out, and if they tried to come any such game on him he knowed of a place six

or seven mile off, to stow me in, where they might hunt till they dropped and they couldn't find me. That made me pretty uneasy again, but only for a minute; I reckoned I wouldn't stay on hand till he got that chance.

The old man made me go to the skiff and fetch the things he had got. There was a fifty-pound sack of corn meal, and a side of bacon, ammunition, and a four-gallon jug of whisky, and an old book and two newspapers for wadding, besides some tow. I tore up a load, and went back and set down on the bow of the skiff to rest. I thought it all over, and I reckoned I would walk off with the gun and some lines, and take to the woods when I run away. I guessed I wouldn't stay in one place, but just tramp right across the country, mostly night times, and hunt and fish to keep alive, and so get so far away that the old man nor the widow couldn't ever find me any more. I judged I would saw out and leave that night if pap got drunk enough, and I reckoned he would. I got so full of it I didn't notice how long I was staying, till the old man hollered and asked me whether I was asleep or drownded.

I got the things all up to the cabin, and then it was about dark. While I was cooking supper the old man took a swig or two and got sort of warmed up, and went to ripping again. He had been drunk over in town, and laid in the gutter all night, and he was a sight to look at. A body would a thought he was Adam, he was just all mud. Whenever his liquor began to work, he most always went for the govment. This time he says:

'Call this a govment! why, just look at it and see what it's like. Here's the law a-standing ready to take a man's son away from him – a man's own son, which he had had all the trouble and all the anxiety and all the expense of raising. Yes, just as that man has got that son raised at last, and ready to go to work and begin to do suthin' for *him* and give him a rest, the law up and goes for him. And they call *that* govment! That ain't all, nuther. The law backs that old Judge Thatcher up and helps him to keep me out o' my property. Here's what the law does. The law takes a man worth six thousand dollars and upwards, and jams him into an old trap of a cabin like this, and lets him go round in clothes that ain't fitten for a hog. They call that govment! A man can't get his rights in a govment like this. Sometimes I've a mighty notion to just leave the country for good and all. Yes, and I *told* 'em so; I told old Thatcher so to his face. Lots of 'em heard me, and can tell what I said. Says I, for two cents I'd leave the blamed country and never come anear it agin. Them's the very words. I says, look at my hat – if you call it a hat – but the lid raises up and the rest of it goes down till it's below my chin, and then it ain't rightly a hat at all, but more like my head was shoved up through a jint o' stove-pipe. Look at it, says I – such a hat for me to wear – one of the wealthiest men in this town, if I could git my rights.

'Oh, yes, this is a wonderful govment, wonderful. Why, looky here. There was a free nigger there, from Ohio; a mulatter, most as white as a white man. He had the whitest shirt on you ever see, too, and the shiniest hat; and there ain't a man in that town that's got as fine clothes as what he had; and he had a gold watch and chain, and a silver-headed cane – the awfullest old grey-headed nabob in the State. And what do you think? they said he was a p'fessor in a college, and could talk all kinds of languages, and knowed everything. And that ain't the wust. They said he could *vote*, when he was at home. Well, that let me out. Thinks I, what is the country a-coming to? It was 'lection day, and I was just about to go and vote, myself, if I warn't too drunk to get there; but when they told me there was a State in this country where they'd let that nigger vote, I drawed out. I says I'll never vote agin. Them's the very words I said; they all heard me; and the country may rot for all me – I'll never vote agin as long as I live. And to see the cool way of that nigger – why, he wouldn't a give me the road if I hadn't shoved him out o' the way. I says to the people, why ain't this nigger put up at auction and sold? – that's what I want to know. And what do you reckon they said? Why, they said he couldn't be sold till he'd been in the State six months, and he hadn't been there that long yet. There, now – that's a specimen. They call that a govment that can't sell a free nigger till he's been in the State six months. Here's a govment that calls itself a govment, and lets on to be a govment, and thinks it is a govment, and yet's got to set stock-still for six whole months before it can take ahold of a prowling, thieving, infernal, white-shirted free nigger, and——'

Pap was a-going on so, he never noticed where his old limber legs was taking him to, so he went head over heels over the tub of salt pork, and barked both shins, and the rest of his speech was all the hottest kind of language – mostly hove at the nigger and the govment, though he give the tubs some, too, all along, here and there. He hopped around the cabin considerable, first on one leg and then on the other, holding first one shin and then the other one, and at last he let out with his left foot all of a sudden and fetched the tub a rattling kick. But it warn't good judgment, because that was the boot that had a couple of his toes leaking out of the front end of it; so now he raised a howl that fairly made a body's hair raise, and down he went in the dirt, and rolled there, and held his toes; and the cussing he done then laid over anything he had ever done previous. He said so his own self, afterwards. He had heard old Sowberry Hagan in his best days, and he said it laid over him, too; but I reckon that was sort of piling it on, maybe.

After supper pap took the jug, and said he had enough whisky there for two drunks and one delirium tremens. That was always his word. I judged he would be blind drunk in about an hour, and then I would steal the key, or saw myself out, one or t'other. He drank and drank, and tumbled down on his blankets, by and by; but luck didn't run my way. He didn't go sound asleep, but was uneasy. He groaned, and moaned, and thrashed around this way and that, for a long time. At last I got so sleepy I couldn't keep my eyes open, all I could do, and so before I knowed what I was about I was sound asleep, and the candle burning.

I don't know how long I was asleep, but all of a sudden there was an awful scream and I was up. There was pap, looking wild and skipping around every which way and yelling about snakes. He said they was crawling up his legs; and then he would give a jump and scream, and say one had bit him on the cheek – but I couldn't see no snakes. He started and run round and round the cabin hollering 'Take him off! take him off! he's biting me on the neck!' I never see a man look so wild in the eyes. Pretty soon he was all fagged out, and fell down panting; then he rolled over and over, wonderful fast, kicking things every which way, and striking and grabbing at the air with his hands, and screaming, and saying there was devils ahold of him. He wore out, by and by, and laid still a while, moaning. Then he laid stiller, and didn't make a sound. I could hear the owls and the wolves, away off in the woods, and it seemed terrible still. He was laying over by the corner. By and by he raised up, part way, and listened, with his head to one side. He says very low:

'Tramp – tramp – tramp; that's the dead; tramp – tramp – tramp; they're coming after me; but I won't go—— Oh, they're here! don't touch me – don't! hands off – they're cold; let go—— Oh, let a poor devil alone!'

Then he went down on all fours and crawled off begging them to let him alone, and he rolled himself up in his blanket and wallowed in under the old pine table, still a-begging; and then he went to crying. I could hear him through the blanket.

By and by he rolled out and jumped up on his feet looking wild, and he see me and went for me. He chased me round and round the place with a clasp-knife, calling me the Angel of Death, and saying he would kill me, and then I couldn't come for him no more. I begged, and told him I was only Huck, but he laughed *such* a screechy laugh, and roared and cussed, and kept on chasing me up. Once when I turned short and dodged under his arm he made a grab and got me by the jacket between my shoulders, and I thought I was gone; but I slid out of the jacket quick as lightning, and saved myself. Pretty soon he was all tired out, and dropped down with his back against the door, and said he would rest a minute and then kill me. He put his knife under him, and said he would sleep and get strong, and then he would see who was who.

So he dozed off, pretty soon. By and by I got the old split-bottom chair and clumb up, as easy as I could, not to make any noise, and got down the gun. I slipped the ramrod down it to make sure it was loaded, and then I laid it across the turnip barrel, pointing towards pap, and set down behind it to wait for him to stir. And how slow and still the time did drag along.

Chapter 7

'Git up! what you 'bout!'

I opened my eyes and looked around, trying to make out where I was. It was after sun-up, and I had been sound asleep. Pap was standing over me, looking sour – and sick, too. He says:

'What you doin' with this gun?'

I judged he didn't know nothing about what he had been doing, so I says:

'Somebody tried to get in, so I was laying for him.'

Why didn't you roust me out?'

'Well, I tried to, but I couldn't; I couldn't budge you.'

'Well, all right. Don't stand there palavering all day, but out with you and see if there's a fish on the lines for breakfast. I'll be along in a minute.'

He unlocked the door and I cleared out, up the river bank. I noticed some pieces of limbs and such things floating down, and a sprinkling of bark; so I knowed the river had begun to rise. I reckoned I would have great times, now, if I was over at the town. The June rise used to be always luck for me; because as soon as that rise begins, here comes cord-wood floating down, and pieces of log rafts – sometimes a dozen logs together; so all you have to do is to catch them and sell them to the wood yards and the sawmill.

I went along up the bank with one eye out for pap and t'other one out for what the rise might fetch along. Well, all at once, here comes a canoe; just a beauty, too, about thirteen or fourteen foot long, riding high like a duck. I shot head first off of the bank, like a frog, clothes and all on, and struck out for the canoe. I just expected there'd be somebody laying down in it, because people often done that to fool folks, and when a chap had pulled a skiff out most to it they'd raise up and laugh at him. But it warn't so this time. It was a drift-canoe, sure enough, and I clumb in and paddled her ashore. Thinks I, the old man will be glad when he sees this – she's worth ten dollars. But when I got to shore pap wasn't in sight yet, and as I was running her into a little creek like a gully, all hung over with vines and willows, I struck another idea; I judged I'd hide her good, and then, stead of taking to the woods when I run off, I'd go down the river about fifty mile and camp in one place for good, and not have such a rough time tramping on foot.

It was pretty close to the shanty, and I thought I heard the old man coming, all the time; but I got her hid; and then I out and looked around a bunch of willows, and there was the old man down the path a piece just drawing a bead on a bird with his gun. So he hadn't seen anything.

When he got along, I was hard at it taking up a 'trot' line. He abused me a little for being so slow, but I told him I fell in the river and that was what made me so long. I knowed he would see I was wet, and then he would be asking questions. We got five cat-fish off of the lines and went home.

While we laid off, after breakfast, to sleep up, both of us being about wore out, I got to thinking that if I could fix up some way to keep pap and the widow from trying to follow me, it would be a certainer thing than trusting to luck to get far enough off before they missed me; you see, all kinds of things might happen. Well, I didn't see no way for a while, but by and by pap raised up a minute, to drink another barrel of water, and he says:

'Another time a man comes a-prowling round here, you roust me out, you hear? That man warn't here for no good. I'd a shot him. Next time, you roust me out, you hear?'

Then he dropped down and went to sleep again – but what he had been saying give me the very idea I wanted. I says to myself, I can fix it now so nobody won't think of following me.

About twelve o'clock we turned out and went along up the bank. The river was coming up pretty fast, and lots of driftwood going by on the rise. By and by, along comes part of a log raft – nine logs fast together. We went out with the skiff and towed it ashore. Then we had dinner. Anybody but pap would a waited and seen the day through, so as to catch more stuff; but that warn't pap's style. Nine logs was enough for one time; he must shove right over to town and sell. So he locked me in and took the skiff and started off towing the raft about half-past three. I judged he wouldn't come back that night. I waited till I reckoned he had got a good start, then I out with my saw and went to work on that log again. Before he was t'other side of the river I was out of the hole; him and his raft was just a speck on the water away off yonder.

I took the sack of corn meal and took it to where the canoe was hid, and shoved the vines and branches apart and put it in; then I done the same with the side of bacon; then the whisky jug; I took all the coffee and sugar there was, and all the ammunition; I took the wadding; I took the bucket and gourd, I took a dipper and a tin cup, and my old saw and two blankets, and the skillet and the coffee-pot. I took fish-lines and matches and other things – everything that was worth a cent. I cleaned out the place. I wanted an axe, but there wasn't any, only the one out at the wood pile, and I knowed why I was going to leave that. I fetched out the gun, and now I was done.

I had wore the ground a good deal, crawling out of the hole and dragging out so many things. So I fixed that as good as I could from the outside by scattering dust on the place, which covered up the smoothness and the sawdust. Then I fixed the piece of log back into its place, and put two rocks under it and one against it to hold it there, – for it was bent up at that place, and didn't quite touch ground. If you stood four or five foot away and didn't know it was sawed, you wouldn't ever notice it; and besides, this was the back of the cabin and it warn't likely anybody would go fooling around there.

It was all grass clear to the canoe; so I hadn't left a track. I followed around to see. I stood on the bank and looked out over the river. All safe. So I took the gun and went up a piece into the woods and was hunting around for some birds, when I see a wild pig; hogs soon went wild in them bottoms after they had got away from the prairie farms. I shot this fellow and took him into camp.

I took the axe and smashed in the door. I beat it and hacked it considerable, a-doing it. I fetched the pig in and took him back nearly to the table and hacked into his throat with the axe, and laid him down on the ground to bleed – I say ground, because it *was* ground – hard packed, and no boards. Well, next I took an old sack and put a lot of big rocks in it – all I could drag – and I started it from the pig and dragged it to the door and through the woods down to the river and dumped it in, and down it sunk, out of sight. You could easy see that something had been dragged over the ground. I did wish Tom Sawyer was there, I knowed he would take an interest in this kind of business, and throw in the fancy touches. Nobody could spread himself like Tom Sawyer in such a thing as that.

Well, last I pulled out some of my hair, and bloodied the axe good, and stuck it on the back side, and slung the axe in the corner. Then I took up the pig and held him to my breast with my jacket (so he couldn't drip) till I got a good piece below the house and then dumped him into the river. Now I thought of something else. So I went and got the bag of meal and my old saw out of the canoe and fetched them to the house. I took the bag to where it used to stand, and ripped a hole in the bottom of it with the saw, for there warn't no knives and forks on the place – pap done everything with his clasp-knife, about the cooking. Then I carried the sack about a hundred yards across the grass and through the willows east of the house, to a shallow lake that was five miles wide and full of rushes – and ducks too, you might say, in the season. There was a slough or a creek leading out of it on the other side, that went miles away, I don't know where, but it didn't go to the river. The meal sifted out and made a little track all the way to the lake. I dropped pap's whetstone there too, so as to look like it had been done by accident. Then I tied up the rip in the meal sack with a string, so it wouldn't leak no more, and took it and my saw to the canoe again.

It was about dark, now; so I dropped the canoe down the river under some willows that hung over the bank, and waited for the moon to rise. I made fast to a willow; then I took a bite to eat, and by and by laid down in the canoe to smoke a pipe and lay out a plan. I says to myself, they'll follow the track of that sackful of rocks to the shore and then drag the river for me. And they'll follow that meal track to the lake and go browsing down the creek that leads out of it to find the robbers that killed me and took the things. They won't ever hunt the river for anything but my dead carcass. They'll soon get tired of that, and won't bother no more about me. All right; I can stop anywhere I want to. Jackson's Island is good enough for me; I know that island pretty well, and nobody ever comes there. And then I can paddle over to town, nights, and slink around and pick up things I want. Jackson's Island's the place.

I was pretty tired, and the first thing I knowed, I was asleep. When I woke up I didn't know where I was, for a minute. I set up and looked around, a little scared. Then I remembered. The river looked miles and miles across. The moon was so bright I could a counted the drift logs that went a-slipping along, black and still, hundreds of yards out from shore. Everything was dead quiet, and it looked late, and *smelt* late. You know what I mean – I don't know the words to put it in.

I took a good gap and a stretch, and was just going to unhitch and start, when I heard a sound away over the water. I listened. Pretty soon I made it out. It was that dull kind of a regular sound that comes from oars working in the rowlocks when it's a still night. I peeped out through the willow branches, and there it was – a skiff, away across the water. I couldn't tell how many was in it. It kept a-coming, and when it was abreast of me I see there warn't but one man in it. Thinks I, maybe it's pap, though I warn't expecting him. He dropped below me, with the current, and by and by he come a-swinging up shore in the easy water, and he went by so close I could a reached out the gun and touched him. Well, it *was* pap, sure enough – and sober, too, by the way he laid to his oars.

I didn't lose no time. The next minute I was a-spinning down stream soft but quick in the shade of the bank. I made two mile and a half, and then struck out a quarter of a mile or more towards the middle of the river, because pretty soon I would be passing the ferry landing and people might see me and hail me. I got out amongst the drift-wood and then laid down in the bottom of the canoe and let her float. I laid there and had a good rest and a smoke out of my pipe, looking away into the sky, not a cloud in it. The sky looks ever so deep when you lay down on your back in the moonshine; I never knowed it before. And how far a body can hear on the water such nights! I heard people talking at the ferry landing. I heard what they said, too, every word of it. One man said it was getting towards the long days and the short nights, now. T'other one said *this* warn't one of the short ones, he reckoned – and then they laughed, and he said it over again, and they laughed again; then they waked up another fellow and told him, and laughed, but he didn't laugh; he ripped out something brisk and said let him alone. The first fellow said he 'lowed to tell it to his old woman – she would think it was pretty good; but he said that warn't nothing to some things he had said in his time. I heard one man say it was nearly three o'clock, and he hoped daylight wouldn't wait more than about a week longer. After that, the talk got further and further away, and I couldn't make out the words any more, but I could hear the mumble; and now and then a laugh, too, but it seemed a long ways off.

I was away below the ferry now. I rose up and there was Jackson's Island, about two mile and a half down stream, heavy-timbered and standing up out of the middle of the river, big and dark and solid, like a steamboat without any lights. There warn't any signs of the bar at the head – it was all under water now.

It didn't take me long to get there. I shot past the head at a ripping rate, the current was so swift, and then I got into the dead water and landed on the side towards the Illinois shore. I run the canoe into a deep dent in the bank that I knowed about; I had to part the willow branches to get in; and when I made fast nobody could a seen the canoe from the outside.

I went up and set down on a log at the head of the island and looked out on the big river and the black drift-wood, and away over to the town, three mile away, where there was three or four lights twinkling. A monstrous big lumber raft was about a mile up stream, coming along down, with a lantern in the middle of it. I watched it come creeping down, and when it was most abreast of where I stood I heard a man say, 'Stern oars, there! heave her head to stabboard!' I heard that just as plain as if the man was by my side.

There was a little grey in the sky, now; so I stepped into the woods and laid down for a nap before breakfast.

Chapter 8

The sun was up so high when I waked, that I judged it was after eight o'clock. I laid there in the grass and the cool shade, thinking about things and feeling rested and ruther comfortable and satisfied. I could see the sun out at one or two holes, but mostly it was big trees all about, and gloomy in there amongst them. There was freckled places on the ground where the light sifted down through the leaves, and the freckled places swapped about a little, showing there was a little breeze up there. A couple of squirrels set on a limb and jabbered at me very friendly.

I was powerful lazy and comfortable – didn't want to get up and cook breakfast. Well, I was dozing off again, when I thinks I hears a deep sound 'boom!' away up the river. I rouses up and rests on my elbow and listens; pretty soon I hears it again. I hopped up and went and looked out at a hole in the leaves, and I see a bunch of smoke laying on the water a long ways up – about abreast the ferry. And there was the ferry-boat full of people, floating along down. I knowed what was the matter, now. 'Boom!' I see the white smoke squirt out of the ferry-boat's side. You see, they was firing cannon over the water, trying to make my carcass come to the top.

I was pretty hungry, but it warn't going to do for me to start a fire, because they might see the smoke. So I set there and watched the cannon-smoke and listened to the boom. The river was a mile wide, there, and it always looks pretty on a summer morning – so I was having a good enough time seeing them hunt for my remainders, if I only had a bit to eat. Well, then I happened to think how they always put quicksilver in loaves of bread and float them off because they always go right to the drownded carcass and stop there. So says I, I'll keep a look-out, and if any of them's floating around after me, I'll give them a show. I changed to the Illinois edge of the island to see what luck I could have, and I warn't disappointed. A big double loaf come along, and I most got it, with a long stick, but my foot slipped and she floated out further. Of course I was where the current set in the closest to the shore – I knowed enough for that. But by and by along comes another one, and this time I won. I took out the plug and shook out the little dab of quicksilver, and set my teeth in. It was 'baker's bread' what the quality eat – none of your low-down corn-pone.

I got a good place amongst the leaves, and set there on a log, munching the bread and watching the ferry-boat, and very well satisfied. And then something struck me. I says, now I reckon the widow or the parson or somebody prayed that this bread would find me, and here it has gone and done it. So there ain't no doubt but there is something in that thing. That is, there's something in it when a body like the widow or the parson prays, but it don't work for me, and I reckon it don't work for only just the right kind.

I lit a pipe and had a good long smoke and went on watching. The ferry-boat was floating with the current, and I allowed I'd have a chance to see who was aboard when she come along, because she would come in close, where the bread did. When she'd got pretty well along down towards me, I put out my pipe and went to where I fished out the bread, and laid down behind a log on the bank in a little open place. Where the log forked I could peep through.

By and by she come along, and she drifted in so close that they could a run out a plank and walked ashore. Most everybody was on the boat. Pap, and Judge Thatcher, and Bessie Thatcher, and Jo Harper, and Tom Sawyer, and his old Aunt Polly, and Sid and Mary, and plenty more. Everybody was talking about the murder, but the captain broke in and says:

'Look sharp, now; the current sets in the closest here, and maybe he's a washed ashore and got tangled among the brush at the water's edge. I hope so, anyway.'

I didn't hope so. They all crowded up and leaned over the rails, nearly in my face, and kept still, watching with all their might. I could see them first-rate, but they couldn't see me. Then the captain sung out:

'Stand away!' and the cannon let off such a blast right before me that it made me deef with the noise and pretty near blind with the smoke, and I judged I was gone. If they'd a had some bullets in, I reckon they'd a got the corpse they was after. Well, I see I warn't hurt, thanks to goodness. The boat floated on and went out of sight around the shoulder of the island. I could hear the booming, now and then, further and further off, and by and by after an hour, I didn't hear it no more. The island was three mile long. I judged they had got to the foot, and was giving it up. But they didn't yet awhile. They turned around the foot of the island and started up the channel on the Missouri side, under steam, and booming once in a while as they went. I crossed over to that side and watched them. When they got abreast the head of the island they quit shooting and dropped over to the Missouri shore and went home to the town.

I knowed I was all right now. Nobody else would come a-hunting after me. I got my traps out of the canoe and made me a nice camp in the thick woods. I made a kind of a tent out of my blankets to put my things under so the rain couldn't get at them. I catched a cat-fish and haggled him open with my saw, and towards sundown I started my camp fire and had supper. Then I set out a line to catch some fish for breakfast.

When it was dark I set by my camp fire smoking, and feeling pretty satisfied; but by and by it got sort of lonesome, and so I went and set on the bank and listened to the currents washing along, and counted the stars and drift-logs and rafts that come down, and then went to bed; there ain't no better way to put in time when you are lonesome; you can't stay so, you soon get over it.

And so for three days and nights. No difference – just the same thing. But the next day I went exploring around down through the island. I was boss of it; it all belonged to me, so to say, and I wanted to know all about it; but mainly I wanted to put in the time. I found plenty strawberries, ripe and prime; and green summer-grapes, and green razberries; and the green blackberries was just beginning to show. They would all come handy by and by, I judged.

Well, I went fooling along in the deep woods till I judged I warn't far from the foot of the island. I had my gun along, but I hadn't shot nothing; it was for protection; thought I would kill some game nigh home. About this time I mighty near stepped on a good-sized snake, and it went sliding off through the grass and flowers, and I after it, trying to get a shot at it. I clipped along, and all of a sudden I bounded right on to the ashes of a camp fire that was still smoking.

My heart jumped up amongst my lungs. I never waited for to look further, but uncocked my gun and went sneaking back on my tiptoes as fast as ever I could. Every now and then I stopped a second, amongst the thick leaves, and listened; but my breath come so hard I couldn't hear nothing else. I slunk along another piece further, then listened again; and so on, and so on; if I see a stump, I took it for a man; if I trod on a stick and broke it, it made me feel like a person had cut one of my breaths in two and I only got half, and the short half, too.

When I got to camp I warn't feeling very brash, there warn't much sand in my craw; but I says, this ain't no time to be fooling around. So I got all my traps into my canoe again so as to have them out of sight, and I put out the fire and scattered the ashes around to look like an old last year's camp, and then clumb a tree.

I reckon I was up in the tree two hours; but I didn't see nothing, I didn't hear nothing – I only *thought* I heard and seen as much as a thousand things. Well, I couldn't stay up there for ever; so at last I got down, but I kept in the thick woods and on the look-out all the time. All I could get to eat was berries and what was left over from breakfast.

By the time it was night I was pretty hungry. So when it was good and dark, I slid out from shore before moonrise and paddled over to the Illinois bank – about a quarter of a mile. I went out in the woods and cooked a supper, and I had about made up my mind I would stay there all night, when I hear a *plunkety-plunk, plunkety-plunk*, and says to myself, horses coming; and next I hear people's voices. I got everything into the canoe as quick as I could, and then went creeping through the woods to see what I could find out. I hadn't got far when I hear a man say:

'We better camp here, if we can find a good place; the horses is about beat out. Let's look around.'

I didn't wait, but shoved out and paddled away easy. I tied up in the old place, and reckoned I would sleep in the canoe.

I didn't sleep much. I couldn't, somehow, for thinking. And every time I waked up I thought somebody had me by the neck. So the sleep didn't do me no good. By and by I says to myself, I can't live this way; I'm a-going to find out who it is that's here on the island with me; I'll find it out or bust. Well, I felt better, right off.

So I took my paddle and slid out from shore just a step or two, and then let the canoe drop along down amongst the shadows. The moon was shining, and outside of the shadows it made it most as light as day. I poked along well on to an hour, everything still as rocks and sound asleep. Well, by this time I was most down to the foot of the island. A little ripply, cool breeze begun to blow, and that was as good as saying the night was about done. I give her a turn with the paddle and brung her nose to shore; then I got my gun and slipped out and into the edge of the woods. I set down there on a log and looked out through the leaves. I see the moon go off watch and the darkness begin to blanket the river. But in a little while I see a pale streak over the tree-tops, and knowed the day was coming. So I took my gun and slipped off towards where I had run across that camp fire, stopping every minute or two to listen. But I hadn't no luck, somehow; I couldn't seem to find the place. But by and by, sure enough, I catched a glimpse of fire, away through the trees. I went for it, cautious and slow. By and by I was close enough to have a look, and there laid a man on the ground. It most give me the fan-tods. He had a blanket around his head, and his head was nearly in the fire. I set there behind a clump of bushes, in about six foot of him, and kept my eyes on him steady. It was getting grey daylight, now. Pretty soon he gapped, and stretched himself, and hove off the blanket, and it was Miss Watson's Jim! I bet I was glad to see him. I says:

'Hallo, Jim!' and skipped out.

He bounced up and stared at me wild. Then he drops down on his knees, and puts his hands together and says:

'Doan' hurt me – don't! I hain't ever done no harm to a ghos'. I awluz liked dead people, en done all I could for 'em. You go en git in de river agin, whah you b'longs, en doan' do nuffn' to Ole Jim, 'at 'uz awluz yo' fren'.'

Well, I warn't long making him understand I warn't dead. I was ever so glad to see Jim. I warn't lonesome, now. I told him I warn't afraid of *him* telling the people where I was. I talked along, but he only set there and looked at me; never said nothing. Then I says:

'It's good daylight. Le's get breakfast. Make up your camp fire good.'

'What's de use er makin' up de camp fire to cook strawbries en sich truck? But you got a gun, hain't you? Den we kin git sumfn' better den strawbries.'

'Strawberries and such truck,' I says. 'Is that what you live on?'

'I couldn' git nuffn' else,' he says.

'Why, how long you been on the island, Jim?'

'I come here de night arter you's killed.'

'What, all that time?'

'Yes-indeedy.'

'And ain't you had nothing but that kind of rubbage to eat?'

'No, sah – nuffn' else.'

'Well, you must be most starved, ain't you?'

'I reck'n I could eat a hoss. I think I could. How long you ben on de islan'?'

'Since the night I got killed.'

'No! W'y, what has you lived on? But you got a gun? Oh, yes, you got a gun. Dat's good. Now you kill sumfn' en I'll make up de fire.'

So we went over to where the canoe was, and while he built a fire in a grassy open place amongst the trees, I fetched meal and bacon and coffee, and coffee-pot and frying-pan, and sugar and tin cups, and the nigger was set back considerable, because he reckoned it was all done with witchcraft. I catched a good big cat-fish, too, and Jim cleaned him with his knife, and fried him.

When breakfast was ready, we lolled on the grass and eat it smoking hot; Jim laid it in with all his might, for he was most about starved. Then when we had got pretty well stuffed, we laid off and lazied.

By and by Jim says:

'But looky here, Huck, who wuz it dat 'uz killed in dat shanty, ef it warn't you?'

Then I told him the whole thing, and he said it was smart. He said Tom Sawyer couldn't get up to no better plan than what I had. Then I says:

'How do you come to be here, Jim, and how'd you get here?'

He looked pretty uneasy, and didn't say nothing for a minute. Then he says:

'Maybe I better not tell.'

'Why, Jim?'

'Well, dey's reasons. But you wouldn' tell on me ef I 'uz to tell you, would you, Huck?'

'Blamed if I would, Jim.'

'Well, I b'lieve you, Huck. I – I *run off*.'

'Jim!'

'But mind, you said you wouldn't tell – you know you said you wouldn't tell, Huck.'

'Well, I did. I said I wouldn't, and I'll stick to it. Honest *injun* I will. People would call me a low down Ablitionist and despise me for keeping mum – but that don't make no difference. I ain't a-going to tell, and I ain't a-going back there anyways. So now, le's know all about it.'

'Well, you see, it 'uz dis way. Ole Missus – dat's Miss Watson – she pecks on me all de time, en treats me pooty rough, but she awluz said she wouldn' sell me down to Orleans. But I noticed dey wuz a nigger trader roun' de place considable, lately, en I begin to git oneasy. Well, one night I creeps to de do', pooty late, en de do' warn't quite shet, en I hear ole missus tell the widder she gwyne to sell me down to Orleans, but she didn' want to, but she could get eight hund'd dollars for me, en it 'uz sich a big stack o' money she couldn' resis'. De widder she try to git her to say she wouldn' do it, but I never waited to hear de res'. I lit out mighty quick, I tell you.

'I tuck out en shin down de hill en 'spec to steal a skift 'long de sho' som'ers 'bove de town, but dey wuz people a-stirrin' yit, so I hid in de ole ṭumbledown cooper shop on de bank to wait for everybody to go 'way. Well, I wuz dah all night. Dey wuz somebody roun' all de time. 'Long 'about six in the mawnin', skifts begin to go by, en 'bout eight or nine every skift dat went 'long wuz talkin' 'bout how yo' pap come over to de town en say you's killed. Dese las' skifts wuz full o' ladies en genlmen a-going' over to see de place. Sometimes dey'd pull up at de sho' en take a res' b'fo' dey started acrost, so by de talk I got to know all 'bout de killin'. I 'uz powerful sorry you's killed, Huck, but I ain't no mo', now.

'I laid dah under de shavin's all day. I 'uz hungry, but I warn't afeard; bekase I knowed ole missus en de widder wuz goin' to start to de camp-meetn' right arter breakfas' en be gone all day, en dey knows I goes off wid de cattle 'bout daylight, so dey wouldn' 'spec to see me roun' de place, en so dey wouldn' miss me tell arter dark in de evenin'. De yuther servants wouldn' miss me, kase dey'd shin out en take holiday, soon as de ole folks 'uz out'n de way.

'Well, when it come dark I tuck out up de river road, en went 'bout two mile er more to whah dey warn't no houses. I'd made up my mine 'bout what I's a-gwyne to do. You see ef I kep' on tryin' to git away afoot, de dogs 'ud track me; ef I stole a skift to cross over, dey'd miss dat skift, you see, en dey'd know 'bout whah I'd lan' on de yuther side en whah to pick up my track. So I says, a raff is what I's arter; it doan' *make* no track.

'I see a light a-comin' roun' de p'int' bymeby, so I wade' in en shove' a log ahead o' me, an swum more'n half-way acrost de river, en got in 'mongst de drift-wood, en kep' my head down low, en kinder swum agin de current tell the raff come along. Den I swum to de stern uv it, en tuck aholt. It clouded up en 'uz pooty dark for a little while. So I clumb up en laid down on de planks. De men 'uz all 'way yonder in de middle, whah de lantern wuz. De river wuz a-risin' en dey wuz a good current; so I reck'n'd 'at by fo' in de mawnin' I'd be twenty-five mile down de river, en den I'd slip in, jis' b'fo' daylight, en swim asho' en take to de woods on de Illinoi side.

'But I didn' have no luck. When we 'uz mos' down to de head er de islan', a man begin to come aft wid de lantern. I see it warn't no use fer to wait, so I slid overboard, en struck out fer de islan'. Well, I had a notion I could lan' mos' anywhers, but I couldn' – bank too bluff. I 'uz mos' to de foot er de islan' b'fo' I foun' a good place. I went into de woods en jedged I wouldn' fool wid raffs no mo, long as dey move de lantern roun' so. I had my pipe en a plug er dog-leg, en some matches in my cap, en dey warn't wet, so I 'uz all right.'

'And so you ain't had no meat nor bread to eat all this time? Why didn't you get mud-turkles?'

'How you gwyne to git'm? You can't slip up on um en grab um; en how's a body gwyne to hit um wid a rock? How could a body do it in de night? en I warn't gwyne to show myself on de bank in de day-time.'

'Well, that's so. You've had to keep in the woods all the time, of course. Did you hear 'em shooting the cannon?'

'Oh, yes. I knowed dey was arter you. I see um go by heah; watched um thoo de bushes.'

Some young birds come along, flying a yard or two at a time and lighting. Jim said it was a sign it was going to rain. He said it was a sign when young chickens flew that way, and so he reckoned it was the same way when young birds done it. I was going to catch some of them, but Jim wouldn't let me. He said it was death. He said his father lay mighty sick once, and some of them catched a bird, and his old granny said his father would die, and he did.

And Jim said you mustn't count the things you are going to cook for dinner, because that would bring bad luck. The same if you shook the table-cloth after sundown. And he said if a man owned a bee-hive, and that man died, the bees must be told about it before sun-up next morning, or else the bees would all weaken down and quit work and die. Jim said bees wouldn't sting idiots; but I didn't believe that, because I had tried them lots of times myself, and they wouldn't sting me.

I had heard about some of these things before, but not all of them. Jim knowed all kinds of signs. He said he knowed most everything. I said it looked to me like all the signs was about bad luck, and so I asked him if there warn't any good luck signs. He says:

'Mighty few – an' *dey* ain' no use to a body. What you want to know when good luck's a-comin' for? want to keep it off?' And he said, 'Ef you's got hairy arms en a hairy breas', it's a sign dat you's a-gwyne to be rich. Well, dey's some use in a sign like dat, 'kase it's so fur ahead. You see, maybe you's got to be po' a long time fust, en so you might git discourage' en kill yo'self 'f you didn' know by de sign dat you gwyne to be rich bymeby.'

'Have you got hairy arms and a hairy breast, Jim?'

'What's de use to axe dat question? don' you see I has?'

'Well, are you rich?'

'No, but I been rich wunst, and gwyne to be rich agin. Wunst I had foteen dollars, but I tuck to speculat'n', en got busted out.'

'What did you speculate in, Jim?'

'Well, fust I tackled stock?'

'What kind of stock?'

'Why, live stock. Cattle, you know. I put ten dollars in a cow. But I ain' gwyne to resk no mo' money in stock. De cow up 'n' died on my han's.'

'So you lost the ten dollars.'

'No, I didn' lose it all. I on'y los' 'bout nine of it. I sole de hide en taller for a dollar en ten cents.'

'You had five dollars and ten cents left. Did you speculate any more?'

'Yes. You know dat one-laigged nigger dat b'longs to old Misto Bradish? well, he sot up a bank, en say anybody dat put in a dollar would git fo' dollars mo' at de en' er de year. Well, all de niggers went in, but dey didn' have much. I wuz de on'y one dat had much. So I stuck out for mo' dan fo' dollars, en I said 'f I didn' git it I'd start a bank mysef. Well, o' course dat nigger want' to keep me out er de business, bekase he say dey warn't business 'nough for two banks, so he say I could put in my five dollars en he pay me thirty-five at de en' er de year.

'So I done it. Den I reck'n'd I'd inves' de thirty-five dollars right off en keep things a-movin'. Dey wuz a nigger name' Bob, dat had ketched a wood-flat, en his marster didn' know it; en I bought it off'n him en told him to take de thirty-five dollars when de en' er de year come; but somebody stole de wood-flat dat night, en nex' day de one-laigged nigger say de bank's busted. So dey didn' none uv us git no money.'

'What did you do with the ten cents, Jim?'

'Well, I 'uz gwyne to spen' it, but I had a dream, en de dream tole me to give it to a nigger name' Balum – Balum's Ass dey call him for short, he's one er dem chuckle-heads, you know. But he's lucky, dey say, en I see I warn't lucky. De dream say let Balum inves' de ten cents en he'd make a raise for me. Well, Balum he tuck de money, en when he wuz in church he hear de preacher say dat whoever give to de po' len' to de Lord, en boun' to git his money back a hund'd times. So Balum he tuck en give de ten cents to de po', en laid low to see what wuz gwyne to come of it.'

'Well, what did come of it, Jim?'

'Nuffn' never come of it. I couldn' manage to k'leck dat money no way;

en Balum he couldn'. I ain't gwyne to len' no mo' money 'dout I see de security. Boun' to git yo' money back a hund'd times, de preacher says! Ef I could git de ten *cents* back, I'd call it squah, en be glad er de chanst.'

'Well, it's all right, anyway, Jim, long as you're going to be rich again some time or other.'

'Yes – en I's rich now, come to look at it. I owns mysef, en I's wuth eight hund'd dollars. I wisht I had de money, I wouldn' want no mo'.'

Chapter 9

I wanted to go and look at a place right about the middle of the island, that I'd found when I was exploring; so we started, and soon got to it, because the island was only three miles long and a quarter of a mile wide.

This place was a tolerable long steep hill or ridge, about forty foot high. We had a rough time getting to the top, the sides was so steep and the bushes so thick. We tramped and clumb around all over it, and by and by found a good big cavern in the rock, most up to the top on the side towards Illinois. The cavern was as big as two or three rooms bunched together, and Jim could stand up straight in it. It was cool in there. Jim was for putting our traps in there, right away, but I said we didn't want to be climbing up and down there all the time.

Jim said if we had the canoe hid in a good place, and had all the traps in the cavern, we could rush there if anybody was to come to the island, and they would never find us without dogs. And besides, he said them little birds had said it was going to rain, and did I want the things to get wet?

So we went back and got the canoe and paddled up abreast the cavern, and lugged all the traps up there. Then we hunted up a place close by to hide the canoe in, amongst the thick willows. We took some fish off the lines and set them again, and begun to get ready for dinner.

The door of the cavern was big enough to roll a hogshead in, and on one side of the door the floor stuck out a little bit and was flat and a good place to build a fire on. So we built it there and cooked dinner.

We spread the blankets inside for a carpet, and eat our dinner in there. We put all the other things handy at the back of the cavern. Pretty soon it darkened up and begun to thunder and lighten; so the birds was right about it. Directly it begun to rain, and it rained like all fury, too, and I never see the wind blow so. It was one of these regular summer storms. It would get so dark that it looked all blue-black outside, and lovely; and the rain would thrash along by so thick that the trees off a little ways looked dim and spider-webby; and here would come a blast of wind that would bend the trees down and turn up the pale underside of the leaves; and then a perfect ripper of a gust would follow along and set the branches to tossing their arms as if they was just wild; and next, when it was just about the bluest and blackest – *fst!* it was as bright as glory and you'd have a little glimpse of tree-tops a-plunging about, away off yonder in the storm, hundreds of yards further than you could see before; dark as sin again in a second, and now you'd hear the thunder let go with an awful crash and then go rumbling, grumbling, tumbling down the sky towards the underside of the world, like rolling empty barrels downstairs, where it's long stairs and they bounce a good deal, you know.

'Jim, this is nice,' I says. 'I wouldn't want to be nowhere else but here. Pass me along another hunk of fish and some hot corn-bread.'

'Well, you wouldn't a ben here, 'f it hadn't a ben for Jim. You'd a ben down dah in de woods widout any dinner, en gittin' mos' drownded, too, dat you would, honey. Chickens knows when it's gwyne to rain, en so do de birds, chile.'

The river went on raising and raising for ten or twelve days, till at last it was over the banks. The water was three or four foot deep on the island in the low places and on the Illinois bottom. On that side it was a good many miles wide; but on the Missouri side it was the same old distance across – a half a mile – because the Missouri shore was just a wall of high bluffs.

Day-times we paddled all over the island in the canoe. It was mighty cool and shady in the deep woods even if the sun was blazing outside. We went winding in and out amongst the trees; and sometimes the vines hung so thick we had to back away and go some other way. Well, on every old broken-down tree you could see rabbits, and snakes, and such things; and when the island had been overflowed a day or two, they got so tame, on account of being hungry, that you could paddle right up and put your hand on them if you wanted to; but not the snakes and turtles – they would slide off in the water. The ridge our cavern was in was full of them. We could a had pets enough if we'd wanted them.

One night we catched a little section of a lumber raft – nice pine planks. It was twelve foot wide and about fifteen or sixteen foot long, and the top stood above water six or seven inches, a solid level floor. We could see saw-logs go by in the daylight, sometimes, but we let them go; we didn't show ourselves in daylight.

Another night, when we was up at the head of the island, just before daylight, here comes a frame house down, on the west side. She was a two-story, and tilted over, considerable. We paddled out and got aboard – clumb in at an upstairs window. But it was too dark to see yet, so we made the canoe fast and set in her to wait for daylight.

The light begun to come before we got to the foot of the island. Then we looked in at the window. We could make out a bed, and a table, and two old chairs, and lots of things around about on the floor; and there was clothes hanging against the wall. There was something laying on the floor in the far corner that looked like a man. So Jim says:

'Hallo, you!'

But it didn't budge. So I hollered again, and then Jim says:

'De man ain't asleep – he's dead. You hold still – I'll go en see.'

He went and bent down and looked, and says:

'It's a dead man. Yes, indeedy; naked, too. He's ben shot in de back. I reck'n he's ben dead two er three days. Come in, Huck, but doan' look at his face – it's too gashly.'

I didn't look at him at all. Jim throwed some old rags over him, but he needn't done it; I didn't want to see him. There was heaps of old greasy cards scattered around over the floor, and old whisky bottles, and a couple of masks made out of black cloth; and over the walls was the ignorantest kind of words and pictures, made with charcoal. There was two old dirty calico dresses, and a sun-bonnet, and some women's underclothes, hanging against the wall, and some men's clothing, too. We put the lot into the canoe; it might come good. There was a boy's old speckled straw hat on the floor; I took that too. And there was a bottle that had had milk in it; and it had a rag stopper for a baby to suck. We would a took the bottle, but it was broke. There was a seedy old chest, and an old hair trunk with the hinges broke. They stood open, but there warn't nothing left in them that was any account. The way things was scattered about, we reckoned the people left in a hurry and warn't fixed so as to carry off most of their stuff.

We got an old tin lantern, and a butcher knife without any handle, and a brand-new Barlow knife worth two bits in any store, and a lot of tallow candles, and a tin candlestick, and a gourd, and a tin cup, and a ratty old bed-quilt off the bed, and a reticule with needles and pins and beeswax and buttons and thread and all such truck in it, and a hatchet and some nails, and a fish-line as thick as my little finger, with some monstrous hooks on it, and a roll of buckskin, and a leather dog-collar, and a horse-shoe, and some vials of medicine that didn't have no label on them; and just as we was leaving I found a tolerable good curry-comb, and Jim he found a ratty old fiddle-bow, and a wooden leg. The straps was broke off of it, but barring that, it was a good enough leg, though it was too long for me and not long enough for Jim, and we couldn't find the other one, though we hunted all around.

And so, take it all around, we made a good haul. When we was ready to shove off, we was a quarter of a mile below the island, and it was pretty broad day; so I made Jim lay down in the canoe and cover up with the quilt, because if he set up, people could tell he was a nigger a good ways off. I paddled over to the Illinois shore, and drifted down most a half a mile doing it. I crept up the dead water under the bank, and hadn't no accidents and didn't see nobody. We got home all safe.

Chapter 10

After breakfast I wanted to talk about the dead man and guess out how he
come to be killed, but Jim didn't want to. He said it would fetch bad luck; and
besides, he said, he might come and ha'nt us; he said a man that warn't buried
was more likely to go a-ha'nting around than one that was planted and
comfortable. That sounded pretty reasonable, so I didn't say no more; but I
couldn't keep from studying over it and wishing I knowed who shot the man,
and what they done it for.

We rummaged the clothes we'd got, and found eight dollars in silver
sewed up in the lining of an old blanket overcoat. Jim said he reckoned the
people in that house stole the coat, because if they'd a knowed the money was
there they wouldn't a left it. I said I reckoned they killed him, too; but Jim
didn't want to talk about that. I says:

'Now you think it's bad luck; but what did you say when I fetched in the
snake-skin that I found on the top of the ridge day before yesterday? You said
it was the worst bad luck in the world to touch a snake-skin with my hands.
Well, here's your bad luck! We've raked in all this truck and eight dollars
besides. I wish we could have some bad luck like this every day, Jim.'

'Never you mind, honey, never you mind. Don't you git too peart. It's a-
comin'. Mind I tell you, it's a-comin'.'

It did come, too. It was a Tuesday that we had that talk. Well, after
dinner Friday, we was laying around in the grass at the upper end of the ridge,
and got out of tobacco. I went to the cavern to get some, and found a
rattlesnake in there. I killed him, and curled him up at the foot of Jim's
blanket, ever so natural, thinking there'd be some fun when Jim found him
there. Well, by night I forgot all about the snake, and when Jim flung himself
down on the blanket while I struck a light, the snake's mate was there, and bit
him.

He jumped up yelling, and the first thing the light showed was the
varmint curled up and ready for another spring. I laid him out in a second
with a stick, and Jim grabbed pap's whisky jug and begun to pour it down.

He was barefooted, and the snake bit him right on the heel. That all
comes of my being such a fool as to not remember that wherever you leave a
dead snake its mate always comes there and curls around it. Jim told me

'*I laid him out in a second with a stick*'

to chop off the snake's head and throw it away, and then skin the body and roast a piece of it. I done it, and he eat it and said it would help cure him. He made me take off the rattles and tie them around his wrist, too. He said that that would help. Then I slid out quiet and throwed the snakes clear away amongst the bushes; for I warn't going to let Jim find out it was all my fault, not if I could help it.

Jim sucked and sucked at the jug, and now and then he got out of his head and pitched around and yelled; but every time he come to himself he went to sucking at the jug again. His foot swelled up pretty big, and so did his leg; but by and by the drunk begun to come, and so I judged he was all right; but I'd druther been bit with a snake than pap's whisky.

Jim was laid up for four days and nights. Then the swelling was all gone and he was around again. I made up my mind I wouldn't ever take aholt of a snake-skin again with my hands, now that I see what had come of it. Jim said he reckoned I would believe him next time. And he said that handling a snake-skin was such awful bad luck that maybe we hadn't got to the end of it yet. He said he druther see the new moon over his left shoulder as much as a thousand times than take up a snake-skin in his hand. Well, I was getting to feel that way myself, though I've always reckoned that looking at the new moon over your left shoulder is one of the carelessest and foolishest things a body can do. Old Hank Bunker done it once, and bragged about it; and in less than two years he got drunk and fell off of the shot-tower and spread himself out so that he was just a kind of a layer, as you may say; and they slid him edgeways between two barn doors for a coffin, and buried him so, so they say, but I didn't see it. Pap told me. But anyway, it all come of looking at the moon that way, like a fool.

Well, the days went along, and the river went down between its banks again; and about the first thing we done was to bait one of the big hooks with a skinned rabbit and set it and catch a cat-fish that was as big as man, being six foot two inches long, and weighed over two hundred pounds. We couldn't handle him, of course; he would a flung us into Illinois. We just set there and watched him rip and tear around till he drownded. We found a brass button in his stomach, and a round ball, and lots of rubbage. We split the ball open with the hatchet, and there was a spool in it. Jim said he'd had it there a long time, to coat it over so and make a ball of it. It was as big a fish as was ever catched in the Mississippi, I reckon. Jim said he hadn't ever seen a bigger one. He would a been worth a good deal over at the village. They peddle out such a fish as that by the pound in the market house there; everybody buys some of him; his meat's as white as snow and makes a good fry.

Next morning I said it was getting slow and dull, and I wanted to get a stirring up, some way. I said I reckoned I would slip over the river and find out what was going on. Jim liked that notion; but he said I must go in the dark and look sharp. Then he studied it over and said, Couldn't I put on some of them old things and dress up like a girl? That was a good notion, too. So we shortened up one of the calico gowns and I turned up my trouser-legs to my knees and got into it. Jim hitched it behind with the hooks, and it was a fair fit. I put on the sun-bonnet and tied it under my chin, and then for a body to look in and see my face was like looking down a joint of stove-pipe. Jim said nobody would know me, even in the day-time, hardly. I practised around all day to get the hang of the things, and by and by I could do pretty well in them, only Jim said I didn't walk like a girl; and he said I must quit pulling up my gown to get at my britches pocket. I took notice, and done better.

I started up the Illinois shore in the canoe just after dark.

I started across to the town from a little below the ferry landing, and the drift of the current fetched me in at the bottom of the town. I tied up and started along the bank. There was a light burning in a little shanty that hadn't been lived in for a long time, and I wondered who had took up quarters there. I slipped up and peeped in at the window. There was a woman about forty year old in there, knitting by a candle that was on a pine table. I didn't know her face; she was a stranger, for you couldn't start a face in that town that I didn't know. Now this was lucky, because I was weakening; I was getting afraid I had come; people might know my voice and find me out. But if this woman had been in such a little town two days she could tell me all I wanted to know; so I knocked at the door, and made up my mind I wouldn't forget I was a girl.

Chapter 11

'Come in,' says the woman, and I did. She says:

'Take a cheer.'

I done it. She looked me all over with her little shiny eyes, and says:

'What might your name be?'

'Sarah Williams.'

'Where'bouts do you live? In this neighbourhood?'

'No'm. In Hookerville, seven mile below. I've walked all the way, and I'm all tired out.'

'Hungry, too, I reckon. I'll find you something.'

'No'm, I ain't hungry. I was so hungry I had to stop two mile below here at a farm; so I ain't hungry no more. It's what makes me so late. My mother's down sick, and out of money and everything, and I come to tell my uncle Abner Moore. He lives at the upper end of the town, she says. I hain't ever been here before. Do you know him?'

'No; but I don't know everybody yet. I haven't lived here quite two weeks. It's a considerable ways to the upper end of the town. You better stay here all night. Take off your bonnet.'

'No,' I says, 'I'll rest awhile, I reckon, and go on. I ain't afeard of the dark.'

She said she wouldn't let me go by myself, but her husband would be in by and by, maybe in a hour and a half, and she'd send him along with me. Then she got to talking about her husband, and about her relations up the river, and her relations down the river, and about how much better off they used to was, and how they didn't know but they'd made a mistake coming to our town, instead of letting well alone – and so on and so on, till I was afeard *I* had made a mistake coming to her to find out what was going on in the town; but by and by she dropped on to pap and the murder, and then I was pretty willing to let her clatter right along. She told about me and Tom Sawyer finding the six thousand dollars (only she got it ten) and all about pap and what a hard lot he was, and what a hard lot I was, and at last she got down to where I was murdered. I says:

'Who done it? We've heard considerable about these goings on, down in Hookerville, but we don't know who 'twas that killed Huck Finn.'

'Well, I reckon there's a right smart chance of people *here* that'd like to know who killed him. Some thinks old Finn done it himself.'

'No – is that so?'

'Most everybody thought it at first. He'll never know how nigh he come to getting lynched. But before night they changed around and judged it was done by a runaway nigger named Jim.'

'Why *he——*'

I stopped. I reckoned I better keep still. She run on, and never noticed I had put in at all.

'The nigger run off the very night Huck Finn was killed. So there's a reward out for him – three hundred dollars. And there's a reward out for old Finn too – two hundred dollars. You see, he come to town the morning after the murder, and told about it, and was out with 'em on the ferry-boat hunt, and right away after he up and left. Before night they wanted to lynch him, but he was gone, you see. Well, next day they found out the nigger was gone; they found out he hadn't ben seen sence ten o'clock the night the murder was done. So then they put it on him, you see, and while they was full of it, next day back comes old Finn and went boo-hooing to Judge Thatcher to get money to hunt for the nigger all over Illinois with. The judge give him some, and that evening he got drunk and was around till after midnight with a couple of mighty hard-looking strangers, and then went off with them. Well, he hain't come back sence, and they ain't looking for him back till this thing blows over a little, for people thinks now that he killed his boy and fixed things so folks would think robbers done it, and then he'd get Huck's money without having to bother a long time with a lawsuit. People do say he warn't any too good to do it. Oh, he's sly, I reckon. If he don't come back for a year, he'll be all right. You can't prove anything on him, you know; everything will be quieted down then, and he'll walk into Huck's money as easy as nothing.'

'Yes, I reckon so, 'm. I don't see nothing in the way of it. Has everybody quit thinking the nigger done it?'

'Oh, no, not everybody. A good many thinks he done it. But they'll get the nigger pretty soon, now, and maybe they can scare it out of him.'

'Why, are they after him yet?'

'Well, you're innocent, ain't you! Does three hundred dollars lay round every day for people to pick up? Some folks thinks the nigger ain't far from here. I'm one of them – but I hain't talked it around. A few days ago I was talking with an old couple that lives next door in the log shanty, and they happened to say hardly anybody ever goes to that island over yonder that they call Jackson's Island. Don't anybody live there? says I. No, nobody, says they. I didn't say any more, but I done some thinking. I was pretty near certain I'd seen smoke over there, about the head of the island, a day or two before that, so I says to myself, like as not that nigger's hiding over there; anyway, says I, it's worth the trouble to give the place a hunt. I hain't seen any smoke sence, so I reckon maybe he's gone, if it was him; but husband's going over to see – him and another man. He was gone up the river; but he got back to-day and I told him as soon as he got here two hours ago.'

I had got so uneasy I couldn't set still. I had to do something with my hands; so I took up a needle off of the table and went to threading it. My hands shook, and I was making a bad job of it. When the woman stopped talking, I looked up, and she was looking at me pretty curious, and smiling a little. I put down the needle and thread and let on to be interested – and I was, too – and says:

'Three hundred dollars is a power of money. I wish my mother could get it. Is your husband going over there tonight?'

'Oh, yes. He went up town with the man I was telling you of, to get a boat and see if they could borrow another gun. They'll go over after midnight.'

'Couldn't they see better if they was to wait till day-time?'

'Yes. And couldn't the nigger see better, too? After midnight he'll likely be asleep, and they can slip around through the woods and hunt up his camp fire all the better for the dark, if he's got one.'

'I didn't think of that.'

The woman kept looking at me pretty curious, and I didn't feel a bit comfortable. Pretty soon she says:

'What did you say your name was, honey?'

'M – Mary Williams.'

Somehow it didn't seem to me that I said it was Mary before, so I didn't look up; seemed to me I said it was Sarah; so I felt sort of cornered, and was afeard maybe I was looking it, too. I wished the woman would say something more; the longer she set still, the uneasier I was. But now she says:

'Honey, I thought you said it was Sarah when you first come in?'

'Oh, yes'm, I did. Sarah Mary Williams. Sarah's my first name. Some calls me Sarah, some calls me Mary.'

'Oh, that's the way of it?'

'Yes'm.'

I was feeling better, then, but I wished I was out of there, anyway. I couldn't look up yet.

Well, the woman fell to talking about how hard times was, and how poor they had to live, and how the rats was as free as if they owned the place, and so forth, and so on, and then I got easy again. She was right about the rats. You'd see one stick his nose out of a hole in the corner every little while. She said she had to have things handy to throw at them when she was alone, or they wouldn't give her no peace. She showed me a bar of lead, twisted up into a knot, and said she was a good shot with it generly, but she'd wrenched her arm a day or two ago, and didn't know whether she could throw true, now. But she watched for a chance, and directly she banged away at a rat, but she missed him wide, and said 'Ouch!' it hurt her arm so. Then she told me to try for the next one. I wanted to be getting away before the old man got back, but of course I didn't let on. I got the thing, and the first rat that showed his nose I let drive, and if he'd a stayed where he was he'd a been a tolerable sick rat. She said that that was first-rate, and she reckoned I would hive the next one. She went and got the lump of lead and fetched it back and brought along a hank of yarn, which she wanted me to help her with. I held up my two hands and she put the hank over them and went on talking about her and her husband's matters. But she broke off to say:

'Keep your eye on the rats. You better have the lead in your lap, handy.'

'So she dropped the lump into my lap, just at that moment, and I clapped my legs together on it and she went on talking. But only about a minute. Then she took off the hank and looked me straight in the face, but very pleasant, and says:

'Come, now – what's your real name?'

'Wh-what, mum?'

'What's your real name? Is it Bill, or Tom, or Bob? – or what is it?'

I reckon I shook like a leaf, and I didn't know hardly what to do. But I says:

'Please to don't poke fun at a poor girl like me, mum. If I'm in the way here, I'll——'

'No, you won't. Set down and stay where you are. I ain't going to hurt you, and I ain't going to tell on you, nuther. You must tell me your secret, and trust me. I'll keep it; and what's more, I'll help you. So'll my old man, if you want him to. You see, you're a runaway 'prentice – that's all. It ain't anything. There ain't any harm in it. You've been treated bad, and you made up your mind to cut. Bless you, child, I wouldn't tell on you. Tell me all about it, now – that's a good boy.'

So I said it wouldn't be no use to try to play it any longer, and I would just make a clean breast and tell her everything, but she mustn't go back on her promise. Then I told her my father and mother was dead, and the law had bound me out to a mean old farmer in the country thirty mile back from the river, and he treated me so bad I couldn't stand it no longer; he went away to be gone a couple of days, and so I took my chance and stole some of his daughter's old clothes, and cleared out, and I had been three nights coming the thirty miles; I travelled nights, and hid day-times and slept, and the bag of bread and meat I carried from home lasted me all the way and I had a plenty. I said I believed my uncle Abner Moore would take care of me, and so that was why I struck out for this town of Goshen.

'Goshen, child? This ain't Goshen. This is St Petersburg. Goshen's ten mile further up the river. Who told you this was Goshen?'

'Why, a man I met at daybreak this morning, just as I was going to turn into the woods for my regular sleep. He told me when the roads forked I must take the right hand, and five mile would fetch me to Goshen.'

'He was drunk, I reckon. He told you just exactly wrong.'

'Well, he did act like he was drunk, but it ain't no matter now. I got to be moving along. I'll fetch Goshen before daylight.'

'Hold on a minute. I'll put you up a snack to eat. You might want it.'

So she put me up a snack, and says:

'Say – when a cow's laying down, which end of her gets up first? Answer up prompt, now – don't stop to study over it. Which end gets up first?'

'The hind end, mum.'

'Well, then, a horse?'

'The for'rard end, mum.'

'Which side of a tree does the most moss grow on?'

'North side.'

'If fifteen cows is browsing on a hillside, how many of them eats with their heads pointed the same direction?'

'The whole fifteen, mum.'

'Well, I reckon you *have* lived in the country. I thought maybe you was trying to hocus me again. What's your real name, now?'

'George Peters, mum.'

'Well, try to remember it, George. Don't forget and tell me it's Elexander before you go, and then get out by saying it's George-Elexander when I catch you. And don't go about women in that old calico. You do a girl tolerable poor, but you might fool men, maybe. Bless you, child, when you set out to thread a needle, don't hold the thread still and fetch the needle up to it; hold the needle still and poke the thread at it – that's the way a woman most always does; but a man always does t'other way. And when you throw at a rat or anything, hitch yourself up a-tiptoe, and fetch your hand up over your head as awkard as you can, and miss your rat about six or seven foot. Throw stiff-armed from the shoulder, like there was a pivot there for it to turn on – like a girl; not from the wrist and elbow, with your arm out to one side, like a boy. And mind you, when a girl tries to catch anything in her lap, she throws her knees apart; she don't clap them together, the way you did when you catched the lump of lead. Why, I spotted you for a boy when you was threading the needle; and I contrived the other things just to make certain. Now trot along to your uncle, Sarah Mary Williams George Elexander Peters, and if you get into trouble you send word to Mrs. Judith Loftus, which is me, and I'll do what I can to get you out of it. Keep the river road, all the way, and next time you tramp, take shoes and socks with you. The river road's a rocky one, and your feet'll be in a condition when you get to Goshen, I reckon.'

I went up the bank about fifty yards, and then I doubled on my tracks and slipped back to where my canoe was, a good piece below the house. I jumped in and was off in a hurry. I went up stream far enough to make the head of the island, and then started across. I took off the sun-bonnet, for I didn't want no blinders on, then. When I was about the middle, I hear the clock begin to strike; so I stops and listens; the sound come faint over the water, but clear – eleven. When I struck the head of the island I never waited to blow, though I was most winded, but I shoved right into the timber where my old camp used to be, and started a good fire there on a high-and-dry spot.

Then I jumped in the canoe and dug out for our place a mile and a half below, as hard as I could go. I landed, and slopped through the timber and up the ridge and into the cavern. There Jim laid, sound asleep on the ground. I roused him out and says:

'Git up and hump yourself, Jim! There ain't a minute to lose. They're after us!'

Jim never asked no questions, he never said a word; but the way he worked for the next half an hour showed about how he was scared. By that time everything we had in the world was on our raft and she was ready to be shoved out from the willow cove where she was hid. We put out the camp fire at the cavern the first thing, and didn't show a candle outside after that.

I took the canoe out from shore a little piece and took a look, but if there was a boat around I couldn't see it, for stars and shadows ain't good to see by. Then we got out the raft and slipped along down in the shade, past the foot of the island dead still, never saying a word.

Chapter 12

It must a been close on to one o'clock when we got below the island at last, and the raft did seem to go mighty slow. If a boat was to come along, we was going to take to the canoe and break for the Illinois shore; and it was well a boat didn't come, for we hadn't ever thought to put the gun into the canoe, or a fishing-line or anything to eat. We was in ruther too much of a sweat to think of so many things. It warn't good judgment to put *everything* on the raft.

If the men went to the island, I just expect they found the camp fire I built, and watched it all night for Jim to come. Anyways, they stayed away from us, and if my building the fire never fooled them it warn't no fault of mine. I played it as low-down on them as I could.

When the first streak of the day begun to show, we tied up to a tow-head in a big bend on the Illinois side, and hacked off cotton-wood branches with the hatchet and covered up the raft with them so she looked like there had been a cave-in in the bank there. A tow-head is a sand-bar that has cotton-woods on it as thick as harrow-teeth.

We had mountains on the Missouri shore and heavy timber on the Illinois side, and the channel was down the Missouri shore at that place, so we warn't afraid of anybody running across us. We laid there all day and watched the rafts and steamboats spin down the Missouri shore, and up-bound steamboats fight the big river in the middle. I told Jim all about the time I had jabbering with that woman; and Jim said she was a smart one, and if she was to start after us herself *she* wouldn't set down and watch a camp fire – no, sir, she'd fetch a dog. Well, then, I said, why couldn't she tell her husband to fetch a dog? Jim said he bet she did think of it by the time the men was ready to start, and he believed they must a gone up town to get a dog, and so they lost all that time, or else we wouldn't be here on a tow-head sixteen or seventeen mile below the village – no, indeedy, we would be in that same old town again. So I said I didn't care what was the reason they didn't get us, as long as they didn't.

When it was beginning to come on dark, we poked our heads out of the cotton-wood thicket and looked up, and down, and across; nothing in sight; so Jim took up some of the top planks of the raft and built a snug wigwam to get under in blazing weather and rainy, and to keep the things dry. Jim made a floor for the wigwam, and raised it a foot or more above the level of the raft, so now the blankets and all the traps was out of the reach of steamboat waves. Right in the middle of the wigwam we made a layer of dirt about five or six inches deep with a frame around it for to hold it to its place; this was to build a fire on in sloppy weather or chilly; the wigwam would keep it from being seen. We made an extra steering oar, too, because one of the others might get broke, on a snag or something. We fixed up a short forked stick to hang the old lantern on; because we must always light the lantern whenever we see a steamboat coming down stream, to keep from getting run over; but we wouldn't have to light it for up-stream boats unless we see we was in what they call a 'crossing'; for the river was pretty high yet, very low banks being still a little under water; so up-bound boats didn't always run the channel, but hunted easy water.

This second night we run between seven and eight hours, with a current that was making over four mile an hour. We catched fish, and talked, and we took a swim now and then to keep off sleepiness. It was kind of solemn, drifting down the big still river, laying on our backs looking up at the stars, and we didn't ever feel like talking loud, and it warn't often that we laughed, only a little kind of a low chuckle. We had mighty good weather, as a general thing, and nothing ever happened to us at all, that night, nor the next, nor the next.

Every night we passed towns, some of them away up on black hillsides, nothing but just a shiny bed of lights, not a house could you see. The fifth night we passed St Louis, and it was like the whole world lit up. In St Petersburg they used to say there was twenty or thirty thousand people in St Louis, but I never believed it till I see that wonderful spread of lights at two o'clock that still night. There warn't a sond there; everybody was asleep.

Every night, now, I used to slip ashore, towards ten o'clock, at some little village, and buy ten or fifteen cents' worth of meal or bacon or other stuff to eat; and sometimes I lifted a chicken that warn't roosting comfortable, and took him along. Pap always said, take a chicken when you get a chance, because if you don't want him yourself you can easy find somebody that does, and a good deed ain't ever forgot. I never see pap when he didn't want the chicken himself, but that is what he used to say, anyway.

Mornings, before daylight, I slipped into corn-fields and borrowed a watermelon, or a mushmelon, or a punkin, or some new corn, or things of that kind. Pap always said it warn't no harm to borrow things, if you was meaning to pay them back, some time; but the widow said it warn't anything but a soft name for stealing, and no decent body would do it. Jim said he reckoned the widow was partly right and pap was partly right; so the best way would be for us to pick out two or three things from the list and say we wouldn't borrow them any more – then he reckoned it wouldn't be no harm to borrow the others. So we talked it over all one night, drifting along down the river, trying to make up our minds whether to drop the watermelons, or the cantelopes, or the mushmelons, or what. But towards daylight we got it all settled satisfactory, and concluded to drop crab-apples and p'simmons. We warn't feeling just right before that, but it was all comfortable now. I was glad the way it came out, too, because crab-apples ain't ever good, and the p'simmons wouldn't be ripe for two or three months yet.

We shot a water-fowl, now and then, that got up too early in the morning or didn't go to bed early enough in the evening. Take it all around, we lived pretty high.

The fifth night below St Louis we had a big storm after midnight, with a power of thunder and lightning, and the rain poured down in a solid sheet. We stayed in the wigwam and let the raft take care of itself. When the lightning glared out we could see a big straight river ahead, and high rocky bluffs on both sides. By and by says I, 'Hal-*lo*, Jim, looky yonder!' It was a steamboat that had killed herself on a rock. We was drifting straight down for her. The lightning showed her very distinct. She was leaning over, with part of her upper deck above water, and you could see every little chimbly-guy clean and clear, and a chair by the big bell, with an old slouch hat hanging on the back of it when the flashes come.

Well, it being away in the night, and stormy, and all so mysterious-like, I felt just the way any other boy would a felt when I see that wreck laying there so mournful and lonesome in the middle of the river. I wanted to get aboard of her and slink around a little, and see what there was there. So I says:

'Le's land on her, Jim.'

But Jim was dead against it, at first. He says:

'I doan' want to go fool'n 'long er no wrack. We's doin' blame' well, en we better let blame' well alone, as de good book says. Like as not dey's a watchman on dat wrack.'

'Watchman your grandmother!' I says; 'there ain't nothing to watch but the texas and the pilot-house; and do you reckon anybody's going to resk his life for a texas and a pilot-house such a night as this, when it's likely to break up and wash off down the river any minute?' Jim couldn't say nothing to that, so he didn't try. 'And besides,' I says, 'we might borrow something worth having, out of the captain's stateroom. Seegars, *I* bet you – and cost five cents apiece, solid cash. Steamboat captains is always rich, and gets sixty dollars a month, and *they* don't care a cent what a thing costs, you know, long as they want it. Stick a candle in your pocket; I can't rest, Jim, till we give her a rummaging. Do you reckon Tom Sawyer would ever go by this thing? Not for pie, he wouldn't. He'd call it an adventure – that's what he'd call it; and he'd land on that wreck if it was his last act. And wouldn't he throw style into it? – wouldn't he spread himself, nor nothing? Why, you'd think it was Christopher C'lumbus discovering Kingdom-Come. I wish Tom Sawyer *was* here.'

Jim he grumbled a little, but give in. He said we mustn't talk any more than we could help, and then talk mighty low. The lightning showed us the wreck again, just in time, and we fetched the stabboard derrick, and made fast there.

The deck was high out, here. We went sneaking down the slope of it to labboard, in the dark, towards the texas, feeling our way slow with our feet, and spreading our hands out to fend off the guys, for it was so dark we couldn't see no sign of them. Pretty soon we struck the forward end of the skylight, and clumb on to it; and the next step fetched us in front of the captain's door, which was open, and by Jimminy, away down through the texas hall we see a light! and all in the same second we seemed to hear low voices in yonder!

Jim whispered and said he was feeling powerful sick, and told me to come along. I says, all right; and was going to start for the raft; but just then I heard a voice wail out and say:

'Oh, please, don't, boys: I swear I won't ever tell!'

Another voice said, pretty loud:

'It's a lie, Jim Turner. You've acted this way before. You always want more'n your share of the truck, and you've always got it, too, because you've swore 't if you didn't you'd tell. But this time you've said it jest one time too many. You're the meanest, treacherousest hound in this country.'

By this time Jim was gone for the raft. I was just a-biling with curiosity; and I says to myself, Tom Sawyer wouldn't back out now, and so I won't either; I'm a-going to see what's going on here. So I dropped on my hands and knees, in the little passage, and crept aft in the dark, till there warn't but about one stateroom betwixt me and the cross-hall of the texas. Then, in there I see a man stretched on the floor and tied hand and foot, and two men standing over him, and one of them had a dim lantern in his hand, and the other one had a pistol. This one kept pointing the pistol at the man's head on the floor and saying:

'I'd *like* to! And I orter, too, a mean skunk!'

The man on the floor would shrivel up, and say, 'Oh, please don't, Bill – I hain't ever goin' to tell.'

And every time he said that, the man with the lantern would laugh and say:

''Deed you *ain't*! You never said no truer thing'n that, you bet you.' And once he said, 'Hear him beg! and yit if we hadn't got the best of him and tied him, he'd a killed us both. And what *for*? Jist for noth'n. Just because we stood on our *rights* – that's what for. But I lay you ain't a-goin' to threaten nobody any more, Jim Turner. Put *up* that pistol, Bill.'

Bill says:

'I don't want to, Jake Packard. I'm for killin' him – and didn't he kill old Hatfield jist the same way – and don't he deserve it?'

'But I don't *want* him killed, and I've got my reasons for it.'

'Bless yo' heart for them words, Jake Packard! I'll never forget you, long's I live!' says the man on the floor, sort of blubbering.

Packard didn't take no notice of that, but hung up his lantern on a nail, and started towards where I was, there in the dark, and motioned Bill to come. I crawfished as fast as I could, about two yards, but the boat slanted so that I couldn't make very good time; so to keep from getting run over and catched I crawled into a stateroom on the upper side. The man come a-pawing along in the dark, and when Packard got to my stateroom, he says:

'Here – come in here.'

And in he came, and Bill after him. But before they got in, I was up in the upper berth, cornered, and sorry I came. Then they stood there, with their hands on the ledge of the berth, and talked. I couldn't see them, but I could tell where they was, by the whisky they'd been having. I was glad I didn't drink whisky; but it wouldn't made much difference, anyway, because most of the time they couldn't a tree'd me because I didn't breathe. I was too scared. And besides, a body *couldn't* breathe, and hear such talk. They talked low and earnest. Bill wanted to kill Turner. He says:

'He's said he'll tell, and he will. If we was to give both our shares to him *now*, it wouldn't make no difference after the row, and the way we've served him. Shore's you're born, he'll turn State's evidence; now you hear *me*. I'm for putting him out of his troubles.'

'So'm I,' says Packard, very quiet.

'Blame it, I'd sorter begun to think you wasn't. Well, then, that's all right. Le's go and do it.'

'Hold on a minute; I ain't had my say yit. You listen to me. Shooting's good, but there's quieter ways if the thing *got* to be done. But what *I* say, is this; it ain't good sense to go court'n around after a halter, if you can git at what you're up to in some way that's jist as good and at the same time don't bring you into no resks. Ain't that so?'

'You bet it is. But how you goin' to manage it this time?'

'Well, my idea is this; we'll rustle around and gether up whatever pickin's we've overlooked in the staterooms, and shove for shore and hide the truck. Then we'll wait. Now I say it ain't a-goin' to be more'n two hours befo' this wrack breaks up and washes off down the river. See? He'll be drownded, and won't have nobody to blame for it but his own self. I reckon that's a considerable sight better'n killin' of him. I'm unfavourable to killin' a man as long as you can git around it; it ain't good sense, it ain't good morals. Ain't I right?'

'Yes – I reck'n you are. But s'pose she *don't* break up and wash off?'

'Well, we can wait the two hours, anyway, and see, can't we?'

'All right, then; come along.

So they started, and I lit out, all in a cold sweat, and scrambled forward. It was dark as pitch there; but I said in a kind of coarse whisper, 'Jim!' and he answered up, right at my elbow, with a sort of moan, and I says:

'Quick, Jim, it ain't no time for fooling around and moaning; there's a gang of murderers in yonder, and if we don't hunt up their boat and set her drifting down the river so these fellows can't get away from the wreck, there's one of 'em going to be in a bad fix. But if we find their boat we can put *all* of 'em in a bad fix – for the sheriff'll get 'em. Quick – hurry! I'll hunt the labboard side, you hunt the stabboard. You start at the raft, and——'

'Oh! my lordy, lordy! *Raf*'? Dey ain' no raf' no mo', she done broke loose en gone! – en here we is!'

Chapter 13

Well, I catched my breath and most fainted. Shut up on a wreck with such a gang as that! But it warn't no time to be sentimentering. We'd *got* to find that boat, now – had to have it for ourselves. So we went a-quaking and shaking down the stabboard side, and slow work it was, too – seemed a week before we got to the stern. No sign of a boat. Jim said he didn't believe he could go any further – so scared he hadn't hardly any strength left, he said. But I said come on, if we get left on this wreck, we are in a fix, sure. So on we prowled, again. We struck for the stern of the texas, and found it, and then scrabbled along forwards on the skylight, hanging on from shutter to shutter, for the edge of the skylight was in the water. When we got pretty close to the cross-hall door, there was the skiff, sure enough! I could just barely see her. I felt ever so thankful. In another second I would a been aboard of her; but just then the door opened. One of the men stuck his head out, only about a couple of foot from me, and I thought I was gone; but he jerked it in again, and says:

'Heave that blame' lantern out o' sight, Bill!'

He flung a bag of something into the boat, and then got in himself, and set down. It was Packard. Then Bill *he* come out and got in. Packard says, in a low voice:

'All ready – shove off.'

I couldn't hardly hang on to the shutters, I was so weak. But Bill says:

'Hold on – 'd you go through him?'

'No. Didn't you?'

'No. So he's got his share o' the cash, yet.'

'Well, then, come along – no use to take truck and leave money.'

'Say – won't he suspicion what we're up to?'

'Maybe he won't. But we got to have it anyway. Come along.'

So they got out and went in.

The door slammed to, because it was on the careened side; and in a half second I was in the boat, and Jim come a-tumbling after me. I out with my knife and cut the rope, and away we went!

We didn't touch an oar, and we didn' speak nor whisper, nor hardly even breathe. We went gliding swift along, dead silent, past the tip of the paddle-box, and past the stern; then in a second or two more we was a hundred yards below the wreck, and the darkness soaked her up, every last sign of her, and we was safe, and knowed it.

When we was three or four hundred yards down stream, we see the lantern show like a little spark at the texas door, for a second, and we knowed by that the rascals had missed their boat, and was beginning to understand that they was in just as much trouble, now, as Jim Turner was.

Then Jim manned the oars, and we took out after our raft. Now was the first time that I begun to worry about the men – I reckon I hadn't had time to before. I began to think how dreadful it was, even for murderers, to be in such a fix. I says to myself, there ain't no telling but I might come to be a murderer myself, yet, and then how would *I* like it? So says I to Jim:

'The first light we see, we'll land a hundred yards below it or above it, in a place where it's a good hiding-place for you and the skiff, and then I'll go and fix up some kind of a yarn, and get somebody to go for that gang and get them out of their scrape, so they can be hung when their time comes.'

But that idea was a failure; for pretty soon it begun to storm again, and this time worse than ever. The rain poured down, and never a light showed; everybody in bed, I reckon. We boomed along down the river, watching for lights and watching for our raft. After a long time the rain let up, but the clouds stayed, and the lightning kept whimpering, and by and by a flash showed us a black thing ahead, floating, and we made for it.

It was the raft, and mighty glad we was to get aboard of it again. We seen a light, now, away down to the right, on shore. So I said I would go for it. The skiff was half full of plunder which that gang had stole, there on the wreck. We hustled it on to the raft in a pile, and I told Jim to float along down, and show a light when he judged he had gone about two miles, and keep it burning till I come; then I manned my oars and shoved for the light. As I got down towards it, three or four more showed – up on a hillside. It was a village. I closed in above the shore-light, and laid on my oars and floated. As I went by, I see it was a lantern hanging on the jackstaff of a double-hull ferry-boat. I skimmed around for the watchman, a-wondering whereabouts he slept; and by and by I found him roosting on the bitts, forward, with his head down between his knees. I give his shoulder two or three little shoves, and begun to cry.

He stirred up, in a kind of a startlish way; but when he see it was only me, he took a good gap and stretched, and then he says:

'Hallo, what's up? Don't cry, bub. What's the trouble?'

I says:

'Pap, and mam, and sis, and——'

Then I broke down. He says:

'Oh, dang it, now, *don't* take on so, we all has to have our troubles and this'n'll come out all right. What's the matter with 'em?'

'They're – they're – are you the watchman of the boat?'

'Yes,' he says, Kind of pretty-well-satisfied like. 'I'm the captain and the owner, and the mate, and the pilot, and watchman, and head deck-hand: and sometimes I'm the freight and passengers. I ain't as rich as old Jim Hornback, and I can't be so blame' generous and good to Tom, Dick, and Harry as what he is, and slam around money the way he does; but I've told him a many a time 't I wouldn't trade places with him; for, says I, a sailor's life's the life for me, and I'm derned if I'd live two mile out o' town, where there ain't nothing ever goin' on, not for all his spondulicks and as much more on top of it. Says I——'

I broke in and says:

'They're in an awful peck of trouble, and——'

'*Who* is?'

'Why, pap, and mam, and sis, and Miss Hooker; and if you'd take your ferry-boat and go up there——'

'Up where? Where are they?'

'On the wreck.'

'What wreck?'

'Why, there ain't but one.'

'What, you don't mean the *Walter Scott?*'

'Yes.'

'Good land! what are they doin' *there*, for gracious sakes?'

'Well, they didn't go there a-purpose.'

'I bet they didn't! Why, great goodness, there ain't no chance for 'em if they don't get off mighty quick! Why, how in the nation did they ever git into such a scrape?'

'Easy enough. Miss Hooker was a-visiting, up there to the town——'

'Yes, Booth's Landing – go on.'

'She was a-visiting, there at Booth's Landing, and just in the edge of the evening she started over with her nigger woman in the horse-ferry, to stay all night at her friend's house, Miss What-you-may-call-her, I disremember her name, and they lost their steering-oar, and swung around and went a-floating down, stern-first, about two mile, and saddle-baggsed on the wreck, and the ferryman and the nigger woman and the horses was all lost, but Miss Hooker she made a grab and got aboard the wreck. Well, about an hour after dark, we come along down in our trading-scow, and it was so dark we didn't notice the wreck till we was right on it; and so *we* saddle-baggsed; but all of us was saved but Bill Whipple – and oh, he *was* the best cretur! – I most wisht it had been me, I do.'

'My George! It's the beatenest thing I ever struck. And *then* what did you all do?'

'Well, we hollered and took on, but it's so wide there, we couldn't make nobody hear. So pap said somebody got to get ashore and get help somehow. I was the only one that could swim, so I made a dash for it, and Miss Hooker she said if I didn't strike help sooner, come here and hunt up her uncle, and he'd fix the thing. I made the land about a mile below, and been fooling along ever since, trying to get people to do something, but they said, "What, in such a night and such a current? there ain't no sense it; go for the steam-ferry." Now if you'll go, and——'

'By Jackson, I'd *like* to, and blame it I don't know but I will; but who in the 'dingnation's a-goin' to *pay* for it? Do you reckon your pap——'

'Why, *that*'s all right. Miss Hooker she told me, *particular*, that her Uncle Hornback——'

'Great guns! is *he* her uncle? Looky here, you break for that light over yonder-way, and turn out west when you git there, and about a quarter of a mile out you'll come to the tavern; tell 'em to dart you out to Jim Hornback's and he'll foot the bill. And don't you fool around any, because he'll want to know the news. Tell him I'll have his niece all safe before he can get to town. Hump yourself, now; I'm a-going up around the corner here, to roust out my engineer.'

I struck for the light, but as soon as he turned the corner I went back and got into my skiff and baled her out and then pulled up shore in the easy water about six hundred yards, and tucked myself in among some woodboats; for I couldn't rest easy till I could see the ferry-boat. But take it all around, I was feeling ruther comfortable on accounts of taking all this trouble for that gang, for not many would a done it. I wished the widow knowed about it. I judged she would be proud of me for helping these rapscallions, because rapscallions and dead beats is the kind the widow and good people takes the most interest in.

Well, before long, here comes the wreck, dim and dusky, sliding along down! A kind of cold shiver went through me, and then I struck out for her. She was very deep, and I see in a minute there warn't much chance for anybody being alive in her. I pulled all around her and hollered a little, but there wasn't any answer; all dead still. I felt a little bit heavy-hearted about the gang, but not much, for I reckoned if they could stand it, I could.

Then here comes the ferry-boat; so I shoved for the middle of the river on a long down-stream slant; and when I judged I was out of eye-reach, I laid on my oars, and looked back and see her go and smell around the wreck for Miss Hooker's remainders, because the captain would know her Uncle Hornback would want them; and then pretty soon the ferry-boat give it up and went for shore, and I laid into my work and went a-booming down the river.

It did seem a powerful long time before Jim's light showed up; and when it did show, it looked like it was a thousand mile off. By the time I got there the sky was beginning to get a little grey in the east; so we struck for an island, and hid the raft, and sunk the skiff, and turned in and slept like dead people.

Chapter 14

By and by, when we got up, we turned over the truck the gang had stole off of the wreck, and found boots, and blankets, and clothes, and all sorts of other things, and a lot of books, and a spy-glass, and three boxes of seegars. We hadn't ever been this rich before, in neither of our lives. The seegars was prime. We laid off all the afternoon in the woods talking, and me reading the books, and having a general good time. I told Jim all about what happened inside the wreck, and at the ferry-boat; and I said these kinds of things was adventures; but he said he didn't want no more adventures. He said that when I went in the texas, and he crawled back to get on the raft and found her gone, he nearly died; because he judged it was all up with *him*, anyway it could be fixed; for if he didn't get saved he would get drownded; and if he did get saved, whoever saved him would send him back home so as to get the reward, and then Miss Watson would sell him South, sure. Well, he was right; he was most always right; he had an uncommon level head, for a nigger.

I read considerable to Jim about kings, and dukes, and earls, and such, and how gaudy they dressed, and how much style they put on, and called each other your majesty, and your grace, and your lordship, and so on, 'stead of mister; and Jim's eyes bugged out, and he was interested. He says:

'I didn't know dey was so many un um. I hain't hearn 'bout none un um, skasely, but ole King Sollermun, onless you counts dem kings dat's in a pack er k'yards. How much do a king git?'

'Get?' I says; 'why, they get a thousand dollars a month if they want it; they can have just as much as they want; everything belongs to them.'

'*Ain't* dat gay? En what dey got to do, Huck?'

'*They* don't do nothing! Why, how you talk. They just set around.'

'No – is dat so?'

'Of course it is. They just set around. Except maybe when there's a war; then they go to the war. But other times they just lazy around; or go hawking – just hawking and Sh! —d'you hear a noise?'

We skipped out and looked; but it warn't nothing but the flutter of a steamboat's wheel, away down coming around the point; so we come back.

'Yes,' says I, 'and other times, when things is dull, they fuss with the parlyment; and if everybody don't go just so he whacks their heads off. But mostly they hang round the harem.'

'Roun' de which?'

'Harem.'

'What's de harem?'

'The place where he keeps his wives. Don't you know about the harem? Solomon had one; he had about a million wives.'

'Why, yes, dat's so; I – I'd done forgot it. A harem's a bo'd'n-house, I reck'n. Mos' likely dey has rackety times in de nussery. En I reck'n de wives quarrels considable; en dat 'crease de racket. Yit dey say Sollermun de wises' man dat ever live'. I doan' take no stock in dat. Bekase why: would a wise man want to live in de mids' er sich a blimblammin' all de time? No – 'deed he wouldn't. A wise man 'ud take en buil' a biler-factry; en den he could shet *down* de biler-factry when he want to res'.'

'Well, but he *was* the wisest man, anyway; because the widow she told me so, her own self.'

'I doan' k'yer what de widder say, he *warn't* no wise man, nuther. He had some er de dad-fetchedes' ways I ever see. Does you know 'bout dat chile-dat he 'uz gwyne to chop in two?'

'Yes, the widow told me all about it.'

'*Well*, den! Warn' dat de beatenes' notion in de worl'? You jes' take en look at it a minute. Dah's de stump, dah— dat's one er de women; heah's you – dat's de yuther one; I's Sollermun; en dish-yer dollar bills' de chile. Bofe un you claims it. What does I do? Does I shin aroun' mongs' de neighbours en fine out which un you de bill *do* b'long to, en han' it over to de right one, all safe an soun', de way dat anybody dat had any gumption would? No – I take en whack de bill in *two*, en give half un it to you, en de yuther half to de yuther woman. Dat's de way Sollermun was gwyne to do wid de chile. Now I want to ast you: what's de use er dat half a bill? – can't buy noth'n wid it. En what use is a half a chile? I would'n give a dern for a million un um.'

'But hang it, Jim, you've clean missed the point – blame it, you've missed it a thousand mile.'

'Who? Me? Go 'long. Doan' talk to *me* 'bout yo' p'ints. I reck'n I knows sense when I sees it; en dey ain' no sense in sich doin's as dat. De 'spute warn't 'bout a half a chile, de 'spute was 'bout a whole chile; en de man dat think he kin settle a 'spute 'bout a whole chile wid a half a chile, doan' know enough to come in out'n de rain. Doan' talk to me 'bout Sollermun, Huck, I knows him by de back.'

'But I tell you you don't get the point.'

'Blame de p'int! I reck'n I knows what I knows. En mine you, de *real* p'int is down furder – it's down deeper. It lays in de way Sollermun was raised. You take a man dat's got on'y one er two chillen; is dat man gwyne to be waseful o' chillen? No, he ain't; he can't 'ford it. *He* know how to value 'em. But you take a man dat's got 'bout five million chillen runnin' roun' de house, en it's diffunt. *He* as soon chop a chile in two as a cat. Dey's plenty mo'. A chile er two, mo' er less, warn't no consekens to Sollermun, dad fetch him!'

I never see such a nigger. If he got a notion in his head once, there warn't no getting it out again. He was the most down on Solomon of any nigger I ever see. So I went to talking about other kings, and let Solomon slide. I told about Louis Sixteenth that got his head cut off in France long time ago; and about his little boy the dolphin, that would a been a king, but they took and shut him up in jail, and some say he died there.

'Po' little chap.'

'But some says he got out and got away, and come to America.'

'Dat's good! But he'll be pooty lonesome – dey ain' no kings here, is dey, Huck?'

'No.'

'Den he can't git no situation. What he gwyne to do?'

'Well, I don't know. Some of them gets on the police, and some of them learns people how to talk French.'

'Why, Huck, doan' de French people talk de same way we does?'

'*No*, Jim; you couldn't understand a word they said – not a single word.'

'Well, now, I be ding-busted! How do dat come?'

'*I* don't know; but it's so. I got some of their jabber out of a book. S'pose a man was to come to you and say *Polly-voo-franzy* – what would you think?'

'I wouldn' think nuff'n; I'd take en bust him over de head. Dat is, if he warn't white. I wouldn't 'low no nigger to call me dat.'

'Shucks, it ain't calling you anything. It's only saying do you know how to talk French.'

'Well, den, why couldn't he *say* it?'

'Why, he *is* a-saying it. That's a Frenchman's *way* of saying it.'

'Well, it's a blame' ridicklous way, en I doan' want to hear no mo' 'bout it. Dey ain' no sense in it.'

'Looky here, Jim; does a cat talk like we do?'

'No, a cat don't.'

'Well, does a cow?'

'No, a cow don't, nuther.'

'Does a cat talk like a cow, or a cow talk like a cat?'

'No, dey don't.'

'It's natural and right for 'em to talk different from each other, ain't it?'

''Course.'

'And ain't it natural and right for a cat and a cow to talk different from *us*?'

'Why, mos' sholy it is.'

'Well, then, why ain't it natural and right for a *Frenchman* to talk different from us? You answer me that.'

'Is a cat a man, Huck?'

'No.'

'Well, den, dey ain't no sense in a cat talkin' like a man. Is a cow a man? – er is a cow a cat?'

'No, she ain't either of them.'

'Well, den, she ain't got no business to talk like either one er de yuther of 'em. Is a Frenchman a man?'

'Yes.'

'*Well*, den! Dad blame it, why doan' he *talk* like a man? You answer me *dat*!'

I see it warn't no use wasting words – you can't learn a nigger to argue. So I quit.

Chapter 15

We judged that three nights more would fetch us to Cairo, at the bottom of Illinois, where the Ohio River comes in, and that was what we was after. We would sell the raft and get on a steamboat and go way up the Ohio amongst the free States, and then be out of trouble.

Well, the second night a fog begun to come on, and we made for a tow-head to tie to, for it wouldn't do to try to run in fog; but when I paddled ahead in the canoe, with the line, to make fast, there warn't anything but little saplings to tie to. I passed the line around one of them right on the edge of the cut bank, but there was a stiff current, and the raft come booming down so lively she tore it out by the roots and away she went. I see the fog closing down, and it made me so sick and scared I couldn't budge for most a half a minute it seemed to me – and then there warn't no raft in sight; you couldn't see twenty yards. I jumped into the canoe and run back to the stern and grabbed the paddle and set her back a stroke. But she didn't come. I was in such a hurry I hadn't untied her. I got up and tried to untie her, but I was so excited my hands shook so I couldn't hardly do anything with them.

As soon as I got started I took out after the raft, hot and heavy, right down the tow-head. That was all right as far as it went, but the tow-head warn't sixty yards long, and the minute I flew by the foot of it I shot out into the solid white fog, and hadn't no more idea which way I was going than a dead man.

Thinks I, it won't do to paddle; first I know I'll run into the bank or a tow-head or something; I got to set still and float, and yet it's mighty fidgety business to have to hold your hands still at such a time. I whooped and listened. Away down there, somewheres, I hears a small whoop, and up comes my spirits. I went tearing after it, listening sharp to hear it again. The next time it come, I see I warn't heading for it but heading away to the right of it. And the next time, I was heading away to the left of it – and not gaining on it much, either, for I was flying around, this way and that and t'other, but it was going straight ahead all the time.

I did wish the fool would think to beat a tin pan, and beat it all the time, but he never did, and it was the still places between the whoops that was making the trouble for me. Well, I fought along, and directly I hears the whoop *behind* me. I was tangled good, now. That was somebody else's whoop, or else I was turned around.

I throwed the paddle down. I heard the whoop again; it was behind me yet, but in a different place; it kept coming, and kept changing its place, and I kept answering, till by and by it was in front of me again and I knowed the current had swung the canoe's head down stream and I was all right, if that was Jim and not some other raftsman hollering. I couldn't tell nothing about voices in a fog, for nothing don't look natural nor sound natural in a fog.

The whooping went on, and in about a minute I come a-booming down on a cut bank with smoky ghosts of big trees on it, and the current throwed me off to the left and shot by, amongst a lot of snags that fairly roared, the current was tearing by them so swift.

In another second or two it was solid white and still again. I set perfectly still, then listening to my heart thump, and I reckon I didn't draw a breath while it thumped a hundred.

I just give up, then. I knowed what the matter was. That cut bank was an island, and Jim had gone down t'other side of it. It warn't no tow-head, that you could float by in ten minutes. It had the big timber of a regular island; it might be five or six mile long and more than a half a mile wide.

I kept quiet, with my ears cocked, about fifteen minutes, I reckon. I was floating along, of course, four or five mile an hour; but you don't ever think of that. No, you *feel* like you are laying dead still on the water; and if a little glimpse of a snag slips by, you don't think to yourself how fast *you're* going, but you catch your breath and think, my! how that snag's tearing along. If you think it ain't dismal and lonesome out in a fog that way, by yourself, in the night, you try it once – you'll see.

Next, for about a half an hour, I whoops now and then; at last I hears the answer a long ways off, and tries to follow it, but I couldn't do it, and directly I judged I'd got into a nest of tow-heads, for I had little dim glimpses of them on both sides of me, sometimes just a narrow channel between; and some that I couldn't see, I knowed was there, because I'd hear the wash of the current against the old dead brush and trash that hung over the banks. Well, I warn't long losing the whoops, down amongst the tow-heads; and I only tried to chase them a little while, anyway, because it was worse than chasing a jack-o'-lantern. You never knowed a sound dodge around so, and swap places so quick and so much.

I had to claw away from the bank pretty lively, four or five times, to keep from knocking the islands out of the river; and so I judged the raft must be butting into the bank every now and then, or else it would get further ahead and clear out of hearing – it was floating a little faster than what I was.

Well, I seemed to be in the open river again, by and by, but I couldn't hear no sign of a whoop nowheres. I reckoned Jim had fetched up on a snag,

'"En you ain' dead – you ain' drownded – you's back agin?"'

maybe, and it was all up with him. I was good and tired, so I laid down in the canoe and said I wouldn't bother no more. I didn't want to go to sleep, of course; but I was so sleepy I couldn't help it; so I thought I would take just one little cat-nap.

But I reckon it was more than a cat-nap, for when I waked up the stars was shining bright, the fog was all gone, and I was spinning down a big bend stern first. First I didn't know where I was; I thought I was dreaming; and when things begun to come back to me, they seemed to come up dim out of last week.

It was a monstrous big river here, with the tallest and the thickest kind of timber on both banks; just a solid wall, as well as I could see, by the stars. I looked away down the stream, and seen a black speck on the water. I took out after it; but when I got to it it warn't nothing but a couple of saw-logs made fast together. Then I see another speck, and chased that; then another, and this time I was right. It was the raft.

When I got to it Jim was sitting there with his head down between his knees, asleep, with his right arm hanging over the steering oar. The other oar was smashed off, and the raft was littered up with leaves and branches and dirt. So she'd had a rough time.

I made fast and laid down under Jim's nose on the raft, and begun to gap, and stretch my fists out against Jim, and says:

'Hallo, Jim, have I been asleep? Why didn't you stir me up?'

'Good gracious, is dat you, Huck? En you ain' dead – you ain' drownded – you's back agin? It's too good for true, honey, it's too good for true. Lemme look at you, chile, lemme feel o' you. No, you ain' dead! you's back agin', live en soun', jis de same ole Huck – de same ole Huck, thanks to goodness!'

'What's the matter with you, Jim? You been a-drinking?'

'Drinkin'? Has I ben a-drinkin'? Has I had a chance to be a-drinkin'?'

'Well, then, what makes you talk so wild?'

'How does I talk wild?'

'*How*? why, hain't you been talking about my coming back, and all that stuff, as if I'd been gone away?'

'Huck – Huck Finn, you look me in de eye; look me in de eye. *Hain't* you ben gone away?'

'Gone away? Why, what in the nation do you mean? *I* hain't been gone anywheres. Where would I go to?'

'Well, looky here, boss, dey's sumf'n wrong, dey is. Is I *me*, or who *is* I? Is I heah, or whah *is* I? Now dat's what I wants to know.'

'Well, I think you're here, plain enough, but I think you're a tangle-headed old fool, Jim.'

'I is, is I? Well, you answer me dis. Didn't you tote out de line in de canoe, fer to make fas' to de tow-head?'

'No, I didn't. What tow-head? I hain't seen no tow-head.'

'You hain't seen no tow-head? Looky here – didn't de line pull loose en de raf' go a-hummin' down de river, en leave you en de canoe behine in de fog?'

'What fog?'

'Why, *de* fog. De fog dat's ben aroun' all night. En didn't you whoop, en didn't I whoop, tell we got mix' up in de islands en one un us got los' en t'other one was jis' as good as los', 'kase he didn' know whah he wuz? En didn't I bust up agin a lot er dem islands en have a turrible time en mos' git drownded? Now ain' dat so, boss – ain' it so? You answer me dat.'

'Well, this is too many for me, Jim. I hain't seen no fog, nor no islands, nor no troubles, nor nothing. I been setting here talking with you all night till you went to sleep about ten minutes ago, and I reckon I done the same. You couldn't a got drunk in that time, so of course you've been dreaming.'

'Dad fetch it, how is I gwyne to dream all dat in ten minutes?'

'Well, hang it all, you did dream it, because there didn't any of it happen.'

'But Huck, it's all jis' as plain to me as——'

'It don't make no difference how plain it is, there ain't nothing in it. I know, because I've been here all the time.'

Jim didn't say nothing for about five minutes, but set there studying over it. Then he says:

'Well, den, I reck'n I did dream it, Huck; but dog my cats ef it ain't de powerfullest dream I ever see. En I hain't ever had no dream b'fo' dat's tired me like dis one.'

'Oh, well, that's all right, because a dream does tire a body like everything, sometimes. But this one was a staving dream – tell me all about it, Jim.'

So Jim went to work and told me the whole thing right through, just as it happened, only he painted it up considerable. Then he said he must start in and ''terpret' it, because it was sent for a warning. He said the first tow-head stood for a man that would try to do us some good, but the current was another man that would get us away from him. The whoops was warnings that would come to us every now and then, and if we didn't try hard to make out to understand them they'd just take us into bad luck, 'stead of keeping us out of it. The lot of tow-heads was troubles we was going to get into with quarrelsome people and all kinds of mean folks, but if we minded our business and didn't talk back and aggravate them, we would pull through and get out of the fog and into the big clear river, which was the free States, and wouldn't have no more trouble.

It had clouded up pretty dark just after I got on to the raft, but it was clearing up again, now.

'Oh, well, that's all interpreted well enough, as far as it goes, Jim,' I says: 'but what does *these* things stand for?'

It was the leaves and rubbish on the raft, and the smashed oar. You could see them first rate, now.

Jim looked at the trash, and then looked at me, and back at the trash again. He had got the dream fixed so strong in his head that he couldn't seem to shake it loose and get the facts back into its place again, right away. But when he did get the thing straightened around, he looked at me steady, without ever smiling, and says:

'What do dey stan' for? I's gwyne to tell you. When I got all wore out wid work, en wid de callin' for you, en went to sleep, my heart wuz mos' broke bekase you wuz los', en I didn't k'yer no mo' what become er me en de raf'. En when I wake up en fine you back agin', all safe en soun', de tears come en I could a got down on my knees en kiss' yo' foot I's so thankful. En all you wuz thinkin 'bout wuz how you could make a fool uv ole Jim wid a lie. Dat truck dah is *trash*; en trash is what people is dat puts dirt on de head er dey fren's en makes 'em ashamed.'

Then he got up slow, and walked to the wigwam, and went in there, without saying anything but that. But that was enough. It made me feel so mean I could almost kissed *his* foot to get him to take it back.

It was fifteen minutes before I could work myself up to go and humble myself to a nigger – but I done it, and I warn't ever sorry for it afterwards, neither. I didn't do him no more mean tricks, and I wouldn't done that one if I'd a knowed it would make him feel that way.

Chapter 16

We slept most all day, and started out at night, a little ways behind a monstrous long raft that was as long going by as a procession. She had four long sweeps at each end, so we judged she carried as many as thirty men, likely. She had five big wigwams aboard, wide apart, and an open camp fire in the middle, and a tall flag-pole at each end. There was a power of style about her. It *amounted* to something being a raftsman on such a craft as that.

We went drifting down into a big bend, and the night clouded up and got hot. The river was very wide, and was walled with solid timber on both sides; you couldn't see a break in it hardly ever, or a light. We talked about Cairo, and wondered whether we would know it when we got to it. I said likely we wouldn't, because I had heard say there warn't but about a dozen houses there, and if they didn't happen to have them lit up, how was we going to know we was passing a town? Jim said if the two big rivers joined together there, that would show. But I said maybe we might think we was passing the foot of an island and coming into the same old river again. That disturbed Jim – and me too. So the question was, what to do? I said, paddle ashore the first time a light showed, and tell them pap was behind, coming along with a trading-scow, and was a green hand at the business, and wanted to know how far it was to Cairo. Jim thought it was a good idea, so we took a smoke on it and waited.

There warn't nothing to do now, but to look out sharp for the town, and not pass it without seeing it. He said he'd be mighty sure to see it, because he'd be a free man the minute he seen it, but if he missed it he'd be in the slave country again and no more show for freedom. Every little while he jumps up and says:

'Dah she is!'

But it warn't. It was jack-o'-lanterns, or lightning-bugs; so he set down again, and went to watching, same as before. Jim said it made him all over trembly and feverish to be so close to freedom. Well, I can tell you it made me all over trembly and feverish, too, to hear him, because I begun to get it through my head that he *was* most free – and who was to blame for it? Why, *me*. I couldn't get that out of my conscience, no how nor no way. It got to troubling me so I couldn't rest; I couldn't stay still in one place. It hadn't ever come home to me, before, what this thing was that I was doing. But now it did; and it stayed with me, and scorched me more and more. I tried to make out to myself that *I* warn't to blame, because *I* didn't run Jim off from his rightful owner; but it warn't no use, conscience up and says, every time, 'But you knowed he was running for his freedom, and you could a paddled ashore and told somebody.' That was so – I couldn't get around that, no way. That was where it pinched. Conscience says to me, 'What had poor Miss Watson done to you, that you could see her nigger go off right under your eyes and never say one single word? What did that poor old woman do to you, that you could treat her so mean? Why, she tried to learn you your book, she tried to learn you your manners, she tried to be good to you every way she knowed how. *That*'s what she done.'

I got to feeling so mean and so miserable I most wished I was dead. I fidgeted up and down the raft, abusing myself to myself, and Jim was fidgeting up and down past me. We neither of us could keep still. Every time he danced around and says, 'Dah's Cairo!' it went through me like a shot, and I thought if it *was* Cairo I reckoned I would die of miserableness.

Jim talked out loud all the time while I was talking to myself. He was saying how the first thing he would do when he got to a free State he would go to saving up money and never spend a single cent, and when he got enough he would buy his wife, which was owned on a farm close to where Miss Watson lived; and then they would both work to buy the two children, and if their master wouldn't sell them, they'd get an Ab'litionist to go and steal them.

It most froze me to hear such talk. He wouldn't ever dared to talk such talk in his life before. Just see what a difference it made in him the minute he judged he was about free. It was according to the old saying, 'Give a nigger an inch and he'll take an ell.' Thinks I, this is what comes of my not thinking. Here was this nigger which I had as good as helped to run away, coming right out flat-footed and saying he would steal his children – children that belonged to a man I didn't even know; a man that hadn't ever done me no harm.

I was sorry to hear Jim say that, it was such a lowering of him. My conscience got to stirring me up hotter than ever, until at last I says to it, 'Let up on me – it ain't too late, yet – I'll paddle ashore at the first light, and tell.' I felt easy, and happy, and light as a feather, right off. All my troubles was gone. I went to looking out sharp for a light, and sort of singing to myself. By and by one showed. Jim sings out:

'We's safe, Huck, we's safe! Jump up and crack yo' heels, dat's de good ole Cairo at las', I jis knows it!'

I says:

'I'll take the canoe and go see, Jim. It mightn't be, you know.'

He jumped and got the canoe ready, and put his old coat in the bottom for me to set on, and give me the paddle; and as I shoved off, he says:

'Pooty soon I'll be a-shout'n for joy, en I'll say, it's all on accounts o' Huck; I's a free man, en I couldn't ever ben free ef it hadn' ben for Huck; Huck done it. Jim won't ever forget you, Huck; you's de bes' fren' Jim's ever had; en you's de *only* fren' ole Jim's got now.'

I was paddling off, all in a sweat to tell on him; but when he says this, it seemed to kind of take the tuck all out of me. I went along slow then, and I warn't right down certain whether I was glad I started or whether I warn't. When I was fifty yards off, Jim says:

'Dah you goes, de ole true Huck; de on'y white genlman dat ever kep' his promise to ole Jim.'

Well, I just felt sick. But I says, I *got* to do it – I can't get *out* of it. Right then, along comes a skiff with two men in it, with guns, and they stopped and I stopped. One of them says:

'What's that, yonder?'

'A piece of a raft.' I says.

'Do you belong on it?'

'Yes, sir.'

'Any men on it?'

'Only one, sir.'

'Well, there's five niggers run off to-night, up yonder above the head of the bend. Is your man white or black?'

I didn't answer up prompt. I tried to, but the words wouldn't come. I tried, for a second or two, to brace up and out with it, but I warn't man enough – hadn't the spunk of a rabbit. I see I was weakening; so I just give up trying, and up and says:

'He's white.'

'I reckon we'll go and see for ourselves.'

'I wish you would,' says I, 'because it's pap that's there, and maybe you'd help me tow the raft ashore where the light is. He's sick – and so is mam and Mary Ann.'

'Oh, the devil! we're in a hurry boy. But I s'pose we've got to. Come – buckle to your paddle, and let's get along.'

I buckled to my paddle and they laid to their oars. When we had made a stroke or two, I says:

'Pap'll be mighty much obleeged to you, I can tell you. Everybody goes away when I want them to help me tow the raft ashore, and I can't do it by myself.'

'Well, that's infernal mean. Odd, too. Say, boy, what's the matter with your father?'

'It's the – a – the – well, it ain't anything much.'

They stopped pulling. It warn't but a mighty ways to the raft, now. One says:

'Boy, that's a lie. What *is* the matter with your pap? Answer up square, now, and it'll be the better for you.'

'I will, sir, I will, honest – but don't leave us, please. It's the – the – gentlemen, if you'll only pull ahead, and let me heave you the head-line, you won't have to come a-near the raft – please do.'

'Set her back John, set her back!' says one. They backed water. 'Keep away, boy – keep to looard. Confound it, I just expect the wind has blowed it to us. Your pap's got the smallpox, and you know it precious well. Why didn't you come out and say so? Do you want to spread it all over?'

'Well,' says I, a-blubbering, 'I've told everybody before, and then they just went away and left us.'

'Poor devil, there's something in that. We are right down sorry for you, but we – well, hang it, we don't want the smallpox, you see. Look here, I'll tell you what to do. Don't you try to land by yourself, or you'll smash everything to pieces. You float along down about twenty miles and you'll come to a town on the left-hand side of the river. It will be long after sun-up, then, and when you ask for help, you tell them your folks are all down with chills and fever. Don't be a fool again, and let people guess what is the matter. Now we're trying to do you a kindness; so you just put twenty miles between us, that's a good boy. It wouldn't do any good to land yonder where the light is – it's only a wood-yard. Say – I reckon your father's poor, and I'm bound to say he's in pretty hard luck. Here – I'll put a twenty dollar gold piece on this board, and you get it when it floats by. I feel mighty mean to leave you, but my kingdom! it won't do to fool with smallpox, don't you see?'

'Hold on, Parker,' says the other man, 'here's a twenty to put on the board for me. Good-bye, boy, you do as Mr. Parker told you, and you'll be all right.'

'That's so, my boy – good-bye, good-bye. If you see any runaway niggers, you get help and nab them, and you can make some money by it.'

'Good-bye, sir,' says I, 'I won't let no runaway niggers get by me if I can help it.'

They went off and I got aboard the raft, feeling bad and low, because I knowed very well I had done wrong, and I see it warn't no use for me to try to learn to do right; a body that don't get *started* right when he's little, ain't got no show – when the pinch comes there ain't nothing to back him up and keep him to his work, and so he gets beat. Then I thought a minute, and says to myself, hold on – s'pose you'd a done right and give Jim up; would you felt better than what you do now? No, says I, I'd feel bad – I'd feel just the same way I do now. Well, then, says I, what's the use you learning to do right, when it's troublesome to do right and ain't no trouble to do wrong, and the wages is just the same? I was stuck. I couldn't answer that. So I reckoned I wouldn't bother no more about it, but after this always do whichever come handiest at the time.

I went into the wigwam; Jim warn't there. I looked all around; he warn't anywhere. I says:

'Jim!'

'Here I is, Huck. Is dey out o' sight yit? Don't talk loud.'

He was in the river, under the stern oar, with just his nose out. I told him they was out of sight, so he come aboard. He says:

'I was a-listenin' to all de talk, en I slips into de river en was gwyne to shove for sho' if dey come aboard. Den I was gwyne to swim to de raf' agin when dey was gone. But lawsy, how you did fool 'em, Huck! Dat *wuz* de smartes' dodge! I tell you, chile, I 'speck it save' ole Jim – ole Jim ain't gwyne to forgit you for dat, honey.'

Then we talked about the money. It was a pretty good raise, twenty dollars apiece. Jim said we could take deck passage on a steamboat now, and the money would last us as far as we wanted to go in the free States. He said twenty mile more warn't far for the raft to go, but he wished he was already there.

Towards daybreak we tied up, and Jim was mighty particular about hiding the raft good. Then he worked all day fixing things in bundles, and getting all ready to quit rafting.

That night about ten we hove in sight of the lights of a town away down in a left-hand bend.

I went off in the canoe, to ask about it. Pretty soon I found a man out in the river with a skiff, setting a trot-line. I ranged up and says:

'Mister, is that town Cairo?'

'Cairo? no. You must be a blame' fool.'

'What town is it, mister?'

'If you want to know, go and find out. If you stay here botherin' around me for about half a minute longer, you'll get something you won't want.'

I paddled to the raft. Jim was awful disappointed, but I said never mind, Cairo would be the next place, I reckoned.

We passed another town before daylight, and I was going out again; but it was high ground, so I didn't go. No high ground about Cairo, Jim said. I had forgot it. We laid up for the day, on a tow-head tolerably close to the left-hand bank. I begun to suspicion something. So did Jim. I says:

'Maybe we went by Cairo in the fog that night.'

He says:

'Doan' less talk about it, Huck. Po' niggers can't have no luck. I awluz 'spected dat rattlesnake skin warn't done wid its work.'

'I wish I'd never seen that snake-skin, Jim – I do wish I'd never laid eyes on it.'

'It ain' yo' fault. Huck; you didn' know. Don' you blame yo'self 'bout it.'

When it was daylight, here was the clear Ohio water in shore, sure enough, and outside was the old regular Muddy! So it was all up with Cairo.

We talked it all over. It wouldn't do to take to the shore; we couldn't take the raft up the stream, of course. There warn't no way but to wait for dark, and start back in the canoe and take the chances. So we slept all day amongst the cotton-wood thicket, so as to be fresh for the work, and when we went back to the raft about dark the canoe was gone!

We didn't say a word for a good while. There warn't anything to say. We both knowed well enough it was some more work of the rattlesnake skin; so what was the use to talk about it? It would only look like we was finding fault, and that would be bound to fetch more bad luck – and keep on fetching it, too, till we knowed enough to keep still.

By and by we talked about what we better do, and found there warn't no way but just to go along down with the raft till we got a chance to buy a canoe to go back in. We warn't going to borrow it when there warn't anybody around, the way pap would do, for that might set people after us.

So we shoved out, after dark, on the raft.

Anybody that don't believe yet, that it's foolishness to handle a snake-skin, after all that that snake-skin done for us, will believe it now, if they read on and see what more it done for us.

The place to buy canoes is off of rafts laying up at shore. But we didn't see no rafts laying up; so we went along during three hours and more. Well, the night got grey, and ruther thick, which is the next meanest thing to fog. You can't tell the shape of the river, and you can't see no distance. It got to be very late and still, and then along comes a steamboat up the river. We lit the lantern, and judged she would see it. Up-stream boats didn't generly come close to us; they go out and follow the bars and hunt for easy water under the reefs; but nights like this they bull right up the channel against the whole river.

We could hear her pounding along, but we didn't see her good till she was close. She aimed right for us. Often they do that and try to see how close they can come without touching; sometimes the wheel bites off a sweep, and then the pilot sticks his head out and laughs, and thinks he's mighty smart. Well, here she comes, and we said she was going to try to shave us; but she didn't seem to be sheering off a bit. She was a big one, and she was coming in a hurry, too, looking like a black cloud with rows of glow-worms around it; but all of a sudden she bulged out, big and scary, with a long row of wide-open furnace doors shining like red-hot teeth, and her monstrous bows and guards hanging right over us. There was a yell at us, and jingling of bells to stop the engines, a pow-wow of cussing and whistling of steam – and as Jim went overboard on one side and I on the other, she come smashing straight through the raft.

I dived – and I aimed to find the bottom, too, for a thirty-foot wheel had got to go over me, and I wanted it to have plenty of room. I could always stay under water a minute; this time I reckon I stayed under water a minute and a half. Then I bounced for the top in a hurry for I was nearly busting. I popped out to my arm-pits and blowed the water out of my nose, and puffed a bit. Of course there was a booming current; and of course that boat started her engines again ten seconds after she stopped them, for they never cared much for raftsmen; so now she was churning along up the river, out of sight in the thick weather, though I could hear her.

I sung out for Jim about a dozen times, but I didn't get any answer; so I grabbed a plank that touched me while I was 'treading water,' and struck out for shore, shoving it ahead of me. But I made out to see that the drift of the current was towards the left-hand shore, which meant that I was in a crossing; so I changed off and went that way.

It was one of these long, slanting, two-mile crossings; so I was a good long time in getting over. I made a safe landing, and clumb up the bank. I couldn't see but a little ways, but I went poking along over rough ground for a quarter of a mile or more, and then I run across a big old-fashioned double log house before I noticed it. I was going to rush by and get away, but a lot of dogs jumped out and went to howling and barking at me, and I knowed better than to move another peg.

Chapter 17

In about half a minute somebody spoke out of a window, without putting his head out, and says:

'Be done, boys! Who's there?'

I says:

'It's me.'

'Who's me?'

'George Jackson, sir.'

'What do you want?'

'I don't want nothing, sir. I only want to go along by, but the dogs won't let me.'

'What are you prowling around here this time of night, for – hey?'

'I warn't prowling around, sir; I fell overboard off of the steamboat.'

'Oh, you did, did you? Strike a light there, somebody. What did you say your name was?'

'George Jackson, sir. I'm only a boy.'

'Look here; if you're telling the truth, you needn't be afraid – nobody'll hurt you. But don't try to budge; stand right where you are. Rouse out Bob and Tom, some of you, and fetch the guns. George Jackson, is there anybody with you?'

'No, sir, nobody.'

I heard the people stirring around in the house, now, and see a light. The man sung out:

'Snatch that light away, Betsy, you old fool – ain't you got any sense? Put it on the floor behind the front door. Bob, if you and Tom are ready, take your places.'

'All ready.'

'Now, George Jackson, do you know the Shepherdsons?'

'No, sir – I never heard of them.'

'Well, that may be so, and it mayn't. Now, all ready. Step forward, George Jackson. And mind, don't you hurry – come mighty slow. If there's anybody with you, let him keep back – if he shows himself he'll be shot. Come along, now. Come slow; push the door open, yourself – just enough to squeeze in, d'you hear?'

I didn't hurry, I couldn't if I'd a wanted to. I took one slow step at a time, and there warn't a sound, only I thought I could hear my heart. The dogs were as still as the humans, but they followed a little behind me. When I got to the three log door-steps, I heard them unlocking and unbarring and unbolting. I put my hand on the door, and pushed it a little and a little more, till somebody said 'There, that's enough – put your head in.' I done it, but I judged they would take it off.

The candle was on the floor, and there they all was, looking at me, and me at them, for about a quarter of a minute. Three big men with guns pointed at me, which made me wince, I tell you; the oldest, grey and about sixty, the other two thirty or more – all of them fine and handsome – and the sweetest old grey-headed lady, and back of her two young women which I couldn't see right well. The old gentleman says:

'There – I reckon it's all right. Come in.'

As soon as I was in, the old gentleman he locked the door and barred it and bolted it, and told the young men to come in with their guns, and they all went in a big parlour that had a new rag carpet on the floor, and got together in a corner that was out of range of the front windows – there warn't none on the side. They held the candle, and took a good look at me, and all said, 'Why *he* ain't a Shepherdson – no, there ain't any Shepherdson about him.' Then the old man said he hoped I wouldn't mind being searched for arms, because he didn't mean no harm by it – it was only to make sure. So he didn't pry into my pockets, but only felt outside with his hands, and said it was all right. He told me to make myself easy and at home, and tell all about myself; but the old lady says:

'Why bless you, Saul, the poor thing's as wet as he can be; and don't you reckon it may be he's hungry?'

'True for you, Rachel – I forgot.'

So the old lady says:

'Betsy' (this was a nigger woman), 'you fly around and get him something to eat, as quick as you can, poor thing; and one of you girls go and wake up Buck and tell him—— Oh, here he is himself. Buck, take this little stranger and get the wet clothes off from him and dress him up in some of yours that's dry.'

Buck looked about as old as me – thirteen or fourteen or along there, though he was a little bigger than me. He hadn't on anything but a shirt, and he was very frowsy-headed. He come in gaping and digging one fist into his eyes, and he was dragging a gun along with the other one. He says:

'Ain't they no Shepherdsons around?'

They said, no, 'twas a false alarm.

'Well,' he says, 'if they'd a ben some, I reckon I'd a got one.'

They all laughed, and Bob says:

'Why, Buck, they might have scalped us all, you've been so slow in coming.'

'Well, nobody come after me, and it ain't right. I'm always kep' down; I don't get no show.'

'Never mind, Buck, my boy,' says the old man, 'you'll have show enough, all in good time, don't you fret about that. Go 'long with you now, and do as your mother told you.'

When we got upstairs to his room, he got me a coarse shirt and a roundabout and pants of his, and I put them on. While I was at it he asked me what my name was, but before I could tell him, he started to telling me about a blue jay and a young rabbit he had catched in the woods day before yesterday, and he asked me where Moses was when the candle went out. I said I didn't know; I hadn't heard about it before, no way.

'Well, guess,' he says.

'How'm I going to guess,' says I, 'when I never heard tell about it before?'

'But you can guess, can't you? It's just as easy.'

'*Which* candle?' I says.

'Why, any candle,' he says.

'I don't know where he was,' says I; 'where was he?'

'Why, he was in the *dark*! That's where he was!'

'Well, if you knowed where he was, what did you ask me for?'

'Why, blame it, it's a riddle, don't you see? Say, how long are you going to stay here? You got to stay always. We can just have booming times – they don't have no school now. Do you own a dog? I've got a dog – and he'll go in the river and bring out chips that you throw in. Do you like to comb up, Sundays, and all that kind of foolishness? You bet I don't, but ma she makes me. Confound these old britches, I reckon I'd better put 'em on, but I'd ruther not, it's so warm. Are you all ready? All right – come along, old hoss.'

Cold corn-pone, cold corn-beef, butter and butter-milk – that is what they had for me down there, and there ain't nothing better than ever I've come across yet. Buck and his ma and all of them smoked cob pipes, except the nigger woman, which was gone, and the two young women. They all smoked and talked, and I eat and talked. The young women had quilts around them, and their hair down their backs. They all asked me questions, and I told them how pap and me and all the family was living on a little farm down at the bottom of Arkansaw, and my sister Mary Ann run off and got married and never was heard of no more, and Bill went to hunt them and he warn't heard of no more, and Tom and Mort died, and then there warn't nobody but just me and pap left, and he was just trimmed down to nothing, on account of his troubles; so when he died I took what there was left, because the farm didn't belong to us, and started up the river, deck passage, and fell overboard; and that was how I come to be here. So they said I could have a home there as long as I wanted it. Then it was most daylight, and everybody went to bed, and I went to bed with Buck, and when I waked up in the morning, drat it all, I had forgot what my name was. So I laid there about an hour trying to think, and when Buck waked up, I says:

'Can you spell, Buck?'

'Yes,' he says.

'I bet you can't spell my name,' says I.

'I bet you what you dare I can,' says he.

'All right,' says I, 'go ahead.'

'G-o-r-g-e J-a-x-o-n – there now,' he says.

'Well,' says I, 'you done it, but I didn't think you could. It ain't no slouch of a name to spell – right off without studying.'

I set it down, private, 'cause somebody might want *me* to spell it, next, and so I wanted to be handy with it and rattle it off like I was used to it.

It was a mighty nice family, and a mighty nice house, too. I hadn't seen no house out in the country before that was so nice and had so much style. It didn't have an iron latch on the front door, nor a wooden one with a buckskin string, but a brass knob to turn, the same as houses in a town. There warn't no bed in the parlour, not a sign of a bed; but heaps of parlours in towns has beds in them. There was a big fire-place that was bricked on the bottom, and the bricks was kept clean and red by pouring water on them and scrubbing them with another brick; sometimes they washed them over with red water-paint that they call Spanish-brown, same as they do in town. They had a big brass dog-irons that could hold up a saw-log. There was a clock on the middle of the mantelpiece, with a picture of a town painted on the bottom half of the glass front, and a round place in the middle of it for the sun, and you could see the pendulum swing behind it. It was beautiful to hear that clock tick; and sometimes when one of these pedlars had been along and scoured her up and got her in good shape, she would start in and strike a hundred and fifty before she got tuckered out. They wouldn't took any money for her.

Well, there was a big outlandish parrot on each side of the clock, made out of something like chalk, and painted up gaudy. By one of the parrots was a cat made of crockery, and a crockery dog by the other; and when you pressed down on them they squeaked, but didn't open their mouths nor look different nor interested. They squeaked through underneath. There was a couple of big wild-turkey-wing fans spread out behind those things. On a table in the middle of the room was a kind of a lovely crockery basket that had apples and oranges and peaches and grapes piled up in it, which was much redder and yellower and prettier than real ones is, but they warn't real because you could see where pieces had got chipped off and showed the white chalk or whatever it was, underneath.

This table had a cover made out of beautiful oil-cloth, with a red and blue spread-eagle painted on it, and a painted border all around. It come all the way from Philadelphia, they said. There was some books too, piled up perfectly exact, on each corner of the table. One was a big family Bible, full of pictures. One was *Pilgrim's Progress*, about a man that left his family it didn't say why. I read considerable in it now and then. The statements was interesting, but tough. Another was *Friendship's Offering*, full of beautiful stuff and poetry; but I didn't read the poetry. Another was *Henry Clay's Speeches*, and another was Dr. Gunn's *Family Medicine*, which told you all about what to do if a body was sick or dead. There was a Hymn Book, and a lot of other books. And there was nice split-bottom chairs, and perfectly sound, too – not bagged down in the middle and busted, like an old basket.

They had pictures hung on the walls – mainly Washingtons and Lafayettes, and battles, and Highland Marys, and one called 'Signing the Declaration.' There was some that they called crayons, which one of the daughters which was dead made her own self when she was only fifteen years old. They was different from any pictures I ever see before; blacker, mostly, than is common. One was a woman in a slim black dress, belted small under the arm-pits, with bulges like a cabbage in the middle of the sleeves, and a large black scoop-shovel bonnet with a black veil, and white slim ankles crossed about with black tape, and very wee black slippers, like a chisel, and she was leaning pensive on a tombstone on her right elbow, under a weeping willow, and her other hand hanging down her side holding a white handkerchief and a reticule, and underneath the picture it said, 'Shall I Never See Thee More Alas?' Another one was a young lady with her hair all combed up straight to the top of her head, and knotted there in front of a comb like a chair-back, and she was crying into a handkerchief and had a dead bird laying on its back in her other hand with its heels up, and underneath the picture it said, 'I Shall Never Hear Thy Sweet Chirrup More Alas!' There was one where a young lady was at a window looking up at the moon, and tears running down her cheeks; and she had an open letter in one hand with a black sealing-wax showing on one edge of it, and she was mashing a locket with a chain to it against her mouth, and underneath the picture it said, 'And Art Thou Gone Yes Thou Art Gone Alas!' These was all nice pictures, I reckon, but I didn't somehow seem to take to them, because if ever I was down a little, they always gave me the fan-tods. Everybody was sorry she died, because she had laid out a lot more of these pictures to do, and a body could see by what she had done what they had lost. But I reckoned, that with her disposition, she was having a better time in the graveyard. She was at work on what they said was her greatest picture when she took sick, and every day and every night it was her prayer to be allowed to live till she got it done, but she never got the chance. It was a picture of a young woman in a long white gown, standing on the rail of a bridge all ready to jump off, with her hair all down her back, and looking up to the moon, with the tears running down her face, and she had two arms folded across her breast, and two arms stretched out in front, and two more reaching up towards the moon – and the idea was, to see which pair would look best and then scratch out all the other arms; but, as I was saying, she died before she got her mind made up, and now they kept this picture over the head of the bed in her room, and every time her birthday come they hung flowers on it. Other times it was hid with a little curtain. The young woman in the picture had a kind of a nice sweet face, but there was so many arms it made her look too spidery, seemed to me.

This young girl kept a scrap-book when she was alive, and used to paste obituaries and accidents and cases of patient suffering in it out of the *Presbyterian Observer*, and write poetry after them out of her own head. It was very good poetry. This is what she wrote about a boy by the name of Stephen Dowling Bots that fell down a well and was drownded:

ODE TO STEPHEN DOWLING BOTS, DEC'D

And did young Stephen sicken,
    And did young Stephen die?
And did the sad hearts thicken,
    And did the mourners cry?

No; such was not the fate of
    Young Stephen Dowling Bots;
Though sad hearts round him thickened,
    'Twas not from sickness' shots.

No whooping-cough did rack his frame,
    Nor measles drear, with spots:
Not these impaired the sacred name
    Of Stephen Dowling Bots.

Despised love struck not with woe
    That head of curly knots,
Nor stomach troubles laid him low,
    Young Stephen Dowling Bots.

Oh no. Then list with tearful eye,
    Whilst I his fate do tell.
His soul did from this cold world fly,
    By falling down a well.

> They got him out and emptied him;
> Alas it was too late;
> His spirit was gone for to sport aloft
> In the realms of the good and great.

If Emmeline Grangerford could make poetry like that before she was fourteen, there ain't no telling what she could a done by and by. Buck said she could rattle off poetry like nothing. She didn't ever have to stop to think. He said she would slap down a line, and if she couldn't find anything to rhyme with it she would scratch it out and slap down another one, and go ahead. She warn't particular, she could write about anything you choose to give her to write about, just so it was sadful. Every time a man died, or a woman died, or a child died, she would be on hand with her 'tribute' before he was cold. She called them tributes. The neighbours said it was the doctor first, then Emmeline, then the undertaker — the undertaker never got in ahead of Emmeline but once, and then she hung fire on a rhyme for the dead person's name, which was Whistler. She warn't ever the same, after that; she never complained, but she kind of pined away and did not live long. Poor thing, many's the time I made myself go up to the little room that used to be hers and get out her poor old scrap-book and read in it when her pictures had been aggravating me and I had soured on her a little. I liked all that family, dead ones and all, and warn't going to let anything come between us. Poor Emmeline made poetry about all the dead people when she was alive, and it didn't seem right that there warn't nobody to make some about her, now she was gone; so I tried to sweat out a verse or two myself, but I couldn't seem to make it go, somehow. They kept Emmeline's room trim and nice and all the things fixed in it just the way she liked to have them when she was alive, and nobody ever slept there. The old lady took care of the room herself, though there was plenty of niggers, and she sewed there a good deal and read her Bible there, mostly.

Well, as I was saying about the parlour, there was beautiful curtains on the windows: white, with pictures painted on them, of castles with vines all down the walls, and cattle coming down to drink. There was a little old piano, too, that had tin pans in it, I reckon, and nothing was ever so lovely as to hear the young ladies sing *The Last Link is Broken* and play *The Battle of Prague* on it. The walls of all the rooms was plastered, and most had carpets on the floors, and the whole house was whitewashed on the outside.

It was a double house, and the big open place betwixt them was roofed and floored, and sometimes the table was set there in the middle of the day, and it was a cool, comfortable place. Nothing couldn't be better. And warn't the cooking good, and just bushels of it too!

Chapter 18

Col. Grangerford was a gentleman, you see. He was a gentleman all over; and so was his family. He was well born, as the saying is, and that's worth as much in a man as it is in a horse, so the Widow Douglas said, and nobody ever denied that she was of the first aristocracy in our town; and pap he always said it, too, Though he warn't no more quality than a mud-cat, himself. Col. Grangerford was very tall and very slim, and had a darkish-paly complexion, not a sign of red in it anywheres; he was clean-shaved every morning, all over his thin face, and he had the thinnest kind of lips, and the thinnest kind of nostrils, and a high nose, and heavy eyebrows, and the blackest kind of eyes, sunk so deep back that they seemed like they was looking out of caverns at you, as you may say. His forehead was high, and his hair was black and straight, and hung to his shoulders. His hands was long and thin, and every day of his life he put on a clean shirt and a full suit from head to foot made out of linen so white it hurt your eyes to look at it; and on Sundays he wore a blue tail-coat with brass buttons on it. He carried a mahogany cane with a silver head to it. There warn't no frivolishness about him, not a bit, and he warn't ever loud. He was as kind as he could be – you could feel that, you know, and so you had confidence. Sometimes he smiled, and it was good to see; but when he straightened himself up like a liberty-pole, and the lightning begun to flicker out from under his eyebrows, you wanted to climb a tree first, and find out what the matter was afterwards. He didn't ever have to tell anybody to mind their manners – everybody was always good-mannered where he was. Everybody loved to have him around, too; he was sunshine most always – I mean he made it seem like good weather. When he turned into a cloud-bank it was awful dark for a half a minute and that was enough; there wouldn't nothing go wrong again for a week.

When him and the old lady come down in the morning, all the family got up out of their chairs and give them good day, and didn't set down again till they had set down. Then Tom and Bob went to the sideboard where the decanters was, and mixed a glass of bitters and handed it to him, and he held it in his hand and waited till Tom's and Bob's was mixed, and then they bowed and said, 'Our duty to you, sir, and madam'; and *they* bowed the least bit in the world and said thank you, and so they drank, all three, and Bob and Tom poured a spoonful of water on the sugar and the mite of whisky or apple brandy in the bottom of their tumblers, and give it to me and Buck, and we drank to the old people too.

Bob was the oldest, and Tom next. Tall, beautiful men with very broad shoulders and brown faces, and long black hair and black eyes. They dressed in white linen from head to foot, like the old gentleman, and wore broad Panama hats.

Then there was Miss Charlotte, she was twenty-five, and tall and proud and grand, but as good as she could be, when she warn't stirred up; but when she was, she had a look that would make you wilt in your tracks, like her father. She was beautiful.

So was her sister, Miss Sophia, but it was a different kind. She was gentle and sweet, like a dove, and she was only twenty.

Each person had their own nigger to wait on them – Buck, too. My nigger had a monstrous easy time, because I warn't used to having anybody do anything for me, but Buck's was on the jump most of the time.

This was all there was of the family, now; but there used to be more – three sons; they got killed; and Emmeline that died.

The old gentleman owned a lot of farms, and over a hundred niggers. Sometimes a stack of people would come there, horseback, from ten to fifteen mile around, and stay five or six days, and have such junketings round about and on the river, and dances and picnics in the woods, day-times, and balls at the house, nights. These people was mostly kin-folks of the family. The men brought their guns with them. It was a handsome lot of quality, I tell you.

There was another clan of aristocracy around there – five or six families – mostly of the name of Shepherdson. They was as high-toned, and well born, and rich and grand, as the tribe of Grangerfords. The Shepherdsons and the Grangerfords used the same steamboat landing, which was about two mile above our house; so sometimes when I went up there with a lot of our folks I used to see a lot of the Shepherdsons there, on their fine horses.

One day Buck and me was away out in the woods, hunting, and heard a horse coming. We was crossing the road. Buck says:

'Quick! Jump for the woods!'

We done it, and then peeped down the woods through the leaves. Pretty soon a splendid young man come galloping down the road, setting his horse easy and looking like a soldier. He had his gun across his pommel. I had seen him before. It was young Harney Shepherdson. I heard Buck's gun go off at my ear, and Harney's hat tumbled off from his head. He grabbed his gun and rode straight to the place where we was hid. But we didn't wait. We started through the woods on a run. The woods warn't thick, so I looked over my shoulder, to dodge the bullet, and twice I seen Harney cover Buck with his gun; and then he rode away the way he come – to get his hat, I reckon, but I couldn't see. We never stopped running till we got home. The old gentleman's eyes blazed a minute – 'twas pleasure, mainly, I judged – then his face sort of smoothed down, and he says, kind of gentle:

'I don't like that shooting from behind a bush. Why didn't you step into the road, my boy?'

'The Shepherdsons don't, father. They always take advantage.'

Miss Charlotte she held her head up like a queen while Buck was telling his tale, and her nostrils spread and her eyes snapped. The two young men looked dark, but never said nothing. Miss Sophia she turned pale, but the colour come back when she found the man warn't hurt.

Soon as I could get Buck down by the corn-cribs under the trees by ourselves, I says:

'Did you want to kill him, Buck?'

'Well, I bet I did.'

'What did he do to you?'

'Him? He never done nothing to me.'

'Well, then, what did you want to kill him for?'

'Why, nothing – only it's on account of the feud.'

'What's a feud?'

'Why, where was you raised? Don't you know what a feud is?'

'Never heard of it before – tell me about it.'

'Well,' says Buck, 'a feud is this way. A man has a quarrel with another man, and kills him; then that other man's brother kills *him*; then the other brothers, on both sides, goes for one another; then the *cousins* chip in – and by and by everybody's killed off, and there ain't no more feud. But it's kind of slow, and takes a long time.'

'Has this one been going on long, Buck?'

'Well, I should *reckon*! it started thirty year ago, or som'ers along there. There was trouble 'bout something and then a lawsuit to settle it; and the suit went agin one of the men, and so he up and shot the man that won the suit – which he would naturally do, of course, Anybody would.'

'What was the trouble about, Buck? – land?'

'I reckon maybe – I don't know.'

'Well, who done the shooting? – was it a Grangerford or a Shepherdson?'

'Laws, how do *I* know? it was so long ago.'

'Don't anybody know?'

'Oh, yes, pa knows, I reckon, and some of the other old folks; but they don't know now what the row was about in the first place.'

'Has there been many killed, Buck?'

'Yes – right smart chance of funerals. But they don't always kill. Pa's got a few buck-shot in him; but he don't mind it 'cuz he don't weigh much anyway. Bob's been carved up some with a bowie, and Tom's been hurt once or twice.'

'Has anybody been killed this year, Buck?'

'Yes, we got one and they got one. 'Bout three months ago, my cousin Bud, fourteen year old, was riding through the woods, on t'other side of the river, and didn't have no weapon with him, which was blame' foolishness, and in a lonesome place he hears a horse a-coming behind him, and sees old Baldy Shepherdson a-linkin' after him with his gun in his hand and his white hair a-flying in the wind; and 'stead of jumping off and taking to the brush, Bud 'lowed he could outrun him; so they had it, nip and tuck, for five mile or more, the old man a-gaining all the time; so at last Bud seen it warn't any use, so he stopped and faced around so as to have the bullet holes in front, you know, and the old man he rode up and shot him down. But he didn't git much chance to enjoy his luck, for inside of a week our folks laid *him* out.'

'I reckon that old man was a coward, Buck.'

'I reckon he *warn't* a coward. Not by a blame' sight. There ain't a coward amongst them Shepherdsons – not a one. And there ain't no cowards amongst the Grangerfords, either. Why, the old man kep' up his end in a fight one day, for a half an hour, against three Grangerfords, and come out winner. They was all a-horseback; he lit off of his horse and got behind a little wood-pile, and kep' his horse before him to stop the bullets; but the Grangerfords stayed on their horses and capered around the old man, and peppered away at him, and he peppered away at them. Him and his horse both went home pretty leaky and crippled, but the Grangerfords had to be *fetched* home – and one of 'em was dead, and another died the next day. No, sir, if a body's out hunting for cowards, he don't want to fool away any time amongst them Shepherdsons, becuz they don't breed any of that *kind*.'

Next Sunday we all went to church, about three mile, everybody a-horseback. The men took their guns along, so did Buck, and kept them between their knees or stood them handy against the wall. The Shepherdsons done the same. It was pretty ornery preaching – all about brotherly love, and such-like tiresomeness; but everybody said it was a good sermon, and they all talked it over going home, and had such a powerful lot to say about faith, and good works, and free grace, and prefore-ordestination, and I don't know what all, that it did seem to me to be one of the roughest Sundays I had run across yet.

About an hour after dinner everybody was dozing around, some in their chairs and some in their rooms, and it got to be pretty dull. Buck and a dog was stretched out on the grass in the sun, sound asleep. I went up to our room, and judged I would take a nap myself. I found that sweet Miss Sophia standing in her door, which was next to ours, and she took me in her room, and shut the door very soft, and asked me if I liked her, and I said I did; and she asked me if I would do something for her and not tell anybody, and I said I would. Then she said she'd forgot her Testament, and left it in the seat at church, between two other books, and would I slip out quiet and go there and fetch it to her, and not say nothing to nobody. I said I would. So I slid out and slipped off up the road, and there warn't anybody at the church, except maybe a hog or two, for there warn't any lock on the door, and hogs likes a puncheon floor in summer-time because it's cool. If you notice, most folks don't go to church only when they've got to; but a hog is different.

Says I to myself something's up – it ain't natural for a girl to be in such a sweat about a Testament; so I give it a shake, and out drops a little piece of paper with '*Half-past-two*' wrote on it with a pencil. I ransacked it, but couldn't find anything else. I couldn't make anything out of that, so I put the paper in the book again, and when I got home and upstairs, there was Miss Sophia in her door waiting for me. She pulled me in and shut the door; then she looked in the Testament till she found the paper, and as soon as she read it she looked glad; and before a body could think, she grabbed me and give me a squeeze, and said I was the best boy in the world, and not to tell anybody. She was mighty red in the face, for a minute, and her eyes lighted up, and it made her powerful pretty. I was a good deal astonished, but when I got my breath I asked her what the paper was about, and she asked me if I had read it, and I said 'no,' and she asked me if I could read writing, and I told her, 'No, only coarse-hand,' and then she said the paper warn't anything but a book-mark to keep her place, and I might go and play now.

I went off down to the river, studying over this thing, and pretty soon I noticed that my nigger was following along behind. When we was out of sight of the house, he looked back and around a second, and then comes a-running, and says:

'Mars Jawge, if you'll come down into de swamp, I'll show you a whole stack o' water-moccasins.'

Thinks I, that's mighty curious; he said that yesterday. He oughter know a body don't love water-moccasins enough to go around hunting for them. What is he up to anyway? So I says:

'All right, trot ahead.'

I followed a half a mile, then he struck out over the swamp and waded ankle deep as much as another half-mile. We come to a little flat piece of land which was dry and very thick with trees and bushes and vines, and he says:

'You shove right in dah, jist a few steps, Mars Jawge, dah's whah dey is. I's seed'm befo', I don't k'yer to see 'em no mo'.'

Then he slopped right along and went away, and pretty soon the trees hid him. I poked into the place a-ways, and come to a little open patch as big as a bedroom, all hung around with vines, and found a man laying there asleep – and by jings it was my old Jim!

I waked him up, and I reckoned it was going to be a grand surprise to him to see me again, but it warn't. He nearly cried, he was so glad, but he warn't surprised. Said he swum along behind me, that night, and heard me yell every time, but dasn't answer, because he didn't want nobody to pick *him* up, and take him into slavery again. Says he:

'I got hurt a little, en couldn't swim fas', so I wuz a considable ways behine you, towards de las'; when you landed I reck'ned I could ketch up wid you on de lan' 'doubt havin' to shout at you, but when I see dat house I begin to go slow. I 'us off too fur to hear what dey say to you – I wuz 'fraid o' de dogs – but when it 'us all quiet agin, I knowed you's in de house, so I struck out for de woods to wait for day. Early in de mawnin' some er de niggers come along, gwyne to de fields, en dey tuck me en showed me dis place, whah de dogs can't track me on account o' de water, en dey brings me truck to eat every night, en tells me how you's a-gitt'n along.'

'Why didn't you tell my Jack to fetch me here sooner, Jim?'

'Well, 'twarn't no use to 'sturb you, Huck, tell we could do sumf'n – but we's all right, now. I ben a-buyin' pots en pans en vittles, as I got a chanst, en a-patchin' up de raf', nights, when——'

'*What* raft, Jim?'

'Our ole raf'.'

'You mean to say our old raft warn't smashed all to flinders?'

'No, she warn't. She was tore up a good deal – one en' of her was – but dey warn't no great harm done, on'y our traps was mos' all los'. Ef we hadn' dive' so deep en swum so fur under water, en de night hadn' ben' so dark, en we warn't so sk'yerd, en ben sich punkin-heads, as de sayin' is, we'd a seed de raf'. But it's jis' as well we didn't, 'kase now she's all fixed up agin mos' as good as new, en we's got a new lot o' stuff, too, in de place o' what 'uz los'.'

'Why, how did you get hold of the raft again, Jim – did you catch her?'

'How I gwyne to ketch her, en I out in de woods? No, some er de niggers foun' her ketched on a snag, along heah in de ben', en dey hid her in a crick, 'mongst de willows, en dey wuz so much jawin' 'bout which un 'um she b'long to de mos', dat I come to heah 'bout it pooty soon, so I ups en settles de trouble by tellin' 'um she don' b'long to none uv um, but to you en me; en I ast'm if dey gwyne to grab a young white genlman's propaty, en git a hid'n for it? Den I gin'm ten cents apiece, en dey 'uz mighty well satisfied, en wisht some mo' raf's 'ud come along en make'm rich agin. Dey's mighty good to me, dese niggers is, en whatever I wants'm to do fur me, I doan' have to ast'm twice, honey. Dat Jack's a good nigger, en pooty smart.

'Yes, he is. He ain't ever told me you was here; told me to come, and he'd show me a lot of water-moccasins. If anything happens, *he* ain't mixed up in it. He can say he never seen us together, and it'll be the truth.'

I don't want to talk much about the next day. I reckon I'll cut it pretty short. I waked up about dawn, and was a-going to turn over and go to sleep again, when I noticed how still it was – didn't seem to be anybody stirring.

That warn't usual. Next I noticed that Buck was up and gone. Well, I gets up, a-wondering, and goes downstairs – nobody around; everything as still as a mouse. Just the same outside; thinks I, what does it mean? Down by the wood-pile I comes across my Jack, and says:

'What's it all about?'

Says he:

'Don't you know, Mars Jawge?'

'No,' says I, 'I don't.'

'Well, den, Miss Sophia's run off! 'deed she has. She run off in de night, some time – nobody don' know jis' when – run off to git married to dat young Harney Shepherdson, you know – leastways, so dey 'spec. De fambly foun' it out, 'bout half an hour ago – maybe a little mo' – en' I *tell* you dey warn't no time los'. Sich another hurryin' up guns en hosses *you* never see! De women folks has gone for to stir up de relations, en ole Mars Saul en de boys tuck dey guns en rode up de river road for to try to ketch dat young man en kill him 'fo' he kin git acrost de river wid Miss Sophia. I reck'n dey's gwyne to be mighty rough times.'

'Buck went off 'thout waking me up.'

'Well, I reck'n he *did*! Dey warn't gwyne to mix you up in it. Mars Buck he loaded up his gun en 'lowed he's gwyne to fetch home a Shepherdson or bust. Well, dey'll be plenty un'm dah, I reck'n, en you bet you he'll fetch one ef he gits a chanst.'

I took up the river road as hard as I could put. By and by I begin to hear guns a good ways off. When I come in sight of the log store and the wood-pile where the steamboats land, I worked along under trees and brush till I got to a good place, and then I clumb up into the forks of a cotton-wood that was out of reach, and watched. There was a wood-rank four foot high, a little ways in front of the tree, and first I was going to hide behind that; but maybe it was luckier I didn't.

There was four or five men cavorting around on their horses in the open place before the log store, cussing and yelling, and trying to get at a couple of young chaps that was behind the wood-rank alongside of the steamboat landing – but they couldn't come it. Every time one of them showed himself on the river side of the wood-pile he got shot at. The two boys was squatting back to back behind the pile, so they could watch both ways.

By and by the men stopped cavorting around and yelling. They started riding towards the store; then up gets one of the boys, draws a steady bead over the wood-rank, and drops one of them out of his saddle. All the men jumped off of their horses and grabbed the hurt one and started to carry him to the store; and that minute the two boys started on the run. They got half-way to the tree I was in before the men noticed. Then the men see them, and jumped on their horses and took out after them. They gained on the boys, but it didn't do no good, the boys had too good a start; they got to the wood-pile that was in front of my tree, and slipped in behind it, and so they had the bulge on the men again. One of the boys was Buck, and the other was a slim young chap about nineteen years old.

The men ripped around awhile, and then rode away. As soon as they was out of sight, I sung out to Buck and told him. He didn't know what to make of my voice coming out of the tree, at first. He was awful surprised. He told me to watch out sharp and let him know when the men came in sight again; said they was up to some devilment or other – wouldn't be gone long. I wished I was out of that tree, but I dasn't come down. Buck begun to cry and rip, and 'lowed that him and his cousin Joe (that was the other young chap) would make up for this day, yet. He said his father and his two brothers was killed, and two or three of the enemy. Said the Shepherdsons laid for them, in ambush. Buck said his father and brothers ought to waited for their relations – the Shepherdsons was too strong for them. I asked him what was become of young Harney and Miss Sophia. He said they'd got across the river and was safe. I was glad of that; but the way Buck did take on because he didn't manage to kill Harney that day he shot at him – I hain't ever heard anything like it.

All of a sudden, bang! bang! bang! goes three or four guns – the men had slipped around through the woods and come in from behind without their horses! The boys jumped for the river – both of them hurt – and as they swum down the current the men run along the bank shouting at them and singing out, 'Kill them, kill them!' It made me so sick I most fell out of the tree. I ain't a-going to tell *all* that happened – it would make me sick again if I was to do that. I wished I hadn't ever come ashore that night, to see such things. I ain't ever going to get shut of them – lots of times I dream about them.

I stayed in the tree till it begun to get dark, afraid to come down. Sometimes I heard guns away off in the woods; and twice I seen little gangs of men gallop past the log store with guns; so I reckoned the trouble was still a-going on. I was mighty down-hearted; so I made up my mind I wouldn't ever go a-near that house again, because I reckoned I was to blame, somehow. I judged that that piece of paper meant that Miss Sophia was to meet Harney somewheres at half-past two and run off; and I judged I ought to told her father about that paper and the curious way she acted, and then maybe he would a locked her up and this awful mess wouldn't ever happened.

When I got down out of the tree, I crept along down the river bank a piece, and found the two bodies laying in the edge of the water, and tugged at them till I got them ashore; then I covered up their faces, and got away as quick as I could. I cried a little when I was covering up Buck's face, for he was mighty good to me.

It was just dark, now. I never went near the house, but struck through the woods and made for the swamp. Jim warn't on his island, so I tramped off in a hurry for the crick, and crowded through the willows, red-hot to jump aboard and get out of that awful country – the raft was gone! My souls, but I was scared! I couldn't get my breath for most a minute. Then I raised a yell. A voice not twenty-five foot from me, says:

'Good lan'! is dat you, honey? Doan' make no noise.'

It was Jim's voice – nothing ever sounded so good before. I run along the bank a piece and got aboard, and Jim he grabbed me and hugged me, he was so glad to see me. He says:

'Laws bless you, chile, I 'uz right down sho' you's dead agin. Jack's been heah, he say he reck'n you's ben shot, kase you didn' come home no mo'; so I's jes' dis minute a-startin' de raf' down towards de mouf er de crick, so's to be all ready for to shove out en leave soon as Jack comes agin en tells me for certain you *is* dead. Lawsy, I's mighty glad to get you back agin, honey.'

I says:

'All right – that's mighty good; they won't find me, and they'll think I've been killed, and floated down the river – there's something up there that'll help them to think so – so don't you lose no time, Jim, but just shove off for the big water as fast as ever you can.'

I never felt easy till the raft was two mile below there and out in the middle of the Mississippi. Then we hung up our signal lantern, and judged that we was free and safe once more. I hadn't had a bit to eat since yesterday; so Jim he got out some corn-dodgers and butter-milk, and pork and cabbage, and greens – there ain't nothing in the world so good, when it's cooked right – and whilst I eat my supper we talked, and had a good time. I was powerful glad to get away from the feuds, and so was Jim to get away from the swamp. We said there warn't no home like a raft, after all. Other places do seem so cramped up and smothery, but a raft don't. You feel mighty free and easy and comfortable on a raft.

Chapter 19

Two or three days and nights went by; I reckon I might say they swum by, they slid along so quiet and smooth and lovely. Here is the way we put in the time. It was a monstrous big river down there – sometimes a mile and a half wide; we run nights, and laid up and hid day-times; soon as night was most gone, we stopped navigating and tied up – nearly always in the dead water under a tow-head; and then cut young cotton-woods and willows and hid the raft with them. Then we set out the lines. Next we slid into the river and had a swim, so as to freshen up and cool off; then we set down on the sandy bottom where the water was about knee-deep, and watched the daylight come. Not a sound anywheres – perfectly still – just like the whole world was asleep, only sometimes the bull-frogs a-clattering, maybe. The first thing to see, looking away over the water, was a kind of dull line – that was the woods on t'other side – you couldn't make nothing else out; then a pale place in the sky; then more paleness, spreading around; then the river softened up, away off, and warn't black any more, but grey; you could see little dark spots drifting along, ever so far away – trading scows, and such things; and long black streaks – rafts; sometimes you could hear a sweep screaking; or jumbled up voices, it was so still, and sounds come so far; and by and by you could see a streak on the water which you know by the look of the streak that there's a snag there in a swift current which breaks on it and makes that streak look that way; and you see the mist curl up off of the water, and the east reddens up, and the river, and you make out a log cabin in the edge of the woods, away on the bank on t'other side of the river, being a wood-yard, likely, and piled by them cheats so you can throw a dog through it anywheres; then the nice breeze springs up, and comes fanning you from over there, so cool and fresh, and sweet to smell, on account of the woods and the flowers; but sometimes not that way, because they've left dead fish laying around, gars, and such, and they do get pretty rank; and next you've got the full day, and everything smiling in the sun, and the song-birds just going it!

A little smoke couldn't be noticed, now, so we would take some fish off of the lines and cook up a hot breakfast. And afterwards we would watch the lonesomeness of the river, and kind of lazy along, and by and by lazy off to sleep. Wake up, by and by, and look to see what done it, and maybe see a

'. . . we would take some fish off the line and cook up a hot breakfast'

steamboat, coughing along up stream, so far off towards the other side you couldn't tell nothing about her only whether she was stern-wheel or side-wheel; then for about an hour there wouldn't be nothing to hear nor nothing to see – just solid lonesomeness. Next you'd see a raft sliding by, away off yonder, and maybe a galoot on it chopping, because they're most always doing it on a raft; you'd see the axe flash, and come down – you don't hear nothing; you see that axe go up again, and by the time it's above the man's head, then you hear the *k'chunk!* – it had took all that time to come over the water. So we would put in the day, lazying around, listening to the stillness. Once there was a thick fog, and the rafts and things that went by was beating tin pans so the steamboats wouldn't run over them. A scow or a raft went by so close we could her them talking and cussing and laughing – heard them plain; but we couldn't see no sign of them; it made you feel crawly, it was like spirits carrying on that way in the air. Jim said he believed it was spirits; but I says:

'No, spirits wouldn't say, "dern the dern fog."'

Soon as it was night, out we shoved; when we got her out to about the middle, we let her alone, and let her float wherever the current wanted her to; then we lit the pipes, and dangled our legs in the water and talked about all kinds of things – we was always naked, day and night, whenever the mosquitoes would let us – the new clothes Buck's folks made for me was too good to be comfortable, and besides I didn't go much on clothes, nohow.

Sometimes we'd have that whole river all to ourselves for the longest time. Yonder was the banks and the islands, across the water; and maybe a spark – which was a candle in a cabin window – and sometimes on the water you could see a spark or two – on a raft or a scow, you know; and maybe you could hear a fiddle or a song coming over from one of them crafts. It's lovely to live on a raft. We had the sky, up there, all speckled with stars, and we used to lay on our backs and look up at them, and discuss about whether they was made, or only just happened – Jim he allowed they was made, but I allowed they happened; I judged it would have took too long to *make* so many. Jim said the moon could a *laid* them; well, that looked kind of reasonable, so I didn't say nothing against it, because I've seen a frog lay most as many, so of course it could be done. We used to watch the stars that fell, too, and see them streak down. Jim allowed they'd got spoiled and was hove out of the nest.

Once or twice of a night we would see a steamboat slipping along in the dark, and now and then she would belch a whole world of sparks up out of her chimbleys, and they would rain down in the river and look awful pretty; then she would turn a corner and her lights would wink out and her pow-wow shut off and leave the river still again; and by and by her waves would get to us, a long time after she was gone, and joggle the raft a bit, and after that you wouldn't hear nothing for you couldn't tell how long, except maybe frogs or something.

After midnight the people on shore went to bed, and then for two or three hours the shores was black – no more sparks in the cabin windows. These sparks was our clock – the first one that showed again meant morning was coming, so we hunted a place to hide and tie up, right away.

One morning about daybreak, I found a canoe and crossed over a chute to the main shore – it was only two hundred yards – and paddled about a mile up a crick amongst the cypress woods, to see if I couldn't get some berries. Just as I was passing a place where a kind of cow-path crossed the crick, here comes a couple of men tearing up the path as tight as they could foot it. I thought I was a goner, for whenever anybody was after anybody I judged it was *me* – or maybe Jim. I was about to dig out from there in a hurry, but they was pretty close to me then, and sung out and begged me to save their lives – said they hadn't been doing nothing, and was being chased for it – said there was men and dogs a-coming. They wanted to jump right in, but I says:

'Don't you do it. I don't hear the dogs and horses yet; you've got time to crowd through the brush and get up the crick a little ways; then you take to the water and wade down to me and get in – that'll throw the dogs off the scent.'

They done it, and soon as they was aboard I lit out for our tow-head, and in about five or ten minutes we heard the dogs and the men away off, shouting. We heard them come along towards the crick, but couldn't see them; they seemed to stop and fool around awhile; then, as we got further and further away all the time, we couldn't hardly hear them at all; by the time we had left a mile of woods behind us and struck the river, everything was quiet, and we paddled over to the tow-head and hid in the cotton-woods and was safe.

One of these fellows was about seventy, or upwards, and had a bald head and very grey whiskers. He had an old battered-up slouch hat on, and a greasy blue woollen shirt, and ragged old blue jeans britches stuffed into his boot tops, and home-knit galluses – no, he only had one. He had an old long-tailed blue jeans coat with slick brass buttons, flung over his arm, and both of them had big fat ratty-looking carpet-bags.

The other fellow was about thirty and dressed about as ornery. After breakfast we all laid off and talked, and the first thing that come out was that these chaps didn't know one another.

'What got you into trouble?' says the baldhead to t'other chap.

'Well, I'd been selling an article to take the tartar off the teeth – and it does take it off, too, and generly the enamel along with it – but I stayed about one night longer than I ought to, and was just in the act of sliding out when I ran across you on the trail this side of town, and you told me they were coming, and begged me to help you to get off. So I told you I was expecting trouble myself and would scatter out *with* you. That's the whole yarn – what's yourn?'

'Well, I'd ben a-runnin' a little temperance revival thar, 'bout a week, and was the pet of the women-folks, big and little, for I was makin' it mighty warm for the rummies, I *tell* you, and takin' as much as five or six dollars a night – ten cents a head, children and niggers free – and business a-growin' all the time; when somehow or another a little report got around, last night, that I had a way of puttin' in my time with a private jug, on the sly. A nigger rousted me out this mornin', and told me the people was getherin' on the quiet, with their dogs and horses, and they'd be along pretty soon and give me 'bout half an hour's start, and then run me down, if they could; and if they got me they'd tar and feather me and ride me on a rail, sure. I didn't wait for no breakfast – I warn't hungry.'

'Old man,' says the young one. 'I reckon we might double-team it together; what do you think?'

'I ain't undisposed. What's your line – mainly?'

'Jour printer, by trade; do a little in patent medicines; theatre-actor – tragedy, you know; take a turn at mesmerism and phrenology when there's a chance; teach singing geography school for a change; sling a lecture, sometimes – oh, I do lots of things – most anything that comes handy, so it ain't work. What's your lay?'

'I've done considerble in the doctoring way in my time. Layin' on o' hands is my best holt – for cancer, and paralysis, and sich things; and I k'n tell a fortune pretty good, when I've got somebody along to find out the facts for me. Preachin's my line, too; and workin' camp-meetin's; and missionaryin' around.'

Nobody never said anything for awhile; then the young man hove a sigh and says:

'Alas!'

'What're you alassin' about?' says the baldhead.

'To think I should have lived to be leading such a life, and be degraded down into such company.' And he begun to wipe the corner of his eye with a rag.

'Dern your skin, ain't the company good enough for you?' says the baldhead, pretty pert and uppish.

'Yes, it *is* good enough for me; it's as good as I deserve; for who fetched me so low, when I was so high? *I* did myself. I don't blame *you*, gentlemen – far from it; I don't blame anybody. I deserve it all. Let the cold world do its worst; one thing I know – there's a grave somewhere for me. The world may go on just as it's always done, and take everything from me – loved ones, property, everything – but it can't take that. Some day I'll lie down in it and forget it all, and my poor broken heart will be at rest.' He went on a-wiping.

'Drot your pore broken heart,' says the baldhead: 'what are you heaving your pore broken heart at *us* f'r? *We* hain't done nothing.'

'No, I know you haven't. I ain't blaming you, gentlemen. I brought myself down – yes, I did it myself. It's right I should suffer – perfectly right – I don't make any moan.'

'Brought you down from what? What was you brought down from?'

'Ah, you would not believe me; the world never believes – let it pass – 'tis no matter. The secret of my birth——'

'The secret of your birth? Do you mean to say——'

'Gentlemen,' says the young man, very solemn, 'I will reveal it to you, for I feel I may have confidence in you. By rights I am a duke!'

Jim's eyes bugged out when he heard that; and I reckon mine did, too. Then the baldhead says: 'No! you can't mean it?'

'Yes. My great-grandfather, eldest son of the Duke of Bridgewater, fled to this country about the end of the last century, to breathe the pure air of freedom; married here, and died, leaving a son, his own father dying about the same time. The second son of the late duke seized the title and estates – the infant real duke was ignored. I am the lineal descendant of that infant – I am the rightful Duke of Bridgewater; and here am I, forlorn, torn from my high estate, hunted of men, despised by the cold world, ragged, worn, heart-broken, and degraded to the companionship of felons on a raft!'

Jim pitied him ever so much, and so did I. We tried to comfort him, but he said it warn't much use, he couldn't be much comforted; said if we was a mind to acknowledge him, that would do him more good than most anything else; so we said we would, if he would tell us how. He said we ought to bow, when we spoke to him, and say 'Your Grace,' or 'My Lord,' or 'Your Lordship' – and he wouldn't mind it if we called him plain 'Bridgewater,' which he said was a title, anyway, and not a name; and one of us ought to wait on him at dinner, and do any little thing for him he wanted done.

Well, that was all easy, so we done it. All through dinner Jim stood around and waited on him, and says, 'Will yo' Grace have some o' dis, or some o' dat?' and so on, and a body could see it was mighty pleasing to him.

But the old man got pretty silent, by and by – didn't have much to say, and didn't look pretty comfortable over all that petting that was going on around the duke. He seemed to have something on his mind. So, along in the afternoon, he says:

'Looky here, Bilgewater,' he says, 'I'm nation sorry for you, but you ain't the only person that's had troubles like that.'

'No?'

'No, you ain't. You ain't the only person that's ben snaked down wrongfully out'n a high place.'

'Alas!'

'No, you ain't the only person that's had a secret of his birth.' And by jings, *he* begins to cry.

'Hold! What do you mean?'

'Bilgewater, kin I trust you?' says the old man, still sort of sobbing.

'To the bitter death!' He took the old man by the hand and squeezed it, and says, 'The secret of your being: speak!'

'Bilgewater, I am the late Dauphin!'

You bet you Jim and me stared, this time. Then the duke says:

'You are what?'

'Yes, my friend, it is too true – your eyes is lookin' at this very moment on the pore disappeared Dauphin, Looy the Seventeen, son of Looy the Sixteen and Marry Antonette.'

'You! At your age! No! You mean you're the late Charlemagne; you must be six or seven hundred years old, at the very least.'

'Trouble has done it, Bilgewater, trouble has done it; trouble has brung these grey hairs and this premature balditude. Yes, gentlemen, you see before you, in blue jeans and misery, the wanderin', exiled, trampled-on, and sufferin' rightful King of France.'

Well, he cried and took on so, that me and Jim didn't know hardly what to do, we was so sorry – and so glad and proud we'd got him with us, too. So we set in, like we done before with the duke, and tried to comfort *him*. But he said it warn't no use, nothing but to be dead and done with it all could do him any good; though he said it often made him feel easier and better for a while if people treated him according to his rights, and got down on one knee to speak to him, and always called him 'Your Majesty,' and waited on him first at meals, and didn't set down in his presence till he asked them. So Jim and me set to majestying him, and doing this and that and t'other for him, and standing up till he told us we might set down. This done him heaps of good, and so he got cheerful and comfortable. But the duke kind of soured on him, and didn't look a bit satisfied with the way things was going; still the king acted real friendly towards him, and said the duke's great-grandfather and all the other Dukes of Bilgewater was a good deal thought of by *his* father, and was allowed to come to the palace considerable; but the duke stayed huffy a good while, till by and by the king says:

'Like as not we got to be together a blamed long time, on this h'yer raft, Bilgewater, and so what's the use o' your bein' sour? It'll only make things oncomfortable. It ain't my fault I warn't born a duke, it ain't your fault you warn't born a king – so what's the use to worry? Make the best o' things the way you find 'em, says I – that's my motto. This ain't no bad thing that we've struck here – plenty grub and an easy life – come, give us your hand, Duke, and less all be friends.'

The duke done it, and Jim and me was pretty glad to see it. It took away all the uncomfortableness, and we felt mighty good over it, because it would a been a miserable business to have any unfriendliness on the raft; for what you want, above all things, on a raft, is for everybody to be satisfied, and feel right and kind towards the others.

It didn't take me long to make up my mind that these liars warn't no kings nor dukes, at all, but just low-down humbugs and frauds. But I never said nothing, never let on; kept it to myself; it's the best way; then you don't have no quarrels, and don't get into no trouble. If they wanted us to call them kings and dukes, I hadn't no objections, 'long as it would keep peace in the family; and it warn't no use to tell Jim, so I didn't tell him. If I never learnt nothing else out of pap I learnt that the best way to get along with his kind of people is to let them have their own way.

Chapter 20

They asked us considerable many questions; wanted to know what we covered up the raft that way for, and laid by in the day-time instead of running – was Jim a runaway nigger? Says I:

'Goodness sakes, would a runaway nigger run *south*?'

No, they allowed he wouldn't. I had to account for things some way, so I says:

'My folks was living in Pike County, in Missouri, where I was born, and they all died off but me and pa and my brother Ike. Pa, he 'lowed he'd break up and go down and live with Uncle Ben, who's got a little one-horse place on the river, forty-four mile below Orleans. Pa was pretty poor, and had some debts; so when he'd squared up there warn't nothing left but sixteen dollars and our nigger, Jim. That warn't enough to take us fourteen hundred mile, deck passage nor no other way. Well, when the river rose, pa had a streak of luck one day; he ketched this piece of a raft; so we reckoned we'd go down to Orleans on it. Pa's luck didn't hold out; a steamboat run over the forrard corner of the raft, one night, and we all went overboard and dove under the wheel; Jim and me come up, all right, but pa was drunk, and Ike was only four years old, so they never come up no more. Well, for the next day or two we had considerable trouble, because people was always coming out in skiffs and trying to take Jim away from me, saying they believed he was a runaway nigger. We don't run day-times no more, now; nights they don't bother us.'

The duke says:

'Leave me alone to cipher out a way so we can run in the day-time if we want to. I'll think the thing over – I'll invent a plan that'll fix it. We'll let it alone for to-day, because of course we don't want to go by that town yonder in daylight – it mightn't be healthy.'

Towards night it begun to darken up and look like rain: the heat lightning was squirting around, low down in the sky, and the leaves was beginning to shiver – it was going to be pretty ugly, it was easy to see that. So the duke and the king went to overhauling our wigwam, to see what the beds was like. My bed was a straw tick – better than Jim's, which was a corn-shuck tick; there's always cobs around about in a shuck tick, and they poke into you and hurt; and when you roll over, the dry shucks sound like you was rolling over in a pile of dead leaves; it makes such a rustling that you wake up. Well, the duke allowed he would take my bed; but the king allowed he wouldn't. He says:

'I should a reckoned the difference in rank would a sejested to you that a corn-shuck bed warn't just fitten for me to sleep on. Your Grace'll take the shuck bed yourself.'

Jim and me was in a sweat again, for a minute, being afraid there was going to be some more trouble amongst them; so we was pretty glad when the duke says:

''Tis my fate to be always ground into the mire under the iron heel of oppression. Misfortune has broken my once haughty spirit; I yield, I submit; 'tis my fate. I am alone in the world – let me suffer; I can bear it.'

We got away as soon as it was good and dark. The king told us to stand well out towards the middle of the river, and not show a light till we got a long ways below the town. We come in sight of the little bunch of lights by and by – that was the town, you know – and slid by, about a half a mile out, all right. When we was three-quarters of a mile below, we hoisted up our signal lantern; and about ten o'clock it come on to rain and blow and thunder and lighten like everything; so the king told us to both stay on watch till the weather got better; then him and the duke crawled into the wigwam and turned in for the night. It was my watch below, till twelve, but I wouldn't a turned in, anyway, if I'd had a bed; because a body don't see such a storm as that every day in the week, not by a long sight. My souls, how the wind did scream along! And every second or two there'd come a glare that lit up the white-caps for half a mile around, and you'd see the islands looking dusty through the rain, and the trees thrashing around in the wind; then comes a *h-wack*! – bum! bum! bumble-umble-um-bum-bum-bum – and the thunder would go rumbling and grumbling away, and quit – and then *rip* comes another flash and another sockdolager. The waves most washed me off the raft, sometimes, but I hadn't any clothes on, and didn't mind. We didn't have no trouble about snags; the lightning was glaring and flittering around so constant that we could see them plenty soon enough to throw her head this way or that and miss them.

I had the middle watch, you know, but I was pretty sleepy by that time, so Jim he said he would stand the first half of it for me; he was always mighty good that way, Jim was. I crawled into the wigwam, but the king and the duke had their legs sprawled around so there warn't no show for me; so I laid outside – I didn't mind the rain, because it was warm, and the waves warn't running so high, now. About two they come up again, though, and Jim was going to call me, but he changed his mind because he reckoned they warn't high enough yet to do any harm; but he was mistaken about that, for pretty soon all of a sudden along comes a regular ripper, and washed me overboard. It most killed Jim a-laughing. He was the easiest nigger to laugh that ever was, anyway.

I took the watch, and Jim he laid down and snored away; and by and by the storm let up for good and all; and the first cabin-light that showed, I rousted him out and we slid the raft into hiding-quarters for the day.

The king got out an old ratty deck of cards, after breakfast, and him and the duke played seven-up a while, five cents a game. Then they got tired of it, and allowed they would 'lay out a campaign,' as they called it. The duke went down into his carpet-bag and fetched up a lot of little printed bills, and read them out loud. One bill said 'The celebrated Dr. Armand de Montalban, of Paris,' would 'lecture on the Science of Phrenology' at such and such a place, on the blank day of blank, at ten cents admission, and 'furnish charts of character at twenty-five cents apiece.' The duke said that was *him*. In another bill he was the 'world-renowned Shakesperean tragedian, Garrick the Younger, of Drury Lane, London.' In other bills he had a lot of other names and done other wonderful things, like finding water and gold with a 'divining rod,' 'dissipating witch-spells,' and so on. By and by he says:

'But the histrionic muse is the darling. Have you ever trod the boards, Royalty?'

'No,' says the king.

'You shall, then, before you're three days older, Fallen Grandeur,' says the duke. 'The first good town we come to, we'll hire a hall and do the sword fight in *Richard III* and the balcony scene in *Romeo and Juliet*. How does that strike you?'

'I'm in, up to the hub, for anything that will pay, Bilgewater, but you see I don't know nothing about play-actn', and hain't ever seen much of it. I was too small when pap used to have 'em at the palace. Do you reckon you can learn me?'

'Easy!'

'All right. I'm jist a-freezn' for something fresh, anyway. Less commence, right away.'

So the duke he told me all about who Romeo was, and who Juliet was, and said he was used to being Romeo, so the king could be Juliet.

'But if Juliet's such a young gal, duke, my peeled head and my white whiskers is goin' to look oncommon odd on her, maybe.'

'No, don't you worry – these country jakes won't ever think of that. Besides, you know, you'll be in costume, and that makes all the difference in the world; Juliet's in a balcony, enjoying the moonlight before she goes to bed, and she's got on her night-gown and her ruffled night-cap. Here are the costumes for the parts.'

He got out two or three curtain-calico suits, which he said was meedyevil armour for Richard III and t'other chap, and a long white cotton night-shirt and a ruffled night-cap to match. The king was satisfied; so the duke got out his book and read the parts over in the most splendid spread-eagle way, prancing around and acting at the same time, to show how it had got to be done; then he give the book to the king and told him to get his part by heart.

There was a little one-horse town about three mile down the bend, and after dinner the duke said he had ciphered out his idea about how to run in daylight without it being dangersome for Jim; so he allowed he would go down to the town and fix that thing. The king allowed he would go too, and see if he couldn't strike something. We was out of coffee, so Jim and I better go along with them in the canoe and get some.

When we got there, there warn't nobody stirring; streets empty, and perfectly dead and still, like Sunday. We found a sick nigger sunning himself in a back yard, and he said everybody that warn't too young or too sick or too old was gone to camp-meeting, about two miles back in the woods. The king got the directions, and allowed he'd go and work that camp-meeting for all it was worth, and I might go, too.

The duke said what he was after was a printing office. We found it; a little bit of a concern, up over a carpenter shop – carpenters and printers all gone to the meeting, and no doors locked. It was a dirty, littered-up place, and had ink marks, and handbills with pictures of horses and runaway niggers on them, all over the walls. The duke shed his coat and said he was all right, now. So me and the king lit out for the camp-meeting.

We got there in about a half an hour, fairly dripping, for it was a most awful hot day. There was as much as a thousand people there, from twenty mile around. The woods was full of teams and wagons, hitched everywheres, feeding out of the wagon troughs and stomping to keep off the flies. There was sheds made out of poles and roofed over with branches, where they had lemonade and gingerbread to sell, and piles of water-melons and green corn and suchlike truck.

The preaching was going on under the same kinds of sheds, only they was bigger and held crowds of people. The benches was made out of outside slabs of logs, with holes bored in the round side to drive sticks into for legs. They didn't have no backs. The preachers had high platforms to stand on, at one end of the sheds. The women had on sun-bonnets; and some had linsey-woolsey frocks, some gingham ones, and a few of the young ones had on calico. Some of the young men was bare-footed, and some of the children didn't have on any clothes but just a tow-linen shirt. Some of the old women was knitting, and some of the young folks was courting on the sly.

The first shed we come to, the preacher was lining out a hymn. He lined out two lines, everybody sung it, and it was kind of grand to hear it, there was so many of them and they done it in such a rousing way; then he lined out two more for them to sing – and so on. The people woke up more and more, and sung louder and louder; and towards the end some begun to groan, and some begun to shout. Then the preacher begun to preach; and begun in earnest, too; and went weaving first to one side of the platform and then the other, and then a-leaning down over the front of it, with his arms and his body going all the time, and shouting his words out with all his might; and every now and then he would hold up his Bible and spread it open, and kind of pass it around this way and that, shouting, 'It's the brazen serpent in the wilderness! Look upon it and live!' And people would shout out, 'Glory! – A-a-*men*!' And so he went on, and the people groaning and crying and saying amen:

'Oh, come to the mourners' bench! come, black with sin! (*amen!*) come, sick and sore! (*amen!*) come, lame and halt, and blind! (*amen!*) come, pore and needy, sunk in shame! (*a-a-men!*) come all that's worn, and soiled, and suffering! – come with a broken spirit! come with a contrite heart! come in your rags and sin and dirt! the waters that cleanse is free, the door of heaven stands open – oh, enter in and be at rest!' (*a-a-men! glory, glory hallelujah!*)

And so on. You couldn't make out what the preacher said, any more, on account of the shouting and crying. Folks got up, everywheres in the crowd, and worked their way, just by main strength, to the mourners' bench, with the tears running down their faces; and when all the mourners had got up there to the front benches in a crowd, they sung, and shouted, and flung themselves down on the straw, just crazy and wild.

Well, the first I knowed, the king got a-going; and you could hear him over everybody; and next he went a-charging up on to the platform and the preacher he begged him to speak to the people, and he done it. He told them he was a pirate – been a pirate for thirty years, out in the Indian Ocean, and his crew was thinned out considerable, last spring, in a fight, and he was home now, to take out some fresh men, and thanks to goodness he'd been robbed last night, and put ashore off of a steamboat without a cent, and he was glad of it, it was the blessedest thing that ever happened to him, because he was a changed man now, and happy for the first time in his life; and poor as he was, he was going to start right off and work his way back to the Indian Ocean and put in the rest of his life trying to turn the pirates into the true path: for he could do it better than anybody else, being acquainted with all the pirate crews in that ocean; and though it would take him a long time to get there without money, he would get there anyway, and every time he convinced a pirate he would say to him, 'Don't you thank me, don't you give me no credit, it all belongs to them dear people in Pokeville camp-meeting, natural brothers and benefactors of the race – and that dear preacher there, the truest friend a pirate ever had!'

And then he busted into tears, and so did everybody. Then somebody sings out, 'Take up a collection for him, take up a collection!' Well, a half a dozen made a jump to do it, but somebody sings out, 'Let *him* pass the hat around!' Then everybody said it, the preacher too.

So the king went all through the crowd with his hat, swabbling his eyes, and blessing the people and praising them and thanking them for being so good to the poor pirates away off there; and every little while the prettiest kind of girls, with the tears running down their cheeks, would up and ask him would he let them kiss him, for to remember him by; and he always done it; and some of them he hugged and kissed as many as five or six times – and he was invited to stay a week; and everybody wanted him to live in their houses, and said they'd think it was an honour; but he said as this was the last day of the camp-meeting he couldn't do no good, and besides he was in a sweat to get to the Indian Ocean right off and go to work on the pirates.

When we got back to the raft and he come to count up, he found he had collected eighty-seven dollars and seventy-five cents. And then he had fetched away a three-gallon jug of whisky, too, that he found under a wagon when we was starting home through the woods. The king said, take it all around, it laid over any day he'd ever put in in the missionarying line. He said it warn't no use talking, heathens don't amount to shucks, alongside of pirates, to work a camp-meeting with.

The duke was thinking *he*'d been doing pretty well, till the king come to show up, but after that he didn't think so so much. He had set up and printed off two little jobs for farmers, in that printing office – horse bills – and took the money, four dollars. And he had got in ten dollars' worth of advertisements for the paper, which he said he would put in for four dollars if they would pay in advance – so they done it. The price of the paper was two dollars a year, but he took in three subscriptions for half a dollar apiece on condition of them paying him in advance; they were going to pay in cord-wood and onions, as usual, but he said he had just bought the concern and knocked down the price as low as he could afford it, and was going to run it for cash. He set up a little piece of poetry which he made, himself, out of his own head – three verses – kind of sweet and saddish – the name of it was, 'Yes, crush, cold world, this breaking heart' – and he left that all set up and ready to print in the paper and didn't charge nothing for it. Well, he took in nine dollars and a half, and said he'd done a pretty square day's work for it.

Then he showed us another little job he'd printed and hadn't charged for, because it was for us. It had a picture of a runaway nigger, with a bundle on a stick, over his shoulder, and '$200 reward' under it. The reading was all about Jim, and just described him to the dot. It said he run away from St Jacques's plantation, forty mile below New Orleans, last winter, and likely went north, and whoever would catch him and send him back, he could have the reward and expenses.

'Now,' says the duke, 'after to-night we can run in the day-time if we want to. Whenever we see anybody coming, we can tie Jim hand and foot with a rope, and lay him in the wigwam and show this handbill and say we captured him up the river, and were too poor to travel on a steamboat, so we got this little raft on credit from our friends and are going down to get the reward. Handcuffs and chains would look still better on Jim, but it wouldn't go well with the story of us being so poor. Too much like jewellery. Ropes are the correct thing – we must preserve the unities, as we say on the boards.'

We all said the duke was pretty smart, and there couldn't be no trouble about running day-times. We judged we could make miles enough that night to get out of the reach of the pow-wow we reckoned the duke's work in the printing office was going to make in that little town – then we coud boom right along, if we wanted to.

We laid low and kept still, and never shoved out till nearly ten o'clock; then we slid by, pretty wide away from the town, and didn't hoist our lanterns till we was clear out of sight of it.

When Jim called me to take the watch at four in the morning, he says: 'Huck, does you reck'n we gwyne to run across any mo' kings on dis trip?'

'No,' I says, 'I reckon not.'

'Well,' says he, 'dat's all right, den. I doan' mine one er two kings, but dat's enough. Dis one's powerful drunk, en de duke ain' much better.'

I found Jim had been trying to get him to talk French, so he could hear what it was like; but he said he had been in this country so long, and had so much trouble, he'd forgot it.

Chapter 21

It was after sun-up, now, but we went right on, and didn't tie up. The king and the duke turned out, by and by, looking pretty rusty; but after they'd jumped overboard and took a swim, it chippered them up a good deal. After breakfast the king he took a seat on a corner of the raft, and pulled off his boots and rolled up his britches, and let his legs dangle in the water, so as to be comfortable, and lit his pipe, and went to getting his *Romeo and Juliet* by heart. When he had got it pretty good, him and the duke begun to practise it together. The duke had to learn him over and over again, how to say every speech; and he made him sigh, and put his hand on his heart, and after a while he said he done it pretty well; 'only,' he says, 'you musn't bellow out *Romeo!* that way, like a bull – you must say it soft, and sick, and languishy, so – R-o-o-meo! that is the idea; for Juliet's a dear sweet mere child of a girl, you know, and she don't bray like a jackass.'

Well, next they got out a couple of long swords that the duke made out of oak laths, and begun to practise the sword-fight – the duke called himself Richard III; and the way they laid on and pranced around the raft was grand to see. But by and by the king tripped and fell overboard, and after that they took a rest, and had a talk about all kinds of adventures they'd had in other times along the river.

After dinner, the duke says:

'Well, Capet, we'll want to make this a first-class show, you know, so I guess we'll add a little more to it. We want a little something to answer encores with, anyway.'

'What's onkores, Bilgewater?'

The duke told him, and then says:

'I'll answer by doing the Highland fling or the sailor's hornpipe; and you – well, let me see – oh, I've got it – you can do Hamlet's soliloquy.'

'Hamlet's which?'

'Hamlet's soliloquy, you know; the most celebrated thing in Shakespeare. Ah, it's sublime, sublime! Always fetches the house. I haven't got it in the book – I've only got one volume – but I reckon I can piece it out from memory. I'll just walk up and down a minute, and see if I can call it back from recollection's vaults.'

So he went to marching up and down, thinking, and frowning horrible every now and then; then he would hoist up his eyebrows; next he would squeeze his hand on his forehead and stagger back and kind of moan; next he would sigh, and next he'd let on to drop a tear. It was beautiful to see him. By and by he got it. He told us to give attention. Then he strikes a most noble attitude, with one leg shoved forwards, and his arms stretched away up, and his head tilted back, looking up at the sky; and then he begins to rip and rave and grit his teeth; and after that, all through his speech he howled, and spread around, and swelled up his chest, and just knocked the spots out of any acting ever *I* see before. This is the speech – I learned it, easy enough, while he was learning it to the king:

To be, or not to be; that is the bare bodkin
That makes calamity of so long life;
For who would fardels bear, till Birnam Wood do come to Dunsinane,
But that the fear of something after death
Murders the innocent sleep,
Great nature's second course,
And makes us rather sling the arrows of outrageous fortune
Than fly to others that we know not of.
There's the respect must give us pause:
Wake Duncan with thy knocking! I would thou couldst:
For who would bear the whips and scorns of time,
The oppressor's wrong, the proud man's contumely,
The law's delay, and the quietus which his pangs might take,
In the dead waste and middle of the night, when churchyards yawn
In customary suits of solemn black,
But that the undiscovered country from whose bourne no traveller returns,
Breathes forth contagion on the world,
And thus the native hue of resolution, like the poor cat i' the adage,
Is sicklied o'er with care,
And all the clouds that lowered o'er our housetops,
With this regard their currents turn awry,
And lose the name of action.
'Tis a consummation devoutly to be wished. But soft you, the fair Ophelia:
Ope not thy ponderous and marble jaws,
But get thee to a nunnery – go!

Well, the old man he liked that speech, and he mighty soon got it so he could do it first rate. It seemed like he was just born for it; and when he had his hand in and was excited, it was perfectly lovely the way he would rip and tear and rair up behind when he was getting it off.

The first chance we got, the duke he had some show bills printed; and after that, for two or three days as we floated along, the raft was a most uncommon lively place, for there warn't nothing but sword-fighting and rehearsing – as the duke called it – going on all the time. One morning, when we was pretty well down the State of Arkansaw, we come in sight of a little one-horse town in a big bend; so we tied up about three-quarters of a mile above it, in the mouth of a crick which was shut in like a tunnel by the cypress trees, and all of us but Jim took the canoe and went down there to see if there was any chance in that place for our show.

We struck it mighty lucky; there was going to be a circus there that afternoon, and the country people was already beginning to come in, in all kinds of old shackly wagons, and on horses. The circus would leave before night, so our show would have a pretty good chance. The duke he hired the court house, and we went around and stuck up our bills. They read like this:

Shaksperean Revival! ! !
Wonderful Attraction!
For One Night Only!

The world renowned tragedians,
David Garrick the younger, of Drury Lane Theatre, London,
and
Edmund Kean the elder, of the Royal Haymarket Theatre, White-
chapel, Pudding Lane, Piccadilly, London, and the
Royal Continental Theatres, in their sublime
Shaksperean Spectacle entitled
The Balcony Scene
in
Romeo and Juliet! ! !
Romeo..Mr. Garrick.
Juliet..Mr. Kean
Assisted by the whole strength of the company!
New costumes, new scenery, new appointments!

Also:

The thrilling, masterly, and blood-curdling
Broad-sword conflict
In Richard III! ! !
Richard III..Mr. Garrick.
Richmond ....Mr. Kean.

also:

(by special request,)
Hamlet's Immortal Soliloquy! ! !
By the Illustrious Kean!
Done by him 300 consecutive nights in Paris!
For One Night Only.
On account of imperative European engagements!

Admission 25 cents; children and servants, 10 cents.

Then we went loafing around the town. The stores and houses was most all old shackly dried-up frame concerns that hadn't ever been painted; they was set up three or four foot above ground on stilts, so as to be out of reach of the water when the river was overflowed. The houses had little gardens around them, but they didn't seem to raise hardly anything in them but jimpson weeds, and sunflowers, and ash-piles, and old curled-up boots and shoes, and pieces of bottles, and rags, and played-out tinware. The fences was made of different kinds of boards, nailed on at different times; and they leaned every which-way, and had gates that didn't generly have but one hinge – a leather one. Some of the fences had been whitewashed, some time or another, but the duke said it was in C'lumbus's time, like enough. There was gerly hogs in the garden, and people driving them out.

All the stores was along one street. They had white-domestic awnings in front, and the country people hitched their horses to the awning-posts. There was empty dry-goods boxes under the awnings, and loafers roosting on them all day long, whittling them with their Barlow knives; and chawing tobacco, and gaping and yawning and stretching – a mighty ornery lot. They generly had on yellow straw hats most as wide as an umbrella, but didn't wear no coats nor waistcoats; they called one another Bill, and Buck, and Hank, and Joe, and Andy, and talked lazy and drawly, and used considerable many cuss-words. There was as many as one loafer leaning up against every awning-post, and he most always had his hands in his britches pockets, except when he fetched them out to lend a chaw of tobacco or scratch. What a body was hearing amongst them, all the time was:

'Gimme a chaw'v tobacker, Hank.'

'Cain't – I haint' got but one chaw left. Ask Bill.'

Maybe Bill he gives him a chaw; maybe he lies and says he ain't got none. Some of them kinds of loafers never has a cent in the world, nor a chaw of tobacco of their own. They get all their chawing by borrowing – they say to a fellow, 'I wisht you'd len' me a chaw, Jack, I just this minute give Ben Thompson the last chaw I had' – which is a lie, pretty much every time; it don't fool nobody but a stranger; but Jack ain't no stranger, so he says:

'*You* give him a chaw, did you? so did your sister's cat's grandmother. You pay me back the chaws you've already borry'd off'n me, Lafe Buckner, then I'll loan you one or two ton of it, won't charge you no back intrust nuther.'

'Well, I *did* pay you back some of it wunst.'

'Yes, you did – 'bout six chaws. You borry'd store tobacker and paid back nigger-head.'

Store tobacco is flat black plug, but these fellows mostly chaws the natural leaf twisted. When they borrow a chaw, they don't generly cut it off with a knife, but they set the plug in between their teeth, and gnaw with their teeth and tug at the plug with their hands till they get it in two – then sometimes the one that owns the tobacco looks mournful at it when it's handed back, and says, sarcastic:

'Here, gimme the *chaw*, and you take the *plug*.'

All the streets and lanes was just mud, they warn't nothing else *but* mud – mud as black as tar, and nigh about a foot deep in some places; and two or three inches deep in *all* the places. The hogs loafed and grunted around, everywheres. You'd see a muddy sow and a litter of pigs come lazying along the street and whollop herself right down in the way, where folks had to walk around her, and she'd stretch out, and shut her eyes, and wave her ears, whilst the pigs was milking her, and look as happy as if she was on salary. And pretty soon you'd hear a loafer sing out, 'Hi! *so* boy! sick him. Tige!' and away the sow would go, squealing most horrible, with a dog or two swinging to each ear, and three or four dozen more a-coming; and then you would see all the loafers get up and watch the thing out of sight, and laugh at the fun and look grateful for the noise. Then they'd settle back again till there was a dog-fight. There couldn't anything wake them up all over, and make them happy all over, like a dog-fight – unless it might be putting turpentine on a stray dog and setting fire to him, or tying a tin pan to his tail and see him run himself to death.

On the river front some of the houses was sticking out over the bank, and they was bowed and bent, and about ready to tumble in. The people had moved out of them. The bank was caved away under one corner of some others, and that corner was hanging over. People lived in them yet, but it was dangersome, because sometimes a strip of land as wide as a house caves in at a time. Sometimes a belt of land a quarter of a mile deep will start in and cave along and cave along till it all caves into the river in one summer. Such a town as that has to be always moving back, and back, and back, because the river's always gnawing at it.

The nearer it got to noon that day, the thicker and thicker was the wagons and horses in the streets, and more coming all the time. Families fetched their dinners with them, from the country, and eat them in the wagons. There was considerable whisky drinking going on, and I seen three fights. By and by somebody sings out:

'Here comes old Boggs! – in from the country for his little old monthly drunk – here he comes, boys!'

All the loafers looked glad – I reckoned they was used to having fun out of Boggs. One of them says:

'Wonder who he's a-gwyne to chaw up this time. If he'd a chawed up all the men he's ben a-gwyne to chaw up in the last twenty year, he'd have considerable ruputation, now.'

Another one says, 'I wisht old Boggs'd threaten me, 'cuz then I'd know I warn't gwyne to die for a thousan' year.'

Boggs comes a-tearing along on his horse, whooping and yelling like an Injun, and singing out:

'Cler the track, thar. I'm on the waw-path, and the price uv coffins is a-gwyne to raise.'

He was drunk, and weaving about in his saddle; he was over fifty year old, and had a very red face. Everybody yelled at him, and laughed at him, and sassed him, and he sassed back, and said he'd attend to them and lay them out in their regular turns, but he couldn't wait now, because he'd come to town to kill old Colonel Sherburn, and his motto was, 'Meat first, and spoon vittles to top off on.'

He see me, and rode up and says:

'Whar'd you come f'm boy? You prepared to die?'

Then he rode on. I was scared; but a man says:

'He don't mean nothing; he's always a carryin' on like that, when he's drunk. He's the best-naturedest old fool in Arkansaw – never hurt nobody, drunk nor sober.'

Boggs rode up before the biggest store in town and bent his head down so he could see under the curtain of the awning, and yells:

'Come out here, Sherburn! Come out and meet the man you've swindled. You're the houn' I'm after, and I'm a-gwyne to have you, too!'

And so he went on, calling Sherburn everything he could lay his tongue to, and the whole street packed with people listening and laughing and going on. By and by a proud-looking man about fifty-five – and he was a heap the best-dressed man in that town, too – steps out of the store, and the crowd drops back on each side to let him come. He says to Boggs, mighty calm and slow – he says:

'I'm tired of this; but I'll endure it till one o'clock. Till one o'clock, mind – no longer. If you open your mouth against me only once, after that time, you can't travel so far but I will find you.'

Then he turns and goes in. The crowd looked mighty sober; nobody stirred, and there warn't no more laughing. Boggs rode off blackguarding

Sherburn as loud as he could yell, all down the street; and pretty soon back he comes and stops before the store, still keeping it up. Some men crowded around him and tried to get him to shut up, but he wouldn't; they told him it would be one o'clock in about fifteen minutes, and so he *must* go home – he must go right away. But it didn't do no good. He cussed away, with all his might, and throwed his hat down in the mud and rode over it, and pretty soon away he went a-raging down the street again, with his grey hair a-flying. Everybody that could get a chance at him tried their best to coax him off of his horse so they could lock him up and get him sober; but it warn't no use – up the street he would tear again, and give Sherburn another cussing. By and by somebody says:

'Go for his daughter! – quick, go for his daughter; sometimes he'll listen to her. If anybody can persuade him, she can.'

So somebody started on a run. I walked down street a ways, and stopped. In about five or ten minutes, here comes Boggs again – but not on his horse. He was a-reeling across the street towards me, bareheaded, with a friend on both sides of him aholt of his arms and hurryin him along. He was quiet, and looked uneasy; and he warn't hanging back any, but was doing some of the hurrying himself. Somebody sings out:

'Boggs!'

I looked over there to see who said it, and it was that Colonel Sherburn. He was standing perfectly still in the street, and had a pistol raised in his right hand – not aiming it, but holding it out with the barrel tilted up towards the sky. The same second I see a young girl coming on the run, and two men with her. Boggs and the men turned round, to see who called him, and when they see the pistol the men jumped to one side, and the pistol barrel come down slow and steady to a level – both barrels cocked. Boggs throws up both of his hands, and says, 'O Lord, don't shoot!' Bang! goes the first shot, and he staggers back clawing at the air – bang! goes the second one, and he tumbles backwards on to the ground, heavy and solid, with his arms spread out. That young girl screamed out, and comes rushing, and down she throws herself on her father, crying, and saying, 'Oh, he's killed him, he's killed him!' The crowd closed up around them, and shouldered and jammed one another, with their necks stretched, trying to see, and people on the inside trying to shove them back, and shouting, 'Back, back! give him air, give him air.'

Colonel Sherburn he tossed his pistol on to the ground, and turned around on his heels and walked off.

They took Boggs to a little drug store, the crowd pressing around, just the same, and the whole town following, and I rushed and got a good place at the window, where I was close to him and could see in. They laid him on the floor, and put one large Bible under his head, and opened another one and spread it on his breast – but they tore open his shirt first, and I seen where one of the bullets went in. He made about a dozen long gasps, his breast lifting the Bible up when he drawed in his breath, and letting it down again when he breathed it out – and after that he laid still; he was dead. Then they pulled his daughter away from him, screaming and crying, and took her off. She was about sixteen, and very sweet and gentle-looking, but awful pale and scared.

Well, pretty soon the whole town was there, squirming and scrouging and pushing and shoving to get at the window and have a look, but people that had the places wouldn't give them up, and folks behind them was saying all the time, 'Say, now, you've looked enough, you fellows; 'taint right and 'taint fair, for you to stay thar all the time, and never give nobody a chance; other folks has their rights as well as you.'

There was considerable jawing back, so I slid out, thinking maybe there was going to be trouble. The streets was full, and everybody was excited. Everybody that seen the shooting was telling how it happened, and there was a big crowd packed around each one of these fellows, stretching their necks and listening. One long lanky man, with long hair and a big white fur stove-pipe hat on the back of his head, and a crooked-handled cane, marked out the places on the ground where Boggs stood, and where Sherburn stood, and the people following him around from one place to t'other and watching everything he done, and bobbing their heads to show they understood, and stooping a little, and resting their hands on their thighs to watch him mark the places on the ground with his cane; and then he stood up straight and stiff where Sherburn had stood, frowning and having his hat-brim down over his eyes, and sung out, 'Boggs!' and then fetched his cane down slow to a dead level, and says 'Bang!' staggered backwards, says 'Bang!' again, and fell down flat on his back. The people that had seen the thing said he done it perfect; said it was just exactly the way it all happened. Then as much as a dozen people got out their bottles and treated him.

Well, by and by somebody said Sherburn ought to be lynched. In about a minute everybody was saying it; so away they went, mad and yelling, and snatching down every clothes-line they come to, to do the hanging with.

Chapter 22

They swarmed up the street towards Sherburn's house, a-whooping and yelling and raging like Injuns, and everything had to clear the way or get run over and tromped to mush, and it was awful to see. Children was heeling it ahead of the mob, screaming and trying to get out of the way; and every window along the road was full of women's heads, and there was nigger boys in every tree, and bucks and wenches looking over every fence; and as soon as the mob would get nearly to them they would break and skaddle back out of reach. Lots of the women and girls was crying and taking on, scared most to death.

They warmed up in front of Sherburn's palings as thick as they could jam together, and you couldn't hear yourself think for the noise. It was a little twenty-foot yard. Some sung out, 'Tear down the fence! tear down the fence!' Then there was a racket of ripping and tearing and smashing, and down she goes, and the front wall of the crowd begins to roll in like a wave.

Just then Sherburn steps out on to the roof of his little front porch, with a double-barrel gun in his hand, and takes his stand perfectly calm and deliberate, not saying a word. The racket stopped, and the wave sucked back.

Sherburn never said a word – just stood there, looking down. The stillness was awful creepy and uncomfortable. Sherburn run his eye slow along the crowd; and wherever it struck, the people tried a little to outgaze him, but they couldn't; they dropped their eyes and looked sneaky. Then pretty soon Sherburn sort of laughed; not the pleasant kind, but the kind that makes you feel like when you are eating bread that's got sand in it.

Then he says, slow and scornful:

'The idea of *you* lynching anybody! It's amusing. The idea of you thinking you had pluck enough, to lynch a *man*! Because you're brave enough to tar and feather poor friendless cast-out women that come along here, did that make you think you had grit enough to lay your hands on a *man*? Why, a *man*'s safe in the hands of ten thousand of your kind – as long as it's day-time and you're not behind him.

'Do I know you? I know you clear through. I was born and raised in the South, and I've lived in the North; so I know the average all around. The average man's a coward. In the North he lets anybody walk over him that wants to, and goes home and prays for a humble spirit to bear it. In the South one man, all by himself, has stopped a stage full of men, in the day-time, and robbed the lot. Your newspapers call you a brave people so much that you think you *are* braver than any other people – whereas you're just *as* brave, and no braver. Why don't your juries hang murderers? Because they're afraid the man's friends will shoot them in the back, in the dark – and it's just what they *would* do.

'So they always acquit; and then a *man* goes in the night, with a hundred masked cowards at his back, and lynches the rascal. Your mistake is, that you didn't bring a man with you; that's one mistake, and the other is that you didn't come in the dark, and fetch your masks. You brought *part* of a man – Buck Harkness, there – and if you hadn't had him to start you, you'd a taken it out in blowing.

'You didn't want to come. The average man don't like trouble and danger. *You* don't like trouble and danger. But if only *half* a man – like Buck Harkness, there – shouts "Lynch him, lynch him!" you're afraid to back down – afraid you'll be found out to be what you are – *cowards* – and so you raise a yell, and hang youselves on to that half-a-man's coat-tail, and come raging up here, swearing what big things you're going to do. The pitifullest thing out is a mob; that's what an army is – a mob; they don't fight with courage that's born in them, but with courage that's borrowed from their mass, and from their officers. But a mob without any *man* at the head of it, is *beneath* pitifulness. Now the thing for *you* to do, is to droop your tails and go home and crawl in a hole. If any real lynching's going to be done, it will be done in the dark, Southern fashion; and when they come they'll bring their masks, and fetch a *man* along. Now *leave* – and take your half-a-man with you' – tossing his gun up across his left arm and cocking it, when he says this.

The crowd washed back sudden, and then broke all apart and went tearing off every which way, and Buck Harkness he heeled it after them, looking tolerable cheap. I could a stayed, if I'd a wanted to, but I didn't want to.

I went to the circus, and loafed around the back side till the watchman went by, and then dived in under the tent. I had my twenty-dollar gold piece and some other money, but I reckoned I better save it, because there ain't no telling how soon you are going to need it, away from home and amongst strangers, that way. You can't be too careful. I ain't opposed to spending money on circuses, when there ain't no other way, but there ain't no use in *wasting* it on them.

It was a real bully circus. It was the splendidest sight that ever was, when they all come riding in, two and two, a gentleman and lady, side by side, the men just in their drawers and under-shirts, and no shoes nor stirrups, and resting their hands on their thighs, easy and comfortable – there must a been twenty of them – and every lady with a lovely complexion, and perfectly beautiful, and looking just like a gang of real sure-enough queens, and dressed in clothes that cost millions of dollars, and just littered with diamonds. It was a powerful fine sight; I never see anything so lovely. And then one by one they got up and stood, and went a-weaving around the ring so gentle and wavy and graceful, the men looking ever so tall and airy and straight, with their heads bobbing and skimming along, away up there under the tent-roof, and every lady's rose-leafy dress flapping soft and silky around her hips, and she looking like the most loveliest parasol.

And then faster and faster they went, all of them dancing first one foot stuck out in the air and then the other, the horses leaning more and more, and the ring-master going round and round the centre-pole, cracking his whip and shouting 'hi! – hi!' and the clown cracking jokes behind him; and by and by all hands dropped the reins, and every lady put her knuckles on her hips and every gentleman folded his arms, and then how the horses did lean over and hump themselves? And so, one after the other they all skipped off into the ring, and made the sweetest bow I ever see, and then scampered out, and everybody clapped their hands and went just about wild.

Well, all through the circus they done the most astonishing things; and all the time that clown carried on so it most killed the people. The ring-master couldn't ever say a word to him but he was back at him quick as a wink with the funniest things a body ever said; and how he ever *could* think of so many of them, and so sudden and so pat, was that I couldn't noway understand. Why, I couldn't a thought of them in a year. And by and by a drunk man tried to get into the ring – said he wanted to ride; said he could ride as well as anybody that ever was. They argued and tried to keep him out, but he wouldn't listen, and the whole show come to a standstill. Then the people begun to holler at him and make fun of him, and that made him mad, and he begun to rip and tear; so that stirred up the people, and a lot of men begun to pile down off of the benches and swarm towards the ring, saying, 'Knock him down! throw him out!' and one or two women begun to scream. So, then, the ring-master he made a little speech, and said he hoped there wouldn't be no disturbance, and if the man would promise he wouldn't make no more trouble, he would let him ride, if he thought he could stay on the horse. So everybody laughed and said all right, and the man got on. The minute he was on, the horse begun to rip and tear and jump and cavort around, with two circus men hanging on to his bridle trying to hold him, and the drunk man hanging on to his neck, and his heels flying in the air every jump, and the whole crowd of people standing up shouting and laughing till the tears rolled down. And at last, sure enough, all the circus men could do, the horse broke loose, and away he went like the very nation, round and round the ring, with that sot laying down on him and hanging to his neck, with first one leg hanging most to the ground on one side, and then t'other one on t'other side, and the people just crazy. It warn't funny to me, though; I was all of a tremble to see his danger. But pretty soon he struggled up astraddle and grabbed the bridle, a-reeling this way and that; and the next minute he sprung up and dropped the bridle and stood! and the horse a-going like a house afire too. He just stood up there, a-sailing around as easy and comfortable as if he warn't ever drunk in his life – and then he begun to pull off his clothes and sling them. He shed them so thick they kind of clogged up the air, and altogether he shed seventeen suits. And then, there he was, slim and handsome, and dressed the gaudiest and prettiest you ever saw, and he lit into that horse with his whip and made him fairly hum – and finally skipped off, and made his bow and danced off to the dressing-room, and everybody just a-howling with pleasure and astonishment.

Then the ring-master he see how he had been fooled, and he *was* the sickest ring-master you ever see, I reckon. Why, it was one of his own men! He had got up that joke all out of his own head, and never let on to nobody. Well, I felt sheepish enough, to be took in so, but I wouldn't a been in that ring-master's place, not for a thousand dollars. I don't know; there may be bullier circuses than what that one was, but I never struck them yet. Anyways it was plenty good enough for *me*; and wherever I run across it, it can have all of *my* custom, every time.

Well, that night we had *our* show; but there warn't only about twelve people there; just enough to pay expenses. And they laughed all the time, and that made the duke mad; and everybody left, anyway, before the show was over, but one boy which was asleep. So the duke said these Arkansaw lunkheads couldn't come up to Shakespeare; what they wanted was low comedy – and maybe something ruther worse than low comedy, he reckoned. He said he could size their style. So next morning he got some big sheets of wrapping-paper and some black paint, and drawed off some handbills and stuck them up all over the village. The bills said:

AT THE COURT HOUSE!

FOR 3 NIGHTS ONLY!

The World-Renowned Tragedians

DAVID GARRICK THE YOUNGER!

AND

EDMUND KEAN THE ELDER!

Of the London and Continental
Theatres,

In their Thrilling Tragedy of

THE KING'S CAMELOPARD

OR

THE ROYAL NONESUCH ! ! !

Admission 50 *cents.*

Then at the bottom was the biggest line of all – which said:

LADIES AND CHILDREN NOT ADMITTED

'There,' says he, 'if that line don't fetch them, I don't know Arkansaw!'

Chapter 23

Well, all day him and the king was hard at it, rigging up a stage, and a curtain, and a row of candles for foot-lights; and that night the house was jam full of men in no time. When the place couldn't hold no more, the duke he quit tending door and went around the back way and come on to the stage and stood up before the curtain, and made a little speech, and praised up this tragedy, and said it was the most thrillingest one that ever was; and so he went on a-bragging about the tragedy, and about Edmund Kean the Elder, which was to play the main principal part in it; and at last when he'd got everybody's expectations up high enough, he rolled up the curtain, and the next minute the king come a-prancing out on all fours, naked; and he was painted all over, ring-streaked-and-striped, all sorts of colours, as splendid as a rainbow. And – but never mind the rest of his outfit, it was just wild, but it was awful funny. The people most killed themselves laughing; and when the king got done capering, and capered off behind the scenes, they roared and clapped and stormed and haw-hawed till he come back and done it over again; and after that, they made him do it another time. Well, it would a made a cow laugh to see the shines that old idiot cut.

Then the duke he lets the curtain down, and bows to the people, and says the great tragedy will be performed only two nights more, on accounts of pressing London engagements, where the seats is all sold already for it in Drury Lane; and then he makes them another bow, and says if he has succeeded in pleasing them and instructing them, he will be deeply obleeged if they will mention it to their friends and get them to come and see it.

Twenty people sings out:

'What, is it over? Is that *all*?'

The duke says 'yes.' Then there was a fine time. Everybody sings out 'sold,' and rose up mad, and was a-going for that stage and them tragedians. But a big, fine-looking man jumps up on a bench, and shouts:

'Hold on! Just a word, gentlemen.' They stopped to listen. 'We are sold – mighty badly sold. But we don't want to be the laughing-stock of this whole town, I reckon, and never hear the last of this thing as long as we live. *No.* What we want, is to go out of here quiet, and talk this show up, and sell the *rest* of the town! Then we'll all be in the same boat. Ain't that sensible?' ('You bet it is! – the jedge is right!' everybody sings out.) 'All right, then – not a word about any sell. Go along home, and advise everybody to come and see the tragedy.'

Next day you couldn't hear nothing around that town but how splendid that show was. House was jammed again, that night, and we sold this crowd the same way. When me and the king and the duke got home to the raft, we all had a supper; and by and by, about midnight, they made Jim and me back her out and float her down the middle of the river and fetch her in and hide her about two mile below town.

The third night the house was crammed again – and they warn't new-comers, this time, but people that was at the show the other two nights. I stood by the duke at the door, and I see that every man that went in had his pockets bulging, or something muffled up under his coat – and I see it warn't no perfumery neither, not by a long sight. I smelt sickly eggs by the barrel, and rotten cabbages, and such things; and if I know the signs of a dead cat being around, and I bet I do, there was sixty-four of them went in. I shoved in there for a minute, but it was too various for me, I couldn't stand it. Well, when the place couldn't hold no more people, the duke he give a fellow a quarter and told him to tend door for him a minute, and then he started around for the stage door, I after him; but the minute we turned the corner and was in the dark, he says:

'Walk fast, now, till you get away from the houses, and then shin for the raft like the dickens was after you!'

I done it, and he done the same. We struck the raft at the same time, and in less than two seconds we was gliding down stream, all dark and still, and edging towards the middle of the river, nobody saying a word. I reckoned the poor king was in for a gaudy time of it with the audience; but nothing of the sort; pretty soon he crawls out from under the wigwam, and says:

'Well, how'd the old thing pan out this time, Duke?'

He hadn't been up town at all.

We never showed a light till we was about ten mile below that village. Then we lit up and had a supper, and the king and the duke fairly laughed their bones loose over the way they'd served them people. The duke says:

'Greenhorns, flatheads! *I* knew the first house would keep mum and let the rest of the town get roped in; and I knew they'd lay for us the third night, and consider it was *their* turn now. Well, it *is* their turn, and I'd give something to know how much they take for it. I *would* just like to know how they're putting in their opportunity. They can turn it into a picnic if they want to – they brought plenty provisions.'

Them rapscallions took in four hundred and sixty-five dollars in that three nights. I never see money hauled in by the wagon-load like that, before.

By and by, when they was asleep and snoring, Jim says:

'Don't it 'sprise you, de way dem kings carries on, Huck?'

'No,' I says, 'it don't.'

'Why don't it, Huck?'

'Well, it don't, because it's in the breed. I reckon they're all alike.'

'But, Huck, dese kings o' ourn is reglar rapscallions; dat's jist what dey is; dey's reglar rapscallions.'

'Well, that's what I'm a-saying; all kings is mostly rapscallions, as fur as I can make out.'

'Is dat so?'

'You read about them once – you'll see. Look at Henry the Eight; this'n's a Sunday school superintendent to *him*. And look at Charles Second, and Louis Fourteen, and Louis Fifteen, and James Second, and Edward Second, and Richard Third, and forty more; besides all them Saxon heptarchies that used to rip around so in old times and raise Cain. My, you ought to see old Henry the Eight when he was in bloom. He *was* a blossom. He used to marry a new wife every day, and chop off her head next morning. And he would do it just as indifferent as if he was ordering up eggs. "Fetch up Nell Gwynn," he says. They fetch her up. Next morning, "Chop off her head!" And they chop it off. "Fetch up Jane Shore," he says; and up she comes. Next morning, "Chop off her head" – and they chop it off. "Ring up Fair Rosamun." Fair Rosamun answers the bell. Next morning, "Chop off her head." And he made every one of them tell him a tale every night; and he kept that up till he had hogged a thousand and one tales that way, and then he put them all in a book, and called it Domesday Book – which was a good name and stated the case. You don't know kings, Jim, but I know them; and this old rip of ourn is one of the cleanest I've struck in history. Well, Henry, he takes a notion he wants to get up some trouble with this country. How does he go at it – give notice? – give the country a show? No. All of a sudden he heaves all the tea in Boston Harbour overboard, and whacks out a declaration of independence, and dares them to come on. That was *his* style – he never give anybody a chance. He had suspicions of his father, the Duke of Wellington. Well, what did he do? – ask him to show up? No – drownded him in a butt of mamsey, like a cat. S'pose people left money laying around where he was – what did he do? He collared it. S'pose he contracted to do a thing; and you paid him, and didn't set down there and see that he done it – what did he do? He always done the other thing. S'pose he opened his mouth – what then? If he didn't shut it up powerful quick, he'd lose a lie, every time. That's the kind of a bug Henry was; and if we'd a had him along 'stead of our kings, he'd a fooled that town a heap worse than ourn done. I don't say that ourn is lambs, because they ain't, when you come right down to the cold facts; but they ain't nothing to *that* old ram, anyway. All I say is, kings is kings, and you got to make allowances. Take them all around, they're a mighty ornery lot. It's the way they're raised.'

'But dis one do *smell* so like de nation, Huck.'

'Well, they all do, Jim. *We* can't help the way a king smells; history don't tell no way.'

'Now de duke, he's a tolerble likely man, in some ways.'

'Yes, a duke's different. But not very different. This one's a middling hard lot for a duke. When he's drunk, there ain't no near-sighted man could tell him from a king.'

'Well, anyways, I doan' hanker for no mo' un um, Huck. Dese is all I kin stan'.'

'It's the way I feel, too, Jim. But we've got them on our hands, and we got to remember what they are, and make allowances. Sometimes I wish we could hear of a country that's out of kings.'

What was the use to tell Jim these warn't real kings and dukes? It wouldn't a done no good; and besides, it was just as I said; you couldn't tell them from the real kind.

I went to sleep, and Jim didn't call me when it was my turn. He often done that. When I waked up, just at day-break, he was setting there with his head down betwixt his knees, moaning and mourning to himself. I didn't take notice, nor let on. I knowed what it was about. He was thinking about his wife and his children, away up yonder, and he was low and homesick; because he hadn't ever been away from home before in his life; and I do believe he cared just as much for his people as white folks does for ther'n. It don't seem natural, but I reckon it's so. He was often moaning and mourning that way, nights, when he judged I was asleep, and saying, 'Po' little 'Lizabeth! po' little Johnny! it's mighty hard; I spec' I ain't ever gwyne to see you no mo', no mo'!' He was a mighty good nigger, Jim was.

But this time I somehow got to talking to him about his wife and young ones; and by and by he says:

'What makes me feel so bad dis time, 'uz bekase I hear sumpn over yonder on de bank like a whack, er a slam, while ago, en it mine me er de time I treat my little 'Lizabeth so ornery. She warn't on'y 'bout fo' year ole, en she tuck de sk'yarlet-fever, en had a powful rough spell; but she got well, en one day she was a-stannin' aroun', en I says to her, I says:

'"Shet de do'."'

'She never done it; jis' stood dah, kiner smilin' up at me. It make me mad; en I says agin' mighty loud, I says:

'"Doan' you hear me? – shet de do'!"'

'She jis' stood de same way, kiner smilin' up. I was a-bilin'! I says:

'"I lay I *make* you mine!"'

'En wid dat I fetch' her a slap side de head dat sont her a-sprawlin'. Den I went into de yuther room, en' uz gone 'bout ten minutes; en when I come back, dah was dat do' a-stannin' open *yit*, en dat chile stannin' mos' right in it, a-lookin' down and mournin', en de tears runnin' down. My, but I *wuz* mad, I was a-gwyne for de chile, but jis' den – it was a do' dat open innerds – jis' den, 'long come de wind en slam it to, behine de chile, ker-*blam*! – en my lan', de chile never move'! My breff mos' hop outer me; en I feel so – so – I doan' know *how* I feel. I crope out, all a-tremblin', en crope aroun' en open de do' easy en slow, en poke my head in behine de chile, sof' en still, en all uv a sudden, I says *pow*! jis' as loud as I could yell. *She never budge!* Oh, Huck, I bust out a-cryin' en grab her up in my arms, en say, "Oh, de po' little thing! de Lord God Almighty fogive po' ole Jim, kaze he never gwyne to fogive hisself as long's he live!' Oh, she was plumb deef en dumb, Huck, plumb deef en dumb – en I'd ben a-treat'n her so!'

Chapter 24

Next day, towards night, we laid up under a little willow tow-head out in the middle, where there was a village on each side of the river, and the duke and the king begun to lay out a plan for working them towns. Jim he spoke to the duke, and said he hoped it wouldn't take but a few hours, because it got mighty heavy and tiresome to him when he had to lay all day in the wigwam tied with the rope. You see, when we left him all alone we had to tie him, because if anybody happened on him all by himself and not tied, it wouldn't look much like he was a runaway nigger, you know. So the duke said it *was* kind of hard to have to lay roped all day, and he'd cipher out some way to get around it.

He was uncommon bright, the duke was, and he soon struck it. He dressed Jim up in King Lear's outfit – it was a long curtain-calico gown, and a white horse-hair wig and whiskers; and then he took his theatre-paint and painted Jim's face and hands and ears and neck all over a dead dull solid blue, like a man that's been drownded nine days. Blamed if he warn't the horriblest looking outrage I ever see. Then the duke took and wrote out a sign on a shingle so –

Sick Arab – but harmless when not out of his head.

And he nailed that shingle to a lath, and stood the lath up four or five foot in front of the wigwam. Jim was satisfied. He said it was a sight better than laying tied a couple of years every day and trembling all over every time there was a sound. The duke told him to make himself free and easy, and if anybody ever come meddling around, he must hop out of the wigwam, and carry on a little, and fetch a howl or two like a wild beast, and he reckoned they would light out and leave him alone. Which was sound enough judgment; but you take the average man, and he wouldn't wait for him to howl. Why, he didn't only look like he was dead, he looked considerable more than that.

These rapscallions wanted to try the Nonesuch again, because there was so much money in it, but they judged it wouldn't be safe, because maybe the news might a worked along down by this time. They couldn't hit no project that suited, exactly; so at last the duke said he reckoned he'd lay off and work his brains an hour or two and see if he couldn't put up something on the Arkansaw village; and the king he allowed he would drop over to t'other village, without any plan, but just trust in Providence to lead him the profitable way – meaning the devil, I reckon. We had all bought store clothes where we stopped last; and now the king put his'n on, and he told me to put mine on. I done it, of course. The king's duds was all black, and he did look real swell and starchy. I never knowed how clothes could change a body before. Why, before, he looked like the orneriest old rip that ever was; but now, when he'd take off his new white beaver and make a bow and do a smile, he looked that grand and good and pious that you'd say he had walked right out of the ark, and maybe was old Leviticus himself. Jim cleaned up the canoe, and I got my paddle ready. There was a big steamboat laying at the shore away up under the point, about three mile above town – been there a couple of hours, taking on freight. Says the king:

'Seein' how I'm dressed, I reckon maybe I better arrive down from St Louis or Cincinnati, or some other big place. Go for the steamboat, Huckleberry; we'll come down to the village on her.'

I didn't have to be ordered twice, to go and take a steamboat ride. I fetched the shore a half a mile above the village, and then went scooting along the bluff bank in the easy water. Pretty soon we come to a nice innocent-looking young country jake setting on a log swabbing the sweat off of his face, for it was powerful warm weather; and he had a couple of big carpet-bags by him.

'Run her nose in shore,' says the king. I done it. 'Wher' you bound for, young man?'

'For the steamboat; going to Orleans.'

'Git aboard,' says the king. 'Hold on a minute, my servant'll he'p you with them bags. Jump out and he'p the gentleman, Adolphus' – meaning me, I see.

I done so, and then we all three started on again. The young chap was mighty thankful; said it was tough work toting his baggage such weather. He asked the king where he was going, and the king told him he'd come down the river and landed at the other village this morning, and how he was going up a few mile to see an old friend on a farm up there. The young fellow says:

'When I first see you, I says to myself, "It's Mr. Wilks, sure, and he come mighty near getting here in time." But then I says again, "No, I reckon it ain't him, or else he wouldn't be paddling up the river." You *ain't* him, are you?'

'No, my name's Blodgett – Alexander Blodgett – *Reverend* Alexander Blodgett, I s'pose I must say, as I'm one o' the Lord's poor servants. But still I'm jist as able to be sorry for Mr. Wilks for not arriving in time, all the same, if he's missed anything by it – which I hope he hasn't.'

'Well, he don't miss any property by it, because he'll get that all right;

but he's missed seeing his brother Peter die – which he mayn't mind, nobody can tell as to that – but his brother would give anything in this world to see *him* before he died; never talked about nothing else all these three weeks; hadn't seen him since they was boys together – and hadn't ever see his brother William at all – that's the deef and dumb one – William ain't more than thirty or thirty-five. Peter and George was the only ones that come out here; George was the married brother; him and his wife both died last year. Harvey and William's the only ones that's left now; and, as I was saying, they haven't got here in time.'

'Did anybody send 'em word?'

'Oh, yes; a month or two ago, when Peter was first took; because Peter said then that he sorter felt like he warn't going to get well this time. You see, he was pretty old, and George's g'yirls was too young to be much company for him, except Mary Jane the red-headed one; and so he was kinder lonesome after George and his wife died, and didn't seem to care much to live. He most desperately wanted to see Harvey – and William too, for that matter – because he was one of them kind that can't bear to make a will. He left a letter behind for Harvey, and said he'd told in it where his money was hid, and how he wanted the rest of the property divided up so George's g'yirls would be all right – for George didn't leave nothing. And that letter was all they could get him to put a pen to.'

'Why do you reckon Harvey don't come? Wher' does he live?'

'Oh, he lives in England – Sheffield – preaches there – hasn't ever been in this country. He hasn't had any too much time – and besides he mightn't a got the letter at all, you know.'

'Too bad, too bad he couldn't a lived to see his brothers, poor soul. You going to Orleans, you say?'

'Yes, but that ain't only a part of it. I'm going in a ship, next Wednesday, for Ryo Janeero, where my uncle lives.'

'It's a pretty long journey. But it'll be lovely; I wisht I was a-going. Is Mary Jane the eldest? How old is the others?'

'Mary Jane's nineteen, Susan's fifteen, and Joanna's about fourteen – that's the one that gives herself to good works and has a hare-lip.'

'Poor things! to be left alone in the cold world so.'

'Well, they could be worse off. Old Peter had friends, and they ain't going to let them come to no harm. There's Hobson, the Babtis' preacher; and Deacon Lot Hovey, and Ben Rucker, and Abner Shackleford, and Levi Bell, the lawyer; and Dr. Robinson, and their wives, and the widow Bartley, and – well, there's a lot of them; but these are the ones that Peter was thickest with, and used to write about sometimes, when he wrote home; so Harvey'll know where to look for friends when he gets here.'

Well, the old man he went on asking questions till he just fairly emptied that young fellow. Blamed if he didn't inquire about everybody and everything in that blessed town, and all about all the Wilkses; and about Peter's business – which was a tanner; and about George's – which was a carpenter; and about Harvey's – which was a dissentering minister; and so on, and so on. Then he says:

'What did you want to walk all the way up to the steamboat for?'

'Because she's a big Orleans boat, and I was afeard she mightn't stop there. When they're deep they won't stop for a hail. A Cincinnati boat will, but this is a St Louis one.'

'Was Peter Wilks well off?'

'Oh, yes, pretty well off. He had houses and land, and it's reckoned he left three or four thousand in cash hid up som'ers.'

'When did you say he died?'

'I didn't say, but it was last night.'

'Funeral to-morrow, likely?'

'Yes, 'bout the middle of the day.'

'Well, it's all terrible sad; but we've all got to go, one time or another. So what we want to do is to be prepared; then we're all right.'

'Yes, sir, it's the best way. Ma used to always say that.'

When we struck the boat, she was about done loading, and pretty soon she got off. The king never said nothing about going aboard, so I lost my ride, after all. When the boat was gone, the king made me paddle up another mile to a lonesome place, then he got ashore, and says:

'Now hustle back, right off, and fetch the duke up here, and the new carpet-bags. And if he's gone over to t'other side, go over there and git him. And tell him to git himself up regardless. Shove along, now.'

I see what *he* was up to; but I never said nothing, of course. When I got back with the duke, we hid the canoe and then they set down on a log, and the king told him everything just like the young fellow had said it – every last word of it. And all the time he was a-doing it, he tried to talk like an Englishman; and done it pretty well too, for a slouch. I can't imitate him, and so I ain't a-going to try to; but he really done it pretty good. Then he says:

'How are you on the deef and dumb, Bilgewater?'

The duke said, leave him alone for that; said he had played a deef and dumb person on the histrionic boards. So then they waited for a steamboat.

About the middle of the afternoon a couple of little boats come along, but they didn't come from high enough up the river; but at last there was a big one, and they hailed her. She sent out her yawl, and we went aboard, and she was from Cincinnati; and when they found we only wanted to go four or five mile, they was booming mad, and give us a cussing, and said they wouldn't land us. But the king was calm. He says:

'If gentlemen kin afford to pay a dollar a mile apiece, to be took on and

'. . . at last there was a big steamboat and they hailed her'

put off in a yawl, a steamboat kin afford to carry 'em, can't it?'

So they softened down and said it was all right; and when we got to the village, they yawled us ashore. About two dozen men flocked down, when they see the yawl a-coming; and when the king says:

'Kin any of you gentlemen tell me wher' Mr. Peter Wilks lives?' they give a glance at one another, and nodded their heads, as much as to say, 'What d' I tell you?' Then one of them says, kind of soft and gentle:

'I'm sorry, sir, but the best we can do is to tell you where he *did* live yesterday evening.'

Sudden as winking, the ornery old cretur went all to smash, and fell up against the man, and put his chin on his shoulder, and cried down his back, and says:

'Alas, alas! our poor brother – gone, and we never got to see him; oh, it's too, *too* hard!

Then he turns around, blubbering, and makes a lot of idiotic signs to the duke on his hands, and blamed if *he* didn't drop a carpet-bag and bust out a-crying. If they warn't the beatenest lot, them two frauds, that ever I struck.

Well, the men gethered around, and sympathized with them, and said all sorts of kind things to them, and carried their carpet-bags up the hill for them, and let them lean on them and cry, and told the king all about his brother's last moments, and the king he told it all over again on his hands to the duke, and both of them took on about that dead tanner like they'd lost the twelve disciples. Well, if ever I struck anything like it, I'm a nigger. It was enough to make a body ashamed of the human race.

Chapter 25

The news was all over the town in two minutes, and you could see the people tearing down on the run, from every which way, some of them putting on their coats as they come. Pretty soon we was in the middle of a crowd, and the noise of the tramping was like a soldier-march. The windows and door-yards was full; and every minute somebody would say, over a fence:

'Is it *them*?'

And somebody trotting along with the gang would answer back and say:

'You bet it is.'

When we got to the house, the street in front of it was packed, and the three girls was standing in the door. Mary Jane *was* red-headed, but that don't make no difference, she was most awful beautiful, and her face and her eyes was all lit up like glory, she was so glad her uncles was come. The king he spread his arms, and Mary Jane she jumped for them, and the hare-lip jumped for the duke, and there they *had* it! Everybody most, leastways women, cried for joy to see them meet again at last and have such good times.

Then the king he hunched the duke, private – I see him do it – and then he looked around and see the coffin, over in the corner on two chairs; so then, him and the duke, with a hand across each other's shoulder, and t'other hand to their eyes, walked slow and solemn over there, everybody dropping back to give them room, and all the talk and noise stopping, people saying 'Sh!' and all the men taking their hats off and drooping their heads, so you could hear a pin fall. And when they got there, they bent over and looked in the coffin, and took one sight, and then they burst out a-crying so you could a heard them to Orleans, most; and then they put their arms around each other's necks, and hung their chins over each other's shoulders; and then for three minutes, or maybe four, I never see two men leak the way they done. And mind you, everybody was doing the same; and the place was that damp I never see anything like it. Then one of them got on one side of the coffin, and t'other on t'other side, and they kneeled down and rested their foreheads on the coffin, and let on to pray all to theirselves. Well, when it come to that, it worked the crowd like you never see anything like it, and so everybody broke down and went to sobbing right out loud – the poor girls, too; and every woman, nearly, went up to the girls, without saying a word, and kissed them, solemn, on the forehead, and then put their hand on their head, and looked up towards the sky, with the tears running down, and then busted out and went off sobbing and swabbing, and give the next woman a show. I never see anything so disgusting.

Well, by and by the king he gets up and comes forward a little, and works himself up and slobbers out a speech, all full of tears and flapdoodle about its being a sore trial for him and his poor brother to lose the diseased, and to miss seeing diseased alive, after the long journey of four thousand mile, but it's a trial that's sweetened and sanctified to us by this dear sympathy and these holy tears, and so he thanks them out of his heart and out of his brother's heart, because out of their mouths they can't, words being too weak and cold, and all that kind of rot and slush, till it was just sickening; and then he blubbers out a pious goody-goody Amen, and turns himself loose and goes to crying fit to bust.

And the minute the words was out of his mouth somebody over in the crowd struck up the doxolojer, and everybody joined in with all their might, and it just warmed you up and made you feel as good as church letting out. Music *is* a good thing; and after all that soul-butter and hogwash, I never see it freshen up things so, and sound so honest and bully.

Then the king begins to work his jaw again, and says how him and his nieces would be glad if a few of the main principal friends of the family would take supper here with them this evening, and help set up with the ashes of the diseased; and says if his poor brother laying yonder could speak, he knows who he would name, for they was names that was very dear to him, and mentioned often in his letters; and so he will name the same, to wit, as follows, viz: Rev. Mr. Hobson, and Deacon Lot Hovey, and Mr. Ben Rucker, and Abner Shackleford, and Levi Bell, and Dr. Robinson, and their wives, and the widow Bartley.

Rev. Hobson and Dr. Robinson was down to the end of the town' a-hunting together; that is, I mean the doctor was shipping a sick man to t'other world, and the preacher was pinting him right. Lawyer Bell was away up to Louisville on some business. But the rest was on hand, and so they all come and shook hands with the king and thanked him and talked to him; and then they shook hands with the duke, and didn't say nothing but just kept a-smiling and bobbing their heads like a passel of sapheads whilst he made all sorts of signs with his hands and said 'Goo-goo – goo-goo-goo,' all the time, like a baby that can't talk.

So the king he blatted along, and managed to inquire about pretty much everybody and dog in town, by his name, and mentioned all sorts of little things that happened one time or another in the town, or to George's family, or to Peter; and he always let on that Peter wrote him the things, but that was a lie, he got every blessed one of them out of that young flat-head that we canoed up to the steamboat.

Then Mary Jane she fetched the letter her father left behind, and the king he read it out loud and cried over it. It give the dwelling-house and three thousand dollars, gold, to the girls; and it give the tanyard (which was doing a good business), along with some other houses and land (worth about seven thousand), and three thousand dollars in gold to Harvey and William, and told where the six thousand cash was hid, down cellar. So these two frauds said they'd go and fetch it up, and have everything square and above board; and told me to come with a candle. We shut the cellar door behind us, and when they found the bag they spilt it out on the floor, and it was a lovely sight, all them yaller-boys. My, the way the king's eyes did shine! He slaps the duke on the shoulder, and says:

'Oh, *this* ain't bully, nor noth'n! Oh, no, I reckon not! Why, Biljy, it beats the Nonesuch, *don't* it?'

The duke allowed it did. They pawed the yaller boys, and sifted them through their fingers and let them jingle down on the floor; and the king says:

'It ain't no use talkin'; bein' brothers to a rich dead man, and representatives of furrin heirs that's got left, is the line for you and me, Bilge. Thish-yer comes of trust'n to Providence. It's the best way, in the long run. I've tried 'em all, and ther' ain't no better way.'

Most everybody would a been satisfied with the pile, and took it on trust; but no, they must count it. So they counts it, and it comes out four hundred and fifteen dollars short. Says the king:

'Dern him, I wonder what he done with that four hundred and fifteen dollars?'

They worried over that a while, and ransacked all around for it. Then the duke says:

'Well, he was a pretty sick man, and likely he made a mistake – I reckon that's the way of it. The best way's to let it go, and keep still about it. We can spare it.'

'Oh, shucks, yes, we can *spare* it. I don't k'yer noth'n 'bout that – it's the *count* I'm thinkin' about. We want to be awful square and open and above-board, here, you know. We want to lug this h-yer money upstairs and count it before everybody – then ther' ain't noth'n suspicious. But when the dead man says there's six thousand dollars, you know, we don't want to——'

'Hold on,' says the duke. 'Less make up the deffisit' – and he begun to haul out yaller-boys out of his pocket.

'It's a most amaz'n' good idea, duke – you *have* got a rattlin' clever head on you,' says the king. 'Blest if the old Nonesuch ain't a-heppin' us out agin' – and *he* begun to haul out yaller-jackets and stack them up.

It most busted them, but they made up the six thousand clean and clear.

'Say,' says the duke, 'I got another idea. Le's go upstairs and count this money, and then take and *give it to the girls.*'

'Good land, duke, lemme hug you! It's the most dazzling idea 'at ever a man struck. You have cert'nly got the most astonishin' head I ever see. Oh, this is the boss dodge, ther' ain't no mistake 'bout it. Let 'em fetch along their suspicions now, if they want to – this'll lay 'em out.'

When we got up stairs, everybody gethered around the table, and the king he counted it and stacked it up, three hundred dollars in a pile – twenty elegant little piles. Everybody looked hungry at it, and licked their chops. Then they raked it into the bag again, and I see the king begin to swell himself up for another speech. He says:

'Friends all, my poor brother that lays yonder has done generous by them that's left behind in the vale of sorrers. He has done generous by these-yer poor little lambs that he loved and sheltered, and that's left fatherless and motherless. Yes, and we that knowed him, knows that he would a done *more* generous by 'em if he hadn't ben afeard o' woundin' his dear William and me. Now, *wouldn't* he? Ther' ain't no question 'bout it, in *my* mind. Well, then – what kind o' brothers would it be, that'd stand in his way at sech a time? And what kind o' uncles would it be that'd rob – yes, *rob* – sech poor sweet lambs as these 'at he loved so, at sech a time? If I know William – and I *think* I do – he – well, I'll jest ask him.' He turns around and begins to make a lot of signs to the duke with his hands; and the duke he looks at him stupid and leather-headed a while, then all of a sudden he seems to catch his meaning, and jumps for the king, goo-gooing with all his might for joy, and hugs him about fifteen times before he lets up. Then the king says, 'I knowed it; I reckon *that*'ll convince anybody the way *he* feels about it. Here, Mary Jane, Susan, Joanner, take the money – take it *all*. It's the gift of him that lays yonder, cold but joyful.'

Mary Jane she went for him, Susan and the hare-lip went for the duke, and then such another hugging and kissing I never see yet. And everybody crowded up with the tears in their eyes, and most shook the hands off of them frauds, saying all the time:

'You *dear* good souls! – how *lovely*! – how *could* you!'

Well, then, pretty soon all hands got to talking about the diseased again, and how good he was, and what a loss he was, and all that; and before long a big iron-jawed man worked himself in there from outside, and stood a-listening and looking, and not saying anything; and nobody saying anything to him either, because the king was talking and they was all busy listening. The king was saying – in the middle of something he'd started in on—

'—they bein' partickler friends o' the diseased. That's why they're invited here this evenin'; but to-morrow we want *all* to come – everybody; for he respected everybody, he liked everybody, and so it's fitten that his funeral orgies sh'd be public.'

And so he went a-mooning on and on, liking to hear himself talk, and every little while he fetched in his funeral orgies again, till the duke he couldn't stand it no more; so he writes on a little scrap of paper, '*obsequies*, you old fool,' and folds it up and goes to goo-gooing and reaching it over people's heads to him. The king he reads it, and puts it in his pocket, and says:

'Poor William, afflicted as he is, his *heart*'s aluz right. Asks me to invite everybody to come to the funeral – wants me to make 'em all welcome. But he needn't a worried – it was jest what I was at.'

Then he weaves along again, perfectly calm, and goes to dropping in his funeral orgies again every now and then, just like he done before. And when he done it the third time, he says:

'I say orgies, not because it's the common term, because it ain't – obsequies bein' the common term – but because orgies is the right term. Obsequies ain't used in England no more, now – it's gone out. We say orgies now, in England. Orgies is better, because it means the thing you're after, more exact. It's a word that's made up out'n the Greek *orgo*, outside, open, abroad; and the Hebrew *jeesum*, to plant, cover up; hence in*ter*. So you see, funeral orgies is an open er public funeral.'

He was the *worst* I ever stuck. Well, the iron-jawed man he laughed right in his face. Everybody was shocked. Everybody says, 'Why *doctor!*' and Abner Shackleford says:

'Why, Robinson, hain't you heard the news? This is Harvey Wilks.'

The king he smiled eager, and shoved out his flapper, and says:

'*Is* it my poor brother's dear good friend and physician? I——'

'Keep your hands off of me!' says the doctor. '*You* talk like an Englishman – *don't* you? It's the worse imitation I ever heard. *You* Peter Wilks's brother? You're a fraud, that's what you are!'

Well, how they all took on! They crowded around the doctor, and tried to quiet him down, and tried to explain to him, and tell him how Harvey'd showed in forty ways that he *was* Harvey, and knowed everybody by name, and the names of the very dogs, and begged and *begged* him not to hurt Harvey's feelings and the poor girls' feelings, and all that; but it warn't no use, he stormed right along, and said any man that pretended to be an Englishman and couldn't imitate the lingo no better than what he did, was a fraud and a liar. The poor girls was hanging to the king and crying; and all of a sudden the doctor ups and turns on *them*. He says:

'I was your father's friend, and I'm your friend; and I warn you *as* a friend, and an honest one, that wants to protect you and keep you out of harm and trouble, to turn your backs on that scoundrel, and have nothing to do with him, the ignorant tramp, with his idiotic Greek and Hebrew as he calls it. He is the thinnest kind of an impostor – has come here with a lot of empty names and facts which he has picked up somewheres, and you take them for *proofs*, and are helped to fool yourselves by these foolish friends here, who ought to know better. Mary Jane Wilks, you know me for your friend, and for your unselfish friend, too. Now listen to me; turn this pitiful rascal out – I *beg* you to do it. Will you?'

Mary Jane straightened herself up, and my, but she was handsome! She says:

'*Here* is my answer.' She hove up the bag of money and put it in the king's hands, and says, 'Take this six thousand dollars, and invest for me and my sisters any way you want to and don't give us no receipt for it.'

Then she put her arm around the king on one side, and Susan and the harelip done the same on the other. Everybody clapped their hands and stomped on the floor like a perfect storm, whilst the king held up his head and smiled proud. The doctor says:

'All right, I wash *my* hands of the matter. But I warn you all that a time's coming when you're going to feel sick whenever you think of this day' – and away he went.

'All right, doctor,' says the king, kinder mocking him, 'we'll try and get 'em to send for you' – which made them all laugh, and they said it was a prime good hit.

Chapter 26

Well, when they was all gone, the king he asks Mary Jane how they was off for spare rooms, and she said she had one spare room, which would do for Uncle William, and she'd give her own room to Uncle Harvey, which was a little bigger, and she would turn into the room with her sisters and sleep on a cot; and up garret was a little cubby, with a pallet in it. The king said the cubby would do for his valley – meaning me.

So Mary Jane took us up, and she showed them their rooms, which was plain but nice. She said she'd have her frocks and a lot of other traps took out of her room if they was in Uncle Harvey's way, but he said they warn't. The frocks was hung along the wall, and before them was a curtain made out of calico that hung down to the floor. There was an old hair trunk in one corner, and a guitar box in another, and all sorts of little knick-knacks and jimcracks around, like girls brisken up a room with. The king said it was all the more homely and more pleasanter for these fixings, and so don't disturb them. The duke's room was pretty small, but plenty good enough, and so was my cubby.

That night they had a big supper, and all them men and women was there, and I stood behind the king and the duke's chairs and waited on them, and the niggers waited on the rest. Mary Jane she set at the head of the table, with Susan alongside of her, and said how bad the biscuits was, and how mean the preserves was, and how ornery and tough the fried chickens was – and all that kind of rot, the way women always do for to force out compliments; and the people all knowed everything was tip-top, and said so – said 'How *do* you get biscuits to brown so nice?' and 'Where, for the land's sake, *did* you get these amaz'n pickles?' and all that kind of humbug talky-talk, just the way people always does at a supper, you know.

And when it was all done, me and the hare-lip had supper in the kitchen off of the leavings, whilst the others was helping the niggers clean up the things. The hare-lip she got to pumping me about England, and blest if I didn't think the ice was getting thin, sometimes. She says:

'Did you ever see the king?'

'Who? William Fourth? Well, I bet I have – he goes to our church.' I knowed he was dead years ago, but I never let on. So when I says he goes to our church, she says:

'What – regular?'

'Yes – regular. His pew's right over opposite ourn – on t'other side the pulpit.'

'I thought he lived in London?'

'Well, he does. Where *would* he live?'

'But I thought *you* lived in Sheffield'

I see I was up a stump. I had to let on to get choked with a chicken bone, so as to get time to think how to get down again. Then I says:

'I mean he goes to our church regular when he's in Sheffield. That's only in the summer-time, when he comes there to take the sea baths.'

'Why, how you talk – Sheffield ain't on the sea.'

'Well, who said it was?'

'Why, you did.'

'I *didn't*, nuther.'

'You did!'

'I didn't.'

'You did.'

'I never said nothing of the kind.'

'Well, what *did* you say, then?'

'Said he come to take the sea *baths* – that's what I said.'

'Well, then! how's he going to take the sea baths if it ain't on the sea?'

'Looky here,' I says; 'did you ever see any Congress water?'

'Yes.'

'Well, did you have to go to Congress to get it?'

'Why, no.'

'Well, neither does William Fourth have to go to the sea to get a sea bath.'

'How does he get it, then?'

'Gets it the way people down here gets Congress water – in barrels. There in the palace at Sheffield they've got furnaces, and he wants his water hot. They can't bile that amount of water off there at the sea. They haven't got no conveniences for it.'

'Oh, I see, now. You might a said that in the first place and saved time.'

When she said that, I see I was out of the woods again, and so I was comfortable and glad. Next, she says:

'Do you go to church, too?'

'Yes – regular.'

'Where do you set?'

'Why in our pew.'

'*Whose* pew?'

'Why, *ourn* – your Uncle Harvey's.'

'His'n? What does *he* want with a pew?'

'Wants it to set in. What did you *reckon* he wanted with it?'

'Why, I thought he'd be in the pulpit.'

Rot him, I forgot he was a preacher. I see I was up a stump again, so I played another chicken bone and got another think. Then I says:

'Blame it, do you suppose there ain't but one preacher to a church?'

'Why, what do they want with more?'

'What! – to preach before a king! I never see such a girl as you. They don't have no less than seventeen.'

'Seventeen! My land! Why, I wouldn't set out such a string as that, not if I *never* got to glory. It must take 'em a week.'

'Shucks, they don't *all* of 'em preach the same day – only *one* of 'em.'

'Well, then, what does the rest of 'em do?'

'Oh, nothing much. Loll around, pass the plate – and one thing or another. But mainly they don't do nothing.'

'Well, then, what are they *for*?'

'Why, they're for *style*. Don't you know nothing?'

'Well, I don't *want* to know no such foolishness as that. How is servants treated in England? Do they treat 'em better'n we treat our niggers?'

'*No!* A servant ain't nobody there. They treat them worse than dogs.'

'Don't they give 'em holidays, the way we do, Christmas and New Year's week, and Fourth of July?'

'Oh, just listen! A body could tell *you* hain't ever been to England by that. Why, Hare-l – why, Joanna, they never see a holiday from year's end to year's end; never go to the circus, nor theatre, nor nigger shows, nor nowheres.'

'Nor church?'

'Nor church.'

'But *you* always went to church?'

Well, I was gone up again. I forgot I was the old man's servant. But next minute I whirled in on a kind of an explanation how a valley was different from a common servant, and *had* to go to church whether he wanted to or not, and set with the family, on account of its being the law. But I didn't do it pretty good, and when I got done I see she warn't satisfied. She says:

'Honest Injun, now, hain't you been telling me a lot of lies?'

'Honest Injun,' says I.

'None of it at all?'

'None of it at all. Not a lie in it,' says I.

'Lay your hand on this book and say it.'

I see it warn't nothing but a dictionary, so I laid my hand on it and said it. So then she looked a little better satisfied, and says:

'Well, then, I'll believe some of it; but I hope to gracious if I'll believe the rest.'

'What is it you won't believe, Joe?' says Mary Jane, stepping in with Susan behind her. 'It ain't right nor kind for you to talk so to him, and him a stranger and so far from his people. How would you like to be treated so?'

'That's always your way, Maim – always sailing in to help somebody before they're hurt. I hain't done nothing to him. He's told some stretchers, I reckon; and I said I wouldn't swallow it all; and that's every bit and grain I *did* say. I reckon he can stand a little thing like that, can't he?'

'I don't care whether 'twas little or whether 'twas big, he's here in our house and a stranger, and it wasn't good of you to say it. If you was in his place, it would make you feel ashamed; and so you oughtn't to say a thing to another person that will make *them* feel ashamed.'

'Why, Maim, he said——'

'It don't make no difference what he *said* – that ain't the thing. The thing is for you to treat him *kind*, and not be saying things to make him remember he ain't in his own country and amongst his own folks.'

I says to myself, *this* is a girl that I'm letting that ole reptile rob her of her money!

Then Susan *she* waltzed in; and if you'll believe me, she did give Hare-lip hark from the tomb!

Says I to myself, And this is *another* one that I'm letting him rob her of her money!

Then Mary Jane she took another inning, and went in sweet and lovely again – which was her way – but when she got done there warn't hardly anything left o' poor Hare-lip. So she hollered.

'All right, then,' says the other girls, 'you just ask his pardon.'

She done it, too. And she done it beautiful. She done it so beautiful it was good to hear; and I wished I could tell her a thousand lies, so she could do it again.

I says to myself, this is *another* one that I'm letting him rob her of her money. And when she got through, they all jest laid themselves out to make me feel at home and know I was amongst friends. I felt so ornery and low down and mean, that I says to myself, My mind's made up; I'll hive that money for them or bust.

So then I lit out – for bed, I said, meaning some time or another. When I got by myself, I went to thinking the thing over. I says to myself, Shall I go to that doctor, private, and blow on these frauds? No – that won't do. He might tell who told him; then the king and the duke would make it warm for me. Shall I go, private, and tell Mary Jane? No – I dasn't do it. Her face would give them a hint, sure; they've got the money, and they'd slide right out and get away with it. If she was to fetch in help, I'd get mixed up in the business, before it was done with, I judge. No, there ain't no good way but one. I got to steal that money, somehow; and I got to steal it some way that they won't suspicion that I done it. They've got a good thing, here; and they ain't a-going to leave till they've played this family and this town for all they're worth, so

I'll find a chance time enough. I'll steal it, and hide it; and by and by, when I'm away down the river, I'll write a letter and tell Mary Jane where it's hid. But I'd better hive it to-night, if I can, because the doctor maybe hasn't let up as much as he lets on he has; he might scare them out of here, yet.

So, thinks I, I'll go and search them rooms. Upstairs the hall was dark, but I found the duke's room, and started to paw around it with my hands; but I recollected it wouldn't be much like the king to let anybody else take care of that money but his own self; so then I went to his room and begun to paw around there. But I see I couldn't do nothing without a candle, and I dasn't light one, of course. So I judged I'd got to do the other thing – lay for them, and eavesdrop. About that time, I hears their footsteps coming, and was going to skip under the bed; I reached for it, but it wasn't where I thought it would be; but I touched the curtain that hid Mary Jane's frocks, so I jumped in behind that and snuggled in amongst the gowns, and stood there perfectly still.

They come in and shut the door; and the first thing the duke done was to get down and look under the bed. Then I was glad I hadn't found the bed when I wanted it. And yet, you know, it's kind of natural to hide under the bed when you are up to anything private. They sets down, then, and the king says:

'Well, what is it? and cut it middlin' short, because it's better for us to be down there a-whoopin'-up the mournin', then up here givin' 'em a chance to talk us over.'

'Well, this is it, Capet. I ain't easy; I ain't comfortable. That doctors lays on my mind. I wanted to know your plans. I've got a notion, and I think it's a sound one.'

'What is it, duke?'

'That we better glide out of this, before three in the morning, and clip it down the river with what we've got. Specially, seeing we got it so easy – *given* back to us, flung at our heads, as you may say, when of course we allowed to have to steal it back. I'm for knocking off and lighting out.'

That made me feel pretty bad. About an hour or two ago, it would a been a little different, but now it made me feel bad and disappointed. The king rips out and says:

'What! And not sell out the rest o' the property? March off like a passel o'' fools and leave eight or nine thous'n' dollars' worth o' property layin' around jest sufferin' to be scooped in? – and all good saleable stuff, too.'

The duke he grumbled; said the bag of gold was enough, and he didn't want to go no deeper – didn't want to rob a lot of orphans of *everything* they had.

'Why, how you talk!' says the king. 'We shan't rob 'em of nothing at all but jest this money. The people that *buys* the property is the suff'rers; because as soon's it's found out 'at we didn't own it – which won't be long after we've slid – the sale won't be valid, and it'll all go back to the estate. These yer orphans'll git their house back again, and that's enough for *them*; they're young and spry, and k'n easy earn a livin'. *They* ain't a-going to suffer. Why, jest think – there's thous'n's and thous'n's that ain't nigh so well off. Bless you, *they* ain't got noth'n to complain of.'

Well, the king he talked him blind; so at last he give in, and said all right, but said he believed it was blame' foolishness to stay, and that doctor hanging over them. But the king says:

'Cuss the doctor! What do we k'yer for *him*? Hain't we got all the fools in town on our side? and ain't that a big enough majority in any town?'

So they got ready to go downstairs again. The duke says:

'I don't think we put that money in a good place.'

That cheered me up. I'd begun to think I warn't going to get a hint of no kind to help me. The king says:

'Why?'

'Because Mary Jane'll be in mourning from this out; and first you know the nigger that does up the rooms will get an order to box these duds up and put 'em away; and do you reckon a nigger can run across money and not borrow some of it?'

'Your head's level agin, duke,' says the king; and he come a-fumbling under the curtain two or three foot from where I was. I stuck tight to the wall, and kept mighty still, though quivery; and I wondered what them fellows would say to me if they catched me; and I tried to think what I'd better do if they did catch me. But the king he got the bag before I could think more than about a half a thought, and he never suspicioned I was around. They took and shoved the bag through a rip in the straw tick that was under the feather bed, and crammed it in a foot or two amongst the straw and said it was all right, now, because a nigger only makes up the feather bed, and don't turn over the straw tick only about twice a year, and so it warn't in no danger of getting stole, now.

But I knowed better. I had it out of there before they was half-way downstairs. I groped along up to my cubby, and hid it there till I could get a chance to do better. I judged I better hide it outside of the house somewheres, because if they missed it they would give the house a good ransacking. I knowed that very well. Then I turned in, with my clothes all on; but I couldn't a gone to sleep, if I'd a wanted to, I was in such a sweat to get through with the business. By and by I heard the king and the duke come up; so I rolled off of my pallet and laid with my chin at the top of my ladder and waited to see if anything was going to happen. But nothing did.

So I held on till all the late sounds had quit and the early ones hadn't begun, yet; and then I slipped down the ladder.

Chapter 27

I crept to their doors and listened; they was snoring, so I tiptoed along, and got downstairs all right. There warn't a sound anywheres. I peeped through a crack of the dining-room door, and see the men that was watching the corpse all sound asleep on their chairs. The door was open into the parlour, where the corpse was laying, and there was a candle in both rooms. I passed along, and the parlour door was open; but I see there warn't nobody in there but the remainders of Peter; so I shoved on by; but the front door was locked, and the key wasn't there. Just then I heard somebody coming down the stairs, back behind me. I run in the parlour, and took a swift look around, and the only place I see to hide the bag was in the coffin. The lid was shoved along about a foot, showing the dead man's face down in there, with a wet cloth over it, and his shroud on. I tucked the money-bag in under the lid, just down beyond where his hands was crossed, which made me creep, they was so cold, and then I run back across the room and in behind the door.

The person coming was Mary Jane. She went to the coffin, very soft, and kneeled down and looked in; then she put up her handkerchief and I see she begun to cry, though I couldn't hear her, and her back was to me. I slid out, and as I passed the dining-room I thought I'd make sure them watchers hadn't seen me; so I looked through the crack and everything was all right. They hadn't stirred.

I slipped up to bed, feeling ruther blue, on accounts of the thing playing out that way after I had took so much trouble and run so much resk about it. Says I, if it could stay where it is, all right; because when we get down the river a hundred mile or two, I could write back to Mary Jane, and she could dig him up again and get it; but that ain't the thing that's going to happen; the thing that's going to happen is, the money'll be found when they come to screw on the lid. Then the king'll get it again, and it'll be a long day before he gives anybody another chance to smouch it from him. Of course I *wanted* to slide down and get it out of there, but I dasn't try it. Every minute it was getting earlier, now, and pretty soon some of them watchers would begin to stir, and I might get catched – catched with six thousand dollars in my hands that nobody hadn't hired me to take care of. I don't wish to be mixed up in no such business as that, I says to myself.

When I got downstairs in the morning the parlour was shut up, and the watchers was gone. There warn't nobody around but the family and the widow Bartley and our tribe. I watched their faces to see if anything had been happening, but I couldn't tell.

Towards the middle of the day the undertaker come, with his man, and they set the coffin in the middle of the room on a couple of chairs, and then set all our chairs in rows, and borrowed more from the neighbours till the hall and the parlour and the dining-room was full. I see the coffin lid was the way it was before, but I dasn't go to look in under it, with folks around.

Then the people begun to flock in, and the beats and the girls took seats in the front row at the head of the coffin, and for a half an hour the people filed around slow, in single rank, and looked down at the dead man's face a minute, and some dropped in a tear, and it was all very still and solemn, only the girls and the beats holding handkerchiefs to their eyes and keeping their heads bent, and sobbing a little. There warn't no other sound but the scraping of the feet on the floor, and blowing noses – because people always blows them more at a funeral than they do at other places except church.

When the place was packed full, the undertaker he slid around in his black gloves with his softy soothering ways, putting on the last touches, and getting people and things all shipshape and comfortable, and making no more sound than a cat. He never spoke; he moved people around, he squeezed in late ones, he opened up passage-ways, and done it all with nods and signs with his hands. Then he took his place over against the wall. He was the softest, glidingest, stealthiest man I ever see; and there warn't no more smile to him than there is to a ham.

They had borrowed a melodeum – a sick one; and when everything was ready, a young woman set down and worked it, and it was pretty skreeky and colicky, and everybody joined in and sung, and Peter was the only one that had a good thing, according to my notion. Then the Reverend Hobson opened up, slow and solemn, and begun to talk; and straight off the most outrageous row busted out in the cellar a body ever heard; it was only one dog, but he made a most powerful racket, and he kept it up, right along; the parson he had to stand there, over the coffin, and wait – you couldn't hear yourself think. It was right down awkward, and nobody didn't seem to know what to do. But pretty soon they see that long-legged undertaker make a sign to the preacher as much as to say, 'Don't you worry – just depend on me.' Then he stooped down and begun to glide along the wall, just his shoulders showing over the people's heads. So he glided along, and the pow-wow and racket getting more and more outrageous all the time; and at last, when he had gone around two sides of the room, he disappears down cellar. Then, in about two seconds we heard a whack, and the dog he finished up with a most amazing howl or two, and then everything was dead still, and the parson begun his solemn talk where he left off. In a minute or two here comes this undertaker's back and shoulders gliding along the wall again; and so he glided, and glided, around three sides of the room, and then rose up, and shaded his mouth with his hands, and stretched his neck out towards the preacher, over the people's heads, and says, in a kind of a coarse whisper, '*He had a rat!*' Then he drooped down and glided along the wall again to his place. You could see it was a great satisfaction to the people, because naturally they wanted to know. A little thing like that don't cost nothing, and it's just the little things that makes a man to be looked up to and liked. There warn't no more popular man in town than what that undertaker was.

Well, the funeral sermon was very good, but pison long and tiresome; and then the king he shoved in and got off some of his usual rubbage, and at last the job was through, and the undertaker begun to sneak up on the coffin with his screwdriver. I was in a sweat then, and watched him pretty keen. But he never meddled at all; just slid the lid along, as soft as mush, and screwed it down tight and fast. So there I was! I didn't know whether the money was in there, or not. So, says I, s'pose somebody has hogged that bag on the sly? – now how do *I* know whether to write to Mary Jane or not? S'pose she dug him up and didn't find nothing – what would she think of me? Blame it, I says, I might get hunted up and jailed; I'd better lay low and keep dark, and not write at all; the thing's awful mixed, now; trying to better it, I've worsened it a hundred times, and I wish to goodness I'd just let it alone, dad fetch the whole business!

They buried him, and we come back home, and I went to watching faces again – I couldn't help it, and I couldn't rest easy. But nothing come of it; the faces didn't tell me nothing.

The king he visited around, in the evening, and sweetened everybody up, and made himself ever so friendly; and he give out the idea that his congregation over in England would be in a sweat about him, so he must hurry and settle up the estate right away, and leave for home. He was very sorry he was so pushed, and so was everybody; they wished he could stay longer, but they said they could see it couldn't be done. And he said of course him and William would take the girls home with them; and that pleased everybody too, because then the girls would be well fixed, and amongst their own relations; and it pleased the girls, too – tickled them so they clean forgot they ever had a trouble in the world; and told him to sell out as quick as he wanted to, they would be ready. Them poor things was that glad and happy it made my heart ache to see them getting fooled and lied to so, but I didn't see no safe way for me to chip in and change the general tune.

Well, blamed if the king didn't bill the house and the niggers and all the property for auction straight off – sale two days after the funeral; but anybody could buy private beforehand if they wanted to.

So the next day after the funeral, along about noontime, the girls' joy got the first jolt; a couple of nigger traders come along, and the king sold them the niggers reasonable, for three-day drafts as they called it, and away they went, the two sons up the river to Memphis, and their mother down the river to Orleans. I thought them poor girls and them niggers would break their hearts for grief; they cried around each other, and took on so it most made me down sick to see it. The girls said they hadn't ever dreamed of seeing the family separated or sold away from the town. I can't ever get it out of my memory, the sight of them poor miserable girls and niggers hanging around each other's necks and crying; and I reckon I couldn't a stood it all but would a had to bust out and tell on our gang if I hadn't knowed the sale warn't no account and the niggers would be back home in a week or two.

The thing made a big stir in the town, too, and a good many come out flat-footed and said it was scandalous to separate the mother and the children that way. It injured the frauds some; but the old fool he bulled right along, spite of all the duke could say or do, and I tell you the duke was powerful uneasy.

Next day was auction day. About broad-day in the morning, the king and the duke come up in the garret and woke me up, and I see by their look that there was trouble. The king says:

'Was you in my room night before last?'

'No, your majesty' – which was the way I always called him when nobody but our gang warn't around.

'Was you in there yesterday er last night?'

'No, your majesty.'

'Honour bright, now – no lies.'

'Honour bright, your majesty, I'm telling you the truth. I hain't been anear your room since Miss Mary Jane took you and the duke and showed it to you.'

The duke says:

'Have you seen anybody else go in there?'

'No, your grace, not as I remember, I believe.'

'Stop and think.'

I studied a while, and see my chance, then I says:

'Well, I see the niggers go in there several times.'

Both of them give a little jump; and looked like they hadn't ever expected it, and then like they *had*. Then the duke says:

'What, *all* of them?'

'No – leastways not all at once. That is, I don't think I ever see them all come *out* at once but just one time.'

'Hallo – when was that?'

'It was the day we had the funeral. In the morning. It warn't early,

'"None o' your business! You keep your head shet'
and mind y'r own affairs——"'

because I overslept. I was just starting down the ladder, and I see them.'

'Well, go on, *go* on – what did they do? How'd they act?'

'They didn't do nothing. And they didn't act any way, much, as fur as I see. They tiptoed away; so I seen, easy enough, that they'd shoved in there to do up your majesty's room, or something, s'posing you was up; and found you *warn't* up, and so they was hoping to slide out of the way of trouble without waking you up, if they hadn't already waked you up.'

'Great guns, *this* is a go!' says the king; and both of them looked pretty sick and tolerable silly. They stood there a-thinking and scratching their heads a minute, and then the duke he bust into a kind of a little raspy chuckle, and says:

'It does beat all, how neat the niggers played their hand. They let on to be *sorry* they was going out of this region! and I believed they *was* sorry. And so did you, and so did everybody. Don't ever tell *me* any more that a nigger ain't got any histrionic talent. Why, the way they played that thing, it would fool *anybody*. In my opinion there's a fortune in 'em. If I had capital and a theatre, I wouldn't want a better lay out than that – and here we've gone and sold 'em for a song. Yes, and ain't privileged to sing the song, yet. Say, where *is* that song? – that draft?'

'In the bank for to be collected. Where *would* it be?'

'Well, *that*'s all right then, thank goodness.'

Says I, kind of timid-like:

'Is something gone wrong?'

The king whirls on me and rips out:

'None o' your business! You keep your head shet, and mind y'r own affairs – if you got any. Long as you're in this town, don't you forgit *that*, you hear?' Then he says to the duke: 'We got to jest swaller it, and say noth'n: mum's the word for *us*.'

As they was starting down the ladder, the duke he chuckles again, and says:

'Quick sales *and* small profits! It's a good business – yes.'

The king snarls around on him and says:

'I was trying to do for the best, in sellin' 'm out so quick. If the profits has turned out to be none, lackin' considable, and none to carry, is it my fault any more'n it's yourn?'

'Well, *they*'d be in this house yet, and we *wouldn't* if I could a got my advice listened to.'

The king sassed back, as much as was safe for him, and then swapped around and lit into *me* again. He give me down the banks for not coming and *telling* him I see the niggers come out of his room acting that way – said any fool would a *knowed* something was up. And then waltzed in and cussed *himself* a while; and said it all come of him not laying late and taking his natural rest that morning, and he'd be blamed if he'd ever do it again. So they went off a-jawing; and I felt dreadful glad I'd worked it all off on to the niggers, and yet hadn't done the niggers no harm by it.

Chapter 28

By and by it was getting-up time; so I come down the ladder and started for downstairs, but as I come to the girls' room, the door was open, and I see Mary Jane setting by her old hair trunk, which was open and she'd been packing things in it – getting ready to go to England. But she had stopped now, with a folded gown in her lap, and had her face in her hands, crying. I felt awful bad to see it; of course anybody would. I went in there, and says:

'Miss Mary Jane, you can't abear to see people in trouble and *I* can't – most always. Tell me about it.'

So she done it. And it was the niggers – I just expected it. She said the beautiful trip to England was most about spoiled for her; she didn't know *how* she was ever going to be happy there, knowing the mother and the children warn't ever going to see each other no more – and then busted out bitterer than ever, and flung up her hands, and says:

'Oh, dear, dear, to think they ain't *ever* going to see each other any more!'

'But they *will* – and inside of two weeks – and I *know* it!' says I.

Laws, it was out before I could think! – and before I could budge, she throws her arms around my neck, and told me to say it *again*, say it *again*, say it *again*!

I see I had spoke too sudden, and said too much, and was in a close place. I asked her to let me think a minute; and she set there, very impatient and excited, and handsome, but looking kind of happy and eased-up, like a person that's had a tooth pulled out. So I went to studying it out. I says to myself, I reckon a body that ups and tells the truth when he is in a tight place, is taking considerable many resks, though I ain't had no experience, and can't say for certain; but it looks so to me, anyway; and yet here's a case where I'm blest if it don't look to me like the truth is better, and actually *safer*, than a lie. I must lay it by in my mind, and think it over some time or other, it's so kind of strange and unregular. I never see nothing like it. Well, I says to myself at last, I'm a-going to chance it; I'll up and tell the truth this time, though it does seem most like setting down on a keg of powder and touching it off just to see where you'll go to. Then I says:

'Miss Mary Jane, is there any place out of town a little ways, where you could go and stay three or four days?'

'Yes – Mr. Lothrop's. Why?'

'Never mind why, yet. If I'll tell you how I know the niggers will see each other again – inside of two weeks – here in this house – and *prove* how I know it – will you go to Mr. Lothrop's and stay four days?'

'Four days!' she says: 'I'll stay a year!'

'All right,' I says, 'I don't want nothing more out of *you* than just your word – I druther have it than another man's kiss-the-Bible.' She smiled, and reddened up very sweet, and I says, 'If you don't mind, I'll shut the door – and bolt it.'

Then I come back and set down again, and says:

'Don't you holler. Just set still, and take it like a man. I got to tell the truth, and you want to brace up, Miss Mary, because it's a bad kind, and going to be hard to take, but there ain't no help for it. These uncles of yourn ain't no uncles at all – they're a couple of frauds – regular dead-beats. There, now we're over the worst of it – you can stand the rest middling easy.'

It jolted her up like everything, of course; but I was over the shoal water now, so I went right along, her eyes a-blazing higher and higher all the time, and told her every blame thing, from where we first struck that young fool going up to the steamboat, clear through to where she flung herself on to the king's breast at the front door, and he kissed her sixteen or seventeen times – and then up she jumps, with her face afire like sunset, and says:

'The brute! Come – don't waste a minute – not a *second* – we'll have them tarred and feathered, and flung in the river!'

Says I:

'Cert'nly. But do you mean, *before* you go to Mr. Lothrop's, or——'

'Oh,' she says, 'what am I *thinking* about!' she says, and set right down again. 'Don't mind what I said – please don't – you *won't*, now, *will* you?' Laying her silky hand on mine in that kind of a way that I said I would die first. 'I never thought, I was so stirred up,' she says; 'now go on, and I won't do so any more. You tell me what to do, and whatever you say, I'll do it.'

'Well,' I says, 'it's a rough gang, them two frauds, and I'm fixed so I got to travel with them a while longer, whether I want to or not – I druther not tell you why – and if you was to blow on them this town would get me out of their claws, and *I'*d be all right, but there'd be another person that you don't know about who'd be in big truble. Well, we got to save *him*, hain't we? Of course. Well, then, we won't blow on them.'

Saying them words put a good idea in my head. I see how maybe I could get me and Jim rid of the frauds; get them jailed here, and then leave. But I didn't want to run the raft in day-time, without anybody aboard to answer questions but me; so I didn't want the plan to begin working till pretty late to-night. I says:

'Miss Mary Jane, I'll tell you what we'll do – and you won't have to stay at Mr. Lothrop's so long, nuther. How fur is it?'

'A little short of four miles – right out in the country, back here.'

'Well, that'll answer. Now you go along out there, and lay low till nine or half-past, to-night, and then get them to fetch you home again – tell them you've thought of something. If you get here before eleven, put a candle in this window, and if I don't turn up, wait *till* eleven, and *then* if I don't turn up it means I'm gone, and out of the way, and safe. Then you come out and spread the news around, and get these beats jailed.'

'Good,' she says, 'I'll do it.'

'And if it just happens so that I don't get away, but get took up along with them, you must up and say I told you the whole thing beforehand, and you must stand by me all you can.'

'Stand by you, indeed I will. They shan't touch a hair of your head!' she says, and I see her nostrils spread and her eyes snap when she said it, too.

'If I get away, I shan't be here,' I says, 'to prove these rapscallions ain't your uncles, and I couldn't do it if I *was* here. I could swear they was beats and bummers, that's all; though that's worth something. Well, there's others can do that better than what I can – and they're people that ain't going to be doubted as quick as I'd be. I'll tell you how to find them. Gimme a pencil and a piece of paper. There – *"Royal Nonesuch, Bricksville."* Put it away, and don't lose it. When the court wants to find out something about these two, let them send up to Bricksville and say they've got the men that played the Royal Nonesuch, and ask for some witnesses – why, you'll have that entire town down here before you can hardly wink, Miss Mary. And they'll come a-biling, too.'

I judged we had got everything fixed about right now. So I says:

'Just let the auction go right along, and don't worry. Nobody don't have to pay for the things they buy till a whole day after the auction, on accounts of the short notice, and they ain't going out of this till they get that money – and the way we've fixed it the sale ain't going to count, and they ain't going to *get* no money. It's just like the way it was with the niggers – it warn't no sale, and the niggers will be back before long. Why, they can't collect the money for the *niggers*, yet – they're in the worst kind of a fix, Miss Mary.'

'Well,' she says, 'I'll run down to breakfast now, and then I'll start straight for Mr. Lothrop's.'

''Deed, *that* ain't the ticket, Miss Mary Jane,' I says, 'by no manner of means; go *before* breakfast.'

'Why?'

'Why did you reckon I wanted you to go at all for, Miss Mary?'

'Well, I never thought – and come to think, I don't know. What was it?'

'Why, it's because you ain't one of these leather-face people. I don't want no better book than what your face is. A body can set down and read it off like

coarse print. Do you reckon you can go and face your uncles, when they come
to kiss you good morning, and never——'

'There, there, don't! Yes, I'll go before breakfast – I'll be glad to. And
leave my sisters with them?'

'Yes – never mind about them. They've got to stand it yet a while. They
might suspicion something if all of you was to go. I don't want you to see
them, nor your sisters, nor nobody in this town – if a neighbour was to ask
how is your uncles this morning, your face would tell something. No, you go
right along, Miss Mary Jane, and I'll fix it with all of them. I'll tell Miss Susan
to give your love to your uncles and say you've went away for a few hours for
to get a little rest and change, or to see a friend, and you'll be back to-night or
early in the morning.'

'Gone to see a friend is all right, but I won't have my love given to them.'

'Well, then, it shan't be.' It was well enough to tell *her* so – no harm in it.
It was only a little thing to do, and no trouble; and it's the little things that
smooths people's roads the most, down here below; it would make Mary Jane
comfortable, and it wouldn't cost nothing. Then I says: 'There's one more
thing – that bag of money.'

'Well, they've got that; and it makes me feel pretty silly to think *how* they
got it.'

'No, you're out, there. They hain't got it.'

'Why, who's got it?'

'I wish I knowed, but I don't. I *had* it, because I stole it from them: and I
stole it to give to you; and I know where I hid it, but I'm afraid it ain't there no
more. I'm awful sorry, Miss Mary Jane, I'm just as sorry as I can be; but I
done the best I could; I did honest. I come nigh getting caught, and I had to
shove it into the first place I come to, and run – and it warn't a good place.'

'Oh, stop blaming yourself – it's too bad to do it, and I won't allow it –
you couldn't help it; it wasn't your fault. Where did you hide it?'

I didn't want to set her to thinking about her troubles again; and I
couldn't seem to get my mouth to tell her what would make her see that corpse
laying in the coffin with that bag of money on his stomach. So for a minute I
didn't say nothing – then I says:

'I'd ruther not *tell* you where I put it, Miss Mary Jane, if you don't mind
letting me off; but I'll write it for you on a piece of paper, and you can read it
along the road to Mr. Lothrop's, if you want to. Do you reckon that'll do?'

'Oh, yes.'

So I wrote: 'I put it in the coffin. It was in there when you was crying
there, away in the night. I was behind the door, and I was mighty sorry for
you, Miss Mary Jane.'

It made my eyes water a little, to remember her crying there all by herself
in the night, and them devils laying there right under her own roof, shaming

her and robbing her; and when I folded it up and give it to her, I see the water come into her eyes, too; and she shook me by the hand, hard, and says:

'*Good*-bye – I'm going to do everything just as you've told me; and if I don't ever see you again I shan't ever forget you, and I'll think of you a many and a many a time, and I'll *pray* for you, too!' – and she was gone.

Pray for me! I reckoned if she knowed me she'd take a job that was more nearer her size. But I bet she done it, just the same – she was just that kind. She had the grit to pray for Judas if she took the notion – there warn't no backdown to her, I judge. You may say what you want to, but in my opinion she had more sand in her than any girl I ever see; in my opinion she was just full of sand. It sounds like flattery, but it ain't no flattery. And when it comes to beauty – and goodness too – she lays over them all. I hain't ever seen her since that time that I see her go out of that door; no, I hain't ever seen her since, but I reckon I've thought of her a many and a many a million times, and of her saying she would pray for me; and if ever I'd a thought it would do any good for me to pray for *her*, blamed if I wouldn't a done it or bust.

Well, Mary Jane she lit out the back way, I reckon; because nobody see her go. When I struck Susan and the hare-lip, I says:

'What's the name of them people over on t'other side of the river that you all goes to see sometimes?'

They says:

'There's several; but it's the Proctors, mainly.'

'That's the name,' I says; 'I most forgot it. Well, Miss Mary Jane she told me to tell you she's gone over there in a dreadful hurry – one of them's sick.'

'Which one?'

'I don't know; leastways I kinder forget; but I think it's——'

'Sakes alive, I hope it ain't *Hanner*!'

'I'm sorry to say it,' I says, 'but Hanner's the very one.'

'My goodness – and she so well only last week! Is she took bad?'

'It ain't no name for it. They set up with her all night, Miss Mary Jane said, and they don't think she'll last many hours.'

'Only think of that, now! What's the matter with her?'

I couldn't think of anything reasonable, right off that way, so I says:

'Mumps.'

'Mumps your granny! They don't set up with people that's got the mumps.'

'They don't, don't they? You better bet they do with *these* mumps. These mumps is different. It's a new kind, Miss Mary Jane said.'

'How's it a new kind?'

'Because it's mixed up with other things.'

'What other things?'

'Well, measles, and whooping-cough, and erysipelas, and consumption, and yaller janders, and brain fever, and I don't know what all.'

'My land! And they call it the *mumps*?'

'That's what Miss Mary Jane said.'

'Well, what in the nation do they call it the *mumps* for?'

'Why, because it *is* the mumps. That's what it starts with.'

'Well, ther' ain't no sense in it. A body might stump his toe, and take pison, and fall down the well, and break his neck, and bust his brains out, and somebody come along and ask what killed him, and some numskull up and say, "Why, he stumped his *toe*." Would ther' be any sense in that? *No*. And ther' ain't no sense in *this*, nuther. Is it ketching?'

'Is it *ketching*? Why, how you talk. Is a *harrow* catching? – in the dark? If you don't hitch on to one tooth, you're bound to on another, ain't you? And you can't get away with that tooth without fetching the whole harrow along, can you? Well, these kind of mumps is a kind of a harrow, as you may say – and it ain't no slouch of a harrow, nuther, you come to get it hitched on good.'

'Well, it's awful, *I* think,' says the hare-lip. 'I'll go to Uncle Harvey and——'

'Oh, yes,' I says, 'I *would*. Of *course* I would. I wouldn't lose no time.'

'Well, why wouldn't you?'

'Just look at it a minute, and maybe you can see. Hain't your uncles obleeged to get along home to England as fast as they can? And do you reckon they'd be mean enough to go off and leave you to go all that journey by yourselves? *You* know they'll wait for you. So fur, so good. Your Uncle Harvey's a preacher, ain't he? Very well, then; is a *preacher* going to deceive a steamboat clerk? is he going to deceive a *ship-clerk*? – so as to get them to let Miss Mary Jane go aboard? Now *you* know he ain't. What *will* he do, then? Why, he'll say, "It's a great pity, but my church matters has got to get along the best way they can; for my niece has been exposed to the dreadful pluribus-unum mumps, and so it's my bounden duty to set down here and wait the three months it takes to show on her if she's got it." But never mind, if you think it's best to tell your Uncle Harvey——'

'Shucks, and stay fooling around here when we could all be having good times in England whilst we was waiting to find out whether Mary Jane's got it or not? Why, you talk like a muggins.'

'Well, anyway, maybe you better tell some of the neighbours.'

'Listen at that, now. You do beat all, for natural stupidity. Can't you *see* that *they*'d go and tell? Ther' ain't no way but just to not tell anybody at *all*.'

'Well, maybe you're right – yes, I judge, you *are* right.'

'But I reckon we ought to tell Uncle Harvey she's gone out awhile, anyway, so he won't be uneasy about her?'

'Yes, Miss Mary Jane she wanted you to do that. She says, "Tell them to give Uncle Harvey and William my love and a kiss, and say I've run over the river to see Mr. – Mr. – what *is* the name of the rich family your Uncle Peter used to think so much of? – I mean the one that——'

'Why, you must mean the Apthorps, ain't it?'

'Of course; bother them kind of names, a body can't ever seem to remember them, half the time, somehow. Yes, she said, say she has run over for to ask the Apthorps to be sure and come to the auction and buy this house, because she allowed her Uncle Peter would ruther they had it than anybody else; and she's going to stick to them till they say they'll come, and then, if she ain't too tired, she's coming home; and if she is, she'll be home in the morning anyway. She said, don't say nothing about the Proctors, but only about the Apthorps – which'll be perfectly true, because she *is* going there to speak about their buying the house; I know it, because she told me so, herself.'

'All right,' they said, and cleared out to lay for their uncles, and give them the love and the kisses, and tell them the message.

Everything was all right now. The girls wouldn't say nothing because they wanted to go to England; and the king and the duke would ruther Mary Jane was off working for the auction than around in reach of Doctor Robinson. I felt very good; I judged I had done it pretty neat – I reckoned Tom Sawyer couldn't a done it no neater himself. Of course he would a throwed more style into it, but I can't do that very handy, not being brung up to it.

Well, they held the auction in the public square, along towards the end of the afternoon, and it strung along and strung along, and the old man he was on hand and looking his level pisonest, up there 'longside of the auctioneer, and chipping in a little Scripture, now and then, or a little goody-goody saying, of some kind, and the duke he was around goo-gooing for sympathy all he knowed how, and just spreading himself generly.

But by and by the thing dragged through, and everything was sold. Everything but a little old trifling lot in the graveyard. So they'd got to work *that* off – I never see such a giraffe as the king was for wanting to swallow *everything*. Well, whilst they was at it, a steamboat landed, and in about two minutes up comes a crowd a-whooping and yelling and laughing and carrying on, and singing out:

'*Here*'s your opposition line! here's your two sets o' heirs to old Peter Wilks – and you pays your money and you takes your choice!'

Chapter 29

They was fetching a very nice-looking old gentleman along, and a nice-looking younger one, with his right arm in a sling. And my souls, how the people yelled, and laughed, and kept it up. But I didn't see no joke about it, and I judged it would strain the duke and the king some to see any. I reckoned they'd turn pale. But no, nary a pale did *they* turn. The duke he never let on he suspicioned what was up, but just went a-goo-gooing around, happy and satisfied, like a jug that's googling out buttermilk; and as for the king, he just gazed and gazed down sorrowful on them newcomers like it give him the stomach-ache in his very heart to think there could be such frauds and rascals in the world. Oh, he done it admirable. Lots of the principal people gethered around the king, to let him see they was on his side. That old gentleman that had just come looked all puzzled to death. Pretty soon he begun to speak, and I see, straight off, he pronounced *like* an Englishman, not the king's way, though the king's *was* pretty good, for an imitation. I can't give the old gent's words, nor I can't imitate him; but he turned around to the crowd, and says, about like this:

'This is a surprise to me which I wasn't looking for; and I'll acknowledge, candid and frank, I ain't very well fixed to meet it and answer it; for my brother and me has had misfortunes, he's broke his arm, and our baggage got put off at a town above here, last night in the night by a mistake. I am Peter Wilks's brother Harvey, and this is his brother William, which can't hear nor speak – and can't even make signs to amount to much, now 't he's only got one hand to work them with. We are who we say we are; and in a day or two, when I get the baggage, I can prove it. But, up till then, I won't say nothing more, but go to the hotel and wait.'

So him and the new dummy started off; and the king he laughs, and blethers out:

'Broke his arm – *very* likely *ain't* it? – and very convenient, too, for a fraud that's got to make signs, and hain't learnt how. Lost their baggage! That's *mighty* good! – and mighty ingenious – under the *circumstances*!'

So he laughed again; and so did everybody else, except three or four, or maybe half a dozen. One of these was that doctor; another one was a sharp-looking gentleman, with a carpet-bag of the old-fashioned kind made out of carpet-stuff, that had just come off the steamboat and was talking to him in a low voice, and glancing towards the king now and then and nodding their heads – it was Levi Bell, the lawyer that was gone up to Louisville; and another one was a big rough husky that come along and listened to all the old gentleman said, and was listening to the king now. And when the king got done, this husky up and says:

'Say, looky here; if you are Harvey Wilks, when'd you come to this town?'

'The day before the funeral, friend,' says the king.

'But what time o' day?'

'In the evenin' – 'bout an hour er two before sundown.'

'*How*'d you come?'

'I come down on the *Susan Powell*, from Cincinnati.'

'Well, then, how'd you come to be up at the Pint in the *mornin*' – in a canoe?'

'I warn't up at the Pint in the mornin'.'

'It's a lie.'

Several of them jumped for him and begged him not to talk that way to an old man and a preacher.

'Preacher be hanged, he's a fraud and a liar. He was up at the Pint that mornin'. I live up there, don't I? Well, I was up there, and he was up there. I *see* him there. He come in a canoe, along with Tim Collins and a boy.'

The doctor he up and says:

'Would you know the boy again if you was to see him, Hines?'

'I reckon I would, but I don't know. Why, yonder he is, now. I know him perfectly easy.'

It was me he pointed at. The doctor says:

'Neighbours, I don't know whether the new couple is frauds or not; but if *these* two ain't frauds, I am an idiot, that's all. I think it's our duty to see that they don't get away from here till we've looked into this thing. Come along, Hines; come along, the rest of you. We'll take these fellows to the tavern and affront them with t'other couple, and I reckon we'll find out *something* before we get through.'

It was nuts for the crowd, though maybe not for the king's friends; so we all started. It was about sundown. The doctor he led me along by the hand, and was plenty kind enough, but he never let *go* my hand.

We all got in a big room in the hotel, and lit up some candles, and fetched in the new couple. First, the doctor says:

'I don't wish to be too hard on these two men, but *I* think they're frauds, and they may have 'complices that we don't know nothing about. If they have, won't the 'complices get away with that bag of gold Peter Wilks left? It ain't unlikely. If these men ain't frauds, they won't object to sending for that money and letting us keep it till they prove they're all right – ain't that so?'

Everybody agreed to that. So I judged they had our gang in a pretty tight place, right at the outstart. But the king he only looked sorrowful, and says:

'Gentlemen, I wish the money was there, for I ain't got no disposition to throw anything in the way of a fair, open, out-and-out investigation o' this misable business; but alas! the money ain't there; you k'n send and see, if you want to.'

'Where is it, then?'

'Well, when my niece give it to me to keep for her, I took and hid it inside o' the straw tick o' my bed, not wishin' to bank it for the few days we'd be here, and considerin' the bed a safe place, we not bein' used to niggers, and suppos'n' 'em honest, like servants in England. The niggers stole it the very next mornin' after I had went downstairs; and when I sold 'em I hadn't missed the money yit, so they got clean away with it. My servant here k'n tell you 'bout it, gentlemen.'

The doctor and several said 'Shucks!' and I see nobody didn't altogether believe him. One man asked me if I see the niggers steal it. I said 'no,' but I see them sneaking out of the room and hustling away, and I never thought nothing, only I reckoned they was afraid they had waked up my master and was trying to get away before he made trouble with them. That was all they asked me. Then the doctor whirls on me and says:

'Are *you* English too?'

I says 'yes'; and him and some others laughed, and said, 'Stuff!'

Well, then they sailed in on the general investigation, and there we had it, up and down, hour in, hour out, and nobody never said a word about supper, nor ever seemed to think about it – and so they kept it up, and kept it up; and it *was* the worst mixed-up thing you ever see. They made the king tell his yarn, and they made the old gentleman tell his'n; and anybody but a lot of prejudiced chuckleheads would a *seen* that the old gentleman was spinning truth and t'other one lies. And by and by they had me up to tell what I knowed. The king he give me a left-handed look out of the corner of his eye, and so I knowed enough to talk on the right side. I begun to tell about Sheffield, and how we lived there, and all about the English Wilkses, and so on; but I didn't get pretty fur till the doctor begun to laugh; and Levi Bell, the lawyer says:

'Set down, my boy, I wouldn't strain myself, if I was you. I reckon you ain't used to lying, it don't seem to come handy; what you want is practice. You do it pretty awkward.'

I didn't care nothing for the compliment, but I was glad to be let off, anyway.

The doctor he started to say something, and turns and says:

'If you'd been in town at first, Levi Bell——'

The king broke in and reached out his hand, and says:

'Why, is this my poor dead brother's old friend that he's wrote so often about?'

The lawyer and him shook hands, and the lawyer smiled and looked pleased, and they talked right along awhile, and then got to one side and talked right along awhile, and then got to one side and talked low; and at last the lawyer speaks up and says:

'That'll fix it. I'll take the order and send it, along with your brother's, and then they'll know it's all right.'

So they got some paper and a pen, and the king he set down and twisted his head to one side, and chawed his tongue, and scrawled off something; and then they give the pen to the duke – and then for the first time, the duke looked sick. But he took the pen and wrote. So then the lawyer turns to the new old gentleman and says:

'You and your brother please write a line or two and sign your names.'

The old gentleman wrote, but nobody couldn't read it. The lawyer looked powerful astonished, and says:

'Well, it beats *me*' – and snaked a lot of old letters out of his pocket, and examined them, and then examined the old man's writing, and then *them* again; and then says, 'These old letters is from Harvey Wilks; and here's *these* two's handwritings, and anybody can see *they* didn't write them' (the king and the duke looked sold and foolish, I tell you, to see how the lawyer had took them in), 'and here's *this* old gentleman's handwriting, and anybody can tell, easy enough, *he* didn't write them – fact is, the scratches he makes ain't properly *writing* at all. Now here's some letters from——'

The new old gentleman says:

'If you please, let me explain. Nobody can read my hand but my brother there – so he copies for me. It's *his* hand you've got there, not mine.'

'*Well!*' says the lawyer, 'this *is* a state of things. I've got some of William's letters too; so if you'll get him to write a line or so we can com——'

'He *can't* write with his left hand,' says the old gentleman. 'If he could use his right hand, you would see that he wrote his own letters and mine too. Look at both, please – they're by the same hand.'

The lawyer done it, and says:

'I believe it's so – and if it ain't so, there's a heap stronger resemblance than I'd noticed before, anyway. Well, well, well! I thought we was right on the track of a s'lution, but it's gone to grass, partly. But anyway, *one* thing is proved – *these* two ain't either of 'em Wilkses' – and he wagged his head towards the king and the duke.

Well, what do you think – that muleheaded old fool wouldn't give in *then*! Indeed he wouldn't. Said it warn't no fair test. Said his brother William was the cussedest joker in the world, and hadn't *tried* to write – *he* see William was going to play one of his jokes the minute he put the pen to paper. And so he warmed up and went warbling and warbling right along, till he was actually beginning to believe what he was saying, *himself* – but pretty soon the new old gentleman broke in, and says:

'I've thought of something. Is there anybody here that helped to lay out my br—— helped to lay out the late Peter Wilks for burying?'

'Yes,' says somebody, 'me and Ab Turner done it. We're both here.'

Then the old man turns towards the king, and says:

'Per'aps this gentleman can tell me what was tattooed on his breast?'

Blamed if the king didn't have to brace up mighty quick, or he'd a squished down like a bluff bank that the river has cut under, it took him so sudden – and mind you, it was a thing that was calculated to make most anybody squish to get fetched such a solid one as that without any notice – because how was *he* going to know what was tattooed on the man? He whitened a little; he couldn't help it; and it was mighty still in there, and everybody bending a little forwards and gazing at him. Says I to myself, *Now* he'll throw up the sponge – there ain't no more use. Well, did he? A body can't hardly believe it, but he didn't. I reckon he thought he'd keep the thing up till he tired them people out, so they'd thin out, and him and the duke could break loose and get away. Anyway, he set there, and pretty soon he begun to smile, and says:

'Mf! It's a *very* tough question, *ain't* it! Yes, sir, I k'n tell you what's tattooed on his breast. It's jest a small, thin, blue arrow – that's what it is; and if you don't look clost, you can't see it. *Now* what do you say – hey?'

Well *I* never see anything like that old blister for clean out-and-out cheek.

The new old gentleman turns brisk towards Ab Turner and his pard, and his eye lights up like he judged he had got the king *this* time, and says:

'There – you've heard what he said! Was there any such mark on Peter Wilks's breast?'

Both of them spoke up and says:

'We didn't see no such mark.'

'Good!' says the old gentleman. 'Now, what you *did* see on his breast was a small dim P, and a B (which is an initial he dropped when he was young), and a W, with dashes between them, so: P – B – W' – and he marked them that way on a piece of paper. 'Come – ain't that what you saw?'

Both of them spoke up again, and says:

'No, we *didn't*. We never seen any marks at all.'

Well, everybody *was* in a state of mind now; and they sings out:

'The whole *bilin'* of 'm's frauds! Le's duck 'em! le's drown 'em! le's ride 'em on a rail!' and everybody was whooping at once, and there was a rattling pow-wow. But the lawyer he jumps on the table and yells, and says:

'Gentlemen – gentle*men*! Hear me just a word – just a *single* word – if you

PLEASE! There's one way yet – let's go and dig up the corpse and look.'

That took them.

'Hooray!' they all shouted; and was starting right off; but the lawyer and the doctor sung out:

'Hold on, hold on! Collar all these four men and the boy, and fetch *them* along, too!'

'We'll do it!' they all shouted; 'and if we don't find them marks we'll lynch the whole gang!'

I *was* scared, now, I tell you. But there warn't no getting away, you know. They gripped us all, and marched us right along, straight for the graveyard, which was a mile and a half down the river, and the whole town at our heels, for we made noise enough, and it was only nine in the evening.

As we went by our house I wished I hadn't sent Mary Jane out of town; because now if I could tip her the wink, she'd light out and save me, and blow on our dead-beats.

Well, we swarmed along down the river road, just carrying on like wild-cats; and to make it more scary, the sky was darking up, and the lightning beginning to wink and flitter, and the wind to shiver amongst the leaves. This was the most awful trouble and most dangersome I ever was in; and I was kinder stunned; everything was going so different from what I had allowed for; 'stead of being fixed so I could take my own time, if I wanted to, and see all the fun, and have Mary Jane at my back to save me and set me free when the close-fit come, there was nothing in the world betwixt me and sudden death but just them tattoo-marks. If they didn't find them——

I couldn't bear to think about it; and yet, somehow, I couldn't think about nothing else. It got darker and darker, and it was a beautiful time to give the crowd the slip; but that big husky had me by the wrist – Hines – and a body might as well try to give Goliar the slip. He dragged me right along, he was so excited; and I had to run to keep up.

When they got there they swarmed into the graveyard and washed over it like an overflow. And when they got to the grave, they found they had about a hundred times as many shovels as they wanted, but nobody hadn't thought to fetch a lantern. But they sailed into digging, anyway, by the flicker of the lightning, and sent a man to the nearest house a half a mile off, to borrow one.

So, they dug and dug, like everything; and it got awful dark, and the rain started, and the wind swished and swushed along, and the lightning come brisker and brisker, and the thunder boomed; but them people never took no notice of it, they was so full of this business; and one minute you could see everything and every face in that big crowd, and the shovelfuls of dirt sailing up out of the grave, and the next second the dark wiped it all out, and you couldn't see nothing at all.

At last they got out the coffin, and begun to unscrew the lid, and then such another crowding, and shouldering, and shoving as there was, to scrouge in and get a sight, you never see; and in the dark, that way, it was awful. Hines he hurt my wrist dreadful, pulling and tugging so, and I reckon he clean forgot I was in the world, he was so excited and panting.

All of a sudden the lightning let go a perfect sluice of white glare, and somebody sings out:

'By the living jingo, here's the bag of gold on his breast!'

Hines let out a whoop, like everybody else, and dropped my wrist and give a big surge to bust his way in and get a look, and the way I lit out and shinned for the road in the dark, there ain't nobody can tell.

I had the road all to myself, and I fairly flew – leastways I had it all to myself except the solid dark, and the now-and-then glares, and the buzzing of the rain, and the thrashing of the wind, and the splitting of the thunder; and sure as you are born I did clip it along!

When I struck the town, I see there warn't nobody out in the storm, so I never hunted for no back streets, but humped it straight through the main one; and when I begun to get towards our house I aimed my eye and set it. No light there; the house all dark – which made me feel sorry and disappointed, I didn't know why. But at last, just as I was sailing by, *flash* comes the light in Mary Jane's window! and my heart swelled up sudden, like to bust; and the same second the house and all was behind me in the dark, and wasn't ever going to be before me no more in this world. She *was* the best girl I ever see, and had the most sand.

The minute I was far enough above the town to see I could make the tow-head, I begun to look sharp for a boat to borrow; and the first time the lightning showed me one that wasn't chained, I snatched it and shoved. It was a canoe, and warn't fastened with nothing but a rope. The tow-head was a rattling big distance off, away out there in the middle of the river, but I didn't lose no time; and when I struck the raft at last, I was so fagged I would a just laid down to blow and gasp if I could afford it. But I didn't. As I sprang aboard I sung out:

'Out with you, Jim, and set her loose! Glory be to goodness, we're shut of them!'

Jim lit out, and was a-coming for me with both arms spread, he was so full of joy; but when I glimpsed him in the lightning, my heart shot up in my mouth, and I went overboard backwards; for I forgot he was old King Lear and a drownded A-rab all in one, and it most scared the livers and lights out of me. But Jim fished me out, and was going to hug me and bless me, and so on, he was so glad I was back and we was shut of the king and the duke, but I says:

'Not now – have it for breakfast, have it for breakfast! Cut loose and let her slide!'

So, in two seconds, away we went, a-sliding down the river, and it *did* seem so good to be free again and all by ourselves on the big river and nobody to bother us. I had to skip around a bit, and jump up and crack my heels a few times, I couldn't help it; but about the third crack I noticed a sound that I knowed mighty well – and held my breath and listened and waited – and sure enough, when the next flash busted out over the water, here they come! – and just a-laying to their oars and making their skiff hum! It was the king and the duke.

So I wilted right down on to the planks, then, and give up; and it was all I could do to keep from crying.

Chapter 30

When they got aboard, the king went for me, and shook me by the collar, and says:

'Tryin' to give us the slip, was ye, you pup! Tired of our company – hey?' I says:

'No, your majesty, we warn't – *please* don't, your majesty!'

'Quick, then, and tell us what *was* your idea, or I'll shake the insides out o' you!'

'Honest, I'll tell you everything, just as it happened, your majesty. The man that had aholt of me was very good to me, and kept saying he had a boy about as big as me that died last year, and he was sorry to see a boy in such a dangerous fix; and when they was all took by surprise by finding the gold, and made a rush for the coffin, he lets go of me and whispers, 'Heel it, now, or they'll hang ye, sure!' and I lit out. It didn't seem no good for *me* to stay – I couldn't do nothing, and I didn't want to be hung if I could get away. So I never stopped running till I found the canoe; and when I got here I told Jim to hurry, or they'd catch me and hang me yet, and said I was afeard you and the duke wasn't alive, now, and I was awful sorry, and so was Jim, and was awful glad when we see you coming, you may ask Jim if I didn't.'

Jim said it was so; and the king told him to shut up, and said, 'Oh, yes, it's *mighty* likely!' and shook me up again, and said he reckoned he'd drownd me. But the duke says:

'Leggo the boy, you old idiot! Would *you* a done any different? Did you inquire around for *him*, when you got loose? *I* don't remember it.'

So the king let go of me, and begun to cuss that town and everybody in it. But the duke says:

'You better a blame' sight give *yourself* a good cussing, for you're the one that's entitled to it most. You hain't done a thing, from the start, that had any sense in it, except coming out so cool and cheeky with that imaginary blue-arrow mark. That *was* bright – it was right down bully; and it was the thing that saved us. For if it hadn't been for that, they'd a jailed us till them Englishmen's baggage come – and then – the penitentiary, you bet! But that trick took 'em to the graveyard, and the gold done us a still bigger kindness; for if the excited fools hadn't let go all holts and made that rush to get a look, we'd a slept in our cravats to-night – cravats warranted to *wear*, too – longer than *we*'d need 'em.'

They was still a minute – thinking – then the king says, kind of absent-minded like:

'Mf! And we reckoned the *niggers* stole it!'

That made me squirm!

'Yes,' says the duke, kinder slow, and deliberate, and sarcastic, '*we* did.'

After about a half a minute, the king drawls out:

'Leastways – *I* did.'

The duke says, the same way:

'On the contrary – *I* did.'

The king kind of ruffles up, and says:

'Looky here, Bilgewater, what'r you referrin' to?'

The duke says, pretty brisk:

'When it comes to that, maybe you'll let me ask, what was *you* referring to?'

'Shucks!' says the king, very sarcastic; 'but *I* don't know – maybe you was asleep, and didn't know what you was about.'

The duke bristles right up now, and says:

'Oh, let *up* on this cussed nonsense – do you take me for a blame' fool? Don't you reckon *I* know who hid that money in that coffin?'

'*Yes*, sir! I know you *do* know – because you done it yourself!'

'It's a lie!' – and the duke went for him. The king sings out:

'Take y'r hands off! – leggo my throat! – I take it all back!'

The duke says:

'Well, you just own up, first, that you *did* hide that money there, intending to give me the slip one of these days, and come back and dig it up, and have it all to yourself.'

'Wait jest a minute, duke – answer me this one question, honest and fair; if you didn't put the money there, say it, and I'll b'lieve you, and take back everything I said.'

'You old scoundrel, I didn't, and you know I didn't. There, now!'

'Well, then, I b'lieve you. But answer me only jest this one more – now *don't* git mad; didn't you have it in your *mind* to hook the money and hide it?'

The duke never said nothing for a little bit; then he says:

'Well – I don't care if I *did*, I didn't *do* it anyway. But you not only had it in mind to do it, but you *done* it.'

'I wisht I may never die if I done it, duke, and that's honest. I won't say I warn't *goin'* to do it, because I *was;* but you – I mean somebody – got in ahead o' me.'

'It's a lie! You done it, and you got to *say* you done it, or——'

The king begun to gurgle, and then he gasps out:

''Nough! – *I own up!*'

I was very glad to hear him say that, it made me feel much more easier than what I was feeling before. So the duke took his hands off, and says:

'If you ever deny it again, I'll drown you. It's *well* for you to set there and blubber like a baby – it's fitten for you, after the way you've acted. I never see such an old ostrich for wanting to gobble everything – and I a-trusting you all the time, like you was my own father. You ought to been ashamed of yourself to stand by and hear it saddled on to a lot of poor niggers and you never say a word for 'em. It makes me feel ridiculous to think I was soft enough to *believe* that rubbage. Cuss you, I can see, now, why you was so anxious to make up the deffersit – you wanted to get what money I'd got out of the Nonesuch, and one thing or another, and scoop it *all*!'

The king says, timid, and still a-snuffling:

'Why, duke, it was you that said make up the deffersit, it warn't me.'

'Dry up! I don't want to hear no more *out* of you!' says the duke. 'And *now* you see what you *got* by it. They've got all their own money back, and all of *ourn* but a shekel or two, *besides*. G'long to bed – and don't you deffersit *me* no more deffersits, long's *you* live!'

So the king sneaked into the wigwam, and took to his bottle for comfort; and before long the duke tackled *his* bottle; and so in about a half an hour they was as thick as thieves again, and the tighter they got, the lovinger they got; and went off a-snoring in each other's arms. They both got powerful mellow, but I noticed the king didn't get mellow enough to forget to remember to not deny about hiding the money-bag again. That made me feel easy and satisfied. Of course when they got to snoring, we had a long gabble, and I told Jim everything.

Chapter 31

We dasn't stop again at any town, for days and days; kept right along down the
river. We was down south in the warm weather, now, and a mighty long ways
from home. We begun to come to trees with Spanish moss on them, hanging
down from the limbs like long grey beards. It was the first I ever see it
growing, and it made the woods look solemn and dismal. So now the frauds
reckoned they was out of danger, and they begun to work the villages again.

First they done a lecture on temperance; but they didn't make enough for
them both to get drunk on. Then in another village they started a dancing
school; but they didn't know no more how to dance than a kangaroo does; so
the first prance they made, the general public jumped in and pranced them
out of town. Another time they tried a go at yellocution; but they didn't
yellocute long till the audience got up and give them a solid good cussing and
made them skip out. They tackled missionarying, and mesmerizering, and
doctoring, and telling fortunes, and a little of everything; but they couldn't
seem to have no luck. So at last they got just about dead broke, and laid
around the raft, as she floated along, thinking, and thinking, and never saying
nothing, by the half a day at a time, and dreadful blue and desperate.

And at last they took a change, and begun to lay their heads together in
the wigwam and talk low and confidential two or three hours at a time. Jim
and me got uneasy. We didn't like the look of it. We judged they was studying
up some kind of worse deviltry than ever. We turned it over and over, and at
last we made up our minds they was going to break into somebody's house or
store, or was going into the counterfeit-money business, or something. So
then we was pretty scared, and made up an agreement that we wouldn't have
nothing in the world to do with such actions, and if we ever got the least show
we would give them the cold shake, and clear out and leave them behind.
Well, early one morning we hid the raft in a good safe place about about two
mile below a little bit of a shabby village, named Pikesville, and the king he
went ashore, and told us all to stay hid whilst he went up to town and smelt
around to see if anybody had got any wind of the Royal Nonesuch there yet.
('House to rob, you *mean*,' says I to myself; 'and when you get through
robbing it you'll come back here and wonder what's become of me and Jim
and the raft – and you'll have to take it out in wondering.') And he said if he

warn't back by midday, the duke and me would know it was all right, and we was to come along.

So we stayed where we was. The duke he fretted and sweated around, and was in a mighty sour way. He scolded us for everything, and we couldn't seem to do nothing right; he found fault with every little thing. Something was a-brewing, sure. I was good and glad when midday come and no king; we could have a change, anyway – and maybe a chance for *the* change, on top of it. So me and the duke went up to the village, and hunted around there for the king, and by and by we found him in the back room of a little low doggery, very tight, and a lot of loafers bullyragging him for sport, and he a cussing and threatening with all his might, and so tight he couldn't walk, and couldn't do nothing to them. The duke he begun to abuse him for an old fool, and the king begun to sass back; and the minute they was fairly at it, I lit out, and shook the reefs out of my hind legs, and spun down the river road like a deer – for I see our chance; and I made up my mind that it would be a long day before they ever see me and Jim again. I got down there all out of breath but loaded up with joy, and sung out:

'Set her loose, Jim, we're all right, now!'

But there warn't no answer, and nobody come out of the wigwam. Jim was gone! I set up a shout – and then another – and then another one; and run this way and that in the woods, whooping and screeching; but it warn't no use – old Jim was gone. Then I set down and cried; I couldn't help it. But I couldn't set still long. Pretty soon I went out on the road, trying to think what I better do, and I run across a boy walking, and asked him if he'd seen a strange nigger, dressed so and so, and he says:

'Yes.'

'Whereabouts?' says I.

'Down to Silas Phelps's place, two mile below here. He's a runaway nigger, and they've got him. Was you looking for him?'

'You bet I ain't. I run across him in the woods about an hour or two ago, and he said if I hollered he'd cut my livers out – and told me to lay down and stay where I was; and I done it. Been there ever since; afeard to come out.'

'Well,' he says, 'you needn't be afeard no more, becuz they've got him. He run f'm down South, som'ers.'

'It's a good job they got him.'

'Well, I *reckon*! There's two hundred dollars reward on him. It's like picking up money out'n the road.'

'Yes, it is – and *I* could a had it if I'd been big enough; I see him *first*. Who nailed him?'

'It was an old fellow – a stranger – and he sold out his chance in him for forty dollars, becuz he's got to go up the river and can't wait. Think o' that, now! You bet *I'd* wait, if it was seven year.'

'That's me, every time,' says I. 'But maybe his chance ain't worth no more than that, if he'll sell it so cheap. Maybe there's something ain't straight about it.'

'But it *is*, though – straight as a string. I see the handbill myself. It tells all about him, to a dot – paints him like a picture, and tells the plantation he's frum, below Newr*leans*. No-sirree-*bob*, they ain't no trouble 'bout *that* speculation, you bet yo. Say, gimme a chaw tobacker, won't ye?'

I didn't have none, so he left. I went to the raft, and set down in the wigwam to think. But I couldn't come to nothing. I thought till I wore my head sore, but I couldn't see no way out of the trouble. After all this long journey, and after all we'd done for them scoundrels, here was it all come to nothing, everything all busted up and ruined, because they could have the heart to serve Jim such a trick as that, and make him a slave again all his life, and amongst strangers, too, for forty dirty dollars.

Once I said to myself it would be a thousand times better for Jim to be a slave at home where his family was, as long as he'd *got* to be a slave, and so I'd better write a letter to Tom Sawyer, and tell him to tell Miss Watson where he was. But I soon give up that notion, for two things: she'd be mad and disgusted at his rascality and ungratefulness for leaving her, and so she'd sell him straight down the river again; and if she didn't, everybody naturally despises an ungrateful nigger, and they'd make Jim feel it all the time, and so he'd feel ornery and disgraced. And then think of *me*! It would get all around that Huck Finn helped a nigger to get his freedom; and if I was to ever see anybody from that town again, I'd be ready to get down and lick his boots for shame. That's just the way; a person does a low-down thing, and then he don't want to take no consequences of it. Thinks as long as he can hide it, it ain't no disgrace. That was my fix exactly. The more I studied about this, the more my conscience went to grinding me, and the more wicked and low-down and ornery I got to feeling. And at last, when it hit me all of a sudden that here was the plain hand of Providence slapping me in the face and letting me know my wickedness was being watched all the time from up there in heaven, whilst I was stealing a poor old woman's nigger that hadn't ever done me no harm, and now was showing me there's One that's always on the look-out, and ain't a-going to allow no such miserable doings to go only just so fur and no further, I most dropped in my tracks I was so scared. Well, I tried the best I could to kinder soften it up somehow for myself, by saying I was brung up wicked, and so I warn't so much to blame; but something inside of me kept saying, 'There was the Sunday school, you could a gone to it; and if you'd a done it they'd a learnt you, there, that people that acts as I'd been acting about that nigger goes to everlasting fire.'

It made me shiver. And I about made up my mind to pray; and see if I couldn't try to quit being the kind of a boy I was, and be better. So I kneeled down. But the words wouldn't come. Why wouldn't they? It warn't no use to try and hide it from Him. Nor from *me*, neither. I knowed very well why they wouldn't come. It was because my heart warn't right; it was because I warn't square; it was because I was playing double. I was letting *on* to give up sin, but away inside of me I was holding on to the biggest one of all. I was trying to make my mouth *say* I would do the right thing and the clean thing, and go and write to that nigger's owner and tell where he was; but deep down in me I knowed it was a lie – and He knowed it. You can't pray a lie – I found that out.

So I was full of trouble, full as I could be, and didn't know what to do. At last I had an idea; and I says, I'll go and write the letter – and *then* see if I can pray. Why, it was astonishing, the way I felt as light as a feather, right straight off, and my troubles all gone. So I got a piece of paper and a pencil, all glad and excited, and set down and wrote:

Miss Watson your runaway nigger Jim is down here two mile below Pikesville and Mr. Phelps has got him and he will give him up for the reward if you send.

HUCK FINN.

I felt good and all washed clean of sin for the first time I had ever felt so in my life, and I knowed I could pray now. But I didn't do it straight off, but laid the paper down and set there thinking – thinking how good it was all this happened so, and how near I come to being lost and going to hell. And went on thinking. And got to thinking over our trip down the river; and I see Jim before me, all the time, in the day, and in the night-time, sometimes moonlight, sometimes storms, and we a-floating along, talking, and singing, and laughing. But somehow I couldn't seem to strike no places to harden me against him, but only the other kind. I'd see him standing my watch on top of his'n, 'stead of calling me, so I could go on sleeping; and see him how glad he was when I come back out of the fog; and when I come to him again in the swamp, up there where the feud was; and such-like times; and would always call me honey, and pet me, and do everything he could think of for me, and how good he always was; and at last I struck the time I saved him by telling the men we had smallpox aboard, and he was so grateful, and said I was the best friend old Jim had in the world, and the *only* one he'd got now; and then I happened to look around, and see that paper.

It was a close place. I took it up, and held it in my hand. I was a-trembling, because I'd got to decide, for ever, betwixt two things, and I knowed it. I studied a minute, sort of holding my breath, and then says to myself:

'All right, then, I'll *go* to hell' – and tore it up.

It was awful thoughts, and awful words, but they was said. And I let them stay said; and never thought no more about reforming. I shoved the whole thing out of my head; and said I would take up wickedness again, which was in my line, being brung up to it, and the other warn't. And for a starter, I would go to work and steal Jim out of slavery again; and if I could think up anything worse, I would do that, too; because as long as I was in, and in for good, I might as well go the whole hog.

Then I set to thinking over how to get at it, and turned over considerable many ways in my mind; and at last fixed up a plan that suited me. So then I took the bearings of a woody island that was down the river a piece, and as soon as it was fairly dark I crept out with my raft and went for it, and hid it there, and then turned in. I slept the night through, and got up before it was light, and had my breakfast, and put on my store clothes, and tied up some others and one thing or another in a bundle, and took the canoe and cleared for shore. I landed below where I judged was Phelps's place, and hid my bundle in the woods, and then filled up the canoe with water, and loaded rocks into her and sunk her where I could find her again when I wanted her, about a quarter of a mile below a little steam sawmill that was on the bank.

Then I struck up the road, and when I passed the mill I see a sign on it, 'Phelps's Sawmill,' and when I come to the farmhouses, two or three hundred yards further along, I kept my eyes peeled, but didn't see nobody around, that it was good daylight, now. But I didn't mind, because I didn't want to see nobody just yet – I only wanted to get the lay of the land. According to my plan, I was going to turn up there from the village, not from below. So I just took a look, and shoved along, straight for town. Well, the very first man I see, when I got there, was the duke. He was sticking up a bill for the Royal Nonesuch – three-night performance – like that other time. *They* had the cheek, them frauds! I was right on him, before I could shirk. He looked astonished, and says:

'Hal-*lo*! Where'd *you* come from?' Then he says, kind of glad and eager, 'Where's the raft? – got her in a good place?'

I says:

'Why, that's just what I was a-going to ask your grace.'

Then he didn't look so joyful – and says:

'What was your idea for asking *me*?' he says.

'Well,' I says, 'when I see the king in that doggery yesterday, I says to myself, we can't get him home for hours, till he's soberer; so I went a-loafing around town to put in the time, and wait. A man up and offered me ten cents to help him pull a skiff over the river and back to fetch a sheep, and so I went along; but when we was dragging him to the boat, and the man left me aholt of the rope and went behind him to shove him along, he was too strong for me, and jerked loose and run, and we after him. We didn't have no dog, and so we had to chase him all over the country till we tired him out. We never got him till dark, then we fetched him over, and I started down for the raft. When I got there and see it was gone, I says to myself, "They've got into trouble and had to leave; and they've took my nigger, which is the only nigger I've got in the world, and now I'm in a strange country, and ain't got no property no more, nor nothing, and no way to make my living"; so I set down and cried. I slept in the woods all night. But what *did* become of the raft then? – and Jim, poor Jim!'

'Blamed if *I* know – that is, what's become of the raft. That old fool had made a trade and got forty dollars, and when we found him in the doggery the loafers had matched half-dollars with him and got every cent but what he'd spent for whisky; and when I got him home late last night and found the raft gone, we said, "That little rascal has stole our raft and shook us, and run off down the river."'

· 'I wouldn't shake my *nigger*, would I? – the only nigger I had in the world, and the only property.'

'We never thought of that. Fact is, I reckon we'd come to consider him *our* nigger; yes, we did consider him so – goodness knows we had trouble enough for him. So when we see the raft was gone, and we flat broke, there warn't anything for it but to try the Royal Nonesuch another shake. And I've pegged along ever since, dry as a powder-horn. Where's that ten cents? Give it here.'

I had considerable money, so I give him ten cents, but begged him to spend it for something to eat, and give me some, because it was all the money I had, and I hadn't had nothing to eat since yesterday. He never said nothing. The next minute he whirls on me and says:

'Do you reckon that nigger would blow on us? We'd skin him if he done that!'

'How can be blow? Hain't he run off?'

'No! That old fool sold him, and never divided with me, and the money's gone.'

'*Sold* him?' I says, and begun to cry; 'why, he was *my* nigger, and that was my money. Where is he? – I want my nigger.'

'Well, you can't *get* your nigger, that's all – so dry up your blubbering. Looky here – do you think *you*'d venture to blow on us? Blamed if I think I'd trust you. Why, if you *was* to blow on us——'

He stopped, but I never see the duke look so ugly out of his eyes before. I went on a-whimpering, and says:

'I don't want to blow on nobody; and I ain't got no time to blow, nohow. I got to turn out and find my nigger.'

He looked kinder bothered, and stood there with his bills fluttering on his arm, thinking, and wrinkling up his forehead. At last he says:

'I'll tell you something. We got to be here three days. If you'll promise you won't blow, and won't let the nigger blow, I'll tell you where to find him.'

So I promised, and he says:

'A farmer by the name of Silas Ph——' and then he stopped. You see he started to tell me the truth; but when he stopped, that way, and begun to study and think again, I reckoned he was changing his mind. And so he was. He wouldn't trust me; he wanted to make sure of having me out of the way the whole three days. So pretty soon he says: 'The man that bought him is named Abram Foster – Abram G. Foster – and he lives forty mile back here in the country, on the road to Lafayette.'

'All right,' I says, 'I can walk it in three days. And I'll start this very afternoon.'

'No, you won't, you'll start *now*; and don't you lose any time about it, neither, nor do any gabbling by the way. Just keep a tight tongue in your head and move right along, and then you won't get into trouble with *us*, d'ye hear?'

That was the order I wanted, and that was the one I played for. I wanted to be left free to work my plans.

'So clear out,' he says; 'and you can tell Mr. Foster whatever you want to. Maybe you can get him to believe that Jim *is* your nigger – some idiots don't require documents – leastways I've heard there's such down South here. And when you tell him the handbill and the reward's bogus, maybe he'll believe you when you explain to him what the idea was for getting 'em out. Go 'long, now, and tell him anything you want to; but mind you don't work your jaw any *between* here and there.'

So I left, and struck for the back country. I didn't look around, but I kinder felt like he was watching me. But I knowed I could tire him out at that. I went straight out in the country as much as a mile, before I stopped; then I doubled back through the woods towards Phelps's. I reckoned I better start in on my plan straight off, without fooling around, because I wanted to stop Jim's mouth till these fellows could get away. I didn't want no trouble with their kind. I'd seen all I wanted to of them, and wanted to get entirely shut of them.

Chapter 32

When I got there it was all still and Sunday-like, and hot and sunshiny – the hands was gone to the fields; and there was them kind of faint droning of bugs and flies in the air that makes it seem so lonesome and like everybody's dead and gone; and if a breeze fans along and quivers the leaves, it makes you feel mournful, because you feel like it's spirits whispering – spirits that's been dead ever so many years – and you always think they're talking about *you*. As a general thing it makes a body wish *he* was dead, too, and done with it all.

Phelps's was one of these little one-horse cotton plantations; and they all look alike. A rail fence round a two-acre yard; a stile, made out of logs sawed off and up-ended, in steps, like barrels of a different length, to climb over the fence with, and for the women to stand on when they are going to jump on to a horse; some sickly grass-patches in the big yard, but mostly it was bare and smooth, like an old hat with the nap rubbed off; big double log house for the white folks – hewed logs, with the chinks stopped up with mud or mortar, and these mud-stripes been whitewashed some time or another; round-log kitchen, with a big broad, open but roofed passage joining it to the house; log smoke-house back of the kitchen; three little log nigger-cabins in a row t'other side the smoke-house; one little hut all by itself away down against the back fence, and some outbuildings down a piece the other side; ash-hopper, and big kettle to bile soap in, by the little hut; bench by the kitchen door, with bucket of water and a gourd; hound asleep there, in the sun; more hounds asleep, round about; about three shade-trees away off in a corner; some currant bushes and gooseberry bushes in one place by the fence; outside of the fence a garden and a water-melon patch; then the cotton fields begins; and after the fields, the woods.

I went around and clumb over the back stile by the ash-hopper, and started for the kitchen. When I got a little ways, I heard the dim hum of a spinning-wheel wailing along up and sinking along down again; and then I knowed for certain I wished I was dead – for that *is* the lonesomest sound in the whole world.

I went right along, not fixing up any particular plan, but just trusting to Providence to put the right words in my mouth when the time come; for I'd noticed that Providence always did put the right words in my mouth, if I left it alone.

When I got half-way, first one hound and then another got up and went for me, and of course I stopped and faced them, and kept still. And such another pow-wow as they made! In a quarter of a minute I was a kind of a hub of a wheel, as you may say – spokes made out of dogs – circle of fifteen of them packed together around me, with their necks and noses stretched up towards me, a-barking and howling; and more a-coming; you could see them sailing over fences and around corners from everywheres.

, A nigger woman come tearing out of the kitchen with a rolling-pin in her hand, singing out, 'Begone! *you* Tige! you Spot! begone, sah!' and she fetched first one and then another of them a clip and sent him howling, and then the rest followed; and the next second, half of them come back, wagging their tails around me and making friends with me. There ain't no harm in a hound, nohow.

And behind the woman comes a little nigger girl and two little nigger boys, without anything on but tow-linen shirts, and they hung on to their mother's gown, and peeped out from behind her at me, bashful, the way they always do. And here comes the white woman running from the house, about forty-five or fifty year old, bareheaded, and her spinning-stick in her hand; and behind her comes her little white children, acting the same way the little niggers was doing. She was smiling all over so she could hardly stand – and says:

'It's *you*, at last! – *ain't* it?'

I out with a 'Yes'm,' before I thought.

She grabbed me and hugged me tight; and then gripped me by both hands and shook and shook; and the tears come in her eyes, and run down over; and she couldn't seem to hug and shake enough, and kept saying, 'You don't look as much like your mother as I reckoned you would, but law sakes, I don't care for that, I'm *so* glad to see you! Dear, dear, it does seem like I could eat you up! Children, it's your Cousin Tom! – tell him howdy.'

But they ducked their heads, and put their fingers in their mouths, and hid behind her. So she run on:

'Lize, hurry up and get him a hot breakfast, right away – or did you get your breakfast on the boat?'

I said I had got it on the boat. So then she started for the house, leading me by the hand, and the children tagging after. When we got there, she set me down in a split-bottomed chair, and set herself down on a little low stool in front of me, holding both of my hands, and says:

'Now I can have a *good* look at you; and laws-a-me, I've been hungry for it a many and a many a time, all these long years, and it's come at last! We been expecting you a couple of days and more. What's kep' you! – boat get aground?'

'Yes'm – she——'

'Don't say yes'm – say Aunt Sally. Where'd she get aground?'

I didn't rightly know what to say, because I didn't know whether the boat would be coming up the river or down. But I go a good deal on instinct; and my instinct said she would be coming up – from down towards Orleans. That didn't help me much, though; for I didn't know the names of bars down that way. I see I'd got to invent a bar, or forget the name of the one we got aground on – or—— Now I struck an idea, and fetched it out:

'It warn't the grounding – that didn't keep us back but a little. We blowed out a cylinder-head.'

'Good gracious! anybody hurt?'

'No'm. Killed a nigger.'

'Well, it's lucky; because sometimes people do get hurt. Two years ago last Christmas, your Uncle Silas was coming up from Newrleans on the old *Lally Rook*, and she blowed out a cylinder-head and crippled a man. And I think he died afterwards. He was a Babtist. Your Uncle Silas knowed a family in Baton Rouge that knowed his people very well. Yes, I remember, now he *did* die. Mortification set in, and they had to amputate him. But it didn't save him. Yes, it was mortification – that was it. He turned blue all over, and died in the hope of a glorious resurrection. They say he was a sight to look at. Your uncle's been up to the town every day to fetch you. And he's gone again, not more'n an hour ago: he'll be back any minute, now. You must a met him on the road, didn't you? – oldish man, with a——'

'No, I didn't see nobody, Aunt Sally. The boat landed just at daylight, and I left my baggage on the wharf-boat and went looking around the town and out a piece in the country, to put in the time and not get here too soon; and so I come down the back way.'

'Who'd you give the baggage to?'

'Nobody.'

'Why, child, it'll be stole!'

'Not where *I* hid it I reckon it won't,' I says.

'How'd you get your breakfast so early on the boat?'

It was kinder thin ice, but I says:

'The captain see me standing around, and told me I better have something to eat before I went ashore; so he took me in the texas to the officers' lunch, and give me all I wanted.'

I was getting so uneasy I couldn't listen good. I had my mind on the children all the time; I wanted to get them out to one side, and pump them a little, and find out who I was. But I couldn't get no show, Mrs. Phelps kept it up and run on so. Pretty soon she made the cold chills streak all down my back, because she says:

'But here we're a-running on this way, and you hain't told me a word about Sis, nor any of them. Now I'll rest my works a little, and you start up yourn; just tell me *everything* – tell me all about'm all – every one of 'm; and how they are, and what they're doing, and what they told you to tell me; and every last thing you can think of.'

Well, I see I was up a stump – and up it good. Providence had stood by me thus fur, all right, but I was hard and right aground, now. I see it warn't a bit of use to try to go ahead – I'd *got* to throw up my hand. So I says to myself, here's another place where I got to resk the truth. I opened my mouth to begin; but she grabbed me and hustled me in behind the bed, and says:

'Here he comes! stick your head down lower – there, that'll do; you can't be seen, now. Don't you let on you're here. I'll play a joke on him. Childern, don't you say a word.'

I see I was in a fix, now. But it warn't no use to worry; there warn't nothing to do but just hold still, and try and be ready to stand from under when the lightning struck.

I had just one little glimpse of the old gentleman when he come in, then the bed hid him. Mrs. Phelps she jumps for him and says:

'Has he come?'

'No,' says her husband.

'Good-*ness* gracious!' she says, 'what in the world *can* have become of him?'

'I can't imagine,' says the old gentleman; 'and I must say, it makes me dreadful uneasy.'

'Uneasy!' she says, 'I'm ready to go distracted! He *must* a come; and you've missed him along the road. I *know* it's so – something *tells* me so.'

'Why, Sally, I *couldn't* miss him along the road – *you* know that.'

'But oh, dear, dear, what *will* Sis say! He must a come! You must a missed him. He——'

'Oh, don't distress me any more'n I'm already distressed. I don't know what in the world to make of it. I'm at my wits' end, and I don't mind acknowledging't I'm right down scared. But there's no hope that he's come! for he *couldn't* come and me miss him. Sally, it's terrible – just terrible – something's happened to the boat, sure!'

'Why, Silas! Look yonder! – up the road! – ain't that somebody coming?'

He sprung to the window at the head of the bed, and that give Mrs. Phelps the chance she wanted. She stooped down quick, at the foot of the bed, and give me a pull, and out I come; and when he turned back from the window, there she stood, a-beaming and a-smiling like a house afire, and I standing pretty meek and sweaty alongside. The old gentleman stared, and says:

'Why, who's that?'

'Who do you reckon't is?'

'I hain't no idea. Who *is* it?'

'It's *Tom Sawyer*!'

By jings, I most slumped through the floor. But there warn't no time to swap knives; the old man grabbed me by the hand and shook, and kept on shaking; and all the time, how the woman did dance around and laugh and cry; and then how they both did fire off questions about Sid, and Mary, and the rest of the tribe.

But if they were joyful, it warn't nothing to what I was; for it was like being born again, I was so glad to find out who I was. Well, they froze to me for two hours; and at last when my chin was so tired it couldn't hardly go, any more, I had told them more about my family – I mean the Sawyer family – than ever happened to any six Sawyer families. And I explained all about how we blowed out a cylinder-head at the mouth of White River and it took us three days to fix it. Which was all right, and worked first rate; because *they* didn't know but what it would take three days to fix it. If I'd a called it a bolt-head it would a done just as well.

Now I was feeling pretty comfortable all down one side, and pretty uncomfortable all up the other. Being Tom Sawyer was easy and comfortable; and it stayed easy and comfortable till by and by I hear a steamboat coughing along down the river – then I says to myself, s'pose Tom Sawyer come down on that boat? – and s'pose he steps in here, any minute, and sings out my name before I can throw him a wink to keep quiet? Well, I couldn't *have* it that way – it wouldn't do at all. I must go up the road and waylay him. So I told the folks I reckoned I would go up to the town and fetch down my baggage. The old gentleman was for going along with me, but I said no, I could drive the horse myself, and I druther he wouldn't take no trouble about me.

Chapter 33

So I started for town, in the wagon, and when I was half-way I see a wagon coming, and sure enough it was Tom Sawyer, and I stopped and waited till he come along. I says, 'Hold on!' and it stopped alongside, and his mouth opened like a trunk, and stayed so; and he swallowed two or three times like a person that's got a dry throat, and then says:

'I hain't ever done you no harm. You know that. So, then, what you want to come back and ha'nt *me* for?'

I says:

'I hain't come back – I hain't been *gone*.'

When he heard my voice, it righted him up some, but he warn't quite satisfied yet. He says:

'Don't you play nothing on me, because I wouldn't on you. Honest injun, now, you ain't a ghost?'

'Honest injun, I ain't,' I says.

'Well – I – I – well, that ought to settle it, of course; but I can't somehow seem to understand it, no way. Looky here, warn't you ever murdered *at all?*'

'No. I warn't ever murdered at all – I played it on them. You come in here and feel of me if you don't believe me.'

So he done it, and it satisfied him; and he was that glad to see me again, he didn't know what to do. And he wanted to know all about it right off; because it was a grand adventure, and mysterious, and so it hit him where he lived. But I said, leave it alone till by and by; and told his driver to wait, and we drove off a little piece, and I told him the kind of a fix I was in, and what did he reckon we better do? He said, let him alone a minute, and don't disturb him. So he thought and thought, and pretty soon he says:

'It's all right, I've got it. Take my trunk in your wagon, and let on it's yourn; and you turn back and fool along slow, so as to get to the house about the time you ought to; and I'll go towards town a piece, and take a fresh start, and get there a quarter or a half an hour after you; and you needn't let on to know me, at first.'

I says:

'All right; but wait a minute. There's one more thing – a thing that *nobody* don't know but me. And that is, there's a nigger here that I'm a-trying to steal out of slavery – and his name is *Jim* – old Miss Watson's Jim.'

He says:

'What! Why Jim is——'

He stopped, and went to studying. I says:

'*I* know what you'll say. You'll say it's dirty low–down business; but what if it is? – *I'*m low down; and I'm a-going to steal him, and I want you to keep mum and not let on. Will you?'

His eye lit up, and he says:

'I'll *help* you steal him!'

Well, I let go all holts then, like I was shot. It was the most astonishing speech I ever heard – and I'm bound to say Tom Sawyer fell, considerable, in my estimation. Only I couldn't believe it. Tom Sawyer a *nigger stealer*!

'Oh, shucks.' I says, 'you're joking.'

'I ain't joking, either.'

'Well, then,' I says, 'joking or no joking, if you hear anything said about a runaway nigger, don't forget to remember that *you* don't know nothing about him, and *I* don't know nothing about him.'

Then we took the trunk and put it in my wagon, and he drove off his way, and I drove mine. But of course I forgot all about driving slow, on accounts of being glad and full of thinking; so I got home a heap too quick for that length of a trip. The old gentleman was at the door, and he says:

'Why, this is wonderful. Who ever would have thought it was in that mare to do it. I wish we'd a timed her. And she hain't sweated a hair – not a hair. It's wonderful. Why, I wouldn't take a hundred dollars for that horse now; I wouldn't, honest; and yet I'd a sold her for fifteen before, and thought 'twas all she was worth.'

That's all he said. He was the innocentest, best old soul I ever see. But it warn't surprising; because he warn't only just a farmer, he was a preacher, too, and had a little one-horse log church down back of the plantation, which he built it himself at his own expense, for a church and school-house, and never charged nothing for his preaching, and it was worth it, too. There was plenty other farmer-preachers like that, and done the same way, down South.

In about half an hour Tom's wagon drove up to the front stile, and Aunt Sally she see it through the window because it was only about fifty yards, and says:

'Why, there's somebody come! I wonder who 'tis? Why, I do believe it's a stranger. Jimmy' (that's one of the children), 'run and tell Lize to put on another plate for dinner.'

Everybody made a rush for the front door, because, of course, a stranger don't come *every* year, and so he lays over the yaller fever, for interest, when he does come. Tom was over the stile and starting for the house; the wagon was spinning up the road for the village, and we was all bunched in the front door. Tom had his store clothes on, and an audience – and that was always nuts for Tom Sawyer. In them circumstances it warn't no trouble to him to throw in an amount of style that was suitable. He warn't a boy to meeky along up that yard like a sheep; no, he come calm and important, like the ram. When he got afront of us, he lifts his hat ever so gracious and dainty, like it was the lid of a box that had butterflies asleep in it, and he didn't want to disturb them, and says:

'Mr. Archibald Nichols, I presume?'

'No, my boy,' says the old gentleman, 'I'm sorry to say't your driver has deceived you; Nichols's place is down a matter of three mile more. Come in, come in.'

Tom he took a look back over his shoulder, and says, 'Too late – he's out of sight.'

'Yes, he's gone, my son, and you must come in and eat your dinner with us; and then we'll hitch up and take you down to Nichols's.'

'Oh, I *can't* make you so much trouble, I couldn't think of it. I'll walk – I don't mind the distance.'

'But we won't *let* you walk – it wouldn't be Southern hospitality to do it. Come right in.'

'Oh, *do*,' says Aunt Sally; 'it ain't a bit of trouble to us, not a bit in the world. You *must* stay. It's a long, dusty three mile, and we *can't* let you walk. And besides, I've already told 'em to put on another plate, when I see you coming; so you mustn't disappoint us. Come right in, and make yourself at home.'

So Tom he thanked them very hearty and handsome, and let himself be persuaded, and come in; and when he was in, he said he was a stranger from Hicksville, Ohio, and his name was William Thompson – and he made another bow.

Well, he run on, and on, and on, making up stuff about Hicksville and everybody in it he could invent, and I getting a little nervous, and wondering how this was going to help me out of my scrape; and at last, still talking along, he reached over and kissed Aunt Sally right on the mouth, and then settled back again in his chair, comfortable, and was going on talking; but she jumped up and wiped it off with the back of her hand, and says:

'You owdacious puppy!'

He looked kind of hurt, and says:

'I'm surprised at you, ma'am.'

'You're s'rp—— Why, what do you reckon *I* am? I've a good notion to take and – say, what do you mean by kissing me?'

He looked kind of humble, and says:

'I didn't mean nothing, ma'm. I didn't mean no harm. I – I – thought you'd like it.'

"'Why, you born fool! . . . what made you think I'd like it?'"

'Why, you born fool!' She took up the spinning-stick, and it looked like it was all she could do to keep from giving him a crack with it. 'What made you think I'd like it?'

'Well, I don't know. Only, they – they – told me you would.'

'*They* told you I would. Whoever told you's *another* lunatic. I never heard the beat of it. Who's *they?*'

'Why – everybody. They all said so, ma'am.'

It was all she could do to hold in; and her eyes snapped, and her fingers worked like she wanted to scratch him; and she says:

'Who's "everybody"? Out with their names – or ther'll be an idiot short.'

He got up and looked distressed, and fumbled his hat, and says:

'I'm sorry, and I warn't expecting it. They told me to. They all told me to. They all said kiss her; and said she'll like it. They all said it – every one of them. But I'm sorry, ma'm, and I won't do it no more – I won't, honest.'

'You won't, won't you? Well, I sh'd *reckon* you won't!'

'No'm, I'm honest about it; I won't ever do it again. Till you ask me.'

'Till I *ask* you! Well, I never see the beat of it in my born days! I lay you'll be the Methusalem-numskull of creation before ever *I* ask you – or the likes of you.'

'Well,' he says, 'it does surprise me so. I can't make it out, somehow. They said you would, and I thought you would. But——' He stopped and looked around slow, like he wished he could run across a friendly eye, somewheres; and fetched up on the old gentleman's, and says, 'Didn't *you* think she'd like me to kiss her, sir?'

'Why, no, I – I – well, no, I b'lieve I didn't.'

Then he looks on around, the same way, to me – and says:

'Tom, didn't *you* think Aunt Sally'd open out her arms and say, "Sid Sawyer——"'

'My land!' she says, breaking in and jumping for him, 'you impudent young rascal, to fool a body so——' and was going to hug him, but he fended her off, and says:

'No, not till you've asked me, first.'

So she didn't lose no time, but asked him; and hugged him and kissed him, over and over again, and then turned him over to the old man, and he took what was left. And after they got a little quiet again, she says:

'Why, dear me, I never see such a surprise. We warn't looking for *you*, at all, but only Tom. Sis never wrote to me about anybody coming but him.'

'It's because it warn't *intended* for any of us to come but Tom,' he says; 'but I begged and begged, and at the last minute she let me come, too; so, coming down the river, me and Tom thought it would be a first-rate surprise for him to come here to the house first, and for me to by and by tag along and drop in and let on to be a stranger. But it was a mistake, Aunt Sally. This ain't no healthy place for a stranger to come.'

'No – not impudent whelps, Sid. You ought to had your jaws boxed; I hain't been so put out since I don't know when. But I don't care, I don't mind the terms – I'd be willing to stand a thousand such jokes to have you here. Well, to think of that performance! I don't deny it, I was most putrified with astonishment when you give me that smack.'

We had dinner out in that broad open passage betwixt the house and the kitchen; and there was things enough on that table for seven families – and all hot, too; none of your flabby tough meat that's laid in a cupboard in a damp cellar all night and tastes like a hunk of cold cannibal in the morning. Uncle Silas he asked a pretty long blessing over it, but it was worth it; and it didn't cool it a bit, neither, the way I've seen them kind of interruptions do, lots of times.

There was a considerable good deal of talk, all the afternoon, and me and Tom was on the look-out all the time, but it warn't no use, they didn't happen to say nothing about any runaway nigger, and we was afraid to try to work up to it. But at supper, at night, one of the little boys says:

'Pa, mayn't Tom and Sid and me go to the show?'

'No,' says the old man, 'I reckon there ain't going to be any; and you couldn't go if there was; because the runaway nigger told Burton and me all about that scandalous show, and Burton said he would tell the people; so I reckon they've drove the owdacious loafers out of town before this time.'

So there it was! – but *I* couldn't help it. Tom and me was to sleep in the same room and bed; so, being tired, we bid good night and went up to bed, right after supper, and clumb out of the window and down the lightning-rod, and shoved for the town; for I didn't believe anybody was going to give the king and the duke a hint, and so, if I didn't hurry up and give them one they'd get into trouble sure.

On the road Tom he told me all about how it was reckoned I was murdered, and how pap disappeared, pretty soon, and didn't come back no more, and what a stir there was when Jim run away; and I told Tom all about our Royal Nonesuch rapscallions, and as much of the raft-voyage as I had time to; and as we struck into the town and up through the middle of it – it was as much as half-after eight, then – here comes a raging rush of people, with torches, and an awful whooping and yelling, and banging tin pans and blowing horns; and we jumped to one side to let them go by; and as they went by, I see they had the king and the duke astraddle of a rail – that is, I knowed it *was* the king and the duke, though they was all over tar and feathers, and didn't look like nothing in the world that was human – just looked like a couple of monstrous big soldier-plumes. Well, it made me sick to see it; and I was sorry for them poor pitiful rascals, it seemed like I couldn't ever feel any hardness against them any more in the world. It was a dreadful thing to see.

Human beings *can* be awful cruel to one another.

We see we was too late – couldn't do no good. We asked some stragglers about it, and they said everybody went to the show looking very innocent; and laid low and kept dark till the poor old king was in the middle of his cavortings on the stage; then somebody gave a signal, and the house rose up and went for them.

So we poked along back home, and I warn't feeling so brash as I was before, but kind of ornery, and humble, and to blame, somehow – though *I* hadn't done nothing. But that's always the way; it don't make no difference whether you do right or wrong, a person's conscience ain't got no sense, and just goes for him *anyway*. If I had a yaller dog that didn't know no more than a person's conscience does, I would pison him. It takes up more room than all the rest of a person's insides, and yet ain't no good, nohow. Tom Sawyer he says the same.

Chapter 34

We stopped talking, and got to thinking. By and by Tom says:

'Looky here, Huck, what fools we are, to not think of it before! I bet I know where Jim is.'

'No! Where?'

'In that hut down by the ash-hopper. Why, looky here. When we was at dinner, didn't you see a nigger man go in there with some vittles?'

'Yes.'

'What did you think the vittles was for?'

'For a dog.'

'So'd I. Well, it wasn't for a dog.'

'Why?'

'Because part of it was watermelon.'

'So it was – I noticed it. Well, it does beat all, that I never thought about a dog not eating watermelon. It shows how a body can see and don't see at the same time.'

'Well, the nigger unlocked the padlock when he went in, and he locked it again when he come out. He fetched uncle a key, about the time we got up from table – same key, I bet. Watermelon shows man, lock shows prisoners; and it ain't likely there's two prisoners on such a little plantation, and where the people's all so kind and good. Jim's the prisoner. All right – I'm glad we found it out detective fashion; I wouldn't give shucks for any other way. Now you work your mind and study out a plan to steal Jim, and I will study out one, too; and we'll take the one we like the best.'

What a head for just a boy to have! If I had Tom Sawyer's head, I wouldn't trade it off to be a duke, nor mate of a steamboat, nor clown in a circus, nor nothing I can think of. I went to thinking out a plan, but only just to be doing something; I knowed very well where the right plan was going to come from. Pretty soon, Tom says:

'Ready?'

'Yes,' I says.

'All right – bring it out.'

'My plan is this,' I says. 'We can easy find out if it's Jim in there. Then get up my canoe to-morrow night, and fetch my raft over from the island.

Then the first dark night that comes, steal the key out of the old man's britches, after he goes to bed, and shove off down the river on the raft, with Jim, hiding day-times and running nights, the way me and Jim used to do before. Wouldn't that plan work?'

'Work? Why cert'nly, it would work, like rats a-fighting. But it's too blame' simple; there ain't nothing *to* it. What's the good of a plan that ain't no more trouble than that? It's as mild as goose-milk. Why, Huck, it wouldn't make no more talk than breaking into a soap factory.'

I never said nothing, because I warn't expecting nothing different; but I knowed mighty well that whenever he got *his* plan ready it wouldn't have none of them objections to it.

And it didn't. He told me what it was, and I see in a minute it was worth fifteen of mine, for style, and would make Jim just as free a man as mine would, and maybe get us all killed besides. So I was satisfied, and said we would waltz in on it. I needn't tell what it was, here, because I knowed it wouldn't stay the way it was. I knowed he would be changing it around, every which way, as we went along, and heaving in new bullinesses wherever he got a chance. And that is what he done.

Well, one thing was dead sure: and that was, that Tom Sawyer was in earnest and was actuly going to help steal that nigger out of slavery. That was the thing that was too many for me. Here was a boy that was respectable, and well brung up; and had a character to lose; and folks at home that had characters; and he was bright and not leather-headed; and knowing and not ignorant; and not mean, but kind; and yet here he was, without any more pride, or rightness, or feeling, than to stoop to this business, and make himself a shame, and his family a shame, before everybody. I *couldn't* understand it, no way at all. It was outrageous, and I knowed I ought to just up and tell him so; and so be his true friend, and let him quit the thing right where he was, and save himself. And I *did* start to tell him; but he shut me up, and says:

'Don't you reckon I know what I'm about? Don't I generly know what I'm about?'

'Yes.'

'Didn't I *say* I was going to help steal the nigger?'

'Yes.'

'Well, then.'

That's all he said, and that's all I said. It warn't no use to say any more; because when he said he'd do a thing, he always done it. But *I* couldn't make out how he was willing to go into this thing; so I just let it go, and never bothered no more about it. If he was bound to have it so, *I* couldn't help it.

When we got home, the house was all dark and still; so we went on down to the hut by the ash-hopper, for to examine it. We went through the yard, so as to see what the hounds would do. They knowed us, and didn't make no more noise than country dogs is always doing when anything comes by in the night. When we got to the cabin, we took a look at the front and the two sides; and on the side I warn't acquainted with – which was the north side – we found a square window-hole, up tolerable high, with just one stout board nailed across it. I says:

'Here's the ticket. This hole's big enough for Jim to get through, if we wrench off the board.'

Tom says:

'It's as simple as tit-tat-toe, three-in-a-row, and as easy as playing hooky. I should *hope* we can find a way that's a little more complicated than *that*, Huck Finn.'

'Well, then,' I says, 'how'll it do to saw him out, the way I done before I was murdered, that time?'

'That's more *like*,' he says. 'It's real mysterious, and troublesome, and good,' he says; 'but I bet we can find a way that's twice as long. There ain't no hurry; le's keep on looking around.'

Betwixt the hut and the fence, on the back side, was a lean-to, that joined the hut at the eaves, and was made out of plank. It was as long as the hut, but narrow – only about six foot wide. The door to it was at the south end, and was padlocked. Tom he went to the soap kettle, and searched around and fetched back the iron thing they lift the lid with; so he took it and prised out one of the staples. The chain fell down, and we opened the door and went in, and shut it, and struck a match, and see the shed was only built against the cabin and hadn't no connection with it; and there warn't no floor to the shed, nor nothing in it but some old rusty played-out hoes, and spades, and picks, and a crippled plow. The match went out, and so did we, and shoved in the staple again, and the door was locked as good as ever. Tom was joyful. He says:

'Now we're all right. We'll *dig* him out. It'll take about a week!'

Then we started for the house, and I went in the back door – you only have to pull a buckskin latch-string, they don't fasten the doors – but that warn't romantical enough for Tom Sawyer: no way would do him but he must climb up the lightning-rod. But after he got up half-way about three times, and missed fire and fell every time, and the last time most busted his brains out, he thought he'd got to give it up; but after he was rested, he allowed he would give her one more turn for luck, and this time he made the trip.

In the morning we was up at break of day, and down to the nigger cabins to pet the dogs and make friends with the nigger that fed Jim – if it *was* Jim that was being fed. The niggers was just getting through breakfast and starting for the fields; and Jim's nigger was piling up a tin pan with bread and meat and things; and whilst the others was leaving, the key come from the house.

This nigger had a good-natured, chuckle-headed face, and his wool was all tied up in little bunches with thread. That was to keep witches off. He said the witches was pestering him awful, these nights, and making him see all kinds of strange things, and hear all kinds of strange words and noises, and he didn't believe he was ever witched so long, before, in his life. He got so worked up, and got to running on so about his troubles, he forgot all about what he'd been a-going to do. So Tom says:

'What's the vittles for? Going to feed the dogs?'

The nigger kind of smiled around graduly over his face, like when you heave a brickbat in a mud puddle, and he says:

'Yes, Mars Sid, *a* dog. Cur'us dog, too. Does you want to go en look at 'im?'

'Yes.'

I hunched Tom, and whispers:

'You going, right here in the daybreak? *That* warn't the plan.'

'No, it warn't – but it's the plan *now*.'

So, drat him, we went along, but I didn't like it much. When we got in, we couldn't hardly see anything, it was so dark; but Jim was there, sure enough, and could see us; and he sings out:

'Why *Huck*! En good *lan'*! ain' dat Misto Tom?'

I just knowed how it would be; I just expected it. *I* didn't know nothing to do; and if I had, I couldn't a done it; because that nigger busted in and says:

'Why, de gracious sakes! do he know you genlmen?'

We could see pretty well, now. Tom he looked at the nigger, steady and kind of wondering, and says:

'Does *who* know us?'

'Why, dish-yer runaway nigger.'

'I don't reckon he does; but what put that into your head?'

'What *put* it dar? Didn' he jis' dis minute sing out like he knowed you?'

Tom says, in a puzzled-up kind of way:

'Well, that's mighty curious. *Who* sung out? *When* did he sing out? *What* did he sing out?' And turns to me, perfectly calm, and says, 'Did *you* hear anybody sing out?'

Of course there warn't nothing to be said but the one thing; so I says:

'No; *I* ain't heard nobody say nothing.'

Then he turns to Jim, and looks him over like he never see him before; and says:

'Did you sing out?'

'No, sah,' says Jim; '*I* hain't said nothing, sah.'

'Not a word?'

'No, sah, I hain't said a word.'

'Did you ever see us before?'

'No, sah; not as *I* knows on.'

So Tom turns to the nigger, which was looking wild and distressed, and says, kind of severe:

'What do you reckon's the matter with you, anyway? What made you think somebody sung out?'

'Oh, it's de dad-blame' witches, sah, en I wisht I was dead, I do. Dey's awluz at it, sah, en dey do mos' kill me, dey sk'yers me so. Please to don't tell nobody 'bout it, sah, er ole Mars Silas he'll scole me; 'kase he says dey *ain't* no witches. I jis' wish to goodness he was heah now – *den* what would he say! I jis' bet he couldn' fine no way to git aroun' it *dis* time. But it's awluz jis' so; people dat's *sot*, stays sot; dey won't look into nothn' en fine it out f'r deyselves, en when *you* fine it out en tell um 'bout it, dey doan' b'lieve you.'

Tom give him a dime, and said we wouldn't tell nobody; and told him to buy some more thread to tie up his wool with; and then looks at Jim, and says:

'I wonder if Uncle Silas is going to hang this nigger. If I was to catch a nigger that was ungrateful enough to run away, *I* wouldn't give him up, I'd hang him.' And whilst the nigger stepped to the door to look at the dime and bite it to see if it was good, he whispers to Jim, and says:

'Don't ever let on to know us. And if you hear any digging going on night, it's us: we're going to set you free.'

Jim only had time to grab us by the hand and squeeze it, then the nigger come back, and we said we'd come again some time if the nigger wanted us to; and he said he would, more particular if it was dark, because the witches went for him mostly in the dark, and it was good to have folks around then.

Chapter 35

It would be most an hour, yet, till breakfast, so we left; and struck down into the woods; because Tom said we got to have *some* light to see how to dig by, and a lantern makes too much, and might get us into trouble; what we must have was a lot of them rotten chunks that's called fox-fire and just makes a soft kind of a glow when you lay them in a dark place. We fetched an armful and hid it in the weeds, and set down to rest, and Tom says, kind of dissatisfied:

'Blame it, this whole thing is just as easy and awkward as it can be. And so it makes it so rotten difficult to get up a difficult plan. There ain't no watchman to be drugged – now there *ought* to be a watchman. There ain't even a dog to give a sleeping-mixture to. And there's Jim chained by one leg, with a ten-foot chain, to the leg of his bed: why, all you got to do is to lift up the bedstead and slip off the chain. And Uncle Silas he trusts everybody; sends the key to the punkin-headed nigger, and don't send nobody to watch the nigger. Jim could a got out of that window-hole before this, only there wouldn't be no use trying to travel with a ten-foot chain on his leg. Why, drat it, Huck, it's the stupidest arrangement I ever see. You got to invent *all* the difficulties. Well, we can't help it, we got to do the best we can with the materials we've got. Anyhow, there's one thing – there's more honour in getting him out through a lot of difficulties and dangers, where there warn't one of them furnished to you by the people who it was their duty to furnish them, and you had to contrive them all out of your own head. Now look at just that one thing of the lantern. When you come down to the cold facts, we simply got to *let* on that a lantern's resky. Why, we could work with a torchlight procession if we wanted to, *I* believe. Now, whilst I think of it, we got to hunt up something to make a saw out of, the first chance we get.'

'What do we want of a saw?'

'What do we *want* of it? Hain't we got to saw the leg of Jim's bed off, so as to get the chain loose?'

'Why, you just said a body could lift up the bedstead and slip the chain off.'

'Well, if that ain't just like you, Huck Finn. You *can* get up the infant-schooliest ways of going at a thing. Why, hain't you ever read any books at all? – Baron Trenck, nor Casanova, nor Benvenuto Challeeny, nor Henri IV, nor none of them heroes? Who ever head of getting a prisoner loose in such an old-maidy way as that? No; the way all the best authorities does, is to saw the bed-leg in two, and leave it just so, and swallow the sawdust, so it can't be found, and put some dirt and grease around the sawed place so the very keenest seneskal can't see no sign of its being sawed, and thinks the bed-leg is perfectly sound. Then, the night you're ready, fetch the leg a kick, down she goes; slip off your chain, and there you are. Nothing to do but hitch your rope-ladder to the battlements, shin down it, break your leg in the moat – because a rope-ladder is nineteen foot too short, you know – and there's your horses and your trusty vassles, and they scoop you up and fling you across a saddle and away you go, to your native Langudoc, or Navarre, or wherever it is. It's gaudy, Huck. I wish there was a moat to this cabin. If we get time, the night of the escape, we'll dig one.'

I says:

'What do we want of a moat, when we're going to snake him out from under the cabin?'

But he never heard me. He had forgot me and everything else. He had his chin in his hand, thinking. Pretty soon, he sighs, and shakes his head; then sighs again, and says:

'No, it wouldn't do – there ain't necessity enough for it.'

'For what?' I says:

'Why, to saw Jim's leg off,' he says.

'Good land!' I says, ' why, there ain't *no* necessity for it. And what would you want to saw his leg off for, anyway?'

'Well, some of the best authorities has done it. They couldn't get the chain off, so they just cut their hand off, and shoved. And a leg would be better still. But we got to let that go. There ain't necessity enough in this case; and besides, Jim's a nigger and wouldn't understand the reasons for it, and how it's the custom in Europe; so we'll let it go. But there's one thing – he can have a rope-ladder; we can tear up our sheets and make him a rope-ladder easy enough. And we can send it to him in a pie; it's mostly done that way. And I've et worse pies.'

'Why, Tom Sawyer, how you talk,' I says; 'Jim ain't got no use for a rope-ladder.'

'He *has* got use for it. How *you* talk; you better say you don't know nothing about it. He's *got* to have a rope-ladder; they all do.'

'What in the nation can he *do* with it?'

'*Do* with it? He can hide it in his bed, can't he? That's what they all do; and *he*'s got to, too. Huck, you don't ever seem to want to do anything that's regular; you want to be starting something fresh all the time. S'pose he *don't* do nothing with it? ain't it there in his bed, for a clew, after he's gone? and don't you reckon they'll want clews? Of course they will. And you wouldn't leave them any? That would be a *pretty* howdy-do, *wouldn't* it! I never heard of such a thing.'

'Well,' I says, 'if it's in the regulations, and he's got to have it, all right, let him have it; because I don't wish to go back on no regulations; but there's one thing, Tom Sawyer – if we go to tearing up our sheets to make Jim a rope-ladder, we're going to get into trouble with Aunt Sally, just as sure as you're born. Now, the way I look at it, a hick'ry-bark ladder don't cost nothing, and don't waste nothing, and is just as good to load up a pie with, and hide in a straw tick, as any rag-ladder you can start; and as for Jim, he ain't had no experience, and so *he* don't care what kind of a——'

'Oh, shucks, Huck Finn, if I was as ignorant as you, I'd keep still – that's what *I'd* do. Who ever heard of a state prisoner escaping by a hick'ry-bark ladder? Why, it's perfectly ridiculous.'

'Well, all right, Tom, fix it your own way; but if you'll take my advice, you'll let me borrow a sheet off of the clothes-line.'

He said that would do. And that give him another idea, and he says:

'Borrow a shirt, too.'

'What do we want of a shirt, Tom?'

'Want it for Jim to keep a journal on.'

'Journal your granny – *Jim* can't write.'

'S'pose he *can't* write – he can make marks on the shirt, can't he, if we make him a pen out of an old pewter spoon or a piece of an old iron barrel-hoop?'

'Why, Tom, we can pull a feather out of a goose and make him a better one; and quicker, too.'

'*Prisoners* don't have geese running around the donjon-keep to pull pens out of, you muggins. They *always* make their pens out of the hardest, toughest, troublesomest piece of old brass candlestick or something like that they can get their hands on; and it takes them weeks and weeks, and months and months to file it out, too, because they've got to do it by rubbing it on the wall. *They* wouldn't use a goose-quill if they had it. It ain't regular.'

'Well, then, what'll we make him the ink out of?'

'Many makes it out of iron-rust and tears; but that's the common sort and women; the best authorities uses their own blood. Jim can do that; and when he wants to send any little common ordinary mysterious message to let the world know where he's captivated, he can write it on the bottom of a tin plate with a fork and throw it out of the window. The Iron Mask always done that, and it's a blame' good way, too.'

'Jim ain't got no tin plates. They feed him in a pan.'

'That ain't anything; we can get him some.'

'Can't nobody *read* his plates?'

'That ain't got nothing to *do* with it, Huck Finn. All *he's* got to do is to write on the plate and throw it out. You don't *have* to be able to read it. Why, half the time you can't read anything a prisoner writes on a tin plate, or anywhere else.'

'Well, then, what's the sense in wasting the plates?'

'Why, blame it all, it ain't the *prisoner's* plates.'

'But it's *somebody's* plates, ain't it?'

'Well, s'pos'n it is? What does the *prisoner* care whose——'

He broke off there, because we heard the breakfast-horn blowing. So we cleared out for the house.

Along during the morning I borrowed a sheet and a white shirt off of the clothes-line; and I found an old sack and put them in it, and we went down and got the fox-fire, and put that in too. I called it borrowing, because that was what pap always called it; but Tom said it warn't borrowing, it was stealing. He said we was representing prisoners; and prisoners don't care how they get a thing so they get it, and nobody don't blame them for it, either. It ain't no crime in a prisoner to steal the thing he needs to get away with, Tom said; it's his right; and so, as long as we was representing a prisoner, we had a perfect right to steal anything on this place we had the least use for, to get ourselves out of prison with. He said if we warn't prisoners it would be a very different thing, and nobody but a mean ornery person would steal when he warn't a prisoner. So we allowed we would steal everything there was that come handy. And yet he made a mighty fuss, one day, after that, when I stole a watermelon out of the nigger patch and eat it; and he made me go and give the niggers a dime, without telling them what it was for. Tom said that what he meant was, we could steal anything we *needed*. Well, I says, I needed the watermelon. But he said I didn't need it to get out of prison with, there's where the difference was. He said if I'd wanted it to hide a knife in, and smuggle it to Jim to kill the seneskal with, it would a been all right. So I let it go at that, though I couldn't see no advantage in my representing a prisoner, if I got to set down and chaw over a lot of gold-leaf distinctions like that, every time I see a chance to hog a watermelon.

Well, as I was saying, we waited that morning till everybody was settled down to business, and nobody in sight around the yard; then Tom he carried the sack into the lean-to whilst I stood off a piece to keep watch. By and by he come out, and we went and set down on the wood-pile, to talk. He says:

'Everything's all right, now, except tools; and that's easy fixed.'

'Tools?' I says.

'Yes.'

'Tools for what?'

'Why, to dig with. We ain't a-going to *gnaw* him out, are we?'

'Ain't them old crippled picks and things in there good enough to dig a nigger out with?' I says.

He turns on me looking pitying enough to make a body cry, and says:

'Huck Finn, did you *ever* hear of a prisoner having picks and shovels, and all the modern conveniences in his wardrobe to dig himself out with? Now I want to ask you – if you got any reasonableness in you at all – what kind of a show would *that* give him to be a hero? Why, they might as well lend him the key, and done it. Picks and shovels – why they wouldn't furnish 'em to a king.'

'Well, then,' I says, 'if we don't want the picks and shovels, what do we want?'

'A couple of case-knives.'

'To dig the foundations out from under that cabin with?'

'Yes.'

'Confound it, it's foolish, Tom.'

'It don't make no difference how foolish it is, it's the *right* way – and it's the regular way. And there ain't no *other* way, that ever *I* heard of, and I've read all the books that gives any information about these things. They always dig out with a case-knife – and not through dirt, mind you; generly it's through solid rock. And it takes them weeks and weeks and weeks, and for ever and ever. Why, look at one of them prisoners in the bottom dungeon of the Castle Deef, in the harbour of Marseilles, that dug himself out that way; how long was *he* at it, you reckon?'

'I don't know.'

'Well, guess.'

'I don't know. A month and a half?'

'*Thirty-seven year* – and he come out in China. *That's* the kind. I wish the bottom of *this* fortress was solid rock.'

'*Jim* don't know nobody in China.'

'What's *that* got to do with it? Neither did that other fellow. But you're always a-wandering off on a side issue. Why can't you stick to the main point?'

'All right – *I* don't care where he comes out, so he *comes* out; and Jim don't, either, I reckon. But there's one thing, anyway – Jim's too old to be dug out with a case-knife. He won't last.'

'Yes he will *last* too. You don't reckon it's going to take thirty-seven years to dig out through a *dirt* foundation, do you?'

'How long will it take, Tom?'

'Well, we can't resk being as long as we ought to, because it mayn't take very long for Uncle Silas to hear from down there by New Orleans. He'll hear Jim ain't from there. Then his next move will be to advertise Jim, or something like that. So we can't resk being as long digging him out as we ought to. By rights I reckon we ought to be a couple of years; but we can't. Things being so uncertain, what I recommend is this: that we really dig right in, as quick as we can; and after that, we can *let on*, to ourselves, that we was at it thirty-seven years. Then we can snatch him out and rush him away the first time there's an alarm. Yes, I reckon that'll be the best way.'

'Now, there's *sense* in that,' I says. 'Letting on don't cost nothing; letting on ain't no trouble· and if it's any object, I don't mind letting on we was at it a hundred and fifty year. It wouldn't strain me none, after I got my hand in. So I'll mosey along now, and smouch a couple of case-knives.'

'Smouch three,' he says; 'we want one to make a saw out of.'

'Tom, if it ain't unregular and irreligious to sejest it,' I says, 'there's an old rusty saw-blade around yonder sticking under the weatherboarding behind the smoke-house.'

He looked kind of weary and discouraged-like, and says:

'It ain't no use to try to learn you nothing, Huck. Run along and smouch the knives – three of them.' So I done it.

Chapter 36

As soon as we reckoned everybody was asleep, that night, we went down the lightning-rod, and shut ourselves up in the lean-to, and got out our pile of fox-fire, and went to work. We cleared everything out of the way, about four or five foot along the middle of the bottom log. Tom said he was right behind Jim's bed now, and we'd dig in under it, and when we got through there couldn't nobody in the cabin ever know there was any hole there, because Jim's counterpin hung down most to the ground, and you'd have to rise it up and look under to see the hole. So we dug and dug, with the case-knives, till most midnight; and then we was dog-tired, and our hands was blistered, and yet you couldn't see we'd done anything, hardly. At last I says:

'This ain't no thirty-seven-year job, this is a thirty-eighty-year job, Tom Sawyer.'

He never said nothing. But he sighed, and pretty soon he stopped digging, and then for a good little while I knowed he was thinking. Then he says:

'It ain't no use, Huck, it ain't a-going to work. If we was prisoners it would, because then we'd have as many years as we wanted, and no hurry; and we wouldn't get but a few minutes to dig, every day, while they was changing watches, and so our hands wouldn't get blistered, and we could keep it up right along, year in and year out, and do it right, and the way it ought to be done. But *we* can't fool along, we got to rush; we ain't got no time to spare. If we was to put in another night this way, we'd have to knock off for a week to let our hands get well – couldn't touch a case-knife with them sooner.'

'Well, then, what we going to do, Tom?'

'I'll tell you. It ain't right, and it ain't moral, and I wouldn't like it to get out – but there ain't only just the one way; we got to dig him out with the picks, and *let on* it's case-knives.'

'*Now* you're *talking*!' I says; 'your head gets leveller and leveller all the time, Tom Sawyer,' I says. 'Picks is the thing, moral or no moral; and as for me, I don't care shucks for the morality of it, nohow. When I start in to steal a nigger, or a watermelon, or a Sunday school book, I ain't no ways particular how it's done so it's done. What I want is my nigger; or what I want is my watermelon; or what I want is my Sunday school book; and if a·pick's the handiest thing, that's the thing I'm a-going to dig that nigger or that watermelon or that Sunday school book out with; and I don't give a dead rat what the authorities thinks about it nuther.'

'Well,' he says, 'there's excuse for picks and letting-on in a case like this; if it warn't so, I wouldn't approve of it, nor I wouldn't stand by and see the rules broke – because right is right, and wrong is wrong, and a body ain't got no business doing wrong when he ain't ignorant and knows better. It might answer for *you* to dig Jim out with a pick, *without* any letting-on, because you don't know no better; but it wouldn't for me, because I do know better. Gimme a case-knife.'

He had his own by him, but I handed him mine. He flung it down, and says:

'Gimme a *case-knife*.'

I didn't know just what to do – but then I thought. I scratched around amongst the old tools, and got a pick-axe and give it to him, and he took it and went to work, and never said a word.

He was always just that particular. Full of principle.

So then I got a shovel, and then we picked and shovelled, turn about, and made the fur fly. We stuck to it about a half an hour, which was as long as we could stand up; but we had a good deal of a hole to show for it. When I got upstairs, I looked out at the window and see Tom doing his level best with the lightning-rod, but he couldn't come it, his hands was so sore. At last he says:

'It ain't no use, it can't be done. What you reckon I better do? Can't you think up no way?'

'Yes,' I says, 'but I reckon it ain't regular. Come up the stairs, and let on it's a lightning-rod.'

So he done it.

Next day Tom stole a pewter spoon and a brass candlestick in the house, for to make some pens for Jim out of, and six tallow candles; and I hung around the nigger cabins, and laid for a chance, and stole three tin plates. Tom said it wasn't enough; but I said nobody wouldn't ever see the plates that Jim throwed out, because they'd fall in the dog-fennel and jimpson weeds under the window-hole – then we could tote them back and he could use them over again. So Tom was satisfied. Then he says:

'Now, the thing to study out is, how to get the things to Jim.'

'Take them in through the hole,' I says, 'when we get it done.'

He only just looked scornful, and said something about nobody ever heard of such an idiotic idea, and then he went to studying. By and by he said he had ciphered out two or three ways, but there warn't no need to decide on any of them yet. Said we'd got to post Jim first.

That night we went down the lightning-rod a little after ten, and took one of the candles along, and listened under the window-hole, and heard Jim snoring; so we pitched it in, and it didn't wake him. Then we whirled in with the pick and shovel, and in about two hours and a half the job was done. We crept in under Jim's bed and into the cabin, and pawed around and found the candle and lit it, and stood over Jim a while, and found him looking hearty and healthy, and then we woke him up gentle and gradual. He was so glad to see us he most cried; and called us honey, and all the pet-names he could think of; and was for having us hunt up a cold chisel to cut the chain off of his leg with, right away, and clearing out without losing any time. But Tom he showed him how unregular it would be, and set down and told him all about our plans, and how we could alter them in a minute any time there was an alarm; and not to be the least afraid, because we would see he got away, *sure*. So Jim he said it was all right, and we set there and talked over old times a while, and then Tom asked a lot of questions, and when Jim told him Uncle Silas come in every day or two to pray with him, and Aunt Sally come in to see if he was comfortable and had plenty to eat, and both of them was kind as they could be, Tom says:

'*Now* I know how to fix it. We'll send you some things by them.'

I said, 'Don't do nothing of the kind; it's one of the most jackass ideas I ever struck'; but he never paid no attention to me; went right on. It was his way when he'd got his plans set.

So he told Jim how we'd have to smuggle in the rope-ladder pie, and other large things, by Nat, the nigger that fed him, and he must be on the look-out, and not be surprised, and not let Nat see him open them; and we would put small things in uncle's coat pockets and he must steal them out; and we would tie things to aunt's apron strings or put them in her apron pocket, if we got a chance; and told him what they would be and what they was for. And told how to keep a journal on the shirt with his blood, and all that. He told him everything. Jim he couldn't see no sense in the most of it, but he allowed we was white folks and knowed better than him; so he was satisfied, and said he would do it all just as Tom said.

Jim had plenty corn-cob pipes and tobacco; so we had a right-down good sociable time; then we crawled out through the hole, and so home to bed, with hands that looked like they'd been chawed. Tom was in high spirits. He said it was the best fun he ever had in his life, and the most intellectural; and said if he only could see his way to it we would keep it up all the rest of our lives and leave Jim to our children to get out; for he believed Jim would come to like it better and better the more he got used to it. He said that in that way it could be strung out to as much as eighty year, and would be the best time on record. And he said it would make us all celebrated that had a hand in it.

In the morning we went out to the wood-pile and chopped up the brass candlestick into handy sizes, and Tom put them and the pewter spoon in his pocket. Then we went to the nigger cabins, and while I got Nat's notice off, Tom shoved a piece of candlestick into the middle of a corn-pone that was in

Jim's pan, and we went along with Nat to see how it would work, and it just worked noble; when Jim bit into it it most mashed all his teeth out; and there warn't ever anything could a worked better. Tom said so himself. Jim he never let on but what it was only just a piece of rock or something like that that's always getting into bread, you know; but after that he never bit into nothing but what he jabbed his fork into it in three or four places, first.

And whilst we was a-standing there in the dimmish light, here comes a couple of the hounds bulging in, from under Jim's bed; and they kept on piling in till there was eleven of them, and there warn't hardly room in there to get your breath. By jings, we forgot to fasten that lean-to door. The nigger Nat he only just hollered 'witches!' once, and keeled over on to the floor amongst the dogs, and begun to groan like he was dying. Tom jerked the door open and flung out a slab of Jim's meat, and the dogs went for it, and in two seconds he was out himself and back again and shut the door, and I knowed he'd fixed the other door too. Then he went to work on the nigger, coaxing him and petting him, and asking him if he'd been imagining he saw something again. He raised up, and blinked his eyes around, and says:

'Mars Sid, you'll say I's a fool, but if I didn't b'lieve I see most a million dogs, er devils, er some'n, I wisht I may die right heah in dese tracks. I did, mos' sholy. Mars Sid, I *felt* um – I *felt* um, sah; dey was all over me. Dad fetch it, I jis' wisht I could git my han's on one er dem witches jis' wunst – on'y jis' wunst – it's all I'd ast. But mos'ly I wisht dey'd lemme 'lone, I does.'

Tom says:

'Well, I tell you what *I* think. What makes them come here just at this runaway nigger's breakfast-time? It's because they're hungry; that's the reason. You make them a witch pie; that's the thing for *you* to do.'

'But my lan', Mars Sid, how's *I* gwyne to make'm a witch pie? I doan' know how to make it. I hain't ever hearn er sich a thing b'fo'.'

'Well, then, I'll have to make it myself.'

'Will you do it, honey? – will you? I'll wusshup de groun' und' yo' foot, I will!'

'All right, I'll do it, seeing it's you, and you've been good to us and showed us the runaway nigger. But you got to be mighty careful. When we come around, you turn your back; and then whatever we've put in the pan, don't you let on you see it at all. And don't you look, when Jim unloads the pan – something might happen, I don't know what. And above all, don't you *handle* the witch-things.'

'*Hannel* 'm, Mars Sid? What *is* you talkin' 'bout? I wouldn' lay de weight er my finger on um, not f'r ten hund'd thous'n' billion dollars, I wouldn't.'

Chapter 37

That was all fixed. So then we went away and went to the rubbage-pile in the back yard where they keep the old boots, and rags, and pieces of bottles, and wore-out tin things, and all such truck, and scratched around and found an old tin wash-pan and stopped up the holes as well as we could, to bake the pie in, and took it down cellar and stole it full of flour, and started for breakfast and found a couple of shingle-nails that Tom said would be handy for a prisoner to scrabble his name and sorrows on the dungeon walls with, and dropped one of them in Aunt Sally's apron pocket which was hanging on a chair, and t'other we stuck in the band of Uncle Silas's hat, which was on the bureau, because we heard the children say their pa and ma was going to the runaway nigger's house this morning, and then went to breakfast, and Tom dropped the pewter spoon in Uncle Silas's coat pocket, and Aunt Sally wasn't come yet, so we had to wait a little while.

And when she come she was hot, and red, and cross, and couldn't hardly wait for the blessing; and then she went to sluicing out coffee with one hand and cracking the handiest child's head with her thimble with the other, and says:

'I've hunted high, and I've hunted low, and it does beat all, what *has* become of your other shirt.'

My heart fell down amongst my lungs and livers and things, and a hard piece of corn-crust started down my throat after it got met on the road with a cough and was shot across the table and took one of the children in the eye and curled him up like a fishing-worm, and let a cry out of him the size of a war-whoop, and Tom he turned kinder blue around the gills, and it all amounted to a considerable state of things for about a quarter of a minute or as much as that, and I would a sold out for half price if there was a bidder. But after that we was all right again – it was the sudden surprise of it that knocked us so kind of cold. Uncle Silas he says;

'It's most uncommon curious, I can't understand it. I know perfectly well I took it *off*, because——'

'Because you hain't got but one *on*. Just *listen* at the man! *I* know you took it off, and I know it by a better way than your wool-gathering memory, too, because it was on the clo'es-line yesterday – I see it there myself. But it's gone

– that's the long and the short of it, and you'll just have to change to a red flann'l one till I can get time to make a new one. And it'll be the third I've made in two years; it just keeps a body on the jump to keep you in shirts; and whatever you do manage to *do* with'm all, is more'n *I* can make out. A body'd think you *would* learn to take some sort of care of 'em, at your time of life.'

'I know it, Sally, and I do try all I can. But it oughtn't to be altogether my fault, because you know I don't see them nor have nothing to do with them except when they're on me; and I don't believe I've ever lost one of them *off* of me.'

'Well, it ain't *your* fault if you haven't, Silas – you'd a done it if you could, I reckon. And the shirt ain't all that's gone, nuther. Ther's a spoon gone; and *that* ain't all. There was ten, and now ther's only nine. The calf got the shirt I reckon, but the calf never took the spoon, *that's* certain.'

'Why, what else is gone, Sally?'

'Ther's six *candles* gone – that's what. The rats could a got the candles, and I reckon they did; I wonder they don't walk off with the whole place, the way you're always going to stop their holes and don't do it; and if they warn't fools they'd sleep in your hair, Silas – *you'd* never find it out; but you can't lay the *spoon* on the rats, and that I *know*.'

'Well, Sally, I'm in fault, and I acknowledge it; I've been remiss; but I won't let to-morrow go by without stopping up them holes.'

'Oh, I wouldn't hurry, next year'll do. Matilda Angelina Araminta *Phelps*!'

Whack comes the thimble, and the child snatches her claws out of the sugar-bowl without fooling around any. Just then, the nigger woman steps on to the passage, and says:

'Missus, dey's a sheet gone.'

'A *sheet* gone! Well, for the land's sake!'

'I'll stop up them holes *to-day*,' says Uncle Silas, looking sorrowful.

'Oh, *do* shet up! – s'pose the rats took the *sheet*? *Where's* it gone, Lize?'

'Clah to goodness I hain't no notion, Miss Sally. She wuz on de clo's-line yistiddy, but she done gone; she ain' dah no mo', now.'

'I reckon the world *is* coming to an end. I *never* see the beat of it, in all my born days. A shirt, and a sheet, and a spoon, and six can——'

'Missus,' comes a young yaller wench, 'dey's a brass cannel-stick miss'n.'

'Cler out from here, you hussy, er I'll take a skillet to ye!'

Well, she was just a-biling. I begun to lay for a chance; I reckoned I would sneak out and go for the woods till the weather moderated. She kept a-raging right along, running her insurrection all by herself, and everybody else mighty meek and quiet; and at last Uncle Silas, looking kind of foolish, fishes up that spoon out of his pocket. She stopped, with her mouth open and her hands up; and as for me, I wished I was in Jerusalem or somewheres. But not long; because she says:

'It's *just* as I expected. So you had it in your pocket all the time; and like as not you've got the other things there, too. How'd it get there?'

'I reely don't know, Sally,' he says, kind of apologizing, 'or you know I would tell. I was a-studying over my text in Acts Seventeen, before breakfast, and I reckon I put it in there, not noticing, meaning to put my Testament in, and it must be so, because my Testament ain't in, but I'll go and see and if the Testament is where I had it, I'll know I didn't put it in, and that will show that I laid the Testament down and took up the spoon, and——'

'Oh, for the land's sake! Give a body a rest! Go 'long now, the whole kit and biling of ye; and don't come nigh me again till I've got back my peace of mind.'

I'd a heard her, if she'd a said it to herself, let alone speaking it out; and I'd a got up and obeyed her, if I'd a been dead. As we was passing through the setting-room, the old man he took up his hat, and the shingle-nail fell out on the floor, and he just merely picked it up and laid it on the mantel-shelf, and never said nothing, and went out. Tom see him do it, and remembered about the spoon, and says:

'Well, it ain't no use to send things by *him* no more, he ain't reliable.' Then he says, 'But he done us a good turn with the spoon, anyway, without knowing it, and so we'll go and do him one without *him* knowing it – stop up his rat-holes.'

There was a noble good lot of them, down cellar, and it took us a whole hour, but we done the job right and good, and shipshape. Then we heard steps on the stairs, and blowed out our light, and hid; and here comes the old man, with a candle in one hand and a bundle of stuff in t'other, looking as absent-minded as year before last. He went a-mooning around, first to one rat-hole and then another, till he'd been to them all. Then he stood about five minutes, picking tallow-drip off of his candle and thinking. Then he turns off slow and dreamy towards the stairs, saying:

'Well, for the life of me I can't remember when I done it. I could show her now that I warn't to blame on account of the rats. But never mind – let it go. I reckon it wouldn't do no good.'

And so he went on a-mumbling upstairs, and then we left. He was a mighty nice old man. And always is.

Tom was a good deal bothered about what to do for a spoon, but he said we'd got to have it; so he took a think. When he had ciphered it out, he told me how we was to do; then we went and waited around the spoon-basket till we see Aunt Sally coming, and then Tom went to counting the spoons and laying them out to one side, and I slid one of them up my sleeve, and Tom says:

'Why, Aunt Sally, there ain't but nine spoons, *yet*.'

She says:

'Go 'long to your play, and don't bother me. I know better, I counted'm myself.'

'Well, I've counted them twice, Aunty, and I can't make but nine.'

She looked out of all patience, but of course she come to count – anybody would.

'I declare to gracious ther' *ain't* but nine!' she says. 'Why, what in the world – plague *take* the things, I'll count'm again.'

So I slipped back the one I had, and when she got done counting, she says:

'Hang the troublesome rubbage, ther's *ten*, now!' and she looked huffy and bothered both. But Tom says:

'Why, Aunty, *I* don't think there's ten.'

'You numskull, didn't you see me *count*'m?'

'I know, but——'

'Well, I'll count'm *again*.'

So I smouched one, and they come out nine same as the other time. Well, she *was* in a tearing way – just a-trembling all over, she was so mad. But she counted and counted, till she got that addled she'd start to count-in the *basket* for a spoon, sometimes; and so, three times they come out right, and three times they come out wrong. Then she grabbed up the basket and slammed it across the house and knocked the cat galley-west; and she said cle'r out and let her have some peace, and if we come bothering around her again betwixt that and dinner, she'd skin us. So we had the odd spoon; and dropped it in her apron pocket whilst she was a giving us our sailing-orders, and Jim got it all right, along with her shingle-nail, before noon. We was very well satisfied with this business, and Tom allowed it was worth twice the trouble it took, because he said *now* she couldn't ever count them spoons twice alike again to save her life; and wouldn't believe she'd counted them right, if she *did*; and said that after she'd about counted her head off, for the next three days, he judged she'd give it up and offer to kill anybody that wanted her to ever count them any more.

So we put the sheet back on the line, that night, and stole one out of her closet: and kept on putting it back and stealing it again, for a couple of days, till she didn't know how many sheets she had, any more, and said she didn't *care*, and warn't a-going to bullyrag the rest of her soul out about it, and wouldn't count them again not to save her life, she druther die first.

So we was all right now, as to the shirt and the sheet and the spoon and the candles, by the help of the calf and the rats and the mixed-up counting; and as to the candlestick, it warn't no consequence, it would blow over by and by.

But that pie was a job; we had no end of trouble with that pie. We fixed it up away down in the woods, and cooked it there; and we got it done at last, and very satisfactory, too; but not all in one day; and we had to use up three wash-pans full of flour, before we got through, and we got burnt pretty much all over, in places, and eyes put out with the smoke; because, you see, we didn't want nothing but a crust, and we couldn't prop it up right, and she would always cave in. But of course we thought of the right way at last; which was to cook the ladder, too, in the pie. So then we laid in with Jim, the second night, and tore up the sheet all in little strings, and twisted them together, and long before daylight we had a lovely rope, that you could a hung a person with. We let on it took nine months to make it.

And in the forenoon we took it down to the woods, but it wouldn't go in the pie. Being made of a whole sheet, that way, there was rope enough for forty pies, if we'd a wanted them, and plenty left over for soup, or sausage, or anything you choose. We could a had a whole dinner.

But we didn't need it. All we needed was just enough for the pie, and so we throwed the rest away. We didn't cook none of the pies in the washpan, afraid the solder would melt; but Uncle Silas he had a noble brass warming-pan which he thought considerable of, because it belonged to one of his ancestors with a long wooden handle that come over from England with William the Conqueror in the *Mayflower* or one of them early ships and was hid away up garret with a lot of other old pots and things that was valuable, not on account of being any account because they warn't, but on account of them being relicts, you know, and we snaked her out, private, and took her down there, but she failed on the first pies, because we didn't know how, but she come up smiling on the last one. We took and lined her with dough, and set her in the coals, and loaded her up with rag-rope, and put on a dough roof, and shut down the lid, and put hot embers on top, and stood off five foot, with the long handle, cool and comfortable, and in fifteen minutes she turned out a pie that was a satisfaction to look at. But the person that et it would want to fetch a couple of kags of toothpicks along, for if that rope-ladder wouldn't cramp him down to business, I don't know nothing what I'm talking about, and lay him in enough stomach-ache to last him till next time, too.

Nat didn't look, when we put the witch-pie in Jim's pan; and we put the three tin plates in the bottom of the pan under the vittles; and so Jim got everything all right, and as soon as he was by himself he busted into the pie and hid the rope-ladder inside of his straw tick, and scratched some marks on a tin plate and throwed it out of the window-hole.

Chapter 38

Making them pens was a distressid-tough job, and so was the saw; and Jim
allowed the inscription was going to be the toughest of all. That's the one
which the prisoner has to scrabble on the wall. But we had to have it; Tom
said we'd *got* to: there warn't no case of a state prisoner not scrabbling his
inscription to leave behind, and his coat of arms.

'Look at Lady Jane Grey,' he says; 'look at Gilford Dudley; look at old
Northumberland! Why, Huck, s'pose it *is* considerble trouble? – what you
going to do? – how you going to get around it? Jim's *got* to do his inscription
and coat of arms. They all do.'

Jim says:

'Why, Mars Tom, I hain't got no coat o' arms; I hain't got nuffn but
dish-yer ole shirt, en you knows I got to keep de journal on dat.'

'Oh, you don't understand, Jim; a coat of arms is very different.'

'Well,' I says, 'Jim's right, anyway, when he says he hain't got no coat of
arms, because he hain't.'

'I reckon *I* knowed that,' Tom says, 'but you bet he'll have one before he
goes out of this – because he's going out *right*, and there ain't going to be no
flaws in his record.

So whilst me and Jim filed away at the pens on a brickbat apiece, Jim a-
making his'n out of the brass and I making mine out of the spoon, Tom set to
work to think out the coat of arms. By and by he said he'd struck so many good
ones he didn't hardly know which to take, but there was one which he
reckoned he'd decide on. He says:

'On the scutcheon we'll have a bend *or* in the dexter base, a saltire *murrey*
in the fess, with a dog, couchant, for common charge, and under his foot a
chain embattled, for slavery, with a chevron *vert* in a chief engrailed, and
three invected lines on a field *azure*, with the nombril points rampant on a
dencette indented; crest, a runaway nigger, *sable*, with his bundle over his
shoulder on a bar sinister: and a couple of gules for supporters, which is you
and me; motto, *Maggiore fretta, minore atto*. Got it out of a book – means, the
more haste, the less speed.'

'Geewhillikins,' I says, 'but what does the rest of it mean?'

'We ain't got no time to bother over that,' he says, 'we got to dig in like all
git-out.'

'Well, anyway,' I says, 'what's *some* of it? What's a fess?'

'A fess – a fess is – *you* don't need to know what a fess is. I'll show him how to make it when he gets to it.'

'Shucks, Tom,' I says, 'Think you might tell a person. What's a bar sinister?'

'Oh, *I* don't know. But he's got to have it. All the nobility does.'

That was just his way. If it didn't suit him to explain a thing to you, he wouldn't do it. You might pump at him a week, it wouldn't make no difference.

He'd got all that coat of arms business fixed, so now he started in to finish up the rest of that part of the work, which was to plan out a mournful inscription – said Jim got to have one, like they all done. He made up a lot, and wrote them out on a paper, and read them off, so:

1. *Here a captive heart busted.*

2. *Here a poor prisoner, forsook by the world and friends, fretted out his sorrowful life.*

3. *Here a lonely heart broke, and a worn spirit went to its rest, after thirty-seven years of solitary captivity.*

4. *Here, homeless and friendless, after thirty-seven years of bitter captivity, perished a noble stranger, natural son of Louis XIV.*

Tom's voice trembled, whilst he was reading, and he most broke down. When he got done, he couldn't no way make up his mind which one for Jim to scrabble on to the wall, they was all so good; but at last he allowed he would let him scrabble them all on. Jim said it would take him a year to scrabble such a lot of truck on to the logs with a nail, and he didn't know how to make letters, besides; but Tom said he would block them out for him, and then he wouldn't have nothing to do but just follow the lines. Then pretty soon he says:

'Come to think, the logs ain't a-going to do; they don't have log walls in a dungeon: we got to dig the inscriptions into a rock. We'll fetch a rock.'

Jim said the rock was worse than the logs; he said it would take him such a pison long time to dig them into a rock, he wouldn't ever get out. But Tom said he would let me help him to do it. Then he took a look to see how me and Jim was getting along with the pens. It was most pesky tedious hard work and slow, and didn't give my hands no show to get well of the sores, and we didn't seem to make no headway, hardly. So Tom says:

'I know how to fix it. We got to have a rock for the coat of arms and mournful inscriptions, and we can kill two birds with that same rock. There's a gaudy big grindstone down at the mill, and we'll smouch it, and carve the things on it, and file out the pens and the saw on it, too.'

It warn't no slouch of an idea; and it warn't no slouch of a grindstone nuther; but we allowed we'd tackle it. It warn't quite midnight, yet, so we cleared out of the mill, leaving Jim at work. We smouched the grindstone, and set out to roll her home, but it was a most nation tough job. Sometimes, do what we could, we couldn't keep her from falling over, and she come mighty near mashing us, every time. Tom said she was going to get one of us, sure, before we got through. We got her half way; and then we was plumb played out, and most drownded with sweat. We see it warn't no use, we got to go and fetch Jim. So he raised up his bed and slid the chain off of the bed-leg, and wrapt it round and round his neck, and we crawled out through our hole and down there, and Jim and me laid into that grindstone and walked her along like nothing; and Tom superintended. He could out-superintend any boy I ever see. He knowed how to do everything.

Our hole was pretty big, but it warn't big enough to get the grindstone through; but Jim he took the pick and soon made it big enough. Then Tom marked out them things on it with the nail, and set Jim to work on them, with the nail for a chisel and an iron bolt from the rubbage in the lean-to for a hammer, and told him to work till the rest of his candle quit on him, and then he could go to bed, and hide the grindstone under his straw tick and sleep on it. Then we helped him fix his chain back on the bed-leg, and was ready for bed ourselves. But Tom thought of something, and says:

'You got any spiders in here, Jim?'

'No, sah, thanks to goodness I hain't, Mars Tom.'

'All right, we'll get you some.'

'But bless you, honey, I doan' *want* none. I's afeard un um. I jis' 's soon have rattlesnakes aroun'.'

Tom thought a minute or two, and says:

'It's a good idea. And I reckon it's been done. It *must* a been done; it stands to reason. Yes, it's a prime good idea. Where could you keep it?'

'Keep what, Mars Tom?'

'Why, a rattlesnake.'

'De goodness gracious alive, Mars Tom! Why, if dey was a rattlesnake to come in heah, I'd take en bust right out thoo dat log wall, I would, wid my head.'

'Why, Jim, you wouldn't be afraid of it, after a little. You could tame it.'

'*Tame* it!'

'Yes – easy enough. Every animal is grateful for kindness and petting, and they wouldn't *think* of hurting a person that pets them. Any book will tell you that. You try – that's all I ask; just try for two or three days. Why, you can get him so, in a little while, that he'll love you; and sleep with you; and won't stay away from you a minute; and will let you wrap him round your neck and put his head in your mouth.'

'*Please*, Mars Tom – *doan'* talk so! I can't *stan'* it! He'd *let* me shove his head in my mouf – fer a favour, hain't it? I lay he'd wait a pow'ful long time 'fo' I *ast* him. En mo' en dat, I doan' *want* him to sleep wid me.'

'Jim, don't act so foolish. A prisoner's *got* to have some kind of dumb pet, and if a rattlesnake hain't ever been tried, why, ther's more glory to be gained in your being the first to ever try it than any other way you could ever think of to save your life.'

'Why, Mars Tom, I doan' *want* no sich glory. Snake take 'n bite Jim's chin off, den *whah* is de glory! No, sah, I doan' want no such doin's.'

'Blame it, can't you *try*? I only *want* you to try – you needn't keep it up if it don't work.'

'But de trouble all *done*, ef de snake bite me while I's a-tryin' him. Mars Tom, I's willin' to tackle mos' anything 'at ain't onreasonable, but ef you en Huck fetches a rattlesnake in heah for me to tame, I's gwyne to *leave*, dat's *shore*.'

'Well, then, let it go, if you're so bullheaded about it. We can get you some garter-snakes and you can tie some buttons on their tails, and let on they're rattlesnakes, and I reckon that'll have to do.'

'I k'n stan' *dem*, Mars Tom, but blame' 'f I couldn' get along widout um, I tell you dat. I never knowed b'fo', 't was so much bother and trouble to be a prisoner.'

'Well, it *always* is, when it's done right. You got any rats around here?'

'No, sah, I hain't seen none.'

'Well, we'll get you some rats.'

'Why, Mars Tom, I doan' *want* no rats. Dey's de dad-blamedest creturs to 'sturb a body, en rustle roun' over 'im, en bite his feet, when he's tryin' to sleep, I ever see. No, sah, gimme g'yarter-snakes 'f I's got to have'm, but doan' gimme no rats, I ain' got no use f'r um, skasely.'

'But Jim, you *got* to have 'em – they all do. So don't make no more fuss about it. Prisoners ain't ever without rats. There ain't no instance of it. And they train them, and pet them, and learn them tricks, and they get to be as sociable as flies. But you got to play music to them. You got anything to play music on?'

'I ain' got nuffn but a coase comb en a piece o' paper, en a juice-harp; but I reck'n dey wouldn' take no stock in a juice-harp.'

'Yes, they would. *They* don't care what kind of music 'tis. A Jew's harp's plenty good enough for a rat. All animals likes music – in a prison they dote on it. Specially, painful music; and you can't get no other kind out of a Jew's harp. It always interests them; they come out to see what's the matter with you. Yes, you're all right; you're fixed very well. You want to set on your bed, nights, before you go to sleep, and early in the mornings, and play your Jew's harp; play *The Last Link is Broken* – that's the thing that'll scoop a rat, quicker'n anything else; and when you've played about two minutes, you'll see all the rats, and the snakes, and spiders, and things begin to feel worried about you, and come. And they'll just fairly swarm over you, and have a noble good time.'

'Yes, *dey* will, I reck'n, Mars Tom, but what kine er time is *Jim* havin'? Blest if I kin see de pint. But I'll do it ef I got to. I reck'n I better keep de animals satisfied, en not have no trouble in de house.'

Tom waited to think over, and see if there wasn't nothing else; and pretty soon he says:

'Oh – there's one thing I forgot. Could you raise a flower here, do you reckon?'

'I doan' know but maybe I could, Mars Tom; but it's tolable dark in heah, en I ain' got no use f'r no flower, nohow, en she'd be a pow'ful sight o' trouble.'

'Well, you try it, anyway. Some other prisoners has done it.'

'One er dem big cat-tail-lookin' mullen-stalks would grow in heah, Mars Tom, I reck'n, but she wouldn' be wuth half de trouble she'd coss.'

'Don't you believe it. We'll fetch you a little one, and you plant it in the corner, over there, and raise it. And don't call it mullen, call it Pitchiola – that's its right name, when it's in a prison. And you want to water it with your tears.'

'Why, I got plenty spring water, Mars Tom.'

'You don't *want* spring water; you want to water it with your tears. It's the way they always do.'

'Why, Mars Tom, I lay I kin raise one er dem mullen-stalks twyste wid spring water whiles another man's a-*start'n* one wid tears.'

'That ain't the idea. You *got* to do it with tears.'

'She'll die on my han's, Mars Tom, she sholy will; kase I doan' skasely ever cry.'

So Tom was stumped. But he studied it over, and then said Jim would have to worry along the best he could with an onion. He promised he would go to the nigger cabins and drop one, private, in Jim's coffee pot in the morning. Jim said he would 'jis' 's soon have tobacker in his coffee'; and found so much fault with it, and with the work and bother of raising the mullen, and Jew's-harping the rats, and petting and flattering up the snakes and spiders and things, on top of all the other work he had to do on pens, and inscriptions, and journals, and things, which made it more trouble and worry and responsibility to be a prisoner than anything he ever undertook, that Tom most lost all patience with him; and said he was just loadened down with more gaudier chances than a prisoner ever had in the world to make a name for himself, and yet he didn't know enough to appreciate them, and they was just about wasted on him. So Jim he was sorry, and said he wouldn't behave so no more, and then me and Tom shoved for bed.

Chapter 39

In the morning we went up to the village and bought a wire rat trap and fetched it down, and unstopped the best rat hole, and in about an hour we had fifteen of the bulliest kind of ones; and then we took it and put it in a safe place under Aunt Sally's bed. But while we was gone for spiders, little Thomas Franklin Benjamin Jefferson Elexander Phelps found it there, and opened the door of it to see if the rats would come out, and they did; and Aunt Sally she come in, and when we got back she was a-standing on top of the bed raising Cain, and the rats was doing what they could to keep off the dull times for her. So she took and dusted us both with the hick'ry, and we was as much as two hours catching another fifteen or sixteen, drat that meddlesome cub, and they warn't the likeliest, nuther, because the first haul was the pick of the flock. I never see a likelier lot of rats than what that first haul was.

We got a splendid stock of sorted spiders, and bugs, and frogs, and caterpillars, and one thing or another; and we like-to got a hornet's nest, but we didn't. The family was at home. We didn't give it right up, but stayed with them as long as we could; because we allowed we'd tire them out or they'd got to tire us out, and they done it. Then we got allycumpain and rubbed on the places, and was pretty near all right again, but couldn't set down convenient. And so we went for the snakes, and grabbed a couple of dozen garters and house-snakes, and put them in a bag, and put it in our room, and by that time it was supper time, and a rattling good honest day's work; and hungry? – oh, no, I reckon not! And there warn't a blessed snake up there, when we went back – we didn't half tie the sack, and they worked out, somehow, and left. But it didn't matter much, because they was still on the premises somewheres. So we judged we could get some of them again. No, there warn't no real scarcity of snakes about the house for a considerble spell. You'd see them dripping from the rafters and places, every now and then; and they generly landed in your plate, or down the back of your neck, and most of the time where you didn't want them. Well, they was handsome, and striped, and there warn't no harm in a million of them; but that never made no difference to Aunt Sally, she despised snakes, be the breed what they might, and she couldn't stand them no way you could fix it; and every time one of them flopped down on her, it didn't make no difference what she was doing, she would just lay that work down and light out. I never see such a woman. And you could hear her whoop to Jericho. You couldn't get her to take aholt of one of them with the tongs. And if she turned over and found one in bed, she would scramble out and lift a howl that you would think the house was afire. She disturbed the old man so, that he said he could most wish there hadn't ever been no snakes created. Why, after every last snake had been gone clear out of the house for as much as a week, Aunt Sally warn't over it yet; she warn't near over it; when she was setting thinking about something, you could touch her on the back of her neck with a feather and she would jump right out of her stockings. It was very curious. But Tom said all women was just so. He said they was made that way; for some reason or other.

We got a licking every time one of our snakes come in her way; and she allowed these lickings warn't nothing to what she would do if we ever loaded up the place again with them. I didn't mind the lickings, because they didn't amount to nothing; but I minded the trouble we had, to lay in another lot. But we got them laid in, and all the other things; and you never see a cabin as blithesome as Jim's was when they'd all swarm out for music and go for him. Jim didn't like the spiders, and the spiders didn't like Jim; and so they'd lay for him and make it mighty warm for him. And he said that between the rats, and the snakes, and the grindstone, there warn't no room in bed for him, skasely; and when there was, a body couldn't sleep, it was so lively, and it was always lively, he said, because *they* never all slept at one time, but took turn about, so when the snakes was asleep the rats was on deck, and when the rats turned in the snakes come on watch, so he always had one gang under him, in his way, and t'other gang having a circus over him, and if he got up to hunt a new place, the spiders would take a chance at him as he crossed over. He said if he ever got out, this time, he wouldn't ever be a prisoner again, not for a salary.

Well, by the end of three weeks, everything was in pretty good shape. The shirt was sent in early, in a pie, and every time a rat bit Jim he would get up and write a little in his journal whilst the ink was fresh; the pens was made, the inscriptions and so on was all carved on the grindstone; the bed-leg was sawed in two, and we had et up the sawdust, and it give us a most amazing stomach-ache. We reckoned we was all going to die, but didn't. It was the most indigestible sawdust I ever see; and Tom said the same. But as I was saying, we'd got all the work done, now, at last; and we was all pretty much fagged out, too, but mainly Jim. The old man had wrote a couple of times to the plantation below Orleans to come and get their runaway nigger, but hadn't got no answer, because there warn't no such plantation; so he allowed he would advertise Jim in the St Louis and New Orleans papers; and when he mentioned the St Louis ones, it give me the cold shivers, and I see we hadn't no time to lose. So Tom said, now for the nonnamous letters.

'What's them?' I says.

'Warnings to the people that something is up. Sometimes it's done one way, sometimes another. But there's always somebody spying around, that gives notice to the governor of the castle. When Louis XVI was going to light out of the Tooleries, a servant-girl done it. It's a very good way, and so is the nonnamous letters. We'll use them both. And it's usual for the prisoner's mother to change clothes with him, and she stays in, and he slides out in her clothes. We'll do that too.'

'But looky here, Tom, what do we want to *warn* anybody for, that something's up? Let them find it out for themselves – it's their look-out.'

'Yes, I know; but you can't depend on them. It's the way they've acted from the very start – left us to do *everything*. They're so confiding and mullet-headed and they don't take notice of nothing at all. So if we don't *give* them notice, there won't be nobody nor nothing to interfere with us, and so after all our hard work and trouble, this escape'll go off perfectly flat; won't amount to nothing – won't be nothing *to* it.'

'Well, as for me, Tom, that's the way I'd like.'

'Shucks,' he says, and looked disgusted. So I says:

'But I ain't going to make no complaint. Any way that suits you suits me. What you going to do about the servant-girl?'

'You'll be her. You slide in, in the middle of the night, and hook that yaller girl's frock.'

'Why, Tom, that'll make trouble next morning; because of course she prob'bly hain't got any but that one.'

'I know; but you don't want it but fifteen minutes, to carry the nonnamous letter and shove it under the front door.'

'All right, then, I'll do it; but I could carry it just as handy in my own togs.'

'You wouldn't look like a servant-girl, *then*, would you?'

'No, but there won't be nobody to see what I look like, *anyway*.'

'That ain't got nothing to do with it. The thing for us to do, is just to do our *duty*, and not worry about whether anybody *sees* us do it or not. Hain't you got no principle at all?'

'All right, I ain't saying nothing; I'm the servant-girl. Who's Jim's mother?'

'I'm his mother. I'll hook a gown from Aunt Sally.'

'Well, then, you'll have to stay in the cabin when me and Jim leaves.'

'Not much. I'll stuff Jim's clothes full of straw and lay it on his bed to represent his mother in disguise, and Jim'll take the nigger woman's gown off of me and wear it, and we'll all evade together. When a prisoner of style escapes, it's called an evasion. It's always called so when a king escapes, f'r instance. And the same with a king's son; it don't make no difference whether he's a natural one or an unnatural one.'

So Tom he wrote the nonnamous letter, and I smouched the yaller wench's frock, that night, and put it on, and shoved it under the front door, the way Tom told me to. It said:

> *Beware. Trouble is brewing. Keep a sharp look-out.*
>
> Unknown Friend.

Next night we stuck a picture which Tom drawed in blood, of a skull and crossbones, on the front door; and next night another one of a coffin, on the back door. I never see a family in such a sweat. They couldn't a been worse scared if the place had a been full of ghosts laying for them behind everything and under the beds and shivering through the air. If a door banged, Aunt Sally she jumped, and said 'ouch!' if anything fell, she jumped, and said 'ouch!' if you happened to touch her, when she warn't noticing, she done the same; she couldn't face noway and be satisfied, because she allowed there was something behind her every time – so she was always a-whirling around, sudden, and saying 'ouch,' and before she'd get two-thirds around, she'd whirl back again, and say it again; and she was afraid to go to bed, but she dasn't set up. So the thing was working very well, Tom said; he said he never see a thing work more satisfactory. He said it showed it was done right.

So he said, now for the grand bulge! So the very next morning at the streak of dawn we got another letter ready, and was wondering what we better do with it, because we heard them say at supper they was going to have a nigger on watch at both doors all night. Tom he went down the lightning-rod to spy around; and the nigger at the back door was asleep, and he stuck it in the back of his neck and come back. This letter said:

> *Don't betray me, I wish to be your friend. There is a desperate gang of cut-throats from over in the Ingean Territory going to steal your runaway nigger to-night, and they have been trying to scare you so as you will stay in the house and not bother them. I am one of the gang, but have got relliggion and wish to quit it and lead a honest life again, and will betray the helish design. They will sneak down from northwards, along the fence, at midnight exact, with a false key, and go in the nigger's cabin to get him. I am to be off a piece and blow a tin horn if I see any danger; but stead of that, I will* BA *like a sheep soon as they get in and not blow at all; then whilst they are getting his chains loose, you slip there and lock them in, and can kill them at your leasure. Don't do anything but just the way I am telling you, if you do they will suspicion something and raise whoopjamboreehoo. I do not wish any reward but to know I have done the right thing.*
>
> Unknown Friend.

Chapter 40

We were feeling pretty good, after breakfast, and took my canoe and went over the river a-fishing, with a lunch, and had a good time, and took a look at the raft and found her all right, and got home late to supper, and found them in such a sweat and worry they didn't know which end they was standing on, and made us go right off to bed the minute we was done supper, and wouldn't tell us what the trouble was, and never let on a word about the new letter, but didn't need to, because we knowed as much about it as anybody did, and as soon as we was half upstairs and her back was turned, we slid for the cellar cubboard and loaded up a good lunch and took it up to our room and went to bed, and got up about half-past eleven, and Tom put on Aunt Sally's dress that he stole and was going to start with the lunch, but says:

'Where's the butter?'

'I laid out a hunk of it.' I says, 'on a piece of a corn-pone.'

'Well, you *left* it laid out, then – it ain't here.'

'We can get along without it,' I says.

'We can get along *with* it, too,' he says; 'just you slide down cellar and fetch it. And then mosey right down the lightning-rod and come along. I'll go and stuff the straw into Jim's clothes to represent his mother in disguise, and be ready to *ba* like a sheep and shove soon as you get there.'

So out he went, and down the cellar went I. The hunk of butter, big as a person's fist, was where I had left it, so I took up the slab of corn-pone with it on, and blowed out my light, and started upstairs, very stealthy, and got up to the main floor all right, but here comes Aunt Sally with a candle, and I clapped the truck in my hat, and clapped my hat on my head, and the next second she see me; and she says:

'You been down cellar?'

'Yes'm.'

'What you been doing down there?'

'Noth'n.'

'*Noth'n!*'

'No'm.'

'Well, then, what possessed you to go down there, this time of night?'

'I don't know'm.'

'You don't *know*? Don't answer me that way, Tom, I want to know what you been *doing* down there.'

'I hain't been doing a single thing, Aunt Sally, I hope to gracious if I have.'

I reckoned she'd let me go, now, and as a generl thing she would; but I s'pose there was so many strange things going on she was just in a sweat about every little thing that warn't yard-stick straight; so she says, very decided:

'You just march into that setting-room and stay there till I come. You been up to something you no business to, and I lay I'll find out what it is before *I*'m done with you.'

So she went away as I opened the door and walked into the setting-room. My, but there was a crowd there! Fifteen farmers, and every one of them had a gun. I was most powerful sick, and slunk to a chair and set down. They was setting around, some of them talking a little, in a low voice, and all of them fidgety and uneasy, but trying to look like they warn't; but I knowed they was, because they was always taking off their hats, and putting them on, and scratching their heads, and changing their seats, and fumbling with their buttons. I warn't easy myself, but I didn't take my hat off, all the same.

I did wish Aunt Sally would come, and get done with me, and lick me, if she wanted to, and let me get away and tell Tom how we'd overdone this thing, and what a thundering hornet's nest we'd got ourselves into, so we could stop fooling around, straight off, and clear out with Jim before these rips got out of patience and come for us.

At last she come, and begun to ask me questions, but I *couldn't* answer them straight, I didn't know which end of me was up; because these men was in such a fidget now, that some was wanting to start right *now* and lay for them desperadoes, and saying it warn't but a few minutes to midnight; and others was trying to get them to hold on and wait for the sheep-signal; and here was aunty pegging away at the questions, and me a-shaking all over and ready to sink down in my tracks I was that scared; and the place getting hotter and hotter, and the butter beginning to melt and run down my neck and behind my ears; and pretty soon, when one of them says, '*I*'m for going and getting in the cabin *first*, and right *now*, and catching them when they come,' I most dropped; and a streak of butter come a-trickling down my forehead, and Aunt Sally she see it, and turns white as a sheet, and says:

'For the land's sake what *is* the matter with the child! – he's got the brain fever as shore as you're born, and they're oozing out!'

And everybody runs to see, and she snatches off my hat, and out comes the bread, and what was left of the butter, and she grabbed me, and hugged me, and says:

'Oh, what a turn you did give me! and how glad and grateful I am it ain't no worse; for luck's against us, and it never rains but it pours, and when I see that truck I thought we'd lost you, for I knowed by the colour and all, it was just like your brains would be if—— Dear, dear, whydn't you *tell* me that was what you'd been down there for, *I* wouldn't a cared. Now cler out to bed, and don't lemme see no more of you till morning!'

I was upstairs in a second, and down the lightning-rod in another one, and shinning through the dark for the lean-to. I couldn't hardly get my words out, I was so anxious; but I told Tom as quick as I could, we must jump for it, now, and not a minute to lose – the house full of men, yonder, with guns!

His eyes just blazed; and he says:

'No! – is that so? *Ain't* it bully! Why, Huck, if it was to do over again, I bet I could fetch two hundred! If we could put it off till——'

'Hurry! *hurry*!' I says. 'Where's Jim?'

'Right at your elbow; if you reach out your arm you can touch him. He's dressed, and everything's ready. Now we'll slide out and give the sheep-signal.'

But then we heard the tramp of men, coming to the door, and heard them begin to fumble with the padlock; and heard a man say:

'I *told* you we'd be too soon; they haven't come – the door is locked. Here, I'll lock some of you into the cabin and you lay for 'em in the dark and kill 'em when they come; and the rest scatter around a piece, and listen if you can hear 'em coming.'

So in they come, but couldn't see us in the dark, and most trod on us whilst we was hustling to get under the bed. But we got under all right, and out through the hole, swift but soft – Jim first, me next, and Tom last, which was according to Tom's orders. Now we was in the lean-to, and heard trampings close by outside. So we crept to the door, and Tom stopped us there and put his eye to the crack, but couldn't make out nothing, it was so dark; and whispered and said he would listen for the steps to get further, and when he nudged us Jim must glide out first, and him last. So he set his ear to the crack and listened, and listened, and listened, and the steps a-scraping around, out there, all the time; and at last he nudged us, and we slid out, and stooped down, not breathing, and not making the least noise, and slipped stealthy towards the fence, in Injun file, and got to it, all right, and me and Jim over it; but Tom's britches catched fast on a splinter on the top rail, and then he hear the steps coming, so he had to pull loose, which snapped the splinter and made a noise; and as he dropped in our tracks and started, somebody sings out:

'Who's that? Answer, or I'll shoot!'

But we didn't answer; we just unfurled our heels and shoved. Then there was a rush, and a *bang, bang, bang*! and the bullets fairly whizzed around us! We heard them sing out:

'Here they are! They've broke for the river! after 'em, boys! And turn loose the dogs!'

'I told Tom . . . we must jump for it . . . the house full of men . . . with guns!'

So here they come, full tilt. We could hear them, because they wore boots, and yelled, but we didn't wear no boots, and didn't yell. We was in the path to the mill; and when they got pretty close on to us, we dodged into the bush and let them go by, and then dropped in behind them. They'd had all the dogs shut up, so they wouldn't scare the robbers; but by this time somebody had let them loose, and here they come, making pow-wow enough for a million; but they was our dogs; so we stopped in our tracks till they catched up; and when they see it warn't nobody but us, and no excitement to offer them, they only just said howdy, and tore right ahead towards the shouting and clattering; and then we up steam again and whizzed along after them till we was nearly to the mill, and then struck up through the bush to where my canoe was tied, and hopped in and pulled for dear life towards the middle of the river, but didn't make no more noise than we was obleeged to. Then we struck out, easy and comfortable, for the island where my raft was; and we could hear them yelling and barking at each other all up and down the bank, till we was so far away the sounds got dim and died out. And when we stepped on to the raft, I says:

'*Now*, old Jim, you're a free man *again*, and I bet you won't ever be a slave no more.'

'En a mighty good job it wuz, too, Huck. It 'uz planned beautiful, en it 'uz *done* beautiful; en dey ain't *nobody* kin git up a plan dat's mo' mixed-up en splendid den what dat one wuz.'

We was all as glad as we could be, but Tom was the gladdest of all, because he had a bullet in the calf of his leg.

When me and Jim heard that, we didn't feel so brash as what we did before. It was hurting him considerable, and bleeding; so we laid him in the wigwam and tore up one of the duke's shirts for to bandage him, but he says:

'Gimme the rags, I can do it myself. Don't stop, now; don't fool around here, and the evasion booming along so handsome; man the sweeps, and set her loose! Boys, we done it elegant! – 'deed we did. I wish *we*'d a had the handling of Louis XVI, there wouldn't a been no "Son of Saint Louis, ascend to heaven!" wrote down in *his* biography: no, sir, we'd a whooped him over the *border* – that's what we'd a done with *him* – and done it just as slick as nothing at all, too. Man the sweeps – man the sweeps!'

But me and Jim was consulting – and thinking. And after we'd thought a minute, I says:

'Say it, Jim.'

So he says:

'Well, den, dis is de way it look to me, Huck. Ef it wuz *him* dat 'uz bein' sot free, en one er de boys wuz to git shot, would he say, "Go on en save me, nemmine 'bout a doctor f'r to save dis one"? Is dat like Mars Tom Sawyer? Would he say dat? You *bet* he wouldn't! *Well*, den, is *Jim* gwyne to say it? No, sah – I doan' budge a step out'n dis place, 'dout a *doctor*; not if it's forty year!'

I knowed he was white inside, and I reckoned he'd say what he did say – so it was all right, now, and I told Tom I was a-going for a doctor. He raised considerble row about it, but me and Jim stuck to it, and wouldn't budge; so he was for crawling out and setting the raft loose himself; but we wouldn't let him. Then he give us a piece of his mind – but it didn't do no good.

So when he sees me getting the canoe ready, he says:

'Well, then, if you're bound to go, I'll tell you the way to do, when you get to the village. Shut the door, and blindfold the doctor tight and fast, and make him swear to be silent as the grave, and put a purse full of gold in his hand, and then take and lead him all around the back alleys and everywheres, in the dark, and then fetch him here in the canoe, in a roundabout way amongst the islands, and search him, and take his chalk away from him, and don't give it back to him till you get him back to the village, or else he will chalk this raft so he can find it again. It's the way they all do.'

So I said I would, and left, and Jim was to hide in the woods when he see the doctor coming, till he was gone again.

Chapter 41

The doctor was an old man; a very nice, kind-looking old man, when I got him up. I told him me and my brother was over on Spanish Island hunting, yesterday afternoon, and camped on a piece of a raft we found, and about midnight he must a kicked his gun in his dreams, for it went off and shot him in the leg, and we wanted him to go over there and fix it and not say nothing about it, nor let anybody know, because we wanted to come home this evening, and surprise the folks.

'Who is your folks?' he says.

'The Phelpses, down yonder.'

'Oh,' he says. And after a minute, he says: 'How'd you say he got shot?'

'He had a dream,' I says, 'and it shot him.'

'Singular dream,' he says.

So he lit up his lantern, and got his saddle-bags, and we started. But when he see the canoe, he didn't like the look of her – said she was big enough for one, but didn't look pretty safe for two. I says:

'Oh, you needn't be afeard, sir, she carried the three of us, easy enough.'

'What three?'

'Why, me and Sid, and – and – and *the guns*; that's what I mean.'

'Oh,' he says.

But he put his foot on the gunnel, and rocked her; and shook his head, and said he reckoned he'd look around for a bigger one. But they was all locked and chained; so he took my canoe, and said for me to wait till he come back, or I could hunt around further, or maybe I better go down home and get them ready for the surprise, if I wanted to. But I said I didn't; so I told him just how to find the raft, and then he started.

I struck an idea, pretty soon. I says to myself, s'pos'n he can't fix that leg just in three shakes of a sheep's tail, as the saying is? s'pos'n it takes him three or four days? What are we going to do? – lay around there till he lets the cat out of the bag? No, sir, I know what *I*'ll do. I'll wait, and when he comes back, if he says he's got to go any more, I'll get down there, too, if I swim; and we'll take and tie him, and keep him, and shove out down the river; and when Tom's done with him, we'll give him what it's worth, or all we got, and then let him get ashore.

So then I crept into a lumber pile to get some sleep; and next time I waked up the sun was away up over my head! I shot out and went for the doctor's house, but they told me he'd gone away in the night, some time or other, and warn't back yet. Well, thinks I, that looks powerful bad for Tom, and I'll dig out for the island, right off. So away I shoved, and turned the corner, and nearly rammed my head into Uncle Silas's stomach! He says:

'Why, *Tom*! Where you been, all this time, you rascal?'

'*I* hain't been nowheres,' I says, 'only just hunting for the runaway nigger – me and Sid.'

'Why, where ever did you go?' he says. 'Your aunt's been mighty uneasy.'

'She needn't,' I says, 'because we was all right. We followed the men and the dogs, but they outrun us, and we lost them; but we thought we heard them on the water, so we got a canoe and took out after them, and crossed over but couldn't find nothing of them; so we cruised along up-shore, till we got kind of tired and beat out; and tied up the canoe and went to sleep, and never waked up till about an hour ago, then we paddled over here to hear the news, and Sid's at the post office to see what he can hear, and I'm a-branching out to get something to eat for us, and then we're going home.'

So then we went to the post office to get 'Sid'; but just as I suspicioned, he warn't there; so the old man he got a letter out of the office, and we waited a while longer but Sid didn't come; so the old man said come along, let Sid foot it home, or canoe it, when he got done fooling around – but we would ride. I couldn't get him to let me stay and wait for Sid; and he said there warn't no use in it, and I must come along, and let Aunt Sally see we was all right.

When we got home, Aunt Sally was that glad to see me she laughed and cried both, and hugged me, and give me one of them lickings of hern that don't amount to shucks, and said she'd serve Sid the same when he come.

And the place was plumb full of farmers and farmers' wives, to dinner; and such another clack a body never heard. Old Mrs. Hotchkiss was the worst; her tongue was a-going all the time. She says:

'Well, Sister Phelps, I've ransacked that-air cabin over an' I b'lieve the nigger was crazy. I says so to Sister Damrell – didn't I, Sister Damrell? – s'I, he's crazy, s'I – them's the very words I said. You all hearn me: he's crazy, s'I, everything shows it, s'I. Look at that-air grindstone, s'I; want to tell *me*'t any cretur 'ts in his right mind's a-goin' to scrabble all them crazy things on to a grindstone, s'I? Here sich 'n' sich a person busted his heart; 'n' here so-'n'-so pegged along for thirty-seven year, 'n' all that – natcherl son o' Louis somebody, 'n' sich everlast'n rubbage. He's plumb crazy, s'I; it's what I says in the fust place, it's what I says in the middle, 'n' it's what I says last 'n' all the time – the nigger's crazy – crazy's Nebokoodneezer, s'I.'

'An' look at that-air ladder made out'n rags, Sister Hotchkiss,' says old

Mrs. Damrell, 'what in the name o' goodness *could* he ever want of——'

'The very words I was a-sayin' no longer ago th'n this minute to Sister Utterback, 'n' she'll tell you so herself. Sh-she, look at that-air rag ladder, sh-she; 'n' s'I, yes, *look* at it, s'I – what *could* he wanted of it, s'I? Sh-she, Sister Hotchkiss, sh-she— —'

'But how in the nation'd they ever *git* that grindstone *in* there, *any*-way? 'n' who dug that-air hole? 'n' who——'

'My very *words*, Brer Penrod! I was a-sayin' – pass that-air sasser o' m'lasses, won't ye? – I was a-sayin' to Sister Dunlap, jist this minute, how *did* they git that grindstone in there, s'I. Without *help*, mind you – 'thout *help*! *That*'s wher' 'tis. Don't tell *me*, s'I; there *wuz* help, s'I; 'n' ther' wuz a *plenty* help, too, s'I; ther's ben a *dozen* a-helpin' that nigger, 'n' I lay I'd skin every last nigger on this place, but *I*'d find out who done it, s'I; 'n' moreover, s'I——'

'A *dozen* says you! – *forty* couldn't a done everything that's been done. Look at them case-knife saws and things, how tedious they've been made; look at that bed-leg sawed off with'm, a week's work for six men; look at that nigger made out'n straw on the bed; and look at——'

'You may *well* say it, Brer Hightower! It's jist as I was a-sayin' to Brer Phelps, his own self. S'e, what do *you* think of it, Sister Hotchkiss, s'e? think o' what, Brer Phelps, s'I? think o' that bed-leg sawed off that a way, s'e? *think* of it, s'I? I lay it never sawed *itself* off, s'I – somebody *sawed* it, s'I; that's my opinion, take it or leave it, it mayn't be no 'count, s'I, but sich as 't is, it's my opinion, s'I, 'n' if anybody k'n start a better one, s'I' let him *do* it, s'I, that's all. I says to Sister Dunlap, s'I——'

'Why, dog my cats, they must a ben a house-full o' niggers in there every night for four weeks, to a done all that work, Sister Phelps. Look at that shirt – every last inch of it kivered over with secret African writ'n done with blood! Must a ben a raft uv 'em at it right along, all the time, a'most. Why, I'd give two dollars to have it read to me; 'n' as for the niggers that wrote it, I 'low I'd take 'n' lash'm t'll——'

'People to *help* him, Brother Marples! Well, I reckon you'd *think* so, if you'd a been in this house for a while back. Why, they've stole everything they could lay their hands on – and we a-watching, all the time, mind you. They stole that shirt right off o' the line! and as for that sheet they made the rag ladder out of ther' ain't no telling how many times they *didn't* steal that; and flour, and candles, and candlesticks, and spoons, and the old warming-pan, and most a thousand things that I disremember, now, and my new calico dress; and me, and Silas, and my Sid and Tom on the constant watch day *and* night, as I was a-telling you, and not a one of us could catch hide nor hair, nor sight nor sound of them; and here at the last minute, lo and behold you, they slides right in under our noses, and fools us, and not only fools *us* but the

Injun Territory robbers too, and actuly gets *away* with that nigger, safe and sound, and that with sixteen men and twenty-two dogs right on their very heels at that very time! I tell you, it just bangs anything I ever *heard* of. Why, *sperits* couldn't a done better, and been no smarter. And I reckon they must a *been* sperits – because, *you* know our dogs, and ther' ain't no better; well, them dogs never even got on the *track* of 'm, once! You explain *that* to me, if you can! – *any* of you!'

'Laws alive, I never——'

'So help me, I wouldn't a be——'

'*House*-thieves as well as——'

'Goodnessgracioussakes, I'd a ben afeard to *live* in sich a——'

''Fraid to *live*! – why, I was that scared I dasn't hardly go to bed, or get up, or lay down, or *set* down, Sister Ridgeway. Why, they'd steal the very – why, goodness sakes, you can guess what kind of a fluster *I* was in by the time midnight come, last night. I hope to gracious if I warn't afraid they'd steal some o' the family! I was just to that pass, I didn't have no reasoning faculties no more. It looks foolish enough, *now*, in the day-time; but I says to myself, there's my two poor boys asleep, 'way upstairs in that lonesome room, and I declare to goodness, I was that uneasy 't I crep' up there and locked 'em in! I *did*. And anybody would. Because, you know, when you get scared, that way, and it keeps running on, and getting worse and worse, all the time, and your wits gets to addling, and you get to doing all sorts o' wild things, and by and by you think to yourself, s'pos'n *I* was a boy, and was away up there, and the door ain't locked, and you——' She stopped, looking kind of wondering, and then she turned her head around slow, and when her eye lit on me – I got up and took a walk.

Says I to myself, I can explain better how we come to not be in that room this morning, if I go out to one side and study over it a little. So I done it. But I dasn't go fur, or she'd a sent for me. And when it was late in the day, the people all went, and then I come in and told her the noise and shooting waked up me and 'Sid,' and the door was locked, and we wanted to see the fun, so we went down the lightning-rod, and both of us got hurt a little, and we didn't never want to try *that* no more. And then I went on and told her all what I told Uncle Silas before; and then she said she'd forgive us, and maybe it was all right enough anyway, and about what a body might expect of boys, for all boys was a pretty harum-scarum lot, as fur as she could see; and so, as long as no harm hadn't come of it, she judged she better put in her time being grateful we was alive and well and she had us still, 'stead of fretting over what was past and done. So then she kissed me and patted me on the head, and dropped into a kind of a brown study; and pretty soon jumps up, and says:

'Why, lawsamercy, it's most night, and Sid not come yet! What *has* become of that boy?'

I see my chance; so I skips up and says:

'I'll run right up to town and get him,' I says.

'No, you won't,' she says. 'You'll stay right wher' you are; *one*'s enough to be lost at a time. If he ain't here to supper, your uncle'll go.'

Well, he warn't there to supper; so right after supper uncle went.

He come back about ten, a little bit uneasy; hadn't run across Tom's track. Aunt Sally was a good *deal* uneasy; but Uncle Silas he said there warn't no occasion to be – boys will be boys, he said, and you'll see this one turn up in the morning, all sound and right. So she had to be satisfied. But she said she'd set up for him a while, anyway, and keep a light burning, so he could see it.

And then when I went up to bed she come up with me and fetched her candle, and tucked me in, and mothered me so good I felt mean, and like I couldn't look her in the face; and she set down on the bed and talked with me a long time, and said what a splendid boy Sid was, and didn't seem to want to ever stop talking about him; and kept asking me every now and then, if I reckoned he could a got lost, or hurt, or maybe drownded, and might be laying at this minute, somewheres, suffering or dead, and she not by him to help him, and so the tears would drip down, silent, and I would tell her that Sid was all right, and would be home in the morning, sure; and she would squeeze my hand, or maybe kiss me, and tell me to say it again, and keep on saying it, because it done her good, and she was in so much trouble. And when she was going away, she looked down in my eyes, so steady and gentle, and says:

'The door ain't going to be locked, Tom; and there's the window and the rod; but you'll be good, *won't* you? And you won't go? For *my* sake.'

Laws knows I *wanted* to go, bad enough, to see about Tom, and was all intending to go; but after that, I wouldn't a went, not for kingdoms.

But she was on my mind, and Tom was on my mind; so I slept very restless. And twice I went down the rod, away in the night, and slipped around front, and see her setting there by her candle in the window with her eyes towards the road and the tears in them; and I wished I could do something for her, but I couldn't, only to swear that I wouldn't never do nothing to grieve her any more. And the third time, I waked up at dawn, and slid down, and she was there yet, and her candle was most out, and her old grey head was resting on her hand, and she was asleep.

Chapter 42

The old man was up town again, before breakfast, but couldn't get no track of Tom; and both of them set at the table, thinking, and not saying nothing, and looking mournful, and their coffee getting cold, and not eating anything. And by and by the old man says:

'Did I give you the letter?'

'What letter?'

'The one I got yesterday out of the post office.'

'No, you didn't give me no letter.'

'Well, I must a forgot it.'

So he rummaged his pockets, and then went off somewheres where he had laid it down, and fetched it, and give it to her. She says:

'Why it's from St Petersburg – it's from Sis.'

I allowed another walk would do me good; but I couldn't stir. But before she could break it open, she dropped it and run – for she see something. And so did I. It was Tom Sawyer on a mattress; and that old doctor; and Jim, in *her* calico dress, with his hands tied behind him; and a lot of people. I hid the letter behind the first thing that come handy, and rushed. She flung herself at Tom, crying, and says:

'Oh, he's dead, he's dead, I know he's dead!'

And Tom he turned his head a little, and muttered something or other, which showed he warn't in his right mind; then she flung up her hands, and says:

'He's alive, thank God! And that's enough!' and she snatched a kiss of him, and flew for the house to get the bed ready, and scattering orders right and left at the niggers and everybody else, as fast as her tongue could go, every jump of the way.

I followed the men to see what they was going to do with Jim; and the old doctor and Uncle Silas followed after Tom into the house. The men was very huffy, and some of them wanted to hang Jim, for an example to all the other niggers around there, so they wouldn't be trying to run away, like Jim done, and making such a raft of trouble, and keeping a whole family scared most to death for days and nights. But the others said, don't do it, it wouldn't answer at all, he ain't our nigger, and his owner would turn up and make us pay for him, sure. So that cooled them down a little, because the people that's always the most anxious for to hang a nigger that hain't done just right, is always the very ones that ain't the most anxious to pay for him when they've got their satisfaction out of him.

They cussed Jim considerable, though, and give him a cuff or two, side the head, once in a while, but Jim never said nothing, and he never let on to know me, and they took him to the same cabin, and put his own clothes on him, and chained him again, and not to no bed-leg, this time, but to a big staple drove into the bottom log, and chained his hands, too, and both legs, and said he warn't to have nothing but bread and water to eat, after this, till his owner come or he was sold at auction, because he didn't come in a certain length of time, and filled up our hole, and said a couple of farmers with guns must stand watch around about the cabin every night, and a bull-dog tied to the door in the day-time; and about this time they was through with the job and was tapering off with a kind of generl good-bye cussing, and then the old doctor comes and takes a look, and says:

'Don't be no rougher on him than you're obleeged to, because he ain't a bad nigger. When I got to where I found the boy, I see I couldn't cut the bullet out without some help, and he warn't in no condition for me to leave, to go and get help; and he got a little worse and a little worse, and after a long time he went out of his head, and wouldn't let me come anigh him, any more, and said if I chalked his raft he'd kill me, and no end of wild foolishness like that, and I see I couldn't do anything at all with him; so I says, I got to have *help*, somehow; and the minute I says it, out crawls this nigger from somewheres, and says he'll help, and he done it, too, and done it very well. Of course I judged he must be a runaway nigger, and there I *was*! and there I had to stick, right straight along all the rest of the day, and all night. It was a fix, I tell you! I had a couple of patients with the chills, and of course I'd of liked to run up to town and see them, but I dasn't, because the nigger might get away, and then I'd be to blame; and yet never a skiff come close enough for me to hail. So there I had to stick, plumb till daylight this morning; and I never see a nigger that was a better nuss or faithfuller, and yet he was resking his freedom to do it, and was all tired out, too, and I see plain enough he'd been worked main hard, lately. I liked the nigger for that; I tell you, gentlemen, a nigger like that is worth a thousand dollars – and kind treatment, too. I had everthing I needed, and the boy was doing as well there as he would a done at home – better, maybe, because it was so quiet; but there I *was*, with both of 'm on my hands; and there I had to stick, till about dawn this morning; then some men in a skiff come by, and as good luck would have it, the nigger was setting by the pallet with his head propped on his knees, sound asleep; so I motioned them in, quiet, and they slipped up on him and grabbed him and tied him before he knowed what he was about, and we never had no trouble. And the boy being in a kind of a flighty sleep, too, we muffled the oars and hitched the raft on, and towed her over very nice and quiet, and the nigger never made the least row nor said a word, from the start. He ain't no bad nigger, gentlemen; that's what I think about him.'

Somebody says:

'Well, it sounds very good, doctor, I'm obleeged to say.'

Then the others softened up a little, too, and I was mighty thankful to that old doctor for doing Jim that good turn; and I was glad it was according to my judgment of him, too; because I thought he had a good heart in him and was a good man, the first time I see him. Then they all agreed that Jim had acted very well, and was deserving to have some notice took of it, and reward. So every one of them promised, right out and hearty, that they wouldn't cuss him no more.

Then they come out and locked him up. I hoped they was going to say he could have one or two of the chains took off, because they was rotten heavy, or could have meat and greens with his bread and water, but they didn't think of it, and I reckoned it warn't best for me to mix in, but I judged I'd get the doctor's yarn to Aunt Sally, somehow or other, as soon as I'd got through the breakers that was laying just ahead of me. Explanations, I mean, of how I forgot to mention about Sid being shot, when I was telling how him and me put in that dratted night paddling around hunting the runaway nigger.

But I had plenty of time. Aunt Sally she stuck to the sick-room all day and all night; and every time I see Uncle Silas mooning around, I dodged him.

Next morning I heard Tom was a good deal better, and they said Aunt Sally was gone to get a nap. So I slips to the sick-room, and if I found him awake I reckoned we could put up a yarn for the family that would wash. But he was sleeping, and sleeping very peaceful, too; and pale, not fire-faced the way he was when he come. So I set down and laid for him to wake. In about a half an hour, Aunt Sally comes gliding in, and there I was, up a stump again! She motioned me to be still, and set down by me, and begun to whisper, and said we could all be joyful now, because all the symptoms was first rate, and he'd been sleeping like that for ever so long, and looking better and peacefuller all the time, and ten to one he'd wake up in his right mind.

So we set there watching, and by and by he stirs a bit, and opened his eyes very natural, and takes a look, and says:

'Hallo, why I'm at *home*! How's that? Where's the raft?'

'It's all right,' I says.

'And *Jim*?'

'The same,' I says, but couldn't say it pretty brash. But he never noticed, but says:

'Good! Splendid! *Now* we're all right and safe! Did you tell aunty?'

I was going to say yes; but she chipped in and says:

'About what, Sid?'

'Why, about the way the whole thing was done.'

'What whole thing?'

'Why, *the* whole thing. There ain't but one; how we set the runaway nigger free – me and Tom.'

'Good land! Set the run—— What *is* the child talking about! Dear, dear, out of his head again!'

'*No*, I ain't out of my HEAD; I know all what I'm talking about. We *did* set him free – me and Tom. We laid out to do it, and we *done* it. And we done it elegant, too.' He'd got a start, and she never checked him up, just set and stared and stared, and let him clip along, and I see it warn't no use for *me* to put in. 'Why, Aunty, it cost us a power of work – weeks of it – hours and hours, every night, whilst you was all asleep. And we had to steal candles, and the sheet, and the shirt, and your dress, and spoons, and tin plates, and case-knives, and the warming-pan, and the grindstone, and flour, and just no end of things, you can't think what work it was to make the saws, and pens, and inscriptions, and one thing or another, and you can't think *half* the fun it was. And we had to make up the pictures of coffins and things, and nonnamous letters from the robbers, and get up and down the lightning-rod, and dig the hole into the cabin, and make the rope-ladder and send it in cooked up in a pie, and send in spoons and things to work with, in your apron pocket –'

'Mercy sakes!'

'– and load up the cabin with rats and snakes and so on, for company for Jim; and then you kept Tom here so long with the butter in his hat that you come near spiling the whole business, because the men come before we was out of the cabin, and we had to rush, and they heard us and let drive at us, and I got my share, and we dodged out of the path and let them go by, and when the dogs come they warn't interested in us, but went for the most noise, and we got our canoe, and made for the raft, and was all safe, and Jim was a free man, and we done it all by ourselves, and *wasn't* it bully, Aunty!'

'Well, I never heard the likes of it in all my born days! So it was *you*, you little rapscallions, that's been making all this trouble, and turned everybody's wits clean inside out and scared us all most to death. I've as good a notion as ever I had in my life, to take it out o' you this very minute. To think, here I've been, night after night, a – *you* just get well once, once, you young scamp, and I lay I'll tan the Old Harry out o' both o' ye!'

But Tom, he *was* so proud and joyful, he just *couldn't* hold in, and his tongue just *went* it – she a-chipping in, and spitting fire all along, and both of them going it at once, like a cat-convention; and she says:

'*Well*, you get all the enjoyment you can out of it *now*, for mind I tell you if I catch you meddling with him again——'

'Meddling with *who*?' Tom says, dropping his smile, and looking surprised.

'With *who*? Why, the runaway nigger, of course. Who'd you reckon?'

Tom looks at me very grave, and says:

'Tom, didn't you just tell me he was all right? Hasn't he got away?'

'*Him?*' says Aunt Sally; 'the runaway nigger? 'Deed he hasn't. They've got him back, safe and sound, and he's in that cabin again, on bread and water, and loaded down with chains, till he's claimed or sold!'

Tom rose square up in bed, with his eye hot, and his nostrils opening and shutting like gills, and sings out to me:

'They hain't no *right* to shut him up! *Shove*! – and don't you lose a minute. Turn him loose! he ain't no slave; he's as free as any cretur that walks this earth!'

'What *does* the child mean?'

'I mean every word I *say*, Aunt Sally, and if somebody don't go, *I*'ll go. I've knowed him all his life, and so has Tom, there. Old Miss Watson died two months ago, and she was ashamed she ever was going to sell him down the river, and *said* so; and she set him free in her will.'

'Then what on earth did *you* want to set him free for, seeing he was already free?'

'Well, that *is* a question, I must say; and *just* like women! Why, I wanted the *adventure* of it; and I'd a waded neck-deep in blood to – goodness alive – AUNT POLLY!'

If she warn't standing right there, just inside the door, looking as sweet and contented as an angel half-full of pie, I wish I may never!

Aunt Sally jumped for her, and most hugged the head off of her, and cried over her, and I found a good enough place for me under the bed, for it was getting pretty sultry for *us*, seemed to me. And I peeped out, and in a little while Tom's Aunt Polly shook herself loose and stood there looking across at Tom over her spectacles – kind of grinding him into the earth, you know. And then she says:

'Yes, you *better* turn y'r head away – I would if I was you, Tom.'

'Oh, deary me!' says Aunt Sally; '*is* he changed so? Why, that ain't *Tom*, it's Sid; Tom's – Tom's – why, where is Tom? He was here a minute ago.'

'You mean where's Huck *Finn* – that's what you mean! I reckon I hain't raised such a scamp as my Tom all these years, not to know him when I *see* him. That *would* be a pretty howdy-do. Come out from under that bed, Huck Finn.'

So I done it. But not feeling brash.

Aunt Sally she was one of the mixed-upest looking persons I ever see; except one, and that was Uncle Silas, when he come in, and they told it all to him. It kind of made him drunk, as you may say, and he didn't know nothing at all the rest of the day, and preached a prayer-meeting sermon that night that give him a rattling ruputation, because the oldest man in the world couldn't a understood it. So Tom's Aunt Polly, she told all about who I was, and what; and I had to up and tell how I was in such a tight place that when Mrs. Phelps took me for Tom Sawyer – she chipped in and says, 'Oh, go on and call me Aunt Sally, I'm used to it, now, and 'tain't no need to change' – that when Aunt Sally took me for Tom Sawyer, I had to stand it – there warn't no other way, and I knowed he wouldn't mind, because it would be nuts for him, being a mystery, and he'd make an adventure out of it and be perfectly satisfied. And so it turned out, and he let on to be Sid, and made things as soft as he could for me.

And his Aunt Polly she said Tom was right about old Miss Watson setting Jim free in her will; and so, sure enough, Tom Sawyer had gone and took all that trouble and bother to set a free nigger free! and I couldn't ever understand, before, until that minute and that talk, how he *could* help a body set a nigger free, with his bringing-up.

Well, Aunt Polly she said that when Aunt Sally wrote to her that Tom and *Sid* had come, all right and safe, she says to herself:

'Look at that, now! I might have expected it, letting him go off that way without anybody to watch him. So now I got to go and trapse all the way down the river, eleven hundred mile, and find out what that creetur's up to, *this* time; as long as I couldn't seem to get any answer out of you about it.'

'Why, I never heard nothing from you,' says Aunt Sally.

'Well, I wonder! Why, I wrote to you twice, to ask you what you could mean by Sid being here.'

'Well, I never got 'em Sis.'

Aunt Polly, she turns slow and severe, and says:

'You, Tom!'

'Well – *what?*' he says, kind of pettish.

'Don't you what *me*, you impudent thing – hand out them letters.'

'What letters?'

'*Them* letters. I be bound, if I have to take aholt of you I'll——'

'They're in the trunk. There, now. And they're just the same as they was when I got them out of the office. I hain't looked into them, I hain't touched them. But I knowed they'd make trouble, and I thought if you warn't in no hurry, I'd——'

'Well, you *do* need skinning, there ain't no mistake about it. And I wrote another one to tell you I was coming; and I s'pose he——'

'No, it come yesterday; I hain't read it yet, but *it's* all right, I've got that one.'

I wanted to offer to bet two dollars she hadn't, but I reckoned maybe it was just as safe to not to. So I never said nothing.

Chapter 43
Chapter the last

The first time I catched Tom, private, I asked him what was his idea, time of the evasion? – what it was he'd planned to do if the evasion worked all right and he managed to set a nigger free that was already free before? And he said, what he had planned in his head, from the start, if we got Jim out all safe, was for us to run him down the river, on the raft, and have adventures plumb to the mouth of the river, and then tell him about his being free, and take him back up home on a steamboat, in style, and pay him for his lost time, and write word ahead and get out all the niggers around, and have them waltz him into town with a torchlight procession and a brass band, and then he would be a hero, and so would we. But I reckoned it was about as well the way it was.

We had Jim out of the chains in no time, and when Aunt Polly and Uncle Silas and Aunt Sally found out how good he helped the doctor nurse Tom, they made a heap of fuss over him, and fixed him up prime, and give him all he wanted to eat, and a good time, and nothing to do. And we had him up to the sick-room; and had a high talk; and Tom give Jim forty dollars for being prisoner for us so patient, and doing it up so good, and Jim was pleased most to death, and busted out, and says:

'*Dah*, now, Huck, what I tell you? – what I tell you up dah on Jackson Islan'? I *tole* you I got a hairy breas', en what's de sign un it; en I *tole* you I ben rich wunst, en gwineter to be rich *agin*; en it's come true; en heah she *is*! *Dah*, now! doan' talk to *me* – signs is *signs*, mine I tell you; en I knowed jis' 's well 'at I 'uz gwineter be rich agin as I's a-stannin' heah dis minute!'

And then Tom he talked along, and talked along, and says, le's all three slide out of here, one of these nights, and get an outfit, and got for howling adventures amongst the Injuns, over in the Territory, for a couple of weeks or so; and I says, all right, that suits me, but I ain't got no money for to buy the outfit, and I reckon I couldn't get none from home, because it's likely pap's been back before now, and got it all away from Judge Thatcher and drunk it up.

'No he hain't,' Tom says; 'it's all there, yet – six thousand dollars and more; and your pap ain't ever been back since. Hadn't when I come away, anyhow.'

Jim, says, kind of solemn:

'He ain't a-comin' back no mo', Huck.'

I says:

'Why, Jim?'

'Nemmine why, Huck – but he ain't comin' back no mo'.'

But I kept at him; so at last he says:

'Doan you 'member de house dat was float'n down de river, en dey wuz a man in dah, kivered up, en I went in en unkivered him and didn' let you come in? Well, den, you k'n git yo' money when you wants it; kase dat wuz him.'

Tom's most well, now, and got his bullet around his neck on a watch-guard for a watch, and is always seeing what time it is, and so there ain't nothing more to write about, and I am rotten glad of it, because if I'd a knowed what a trouble it was to make a book I wouldn't a tackled it and ain't a-going to no more, But I reckon I got to light out for the Territory ahead of the rest, because Aunt Sally she's going to adopt me and civilize me, and I can't stand it. I been there before.

THE END
YOURS TRULY
HUCK FINN

THE PRINCE AND THE PAUPER

THE PRINCE AND THE PAUPER

A Tale for Young People of all ages

Mark Twain

Contents

List of Illustrations

Dedication

Preface

I will set down a tale as it was told to me by one who had it of his father, which latter had it of *his* father, this last having in like manner had it of *his* father – and so on, back and still back, three hundred years and more, the fathers transmitting it to the sons and so preserving it. It may be history, it may be only legend, a tradition. It may have happened, it may not have happened: but it *could* have happened. It may be that the wise and the learned believed it in the old days; it may be that only the unlearned and the simple loved it and credited it.

HUGH LATIMER, *Bishop of Worcester, to* LORD CROMWELL, *on the birth of the* PRINCE OF WALES (*afterward* EDWARD VI.)

FROM THE NATIONAL MANUSCRIPTS PRESERVED BY THE BRITISH GOVERNMENT

HUGH LATIMER, *Bishop of Worcester, to* LORD CROMWELL, *on the birth of the* PRINCE OF WALES (*afterward* EDWARD VI.)

FROM THE NATIONAL MANUSCRIPTS PRESERVED BY THE BRITISH GOVERNMENT

Ryght honorable, *Salutem in Christo Jesu*, and Syr here ys no lesse joynge and rejossynge in thes partees for the byrth of our prynce, hoom we hungurde for so longe, then ther was (I trow), *inter vicinos* att the byrth of S.I. Baptyste, as thys berer, Master Erance, can telle you. Gode gyffe us alle grace, to yelde dew thankes to our Lorde gode, Gode of Inglonde, for verely He hathe shoyd Hym selff Gode of Inglonde, or rather an Inglyssh Gode, yf we consydyr and pondyr welle alle Hys procedynges with us from tyme to tyme. He hath overcumme alle our yllnesse with Hys excedynge goodnesse, so that we ar now moor then compellyd to serve Hym, seke Hys glory, promott Hys wurde, yf the Devylle be natt in us. We have now the stooppe of vayne trustes ande the stey of vayne expectations; lett us alle pray for hys preservatione. And I for my partt wylle wyssh that hys Grace allways have, and evyn now from the begynynge, Governares, Instructores and offyceres of ryght jugmente, *ne optimun ingenium non optimâ educatione depravetur*.

Butt whatt a grett fowlle am I! So, whatt devotione shoyth many tymys butt lytelle dyscretione! Ande thus the Gode of Inglonde be ever with you in alle your procedynges.

The 19 of October.

Youres, H. L. B. of Wurcestere, now att Hartlebury.

Yf you wolde excytt thys berere to be moore hartye ayen the abuse of ymagry or mor forwarde to promotte the veryte, ytt myght doo goode. Natt that ytt came of me, butt of your selffe, &c.

(*Addressed*) To the Ryght Honorable Loorde P. Sealle hys synguler gode Lorde.

1 The Birth of the Prince and the Pauper

In the ancient city of London, on a certain autumn day in the second quarter of the sixteenth century, a boy was born to a poor family of the name of Canty, who did not want him. On the same day another English child was born to a rich family of the name of Tudor, who did want him. All England wanted him too. England had so longed for him, and hoped for him, and prayed God for him that now that he was really come, the people went nearly mad for joy. Mere acquaintances hugged and kissed each other and cried. Everybody took a holiday, and high and low, rich and poor, feasted and danced and sang, and got very mellow; and they kept this up for days and nights together. By day London was a sight to see, with gay banners waving from every balcony and housetop and splendid pageants marching along. By night it was again a sight to see, with its great bonfires at every corner and its troops of revellers making merry around them. There was no talk in all of England but of the new baby, Edward Tudor, Prince of Wales, who lay lapped in silks and satins, unconscious of all this fuss, and not knowing that great lords and ladies were tending him and watching over him – and not caring either. But there was no talk about the other baby, Tom Canty, lapped in his poor rags, except among the family of paupers whom he had just come to trouble with his presence.

2 Tom's Early Life

Let us skip a number of years.

London was fifteen hundred years old, and was a great town – for that day. It had a hundred thousand inhabitants – some think double as many. The streets were very narrow, and crooked, and dirty, especially in that part where Tom Canty lived, which was not far from London Bridge. The houses were of wood, with the second story projecting over the first, and the third sticking its elbows out beyond the second. The higher the houses grew, the broader they grew. They were skeletons of strong criss-cross beams, with solid material between coated with plaster. The beams were painted red or blue or black, according to the owner's taste, and this gave the houses a very picturesque look. The windows were small, glazed with little diamond-shaped panes, and they opened outward on hinges like doors.

The house which Tom's father lived in was up a foul little pocket called Offal Court, out of Pudding Lane. It was small, decayed, and rickety, but it was packed full of wretchedly poor families. Canty's tribe occupied a room on the third floor. The mother and father had a sort of bedstead in the corner; but Tom, his grandmother, and his two sisters, Bet and Nan, were not restricted – they had all the floor to themselves and might sleep where they chose. There were the remains of a blanket or two and some bundles of ancient and dirty straw, but these could not rightly be called beds, for they were not organized; they were kicked into a general pile in the mornings, and selections made from the mass at night for service.

Bet and Nan were fifteen years old – twins. They were goodhearted girls, unclean, clothed in rags, and profoundly ignorant. Their mother was like them. But the father and the grandmother were a couple of fiends. They got drunk whenever they could; then they fought each other or anybody else who came in the way; they cursed and swore always, drunk or sober; John Canty was a thief, and his mother a beggar. They made beggars of the children but failed to make thieves of them. Among, but not of, the dreadful rabble that inhabited the house was a good old priest whom the king had turned out of house and home with a pension of a few farthings, and he used to get the children aside and teach them right ways secretly. Father Andrew also taught Tom a little Latin and how to read and write, and would have done the same with the girls, but they were afraid of the jeers of their friends, who could not have endured such a queer accomplishment in them.

All Offal Court was just such another hive as Canty's house. Drunkenness, riot, and brawling were the order there every night and nearly all night long. Broken heads were as common as hunger in that place. Yet little Tom was not unhappy. He had a hard time of it, but did not know it. It was the sort of time that all the Offal Court boys had; therefore he supposed it was the correct and comfortable thing. When he came home empty-handed at night, he knew his father would curse him and thrash him first, and that when he was done the awful grandmother would do it all over again and improve on it, and that away in the night his starving mother would slip to him stealthily with any miserable scrap or crust she had been able to save for him by going hungry herself, notwithstanding she was often caught in that sort of treason and soundly beaten for it by her husband.

No, Tom's life went along well enough, especially in summer. He only begged just enough to save himself, for the the laws against mendicancy were stringent and the penalties heavy; so he put in a good deal of his time listening to good Father Andrew's charming old tales and legends about giants and fairies, dwarfs and genii, and enchanted castles, and gorgeous kings and princes. His head grew to be full of these wonderful things, and many a night as he lay in the dark on his scant and offensive straw, tired, hungry, and smarting from a thrashing, he unleashed his imagination and soon forgot his aches and pains in delicious picturings to himself of the charmed life of a petted prince in a regal palace. One desire came in time to haunt him day and night: it was to see a real prince, with his own eyes. He spoke of it once to some of his Offal Court comrades, but they jeered at him and scoffed him so unmercifully that he was glad to keep his dream to himself after that.

He often read the priest's old books and got him to explain and enlarge upon them. His dreamings and readings worked certain changes in him by and by. His dream people were so fine that he grew to lament his shabby clothing and his dirt and to wish to be clean and better clad. He went on playing in the mud just the same, and enjoying it too; but instead of splashing around in the Thames solely for the fun of it, he began to find an added value in it because ot the washings and cleansings it afforded.

Tom could always find something going on around the Maypole in Cheapside and at the fairs; and now and then he and the rest of London had a chance to see a military parade when some famous unfortunate was carried prisoner to the Tower by land or boat. One summer's day he saw poor Anne Askew and three men burned at the stake in Smithfield and heard an ex-bishop preach a sermon to them which did not interest him. Yes, Tom's life was varied and pleasant enough on the whole.

By and by Tom's reading and dreaming about princely life wrought such a strong effect upon him that he began to *act* the prince, unconsciously. His speech and manners became curiously ceremonious and courtly, to the vast admiration and amusement of his intimates. But Tom's influence among these young people began to grow now day by day, and in time he came to be looked up to by them, with a sort of wondering awe, as a superior being. He seemed to know so much! And he could do and say such marvellous things! And withal, he was so deep and wise! Tom's remarks and Tom's performances were reported by the boys to their elders; and these also presently began to discuss Tom Canty and to regard him as a most gifted and extraordinary creature. Full-grown people brought their perplexities to Tom for solution and were often astonished at the wit and wisdom of his decisions. In fact he was become a hero to all who knew him except his own family – these only saw nothing in him.

Privately, after a while, Tom organized a royal court! He was the prince; his special comrades were guards, chamberlains, equerries, lords- and ladies-in-waiting, and the royal family. Daily the mock prince was received with elaborate ceremonials borrowed by Tom from his romantic readings; daily the great affairs of the mimic kingdom were discussed in the royal council; and daily his mimic highness issued decrees to his imaginary armies, navies, and vice-royalties.

After which, he would go forth in his rags and beg a few farthings, eat his poor crust, take his customary cuffs and abuse, and then stretch himself upon his handful of foul straw and resume his empty grandeurs in his dreams.

And still his desire to look just once upon a real prince in the flesh grew upon him, day by day, and week by week, until at last it absorbed all other desires and became the one passion of his life.

One January day, on his usual begging tour, he tramped despondently up and down the region round about Mincing Lane and Little East Cheap, hour after hour, barefooted and cold, looking in at cookshop windows and longing for the dreadful pork pies and other deadly inventions displayed there; for to him these were dainties fit for the angels; that is, judging by the smell they were, for it had never been his good luck to own and eat one. There was a cold drizzle of rain; the atmosphere was murky; it was a melancholy day. At night Tom reached home so wet and tired and hungry that it was not possible for his father and grandmother to observe his forlorn condition and not be moved – after their fashion; wherefore they gave him a brisk cuffing at once and sent him to bed. For a long time his pain and hunger and the swearing and fighting going on in the building kept him awake; but at last his thoughts drifted away to far, romantic lands, and he fell asleep in the company of jewelled and gilded princelings who lived in vast palaces and had servants salaaming before them or flying to execute their orders. And then as usual, he dreamed that *he* was a princeling himself.

All night long the glories of his royal estate shone upon him: he moved among great lords and ladies in a blaze of light, breathing perfumes, drinking in delicious music, and answering the reverent obeisances of the glittering throng as it parted to make way for him, with here a smile and there a nod of his princely head.

And when he awoke in the morning and looked upon the wretchedness about him, his dream had had its usual effect: it had intensified the sordidness of his surroundings a thousandfold. Then came bitterness, and heartbreak, and tears.

3 Tom's Meeting with the Prince

Tom got up hungry, and sauntered hungry away, but with his thoughts busy with the shadowy splendours of his night's dreams. He wandered here and there in the city, hardly noticing where he was going or what was happening around him. People jostled him, and some gave him rough speech; but it was all lost on the musing boy. By and by he found himself at Temple Bar, the farthest from home he had ever travelled in that direction. He stopped and considered a moment, then fell into his imaginings again, and passed on outside the walls of London. The Strand had ceased to be a country road then and regarded itself as a street, but by a strained construction; for though there was a tolerably compact row of houses on one side of it, there were only some scattering great buildings on the other, these being palaces of rich nobles, with ample and beautiful grounds stretching to the river – grounds that are now closely packed with grim acres of brick and stone.

Tom discovered Charing Village presently and rested himself at the beautiful cross built there by a bereaved king of earlier days; then idled down a quiet, lovely road past the great cardinal's stately palace, toward a far more mighty and majestic palace beyond – Westminster. Tom stared in glad wonder at the vast pile of masonry, the wide-spreading wings, the frowning bastions and turrets, the huge stone gateway, with its gilded bars and its magnificent array of colossal granite lions, and the other signs and symbols of English royalty. Was the desire of his soul to be satisfied at last? Here indeed was a king's palace. Might he not hope to see a prince now, a prince of flesh and blood, if heaven were willing?

At each side of the gilded gate stood a living statue, that is to say, an erect and stately and motionless man-at-arms clad from head to heel in shining steel armour. At a respectful distance were many country folk and people from the city waiting for any chance glimpse of royalty that might offer. Splendid carriages with splendid people in them and splendid servants outside were arriving and departing by several other noble gateways that pierced the royal enclosure.

Poor little Tom, in his rags, approached and was moving slowly and timidly past the sentinels, with a beating heart and a rising hope, when all at once he caught sight through the golden bars of a spectacle that almost made him shout for joy. Within was a comely boy, tanned and brown with sturdy outdoor sports and exercises, whose clothing was all of lovely silks and satins, shining with jewels – at his hip a little jewelled sword and dagger, dainty buskins on his feet, with red heels, and on his head a jaunty crimson cap with drooping plumes fastened with a great sparkling gem. Several gorgeous gentlemen stood near – his servants, without a doubt. Oh! He was a prince – a prince, a living prince, a real prince – without the shadow of a question; and the prayer of the pauper-boy's heart was answered at last.

Tom's breath came quick and short with excitement, and his eyes grew big with wonder and delight. Everything gave way in his mind instantly to one desire: that was to get close to the prince and have a good, devouring look at him. Before he knew what he was about, he had his face against the gate bars. The next instant one of the soldiers snatched him rudely away and sent him spinning among the gaping crowd of country gawks and London idlers.

The soldier said, 'Mind thy manners, thou young beggar!'

The crowd jeered and laughed, but the young prince sprang to the gate with his face flushed and his eyes flashing with indignation and cried out, 'How darst thou use a poor lad like that! How darst thou use the king my father's meanest subject so! Open the gates and let him in!'

You should have seen that fickle crowd snatch off their hats then. You should have heard them cheer and shout, 'Long live the Prince of Wales!'

The soldiers presented arms with their halberds, opened the gates, and presented again as the little Prince of Poverty passed in, in his fluttering rags, to join hands with the Prince of Limitless Plenty.

Edward Tudor said, 'Thou lookest tired and hungry: thou'st been treated ill. Come with me.'

Half a dozen attendants sprang forward to – I don't know what; interfere, no doubt. But they were waved aside with a right royal gesture, and they stopped stock-still where they were, like so many statues. Edward took Tom to a rich apartment in the palace, which he called his cabinet. By his command a repast was brought such as Tom had never encountered before except in books. The prince, with princely delicacy and breeding, sent away the servants so that his humble guest might not be embarrassed by their critical presence; then he sat nearby and asked questions while Tom ate.

'What is thy name, lad?'

'Tom Canty, an' it please thee, sir.'

''Tis an odd one. Where dost live?'

'In the city, please thee, sir. Offal Court, out of Pudding Lane.'

'Offal Court! Truly 'tis another odd one. Hast parents?'

'Parents have I, sir, and a grandam likewise that is but indifferently precious to me – God forgive me if it be offence to say it – also twin sisters, Nan and Bet.'

'Then is thy grandam not over kind to thee, I take it.'

'Neither to any other is she, so please your Worship. She hath a wicked heart and worketh evil all her days.'

'Doth she mistreat thee?'

'There be times when she stayeth her hand, being asleep or overcome with drink; but when she hath her judgment clear again, she maketh it up to me with goodly beatings.'

A fierce look came into the little prince's eyes, and he cried out, 'What! Beatings?'

'Oh, indeed, yes, please you, sir.'

'*Beatings*! And thou so frail and little. Hark ye; before the night come she shall hie her to the Tower. The king my father——'

'In sooth, you forget, sir, her low degree. The Tower is for the great alone.

'True, indeed. I had not thought of that. I will consider of her punishment. Is thy father kind to thee?'

'Not more than Gammer Canty, sir.'

'Fathers be alike, mayhap. Mine hath not a doll's temper. He smiteth with a heavy hand, yet spareth me; he spareth me not always with his tongue, though, sooth to say. How doth thy mother use thee?'

'She is good, sir, and giveth me neither sorrow nor pain of any sort. And Nan and Bet are like to her in this.'

'How old be these?'

'Fifteen, an' it please you, sir.'

'The lady Elizabeth, my sister, is fourteen, and the lady Jane Grey, my cousin, is of mine own age, and comely and gracious withal; but my sister the lady Mary, with her gloomy mien and—— Look you; do thy sisters forbid their servants to smile, lest the sin destroy their souls?'

'They? Oh, dost think, sir, that *they* have servants?'

The little prince contemplated the little pauper gravely a moment, then said, 'And prithee, why not? Who helpeth them undress at night? Who attireth them when they rise?'

'None, sir. Wouldst have them take off their garment and sleep without —' like beasts?'

'Their garment! Have they but one?'

'Ah, good your Worship, what would they do with more? Truly they have not two bodies each.'

'It is a quaint and marvellous thought! Thy pardon, I had not meant to laugh. But thy good Nan and thy Bet shall have raiment and lackeys enow, and that soon too; my cofferer shall look to it. No, thank me not; 'tis nothing. Thou speakest well; thou hast an easy grace in it. Art learned?'

'I know not if I am or not, sir. The good priest that is called Father

'The two went and stood side by side before a great mirror'

Andrew taught me, of his kindness, from his books.'

'Knowst thou the Latin?'

'But scantly, sir, I doubt.'

'Learn it, lad; 'tis hard only at first. The Greek is harder; but neither these nor any tongues else, I think, are hard to the lady Elizabeth and my cousin. Thou shouldst hear those damsels at it! But tell me of thy Offal Court. Hast thou a pleasant life there?'

'In truth, yes, so please you, sir, save when one is hungry. There be Punch-and-Judy shows, and monkeys – oh, such antic creatures, and so bravely dressed! – and there be plays wherein they that play do shout and fight till all are slain, and 'tis so fine to see, and costeth but a farthing, albeit 'tis main hard to get the farthing, please your Worship.'

'Tell me more.'

'We lads of Offal Court do strive against each other with the cudgel, like to the fashion of the 'prentices, sometimes.'

The prince's eyes flashed. Said he, 'Marry, that would not I mislike. Tell me more.'

'We strive in races, sir, to see who of us shall be fleetest.'

'That I would like also. Speak on.'

'In summer, sir, we wade and swim in the canals and in the river, and each doth duck his neighbour, and spatter him with water, and dive and shout and tumble and——'

'Twould be worth my father's kingdom but to enjoy it once! Prithee go on.'

'We dance and sing about the Maypole in Cheapside; we play in the sand, each covering his neighbour up; and times we make mud pastry – oh, the lovely mud, it hath not its like for delightfulness in all the world! – we do fairly wallow in the mud, sir, saving your worship's presence.'

'Oh, prithee say no more; 'tis glorious! If that I could but clothe me in raiment like to thine, and strip my feet, and revel in the mud once, just once, with none to rebuke me or forbid, meseemeth I could forgo the crown!'

'And if that I could clothe me once, sweet sir, as thou are clad, just once——'

'Oho, wouldst like it? Then so shall it be. Doff thy rags and don these splendours, lad! It is a brief happiness, but will be not less keen for that. We will have it while we may, and change again before any come to molest.'

A few minutes later the little Prince of Wales was garlanded with Tom's fluttering odds and ends, and the little Prince of Pauperdom was tricked out in the gaudy plumage of royalty. The two went and stood side by side before a great mirror, and lo, a miracle: there did not seem to have been any change made! They stared at each other, then at the glass, then at each other again. At last the puzzled princeling said, 'What dost thou make of this?'

'Ah, good your worship, require me not to answer. It is not meet that one of my degree should utter the thing.'

'Then will *I* utter it. Thou hast the same hair, the same eyes, the same voice and manner, the same form and stature, the same face and countenance that I bear. Fared we forth naked, there is none could say which was you, and which the Prince of Wales. And now that I am clothed as thou wert clothed, it seemeth I should be able the more nearly to feel as thou didst when the brute soldier—— Hark ye, is not this a bruise upon your hand?'

'Yes; but it is a slight thing, and your Worship knoweth that the poor man-at-arms——'

'Peace! It was a shameful thing and a cruel!' cried the little prince, stamping his bare foot. 'If the king—— Stir not a step till I come again! It is a command!'

In a moment he had snatched up and put away an article of national importance that lay upon a table, and was out at the door and flying through the palace grounds in his bannered rags, with a hot face and glowing eyes. As soon as he reached the great gate, he seized the bars and tried to shake them, shouting, 'Open! Unbar the gates!'

The soldier that had maltreated Tom obeyed promptly; and as the prince burst through the portal, half smothered with royal wrath, the soldier fetched him a sounding box on the ear that sent him whirling to the roadway and said, 'Take that, thou beggar's spawn, for what thou got'st me from his Highness!'

The crowd roared with laughter. The prince picked himself out of the mud and made fiercely at the sentry, shouting, 'I am the Prince of Wales, my person is sacred; and thou shalt hang for laying thy hand upon me!'

The soldier brought his halberd to a present arms and said mockingly, 'I salute your gracious Highness.' Then angrily, 'Be off, thou crazy rubbish!'

Here the jeering crowd closed around the poor little prince and hustled him far down the road, hooting him and shouting, 'Way for his royal Highness! Way for the Prince of Wales!'

4 The Prince's Troubles Begin

After hours of persistent pursuit and persecution, the little prince was at last deserted by the rabble and left to himself. As long as he had been able to rage against the mob, and threaten it royally, and royally utter commands that were good stuff to laugh at, he was very entertaining; but when weariness finally forced him to be silent, he was no longer of use to his tormentors and they sought amusement elsewhere. He looked about him now but could not recognize the locality. He was within the city of London – that was all he knew. He moved on aimlessly, and in a little while the houses thinned and the passers-by were infrequent. He bathed his bleeding feet in the brook which flowed then where Farrington Street now is, rested a few moments, then passed on, and presently came upon a great space with only a few scattered houses in it and a prodigious church. He recognized this church. Scaffoldings were about everywhere, and swarms of workmen, for it was undergoing elaborate repairs. The prince took heart at once; he felt that his troubles were at an end now. He said to himself, 'It is the ancient Grey Friars' Church, which the king my father hath taken from the monks and given for a home forever for poor and forsaken children, and new-named it Christ's Church. Right gladly will they serve the son of him who hath done so generously by them, and the more that that son is himself as poor and as forlorn as any that be sheltered here this day, or ever shall be.'

He was soon in the midst of a crowd of boys who were running, jumping, playing at ball and leapfrog, and otherwise disporting themselves, and right noisily too. They were all dressed alike, and in the fashion which in that day prevailed among servingmen and 'prentices[1] – that is to say, each had on the crown of his head a flat black cap about the size of a saucer, which was not useful as a covering, it being of such scanty dimensions; neither was it ornamental; from beneath it the hair fell, unparted, to the middle of the forehead, and was cropped straight around; a clerical band at the neck; a blue gown that fitted closely and hung as low as the knees or lower; full sleeves; a broad red belt; bright-yellow stockings, gartered above the knees; low shoes with large metal buckles. It was a sufficiently ugly costume.

The boys stopped their play and flocked about the prince, who said with native dignity, 'Good lads, say to your master that Edward, Prince of

Wales, desireth speech with him.'

A great shout went up at this, and one rude fellow said, 'Marry, art thou his Grace's messenger, beggar?'

The prince's face flushed with anger, and his ready hand flew to his hip, but there was nothing there. There was a storm of laughter, and one boy said, 'Didst mark that? He fancied he had a sword – belike he is the prince himself.'

This sally brought more laughter. Poor Edward drew himself up proudly and said, 'I am the prince, and it ill beseemeth you that feed upon the king my father's bounty to use me so.'

This was vastly enjoyed, as the laughter testified. The youth who had first spoken shouted to his comrades, 'Ho, swine, slaves, pensioners of his Grace's princely father, where be your manners? Down on your marrow-bones, all of ye, and do reverence to his kingly port and royal rags!'

With boisterous mirth they dropped upon their knees in a body and did mock homage to their prey. The prince spurned the nearest boy with his foot and said fiercely, 'Take thou that till the morrow come and I build thee a gibbet!'

Ah, but this was not a joke; this was going beyond fun. The laughter ceased on the instant, and fury took its place. A dozen shouted, 'Hale him forth! To the horse-pond, to the horse-pond! Where be the dogs? Ho, there, Lion! Ho, Fangs!'

Then followed such a thing as England had never seen before – the sacred person of the heir to the throne rudely buffeted by plebeian hands and set upon and torn by dogs.

As night drew to a close that day, the prince found himself far down in the close-built portion of the city. His body was bruised, his hands were bleeding, and his rags were all besmirched with mud. He wandered on and on, and grew more and more bewildered, and so tired and faint he could hardly drag one foot after the other. He had ceased to ask questions of anyone, since they brought him only insult instead of information. He kept muttering to himself, 'Offal Court – that is the name; if I can but find it before my strength is wholly spent and I drop, then am I saved, for his people will take me to the palace and prove that I am none of theirs, but the true prince, and I shall have mine own again.' And now and then his mind reverted to his treatment by those rude Christ's Hospital boys, and he said, 'When I am king, they shall not have bread and shelter only, but also teachings out of books, for a full belly is little worth where the mind is starved, and the heart. I will keep this diligently in my remembrance, that this day's lesson be not lost upon me, and my people suffer thereby; for learning softeneth the heart and breedeth gentleness and charity.'[2]

The lights began to twinkle, it came on to rain, the wind rose, and a raw and gusty night set in. The houseless prince, the homeless heir to the throne of England, still moved on, drifting deeper into the maze of squalid alleys where the swarming hives of poverty and misery were massed together.

Suddenly a great drunken ruffian collared him and said, 'Out to this time of night again, and hast not brought a farthing home, I warrant me! If it be so, an' I do not break all the bones in thy lean body, then am I not John Canty, but some other.'

The prince twisted himself loose, unconsciously brushed his profaned shoulder, and eagerly said, 'Oh, art *his* father, truly? Sweet heaven grant it be so; then wilt thou fetch him away and restore me!'

'*His* father? I know not what thou meanst; I but know I am *thy* father, as thou shalt soon have cause to——'

'Oh, jest not, palter not, delay not! I am worn, I am wounded, I can bear no more. Take me to the king my father, and he will make thee rich beyond thy wildest dreams. Believe me, man, believe me! I speak no lie, but only the truth! Put forth thy hand and save me! I am indeed the Prince of Wales!'

The man stared down, stupefied, upon the lad, then shook his head and muttered, 'Gone stark mad as any Tom o' Bedlam!' – then collared him once more and said with a coarse laugh and an oath, 'But mad or no mad, I and thy Gammer Canty will soon find where the soft places in thy bones lie, or I'm no true man!'

With this he dragged the frantic and struggling prince away and disappeared up a front court followed by a delighted and noisy swarm of human vermin.

1 See Note 1 at end of volume.
2 See Note 2 at end of volume.

5 Tom as a Patrician

Tom Canty, left alone in the prince's cabinet, made good use of his opportunity. He turned himself this way and that before the great mirror, admiring his finery; then walked away, imitating the prince's high-bred carriage, and still observing results in the glass. Next he drew the beautiful sword and bowed, kissing the blade and laying it across his breast as he had seen a noble knight do, by way of salute to the lieutenant of the Tower, five or six weeks before, when delivering the great lords of Norfolk and Surrey into his hands for captivity. Tom played with the jewelled dagger that hung upon his thigh; he examined the costly and exquisite ornaments of the room; he tried each of the sumptuous chairs and thought how proud he would be if the Offal Court herd could only peep in and see him in his grandeur. He wondered if they would believe the marvellous tale he should tell when he got home or if they would shake their heads and say his overtaxed imagination had at last upset his reason.

At the end of half an hour it suddenly occurred to him that the prince was gone a long time; then right away he began to feel lonely; very soon he fell to listening and longing, and ceased to toy with the pretty things about him; he grew uneasy, then restless, then distressed. Suppose someone should come and catch him in the prince's clothes, and the prince not there to explain. Might they not hang him at once and inquire into his case afterward? He had heard that the great were prompt about small matters. His fears rose higher and higher, and trembling, he softly opened the door to the antechamber, resolved to fly and seek the prince, and through him, protection and release. Six gorgeous gentlemen servants and two young pages of high degree, clothed like butterflies, sprung to their feet and bowed low before him. He stepped quickly back and shut the door. He said, 'Oh, they mock at me! They will go and tell. Oh! Why came I here to cast away my life?'

He walked up and down the floor, filled with nameless fears, listening, starting at every trifling sound. Presently the door swung open and a silken page said, 'The lady Jane Grey.'

The door closed, and a sweet young girl, richly clad, bounded towards him. But she stopped suddenly and said in a distressed voice, 'Oh, what aileth thee, my lord?'

Tom's breath was nearly failing him, but he made shift to stammer out, 'Ah, be merciful, thou! In sooth I am no lord, but only poor Tom Canty of Offal Court in the city. Prithee let me see the prince, and he will of his grace restore to me my rags and let me hence unhurt. Oh, be thou merciful and save me!'

By this time the boy was on his knees and supplicating with his eyes and uplifted hands as well as with his tongue. The young girl seemed horror-stricken. She cried out, 'Oh, my lord, on thy knees? And to *me*!'

Then she fled away in fright; and Tom, smitten with despair, sank down, murmuring, 'There is no help, there is no hope. Now will they come and take me.'

Whilst he lay there benumbed with terror, dreadful tidings were speeding through the palace. The whisper, for it was whispered always, flew from menial to menial, from lord to lady, down all the long corridors, from story to story, from saloon to saloon, 'The prince hath gone mad, the prince hath gone mad!' Soon every saloon, every marble hall, had its group of glittering lords and ladies and other groups of dazzling lesser folk, talking earnestly together in whispers, and every face had in it dismay. Presently a splendid official came marching by these groups, making solemn proclamation, 'In the name of the king! Let none list to this false and foolish matter, upon pain of death, nor discuss the same, nor carry it abroad. In the name of the king!'

The whisperings ceased as suddenly as if the whisperers had been stricken dumb.

Soon there was a general buzz along the corridors of, 'The prince! See, the prince comes!'

Poor Tom came slowly walking past the low-bowing groups, trying to bow in return, and meekly gazing upon his strange surroundings with bewildered and pathetic eyes. Great nobles walked upon each side of him, making him lean upon them, and so steady his steps. Behind him followed the court physicians and some servants.

Presently Tom found himself in a noble apartment of the palace and heard the door close behind him. Around him stood those who had come with him. Before him, at a little distance, reclined a very large and very fat man with a wide, pulpy face and a stern expression. His large head was very grey; and his whiskers, which he wore only around his face, like a frame, were grey also. His clothing was of rich stuff, but old and slightly frayed in places. One of his swollen legs had a pillow under it and was wrapped in bandages. There was silence now, and there was no head there but was bent in reverence, except this man's. This stern-countenanced invalid was the dread Henry VIII. He said – and his face grew gentle as he began to speak – 'How now, my lord Edward, my prince? Hast been minded to cozen me, the good king thy father, who loveth thee and kindly useth thee, with a sorry jest?'

Poor Tom was listening, as well as his dazed faculties would let him, to the beginning of this speech; but when the words 'me, the good king' fell upon his ear, his face blanched and he dropped as instantly upon his knees as if a shot had brought him there. Lifting up his hands, he exclaimed, 'Thou the *king*? Then am I undone indeed!'

This speech seemed to stun the king. His eyes wandered from face to face aimlessly, then rested, bewildered, upon the boy before him. Then he said in a tone of deep disappointment, 'Alack, I had believed the rumour disproportioned to the truth, but I fear me 'tis not so.' He breathed a heavy sigh and said in a gentle voice, 'Come to thy father, child; thou art not well.'

Tom was assisted to his feet, and approached the Majesty of England, humble and trembling. The king took the frightened face between his hands and gazed earnestly and lovingly into it awhile, as if seeking some grateful sign of returning reason there, then pressed the curly head against his breast and patted it tenderly. Presently he said, 'Dost not know thy father, child? Break not mine old heart; say thou knowst me. Thou *dost* know me, dost thou not?'

'Yea, thou art my dread lord the king, whom God preserve!'

'True, true – that is well – be comforted, tremble not so; there is none here would hurt thee; there is none here but loves thee. Thou art better now; thy ill dream passeth; is't not so? And thou knowest thyself now also; is't not so? Thou wilt not miscall thyself again, as they say thou didst a little while agone?'

'I pray thee of thy Grace believe me, I did but speak the truth, most dread lord, for I am the meanest among thy subjects, being a pauper born, and 'tis by a sore mischance and accident I am here, albeit I was therein nothing blameful. I am but young to die, and thou canst save me with one little word. Oh, speak it, sir!'

'Die? Talk not so, sweet prince; peace, peace, to thy troubled heart; thou shalt not die!'

Tom dropped upon his knees with a glad cry, 'God requite thy mercy, O my king, and save thee long to bless thy land!' Then springing up, he turned a joyful face toward the two lords-in-waiting and exclaimed, 'Thou heardst it! I am not to die; the king hath said it!' There was no movement, save that all bowed with grave respect; but no one spoke. He hesitated, a little confused, then turned timidly toward the king, saying, 'I may go now?'

'Go? Surely, if thou desirest. But why not tarry yet a little? Whither wouldst go?'

Tom dropped his eyes and answered humbly, 'Peradventure I mistook; but I did think me free, and so was I moved to seek again the kennel where I was born and bred to misery, yet which harboureth my mother and my sisters, and so is home to me; whereas these pomps and splendours whereunto

I am not used – Oh, please you, sir, to let me go!'

The king was silent and thoughtful awhile, and his face betrayed a growing distress and uneasiness. Presently he said, with something of hope in his voice, 'Perchance he is but mad upon this one strain and hath his wits unmarred as toucheth other matter. God send it may be so! We will make trial.'

Then he asked Tom a question in Latin, and Tom answered him lamely in the same tongue. The king was delighted, and showed it. The lords and doctors manifested their gratification also. The king said, ''Twas not according to his schooling and ability, but sheweth that his mind is but diseased, not stricken fatally. How say you, sir?'

The physician addressed bowed low and replied, 'It jumpeth with mine own conviction, sire, that thou hast divined aright.'

The king looked pleased with this encouragement, coming as it did from so excellent authority, and continued with good heart, 'Now mark ye all; we will try him further.'

He put a question to Tom in French. Tom stood silent a moment, embarrassed by having so many eyes centred upon him, then said diffidently, 'I have no knowledge of this tongue, so please your majesty.'

The king fell back upon his couch. The attendants flew to his assistance; but he put them aside and said, 'Trouble me not – it is nothing but a scurvy faintness. Raise me! There, 'tis sufficient. Come hither, child; there, rest thy poor troubled head upon thy father's heart and be at peace. Thou'lt soon be well; 'tis but a passing fantasy. Fear thou not; thou'lt soon be well.' Then he turned toward the company; his gentle manner changed, and baleful lightnings began to play from his eyes. He said, 'List ye all! This my son is mad, but it is not permanent. Overstudy hath done this, and somewhat too much of confinement. Away with his books and teachers! See ye to it. Pleasure him with sports, beguile him in wholesome ways, so that his health come again.' He raised himself higher still and went on with energy, 'He is mad, but he is my son and England's heir, and mad or sane, still shall he reign! And hear ye further, and proclaim it: whoso speaketh of this his distemper worketh against the peace and order of these realms and shall to the gallows! Give me to drink – I burn: this sorrow sappeth my strength. There, take away the cup. Support me. There, that is well. Mad, is he? Were he a thousand times mad, yet is he Prince of Wales, and I the king will confirm it. This very morrow shall he be installed in his princely dignity in due and ancient form. Take instant order for it, my lord Hertford.'

One of the nobles knelt at the royal couch and said, 'The king's majesty knoweth that the Hereditary Great Marshal of England lieth attainted in the Tower. It were not meet that one attainted——'

'Peace! Insult not mine ears with his hated name. Is this man to live forever? Am I to be balked of my will? Is the prince to tarry uninstalled because, forsooth, the realm lacketh an earl marshal free of treasonable taint to invest him with his honours? No, by the splendour of God! Warn my Parliament to bring me Norfolk's doom before the sun rise again, else shall they answer for it grievously!'[1]

Lord Hertford said, 'The king's will is law," and rising, returned to his former place.

Gradually the wrath faded out of the old king's face, and he said, 'Kiss me, my prince. There. What fearest thou? Am I not thy loving father?'

'Thou art good to me that am unworthy, O mighty and gracious lord; that in truth I know. But – but – it grieveth me to think of him that is to die, and——'

'Ah, 'tis like thee, 'tis like thee! I know thy heart is still the same, even though thy mind hath suffered hurt, for thou wert ever of a gentle spirit. But this duke standeth between thee and thine honours; I will have another in his stead that shall bring no taint to his great office. Comfort thee, my prince; trouble not thy poor head with this matter.'

'But is it not I that speed him hence, my liege? How long might he not live, but for me?'

'Take no thought of him, my prince; he is not worthy. Kiss me once again and go to thy trifles and amusements, for my malady distresseth me. I am aweary and would rest. Go with thine uncle Hertford and thy people, and come again when my body is refreshed.'

Tom, heavy-hearted, was conducted from the presence, for this last sentence was a death-blow to the hope he had cherished that now he would be set free. Once more he heard the buzz of low voices exclaiming, 'The prince, the prince comes!'

His spirits sank lower and lower as he moved between the glittering files of bowing courtiers, for he recognized that he was indeed a captive now and might remain forever shut up in this gilded cage, a forlorn and friendless prince, except God in his mercy take pity on him and set him free.

And turn where he would, he seemed to see floating in the air the severed head and the remembered face of the great Duke of Norfolk, the eyes fixed on him reproachfully.

His old dreams had been so pleasant, but this reality was so dreary!

---

1 See note 3 at end of volume.

6 Tom Receives Instructions

Tom was conducted to the principal apartment of a noble suite and made to sit down, a thing which he was loath to do since there were elderly men and men of high degree about him. He begged them to be seated also, but they only bowed their thanks or murmured them and remained standing. He would have insisted, but his 'uncle' the Earl of Hertford whispered in his ear, 'Prithee, insist not, my lord; it is not meet that they sit in thy presence.'

The lord St John was announced, and after making obeisance to Tom, he said, 'I come upon the king's errand, concerning a matter which requireth privacy. Will it please your royal Highness to dismiss all that attend you here, save my lord the Earl of Hertford?'

Observing that Tom did not seem to know how to proceed, Hertford whispered him to make a sign with his hand and not trouble himself to speak unless he chose. When the waiting gentlemen had retired, Lord St John said, 'His Majesty commandeth that for due and weighty reasons of state, the prince's grace shall hide his infirmity in all ways that be within his power till it be passed and he be as he was before. To wit, that he shall deny to none that he is the true prince and heir to England's greatness; that he shall uphold his princely dignity and shall receive, without word or sign of protest, that reverence and observance which unto it do appertain of right and ancient usage; that he shall cease to speak to any of that lowly birth and life his malady hath conjured out of the unwholesome imaginings of o'erwrought fancy; that he shall strive with diligence to bring unto his memory again those faces which he was wont to know – and where he faileth he shall hold his peace, neither betraying by semblance of surprise or other sign that he hath forgot; that upon occasions of state, whensoever any matter shall perplex him as to the thing he should do or the utterance he should make, he shall show nought of unrest to the curious that look on, but take advice in that matter of the lord Hertford or my humble self, which are commanded of the king to be upon this service and close at call till this commandment be dissolved. Thus saith the king's majesty, who sendeth greeting to your royal Highness and prayeth that God will of his mercy quickly heal you and have you now and ever in his holy keeping.'

The lord St John made reverence and stood aside. Tom replied resignedly, 'The king hath said it. None may palter with the king's command or fit it to his ease, where it doth chafe, with deft evasions. The king shall be obeyed.'

Lord Hertford said, 'Touching the king's majesty's ordainment concerning books and such like serious matters, it may peradventure please your Highness to ease your time with lightsome entertainment, lest you go wearied to the banquet and suffer harm thereby.'

Tom's face showed inquiring surprise, and a blush followed when he saw Lord St John's eyes bent sorrowfully upon him. His lordship said, 'Thy memory still wrongeth thee, and thou hast shown surprise; but suffer it not to trouble thee, for 'tis a matter that will not bide, but depart with thy mending malady. My lord of Hertford speaketh of the city's banquet which the king's majesty did promise, some two months flown, your Highness should attend. Thou recallest it now?'

'It grieves me to confess it had indeed escaped me,' said Tom in a hesitating voice, and blushed again.

At this moment the lady Elizabeth and the lady Jane Grey were announced. The two lords exchanged significant glances, and Hertford stepped quickly toward the door. As the young girls passed him, he said in a low voice, 'I pray ye, ladies, seem not to observe his humours nor show surprise when his memory doth lapse, it will grieve you to note how it doth stick at every trifle.'

Meantime Lord St John was saying in Tom's ear, 'Please you, sir, keep diligently in mind his Majesty's desire. Remember all thou canst, *seem* to remember all else. Let them not perceive that thou art much changed from thy wont, for thou knowest how tenderly thy old play-fellows bear thee in their hearts and how 'twould grieve them. Art willing, sir that I remain? And thine uncle?'

Tom signified assent with a gesture and a murmured word, for he was already learning, and in his simple heart was resolved to acquit himself as best he might, according to the king's command.

In spite of every precaution, the conversation among the young people became a little embarrassing at times. More than once, in truth, Tom was near to breaking down and confessing himself unequal to his tremendous part; but the tact of the princess Elizabeth saved him, or a word from one or the other of the vigilant lords, thrown in apparently by chance, had the same happy effect. Once the little lady Jane turned to Tom and dismayed him with this question, 'Hast paid thy duty to the queen's majesty today, my lord?'

Tom hesitated, looked distressed, and was about to stammer out something at hazard when Lord St John took the word and answered for him with the easy grace of a courtier accustomed to encounter delicate difficulties and to be ready for them, 'He hath indeed, madam, and she did greatly hearten him, as touching his Majesty's condition; is it not so, your Highness?'

Tom mumbled something that stood for assent, but felt that he was getting upon dangerous ground. Somewhat later it was mentioned that Tom was to study no more at present, whereupon her little ladyship exclaimed, ''Tis a pity, 'tis such a pity! Thou wert proceeding bravely. But bide thy time in patience; it will not be for long. Thou'lt yet be graced with learning like thy father, and make thy tongue master of as many languages as his, good my prince.'

'My father!' cried Tom, off his guard for a moment. 'I trow he cannot speak his own so that any but the swine that wallow in the sties may tell his meaning; and as for learning of any sort soever——'

He looked up and encountered a solemn warning in my lord St John's eyes.

He stopped, blushed, then continued low and sadly, 'Ah, my malady persecuteth me again, and my mind wandereth. I meant the king's grace no irreverence.'

'We know it, sir,' said the princess Elizabeth, taking her 'brother's' hand between her two palms, respectfully but caressingly; 'trouble not thyself as to that. The fault is none of thine, but thy distemper's'

'Thou'rt a gentle comforter, sweet lady,' said Tom gratefully, 'and my heart moveth me to thank thee for't, an' I may be so bold.'

Once the giddy little lady Jane fired a simple Greek phrase at Tom. The princess Elizabeth's quick eye saw by the serene blankness of the target's front that the shaft was overshot, so she tranquilly delivered a return volley of sounding Greek on Tom's behalf and then straightway changed the talk to other matters.

Time wore on pleasantly, and likewise smoothly, on the whole. Snags and sandbars grew less and less frequent, and Tom grew more and more at his ease, seeing that all were so lovingly bent upon helping him and overlooking his mistakes. When it came out that the little ladies were to accompany him to the Lord Mayor's banquet in the evening, his heart gave a bound of relief and delight, for he felt that he should not be friendless now among that multitude of strangers, whereas an hour earlier the idea of their going with him would have been an insupportable terror to him.

Tom's guardian angels, the two lords, had had less comfort in the interview than the other parties to it. They felt much as if they were piloting a great ship through a dangerous channel; they were on the alert constantly, and found their office no child's play. Wherefore, at last, when the ladies' visit was drawing to a close and the lord Guilford Dudley was announced, they not only felt that their charge had been sufficiently taxed for the present, but also that they themselves were not in the best condition to take their ship back and make their anxious voyage all over again. So they respectfully advised Tom to excuse himself, which he was very glad to do, although a slight shade of disappointment might have been observed upon my lady Jane's face when she heard the splendid stripling denied admittance.

There was a pause now, a sort of waiting silence which Tom could not understand. He glanced at Lord Hertford, who gave him a sign, but he failed to understand that also. The ready Elizabeth came to the rescue with her usual easy grace. She made reverence and said, 'Have we leave of the prince's grace my brother to go?'

Tom said, 'Indeed your ladyships can have whatsoever of me they will for the asking; yet would I rather give them any other thing that in my poor power lieth than leave to take the light and blessing of their presence hence. Give ye good den, and God be with ye!' Then he smiled inwardly at the thought; ''Tis not for nought I have dwelt but among princes in my reading and taught my tongue some slight trick of their broidered and gracious speech withal!'

When the illustrious maidens were gone, Tom turned wearily to his keepers and said, 'May it please your lordships to grant me leave to go into some corner and rest me?'

Lord Hertford said, 'So please your Highness, it is for you to command, it is for us to obey. That thou shouldst rest is indeed a needful thing, since thou must journey to the city presently.'

He touched a bell, and a page appeared, who was ordered to desire the presence of Sir William Herbert. This gentleman came straightway and conducted Tom to an inner apartment. Tom's first movement there was to reach for a cup of water; but a silk-and-velvet servitor seized it, dropped upon one knee, and offered it to him on a golden salver.

Next the tired captive sat down and was going to take off his buskins, timidly asking leave with his eye, but another silk-and-velvet discomforter went down upon his knees and took the office from him. He made two or three further efforts to help himself, but being promptly forestalled each time, he finally gave up with a sigh of resignation and a murmured, 'Beshrew me but I marvel they do not require to breathe for me also!' Slippered and wrapped in a sumptuous robe, he laid himself down at last to rest, but not to sleep, for his head was too full of thoughts and the room too full of people. He could not dismiss the former, so they stayed; he did not know enough to dismiss the latter, so they stayed also, to his vast regret – and theirs.

Tom's departure had left his two noble guardians alone. They mused awhile, with much headshaking and walking the floor; then Lord St John said, 'Plainly, what dost thou think?'

'Plainly, then, this. The king is near his end, my nephew is mad, mad will mount the throne, and mad remain. God protect England, since she will need it!'

'Verily it promiseth so, indeed. But – have you no misgivings as to – as to——'

The speaker hesitated and finally stopped. He evidently felt that he was upon delicate ground. Lord Hertford stopped before him, looked into his face with a clear, frank eye, and said, 'Speak on; there is none to hear but me. Misgivings as to what?'

'I am full loath to word the thing that is in my mind, and thou so near to him in blood, my lord. But craving pardon if I do offend, seemeth it not strange that madness could so change his port and manner! Not but that his port and speech are princely still, but that they *differ* in one unweighty trifle or another from what his custom was aforetime. Seemeth it not strange that madness should filch from his memory his father's very lineaments; the customs and observances that are his due from such as be about him; and, leaving him his Latin, strip him of his Greek and French? My Lord, be not offended, but ease my mind of its disquiet and receive my grateful thanks. It haunteth me, his saying he was not the prince, and so——'

'Peace, my lord, thou utterest treason! Hast forgot the king's command? Remember I am party to thy crime if I but listen.'

St John paled and hastened to say, 'I was in fault, I do confess it. Betray me not, grant me this grace out of thy courtesy, and I will neither think nor speak of this thing more. Deal not hardly with me, sir, else am I ruined.'

'I am content, my lord. So thou offend not again, here or in the ears of others, it shall be as though thou hadst not spoken. But thou needst not have misgivings. He is my sister's son; are not his voice, his face, his form, familiar to me from his cradle? Madness can do all the odd conflicting things thou seest in him, and more. Dost not recall how that the old baron Marley, being mad, forgot the favour of his own countenance that he had known for sixty years, and held it was another's; nay, even claimed he was the son of Mary Magdalene and that his head was made of Spanish glass; and sooth to say, he suffered none to touch it, lest by mischance some heedless hand might shiver it. Give thy misgivings easement, good my lord. This is the very prince, I know him well – and soon will be thy king; it may advantage thee to bear this in mind and more dwell upon it than the other.'

After some further talk, in which the lord St John covered up his mistake as well as he could by repeated protests that his faith was thoroughly grounded now and could not be assailed by doubts again, the lord Hertford relieved his fellow keeper and sat down to keep watch and ward alone. He was soon deep in meditation. And evidently the longer he thought, the more he was bothered. By and by he began to pace the floor and mutter.

'Tush, he *must* be the prince! Will any he in all the land maintain there can be two, not of one blood and birth, so marvellously twinned? And even were it so, 'twere yet a stranger miracle that chance should cast the one into the other's place. Nay, 'tis folly, folly, folly!'

Presently he said, 'Now were he impostor and called himself prince, look you *that* would be natural; that would be reasonable. But lived ever an impostor yet who, being called prince by the king, prince by the court, prince by all, *denied* his dignity and pleaded against his exaltation? *No!* By the soul of St Swithin, no! This is the true prince, gone mad!'

7 Tom's First Royal Dinner

Somewhat after one in the afternoon, Tom resignedly underwent the ordeal of being dressed for dinner. He found himself as finely clothed as before, but everything different, everything changed, from his ruff to his stockings. He was presently conducted with much state to a spacious and ornate apartment, where a table was already set for one. Its furniture was all of massy gold, and beautified with designs which well-nigh made it priceless, since they were the work of Benvenuto. The room was half filled with noble servitors. A chaplain said grace, and Tom was about to fall to, for hunger had long been constitutional with him, but was interrupted by my lord the Earl of Berkeley, who fastened a napkin about his neck, for the great post of Diaperers to the Princes of Wales was hereditary in this nobleman's family. Tom's cupbearer was present and forestalled all his attempts to help himself to wine. The Taster to his Highness the Prince of Wales was there also, prepared to taste any suspicious dish upon requirement and run the risk of being poisoned. He was only an ornamental appendage at this time and was seldom called upon to exercise his function; but there had been times, not many generations past, when the office of taster had its perils and was not a grandeur to be desired. Why they did not use a dog or a plumber seems strange, but all the ways of royalty are strange. My lord D'Arcy, First Groom of the Chamber, was there to do goodness knows what; but there he was – let that suffice. The Lord Chief Butler was there and stood behind Tom's chair, overseeing the solemnities under command of the Lord Great Steward and the Lord Head Cook, who stood near. Tom had three hundred and eighty-four servants beside these, but they were not all in that room, of course, nor the quarter of them; neither was Tom aware yet that they existed.

All those that were present had been well drilled within the hour to remember that the prince was temporarily out of his head and to be careful to show no surprise at his vagaries. These 'vagaries' were soon on exhibition before them, but they only moved their compassion and their sorrow, not their mirth. It was a heavy affliction to them to see the beloved prince so stricken.

Poor Tom ate with his fingers mainly, but no one smiled at it or even seemed to observe it. He inspected his napkin curiously and with deep interest, for it was of a very dainty and beautiful fabric; then said with simplicity, 'Prithee take it away, lest in mine unheedfulness it be soiled.'

The Hereditary Diaperer took it away with reverent manner and without word or protest of any sort.

Tom examined the turnips and the lettuce with interest, and asked what they were and if they were to be eaten, for it was only recently that men had begun to raise these things in England in place of importing them as luxuries from Holland.[1] His question was answered with grave respect, and no surprise manifested. When he had finished his dessert, he filled his pockets with nuts; but nobody appeared to be aware of it or disturbed by it. But the next moment he was himself disturbed by it and showed discomposure, for this was the only service he had been permitted to do with his own hands during the meal, and he did not doubt that he had done a most improper and unprincely thing. At that moment the muscles of his nose began to twitch, and the end of that organ to lift and wrinkle. This continued, and Tom began to evince a growing distress. He looked appealingly, first at one and then another of the lords about him, and tears came into his eyes. They sprang forward with dismay in their faces and begged to know his trouble. Tom said with genuine anguish, 'I crave your indulgence; my nose itcheth cruelly. What is the custom and usage in this emergence? Prithee speed, for 'tis but a little time that I can bear it.'

None smiled, but all were sore perplexed and looked one to the other in deep tribulation for counsel. But behold, here was a dead wall, and nothing in English history to tell how to get over it. The Master of Ceremonies was not present; there was no one who felt safe to venture upon this uncharted sea or risk the attempt to solve this solemn problem. Alas! There was no Hereditary Scratcher. Meantime the tears had overflowed their banks and begun to trickle down Tom's cheeks. His twitching nose was pleading more urgently than ever for relief. At last nature broke down the barriers of etiquette: Tom lifted up an inward prayer for pardon if he was doing wrong and brought relief to the burdened hearts of his court by scratching his nose himself.

His meal being ended, a lord came and held before him a broad, shallow, golden dish with fragrant rose water in it to cleanse his mouth and fingers with; and my lord the Hereditary Diaperer stood by with a napkin for his use. Tom gazed at the dish a puzzled moment or two, then raised it to his lips and gravely took a draught. Then he returned it to the waiting lord and said 'Nay, it likes me not, my lord; it hath a pretty flavour, but it wanteth strength.'

This new eccentricity of the prince's ruined mind made all the hearts about him ache, but the sad sight moved none to merriment.

Tom's next unconscious blunder was to get up and leave the table just when the chaplain had taken his stand behind his chair, and with uplifted hands and closed, uplifted eyes was in the act of beginning the blessing. Still nobody seemed to perceive that the prince had done a thing unusual.

By his own request, our small friend was now conducted to his private cabinet and left there alone to his own devices. Hanging upon hooks in the oaken wainscotting were the several pieces of a suit of shining steel armour, covered all over with beautiful designs exquisitely inlaid in gold. This martial panoply belonged to the true prince, a recent present from Madam Parr, the queen. Tom put on the greaves, the gauntlets, the plumed helmet, and such other pieces as he could don without assistance, and for a while was minded to call for help and complete the matter, but bethought him of the nuts he had brought away from dinner and the joy it would be to èat them with no crowd to eye him and no Grand Hereditaries to pester him with undesired services; so he restored the pretty things to their several places and soon was cracking nuts and feeling almost naturally happy for the first time since God for his sins had made him a prince. When the nuts were all gone, he stumbled upon some inviting books in a closet, among them one about the etiquette of the English court. This was a prize. He lay down upon a sumptuous divan and proceeded to instruct himself with honest zeal. Let us leave him there for the present.

1 See Note 4 at end of volume.

8 The Question of the Seal

About five o'clock Henry VIII awoke out of an unrefreshing nap and muttered to himself, 'Troublous dreams, troublous dreams! Mine end is now at hand; so say these warnings, and my failing pulses do confirm it.' Presently a wicked light flamed up in his eye, and he muttered, 'Yet will not I die till *he* go before.'

His attendants perceiving that he was awake, one of them asked his pleasure concerning the Lord Chancellor, who was waiting without.

'Admit him, admit him!' exclaimed the king eagerly.

The Lord Chancellor entered and knelt by the king's couch, saying, 'I have given order, and according to the king's command, the peers of the realm, in their robes, do now stand at the bar of the House, where, having confirmed the Duke of Norfolk's doom, they humbly wait his Majesty's further pleasure in the matter.'

The king's face lit up with a fierce joy. Said he, 'Lift me up! In mine own person will I go before my Parliament, and with mine own hand will I seal the warrant that rids me of——'

His voice failed, an ashen pallor swept the flush from his cheeks, and the attendants eased him back upon his pillows and hurriedly assisted him with restoratives. Presently he said sorrowfully, 'Alack, how have I longed for this sweet hour! And lo, too late it cometh, and I am robbed of this so coveted chance. But speed ye, speed ye! Let others do this happy office sith 'tis denied to me. I put my Great Seal in commission; choose thou the lords that shall compose it, and get ye to your work. Speed ye, man! Before the sun shall rise and set again, bring me his head, that I may see it.'

'According to the king's command, so shall it be. Will't please your Majesty to order that the Seal be now restored to me, so that I may forth upon the business?'

'The Seal? Who keepeth the Seal but thou?'

'Please your Majesty, you did take it from me two days since, saying it should no more do its office till your own royal hand should use it upon the Duke of Norfolk's warrant.'

'Why, so in sooth I did; I do remember it. What did I with it? I am very feeble. So oft these days doth my memory play the traitor with me. 'Tis

'The King . . . tried to recollect what he had done with the seal'

strange, strange———'

The king dropped into inarticulate mumblings, shaking his grey head weakly from time to time and gropingly trying to recollect what he had done with the Seal.

At last my lord Hertford ventured to kneel and offer information, 'Sire, if that I may be so bold, here be several that do remember with me how that you gave the Great Seal into the hands of his Highness the Prince of Wales to keep against the day that———'

'True, most true!' interrupted the king. 'Fetch it! Go; time flieth!'

Lord Hertford flew to Tom, but returned to the king before very long troubled and empty-handed. He delivered himself to this effect: 'It grieveth me, my lord the king, to bear so heavy and unwelcome tidings; but it is the will of God that the prince's affliction abideth still, and he cannot recall to mind that he received the Seal. So came I quickly to report, thinking it were waste of precious time and little worth withal that any should attempt to search the long array of chambers and saloons that belong unto his royal High———'

A groan from the king interrupted my lord at this point. After a little while his Majesty said, with a deep sadness in his tone, 'Trouble him no more, poor child. The hand of God lieth heavy upon him, and my heart goeth out in loving compassion for him, and sorrow that I may not bear his burden on mine own old trouble-weighted shoulders, and so bring him peace.'

He closed his eyes, fell to mumbling, and presently was silent. After a time he opened his eyes again and gazed vacantly around until his glance rested upon the kneeling Lord Chancellor. Instantly his face flushed with wrath: 'What, thou here yet! By the glory of God, an' thou gettest not about that traitor's business, thy mitre shall have holiday the morrow for lack of a head to grace withal!'

The trembling Chancellor answered, 'Good your Majesty, I cry you mercy! I but waited for the Seal.'

'Man, hast lost thy wits? The small Seal which aforetime I was wont to take with me abroad lieth in my treasury. And since the Great Seal hath flown away, shall not it suffice? Hast lost thy wits? Begone! And hark ye; come no more till thou do bring his head.'

The poor Chancellor was not long in removing himself from this dangerous vicinity, nor did the commission waste time in giving the royal assent to the work of the slavish Parliament and appointing the morrow for the beheading of the premier peer of England, the luckless Duke of Norfolk.[1]

---

1 See Note 5 at end of volume.

9 The River Pageant

At nine in the evening the whole vast river-front of the palace was blazing with light. The river itself, as far as the eye could reach citywards, was so thickly covered with watermen's boats and with pleasure barges, all fringed with coloured lanterns and gently agitated by the waves, that it resembled a glowing and limitless garden of flowers stirred to soft motion by summer winds. The grand terrace of stone steps leading down to the water, spacious enough to mass the army of a German principality upon, was a picture to see, with its ranks of royal halberdiers in polished armour and its troops of brilliantly costumed servitors flitting up and down, and to and fro, in the hurry of preparation.

Presently a command was given, and immediately all living creatures vanished from the steps. Now the air was heavy with the hush of suspense and expectancy. As far as one's vision could carry, he might see the myriads of people in the boats rise up, and shade their eyes from the glare of lanterns and torches, and gaze toward the palace.

A file of forty or fifty state barges drew up to the steps. They were richly gilt, and their lofty prows and sterns were elaborately carved. Some of them were decorated with banners and streamers, some with cloth of gold and arras embroidered with coats of arms, others with silken flags that had numberless little silver bells fastened to them which shook out tiny showers of joyous music whenever the breezes fluttered them; others of yet higher pretensions, since they belonged to nobles in the prince's immediate service, had their sides picturesquely fenced with shields gorgeously emblazoned with armorial bearings. Each state barge was towed by a tender. Besides the rowers, these tenders carried each a number of men-at-arms in glossy helmet and breastplate, and a company of musicians.

The advance guard of the expected procession now appeared in the great gateway, a troop of halberdiers. They were dressed in striped hose of black and tawny, velvet caps graced at the sides with silver roses, and doublets of murrey-and-blue cloth embroidered on the front and back with the three feathers, the prince's blazon, woven in gold. Their halberd staves were covered with crimson velvet, fastened with gilt nails, and ornamented with gold tassels. Filing off on the right and left, they formed two long lines, extending from the gateway of the palace to the water's edge. A thick, rayed cloth, or carpet, was then unfolded and laid down between them by attendants in the gold-and-crimson liveries of the prince. This done, a flourish of trumpets resounded from within. A lively prelude arose from the musicians on the water, and two ushers with white wands marched with a slow and stately pace from the portal. They were followed by an officer bearing the civic mace, after whom came another carrying the city's sword; then several sergeants of the city guard, in their full accoutrements and with badges on their sleeves; then the garter king-at-arms, in his tabard; then several knights of the bath, each with a white lace on his sleeve; then their esquires; then the judges, in their robes of scarlet and coifs; then the lord High Chancellor of England, in a robe of scarlet, open before and purfled with miniver; then a deputation of aldermen, in their scarlet cloaks; and then the heads of the different civic companies, in their robes of state. Now came twelve French gentlemen, in splendid habiliments, consisting of pourpoints of white damask barred with gold, short mantles of crimson velvet lined with violet taffeta, and carnation-coloured *hauts-de-chausses*, and took their way down the steps. They were of the suite of the French ambassador, and were followed by twelve cavaliers of the suite of the Spanish ambassador, clothed in black velvet unrelieved by any ornament. Following these came several great English nobles with their attendants.

There was a flourish of trumpets within; and the prince's uncle, the future great Duke of Somerset, emerged from the gateway arrayed in a doublet of black cloth of gold and a cloak of crimson satin flowered with gold and ribanded with nets of silver. He turned, doffed his plumed cap, bent his body in a low reverence, and began to step backward, bowing at each step. A prolonged trumpet blast followed, and a proclamation, 'Way for the high and mighty, the lord Edward, Prince of Wales!' High aloft on the palace walls a long line of red tongues of flame leaped forth with a thundercrash; the massed world on the river burst into a mighty roar of welcome; and Tom Canty, the cause and hero of it all, stepped into view and slightly bowed his princely head.

He was magnificently habited in a doublet of white satin, with a frontpiece of purple cloth of tissue, powdered with diamonds, and edged with ermine. Over this he wore a mantle of white cloth of gold pounced with the triple-feather crest, lined with blue satin, set with pearls and precious stones, and fastened with a clasp of brilliants. About his neck hung the Order of the Garter and several princely foreign orders, and wherever light fell upon him jewels responded with a blinding flash. O Tom Canty, born in a hovel, bred in the gutters of London, familiar with rags and dirt and misery, what a spectacle is this!

10 The Prince in the Toils

We left John Canty dragging the rightful prince into Offal Court, with a noisy and delighted mob at his heels. There was but one person in it who offered a pleading word for the captive, and he was not heeded; he was hardly even heard, so great was the turmoil. The prince continued to struggle for freedom and to rage against the treatment he was suffering, until John Canty lost what little patience was left in him and raised his oaken cudgel in a sudden fury over the prince's head. The single pleader for the lad sprang to stop the man's arm, and the blow descended upon his own wrist. Canty roared out, 'Thou'lt meddle, wilt thou? Then have thy reward.'

His cudgel crashed down upon the meddler's head; there was a groan, a dim form sank to the ground among the feet of the crowd, and the next moment it lay there in the dark alone. The mob pressed on, their enjoyment nothing disturbed by this episode.

Presently the prince found himself in John Canty's abode, with the door closed against the outsiders. By the vague light of a tallow candle which was thrust into a bottle he made out the main features of the loathsome den and also the occupants of it. Two frowzy girls and a middle-aged woman cowered against the wall in one corner with the aspect of animals habituated to harsh usage and expecting and dreading it now. From another corner stole a withered hag with streaming grey hair and malignant eyes. John Canty said to this one, 'Tarry! There's fine mummeries here. Mar them not till thou'st enjoyed them; then let thy hand be heavy as thou wilt. Stand forth, lad. Now say thy foolery again, an' thou'st not forgot it. Name thy name. Who art thou?'

The insulted blood mounted to the little prince's cheek once more, and he lifted a steady and indignant gaze to the man's face and said, ''Tis but ill breeding in such as thou to command me to speak. I tell thee now, as I told thee before, I am Edward, Prince of Wales, and none other.'

The stunning surprise in this reply nailed the hag's feet to the floor where she stood, and almost took her breath. She stared at the prince in stupid amazement, which so amused her ruffianly son that he burst into a roar of laughter. But the effect upon Tom Canty's mother and sisters was different. Their dread of bodily injury gave way at once to distress of a different sort.

They ran forward with woe and dismay in their faces, exclaiming, 'O poor Tom, poor lad!'

The mother fell on her knees before the prince, put her hands upon his shoulders, and gazed yearningly into his face through her rising tears. Then she said, 'O my poor boy! Thy foolish reading hath wrought its woeful work at last and ta'en thy wit away. Ah! Why didst thou cleave to it when I so warned thee 'gainst it? Thou'st broke thy mother's heart.'

The prince looked into her face and said gently, 'Thy son is well and hath not lost his wits, good dame. Comfort thee; let me to the palace where he is, and straightway will the king my father restore him to thee.'

'The king thy father! O my child! Unsay these words that be freighted with death for thee and ruin for all that be near to thee. Shake off this gruesome dream. Call back thy poor wandering memory. Look upon me. Am not I thy mother that bore thee and loveth thee?'

The prince shook his head and reluctantly said, 'God knoweth I am loath to grieve thy heart, but truly have I never looked upon thy face before.'

The woman sank back to a sitting posture on the floor, and covering her eyes with her hands, gave way to heart-broken sobs and wailings.

'Let the show go on!' shouted Canty. 'What, Nan! What, Bet! Mannerless wenches! Will ye stand in the prince's presence? Upon your knees, ye pauper scum, and do him reverence!'

He followed this with another horse-laugh. The girls began to plead timidly for their brother, and Nan said, 'An' thou wilt but let him to bed, Father, rest and sleep will heal his madness; prithee, do.'

'Do, Father,' said Bet; 'he is more worn than is his wont. Tomorrow will he be himself again, and will beg with diligence, and come not empty home again.'

This remark sobered the father's joviality and brought his mind to business. He turned angrily upon the prince and said, 'The morrow must we pay two pennies to him that owns this hole; two pennies, mark ye – all this money for a half year's rent, else out of this we go. Show what thou'st gathered with thy lazy begging.'

The prince said, 'Offend me not with thy sordid matters. I tell thee again I am the king's son.'

A sounding blow upon the prince's shoulder from Canty's broad palm sent him staggering into goodwife Canty's arms, who clasped him to her breast and sheltered him from a pelting rain of cuffs and slaps by interposing her own person. The frightened girls retreated to their corner, but the grandmother stepped eagerly forward to assist her son. The prince sprang away from Mrs. Canty, exclaiming, 'Thou shalt not suffer for me, madam. Let these swine do their will upon me alone.'

This speech infuriated the swine to such a degree that they set about their work without waste of time. Between them they belaboured the boy right soundly, and then gave the girls and their mother a beating for showing sympathy for the victim.

'Now,' said Canty, 'to bed, all of ye. The entertainment has tired me.'

The light was put out, and the family retired. As soon as the snorings of the head of the house and his mother showed that they were asleep, the young girls crept to where the prince lay and covered him tenderly from the cold with straw and rags; and their mother crept to him also and stroked his hair, and cried over him, whispering broken words of comfort and compassion in his ear the while. She had saved a morsel for him to eat also, but the boy's pains had swept away all appetite, at least for black and tasteless crusts. He was touched by her brave and costly defence of him and by her commiseration, and he thanked her in very noble and princely words, and begged her to go to her sleep and try to forget her sorrows. And he added that the king his father would not let her loyal kindness and devotion go unrewarded. This return to his 'madness' broke her heart anew, and she strained him to her breast again and again and then went back, drowned in tears, to her bed.

As she lay thinking and mourning, the suggestion began to creep into her mind that there was an undefinable something about this boy that was lacking in Tom Canty, mad or sane. She could not describe it, she could not tell just what it was, and yet her sharp mother instinct seemed to detect it and perceive it. What if the boy were really not her son after all? Oh, absurd! She almost smiled at the idea, spite of her griefs and troubles. No matter, she found that it was an idea that would not 'down,' but persisted in haunting her. It pursued her, it harassed her, it clung to her, and refused to be put away or ignored. At last she perceived that there was not going to be any peace for her until she should devise a test that should prove, clearly and without question, whether this lad was her son or not, and so banish these wearing and worrying doubts. Ah yes, this was plainly the right way out of the difficulty; therefore she set her wits to work at once to contrive that test. But it was an easier thing to propose than to accomplish. She turned over in her mind one promising test after another, but was obliged to relinquish them all: none of them were absolutely sure, absolutely perfect; and an imperfect one could not satisfy her. Evidently she was racking her head in vain; it seemed manifest that she must give the matter up. While this depressing thought was passing through her mind, her ear caught the regular breathing of the boy, and she knew he had fallen asleep. And while she listened, the measured breathing was broken by a soft, startled cry, such as one utters in a troubled dream. This chance occurrence furnished her instantly with a plan worth all her laboured tests combined. She at once set herself feverishly but noiselessly to work to relight her candle, muttering to herself, 'Had I but seen him *then*, I should have known! Since that day, when he was little, that the powder burst in his face, he hath never been startled of a sudden out of his dreams or out of his thinkings, but he hath cast his hand before his eyes, even as he did that day; and not as others would do it, with the palm inward, but always with the palm turned outward. I have seen it a hundred times, and it hath never varied nor even failed. Yes, I shall soon know now!'

By this time she had crept to the slumbering boy's side with the candle, shaded, in her hand. She bent heedfully and warily over him, scarcely breathing in her suppressed excitement, and suddenly flashed the light in his face and struck the floor by his ear with her knuckles. The sleeper's eyes sprung wide open, and he cast a startled stare about him, but he made no special movement with his hands.

The poor woman was smitten almost helpless with surprise and grief, but she contrived to hide her emotions and to soothe the boy to sleep again; then she crept apart and communed miserably with herself upon the disastrous result of her experiment. She tried to believe that her Tom's madness had banished this habitual gesture of his, but she could not do it. 'No,' she said. 'his *hands* are not mad; they could not unlearn so old a habit in so brief a time. Oh, this is a heavy day for me!'

Still, hope was as stubborn now as doubt had been before; she could not bring herself to accept the verdict of the test; she must try the thing again: the failure must have been only an accident; so she startled the boy out of his sleep a second and a third time, at intervals, with the same result which had marked the first test; then she dragged herself to bed and fell sorrowfully asleep, saying, 'But I cannot give him up. Oh, no, I cannot, I cannot; he *must* be my boy!'

The poor mother's interruptions having ceased and the prince's pains having gradually lost their power to disturb him, utter weariness at last sealed his eyes in a profound and restful sleep. Hour after hour slipped away, and still he slept like the dead. Thus four or five hours passed. Then his stupor began to lighten. Presently while half asleep and half awake, he murmured, 'Sir William!'

After a moment, 'Ho, Sir William Herbert! Hie thee hither, and list to the strangest dream that ever. Sir William! Dost hear? Man, I did think me changed to a pauper, and—— Ho there! Guards! Sir William! What! Is there no groom of the chamber in waiting? Alack, it shall go hard with——'

'What aileth thee?' asked a whisper near him. 'Who art thou calling?'

'Sir William Herbert. Who art thou?'

'I? Who should I be but thy sister Nan? Oh, Tom, I had forgot! Thou'rt mad yet; poor lad thou'rt mad yet; would I had never woke to know it again! But prithee master thy tongue, lest we be all beaten till we die!'

The startled prince sprang partly up, but a sharp reminder from his stiffened bruises brought him to himself, and he sunk back among his foul straw with a moan and the ejaculation, 'Alas, it was no dream then!'

In a moment all the heavy sorrow and misery which sleep had banished were upon him again, and he realized that he was no longer a petted prince in a palace with the adoring eyes of a nation upon him, but a pauper, an outcast, clothed in rags, prisoner in a den fit only for beasts, and consorting with beggars and thieves.

In the midst of his grief he began to be conscious of hilarious noises and shoutings, apparently but a block or two away. The next moment there were several sharp raps at the door; John Canty ceased from snoring and said, 'Who knocketh?' What wilt thou?'

A voice answered, 'Knowst thou who it was thou laid thy cudgel on?'

'No. Neither know I, nor care.'

'Belike thou'lt change thy note eftsoons. An' thou would save thy neck, nothing but flight may stead thee. The man is this moment delivering up the ghost. 'Tis the priest Father Andrew!'

'God-a-mercy!' exclaimed Canty. He roused his family and hoarsely commanded, 'Up with ye all and fly, or bide where ye are and perish!'

Scarcely five minutes later the Canty household were in the street and flying for their lives. John Canty held the prince by the wrist and hurried him along the dark way, giving him his caution in a low voice, 'Mind thy tongue, thou mad fool, and speak not our name. I will choose me a new name speedily to throw the law's dogs off the scent. Mind thy tongue, I tell thee!' He growled these words to the rest of the family: 'If it so chance that we be separated, let each make for London Bridge; whoso findeth himself as far as the last linen-draper's shop on the bridge, let him tarry there till the others be come; then will we flee into Southwark together.'

At this moment the party burst suddenly out of darkness into light, and not only into light, but into the midst of a multitude of singing, dancing, and shouting people massed together on the river frontage. There was a line of bonfires stretching as far as one could see, up and down the Thames; London Bridge was illuminated; Southwark Bridge likewise; the entire river was aglow with the flash and sheen of coloured lights; and constant explosions of fireworks filled the skies with an intricate commingling of shooting splendours and a thick rain of dazzling sparks that almost turned night into day; everywhere were crowds of revellers; all London seemed to be at large.

John Canty delivered himself of a furious curse and commanded a retreat, but it was too late. He and his tribe were swallowed up in that swarming hive of humanity and hopelessly separated from each other in an instant. We are not considering that the prince was one of his tribe; Canty still kept his grip upon him. The prince's heart was beating high with hopes of escape now. A burly waterman, considerably exalted with liquor, found himself rudely shoved by Canty in his efforts to plough through the crowd;

he laid his great hand on Canty's shoulder and said, 'Nay, whither so fast, friend? Dost canker thy soul with sordid business when all that be leal men and true make holiday?'

'Mine affairs are mine own; they concern thee not,' answered Canty roughly; 'take away thy hand and let me pass.'

'Sith that is thy humour, thou'lt *not* pass till thou'st drunk to the Prince of Wales, I tell thee that,' said the waterman, barring the way resolutely.

'Give me the cup, then, and make speed, make speed!'

Other revellers were interested by this time. They cried out, 'The loving cup, the loving cup! Make the sour knave drink the loving cup, else will we feed him to the fishes.'

So a huge loving cup was brought; the waterman, grasping it by one of its handles, and with his other hand bearing up the end of an imaginary napkin, presented it in due and ancient form to Canty, who had to grasp the opposite handle with one of his hands and take off the lid with the other, according to ancient custom.[1] This left the prince hand-free for a second of course. He wasted no time, but dived among the forest of legs about him and disappeared. In another moment he could not have been harder to find under that tossing sea of life if its billows had been the Atlantic's and he a lost sixpence.

He very soon realized this fact and straightway busied himself about his own affairs without further thought of John Canty. He quickly realized another thing too. To wit, that a spurious Prince of Wales was being feasted by the city in his stead. He easily concluded that the pauper lad, Tom Canty, had deliberately taken advantage of his stupendous opportunity and become a usurper.

Therefore there was but one course to pursue – find his way to the Guildhall, make himself known, and denounce the impostor. He also made up his mind that Tom should be allowed a reasonable time for spiritual preparation and then be hanged, drawn, and quartered according to the law and usage of the day in cases of high treason.

1 See Note 6 at end of volume.

11 At Guildhall

The royal barge, attended by its gorgeous fleet, took its stately way down the Thames through the wilderness of illuminated boats. The air was laden with music; the river banks were beruffled with joy flames; the distant city lay in a soft luminous glow from its countless invisible bonfires; above it rose many a slender spire into the sky, encrusted with sparkling lights, wherefore in their remoteness they seemed like jewelled lances thrust aloft; as the fleet swept along, it was greeted from the banks with a continuous hoarse roar of cheers and the ceaseless flash and boom of artillery.

To Tom Canty, half buried in his silken cushions, these sounds and this spectacle were a wonder unspeakably sublime and astonishing. To his little friends at his side, the princess Elizabeth and the lady Jane Grey, they were nothing.

Arrived at the Dowgate, the fleet was towed up the limpid Walbrook (whose channel has now been for two centuries buried out of sight under acres of buildings) to Bucklersbury, past houses and under bridges populous with merrymakers and brilliantly lighted, and at last came to a halt in a basin where now is Barge Yard, in the centre of the ancient city of London. Tom disembarked, and he and his gallant procession crossed Cheapside and made a short march through the Old Jewry and Basinghall street to the Guildhall.

Tom and his little ladies were received with due ceremony by the Lord Mayor and the Fathers of the city, in their gold chains and scarlet robes of state, and conducted to a rich canopy of estate at the head of the great hall, preceded by heralds making proclamation, and by the mace and the city sword. The lords and ladies who were to attend upon Tom and his two small friends took their places behind their chairs.

At a lower table the court grandees and other guests of noble degree were seated with the magnates of the city; the commoners took places at a multitude of tables on the main floor of the hall. From their lofty vantage ground the giants Gog and Magog, the ancient guardians of the city, contemplated the spectacle below them with eyes grown familiar to it in forgotten generations. There was a bugle blast and a proclamation, and a fat butler appeared in a high perch in the leftward wall, followed by his servitors bearing with impressive solemnity a royal Baron of Beef, smoking hot and ready for the knife.

After grace, Tom (being instructed) rose -- and the whole house with him – and drank from a portly golden loving cup with the princess Elizabeth; from her it passed to the lady Jane and then traversed the general assemblage. So the banquet began.

By midnight the revelry was at its height. Now came one of those picturesque spectacles so admired in that old day. A description of it is still extant in the quaint wording of a chronicler who witnessed it:

'Space being made, presently entered a baron and an earl apparelled after the Turkish fashion in long robes of bawdkin powdered with gold, hats on their heads of crimson velvet, with great rolls of gold, girded with two swords called scimitars hanging by great bawdricks of gold. Next came yet another baron and another earl, in two long gowns of yellow satin, traversed with white satin, and in every bend of white was a bend of crimson satin, after the fashion of Russia, with furred hats of grey on their heads, either of them having an hatchet in their hands and boots with pikes' (points a foot long), 'turned up. And after them came a knight, then the Lord High Admiral, and with him five nobles, in doublets of crimson velvet, voyded low on the back and before to the cannell-bone, laced on the breasts with chains of silver; and over that, short cloaks of crimson satin, and on their heads hats after the dancers' fashion, with pheasants' feathers in them. These were apparelled after the fashion of Prussia. The torchbearers, which were about an hundred, were apparelled in crimson satin and green, like Moors, their faces black. Next came in a *mommarye*. Then the minstrels, which were disguised, danced; and the lords and ladies did wildly dance also, that it was a pleasure to behold.'

And while Tom, in his high seat, was gazing upon this 'wild' dancing, lost in admiration of the dazzling commingling of kaleidoscopic colours which the whirling turmoil of gaudy figures below him presented, the ragged but real little Prince of Wales was proclaiming his rights and his wrongs, denouncing the impostor, and clamouring for admission at the gates of Guildhall! The crowd enjoyed this episode prodigiously and pressed forward and craned their necks to see the small rioter. Presently they began to taunt him and mock at him, purposely to goad him to a higher and still more entertaining fury. Tears of mortification sprung to his eyes, but he stood his ground and defied the mob right royally. Other taunts followed, added mockings stung him, and he exclaimed, 'I tell ye again, you pack of unmannerly curs, I am the Prince of Wales! And all forlorn and friendless as I be, with none to give me word of grace or help me in my need, yet will not I be driven from my ground, but will maintain it!'

'Though thou be prince or no prince, 'tis all one; thou be'st a gallant lad, and not friendless neither! Here stand I by thy side to prove it; and mind I tell thee thou mightst have a worser friend than Miles Hendon and yet not tire thy legs with seeking. Rest thy small jaw, my child; I talk the language of these base kennel-rats like to a very native.'

The speaker was a sort of Don Caesar de Bazan in dress, aspect, and bearing. He was tall, trim-built, muscular. His doublet and trunks were of rich material, but faded and threadbare, and their gold-lace adornments were sadly tarnished; his ruff was rumpled and damaged; the plume in his slouched hat was broken and had a bedraggled and disreputable look; at his side he wore a long rapier in a rusty iron sheath; his swaggering carriage marked him at once as a ruffler of the camp. The speech of this fantastic figure was received with an explosion of jeers and laughter. Some cried, ''Tis another prince in disguise!' ''Ware thy tongue, friend; belike he is dangerous!' 'Marry, he looketh it; mark his eye!' 'Pluck the lad from him; to the horse-pond wi' the cub!'

Instantly a hand was laid upon the prince, under the impulse of this happy thought; as instantly the stranger's long sword was out and the meddler went to the earth under a sounding thump with the flat of it. The next moment a score of voices shouted, 'Kill the dog! Kill him! Kill him!' And the mob closed in on the warrior, who backed himself against a wall and began to lay about him with his long weapon like a madman. His victims sprawled this way and that, but the mobtide poured over their prostrate forms and dashed itself against the champion with undiminished fury. His moments seemed numbered, his destruction certain, when suddenly a trumpet blast sounded, a voice shouted, 'Way for the king's messenger!' and a troop of horsemen came charging down upon the mob, who fled out of harm's reach as fast as their legs could carry them. The bold stranger caught up the prince in his arms and was soon far away from danger and the multitude.

Return we within the Guildhall. Suddenly, high above the jubilant roar and thunder of the revel, broke the clear peal of a bugle note. There was instant silence, a deep hush; then a single voice rose – that of the messenger from the palace – and began to pipe forth a proclamation, the whole multitude standing, listening.

The closing words, solemnly pronounced, were, 'The king is dead!'

The great assemblage bent their heads upon their breasts with one accord, remained so in profound silence a few moments; then all sunk upon their knees in a body, stretched out their hands toward Tom; and a mighty shout burst forth that seemed to shake the building, 'Long live the king!'

Poor Tom's dazed eyes wandered abroad over this stupefying spectacle and finally rested dreamily upon the kneeling princesses beside him a moment, then upon the Earl of Hertford. A sudden purpose dawned in his face. He said in a low tone at Lord Hertford's ear, 'Answer me truly, on thy faith and honour! Uttered I here a command, the which none but a king might hold privilege and prerogative to utter, would such commandment be obeyed, and none rise up to say me nay?'

'None, my liege, in all these realms. In thy person bides the majesty of. England. Thou art the king; thy word is law.'

Tom responded in a strong, earnest voice, and with great animation, 'Then shall the king's law be law of mercy from this day, and never more be law of blood! Up from thy knees and away! To the Tower and say the king decrees the Duke of Norfolk shall not die!'[1]

The words were caught up and carried eagerly from lip to lip far and wide over the hall, and as Hertford hurried from the presence, another prodigious shout burst forth, 'The reign of blood is ended! Long live Edward, King of England!'

1 See Note 7 at end of volume.

12 The Prince and His Deliverer

As soon as Miles Hendon and the little prince were clear of the mob, they struck down through back lanes and alleys toward the river. Their way was unobstructed until they approached London Bridge; then they ploughed into the multitude again, Hendon keeping a fast grip upon the prince's – no, the king's – wrist. The tremendous news was already abroad, and the boy learned it from a thousand voices at once – 'The king is dead!' The tidings struck a chill to the heart of the poor little waif and sent a shudder through his frame. He realized the greatness of his loss and was filled with a bitter grief, for the grim tyrant who had been such a terror to others had always been gentle with him. The tears sprung to his eyes and blurred all objects. For an instant he felt himself the most forlorn, outcast, and forsaken of God's creatures; then another cry shook the night with its far-reaching thunder, 'Long live King Edward the Sixth!' And this made his eyes kindle and thrilled him with pride to his finger's ends. 'Ah,' he thought, 'how grand and strange it seems – I AM KING!'

Our friends threaded their way slowly through the throngs upon the bridge. This structure, which had stood for six hundred years and had been a noisy and populous thoroughfare all that time, was a curious affair, for a closely packed rank of stores and shops, with family quarters overhead, stretched along both sides of it, from one bank of the river to the other. The bridge was a sort of town to itself; it had its inns, its beer houses, its bakeries, its haberdasheries, its food markets, its manufacturing industries, and even its church. It looked upon the two neighbours which it linked together – London and Southwark – as being well enough as suburbs, but not otherwise particularly important. It was a close corporation, so to speak; it was a narrow town, of a single street a fifth of a mile long; its population was but a village population, and everybody in it knew all his fellow townsmen intimately and had known their fathers and mothers before them – and all their little family affairs into the bargain. It had its aristocracy, of course – its fine old families of butchers, and bakers, and what-not, who had occupied the same old premises for five or six hundred years and knew the great history of the bridge from beginning to end, and all its strange legends, and who always talked bridgy talk, and thought bridgy thoughts, and lied in a long, level, direct, substantial bridgy way. It was just the sort of population to be narrow and ignorant and self-conceited. Children were born on the bridge, were reared there, grew to old age and finally died without ever having set a foot upon any part of the world but London Bridge alone. Such people would naturally imagine that the mighty and interminable procession which moved through its street night and day, with its confused roar of shouts and cries, its neighings and bellowings and bleatings and its muffled thunder-tramp, was the one great thing in this world, and themselves somehow the proprietors of it. And so they were in effect; at least they could exhibit it from their windows, and did – for a consideration – whenever a returning king or hero gave it a fleeting splendour, for there was no place like it for affording a long, straight, uninterrupted view of marching columns.

Men born and reared upon the bridge found life unendurably dull and inane elsewhere. History tells of one of these who left the bridge at the age of seventy-one and retired to the country. But he could only fret and toss in his bed; he could not go to sleep, the deep stillness was so painful, so awful, so oppressive. When he was worn out with it at last, he fled back to his old home, a lean and haggard spectre, and fell peacefully to rest and pleasant dreams under the lulling music of the lashing waters and the boom and crash and thunder of London Bridge.

In the times of which we are writing, the bridge furnished 'object lessons' in English history for its children, namely, the livid and decaying heads of renowned men impaled upon iron spikes atop of its gateways. But we digress.

Hendon's lodgings were in the little inn on the bridge. As he neared the door with his small friend, a rough voice said, 'So, thou'rt come at last! Thou'lt not escape again, I warrant thee; and if pounding thy bones to a pudding can teach thee somewhat, thou'lt not keep us waiting another time, mayhap.' And John Canty put out his hand to seize the boy.

Miles Hendon stepped in the way and said, 'Not too fast, friend. Thou art needlessly rough, methinks. What is the lad to thee?'

'If it be any business of thine to make and meddle in others' affairs, he is my son.'

''Tis a lie!' cried the little king hotly.

'Boldly said, and I believe thee, whether thy small headpiece be sound or cracked, my boy. But whether this scurvy ruffian be thy father or no, 'tis all one; he shall not have thee to beat thee and abuse, according to his threat, so thou prefer to bide with me.'

'I do, I do – I know him not, I loathe him, and will die before I will go with him.'

'Then 'tis settled, and there is nought more to say.'

'We will see as to that!' exclaimed John Canty, striding past Hendon to get at the boy. 'By force shall he——'

'If thou do but touch him, thou animated offal, I will spit thee like a goose!' said Hendon, barring the way and laying his hand upon his sword hilt. Canty drew back. 'Now mark ye,' continued Hendon, 'I took this lad under my protection when a mob of such as thou would have mishandled him, mayhap killed him; dost imagine I will desert him now to a worser fate? For whether thou art his father or no – and sooth to say, I think it is a lie – a decent swift death were better for such a lad than life in such brute hands as thine. So go thy ways, and set quick about it, for I like not much bandying of words, being not overpatient in my nature.'

John Canty moved off, muttering threats and curses, and was swallowed from sight in the crowd. Hendon ascended three flights of stairs to his room, with his charge, after ordering a meal to be sent thither. It was a poor apartment, with a shabby bed and some odds and ends of old furniture in it, and was vaguely lighted by a couple of sickly candles. The little king dragged himself to the bed and lay down upon it, almost exhausted with hunger and fatigue. He had been on his feet a good part of a day and a night, for it was now two or three o'clock in the morning, and had eaten nothing meantime. He murmured drowsily, 'Prithee call me when the table is spread,' and sunk into a deep sleep immediately.

A smile twinkled in Hendon's eye, and he said to himself, 'By the mass, the little beggar takes to one's quarters and usurps one's bed with as natural and easy a grace as if he owned them – with never a by-your-leave or so-please-it-you, or anything of the sort. In his diseased ravings he called himself the Prince of Wales, and bravely doth he keep up the character. Poor little friendless rat, doubtless his mind has been disordered with ill usage. Well, I will be his friend; I have saved him, and it draweth me strongly to him; already I love the bold-tongued little rascal. How soldier-like he faced the smutty rabble and flung back his high defiance! And what a comely, sweet and gentle face he hath, now that sleep hath conjured away its troubles and its griefs. I will teach him, I will cure his malady; yea, I will be his elder brother, and care for him and watch over him; and whoso would shame him or do him hurt may order his shroud, for though I be burnt for it he shall need it!'

He bent over the boy and contemplated him with kind and pitying interest, tapping the young cheek tenderly and smoothing back the tangled curls with his great brown hand. A slight shiver passed over the boy's form. Hendon muttered, 'See, now, how like a man it was to let him lie here uncovered and fill his body with deadly rheums. Now what shall I do? 'Twill wake him to take him up and put him within the bed, and he sorely needeth sleep.'

He looked about for extra covering, but finding none, doffed his doublet and wrapped the lad in it, saying, 'I am used to nipping air and scant apparel; 'tis little I shall mind the cold'; then walked up and down the room to keep his blood in motion, soliloquizing as before. 'His injured mind persuades him he is Prince of Wales; 'twill be odd to have a Prince of Wales with us, now that he that *was* the prince is prince no more, but king – for this poor mind is set upon the one fantasy and will not reason out that now it should cast by the prince and call itself the king. If my father liveth still, after these seven years that I have heard nought from home in my foreign dungeon, he will welcome the poor lad and give him generous shelter for my sake; so will my good elder brother, Arthur; my other brother, Hugh – but I will crack his crown, an' *he* interfere, the fox-hearted, ill-conditioned animal! Yes, thither will we fare – and straightway too.'

A servant entered with a smoking meal, disposed it upon a small deal table, placed the chairs, and took his departure, leaving such cheap lodgers as these to wait upon themselves. The door slammed after him, and the noise woke the boy, who sprung to a sitting posture and shot a glad glance about him; then a grieved look came into his face and he murmured to himself with a deep sigh, 'Alack, it was but a dream, woe is me.' Next he noticed Miles Hendon's doublet – glanced from that to Hendon, comprehended the sacrifice that had been made for him, and said gently, 'Thou art good to me; yes, thou art very good to me. Take it and put it on; I shall not need it more.'

Then he got up and walked to the washstand in the corner, and stood there, waiting. Hendon said in a cheery voice, 'We'll have a right hearty sup and bite now, for everything is savoury and smoking hot, and that and thy nap together will make thee a little man again, never fear!'

The boy made no answer, but bent a steady look that was filled with grave surprise and also somewhat touched with impatience upon the tall knight of the sword. Hendon was puzzled and said, 'What's amiss?'

'Good sir, I would wash me.'

'Oh, is that all! Ask no permission of Miles Hendon for aught thou cravest. Make thyself perfectly free here, and welcome, with all that are his belongings.'

Still the boy stood, and moved not; more, he tapped the floor once or twice with his small impatient foot. Hendon was wholly perplexed. Said he, 'Bless us, what is it?'

'Prithee pour the water, and make not so many words!'

Hendon, suppressing a horse-laugh and saying to himself, 'By all the saints, but this is admirable!' stepped briskly forward and did the small insolent's bidding; then stood by in a sort of stupefaction until the command, 'Come, the towel!' woke him sharply up. He took up a towel from under the boy's nose and handed it to him without comment. He now proceeded to comfort his own face with a wash, and while he was at it his adopted child seated himself at the table and prepared to fall to. Hendon dispatched his ablutions with alacrity, then drew back the other chair and was about to place himself at table when the boy said indignantly, 'Forbear! Wouldst sit in the presence of the king?'

This blow staggered Hendon to his foundations. He muttered to himself, 'Lo, the poor thing's madness is up with the time! It hath changed with the great change that is come to the realm, and now in fancy is he *king*! Good lack, I must humour the conceit too – there is no other way – faith, he would order me to the Tower, else!'

And pleased with this jest, he removed the chair from the table, took his stand behind the king, and proceeded to wait upon him in the courtliest way he was capable of.

While the king ate, the rigour of his royal dignity relaxed a little, and with his growing contentment came a desire to talk. He said, 'I think thou callest thyself Miles Hendon, if I heard thee aright?'

'Yes, sire,' Miles replied; then observed, 'If I *must* humour the poor lad's madness, I must sire him, I must majesty him, I must not go by halves, I must stick at nothing that belongeth to the part I play, else shall I play it ill and work evil to this charitable and kindly cause.'

The king warmed his heart with a second glass of wine and said, 'I would know thee – tell me thy story. Thou hast a gallant way with thee, and a noble – art nobly born?'

'We are of the tail of the nobility, good your Majesty. My father is a baronet – one of the smaller lords, by knight service[1] – Sir Richard Hendon, of Hendon Hall, by Monk's Holm, in Kent.'

'Thy name has escaped my memory. Go on – tell me thy story.'

''Tis not much, your Majesty, yet perchance it may beguile a short half hour for want of a better. My father, Sir Richard, is very rich and of a most generous nature. My mother died whilst I was yet a boy. I have two brothers: Arthur, my elder, with a soul like to his father's; and Hugh, younger than I, a mean spirit, covetous, treacherous, vicious, underhanded – a reptile. Such was he from the cradle; such was he ten years past, when I last saw him – a ripe rascal at nineteen, I being twenty then and Arthur twenty-two. There is none other of us but the lady Edith, my cousin – she was sixteen then – beautiful, gentle, good, the daughter of an earl, the last of her race, heiress of a great fortune and a lapsed title. My father was her guardian. I loved her and she loved me, but she was betrothed to Arthur from the cradle, and Sir Richard would not suffer the contract to be broken. Arthur loved another maid and bade us be of good cheer and hold fast to the hope that delay and luck together would some day give success to our several causes. Hugh loved the lady Edith's fortune, though in truth he said it was herself he loved; but then 'twas his way, always, to say the one thing and mean the other. But he lost his arts upon the girl; he could deceive my father, but none else. My father loved him best of us all and trusted and believed him, for he was the

'*And pleased with this jest ... Hendon took his stand behind the King*'

youngest child and others hated him – these qualities being in all ages sufficient to win a parent's dearest love; and he had a smooth persuasive tongue, with an admirable gift of lying – and these be qualities which do mightily assist a blind affection to cozen itself. I was wild – in troth I might go yet farther and say *very* wild, though 'twas a wildness of an innocent sort, since it hurt none but me, brought shame to none, nor loss, nor had in it any taint of crime or baseness or what might not beseem mine honourable degree.

'Yet did my brother Hugh turn these faults to good account, he seeing that our brother Arthur's health was but indifferent, and hoping the worst might work him profit were I swept out of the path – But 'twere a long tale, good my liege, and little worth the telling. Briefly, then, this brother did deftly magnify my faults and make them crimes, ending his base work with finding a silken ladder in mine apartments – conveyed thither by his own means – and did convince my father by this and suborned evidence of servants and other lying knaves that I was minded to carry off my Edith and marry her in rank defiance of his will.

'Three years of banishment from home and England might make a soldier and a man of me, my father said, and teach me some degree of wisdom. I fought out my long probation in the continental wars, tasting sumptuously of hard knocks, privation, and adventure; but in my last battle I was taken captive, and during the seven years that have waxed and waned since then, a foreign dungeon hath harboured me. Through wit and courage I won to the free air at last and fled hither straight, and am but just arrived, right poor in purse and raiment, and poorer still in knowledge of what these dull seven years have wrought at Hendon Hall, its people and belongings. So please you, sir, my meagre tale is told.'

'Thou hast been shamefully abused!' said the little king with a flashing eye. 'But I will right thee – by the cross will I! The king hath said it.'

Then, fired by the story of Miles' wrongs, he loosed his tongue and poured the history of his own recent misfortunes into the ears of the astonished listener.

When he had finished, Miles said to himself, 'Lo, what an imagination he hath! Verily this is no common mind, else, crazed or sane, it could not weave so straight and gaudy a tale as this out of the airy nothings wherewith it hath wrought this curious romaunt. Poor ruined little head, it shall not lack friend or shelter whilst I bide with the living. He shall never leave my side; he shall be my pet, my little comrade. And he shall be cured! Aye, made whole and sound; then he will make himself a name; and proud shall I be to say, 'Yes, he is mine – I took him, a homeless little ragamuffin, but I saw what was in him, and I said his name would be heard some day – behold him, observe him – was I right?''

The king spoke in a thoughtful, measured voice, 'Thou didst save me injury and shame, perchance my life, and so my crown. Such service demandeth rich reward. Name thy desire, and so it be within the compass of my royal power, it is thine.'

This fantastic suggestion startled Hendon out of his reverie. He was about to thank the king and put the matter aside with saying he had only done his duty and desired no reward, but a wiser thought came into his head, and he asked leave to be silent a few moments and consider the gracious offer – an idea which the king gravely approved, remarking that it was best to be not too hasty with a thing of such great import.

Miles reflected during some moments, then said to himself, 'Yes, that is the thing to do; by any other means it were impossible to get at it, and certes, this hour's experience has taught me 'twould be most wearing and inconvenient to continue as it is. Yes, I will propose it; 'twas a happy accident that I did not throw the chance away.' Then he dropped upon one knee and said, 'My poor service went not beyond the limit of a subject's simple duty and therefore hath no merit, but since your Majesty is pleased to hold it worthy some reward, I take heart of grace to make petition to this effect. Near four hundred years ago, as your Grace knoweth, there being ill blood betwixt John, king of England, and the king of France, it was decreed that two champions should fight together in the lists and so settle the dispute by what is called the arbitrament of God. These two kings, and the Spanish king, being assembled to witness and judge the conflict, the French champion appeared; but so redoubtable was he that our English knights refused to measure weapons with him. So the matter, which was a weighty one, was like to go against the English monarch by default. Now in the Tower lay the lord De Courcy, the mightiest arm in England, stripped of his honours and possessions, and wasting with long captivity. Appeal was made to him; he gave assent and came forth arrayed for battle; but no sooner did the Frenchman glimpse his huge frame and hear his famous name but he fled away, and the French king's cause was lost. King John restored De Courcy's titles and possessions and said, 'Name thy wish and thou shalt have it, though it cost me half my kingdom'; whereat De Courcy, kneeling, as I do now, made answer, 'This, then, I ask, my liege; that I and my successors may have and hold the privilege of remaining covered in the presence of the kings of England, henceforth while the throne shall last.' The boon was granted, as your Majesty knoweth; and there hath been no time these four hundred years that that line has failed of an heir; and so, even unto this day, the head of that ancient house still weareth his hat or helm before the king's majesty, without let or hindrance, and this none other may do.[2] Invoking this precedent in aid of my prayer, I beseech the king to grant me but this one grace and privilege – to my more than sufficient reward – and none other, to wit: that I and my heirs forever may *sit* in the presence of the Majesty of England!'

'Rise, Sir Miles Hendon, knight,' said the king gravely, giving the accolade with Hendon's sword; 'rise, and seat thyself. Thy petition is granted. Whilst England remains, and the crown continues, the privilege shall not lapse.'

His Majesty walked apart, musing, and Hendon dropped into a chair at table, observing to himself, ''Twas a brave thought and hath wrought me a mighty deliverance; my legs are grievously wearied. An' I had not thought of that, I must have had to stand for weeks, till my poor lad's wits are cured.' After a little, he went on, 'And so I am become a knight of the Kingdom of Dreams and Shadows! A most odd and strange position truly for one so matter-of-fact as I. I will not laugh – no, God forbid, for this thing which is so substanceless to me is *real* to him. And to me also, in one way, it is not a falsity, for it reflects with truth the sweet and generous spirit that is in him.' After a pause: 'Ah, what if he should call me by my fine title before folk! There'd be a merry contrast betwixt my glory and my raiment! But no matter; let him call me what he will, so it please him, I shall be content.'

1 He refers to the order of baronets or baronettes – the *barones minores*, as distinct from the parliamentary barons – not, it need hardly be said, the baronets of later creation.

2 The lords of Kingsale, descendants of De Courcy, still enjoy this curious privilege.

13 The Disappearance of the Prince

A heavy drowsiness presently fell upon the two comrades. The king said, 'Remove these rags,' meaning his clothing.

Hendon disapparelled the boy without dissent or remark, tucked him up in bed, then glanced about the room, saying to himself ruefully, 'He hath taken my bed again, as before; marry, what shall *I* do?'

The little king observed his perplexity and dissipated it with a word. He said sleepily, 'Thou wilt sleep athwart the door and guard it.' In a moment more he was out of his troubles, in a deep slumber.

'Dear heart, he should have been born a king!' muttered Hendon admiringly. 'He playeth the part to a marvel.'

Then he stretched himself across the door, on the floor, saying contentedly, 'I have lodged worse for seven years; 'twould be but ill gratitude to Him above to find fault with this.'

He dropped asleep as the dawn appeared. Toward noon he rose, uncovered his unconscious ward – a section at a time – and took his measure with a string. The king awoke just as he had completed his work, complained of the cold, and asked what he was doing.

''Tis done now, my liege,' said Hendon; 'I have a bit of business outside, but will presently return; sleep thou again – thou needest it. There – let me cover thy head also – thou'lt be warm the sooner.'

The king was back in dreamland before this speech was ended. Miles slipped softly out and slipped as softly in again in the course of thirty or forty minutes, with a complete second-hand suit of boy's clothing, of cheap material and showing signs of wear, but tidy and suited to the season of the year. He seated himself and began to overhaul his purchase, mumbling to himself, 'A longer purse would have got a better sort, but when one has not the long purse one must be content with what a short one may do:

> There was a woman in our town
> In our town did dwell——

He stirred, methinks. I must sing in a less thunderous key; 'tis not good to mar his sleep, with this journey before him and he so wearied out, poor chap. This garment – 'tis well enough – a stitch here and another there will set it aright. This other is better, albeit a stitch or two will not come amiss in it likewise. *These* be very good and sound, and will keep his small feet warm and dry – an odd new thing to him, belike, since he has doubtless been used to foot it bare, winters and summers the same. Would thread were bread, seeing one getteth a year's sufficiently for a farthing, and such a brave big needle without cost, for mere love. Now shall I have the demon's own time to thread it!'

And so he had. He did as men have always done, and probably always will do, to the end of time – held the needle still and tried to thrust the thread through the eye, which is the opposite of a woman's way. Time and time again the thread missed the mark, going sometimes on one side of the needle, sometimes on the other, sometimes doubling up against the shaft; but he was patient, having been through these experiences before when he was soldiering. He succeeded at last and took up the garment that had lain waiting meantime across his lap and began his work.

'The inn is paid – the breakfast that is to come, included – and there is wherewithal left to buy a couple of donkeys and meet our little costs for the two or three days betwixt this and the plenty that awaits us at Hendon Hall:

> She loved her hus——

Body o' me! I have driven the needle under my nail! It matters little – 'tis not a novelty – yet 'tis not a convenience neither. We shall be merry there, little one, never doubt it! Thy troubles will vanish, there, and likewise thy sad distemper:

> She loved her husband dearilee,
> But another man——

These be noble large stitches!' – holding the garment up and viewing it admiringly. 'They have a grandeur and a majesty that do cause these small stingy ones of the tailorman to look mightily paltry and plebeian:

> She loved her husband dearilee,
> But another man he loved she——

Marry, 'tis done – a goodly piece of work, too, and wrought with expedition. Now will I wake him, apparel him, pour for him, feed him, and then will we hie us to the mart by the Tabard Inn in Southwark and – be pleased to rise, my liege! – he answereth not – what ho, my liege! – of a truth must I profane his sacred person with a touch, sith his slumber is deaf to speech. What!'

He threw back the covers; the boy was gone!

He stared about him in speechless astonishment for a moment, noticed for the first time that his ward's ragged raiment was also missing; then he began to rage and storm and shout for the innkeeper. At that moment a servant entered with the breakfast.

'Explain, thou limb of Satan, or thy time is come!' roared the man of war, and made so savage a spring toward the waiter that this latter could not find his tongue for the instant, for fright and surprise. 'Where is the boy?'

In disjointed and trembling syllables the man gave the information desired.

'You were hardly gone from the place, your worship, when a youth came running and said it was your worship's will that the boy come to you straight, at the bridge end of the Southwark side. I brought him hither, and when he woke the lad and gave his message, the lad did grumble some little for being disturbed 'so early,' as he called it, but straightway trussed on his rags and went with the youth, only saying it had been better manners that your worship came yourself, not sent a stranger; and so——'

'And so thou'rt a fool: a fool, and easily cozened; hang all thy breed! Yet mayhap no hurt is done. Possibly no harm is meant the boy. I will go fetch him. Make the table ready. Stay! The coverings of the bed were disposed as if one lay beneath them; happened that by accident?'

'I know not, good your worship. I saw the youth meddle with them – he that came for the boy.'

'Thousand deaths! 'Twas done to deceive me – 'tis plain 'twas done to gain time. Hark ye! Was that youth alone?'

'All alone, your worship.'

'Art sure?'

'Sure, your worship.'

'Collect thy scattered wits – bethink thee – take time, man.'

After a moment's thought the servant said, 'When he came, none came with him; but now I remember me that as the two stepped into the throng of the bridge, a ruffian-looking man plunged out from some near place; and just as he was joining them——'

'What *then*? Out with it!' thundered the impatient Hendon, interrupting.

''Just then the crowd lapped them up and closed them in, and I saw no more, being called by my master, who was in a rage because a joint that the scrivener had ordered was forgot, though I take all the saints to witness that to blame *me* for that miscarriage were like holding the unborn babe to judgment for sins com——'

'Out of my sight, idiot! Thy prating drives me mad! Hold! Whither art flying? Canst not bide still an instant? Went they toward Southwark?'

'Even so, your worship; for, as I said before, as to the detestable joint, the babe unborn is no whit more blameless than——'

'Art here *yet*! And prating still? Vanish, lest I throttle thee!' The servitor vanished. Hendon followed after him, passed him, and plunged down the stairs two steps at a stride, muttering, ''Tis that scurvy villain that claimed he was his son. I have lost thee, my poor little mad master – it is a bitter thought – and I had come to love thee so! No! By book and bell, *not* lost! Not lost, for I will ransack the land till I find thee again. Poor child, yonder is his breakfast and mine, but I have no hunger now; so let the rats have it. Speed, speed! That is the word!' As he wormed his swift way through the noisy multitudes upon the bridge, he several times said to himself, clinging to the thought, as if it were a particularly pleasing one, 'He grumbled, but he *went* – he went, yes, because he thought Miles Hendon asked it, sweet lad – he would ne'er have done it for another, I know it well.'

14 'Le Roi Est Mort – Vive le Roi'

Toward daylight of the same morning, Tom Canty stirred out of a heavy sleep and opened his eyes in the dark. He lay silent a few moments, trying to analyse his confused thoughts and impressions and get some sort of meaning out of them; then suddenly he burst out in a rapturous but guarded voice, 'I see it all, I see it all! Now God be thanked, I am indeed awake at last! Come, joy! Vanish, sorrow! Ho, Nan! Bet! Kick off your straw and hie ye hither to my side, till I do pour into your unbelieving ears the wildest madcap dream that ever the spirits of night did conjure up to astonish the soul of man withal! Ho, Nan, I say! Bet!'

A dim form appeared at his side, and a voice said, 'Wilt deign to deliver thy commands?'

'Commands? Oh, woe is me, I know thy voice! Speak, thou – who am I?'

'Thou? In sooth, yesternight wert thou the prince of Wales; today art thou my most gracious liege, Edward, king of England.'

Tom buried his head among his pillows, murmuring plaintively, 'Alack, it was no dream! Go to thy rest, sweet sir; leave me to my sorrows.'

Tom slept again, and after a time he had this pleasant dream. He thought it was summer and he was playing all alone in the fair meadow called Goodman's Fields, when a dwarf only a foot high, with long red whiskers and a humped back, appeared to him suddenly and said, 'Dig, by that stump.' He did so and found twelve bright new pennies – wonderful riches! Yet this was not the best of it, for the dwarf said, 'I know thee. Thou art a good lad and a deserving; thy distresses shall end, for the day of thy reward is come. Dig here every seventh day, and thou shalt find always the same treasure, twelve bright new pennies. Tell none – keep the secret.' Then the dwarf vanished, and Tom flew to Offal Court with his prize, saying to himself, 'Every night will I give my father a penny; he will think I begged it, it will glad his heart, and I shall no more be beaten. One penny every week the good priest that teacheth me shall have; Mother, Nan, and Bet the other four. We be done with hunger and rags now, done with fears and frets and savage usage.'

In his dream he reached his sordid home all out of breath, but with eyes dancing with grateful enthusiasm, cast four of his pennies into his mother's lap, and cried out, 'They are for thee! All of them, every one! For thee and

Nan and Bet – and honestly come by, not begged nor stolen!'

The happy and astonished mother strained him to her breast and exclaimed, 'It waxeth late; may it please your Majesty to rise?'

Ah, that was not the answer he was expecting. The dream had snapped asunder – he was awake.

He opened his eyes; the richly clad First Lord of the Bedchamber was kneeling by his couch. The gladness of the lying dream faded away; the poor boy recognized that he was still a captive and a king. The room was filled with courtiers clothed in purple mantles – the mourning colour – and with noble servants of the monarch. Tom sat up in bed and gazed out from the heavy silken curtains upon this fine comapny.

The weighty business of dressing began, and one courtier after another knelt and paid his court and offered to the little king his condolences upon his heavy loss whilst the dressing proceeded. In the beginning, a shirt was taken up by the Chief Equerry-in-Waiting, who passed it to the First Lord of the Buckhounds, who passed it to the Second Gentleman of the Bedchamber, who passed it to the Head Ranger of Windsor Forest, who passed it to the Third Groom of the Stole, who passed it to the Chancellor Royal of the Duchy of Lancaster, who passed it to Norroy King-at-Arms, who passed it to the Constable of the Tower, who passed it to the Hereditary Grand Diaperer, who passed it to the Lord High Admiral of England, who passed it to the Archbishop of Canterbury, who passed it to the First Lord of the Bedchamber, who took what was left of it and put it on Tom. Poor little wandering chap, it reminded him of passing buckets at a fire.

Each garment in its turn had to go through this slow and solemn process; consequently Tom grew very weary of the ceremony, so weary that he felt an almost gushing gratefulness when he at last saw his long silken hose begin the journey down the line and knew that the end of the matter was drawing near. But he exulted too soon. The First Lord of the Bedchamber received the hose and was about to encase Tom's legs in them when a sudden flush invaded his face and he hurriedly hustled the things back into the hands of the Archbishop of Canterbury with an astounded look and a whispered, 'See, my lord!' – pointing to a something connected with the hose. The Archbishop paled, then flushed, and passed the hose to the Lord High Admiral, whispering, 'See, my lord!' The admiral passed the hose to the Hereditary Grand Diaperer and had hardly breath enough in his body to ejaculate, 'See, my lord!' The hose drifted backward along the line, to the Chief Steward of the Household, the Constable of the Tower, Norroy King-at-Arms, the Master of the Wardrobe, the Chancellor Royal of the Duchy of Lancaster, the Third Groom of the Stole, the Head Ranger of Windsor Forest, the Second Gentleman of the Bedchamber, the First Lord of the Buckhounds, accompanied always with that amazed and frightened 'See! see!' – till they finally reached the hands of the Chief Equerry-in-Waiting, who gazed a moment, then hoarsely whispered, 'Body of my life, a tag gone from a trusspoint! To the Tower with the Head Keeper of the King's Hose!' – after which he leaned upon the shoulder of the First Lord of the Buckhounds to regather his vanished strength whilst fresh hose, without any damaged strings to them, were brought.

But all things must have an end, and so in time Tom Canty was in a condition to get out of the bed. The proper official poured water, the proper official engineered the washing, the proper official stood by with a towel, and by and by Tom got safely through the purifying stage and was ready for the services of the Hairdresser Royal. When he at length emerged from this master's hands, he was a gracious figure and as pretty as a girl in his mantle and trunks of purple satin and purple-plumed cap. He now moved in state toward his breakfast room through the midst of the courtly assemblage; and as he passed, these fell back, leaving his way free, and dropped upon their knees.

After breakfast he was conducted, with regal ceremony, attended by his great officers and his guard of fifty Gentlemen Pensioners bearing gilt battle axes, to the throne room, where he proceeded to transact business of state. His 'uncle' Lord Hertford, took his stand by the throne to assist the royal mind with wise counsel.

The body of illustrious men named by the late king as his executors appeared to ask Tom's approval of certain acts of theirs – rather a form, and yet not wholly a form, since there was no Protector as yet. The Archbishop of Canterbury made report of the decree of the Council of Executors concerning the obsequies of his late most illustrious Majesty and finished by reading the signatures of the executors, to wit: the Archbishop of Canterbury, the Lord Chancellor of England, William Lord St John, John Lord Russell, Edward Earl of Hertford, John Viscount Lisle, Cuthbert Bishop of Durham——

Tom was not listening; an earlier clause of the document was puzzling him. At this point he turned and whispered to Lord Hertford, 'What day did he say the burial hath been appointed for?'

'The sixteenth of the coming month, my liege.'

''Tis a strange folly. Will he keep?'

Poor chap, he was still new to the customs of royalty; he was used to seeing the forlorn dead of Offal Court hustled out of the way with a very different sort of expedition. However, the lord Hertford set his mind at rest with a word or two.

A secretary of state presented an order of the council appointing the morrow at eleven for the reception of the foreign ambassadors, and desired the king's assent.

Tom turned an inquiring look toward Hertford, who whispered, 'Your

Majesty will signify consent. They come to testify their royal masters' sense of the heavy calamity which hath visited your Grace and the realm of England.'

Tom did as he was bidden. Another secretary began to read a preamble concerning the expenses of the late king's household, which had amounted to £28,000 during the preceding six months – a sum so vast that it made Tom Canty gasp; he gasped again when the fact appeared that £20,000 of this money were still owing and unpaid[1], and once more when it appeared that the king's coffers were about empty and his twelve hundred servants much embarrassed for lack of the wages due them. Tom spoke out with lively apprehension, 'We be going to the dogs, 'tis plain. 'tis meet and necessary that we take a smaller house and set the servants at large, sith they be of no value but to make delay, and trouble one with offices that harass the spirit and shame the soul, they misbecoming any but a doll, that hath nor brains nor hands to help itself withal. I remember me of a small house that standeth over against the fish market, by Billingsgate——'

A sharp pressure upon Tom's arm stopped his foolish tongue and sent a blush to his face; but no countenance there betrayed any sign that this strange speech had been remarked or given concern.

A secretary made report that forasmuch as the late king had provided in his will for conferring the ducal degree upon the Earl of Hertford and raising his brother, Sir Thomas Seymour, to the peerage, and likewise Hertford's son to an earldom, together with similar aggrandizements to other great servants of the Crown, the council had resolved to hold a sitting on the sixteenth of February for the delivering and confirming of these honours; and that meantime, the late king not having granted in writing estates suitable to the support of these dignities, the council, knowing his private wishes in that regard, had thought proper to grant to Seymour '£500 lands,' and to Hertford's son '800 pound lands and 300 pound of the next bishop's lands which should fall vacant,'[1] his present Majesty being willing.

Tom was about to blurt out something about the propriety of paying the late king's debts first before squandering all this money, but a timely touch upon his arm from the thoughtful Hertford saved him this indiscretion, wherefore he gave the royal assent, without spoken comment but with much inward discomfort. While he sat reflecting a moment over the ease with which he was doing strange and glittering miracles, a happy thought shot into his mind: why not make his mother Duchess of Offal Court and give her an estate? But a sorrowful thought swept it instantly away: he was only a king in name, these grave veterans and great nobles were his masters; to them his mother was only the creature of a diseased mind; they would simply listen to his project with unbelieving ears, then send for the doctor.

The dull work went tediously on. Petitions were read, and proclamations, patents, and all manner of wordy, repetitious, and wearisome papers relating to the public business; and at last Tom sighed pathetically and murmured to himself, 'In what have I offended, that the good God should take me away from the fields and the free air and the sunshine to shut me up here and make me a king and afflict me so?' Then his poor muddled head nodded awhile and presently drooped to his shoulder, and the business of the empire came to a standstill for want of that august factor the ratifying power. Silence ensued around the slumbering child, and the sages of the realm ceased from their deliberations.

During the forenoon Tom had an enjoyable hour, by permission of his keepers, Hertford and St John, with the lady Elizabeth and the little lady Jane Grey, though the spirits of the princesses were rather subdued by the mighty stroke that had fallen upon the royal house; and at the end of the visit his 'elder sister' – afterwards the 'Bloody Mary' of history – chilled him with a solemn interview which had but one merit in his eyes, its brevity. He had a few moments to himself, and then a slim lad of about twelve years of age was admitted to his presence, whose clothing, except his snowy ruff and the laces about his wrists, was of black – doublet, hose and all. He bore no badge of mourning but a knot of purple ribbon on his shoulder. He advanced hesitatingly with head bowed and bare and dropped upon one knee in front of Tom. Tom sat still and contemplated him soberly a moment. Then he said, 'Rise, lad. Who art thou? What wouldst have?'

The boy rose and stood at graceful ease, but with an aspect of concern in his face. He said 'Of a surety thou must remember me, my lord. I am thy whipping boy.'

'My *whipping* boy?'

'The same, your Grace. I am Humphrey – Humphrey Marlow.'

Tom perceived that here was someone whom his keepers ought to have posted him about. The situation was delicate. What should he do? Pretend he knew this lad, and then betray by his every utterance that he had never heard of him before? No, that would not do. An idea came to his relief: accidents like this might be likely to happen with such frequency now that business urgencies would often call Hertford and St John from his side, they being members of the council of executors; therefore perhaps it would be well to strike out a plan himself to meet the requirements of such emergencies. Yes, that would be a wise course; he would practise on this boy, and see what sort of success he might achieve. So he stroked his brow perplexedly a moment or two and presently said, 'Now I seem to remember thee somewhat, but my wit is clogged and dim with suffering——'

'Alack, my poor master!' ejaculated the whipping boy with feeling, adding to himself, 'In truth 'tis as they said – his mind is gone; alas, poor soul! But misfortune catch me, how am I forgetting! They said one must not seem to observe that aught is wrong with him.'

''Tis strange how my memory doth wanton with me these days,' said Tom. 'But mind it not – I mend apace – a little clue doth often serve to bring me back again the things and names which had escaped me. [And not they only, forsooth, but e'en such as I ne'er heard before – as this lad shall see.] Give thy business speech.'

''Tis matter of small weight, my liege, yet will I touch upon it an' it please your Grace. Two days gone by, when your Majesty faulted thrice in your Greek in the morning lessons – dost remember it?'

'Y-e-s – methinks I do. [It is not much of a lie – an' I had meddled with the Greek at all, I had not faulted simply thrice, but forty times.] Yes, I do recall it now; go on.'

'The master, being wroth with what he termed such slovenly and doltish work, did promise that he would soundly whip me for it, and——'

'Whip *thee*!' said Tom, astonished out of his presence of mind. 'Why should he whip *thee* for faults of mine?'

'Ah, your Grace forgetteth again. He always scourgeth me when thou dost fail in thy lessons.'

'True, true – I had forgot. Thou teachest me in private; then if I fail, he argueth that thy office was lamely done, and——'

'Oh, my liege, what words are these? I, the humblest of thy servants, presume to teach *thee*?'

'Then where is thy blame? What riddle is this? Am I in truth gone mad, or is it thou? Explain – speak out.'

'But good your Majesty, there's nought that needeth simplifying. None may visit the sacred person of the Prince of Wales with blows, wherefore when he faulteth, 'tis I that take them; and meet it is and right, for that it is mine office and my livelihood.'[2]

Tom stared at the tranquil boy, observing to himself, 'Lo, it is a wonderful thing – a most strange and curious trade; I marvel they have not hired a boy to take my combings and my dressings for me – would heaven they would! – an' they will do this thing, I will take my lashings in mine own person, giving God thanks for the change.' Then he said aloud, 'And hast thou been beaten, poor friend, according to the promise?'

'No, good your Majesty, my punishment was appointed for this day, and peradventure it may be annulled as unbefitting the season of mourning that is come upon us; I know not, and so have made bold to come hither and remind your Grace about your gracious promise to intercede in my behalf——'

'With the master? To save thee thy whipping?'

'Ah, thou dost remember!'

'My memory mendeth, thou seest. Set thy mind at ease; thy back shall go unscathed; I will see to it.'

'Oh, thanks, my good lord!' cried the boy, dropping upon his knee again. 'Mayhap I have ventured far enow; and yet——'

Seeing Master Humphrey hesitate, Tom encouraged him to go on, saying he was 'in the granting mood.'

'Then will I speak it out, for it lieth near my heart. Sith thou art no more Prince of Wales, but king, thou canst order matters as thou wilt, with none to say thee nay; wherefore it is not in reason that thou wilt longer vex thyself with dreary studies, but wilt burn thy books and turn thy mind to things less irksome. Then am I ruined, and mine orphan sisters with me!'

'Ruined? Prithee how?'

'My back is my bread, O my gracious liege! If it go idle, I starve. An' thou cease from study, mine office is gone, thou'lt need no whipping boy. Do not turn me away!'

Tom was touched with this pathetic distress. He said, with a right royal burst of generosity, 'Discomfort thyself no further, lad. Thine office shall be permanent in thee and thy line forever.' Then he struck the boy a light blow on the shoulder with the flat of his sword, exclaiming, 'Rise, Humphrey Marlow, Hereditary Grand Whipping Boy to the royal house of England! Banish sorrow; I will betake me to my books again and study so ill that they must in justice treble thy wage, so mightily shall the business of thine office be augmented.'

The grateful Humphrey responded fervidly, 'Thanks, O most noble master; this princely lavishness doth far surpass my most distempered dreams of fortune. Now shall I be happy all my days, and all the house of Marlow after me.'

Tom had wit enough to perceive that here was a lad who could be useful to him. He encouraged Humphrey to talk, and he was nothing loath. He was delighted to believe that he was helping in Tom's 'cure', for always, as soon as he had finished calling back to Tom's diseased mind the various particulars of his experiences and adventures in the royal schoolroom and elsewhere about the palace, he noticed that Tom was then able to 'recall' the circumstances quite clearly. At the end of an hour Tom found himself well freighted with very valuable information concerning personages and matters pertaining to the court, so he resolved to draw instruction from this source daily, and to this end he would give order to admit Humphrey to the royal closet whenever he might come, provided the majesty of England was not engaged with other people. Humphrey had hardly been dismissed when my lord Hertford arrived with more trouble for Tom.

He said that the lords of the council, fearing that some overwrought report of the king's damaged health might have leaked out and got abroad, they deemed it wise and best that his Majesty should begin to dine in public after a day or two – his wholesome complexion and vigorous step, assisted by a carefully guarded repose of manner and ease and grace of demeanour, would more surely quiet the general pulse, in case any evil rumours *had* gone about, than any other scheme that could be devised.

Then the earl proceeded very delicately to instruct Tom as to the observances proper to the stately occasion, under the rather thin disguise of 'reminding' him concerning things already known to him; but to his vast gratification it turned out that Tom needed very little help in this line: he had been making use of Humphrey in that direction, for Humphrey had mentioned that within a few days he was to begin to dine in public, having gathered it from the swift-winged gossip of the court. Tom kept these facts to himself, however.

Seeing the royal memory so improved, the earl ventured to apply a few tests to it, in an apparently casual way, to find out how far its amendment had progressed. The results were happy, here and there, in spots – spots where Humphrey's tracks remained; and on the whole my lord was greatly pleased and encouraged. So encouraged was he, indeed, that he spoke up and said in a quite hopeful voice, 'Now am I persuaded that if your Majesty will but tax your memory yet a little further, it will resolve the puzzle of the Great Seal – a loss which was of moment yesterday, although of none today, since its term of service ended with our late lord's life. May it please your Grace to make the trial?'

Tom was at sea – a Great Seal was a something which he was totally unacquainted with. After a moment's hesitation he looked up innocently and asked, 'What was it like, my lord?'

The earl started, almost imperceptibly, muttering to himself, 'Alack, his wits are flown again! It was ill wisdom to lead him on to strain them.' Then he deftly turned the talk to other matters, with the purpose of sweeping the unlucky Seal out of Tom's thoughts – a purpose which easily succeeded.

1 Hume.
2 See Note 8 at end of volume.

15 Tom as King

The next day the foreign ambassadors came, with their gorgeous trains; and Tom, throned in awful state, received them. The splendours of the scene delighted his eye and fired his imagination at first, but the audience was long and dreary, and so were most of the addresses; wherefore, what began as a pleasure grew into weariness and homesickness by and by. Tom said the words which Hertford put into his mouth from time to time and tried hard to acquit himself satisfactorily, but he was too new to such things and too ill at ease to accomplish more than a tolerable success. He looked sufficiently like a king, but he was ill able to feel like one. He was cordially glad when the ceremony was ended.

The larger part of his day was 'wasted' – as he termed it in his own mind – in labours pertaining to his royal office. Even the two hours devoted to certain princely pastimes and recreations were rather a burden to him than otherwise, they were so fettered by restrictions and ceremonious observances. However, he had a private hour with his whipping boy, which he counted clear gain, since he got both entertainment and needful information out of it.

The third day of Tom Canty's kingship came and went much as the others had done, but there was a lifting of his cloud in one way: he felt less uncomfortable than at first; he was getting a little used to his circumstances and surroundings; his chains still galled, but not all the time; he found that the presence and homage of the great afflicted and embarrassed him less and less sharply with every hour that drifted over his head.

But for one single dread, he could have seen the fourth day approach without serious distress – the dining in public; it was to begin that day. There were greater matters in the programme, for on that day he would have to preside at a council which would take his views and commands concerning the policy to be pursued toward various foreign nations scattered far and near over the great globe; on that day too, Hertford would be formally chosen to the grand office of Lord Protector; other things of note were appointed for that fourth day also, but to Tom they were all insignificant compared with the ordeal of dining all by himself with a multitude of curious eyes fastened upon him and a multitude of mouths whispering comments upon his performance – and upon his mistakes, if he should be so unlucky as to make any.

Still, nothing could stop that fourth day, and so it came. It found poor Tom low-spirited and absent-minded, and this mood continued; he could not shake it off. The ordinary duties of the morning dragged upon his hands and wearied him. Once more he felt the sense of captivity heavy upon him.

Late in the forenoon he was in a large audience chamber, conversing with the Earl of Hertford and dully awaiting the striking of the hour appointed for a visit of ceremony from a considerable number of great officials and courtiers.

After a little while Tom, who had wandered to a window and become interested in the life and movement of the great highway beyond the palace gates – and not idly interested, but longing with all his heart to take part in person in its stir and freedom – saw the van of a hooting and shouting mob of disorderly men, women, and children of the lowest and poorest degree approaching from up the road.

'I would I knew what 'tis about!' he exclaimed with all a boy's curiosity in such happenings.

'Thou art the king!' solemnly responded the earl with a reverence. 'Have I your Grace's leave to act?'

'Oh, blithely, yes! Oh, gladly, yes!' exclaimed Tom excitedly, adding to himself with a lively sense of satisfaction, 'In truth, being a king is not all dreariness; it hath its compensations and conveniences.'

The earl called a page and sent him to the captain of the guard with the order, 'Let the mob be halted, and inquiry made concerning the occasion of its movement. By the king's command!'

A few seconds later a long rank of the royal guards, cased in flashing steel, filed out at the gates and formed across the highway in front of the multitude. A messenger returned to report that the crowd were following a man, a woman, and a young girl to execution for crimes committed against the peace and dignity of the realm.

Death – and a violent death – for these poor unfortunates! The thought wrung Tom's heartstrings. The spirit of compassion took control of him, to the exclusion of all other considerations: he never thought of the offended laws or of the grief or loss which these three criminals had inflicted upon their victims, he could think of nothing but the scaffold and the grisly fate hanging over the heads of the condemned. His concern made him even forget for the moment that he was but the false shadow of a king, not the substance; and before he knew it he had blurted out the command, 'Bring them here!'

Then he blushed scarlet, and a sort of apology sprung to his lips; but observing that his order had wrought no sort of surprise in the earl or the waiting page, he suppressed the words he was about to utter. The page, in the most matter-of-fact way, made a profound obeisance and retired backwards out of the room to deliver the command. Tom experienced a glow of pride and a renewed sense of the compensating advantages of the kingly office. He said to himself, 'Truly it is like what I was used to feel when I read the old priest's tales and did imagine mine own self a prince, giving law and command to all, saying, "Do this, do that," whilst none durst offer let or hindrance to my will.'

Now the doors swung open; one high-sounding title after another was announced, the personages owning them followed, and the place was quickly half filled with noble folk and finery. But Tom was hardly conscious of the presence of these people, so wrought up was he and so intensely absorbed in that other and more interesting matter. He seated himself absently in his chair of state and turned his eyes upon the door with manifestations of impatient expectancy, seeing which, the company forebore to trouble him and fell to chatting a mixture of public business and court gossip one with another.

In a little while the measured tread of military men was heard approaching, and the culprits entered the presence in charge of an under-sheriff and escorted by a detail of the king's guard. The civil officer knelt before Tom, then stood aside; the three doomed persons knelt also and remained so; the guard took position behind Tom's chair. Tom scanned the prisoners curiously. Something about the dress or appearance of the man had stirred a vague memory in him. 'Methinks I have seen this man ere now, but the when or the where fail me——' Such was Tom's thought. Just then the man glanced quickly up, and quickly dropped his face again, not being able to endure the awful port of sovereignty; but the one full glimpse of the face which Tom got was sufficient. He said to himself, 'Now is the matter clear; this is the stranger that plucked Giles Witt out of the Thames and saved his life that windy, bitter, first day of the new year – a brave good deed; pity he hath been doing baser ones and got himself in this sad case. I have not forgot the day, neither the hour; by reason that an hour after, upon the stroke of eleven, I did get a hiding by the hand of Gammer Canty which was of so goodly and admired severity that all that went before or followed after it were but fondlings and caresses by comparison.'

Tom now ordered that the woman and the girl be removed from the presence for a little time, then addressed himself to the under-sheriff, saying, 'Good sir, what is this man's offence?'

The officer knelt and answered, 'So please your Majesty, he hath taken the life of a subject by poison.'

Tom's compassion for the prisoner and admiration of him as the daring rescuer of a drowning boy experienced a most damaging shock.

'The thing was proven upon him?' he asked.

'Most clearly, sire.'

Tom sighed and said, 'Take him away – he hath earned his death. 'Tis a pity, for he was a brave heart – na – na, I mean he hath the *look* of it!'

The prisoner clasped his hands together with sudden energy and wrung them despairingly, at the same time appealing imploringly to the 'king' in broken and terrified phrases, 'O my lord the king, an' thou canst pity the lost, have pity upon me! I am innocent – neither hath that wherewith I am charged been more than but lamely proved – yet I speak not of that; the judgment is gone forth against me and may not suffer alteration; yet in mine extremity I beg a boon, for my doom is more than I can bear. A grace, a grace, my lord the king! In thy royal compassion grant my prayer; give commandment that I be hanged!'

Tom was amazed. This was not the outcome he had looked for.

'Odds my life, a strange *boon*! Was it not the fate intended thee?'

'O good my liege, not so! It is ordered that I be *boiled alive*!'

The hideous surprise of these words almost made Tom spring from his chair. As soon as he could recover his wits he cried out, 'Have thy wish, poor soul! An' thou had poisoned a hundred men thou shouldst not suffer so miserable a death.'

The prisoner bowed his face to the ground and burst into passionate expressions of gratitude, ending with, 'If ever thou shouldst know misfortune – which God forefend! – may thy goodness to me this day be remembered and requited!'

Tom turned to the Earl of Hertford and said, 'My lord, is it believable that there was warrant for this man's ferocious doom?'

'It is the law, your Grace – for poisoners. In Germany coiners be boiled to death in *oil* – not cast in of a sudden, but by a rope let down into the oil by degrees, and slowly; first the feet, then the legs, then——'

'Oh, prithee no more, my lord; I cannot bear it!' cried Tom, covering his eyes with his hands to shut out the picture. 'I beseech your good lordship that order be taken to change this law. Oh, let no more poor creatures be visited with its tortures.'

The earl's face showed profound gratification, for he was a man of merciful and generous impulses – a thing not very common with his class in that fierce age. He said 'These your Grace's noble words have sealed its doom. History will remember it to the honour of your royal house.'

The under-sheriff was about to remove his prisoner; Tom gave him a sign to wait; then he said, 'Good sir, I would look into this matter further. The man has said his deed was but lamely proved. Tell me what thou knowest.'

'If the king's grace please, it did appear upon the trial that this man entered into a house in the hamlet of Islington where one lay sick – three witnesses say it was at ten of the clock in the morning and two say it was some minutes later – the sick man being alone at the time, and sleeping; and presently the man came forth again and went his way. The sick man died within the hour, being torn with spasms and retchings.'

'"*It is ordered that I be* boiled alive!*"*'

'Did any see the poison given? Was poison found?'

'Marry, no, my liege.'

'Then how doth one know there was poison given at all?'

'Please your Majesty, the doctors testified that none die with such symptoms but by poison.'

Weighty evidence, this – in that simple age. Tom recognized its formidable nature and said, 'The doctor knoweth his trade; belike they were right. The matter hath an ill look for this poor man.'

'Yet was not this all, your Majesty; there is more and worse. Many testified that a witch, since gone from the village, none know whither, did foretell, and speak it privately in their ears, that the sick man *would die by poison*, and more, that a stranger would give it – a stranger with brown hair and clothed in a worn and common garb; and surely this prisoner doth answer woundily to the bill. Please your Majesty to give the circumstance that solemn weight which is its due, seeing it was *foretold*.'

This was an argument of tremendous force in that superstitious day. Tom felt that the thing was settled; if evidence was worth anything, this poor fellow's guilt was proved. Still he offered the prisoner a chance, saying, 'If thou canst say aught in thy behalf, speak.'

'Nought that will avail, my king. I am innocent, yet cannot I make it appear. I have no friends, else might I show that I was not in Islington that day; so also might I show that at that hour they name I was above a league away, seeing I was at Wapping Old Stairs; yea more, my king, for I could show that whilst they say I was *taking* life, I was *saving* it. A drowning boy——'

'Peace! Sheriff, name the day the deed was done!'

'At ten in the morning, or some minutes later, the first day of the new year, most illustrious——'

'Let the prisoner go free; it is the king's will!'

Another blush followed this unregal outburst, and he covered his indecorum as well as he could by adding, 'It enrageth me that a man should be hanged upon such idle, harebrained evidence!'

A low buzz of admiration swept through the assemblage. It was not admiration of the decree that had been delivered by Tom, for the propriety or expediency of pardoning a convicted poisoner was a thing which few there would have felt justified in either admitting or admiring – no the admiration was for the intelligence and spirit which Tom had displayed. Some of the low-voiced remarks were to this effect: 'This is no mad king; he hath his wits sound.' 'How sanely he put his questions; how like his former natural self was this abrupt, imperious disposal of the matter!' 'God be thanked his infirmity is spent! This is no weakling, but a king. He hath borne himself like to his own father.'

The air being filled with applause, Tom's ear necessarily caught a little of it. The effect which this had upon him was to put him greatly at his ease and also to charge his system with very gratifying sensations.

However, his juvenile curiosity soon rose superior to these pleasant thoughts and feelings; he was eager to know what sort of deadly mischief the woman and the little girl could have been about; so, by his command the two terrified and sobbing creatures were brought before him.

'What is it that these have done?' he inquired of the sheriff.

'Please your Majesty, a black crime is charged upon them, and clearly proven; wherefore the judges have decreed, according to the law, that they be hanged. They sold themselves to the devil; such is their crime.'

Tom shuddered. He had been taught to abhor people who did this wicked thing. Still, he was not going to deny himself the pleasure of feeding his curiosity, for all that; so he asked, 'Where was this done? And when?'

'On a midnight, in December, in a ruined church, your Majesty.'

Tom shuddered again.

'Who was there present?'

'Only these two, your Grace – and *that other*.'

'Have these confessed?'

'Nay, not so, sire; they do deny it.'

'Then prithee, how was it known?'

'Certain witnesses did see them wending thither, good your Majesty; this bred the suspicion, and dire effects have since confirmed and justified it. In particular, it is in evidence that through the wicked power so obtained, they did invoke and bring about a storm that wasted all the region round about. Above forty witnesses have proved the storm; and sooth one might have had a thousand, for all had reason to remember it, sith all had suffered by it.'

'Certes this is a serious matter.' Tom turned this dark piece of scoundrelism over in his mind awhile, then asked, 'Suffered the woman also by the storm?'

Several old heads among the assemblage nodded their recognition of the wisdom of this question. The sheriff, however, saw nothing consequential in the inquiry; he answered with simple directness, 'Indeed did she, your Majesty, and most righteously, as all aver. Her habitation was swept away, and herself and child left shelterless.'

'Methinks the power to do herself so ill a turn was dearly bought. She had been cheated had she paid but a farthing for it; that she paid her soul, and her child's, argueth that she is mad; if she is mad she knoweth not what she doth, therefore sinneth not.'

The elderly heads nodded recognition of Tom's wisdom once more, and one individual murmured, 'An' the king be mad himself, according to report, then is it a madness of a sort that would improve the sanity of some I wot of, if by the gentle providence of God they could but catch it.'

'What age hath the child?'

'Nine years, please your Majesty.'

'By the law of England may a child enter into covenant and sell itself, my lord?' asked Tom, turning to a learned judge.

'The law doth not permit a child to make or meddle in any weighty matter, good my liege, holding that its callow wit unfitteth it to cope with the riper wit and evil schemings of them that are its elders. The *devil* may buy a child if he so choose, and the child agree thereto, but not an Englishman; in this latter case the contract would be null and void.'

'It seemeth a rude, unchristian thing, and ill-contrived, that English law denieth privileges to Englishmen, to waste them on the devil!' cried Tom with honest heat.

This novel view of the matter excited many smiles, and was stored away in many heads to be repeated about the court as evidence of Tom's originality as well as progress toward mental health.

The elder culprit had ceased from sobbing and was hanging upon Tom's words with an excited interest and a growing hope. Tom noticed this, and it strongly inclined his sympathies toward her in her perilous and unfriended situation. Presently he asked, 'How wrought they to bring the storm?'

'*By pulling of their stockings*, sir.'

This astonished Tom and also fired his curiosity to fever heat. He said eagerly, 'It is wonderful! Hath it always this dread effect?'

'Always, my liege, at least if the woman desire it and utter the needful words, either in her mind or with her tongue.'

Tom turned to the woman and said with impetuous zeal, 'Exert thy power; I would see a storm!'

There was a sudden paling of cheeks in the superstitious assemblage, and a general though unexpressed desire to get out of the place, all of which was lost upon Tom, who was dead to everything but the proposed cataclysm. Seeing a puzzled and astonished look in the woman's face, he added excitedly, 'Never fear; thou shalt be blameless. More, thou shalt go free; none shall touch thee. Exert thy power.'

'Oh, my lord the king, I have it not; I have been falsely accused.'

'Thy fears stay thee. Be of good heart; thou shalt suffer no harm. Make a storm; it mattereth not how small a one – I require nought great or harmful, but indeed prefer the opposite; do this and thy life is spared; thou shalt go out free, with thy child, bearing the king's pardon, and safe from hurt or malice from any in the realm.'

The woman prostrated herself and protested with tears that she had no power to do the miracle, else she would gladly win her child's life alone and be content to lose her own, if by obedience to the king's command so precious a grace might be acquired.

Tom urged; the woman still adhered to her declarations. Finally he said, 'I think the woman hath said true. An' *my* mother were in her place and gifted with the devil's functions, she had not stayed a moment to call her storms and lay the whole land in ruins if the saving of my forfeit life were the price she got! It is argument that other mothers are made in like mould. Thou art free, goodwife – thou and thy child – for I do think thee innocent *Now* thou'st nought to fear, being pardoned, pull of thy stockings! An' thou canst make me a storm, thou shalt be rich!'

The redeemed creature was loud in her gratitude and proceeded to obey, whilst Tom looked on with eager expectancy, a little marred by apprehension, the courtiers at the same time manifesting decided discomfort and uneasiness. The woman stripped her own feet and her little girl's also, and plainly did her best to reward the king's generosity with an earthquake, but it was all a failure and a disappointment.

Tom sighed and said, 'There, good soul, trouble thyself no further; thy power is departed out of thee. Go thy way in peace; and if it return to thee at any time, forget me not, but fetch me a storm.'[1]

1 See Notes to Chapter 15 at end of volume.

16 The State Dinner

The dinner hour drew near, yet strangely enough the thought brought but slight discomfort to Tom, and hardly any terror. The morning's experiences had wonderfully built up his confidence; the poor little ash-cat was already more wonted to his strange garret after four days' habit than a mature person could have become in a full month. A child's facility in accommodating itself to circumstances was never more strikingly illustrated.

Let us privileged ones hurry to the great banqueting room and have a glance at matters there whilst Tom is being made ready for the imposing occasion. It is a spacious apartment, with gilded pillars and pilasters, and pictured walls and ceilings. At the door stand tall guards, as rigid as statues, dressed in rich and picturesque costumes, and bearing halberds. In a high gallery which runs all around the place is a band of musicians and a packed company of citizens of both sexes in brilliant attire. In the centre of the room, upon a raised platform, is Tom's table. Now let the ancient chronicler speak:

'A gentleman enters the room bearing a rod, and along with him another bearing a tablecloth, which, after they have both kneeled three times with the utmost veneration, he spreads upon the table, and after kneeling again they both retire; then come two others, one with the rod again, the other with a salt cellar, a plate, and bread; when they have kneeled as the others have done and placed what was brought upon the table, they too retire with the same ceremonies performed by the first; at last come two nobles, richly clothed, one bearing a tasting knife, who, after prostrating themselves three times in the most graceful manner, approach and rub the table with bread and salt with as much awe as if the king had been present.'[1]

So end the solemn preliminaries. Now, far down the echoing corridors we hear a bugle blast and the indistinct cry, 'Place for the king! Way for the king's most excellent majesty!' These sounds are momently repeated – they grow nearer and nearer – and presently, almost in our faces, the martial note peals and the cry rings out, 'Way for the king!' At this instant the shining pageant appears and files in at the door with a measured march. Let the chronicler speak again:

'First come gentlemen, barons, earls, knights of the Garter, all richly dressed and bareheaded; next comes the Chancellor, between two, one of which carries the royal sceptre, the other the Sword of State in a red scabbard studded with golden fleurs-de-lis, the point upwards; next comes the king himself, whom, upon his appearing, twelve trumpets and many drums salute with a great burst of welcome, whilst all in the galleries rise in their places, crying, 'God save the king!' After him come nobles attached to his person, and on his right and left march his guard of honour, his fifty gentlemen pensioners, with gilt battle-axes.'

This was all fine and pleasant. Tom's pulse beat high, and a glad light was in his eyes. He bore himself right gracefully, and all the more so because he was not thinking of how he was doing it, his mind being charmed and occupied with the blithe sights and sounds about him; and besides, nobody can be very ungraceful in nicely fitting beautiful clothes after he has grown a little used to them, especially if he is for the moment unconscious of them. Tom remembered his instructions and acknowledged his greeting with a slight inclination of his plumed head and a courteous, 'I thank ye, my good people.'

He seated himself at table without removing his cap, and did it without the least embarrassment, for to eat with one's cap on was the one solitary royal custom upon which the kings and the Cantys met upon common ground, neither party having any advantage over the other in the matter of old familiarity with it. The pageant broke up and grouped itself picturesquely, and remained bareheaded.

Now, to the sound of gay music, the yeoman of the guard entered, 'the tallest and mightiest men in England, they being carefully selected in this regard.' But we will let the chronicler tell about it:

'The yeomen of the guard entered, bareheaded, clothed in scarlet, with golden roses upon their backs; and these went and came, bringing in each turn a course of dishes, served in plate. These dishes were received by a gentleman in the same order they were brought, and placed upon the table, while the taster gave to each guard a mouthful to eat of the particular dish he had brought, for fear of any poison.'

Tom made a good dinner, notwithstanding he was conscious that hundreds of eyes followed each morsel to his mouth and watched him eat it with an interest which could not have been more intense if it had been a deadly explosive and was expected to blow him up and scatter him all about the place. He was careful not to hurry, and equally careful not to do anything whatever for himself, but wait till the proper official knelt down and did it for him. He got through without a mistake – flawless and precious triumph.

When the meal was over at last and he marched away in the midst of his bright pageant, with the happy noises in his ears of blaring bugles, rolling drums, and thundering acclamations, he felt that if he had seen the worst of dining in public, it was an ordeal which he would be glad to endure several times a day if by that means he could but buy himself free from some of the more formidable requirements of his royal office.

1 Leigh Hunt's *The Town*, p. 408, quotation from an earlier tourist.

17 Foo-foo the First

Miles Hendon hurried along toward the Southwark end of the bridge, keeping a sharp lookout for the persons he sought and hoping and expecting to overtake them presently. He was disappointed in this, however. By asking questions, he was enabled to track them part of the way through Southwark; then all traces ceased, and he was perplexed as to how to proceed. Still, he continued his efforts as best he could during the rest of the day. Nightfall found him leg-weary, half famished, and his desire as far from accomplishment as ever; so he supped at the Tabard Inn and went to bed, resolved to make an early start in the morning and give the town an exhaustive search. As he lay thinking and planning, he presently began to reason thus: The boy would escape from the ruffian, his reputed father, if possible; would he go back to London and seek his former haunts? No, he would not do that; he would avoid recapture. What, then, would he do? Never having had a friend in the world or a protector until he met Miles Hendon, he would naturally try to find that friend again, provided the effort did not require him to go toward London and danger. He would strike for Hendon Hall, that is what he would do, for he knew Hendon was homeward bound and there he might expect to find him. Yes, the case was plain to Hendon – he must lose no more time in Southwark, but move at once through Kent, toward Monk's Holm, searching the wood and inquiring as he went. Let us return to the vanished little king now.

The ruffian whom the waiter at the inn on the bridge saw 'about to join' the youth and the king did not exactly join them, but fell in close behind them and followed their steps. He said nothing. His left arm was in a sling, and he wore a large green patch over his left eye; he limped slightly and used an oaken staff as a support. The youth led the king a crooked course through Southwark, and by and by struck into the high road beyond. The king was irritated now and said he would stop here – it was Hendon's place to come to him, not his to go to Hendon. He would not endure such insolence; he would stop where he was. The youth said, 'Thou'lt tarry here, and thy friend lying wounded in the wood yonder? So be it then.'

The king's manner changed at once. He cried out, 'Wounded? And who hath dared to do it? But that is apart; lead on, lead on! Faster, sirrah! Art shod with lead? Wounded, is he? Now though the doer of it be a duke's son, he shall rue it!'

It was some distance to the wood, but the space was speedily traversed. The youth looked about him, discovered a bough sticking in the ground, with a small bit of rag tied to it, then led the way into the forest, watching for similar boughs and finding them at intervals: they were evidently guides to the point he was aiming at. By and by an open place was reached, where were the charred remains of a farmhouse, and near them a barn which was falling to ruin and decay. There was no sign of life anywhere, and utter silence prevailed. The youth entered the barn, the king following eagerly upon his heels. No one there! The king shot a surprised and suspicious glance at the youth and asked, 'Where is he?'

A mocking laugh was his answer. The king was in a rage in a moment; he seized a billet of wood and was in the act of charging upon the youth when another mocking laugh fell upon his ear. It was from the lame ruffian who had been following at a distance. The king turned and said angrily, 'Who art thou? What is thy business here?'

'Leave thy foolery,' said the man, 'and quiet thyself. My disguise is none so good that thou canst pretend thou knowest not thy father through it.'

'Thou art not my father. I know thee not. I am the king. If thou hast hid my servant, find him for me, or thou shalt sup sorrow for what thou hast done.'

John Canty replied in a stern and measured voice, 'It is plain thou art mad, and I am loath to punish thee; but if thou provoke me, I must. Thy prating doth no harm here, where there are no ears that need to mind thy follies, yet is it well to practise thy tongue to wary speech, that it may do no hurt when our quarters change. I have done a murder and may not tarry at home; neither shalt thou, seeing I need thy service. My name is changed, for wise reasons; it is Hobbs – John Hobbs; thine is Jack; charge thy memory accordingly. Now then, speak. Where is thy mother? Where are thy sisters? They came not to the place appointed; knowest thou whither they went?'

The king answered sullenly, 'Trouble me not with these riddles. My mother is dead; my sisters are in the palace.'

The youth nearby burst into a derisive laugh, and the king would have assaulted him, but Canty – or Hobbs, as he now called himself – prevented him, and said, 'Peace, Hugo, vex him not; his mind is astray, and thy ways fret him. Sit thee down, Jack, and quiet thyself; thou shalt have a morsel to eat, anon.'

Hobbs and Hugo fell to talking together in low voices, and the king removed himself as far as he could from their disagreeable company. He withdrew into the twilight of the farther end of the barn, where he found the earthen floor bedded a foot deep with straw. He lay down here, drew straw over himself in lieu of blankets, and was soon absorbed in thinking. He had many griefs, but the minor ones were swept almost into forgetfulness by the supreme one, the loss of his father. To the rest of the world the name of Henry VIII brought a shiver and suggested an ogre whose nostrils breathed destruction and whose hand dealt scourgings and death; but to this boy the name brought only sensations of pleasure, the figure it invoked wore a countenance that was all gentleness and affection. He called to mind a long succession of loving passages between his father and himself and dwelt fondly upon them, his unstinted tears attesting how deep and real was the grief that possessed his heart. As the afternoon wasted away, the lad, wearied with his troubles, sunk gradually into a tranquil and healing slumber.

After a considerable time – he could not tell how long – his senses struggled to a half consciousness, and as he lay with closed eyes vaguely wondering where he was and what had been happening, he noted a murmurous sound, the sullen beating of rain upon the roof. A snug sense of comfort stole over him, which was rudely broken the next moment by a chorus of piping cackles and coarse laughter. It startled him disagreeably, and he unmuffled his head to see whence this interruption proceeded. A grim and unsightly picture met his eye. A bright fire was burning in the middle of the floor at the other end of the barn; and around it, and lit weirdly up by the red glare, lolled and sprawled the motliest company of tattered gutter scum and ruffians, of both sexes, he had ever read or dreamed of. There were huge, stalwart men, brown with exposure, long-haired, and clothed in fantastic rags; there were middle-sized youths of truculent countenance, and similarly clad; there were blind mendicants with patched or bandaged eyes, crippled ones with wooden legs and crutches; there was a villain-looking peddler with his pack, a knife-grinder, a tinker, and a barber-surgeon with the implements of their trades; some of the females were hardly grown girls, some were at prime, some were old and wrinkled hags, and all were loud, brazen, foul-mouthed; and all soiled and slatternly; there were three sore-faced babies; there were a couple of starveling curs, with strings about their necks, whose office was to lead the blind.

The night was come, the gang had just finished feasting, an orgy was beginning, the can of liquor was passing from mouth to mouth. A general cry broke forth, 'A song! A song from the Bat and Dick Dot-and-Go-One!'

One of the blind men got up and made ready by casting aside the patches that sheltered his excellent eyes and the pathetic placard which recited the cause of his calamity. Dot-and-Go-One disencumbered himself of his timber leg and took his place, upon sound and healthy limbs, beside his fellow rascal; then they roared out a rollicking ditty, and were re-enforced by the whole crew at the end of each stanza in a rousing chorus. By the time the last stanza was reached, the half-drunken enthusiasm had risen to such a pitch that everybody joined in and sang it clear through from the beginning, producing a volume of villainous sound that made the rafters quake. These were the inspiring words:

> Bien Darkmans then, Bouse Mort and Ken,
> The bien Coves bings awast,
> On Chates to trine by Rome Coves dine
> For his long lib at last.
>
> Bing'd out bien Morts and toure, and toure,
> Bing out of the Rome vile bine,
> And toure the Cove that cloy'd your duds,
> Upon the Chates to trine.[1]

Conversation followed; not in the thieves' dialect of the song, for that was only used in talk when unfriendly ears might be listening. In the course of it, it appeared that 'John Hobbs' was not altogether a new recruit, but had trained in the gang at some former time. His later history was called for, and when he said he had 'accidentally' killed a man, considerable satisfaction was expressed; when he added that the man was a priest, he was roundly applauded and had to take a drink with everybody. Old acquaintances welcomed him joyously, and new ones were proud to shake him by the hand. He was asked why he had 'tarried away so many months.' He answered, 'London is better than the country, and safer these late years, the laws be so bitter and so diligently enforced. An' I had not had that accident, I had stayed there. I had resolved to stay and never more venture countrywards, but the accident has ended that.'

He inquired how many persons the gang numbered now. The 'Ruffler,' or chief, answered, 'Five and twenty sturdy budges, bulks, files, clapperdogeons and maunders, counting the dells and doxies and other morts.[2] Most are here; the rest are wandering eastward along the winter lay. We follow at dawn.'

'I do not see the Wen among the honest folk about me. Where may he be?'

'Poor lad, his diet is brimstone now, and over hot for a delicate taste. He was killed in a brawl, somewhere about midsummer.'

I sorrow to hear that; the Wen was a capable man, and brave.'

'That was he, truly. Black Bess, his dell, is of us yet, but absent on the eastward tramp; a fine lass, of nice ways and orderly conduct, none ever seeing her drunk above four days in the seven.'

'She was ever strict – I remember it well – a goodly wench and worthy all commendation. Her mother was more free and less particular, a troublesome and ugly tempered beldame, but furnished with a wit above the common.'

'We lost her through it. Her gift of palmistry and other sorts of fortune-telling begot for her at last a witch's name and fame. The law roasted her to death at a slow fire. It did touch me to a sort of tenderness to see the gallant way she met her lot – cursing and reviling all the crowd that gaped and gazed around her, whilst the flames licked upward toward her face and catched her thin locks and crackled about her old grey head. Cursing them, said I? Cursing them! Why, an' thou shouldst live a thousand years thou'dst never hear so masterful a cursing. Alack, her art died with her. There be base and weakling imitations left, but no true blasphemy.'

The Ruffler sighed; the listeners sighed in sympathy; a general depression fell upon the company for a moment, for even hardened outcasts like these are not wholly dead to sentiment, but are able to feel a fleeting sense of loss and affliction at wide intervals and under peculiarly favouring circumstances – as in cases like to this, for instance, when genius and culture depart and leave no heir. However, a deep drink all round soon restored the spirits of the mourners.

'Have any others of our friends fared hardly?' asked Hobbs.

'Some – yes. Particularly newcomers, such as small husbandmen turned shiftless and hungry upon the world because their farms were taken from them to be changed to sheep ranges. They begged, and were whipped at the cart's tail, naked from the girdle up, till the blood ran, then set in the stocks to be pelted; they begged again, were whipped again, and deprived of an ear; they begged a third time – poor devils, what else could they do? – and were branded on the cheek with a red-hot iron, then sold for slaves; they ran away, were hunted down, and hanged. 'Tis a brief tale, and quickly told. Others of us have fared less hardly. Stand forth, Yokel, Burns, and Hodge – show your adornments!'

These stood up and stripped away some of their rags, exposing their backs, criss-crossed with ropy old welts left by the lash; one turned up his hair and showed the place where a left ear had once been; another showed a brand upon his shoulder – the letter V – and a mutilated ear; the third said, 'I am Yokel, once a farmer and prosperous, with loving wife and kids, now am I somewhat different in estate and calling, and the wife and kids are gone; mayhap they are in heaven, mayhap in – in the other place; but the kindly God be thanked, they bide no more in *England*! My good old blameless mother strove to earn bread by nursing the sick; one of these died, the doctors knew not how, so my mother was burnt for a witch, whilst my babes looked on and wailed. English law! Up, all, with your cups! Now altogether and with a cheer! Drink to the merciful English law that delivered *her* from the English hell! Thank you, mates, one and all. I begged, from house to house – I and the wife – bearing with us the hungry kids; but it was crime to be hungry in England, so they stripped us and lashed us through three towns. Drink ye all again to the merciful English law! For its lash drank deep of my Mary's blood and its blessed deliverance came quick. She lies there, in the potter's field, safe from all harms. And the kids – well, whilst the law lashed me from town to town, they starved. Drink lads – only a drop – a drop to the poor kids, that never did any creature harm. I begged again – begged for a crust, and got the stocks and lost an ear – see, here bides the stump; I begged again, and here is the stump of the other to keep me minded of it. And still I begged again, and was sold for a slave – here on my cheek under this stain, if I washed it off, ye might see the red S the branding iron left there! A *slave*! Do ye understand that word! An English *slave*! That is he that stands before ye. I have run from my master, and when I am found – the heavy curse of heaven fall on the law of the land that hath commanded it! – I shall hang!'[3]

A ringing voice came through the murky air, 'Thou shalt *not*! And this day the end of that law is come!'

All turned and saw the fantastic figure of the little king approaching hurriedly; as it emerged into the light and was clearly revealed, a general explosion of inquiries broke out: 'Who is it? *What* is it? Who art thou, manikin?'

The boy stood unconfused in the midst of all those surprised and questioning eyes and answered with princely dignity, 'I am Edward, king of England.'

A wild burst of laughter followed, partly of derision and partly of delight in the excellence of the joke. The king was stung. He said sharply, 'Ye mannerless vagrants, is this your recognition of the royal boon I have promised?'

He said more, with angry voice and excited gesture, but it was lost in a whirlwind of laughter and mocking exclamations. 'John Hobbs' made several attempts to make himself heard above the din, and at last succeeded, saying, 'Mates, he is my son, a dreamer, a fool, and stark mad; mind him not – he thinketh he *is* the king.'

'I *am* the king,' said Edward, turning toward him, 'as thou shalt know to thy cost, in good time. Thou hast confessed a murder – thou shalt swing for it.'

'*Thou'lt* betray me? *Thou*? An' I get my hands upon thee——'

'Tut-tut!' said the burly Ruffler, interposing in time to save the king, and emphasizing this service by knocking Hobbs down with his fist. 'Hast respect for neither king *nor* Rufflers? An' thou insult my presence so again, I'll hang thee up myself.' Then he said to his Majesty, 'Thou must make no threats against thy mates, lad; and thou must guard thy tongue from saying evil of them elsewhere. *Be* king, if it please thy mad humour, but be not harmful in it. Sink the title thou hast uttered – 'tis treason; we be bad men in some few trifling ways, but none among us is so base as to be traitor to his king; we be loving and loyal hearts in that regard. Note if I speak truth. Now, all together: 'Long Live Edward, king of England!'

'*Long live Edward, king of England!*'

The response came with such a thundergust from the motley crew that the crazy building vibrated to the sound. The little king's face lighted with pleasure for an instant, and he slightly inclined his head and said with grave simplicity, 'I thank you, my good people.'

This unexpected result threw the company into convulsions of merriment. When something like quiet was presently come again, the Ruffler said firmly but with an accent of good nature, 'Drop it, boy; 'tis not wise nor well. Humour thy fancy if thou must, but choose some other title.'

A tinker shrieked out a suggestion, 'Foo-foo the First, king of the Mooncalves!'

The title 'took' at once, every throat responded, and a roaring shout went up of 'Long live Foo-foo the First, king of the Mooncalves!' followed by hootings, catcalls, and peals of laughter.

'Hale him forth and crown him!'

'Robe him!'

'Sceptre him!'

'Throne him!'

These and twenty other cries broke out at once; and almost before the poor little victim could draw a breath he was crowned with a tin basin, robed in a tattered blanket, throned upon a barrel, and sceptred with the tinker's soldering iron. Then all flung themselves upon their knees about him and sent up a chorus of ironical wailings and mocking supplications, whilst they swabbed their eyes with their soiled and ragged sleeves and aprons: 'Be gracious to us, O sweet king!!' 'Trample not upon thy beseeching worms, O noble Majesty!' 'Pity thy slaves, and comfort them with a royal kick!' 'Cheer us and warm us with thy gracious rays, O flaming sun of sovereignty!' 'Sanctify the ground with the touch of thy foot, that we may eat the dirt and be ennobled!' 'Deign to spit upon us, O sire, that our children's children may tell of thy princely condescension, and be proud and happy forever!'

But the humorous tinker made the 'hit' of the evening and carried off the honours. Kneeling, he pretended to kiss the king's foot, and was indignantly spurned; whereupon he went about begging for a rag to paste over the place upon his face which had been touched by the foot, saying it must be preserved from contact with the vulgar air and that he should make his fortune by going to the highway and exposing it to view at the rate of a hundred shillings a sight. He made himself so killingly funny that he was the envy and admiration of the whole mangy rabble.

Tears of shame and indignation stood in the little monarch's eyes; and the thought in his heart was, 'Had I offered them a deep wrong they could not be more cruel; yet have I proffered nought but to do them a kindness, and it is thus they use me for it!'

1 From *The English Rogue;* London, 1665.
2 Canting terms for various kinds of thieves, beggars, and vagabonds and their female companions.
3 See Note 10 at end of volume.

18 The Prince with the Tramps

The troop of vagabonds turned out at early dawn and set forward on their march. There was a lowering sky overhead, sloppy ground underfoot, and a winter chill in the air. All gaiety was gone from the company; some were sullen and silent, some were irritable and petulant, none were gentle-humoured, all were thirsty.

The Ruffler put 'Jack' in Hugo's charge, with some brief instructions, and commanded John Canty to keep away from him and let him alone; he also warned Hugo not to be too rough with the lad.

After a while the weather grew milder and the clouds lifted somewhat. The troop ceased to shiver, and their spirits began to improve. They grew more and more cheerful and finally began to chaff each other and insult passengers along the highway. This showed that they were awaking to an appreciation of life and its joys once more. The dread in which their sort was held was apparent in the fact that everybody gave them the road and took their ribald insolences meekly, without venturing to talk back. They snatched linen from the hedges occasionally, in full view of the owners, who made no protest but only seemed grateful that they did not take the hedges too.

By and by they invaded a small farmhouse and made themselves at home while the trembling farmer and his people swept the larder clean to furnish a breakfast for them. They chucked the housewife and her daughters under the chin whilst receiving the food from their hands, and made coarse jests about them, accompanied with insulting epithets and bursts of horse-laughter. They threw bones and vegetables at the farmer and his sons, kept them dodging all the time, and applauded uproariously when a good hit was made. They ended by buttering the head of one of the daughters who resented some of their familiarities. When they took their leave they threatened to come back and burn the house over the heads of the family if any report of their doings got to the ears of the authorities.

About noon, after a long and heavy tramp, the gang came to a halt behind a hedge on the outskirts of a considerable village. An hour was allowed for rest, then the crew scattered themselves abroad to enter the village at different points to ply their various trades.

'Jack' was sent with Hugo. They wandered hither and thither for some time, Hugo watching for opportunities to do a stroke of business but finding none; so he finally said, 'I see nought to steal; it is a paltry place. Wherefore we will beg.'

'*We*, forsooth! Follow thy trade – it befits thee. But *I* will not beg.'

'Thou'lt not beg!' exclaimed Hugo, eyeing the king with surprise. 'Prithee, since when hast thou reformed?'

'What dost thou mean?'

'Mean? Hast thou not begged the streets of London all thy life?'

'I? Thou idiot!'

'Spare thy compliments – thy stock will last longer. Thy father says thou hast begged all thy days. Mayhap he lied. Peradventure you will even make so bold as to *say* he lied,' scoffed Hugo.

'Him *you* call my father? Yes, he lied.'

'Come, play not thy merry game of madman so far, mate; use it for thy amusement, not thy hurt. An' I tell him this, he will scorch thee finely for it.'

'Save thyself the trouble. I will tell him.'

'I like thy spirit, I do in truth; but I do not admire thy judgment. Bone-rackings and bastings be plenty enow in this life without going out of one's way to invite them. But a truce to these matters; *I* believe your father. I doubt not he can lie; I doubt not he *doth* lie upon occasion, for the best of us do that; but there is no occasion here. A wise man does not waste so good a commodity as lying for nought. But come; sith it is thy humour to give over begging, wherewithal shall we busy ourselves? With robbing kitchens?'

The king said impatiently, 'Have done with this folly; you weary me!'

Hugo replied with temper, 'Now harkee, mate; you will not beg, you will not rob; so be it. But I will tell you what you *will* do. You will play decoy whilst *I* beg. Refuse, an' you think you may venture!'

The king was about to reply contemptuously when Hugo said, interrupting, 'Peace! Here comes one with a kindly face. Now will I fall down in a fit. When the stranger runs to me, set you up a wail and fall upon your knees, seeming to weep; then cry out as all the devils of misery were in your belly and say, 'Oh, sir, it is my poor afflicted brother, and we be friendless; o' God's name cast through your merciful eyes one pitiful look upon a sick, forsaken, and most miserable wretch; bestow one little penny of thy riches upon one smitten of God and ready to perish!' And mind you, keep you *on* wailing, and abate not till we bilk him of his penny, else shall you rue it.'

Then immediately Hugo began to moan, and groan, and roll his eyes, and reel and totter about; and when the stranger was close at hand, down he sprawled before him, with a shriek, and began to writhe and wallow in the dirt, in seeming agony.

'Oh dear, oh dear!' cried the benevolent stranger. 'Oh, poor soul, poor soul, how he doth suffer! There, let me help thee up.'

'"I am not his brother," said the King interrupting'

'Oh, noble sir, forbear, and God love you for a princely gentleman – but it giveth me cruel pain to touch me when I am taken so. My brother there will tell your worship how I am racked with anguish when these fits be upon me. A penny, dear sir, a penny to buy a little food; then leave me to my sorrows.'

'A penny! Thou shalt have three, thou hapless creature' – and he fumbled in his pocket with nervous haste and got them out. 'There, poor lad, take them, and most welcome. Now come hither, my boy, and help me carry thy stricken brother to yon house, where——'

'I am not his brother,' said the king, interrupting.

'What! Not his brother?'

'Oh, hear him!' groaned Hugo, then privately ground his teeth. 'He denies his own brother – and he with one foot in the grave!'

'Boy, thou art indeed hard of heart if this is thy brother. For shame! And he scarce able to move hand or foot. If he is not thy brother, who is he then?'

'A beggar and a thief! He has got your money and has picked your pocket likewise. An' thou wouldst do a healing miracle, lay thy staff over his shoulders, and trust Providence for the rest.'

But Hugo did not tarry for the miracle. In a moment he was up and off like the wind, the gentleman following after and raising the hue and cry lustily as he went. The king, breathing deep gratitude to heaven for his own release, fled in the opposite direction and did not slacken his pace until he was out of harm's reach. He took the first road that offered and soon put the village behind him. He hurried along as briskly as he could during several hours, keeping a nervous watch over his shoulder for pursuit; but his fears left him at last, and a grateful sense of security took their place. He recognized now that he was hungry, and also very tired. So he halted at a farmhouse, but when he was about to speak he was cut short and driven rudely away. His clothes were against him.

He wandered on, wounded and indignant, and was resolved to put himself in the way of like treatment no more. But hunger is pride's master; so as the evening drew near, he made an attempt at another farmhouse, but here he fared worse than before, for he was called hard names and was promised arrest as a vagrant except he moved on promptly.

The night came on, chilly and overcast; and still the footsore monarch laboured slowly on. He was obliged to keep moving, for every time he sat down to rest he was soon penetrated to the bone with the cold. All his sensations and experiences as he moved through the solemn gloom and the empty vastness of the night were new and strange to him. At intervals he heard voices approach, pass by, and fade into silence; and as he saw nothing more of the bodies they belonged to than a sort of formless drifting blur, there was something spectral and uncanny about it all that made him shudder. Occasionally he caught the twinkle of a light – always far away apparently, almost in another world; if he heard the tinkle of a sheep's bell, it was vague, distant, indistinct; the muffled lowing of the herds floated to him on the night wind in vanishing cadences, a mournful sound; now and then came the complaining howl of a dog over viewless expanses of field and forest; all sounds were remote; they made the little king feel that all life and activity were far removed from him and that he stood solitary, companionless, in the centre of a measureless solitude.

He stumbled along through the gruesome fascinations of this new experience, startled occasionally by the soft rustling of the dry leaves overhead, so like human whispers they seemed to sound; and by and by he came suddenly upon the freckled light of a tin lantern near at hand. He stepped back into the shadows and waited. The lantern stood by the open door of a barn. The king waited some time; there was no sound, and nobody stirring. He got so cold, standing still, and the hospitable barn looked so enticing that at last he resolved to risk everything and enter. He started swiftly and stealthily, and just as he was crossing the threshold he heard voices behind him. He darted behind a cask within the barn and stooped down. Two farm labourers came in, bringing the lantern with them, and fell to work, talking meanwhile. Whilst they moved about with the light, the king made good use of his eyes and took the bearings of what seemed to be a good-sized stall at the further end of the place, purposing to grope his way to it when he should be left to himself. He also noted the position of a pile of horse blankets, midway of the route, with the intent to levy upon them for the service of the Crown of England for one night.

By and by the men finished and went away, fastening the door behind them and taking the lantern with them. The shivering king made for the blankets with as good speed as the darkness would allow, gathered them up, and then groped his way safely to the stall. Of two of the blankets he made a bed, then covered himself with the remaining two. He was a glad monarch now, though the blankets were old and thin and not quite warm enough, and besides, gave out a pungent horsey odour that was almost suffocatingly powerful.

Although the king was hungry and chilly, he was also so tired and so drowsy that these latter influences soon began to get the advantage of the former, and he presently dozed off into a state of semi-consciousness. Then, just as he was on the point of losing himself wholly, he distinctly felt something touching him! He was broad awake in a moment, and gasping for breath. The cold horror of that mysterious touch in the dark almost made his heart stand still. He lay motionless and listened, scarcely breathing. But nothing stirred, and there was no sound. He continued to listen and wait during what seemed a long time, but still nothing stirred, and there was no sound. So he began to drop into a drowse once more at last; and all at once he felt that mysterious touch again! It was a grisly thing, this light touch from this noiseless and invisible presence; it made the boy sick with ghostly fears. What should he do? That was the question, but he did not know how to answer it. Should he leave these reasonably comfortable quarters and fly from this inscrutable horror? But fly whither? He could not get out of the barn, and the idea of scurrying blindly hither and thither in the dark within the captivity of the four walls, with this phantom gliding after him and visiting him with that soft, hideous touch upon cheek or shoulder at every turn, was intolerable. But to stay where he was and endure this living death all night? Was that better? No. What, then, was there left to do? Ah, there was but one course; he knew it well – he must put out his hand and find that thing!

It was easy to think this, but it was hard to brace himself up to try it. Three times he stretched his hand a little way out into the dark, gingerly, and snatched it suddenly back, with a gasp – not because it had encountered anything, but because he had felt so sure it was just *going* to. But the fourth time, he groped a little further, and his hand lightly swept against something soft and warm. This petrified him, nearly, with fright; his mind was in such a state that he could imagine the thing to be nothing else than a corpse newly dead and still warm. He thought he would rather die than touch it again. But he thought this false thought because he did not know the immortal strength of human curiosity. In no long time his hand was tremblingly groping again – against his judgment, and without his consent, but groping persistently on just the same. It encountered a bunch of long hair; he shuddered, but followed up the hair and found what seemed to be a warm rope; followed up the rope and found an innocent calf! For the rope was not a rope at all, but a calf's tail.

The king was cordially ashamed of himself for having got all that fright and misery out of so paltry a matter as a slumbering calf; but he need not have felt so about it, for it was not the calf that frightened him but a dreadful non-existent something which the calf stood for; and any other boy in those superstitious times would have acted and suffered just as he had done.

The king was not only delighted to find that the creature was only a calf, but delighted to have the calf's company, for he had been feeling so lonesome and friendless that the company and comradeship of even this humble animal was welcome. And he had been so buffeted, so rudely entreated by his own kind, that it was a real comfort to him to feel that he was at last in the society of a fellow creature that had at least a soft heart and a gentle spirit, whatever loftier attributes might be lacking. So he resolved to waive rank and make friends with the calf.

While stroking its sleek warm back – for it lay near him and within easy reach – it occurred to him that this calf might be utilized in more ways than one. Whereupon he rearranged his bed, spreading it down close to the calf;

then he cuddled himself up to the calf's back, drew the covers up over himself and his friend, and in a minute or two was as warm and comfortable as he had ever been in the downy couches of the regal palace of Westminster.

Pleasant thoughts came at once; life took on a cheerfuller seeming. He was free of the bonds of servitude and crime, free of the companionship of base and brutal outlaws; he was warm, he was sheltered; in a word, he was happy. The night wind was rising; it swept by in fitful gusts that made the old barn quake and rattle; then its forces died down at intervals and went moaning and wailing around corners and projections; but it was all music to the king, now that he was snug and comfortable: let it blow and rage, let it batter and bang, let it moan and wail, he minded it not, he only enjoyed it. He merely snuggled the closer to his friend, in a luxury of warm contentment, and drifted blissfully out of consciousness into a deep and dreamless sleep that was full of serenity and peace. The distant dogs howled, the melancholy kine complained, and the winds went on raging, whilst furious sheets of rain drove along the roof; but the Majesty of England slept on, undisturbed, and the calf did the same, it being a simple creature and not easily troubled by storms or embarrassed by sleeping with a king.

19 The Prince with the Peasants

When the king awoke in the early morning, he found that a wet but thoughtful rat had crept into the place during the night and made a cosy bed for itself in his bosom. Being disturbed now, it scampered away. The boy smiled and said, 'Poor fool, why so fearful? I am as forlorn as thou. 'Twould be a shame in me to hurt the helpless, who am myself so helpless. Moreover, I owe you thanks for a good omen; for when a king has fallen so low that the very rats do make a bed of him, it surely meaneth that his fortunes be upon the turn, since it is plain he can no lower go.'

He got up and stepped out of the stall, and just then he heard the sound of children's voices. The barn door opened and a couple of little girls came in. As soon as they saw him their talking and laughing ceased, and they stopped and stood still, gazing at him with strong curiosity; they presently began to whisper together, then they approached nearer, and stopped again to gaze and whisper. By and by they gathered courage and began to discuss him aloud. One said, 'He hath a comely face.'

The other added, 'And pretty hair.'

'But is ill-clothed enow.'

'And how starved he looketh.'

They came still nearer, sidling shyly around and about him, examining him minutely from all points as if he were some strange new kind of animal, but warily and watchfully the while, as if they half feared he might be a sort of animal that would bite upon occasion. Finally they halte before him, holding each other's hands for protection, and took a good satisfying stare with their innocent eyes; then one of them plucked up all her courage and inquired with honest directness, 'Who art thou, boy?'

'I am the king,' was the grave answer.

The children gave a little start, and their eyes spread themselves wide open and remained so during a speechless half minute. Then curiosity broke the silence. 'The *king*? What king?'

'The king of England.'

The children looked at each other, then at him, then at each other again – wonderingly, perplexedly; then one said, 'Didst hear him, Margery? He saith he is the king. Can that be true?'

'How can it be else but true, Prissy? Would he say a lie? For look you, Prissy, an' it were not true, it *would* be a lie. It surely would be. Now think on't. For all things that be not true be lies; thou canst make nought else out of it.'

It was a good tight argument, without a leak in it anywhere; and it left Prissy's half doubts not a leg to stand on. She considered a moment, then put the king upon his honour with the simple remark, 'If thou art truly the king, then I believe thee.'

'I am truly the king.'

This settled the matter. His Majesty's royalty was accepted without further question or discussion, and the two little girls began at once to inquire into how he came to be where he was, and how he came to be so unroyally clad, and whither he was bound, and all about his affairs. It was a mighty relief to him to pour out his troubles where they would not be scoffed at or doubted, so he told his tale with feeling, forgetting even his hunger for the time; and it was received with the deepest and tenderest sympathy by the gentle little maids. But when he got down to his latest experiences and they learned how long he had been without food, they cut him short and hurried him away to the farmhouse to find a breakfast for him.

The king was cheerful and happy now and said to himself, 'When I am come to mine own again, I will always honour little children, remembering how that these trusted me and believed in me in my time of trouble, whilst they that were older and thought themselves wiser mocked at me and held me for a liar.'

The children's mother received the king kindly and was full of pity, for his forlorn condition and apparently crazed intellect touched her womanly heart. She was a widow and rather poor; consequently she had seen trouble enough to enable her to feel for the unfortunate. She imagined that the demented boy had wandered away from his friends or keepers, so she tried to find out whence he had come in order that she might take measures to return him; but all her references to neighbouring towns and villages, and all her inquiries in the same line, went for nothing: the boy's face, and his answers too, showed that the things she was talking of were not familiar to him. He spoke earnestly and simply about court matters and broke down more than once when speaking of the late king 'his father'; but whenever the conversation changed to baser topics, he lost interest and became silent.

The woman was mightily puzzled, but she did not give up. As she proceeded with her cooking, she set herself to contriving devices to surprise the boy into betraying his real secret. She talked about cattle – he showed no concern; then about sheep – the same result, so her guess that he had been a shepherd boy was an error; she talked about mills; and about weavers, tinkers, smiths, trades, and tradesmen of all sorts; and about Bedlam, and jails, and charitable retreats; but no matter, she was baffled at all points. Not altogether, either, for she argued that she had narrowed the thing down to domestic service. Yes, she was sure she was on the right track now; he must have been a house servant. So she led up to that. But the result was discouraging. The subject of sweeping appeared to weary him; firebuilding failed to stir him; scrubbing and scouring awoke no enthusiasm. Then the goodwife touched, with a perishing hope, and rather as a matter of form, upon the subject of cooking. To her surprise and her vast delight, the king's face lighted at once! Ah, she had hunted him down at last, she thought; and she was right proud too of the devious shrewdness and tact which had accomplished it.

Her tired tongue got a chance to rest now, for the king's, inspired by gnawing hunger and the fragrant smells that came from the sputtering pots and pans, turned itself loose and delivered itself up to such an eloquent dissertation upon certain toothsome dishes that within three minutes the woman said to herself, 'Of a truth I was right – he hath holpen in a kitchen!' Then he broadened his bill of fare, and discussed it with such appreciation and animation that the goodwife said to herself, 'Good lack! How can he know so many dishes, and so fine ones withal? For these belong only upon the tables of the rich and great. Ah, now I see! Ragged outcast as he is, he must have served in the palace before his reason went astray; yes, he must have helped in the very kitchen of the king himself! I will test him.'

Full of eagerness to prove her sagacity, she told the king to mind the cooking a moment, hinting that he might manufacture and add a dish or two if he chose; then she went out of the room and gave her children a sign to follow after. The king muttered, 'Another English king had a commission like to this in a bygone time; it is nothing against my dignity to undertake an office which the great Alfred stooped to assume. But I will try to better serve my trust than he, for he let the cakes burn.'

The intent was good, but the performance was not answerable to it; for this king, like the other one, soon fell into deep thinkings concerning his vast affairs, and the same calamity resulted – the cookery got burned. The woman returned in time to save the breakfast from entire destruction, and she promptly brought the king out of his dreams with a brisk and cordial tongue-lashing. Then, seeing how troubled he was over his violated trust, she softened at once and was all goodness and gentleness toward him.

The boy made a hearty and satisfying meal, and was greatly refreshed and gladdened by it. It was a meal which was distinguished by this curious feature, that rank was waived on both sides; yet neither recipient of the favour was aware that it had been extended. The goodwife had intended to feed this young tramp with broken victuals in a corner like any other tramp or like a dog, but she was so remorseful for the scolding she had given him that she did what she could to atone for it by allowing him to sit at the family table and eat with his betters, on ostensible terms of equality with them; and the king, on his side, was so remorseful for having broken his trust after the family had been so kind to him that he forced himself to atone for it by humbling himself to the family level, instead of requiring the woman and her children to stand and wait upon him while he occupied their table in the solitary state due his birth and dignity. It does us all good to unbend sometimes. This good woman was made happy all the day long by the applauses which she got out of herself for her magnanimous condescension to a tramp, and the king was just as self-complacent over his gracious humility toward a humble peasant woman.

When breakfast was over, the housewife told the king to wash up the dishes. This command was a staggerer for a moment, and the king came near rebelling; but then he said to himself, 'Alfred the Great watched the cakes; doubtless he would have washed the dishes too; therefore will I essay it.'

He made a sufficiently poor job of it; and to his surprise too, for the cleaning of wooden spoons and trenchers had seemed an easy thing to do. It was a tedious and troublesome piece of work, but he finished it at last. He was becoming impatient to get away on his journey now; however, he was not to lose this thrifty dame's society so easily. She furnished him some little odds and ends of employment, which he got through with after a fair fashion and with some credit. Then she set him and the little girl to paring some winter apples, but he was so awkward at this service that she retired him from it and gave him a butcher knife to grind. Afterward she kept him carding wool until he began to think he had laid the good king Alfred about far enough in the shade for the present in the matter of showy menial heroisms that would read picturesquely in storybooks and histories, and so he was half minded to resign. And when, just after the noonday dinner, the goodwife gave him a basket of kittens to drown, he did resign. At least he was just going to resign – for he felt that he must draw the line somewhere, and it seemed to him that to draw it at kitten drowning was about the right thing – when there was an interruption. The interruption was John Canty, with a peddler's pack on his back, and Hugo!

The king discovered these rascals approaching the front gate before they had had a chance to see him; so he said nothing about drawing the line, but took up his basket of kittens and stepped quietly out the back way, without a word. He left the creatures in an outhouse and hurried on into a narrow lane at the rear.

20 The Prince and the Hermit

The high hedge hid him from the house now, and so under the impulse of a deadly fright he let out all his forces and sped toward a wood in the distance. He never looked back until he had almost gained the shelter of the forest; then he turned and descried two figures in the distance. That was sufficient; he did not wait to scan them critically, but hurried on, and never abated his pace till he was far within the twilight depths of the wood. Then he stopped, being persuaded that he was now tolerably safe. He listened intently, but the stillness was profound and solemn – awful, even, and depressing to the spirits. At wide intervals his straining ear did detect sounds, but they were so remote, and hollow, and mysterious that they seemed not to be real sounds, but only the moaning and complaining ghosts of departed ones. So the sounds were yet more dreary than the silence which they interrupted.

It was his purpose, in the beginning, to stay where he was the rest of the day; but a chill soon invaded his perspiring body, and he was at last obliged to resume movement in order to get warm. He struck straight through the forest, hoping to pierce to a road presently, but he was disappointed in this. He travelled on and on, but the farther he went, the denser the wood became apparently. The gloom began to thicken by and by, and the king realized that the night was coming on. It made him shudder to think of spending it in such an uncanny place; so he tried to hurry faster, but he only made the less speed, for he could not now see well enough to choose his steps judiciously; consequently he kept tripping over roots and tangling himself in vines and briers.

And how glad he was when at last he caught the glimmer of a light! He approached it warily, stopping often to look about him and listen. It came from an unglazed window opening in a shabby little hut. He heard a voice now and felt a disposition to run and hide; but he changed his mind at once, for this voice was praying evidently. He glided to the one window of the hut, raised himself on tiptoes, and stole a glance within. The room was small; its floor was the natural earth, beaten hard by use; in a corner was a bed of rushes and a ragged blanket or two; near it was a pail, a cup, a basin, and two or three pots and pans; there was a short bench and a three-legged stool; on the hearth the remains of a fagot fire were smouldering; before a shrine, which was lighted by a single candle, knelt an aged man; and on an old wooden box at his side lay an open book and a human skull. The man was of large, bony frame; his hair and whiskers were very long and snowy white; he was clothed in a robe of sheepskins which reached from his neck to his heels.

'A holy hermit!' said the king to himself. 'Now am I indeed fortunate.'

The hermit rose from his knees; the king knocked. A deep voice responded, 'Enter! But leave sin behind, for the ground whereon thou shalt stand is holy!'

The king entered and paused. The hermit turned a pair of gleaming, unrestful eyes upon him and said, 'Who art thou?'

'I am the king,' came the answer, with placid simplicity.

'Welcome, king!' cried the hermit with enthusiasm. Then, bustling about with feverish activity and constantly saying 'Welcome, welcome,' he arranged his bench, seated the king on it, by the hearth, threw some fagots on the fire, and finally fell to pacing the floor with a nervous stride.

'Welcome! Many have sought sanctuary here, but they were not worthy, and were turned away. But a king who casts his crown away, and despises the vain splendours of his office, and clothes his body in rags to devote his life to holiness and the mortification of the flesh – he is worthy, he is welcome! Here shall he abide all his days till death come.' The king hastened to interrupt and explain, but the hermit paid no attention to him, did not even hear him apparently, but went right on with his talk with a raised voice and a growing energy. 'And thou shalt be at peace here. None shall find out thy refuge to disquiet thee with supplications to return to that empty and foolish life which God hath moved thee to abandon. Thou shalt pray here; thou shalt study the Book; thou shalt meditate upon the follies and delusions of this world, and upon the sublimities of the world to come; thou shalt feed upon crusts and herbs, and scourge thy body with whips daily to the purifying of thy soul. Thou shalt wear a hair shirt next thy skin; thou shalt drink water only; and thou shalt be at peace, yes, wholly at peace, for whoso comes to seek thee shall go his way again, baffled; he shall not find thee, he shall not molest thee.'

The old man, still pacing back and forth, ceased to speak aloud and began to mutter. The king seized this opportunity to state his case, and he did it with an eloquence inspired by uneasiness and apprehension. But the hermit went on muttering and gave no heed. And still muttering, he approached the king and said impressively, 'Sh! I will tell you a secret!' He bent down to impart it, but checked himself and assumed a listening attitude. After a moment or two he went on tiptoe to the window opening, put his head out and peered around in the gloaming, then came tiptoeing back again, put his face close down to the king's, and whispered, 'I am an archangel!'

The king started violently and said to himself, 'Would God I were with the outlaws again; for lo, now am I the prisoner of a madman!' His apprehensions were heightened, and they showed plainly in his face.

In a low, excited voice the hermit continued, 'I see you feel my atmosphere! There's awe in your face! None may be in this atmosphere and not be thus affected, for it is the very atmosphere of heaven. I go thither and return in the twinkling of an eye. I was made an archangel on this very spot, it is five years ago, by angels sent from heaven to confer that awful dignity. Their presence filled this place with an intolerable brightness. And they knelt to me, king! Yes, they knelt to me! For I was greater than they. I have walked in the courts of heaven and held speech with the patriarchs. Touch my hand – be not afraid – touch it. There, now thou hast touched a hand which has been clasped by Abraham and Isaac and Jacob! For I have walked in the golden courts, I have seen the Deity face to face!' He paused to give this speech effect; then his face suddenly changed, and he started to his feet again, saying with angry energy, 'Yes, I am an archangel, *a mere archangel*! I that might have been pope! It is verily true. I was told it from heaven in a dream twenty years ago; ah, yes, I was to be pope! And I *should* have been pope, for heaven had said it, but the king dissolved my religious house, and I, poor, obscure, unfriended monk, was cast homeless upon the world, robbed of my mighty destiny!' Here he began to mumble again and beat his forehead in futile rage with his fist, now and then articulating a venomous curse, and now and then a pathetic, 'Wherefore I am nought but an archangel – I that should have been pope!'

So he went on for an hour, whilst the poor little king sat and suffered. Then all at once the old man's frenzy departed and he became all gentleness. His voice softened, he came down out of his clouds and fell to prattling along so simply and so humanly that he soon won the king's heart completely. The old devotee moved the boy nearer to the fire and made him comfortable, doctored his small bruises and abrasions with a deft and tender hand, and then set about preparing and cooking a supper, chatting pleasantly all the time and occasionally stroking the lad's cheek or patting his head in such a gently caressing way that in a little while all the fear and repulsion inspired by the archangel were changed to reverence and affection for the man.

This happy state of things continued while the two ate the supper; then, after a prayer before the shrine, the hermit put the boy to bed in a small adjoining room, tucking him in as snugly and lovingly as a mother might; and so, with a parting caress, left him and sat down by the fire and began to poke the brands about in an absent and aimless way. Presently he paused, then tapped his forehead several times with his fingers as if trying to recall some thought which had escaped from his mind. Apparently he was unsuccessful. Now he started quickly up and entered his guest's room and said, 'Thou art king?'

'Yes,' was the response drowsily uttered.

'What king?'

'Of England.'

'Of England! Then Henry is gone!'

'Alack, it is so. I am his son.'

A black frown settled down upon the hermit's face, and he clenched his bony hands with a vindictive energy. He stood a few moments, breathing fast and swallowing repeatedly, then said in a husky voice, 'Dost know it was he that turned us out into the world houseless and homeless?'

There was no response. The old man bent down and scanned the boy's reposeful face and listened to his placid breathing. 'He sleeps – sleeps soundly'; and the frown vanished away and gave place to an expression of evil satisfaction. A smile flitted across the dreaming boy's features. The hermit muttered, 'So, his heart is happy,' and he turned away. He went stealthily about the place, seeking here and there for something, now and then halting to listen, now and then jerking his head around and casting a quick glance toward the bed, and always muttering, always mumbling to himself. At last he found what he seemed to want – a rusty old butcher's knife and a whetstone. Then he crept to his place by the fire, sat himself down, and began to whet the knife softly on the stone, still muttering, mumbling, ejaculating. The winds sighed around the lonely place, the mysterious voices of the night floated by out of the distances. The shining eyes of venturesome mice and rats peered out at the old man from cracks and coverts, but he went on with his work, rapt absorbed, and noted none of these things.

At long intervals he drew his thumb along the edge of his knife and nodded his head with satisfaction. 'It grows sharper,' he said; 'yes, it grows sharper.'

He took no note of the flight of time, but worked tranquilly on, entertaining himself with his thoughts, which broke out occasionally in articulate speech: 'His father wrought us evil, he destroyed us – and is gone down into the eternal fires! Yes, down in to the eternal fires! He escaped us, but it was God's will, yes, it was God's will, we must not repine. But he hath not escaped the fires! No, he hath not escaped the fires, the consuming, unpitying, remorseless fires – and *they* are everlasting!'

And so he wrought, and still wrought, mumbling – chuckling a low rasping chuckle at times, and at times breaking again into words: 'It was his father that did it all. I am but an archangel; but for him, I should be pope!'

The king stirred. The hermit sprang noiselessly to the bedside and went down upon his knees, bending over the prostrate form with his knife uplifted. The boy stirred again; his eyes came open for an instant, but there was no speculation in them, they saw nothing; the next moment his tranquil breathing showed that his sleep was sound once more.

The hermit watched and listened for a time, keeping his position and scarcely breathing; then he slowly lowered his arm and presently crept away, saying, 'It is long past midnight; it is not best that he should cry out, lest by accident someone be passing.'

He glided about his hovel, gathering a rag here, a thong there, and another one yonder; then he returned, and by careful and gentle handling he managed to tie the king's ankles together without waking him. Next he essayed to tie the wrists; he made several attempts to cross them, but the boy always drew one hand or the other away just as the cord was ready to be applied; but at last, when the archangel was almost ready to despair, the boy crossed his hands himself, and the next moment they were bound. Now a bandage was passed under the sleeper's chin and brought up over his head and tied vast; and so softly, so gradually, and so deftly were the knots drawn together and compacted that the boy slept peacefully through it all without stirring.

21 Hendon to the Rescue

The old man glided away, stooping, stealthy, catlike, and brought the low bench. He seated himself upon it, half his body in the dim and flickering light and the other half in shadow; and so, with his craving eyes bent upon the slumbering boy, he kept his patient vigil there, heedless of the drift of time, and softly whetted his knife and mumbled and chuckled; and in aspect and attitude he resembled nothing so much as a grisly, monstrous spider gloating over some hapless insect that lay bound and helpless in his web.

After a long while the old man, who was still gazing, yet not seeing, his mind having settled into a dreamy abstraction, observed on a sudden that the boy's eyes were open – wide open and staring, staring up in frozen horror at the knife! The smile of a gratified devil crept over the old man's face, and he said, without changing his attitude or his occupation, 'Son of Henry the Eighth, hast thou prayed?'

The boy struggled helplessly in his bonds and at the same time forced a smothered sound through his closed jaws, which the hermit chose to interpret as an affirmative answer to his question.

'Then pray again. Pray the prayer for the dying!'

A shudder shook the boy's frame, and his face blenched. Then he struggled again to free himself, turning and twisting himself this way and tat, tugging frantically, fiercely, desperately – but uselessly – to burst his fetters; and all the while, the old ogre smiled down upon him, and nodded his head, and placidly whetted his knife, mumbling from time to time. 'The moments are precious; they are few and precious; pray the prayer for the dying!'

The boy uttered a despairing groan and ceased from his struggles, panting. The tears came then and trickled, one after the other, down his face; but this piteous sight wrought no softening effect upon the savage old man.

The dawn was coming now; the hermit observed it and spoke up sharply with a touch of nervous apprehension in his voice, 'I may not indulge this ecstasy longer! The night is already gone. It seems but a moment, only a moment; would it had endured a year! Seed of the Church's spoiler, close thy perishing eyes, an' thou fearest to look upon——'

The rest was lost in inarticulate mutterings. The old man sunk upon his knees, his knife in his hand, and bent himself over the moaning boy.

Hark! There was a sound of voices near the cabin; the knife dropped from the hermit's hand; he cast a sheepskin over the boy and started up, trembling. The sounds increased, and presently the voices became rough and angry; then came blows, and cries for help; then a clatter of swift footsteps retreating. Immediately came a succession of thundering knocks upon the cabin door, followed by, 'Hullo-o-o! Open! And dispatch, in the name of all the devils!'

Oh, this was the blessedest sound that had ever made music in the king's ears, for it was Miles Hendon's voice!

The hermit, grinding his teeth in impotent rage, moved swiftly out of the bedchamber, closing the door behind him; and straightway the king heard a talk to this effect proceeding from the 'chapel':

'Homage and greeting, reverend sir! Where is the boy – *my* boy?'

'What boy, friend?'

'What boy! Lie me no lies, sir priest, play me no deceptions! I am not in the humour for it. Near to this place I caught the scoundrels who I judged did steal him from me, and I made them confess; they said he was at large again, and they had tracked him to your door. They showed me his very footprints. Now palter no more; for look you, holy sir, an' thou produce him not—— Where is the boy?'

'Oh, good sir, peradventure you mean the ragged regal vagrant that tarried here the night. If such as you take interest in such as he, know then that I have sent him of an errand. He will be back anon.'

'How soon? How soon? Come, waste not the time; cannot I overtake him? How soon will he be back?'

'Thou needst not stir; he will return quickly.'

'So be it then. I will try to wait. But stop! *You* sent him of an errand? You! Verily this is a lie – he would not go. He would pull thy old beard, an' thou didst offer him such an insolence. Thou hast lied, friend; thou hast surely lied! He would not go for thee nor for any man.'

'For any *man*, no; haply not. But I am not a man.'

'*What*! Now o' God's name what art thou then?'

'It is a secret; mark thou reveal it not. I am an archangel!'

There was a tremendous ejaculation from Miles Hendon – not altogether unprofane – followed by, 'This doth well and truly account for his complaisance! Right well I knew he would budge nor hand nor foot in the menial service of any mortal; but lord, even a king must obey when an archangel gives the word o' command! Let me—— sh! What noise was that?'

All this while the little king had been yonder, alternately quaking with terror and trembling with hope; and all the while too he had thrown all the strength he could into his anguished moanings, constantly expecting them to reach Hendon's ear but always realizing, with bitterness, that they failed, or at least made no impression. So this last remark of his servant came as comes a reviving breath from fresh fields to the dying; and he exerted himself once more, and with all his energy, just as the hermit was saying, 'Noise? I hear only the wind.'

'Mayhap it was. Yes, doubtless that was it. I have been hearing it faintly all the—— There it is again! It is not the wind! What an odd sound! Come, we will hunt it out!'

Now the king's joy was nearly insupportable. His tired lungs did their utmost – and hopefully, too – but the sealed jaws and the muffling sheepskin sadly crippled the effort. Then the poor fellow's heart sank to hear the hermit say, 'Ah, it came from without – I think from the copse yonder. Come, I will lead the way.'

The king heard the two pass out, talking; heard their footsteps die quickly away; then he was alone with a boding, brooding, awful silence.

It seemed an age till he heard the steps and voices approaching again, and this time he heard an added sound – the trampling of hoofs apparently. Then he heard Hendon say, 'I will not wait longer. I *cannot* wait longer. He has lost his way in this thick wood. Which direction took he? Quick, point it out to me.'

'He—— But wait; I will go with thee.'

'Good – good! Why, truly thou art better than thy looks. Marry I do not think there's not another archangel with so right a heart as thine. Wilt ride? Wilt take the wee donkey that's for my boy, or wilt thou fork thy holy legs over this ill-conditioned slave of a mule that I have provided for myself? And had been cheated in too, had he cost but the indifferent sum of a month's usury on a brass farthing let to a tinker out of work.'

'No, ride thy mule and lead thine ass; I am surer on mine own feet and will walk.'

'Then prithee mind the little beast for me while I take my life in my hands and make what success I may toward mounting the big one.'

Then followed a confusion of kicks, cuffs, tramplings, and plungings, accompanied by a thunderous intermingling of volleyed curses, and finally a bitter apostrophe to the mule, which must have broken its spirit, for hostilities seemed to cease from that moment.

With unutterable misery the fettered little king heard the voices and footsteps fade away and die out. All hope forsook him now for the moment, and a dull despair settled down upon his heart. 'My only friend is deceived and got rid of,' he said; 'the hermit will return and——' He finished with a gasp, and at once fell to struggling so frantically with his bonds again that he shook off the smothering sheepskin.

And now he heard the door open! The sound chilled him to the marrow;

already he seemed to feel the knife at his throat. Horror made him close his eyes; horror made him open them again – and before him stood John Canty and Hugo!

He would have said, 'Thank God!' if his jaws had been free.

A moment or two later his limbs were at liberty, and his captors, each gripping him by an arm, were hurrying him with all speed through the forest.

22 A Victim of Treachery

Once more 'King Foo-foo the First' was roving with the tramps and outlaws, a butt for their coarse jests and dull-witted railleries, and sometimes the victim of small spitefulnesses at the hands of Canty and Hugo when the Ruffler's back was turned. None but Canty and Hugo really disliked him. Some of the others liked him, and all admired his pluck and spirit. During two or three days, Hugo, in whose ward and charge the king was, did what he covertly could to make the boy uncomfortable; and at night, during the customary orgies, he amused the company by putting small indignities upon him – always as if by accident. Twice he stepped upon the king's toes – accidentally – and the king, as became his royalty, was contemptuously unconscious of it and indifferent to it; but the third time Hugo entertained himself in that way, the king felled him to the ground with a cudgel, to the prodigious delight of the tribe. Hugo, consumed with anger and shame, sprang up, seized a cudgel, and came at his small adversary in a fury. Instantly a ring was formed around the gladiators, and the betting and cheering began. But poor Hugo stood no chance whatever. His frantic and lubberly 'prenticework found but a poor market for itself when pitted against an arm which had been trained by the first masters of Europe in single-stick, quarter-staff, and every art and trick of swordmanship. The little king stood, alert but at graceful ease, and caught and turned aside the thick rain of blows with a facility and precision which set the motley onlookers wild with admiration; and every now and then, when his practised eye detected an opening, and a lightning-swift rap upon Hugo's head followed as a result, the storm of cheers and laughter that swept the place was something wonderful to hear. At the end of fifteen minutes, Hugo, all battered, bruised, and the target for a pitiless bombardment of ridicule, slunk from the field; and the unscathed hero of the fight was seized and borne aloft upon the shoulders of the joyous rabble to the place of honour beside the Ruffler, where with vast ceremony he was crowned king of the Gamecocks, his meaner title being at the same time solemnly cancelled and annulled, and a decree of banishment from the gang pronounced against any who should thenceforth utter it.

All attempts to make the king serviceable to the troop had failed. He had stubbornly refused to act; moreover, he was always trying to escape. He had been thrust into an unwatched kitchen the first day of his return; he not only came forth empty-handed, but tried to rouse the house-mates. He was sent out with a tinker to help him at his work; he would not work; moreover, he threatened the tinker with his own soldering iron; and finally both Hugo and the tinker found their hands full with the mere matter of keeping him from getting away. He delivered the thunders of his royalty upon the heads of all who hampered his liberties or tried to force him to service. He was sent out, in Hugo's charge, in company with a slatternly woman and a diseased baby to beg; but the result was not encouraging: he declined to plead for the mendicants or be a party to their cause in any way.

Thus several days went by; and the miseries of this tramping life, and the weariness and sordidness and meanness and vulgarity of it, became gradually and steadily so intolerable to the captive that he began at last to feel that his release from the hermit's knife must prove only a temporary respite from death at best.

But at night, in his dreams, these things were forgotten, and he was on his throne, and master again. This, of course, intensified the sufferings of the awakening, so the mortifications of each succeeding morning of the few that passed between his return to bondage and the combat with Hugo grew bitterer and bitterer, and harder and harder to bear.

The morning after that combat, Hugo got up with a heart filled with vengeful purposes against the king. He had two plans in particular. One was to inflict upon the lad what would be, to his proud spirit and 'imagined' royalty, a peculiar humiliation; and if he failed to accomplish this, his other plan was to put a crime of some kind upon the king and then betray him into the implacable clutches of the law.

In pursuance of the first plan, he purposed to put a 'clime' upon the king's leg, rightly judging that that would mortify him to the last and perfect degree; and as soon as the clime should operate, he meant to get Canty's help, and *force* the king to expose his leg in the highway and beg for alms. 'Clime' was the cant term for a sore artificially created. To make a clime, the operator made a paste or poultice of unslaked lime, soap, and the rust of old iron, and spread it upon a piece of leather, which was then bound tightly upon the leg. This would presently fret off the skin and make the flesh raw and angry looking; blood was then rubbed upon the limb, which being fully dried, took on a dark and repulsive colour. Then a bandage of soiled rags was put on in a cleverly careless way which would allow the hideous ulcer to be seen and move the compassion of the passer-by.[1]

Hugo got the help of the tinker whom the king had cowed with the soldering iron; they took the boy on a tinkering tramp, and as soon as they were out of sight of the camp they threw him down and the tinker held him while Hugo bound the poultice tight and fast upon his leg.

The king raged and stormed and promised to hang the two the moment the sceptre was in his hand again, but they kept a firm grip upon him and enjoyed his impotent struggling and jeered at his threats. This continued until the poultice began to bite, and in no long time its work would have been perfected if there had been no interruption. But there was, for about this time the 'slave' who had made the speech denouncing England's laws appeared on the scene and put an end to the enterprise and stripped off the poultice and bandage.

The king wanted to borrow his deliverer's cudgel and warm the jackets of the two rascals on the spot; but the man said no, it would bring trouble – leave the matter till night; the whole tribe being together then, the outside world would not venture to interfere or interrupt. He marched the party back to camp and reported the affair to the Ruffler, who listened, pondered, and then decided that the king should not be again detailed to beg, since it was plain he was worthy of something higher and better, wherefore, on the spot he promoted him from the mendicant rank and appointed him to steal!

Hugo was overjoyed. He had already tried to make the king steal and failed, but there would be no more trouble of that sort now, for of course the king would not dream of defying a distinct command delivered directly from headquarters. So he planned a raid for that very afternoon, purposing to get the king in the law's grip in the course of it; and to do it, too, with such ingenious strategy that it should seem to be accidental and unintentional, for the king of the Gamecocks was popular now, and the gang might not deal over gently with an unpopular member who played so serious a treachery upon him as the delivering him over to the common enemy, the law.

Very well. All in good time Hugo strolled off to a neighbouring village with his prey; and the two drifted slowly up and down one street after another, the one watching sharply for a sure chance to achieve his evil purpose, and the other watching as sharply for a chance to dart away and get free of his infamous captivity forever.

Both threw away some tolerably fair-looking opportunities; for both, in their secret hearts, were resolved to make absolutely sure work this time, and neither meant to allow his fevered desires to seduce him into any venture that had much uncertainty about it.

Hugo's chance came first. For at last a woman approached who carried a fat package of some sort in a basket. Hugo's eyes sparkled with sinful pleasure as he said to himself, 'Breath o' my life an' I can but put *that* upon him, 'tis good den and God keep thee, king of the Gamecocks!' He waited and watched, outwardly patient but inwardly consuming with excitement, till the woman had passed by and the time was ripe; then said in a low voice, 'Tarry here till I come again,' and darted stealthily after the prey.

The king's heart was filled with joy: he could make his escape now if

'Hugo thrust the bundle into the King's hands without halting'

Hugo's quest only carried him far enough away.

But he was to have no such luck. Hugo crept behind the woman, snatched the package, and came running back, wrapping it in an old piece of blanket which he carried on his arm. The hue and cry was raised in a moment by the woman, who knew her loss by the lightening of her burden, although she had not seen the pilfering done. Hugo thrust the bundle into the king's hands without halting, saying 'Now speed ye after me with the rest, and cry 'Stop, thief!' but mind ye lead them astray!'

The next moment Hugo turned a corner and darted down a crooked alley, and in another moment or two he lounged into view again, looking innocent and indifferent, and took up a position behind a post to watch results.

The insulted king threw the bundle on the ground, and the blanket fell away from it just as the woman arrived with an augmenting crowd at her heels; she seized the king's wrist with one hand, snatched up her bundle with the other, and began to pour out a tirade of abuse upon the boy while he struggled, without success, to free himself from her grip.

Hugo had seen enough – his enemy was captured and the law would get him now – so he slipped away, jubilant and chuckling, and wended campwards, framing a judicious version of the matter to give to the Ruffler's crew as he strode along.

The king continued to struggle in the woman's strong grasp, and now and then cried out in vexation, 'Unhand me, thou foolish creature; it was not I that bereaved thee of thy paltry goods.'

The crowd closed around, threatening the king and calling him names; a brawny blacksmith in leather apron and sleeves rolled to his elbows made a reach for him, saying he would trounce him well for a lesson; but just then a long sword flashed in the air and fell with convincing force upon the man's arm, flat side down, the fantastic owner of it remarking pleasantly at the same time, 'Marry, good souls, let us proceed gently, not with ill blood and uncharitable words. This is a matter for the law's consideration, not private and unofficial handling. Loose thy hold from the boy, goodwife.'

The blacksmith averaged the stalwart soldier with a glance, then went muttering away, rubbing his arm; the woman released the boy's wrist reluctantly; the crowd eyed the stranger unlovingly, but prudently closed their mouths. The king sprang to his deliverer's side, with flushed cheeks and sparkling eyes, exclaiming, 'Thou hast lagged sorely, but thou comest in good season now, Sir Miles; carve me this rabble to rags!'

1 From *The English Rogue*; London, 1665.

23 The Prince a Prisoner

Hendon forced back a smile and bent down and whispered in the king's ear, 'Softly, softly, my prince; wag thy tongue warily; nay, suffer it not to wag at all. Trust in me – all shall go well in the end.' Then he added to himself: '*Sir* Miles! Bless me, I had totally forgot I was a knight! Lord how marvellous a thing it is, the grip his memory doth take upon his quaint and crazy fancies! An empty and foolish title is mine, and yet it is something to have deserved it, for I think it is more honour to be held worthy to be a spectre-knight in his Kingdom of Dreams and Shadows, than to be held base enough to be an earl in some of the *real* kingdoms of this world.'

The crowd fell apart to admit a constable, who approached and was about to lay his hand upon the king's shoulder when Hendon said, 'Gently, good friend, withhold your hand; he shall go peaceably; I am responsible for that. Lead on, we will follow.'

The officer led, with the woman and her bundle; Miles and the king followed after, with the crowd at their heels. The king was inclined to rebel, but Hendon said to him in a low voice, 'Reflect, sire; your laws are the wholesome breath of your own royalty; shall their source resist them, yet require the branches to respect them? Apparently one of these laws has been broken; when the king is on the throne again, can it ever grieve him to remember that when he was seemingly a private person he loyally sunk the king in the citizen and submitted to its authority?'

'Thou art right; say no more; thou shalt see that whatsoever the king of England requires a subject to suffer under the law, he will himself suffer while he holdeth the station of a subject.'

When the woman was called upon to testify before the justice of the peace, she swore that the small prisoner at the bar was the person who had committed the theft; there was none able to show the contrary, so the king stood convicted. The bundle was now unrolled, and when the contents proved to be a plump little dressed pig, the judge looked troubled, whilst Hendon turned pale, and his body was thrilled with an electric shiver of dismay; but the king remained unmoved, protected by his ignorance. The judge meditated during an ominous pause, then turned to the woman with the question, 'What dost thou hold this property to be worth?'

The woman courtesied and replied, 'Three shillings and eightpence, your worship; I could not abate a penny and set forth the value honestly.'

The justice glanced around uncomfortably upon the crowd, then nodded to the constable and said, 'Clear the court and close the doors.'

It was done. None remained but the two officials, the accused, the accuser, and Miles Hendon. This latter was rigid and colourless, and on his forehead big drops of cold sweat gathered, broke and blended together, and trickled down his face. The judge turned to the woman again and said in a compassionate voice, ' 'Tis a poor ignorant lad, and mayhap was driven hard by hunger, for these be grievous times for the unfortunate; mark you, he hath not an evil face, but when hunger driveth—— Good woman! Dost know that when one steals a thing above the value of thirteen pence ha'penny the law saith he shall *hang* for it!'

The little king started, wide-eyed with consternation, but controlled himself and held his peace; but not so the woman. She sprang to her feet, shaking with fright, and cried out, 'Oh, good lack, what have I done! God-a-mercy, I would not hang the poor thing for the whole world! Ah, save me from this, your worship; what shall I do, what *can* I do?'

The justice maintained his judicial composure and simply said, 'Doubtless it is allowable to revise the value, since it is not yet writ upon the record.'

'Then in God's name call the pig eightpence, and heaven bless the day that freed my conscience of this awesome thing!'

Miles Hendon forgot all decorum in his delight, and surprised the king and wounded his dignity by throwing his arms around him and hugging him. The woman made her grateful adieux and started away with her pig; and when the constable opened the door for her, he followed her out into the narrow hall. The justice proceeded to write in his record book. Hendon, always alert, thought he would like to know why the officer followed the woman out; so he slipped softly into the dusky hall and listened. He heard a conversation to this effect:

'It is a fat pig and promises good eating; I will buy it of thee; here is the eightpence.'

'Eightpence, indeed! Thou'lt do no such thing. It cost me three shillings and eightpence, good honest coin of the last reign, that old Harry that's just dead ne'er touched nor tampered with. A fig for thy eightpence!'

'Stands the wind in that quarter? Thou wast under oath, and so swore falsely when thou saidst the value was but eightpence. Come straightway back with me before his worship and answer for the crime! And then the lad will hang.'

'There, there, dear heart, say no more, I am content. Give me the eightpence, and hold thy peace about the matter.'

The woman went off crying; Hendon slipped back into the courtroom, and the constable presently followed, after hiding his prize in some convenient place. The justice wrote a while longer, then read the king a wise and kindly lecture and sentenced him to a short imprisonment in the common jail, to be followed by a public flogging. The astounded king opened his mouth and was probably going to order the good judge to be beheaded on the spot, but he caught a warning sign from Hendon and succeeded in closing his mouth again before he lost anything out of it. Hendon took him by the hand now, made reverence to the justice, and the two departed in the wake of the constable toward the jail. The moment the street was reached, the inflamed monarch halted, snatched away his hand, and exclaimed, 'Idiot, dost imagine I will enter a common jail *alive?*'

Hendon bent down and said somewhat sharply, *'Will* you trust in me? Peace! And forbear to worsen our chances with dangerous speech. What God wills, will happen; thou canst not hurry it, thou canst not alter it; therefore wait, and be patient; 'twill be time enow to rail or rejoice when what is to happen has happened.'[1]

[1] See Notes to Chapter 23 at end of volume.

24 The Escape

The short winter day was nearly ended. The streets were deserted save for a few random stragglers, and these hurried straight along, with the intent look of people who were only anxious to accomplish their errands as quickly as possible and then snugly house themselves from the rising wind and the gathering twilight. They looked neither to the right nor to the left; they paid no attention to our party; they did not even seem to see them. Edward the Sixth wondered if the spectacle of a king on his way to jail had ever encountered such marvellous indifference before. By and by the constable arrived at a deserted market square and proceeded to cross it. When he had reached the middle of it, Hendon laid his hand upon his arm and said in a low voice, 'Bide a moment, good sir; there is none in hearing, and I would say a word to thee.'

'My duty forbids it, sir; prithee hinder me not; the night comes on.'

'Stay, nevertheless, for the matter concerns thee nearly. Turn thy back a moment and seem not to see: *let this poor lad escape.*'

'This to me, sir! I arrest thee in——'

'Nay, be not too hasty. See thou be careful and commit no foolish error' – then he shut his voice down to a whisper and said in the man's ear— 'the pig thou hast purchased for eightpence may cost thee thy neck, man!'

The poor constable, taken by surprise, was speechless at first, then found his tongue and fell to blustering and threatening; but Hendon was tranquil and waited with patience till his breath was spent; then said, 'I have a liking to thee, friend, and would not willingly see thee come to harm. Observe, I heard it all – every word. I will prove it to thee.' Then he repeated the conversation which the officer and the woman had had together in the hall, word for word, and ended with, 'There, have I set it forth correctly? Should not I be able to set it forth correctly before the judge, if occasion required?'

The man was dumb with fear and distress for a moment; then he rallied and said with forced lightness, ''Tis making a mighty matter indeed out of a jest; I but plagued the woman for mine amusement.'

'Kept you the woman's pig for amusement?'

The man answered sharply, 'Nought else, good sir. I tell thee 'twas but a jest.'

'I do begin to believe thee,' said Hendon with a perplexing mixture of mockery and half conviction in his tone; 'but tarry thou here a moment whilst I run and ask his worship, for nathless, he being a man experienced in law, in jests, in——'

He was moving away, still talking; the constable hesitated, fidgeted, spat out an oath or two, then cried out, 'Hold, hold, good sir; prithee wait a little – the judge! Why, man, he hath no more sympathy with a jest than hath a dead corpse! Come, and we will speak further. Ods body! I seem to be in evil case, and all for an innocent and thoughtless pleasantry. I am a man of family; and my wife and little ones—— List to reason, good your worship; what wouldst thou of me?'

'Only that thou be blind and dumb and paralytic whilst one may count a hundred thousand, counting slowly,' said Hendon with the expression of a man who asks but a reasonable favour, and that a very little one.

'It is my destruction!' said the constable despairingly. 'Ah, be reasonable, good sir; only look at this matter on all its sides, and see how mere a jest it is – how manifestly and how plainly it is so. And even if one granted it were not a jest, it is a fault so small that e'en the grimmest penalty it could call forth would be but a rebuke and warning from the judge's lips.'

Hendon replied with a solemnity which chilled the air about him, 'This jest of thine hath a name in law; wot you what it is?'

'I knew it not! Peradventure I have been unwise. I never dreamed it had a name; as, sweet heaven, I thought it was original.'

'Yes, it hath a name. In the law this crime is called *Non compos mentis lex talionis sic transit gloria mundi.*'

'Ah, my God!'

'And the penalty is death!'

'God be merciful to me, a sinner!'

'By advantage taken of one in fault, in dire peril, and at thy mercy, thou hast seized goods above thirteen pence ha'penny, paying but a trifle for the same; and this, in the eye of the law, is constructive barratry, misprision of treason, malfeasance in office, *ad hominem expurgatis in statu quo* – and the penalty is death by the halter, without ransom, commutation, or benefit of clergy.'

'Bear me up, bear me up, sweet sir, my legs do fail me! Be thou merciful; spare me this doom, and I will turn my back and see nought that shall happen.'

'Good! Now thou'rt wise and reasonable. And thou'lt restore the pig?'

'I will, I will indeed, nor ever touch another, though heaven send it and an archangel fetch it. Go – I am blind for thy sake – I see nothing. I will say thou didst break in and wrest the prisoner from my hands by force. It is but a crazy, ancient door; I will batter it down myself betwixt midnight and the morning.'

'Do it, good soul; no harm will come of it; the judge hath a loving charity for this poor lad and will shed no tears and break no jailer's bones for his escape.'

25 Hendon Hall

As soon as Hendon and the king were out of sight of the constable, his Majesty was instructed to hurry to a certain place outside the town and wait there whilst Hendon should go to the inn and settle his account. Half an hour later the two friends were blithely jogging eastward on Hendon's sorry steeds. The king was warm and comfortable now, for he had cast his rags and clothed himself in the second-hand suit which Hendon had bought on London Bridge.

Hendon wished to guard against over-fatiguing the boy; he judged that hard journeys, irregular meals, and illiberal measures of sleep would be bad for his crazed mind, whilst rest, regularity, and moderate exercise would be pretty sure to hasten its cure; he longed to see the stricken intellect made well again and its diseased visions driven out of the tormented little head; therefore he resolved to move by easy stages toward the home whence he had so long been banished, instead of obeying the impulse of his impatience and hurrying along night and day.

When he and the king had journeyed about ten miles, they reached a considerable village and halted there for the night at a good inn. The former relations were resumed; Hendon stood behind the king's chair while he dined, and waited upon him; undressed him when he was ready for bed; then took the floor for his own quarters and slept athwart the door rolled up in a blanket.

The next day, and the day after, they jogged lazily along talking over the adventures they had met since their separation, and mightily enjoying each other's narratives. Hendon detailed all his wide wanderings in search of the king and described how the archangel had led him a fool's journey all over the forest and taken him back to the hut finally when he found he could not get rid of him. Then, he said, the old man went into the bedchamber and came staggering back looking broken hearted and saying he had expected to find that the boy had returned and lain down in there to rest, but it was not so. Hendon had waited at the hut all day; hope of the king's return died out then, and he departed upon the quest again.

'And old Sanctum Sanctorum *was* truly sorry your Highness came not back,' said Hendon; 'I saw it in his face.'

'Marry I will never doubt *that*!' said the king; and then told his own story, after which Hendon was sorry he had not destroyed the archangel.

During the last day of the trip Hendon's spirits were soaring. His tongue ran constantly. He talked about his old father and his brother Arthur, and told of many things which illustrated their high and generous characters; he went into loving frenzies over his Edith, and was so glad hearted that he was even able to say some gentle and brotherly things about Hugh. He dwelt a deal on the coming meeting at Hendon Hall; what a surprise it would be to everybody, and what an outburst of thanksgiving and delight there would be.

It was a fair region, dotted with cottages and orchards, and the road led through broad pasturelands whose receding expanses, marked with gentle elevations and depressions, suggested the swelling and subsiding undulations of the sea. In the afternoon the returning prodigal made constant deflections from his course to see if by ascending some hillock he might not pierce the distance and catch a glimpse of his home. At last he was successful and cried out excitedly, 'There is the village, my prince, and there is the Hall close by! You may see the towers from here; and that wood there – that is my father's park. Ah, *now* thou'lt know what state and grandeur be! A house with seventy rooms – think of that! – and seven and twenty servants! A brave lodging for such as we, is it not so? Come, let us speed; my impatience will not brook further delay.'

All possible hurry was made; still, it was after three o'clock before the village was reached. The travellers scampered through it, Hendon's tongue going all the time. 'Here is the church – covered with the same ivy, none gone, none added.' 'Yonder is the inn, the old Red Lion; and yonder is the market-place.' 'Here is the Maypole, and here the pump; nothing is altered – nothing but the people, at any rate; ten years make a change in people; some of these I seem to know, but none know me.' So his chat ran on. The end of the village was soon reached; then the travellers struck into a crooked, narrow road, walled in with tall hedges, and hurried briskly along it for a half mile, then passed into a vast flower garden through an imposing gateway whose huge stone pillars bore sculptured armorial devices. A noble mansion was before them.

'Welcome to Hendon Hall my king!' exclaimed Miles. 'Ah, 'tis a great day! My father and my brother, and the lady Edith will be so mad with joy that they will have eyes and tongue for none but me in the first transports of the meeting, and so thou'lt seem but coldly welcomed; but mind it not; 'twill soon seem otherwise, for when I say thou art my ward and tell them how costly is my love for thee, thou'lt see them take thee to their breasts for Miles Hendon's sake and make their house and hearts thy home forever after!'

The next moment Hendon sprang to the ground before the great door, helped the king down, then took him by the hand and rushed within. A few steps brought him to a spacious apartment; he entered, seated the king with more hurry than ceremony, then ran toward a young man who sat at a writing table in front of a generous fire of logs.

'Embrace me, Hugh,' he cried, 'and say thou'rt glad I am come again! And call our father, for home is not home till I shall touch his hand, and see his face, and hear his voice once more!'

But Hugh only drew back, after betraying a momentary surprise, and bent a grave stare upon the intruder – a stare which indicated somewhat of offended dignity at first, then changed, in response to some inward thought or purpose, to an expression of marvelling curiosity mixed with a real or assumed compassion. Presently he said in a mild voice, 'Thy wits seem touched, poor. stranger; doubtless thou hast suffered privations and rude buffetings at the world's hands; thy looks and dress betoken it. Whom dost thou take me to be?'

'Take thee? Prithee for whom else than whom thou art? I take thee to be Hugh Hendon,' said Miles sharply.

The other continued in the same soft tone, 'And whom dost thou imagine thyself to be?'

'Imagination hath nought to do with it! Dost thou pretend thou knowest me not for thy brother Miles Hendon?'

An expression of pleased surprise flitted across Hugh's face, and he exclaimed, 'What! Thou art not jesting? Can the dead come to life? God be praised if it be so! Our poor lost boy restored to our arms after all these cruel years! Ah, it seems too good to be true, it *is* too good to be true; I charge thee, have pity, do not trifle with me! Quick, come to the light – let me scan thee well!'

He seized Miles by the arm, dragged him to the window, and began to devour him from head to foot with his eyes, turning him this way and that and stepping briskly around him and about him to prove him from all points of view, whilst the returned prodigal, all aglow with gladness, smiled, laughed, and kept nodding his head and saying, 'Go on, brother, go on, and fear not; thou'lt find nor limb nor feature that cannot bide the test. Scour and scan me to thy content, my good old Hugh. I am indeed thy old Miles, thy same old Miles, thy lost brother, is't not so? Ah, 'tis a great day – I *said* 'twas a great day! Give me thy hand, give me thy cheek; lord, I am like to die of very joy!'

He was about to throw himself upon his brother, but Hugh put up his hand in dissent, then dropped his chin mournfully upon his breast, saying with emotion, 'Ah, God of his mercy give me strength to bear this grievous disappointment!'

Miles, amazed, could not speak for a moment; then he found his tongue and cried out, *'What* disappointment? Am I not thy brother?'

Hugh shook his head sadly and said, 'I pray heaven it may prove so, and that other eyes may find the resemblances that are hid from mine. Alack, I fear me the letter spoke but too truly.'

'What letter?'

'One that came from over sea, some six or seven years ago. It said my brother died in battle.'

'It was a lie! Call thy father; he will know me.'

'One may not call the dead.'

'Dead?' Miles's voice was subdued, and his lips trembled. 'My father dead! Oh, this is heavy news. Half my new joy is withered now. Prithee let me see my brother Arthur; he will know me; he will know me and console me.'

'He also is dead.'

'God be merciful to me, a stricken man! Gone, both gone – the worthy taken and the worthless spared, in me! Ah! I crave your mercy! Do not say the lady Edith——'

'Is dead? No, she lives.'

'Then, God be praised, my joy is whole again! Speed thee, brother, let her come to me! An' *she* say I am not myself, but she will not; no, no, *she* will know me; I were a fool to doubt it. Bring her, bring the old servants; they too will know me.'

'All are gone but five – Peter, Halsey, David, Bernard, and Margaret.'

So saying, Hugh left the room. Miles stood musing a while, then began to walk the floor, muttering, 'The five arch villains have survived the two and twenty leal and honest – 'tis an odd thing.'

He continued walking back and forth, muttering to himself; he had forgotten the king entirely. By and by his Majesty said gravely, and with a touch of genuine compassion, though the words themselves were capable of being interpreted ironically, 'Mind not thy mischance, good man; there be others in the world whose identity is denied and whose claims are derided. Thou hast company.'

'Ah, my king,' cried Hendon, colouring slightly, 'do not thou condemn me; wait, and thou shalt see. I am no impostor; she will say it; you shall hear it from the sweetest lips in England. I an impostor? Why, I know this old hall, these pictures of my ancestors, and all things that are about us as a child knoweth its own nursery. Here was I born and bred, my lord; I speak the truth; I would not deceive thee; and should none else believe, I pray thee do not *thou* doubt me; I could not bear it.'

'I do not doubt thee,' said the king with a child-like simplicity and faith.

'I thank thee out of my heart!' exclaimed Hendon with a fervency which showed that he was touched. The king added, with the same gentle simplicity, 'Dost thou doubt *me*?'

A guilty confusion seized upon Hendon, and he was grateful that the door opened to admit Hugh at that moment and saved him the necessity of replying.

A beautiful lady, richly clothed, followed Hugh, and after her came several liveried servants. The lady walked slowly, with her head bowed and her eyes fixed upon the floor. The face was unspeakably sad. Miles Hendon sprang forward, crying out, 'Oh, my Edith, my darling——'

But Hugh waved him back gravely and said to the lady, 'Look upon him. Do you know him?'

At the sound of Miles's voice the woman had started slightly and her cheeks had flushed; she was trembling now. She stood still during an impressive pause of several moments, then slowly lifted up her head and looked into Hendon's eyes with a stony and frightened gaze; the blood sank out of her face, drop by drop, till nothing remained but the grey pallor of death; then she said, in a voice as dead as the face, 'I know him not!' and turned, with a moan and a stifled sob, and tottered out of the room.

Miles Hendon sank into a chair and covered his face with his hands. After a pause, his brother said to the servants, 'You have observed him. Do you know him?'

They shook their heads; then the master said. 'The servants know you not, sir. I fear there is some mistake. You have seen that my wife knew you not.'

'Thy *wife*!' In an instant Hugh was pinned to the wall with an iron grip about his throat. 'Oh, thou fox-hearted slave, I see it all! Thou'st writ the lying letter thyself, and my stolen bride and goods are its fruit. There, now get thee gone, lest I shame mine honourable soldiership with the slaying of so pitiful a manikin!'

Hugh, red-faced and almost suffocated, reeled to the nearest chair and commanded the servants to seize and bind the murderous stranger. They hesitated, and one of them said, 'He is armed, Sir Hugh, and we are weaponless.'

'Armed? What of it, and ye so many? Upon him, I say!'

But Miles warned them to be careful what they did, and added, 'Ye know me of old – I have not changed; come on, an' it like you.'

This reminder did not hearten the servants much; they held back.

'Then go, ye paltry cowards, and arm yourselves and guard the doors, whilst I send one to fetch the watch,' said Hugh. He turned at the threshold and said to Miles, 'You'll find it to your advantage to offend not with useless endeavours at escape.'

'Escape? Spare thyself discomfort, an' that is all that troubles thee. For Miles Hendon is master of Hendon Hall and all its belongings. He will remain; doubt it not.'

26 Disowned

The king sat musing a few moments, then looked up and said, "'Tis strange – most strange. I cannot account for it.'

'No, it is not strange, my liege. I know him, and this conduct is but natural. He was a rascal from his birth.'

'Oh, I spake not of *him*, Sir Miles.'

'Not of him? Then of what? What is it that is strange?'

'That the king is not missed.'

'How? Which? I doubt I do not understand.'

'Indeed? Doth it not strike you as being passing strange that the land is not filled with couriers and proclamations describing my person and making search for me? Is it no matter for commotion and distress that the head of the state is gone, that I am vanished away and lost?'

'Most true, my king, I had forgot.' Then Hendon sighed and muttered to himself, 'Poor ruined mind – still busy with its pathetic dream.'

'But I have a plan that shall right us both. I will write a paper in three tongues – Latin, Greek and English – and thou shalt haste away with it to London in the morning. Give it to none but my uncle the lord Hertford; when he shall see it, he will know and say I wrote it. Then he will send for me.'

'Might it not be best, my prince, that we wait here until I prove myself and make my rights secure to my domains? I should be so much the better able then to——'

The king interrupted him imperiously, 'Peace! What are thy paltry domains, thy trivial interests, contrasted with matters which concern the weal of a nation and the integrity of a throne!' Then he added in a gentle voice, as if he were sorry for his severity, 'Obey, and have no fear; I will right thee, I will make thee whole – yes, more than whole. I shall remember, and requite.'

So saying, he took the pen and set himself to work. Hendon contemplated him lovingly awhile, then said to himself, 'An' it were dark, I should think it *was* a king that spoke; there's no denying it, when the humour's upon him he doth thunder and lighten like your true king; now where got he that trick? See him scribble and scratch away contentedly at his meaningless pothooks, fancying them to be Latin and Greek; and except my wit shall serve me with a lucky device for diverting him from his purpose. I shall be forced to pretend to post away tomorrow on this wild errand he hath invented for me.'

The next moment Sir Miles's thoughts had gone back to the recent episode. So absorbed was he in his musings that when the king presently handed him the paper which he had been writing, he received it and pocketed it without being conscious of the act. 'How marvellous strange she acted,' he muttered, 'I think she knew me, and I think she did *not* know me. These opinions do conflict, I perceive it plainly; I cannot reconcile them; neither can I by argument dismiss either of the two or even persuade one to outweigh the other. The matter standeth simply thus: she *must* have known my face, my figure, my voice, for how could it be otherwise? Yet she *said* she knew me not, and that is proof perfect, for she cannot lie. But stop – I think I begin to see. Peradventure he hath influenced her – commanded her – compelled her to lie. That is the solution! The riddle is unriddled. She seemed dead with fear; yes, she was under his compulsion. I will seek her; I will find her; now that he is away, she will speak her true mind. She will remember the old times when we were little playfellows together, and this will soften her heart, and she will no more betray me, but will confess me. There is no treacherous blood in her; no, she was always honest and true. She has loved me in those old days; this is my security, for whom one has loved one cannot betray.'

He stepped eagerly toward the door; at that moment it opened, and the lady Edith entered. She was very pale, but she walked with a firm step, and her carriage was full of grace and gentle dignity. Her face was sad as before.

Miles sprang forward with a happy confidence to meet her, but she checked him with a hardly perceptible gesture, and he stopped where he was. She seated herself and asked him to do likewise. Thus simply did she take the sense of old comradeship out of him and transform him into stranger and a guest. The surprise of it, the bewildering unexpectedness of it, made him begin to question, for a moment, if he *was* the person he was pretending to be after all.

The lady Edith said, 'Sir, I have come to warn you. The mad cannot be persuaded out of their delusions, perchance; but doubtless they may be persuaded to avoid perils. I think this dream of yours hath the seeming of honest truth to you, and therefore is not criminal; but do not tarry here with it, for here it is dangerous.' She looked steadily into Miles's face a moment, then added impressively, 'It is the more dangerous for that you *are* much like what our lost lad must have grown to be if he had lived.'

'Heavens, madam, but I *am* he!'

'I truly think you think it, sir. I question not your honesty in that; I but warn you, that is all. My husband is master in this region; his power hath hardly any limit; the people prosper or starve as he wills. If you resembled not the man whom you profess to be, my husband might bid you pleasure yourself with your dream in peace; but trust me, I know him well, I know what he will do; he will say to all that you are but a mad impostor, and straightway all will echo him.' She bent upon Miles that same steady look once more and added, 'If you *were* Miles Hendon, and he knew it and all the region knew it – consider what I am saying, weigh it well – you would stand in the same peril, your punishment would be no less sure; he would deny you and denounce you, and none would be bold enough to give you countenance.'

'Most truly I believe it,' said Miles bitterly. 'The power that can command one lifelong friend to betray and disown another be obeyed, may well look to be obeyed in quarters where bread and life are on the stake and no cobweb ties of loyalty and honour are concerned.'

A faint tinge appeared for a moment in the lady's cheek, and she dropped her eyes to the floor; but her voice betrayed no emotion which she proceeded, 'I have warned you, I must still warn you, to go hence. This man will destroy you, else. He is a tyrant who knows no pity. I, who am his fettered slave, know this. Poor Miles, and Arthur, and my dear guardian, Sir Richard, are free of him and at rest; better that you were with them than that you bide here in the clutches of this miscreant. Your pretensions are a menace to his title and possessions; you have assaulted him in his own house; you are ruined if you stay. Go – do not hesitate. If you lack money, take this purse, I beg of you, and bribe the servants to let you pass. Oh, be warned, poor soul, and escape while you may.'

Miles declined the purse with a gesture and rose up and stood before her.

'Grant me one thing,' he said. 'Let your eyes rest upon mine so that I may see if they be steady. There, now answer me. Am I Miles Hendon?'

'No. I know you not.'

'Swear it!'

The answer was low but distinct, 'I swear.'

'Oh, this passes belief!'

'Fly! Why will you waste the precious time? Fly, and save yourself.'

At that moment the officers burst into the room, and a violent struggle began; but Hendon was soon overpowered and dragged away. The king was taken also, and both were bound and led to prison.

27 In Prison

The cells were all crowded, so the two friends were chained in a large room where persons charged with trifling offences were commonly kept. They had company, for there were some twenty manacled and fettered prisoners here, of both sexes and of varying ages – an obscene and noisy gang. The king chafed bitterly over the stupendous indignity thus put upon his royalty, but Hendon was moody and taciturn. He was pretty thoroughly bewildered. He had come home a jubilant prodigal expecting to find everybody wild with joy over his return, and instead had got the cold shoulder and a jail. The promise and the fulfillment differed so widely that the effect was stunning; he could not decide whether it was most tragic or most grotesque. He felt much as a man might who had danced blithely out to enjoy a rainbow and got struck by lightning.

But gradually his confused and tormenting thoughts settled down into some sort of order, and then his mind centred itself upon Edith. He turned her conduct over and examined it in all lights, but he could not make anything satisfactory out of it. Did she know him? Or didn't she know him? It was a perplexing puzzle and occupied him a long time, but he ended finally with the conviction that she did know him and had repudiated him for interested reasons. He wanted to load her name with curses now, but this name had so long been sacred to him that he found he could not bring his tongue to profane it.

Wrapped in prison blankets of a soiled and tattered condition, Hendon and the king passed a troubled night. For a bribe the jailer had furnished liquor to some of the prisoners; singing of ribald songs, fighting, shouting, and carousing was the natural consequence. At last, a while after midnight, a man attacked a woman and nearly killed her by beating her over the head with his manacles before the jailer could come to the rescue. The jailer restored peace by giving the man a sound clubbing about the head and shoulders; then the carousing ceased, and after that all had an opportunity to sleep who did not mind the annoyance of the moanings and groanings of the two wounded people.

During the ensuing week, the days and nights were of a monotonous sameness as to events; men whose faces Hendon remembered more or less distinctly came by day to gaze at the 'impostor' and repudiate and insult him; and by night the carousing and brawling went on with symmetrical regularity.

However, there was a change of incident at last. The jailer brought in an old man and said to him, 'The villain is in this room; cast thy old eyes about and see if thou canst say which is he.'

Hendon glanced up and experienced a pleasant sensation for the first time since he had been in the jail. He said to himself, 'This is Blake Andrews, a servant all his life in my father's family – a good honest soul, with a right heart in his breast. That is, formerly. But none are true now; all are liars. This man will know me – and will deny me too, like the rest.'

The old man gazed around the room, glanced at each face in turn, and finally said, 'I see none here but paltry knaves, scum o' the streets. Which is he?'

The jailer laughed.

'Here,' he said; 'scan this big animal, and grant me an opinion.'

The old man approached and looked Hendon over long and earnestly, then shook his head and said, 'Marry, *this* is no Hendon – nor ever was!'

'Right! Thy old eyes are sound yet. An' I were Sir Hugh, I would take the shabby carl and——'

The jailer finished by lifting himself atiptoe with an imaginary halter, at the same time making a gurgling noise in his throat suggestive of suffocation. The old man said vindictively, 'Let him bless God an' he fare no worse. An' *I* had the handling o' the villain, he should roast, or I am no true man!'

The jailer laughed a pleasant hyena laugh and said, 'Give him a piece of thy mind, old man; they all do it. Thou'lt find it good diversion.'

Then he sauntered toward his ante-room and disappeared. The old man dropped upon his knees and whispered, 'God be thanked, thou'rt come again, my master! I believed thou wert dead these seven years, and lo, here thou art alive! I knew thee the moment I saw thee; and main hard work it was to keep a stony countenance and seem to see none here but tuppenny knaves and rubbish o' the streets. I am old and poor, Sir Miles; but say the word and I will go forth and proclaim the truth, though I be strangled for it.'

'No,' said Hendon; 'thou shalt not. It would ruin thee, and yet help but little in my cause. But I thank thee, for thou hast given me back somewhat of my lost faith in my kind.'

The old servant became very valuable to Hendon and the king, for he dropped in several times a day to 'abuse' the former and always smuggled in a few delicacies to help out the prison bill of fare; he also furnished the current news. Hendon reserved the dainties for the king; without them his Majesty might not have survived, for he was not able to eat the coarse and wretched food provided by the jailer. Andrews was obliged to confine himself to brief visits in order to avoid suspicion, but he managed to impart a fair degree of information each time – information delivered in a low voice for Hendon's benefit, and interlarded with insulting epithets delivered in a louder voice for the benefit of other hearers.

So little by little the story of the family came out. Arthur had been dead six years. This loss, with the absence of news from Hendon, impaired the father's health; he believed he was going to die, and he wished to see Hugh and Edith settled in life before he passed away; but Edith begged hard for delay, hoping for Miles's return; then the letter came which brought the news of Miles's death; the shock prostrated Sir Richard; he believed his end was very near, and he and Hugh insisted upon the marriage; Edith begged for and obtained a month's respite; then another and finally a third; the marriage then took place by the deathbed of Sir Richard. It had not proved a happy one. It was whispered about the country that shortly after the nuptials the bride found among her husband's papers several rough and incomplete drafts of the fatal letter and had accused him of precipitating the marriage, and Sir Richard's death too, by a wicked forgery. Tales of cruelty to the lady Edith and the servants were to be heard on all hands; and since the father's death Sir Hugh had thrown off all soft disguises and become a pitiless master toward all who in any way depended upon him and his domains for bread.

There was a bit of Andrews' gossip which the king listened to with a lively interest, 'There is rumour that the king is mad. But in charity forbear to say *I* mentioned it, for 'tis death to speak of it, they say.'

His Majesty glared at the old man and said, 'The king is *not* mad, good man, and thou'lt find it to thy advantage to busy thyself with matters that nearer concern thee than this seditious prattle.'

'What doth the lad mean?' said Andrews, surprised at this brisk assault from an unexpected quarter. Hendon gave a sign, and he did not pursue his question, but went on with his budget, 'The late king is to be buried at Windsor in a day or two – the sixteenth of the month – and the new king will be crowned at Westminster the twentieth'

"Methinks they must needs find him first,' muttered his Majesty; then added confidently, 'but they will look to that – and also shall I.'

'In the name of——'

But the old man got no further: a warning sign from Hendon checked his remark. He resumed the thread of his gossip, 'Sir Hugh goeth to the coronation, and with grand hopes. He confidently looketh to come back a peer, for he is high in favour with the Lord Protector.'

'What Lord Protector?' asked his Majesty.

'His grace the Duke of Somerset.'

'What Duke of Somerset?'

'Marry, there is but one – Seymour, Earl of Hertford.'

The king asked sharply, 'Since when is *he* a duke, and Lord Protector?'
'Since the last day of January.'
'And prithee who made him so?'
'Himself and the Great Council, with help of the king.'
His Majesty started violently. 'The *king!*' he cried. *'What* king, good sir?'
'What king, indeed! (God-a-mercy, what aileth the boy?) Sith we have but one, 'tis not difficult to answer – his most sacred Majesty King Edward the Sixth, whom God preserve! Yea, and a dear and gracious little urchin is he too; and whether he be mad or no – and they say he mendeth daily – his praises are on all men's lips; and all bless him, likewise, and offer prayers that he may be spared to reign long in England, for he began humanely with saving the old Duke of Norfolk's life, and now is he bent on destroying the cruellest of the laws that harry and oppress the people.'

This news struck his Majesty dumb with amazement and plunged him into so deep dismal a reverie that he heard no more of the old man's gossip. He wondered if the 'little urchin' was the beggar boy whom he left dressed in his own garments in the palace. It did not seem possible that this could be, for surely his manners and speech would betray him if he pretended to be the Prince of Wales; then he would be driven out, and search made for the true prince. Could it be that the court had set up some sprig of the nobility in his place? No, for his uncle would not allow that; he was all-powerful and could and would crush such a movement, of course. The boy's musings profited him nothing; the more he tried to unriddle the mystery, the more perplexed he became, the more his head ached, and the worse he slept. His impatience to get to London grew hourly, and his captivity became almost unendurable.

Hendon's arts all failed with the king – he could not be comforted; but a couple of women who were chained near him succeeded better. Under their gentle ministrations he found peace and learned a degree of patience. He was very grateful and came to love them dearly and to delight in the sweet and soothing influence of their presence. He asked them why they were in prison, and when they said they were Baptists, he smiled and inquired, 'Is that a crime to be shut up for, in a prison? Now I grieve, for I shall lose ye – they will not keep ye long for such a little thing.'

They did not answer, and something in their faces made him uneasy. He said eagerly, 'You do not speak; be good to me and tell me – there will be no other punishment? Prithee tell me there is no fear of that.'

They tried to change the topic, but his fears were aroused, and he pursued it, 'Will they scourge thee? No, no, they would not be so cruel! Say they would not. Come, they *will* not, will they?'

The women betrayed confusion and distress, but there was no avoiding an answer, so one of them said in a voice choked with emotion, 'Oh, thou'lt break our hearts, thou gentle spirit! God will help us to bear our——'

'It is a confession!' the king broke in. 'Then they *will* scourge thee, the stonyhearted wretches! But oh, thou must not weep; I cannot bear it. Keep up thy courage; I shall come to my own in time to save thee from this bitter thing, and I will do it!'

When the king awoke in the morning, the women were gone.

'They are saved!' he said, joyfully; then added despondently, 'but woe is me, for they were my comforters.'

Each of them had left a shred of ribbon pinned to his clothing in token of remembrance. He said he would keep these things always and that soon he would seek out these dear good friends of his and take them under his protection.

Just then the jailer came in with some subordinates and commanded that the prisoners be conducted to the jailyard. The king was overjoyed: it would be a blessed thing to see the blue sky and breathe the fresh air once more. He fretted and chafed at the slowness of the officers, but his turn came at last and he was released from his stable and ordered to follow the other prisoners, with Hendon.

The court, or quadrangle, was stone-paved and open to the sky. The prisoners entered it through a massive archway of masonry, and were placed in file, standing with their backs against the wall. A rope was stretched in front of them, and they were also guarded by their officers. It was a chill and lowering morning, and light snow which had fallen during the night whitened the great empty space and added to the general dismalness of its aspect. Now and then a wintry wind shivered through the place and sent the snow eddying hither and thither.

In the centre of the court stood two women, chained to posts. A glance showed the king that these were his good friends. He shuddered and said to himself, 'Alack, they are not gone free, as I had thought. To think that such as these should know the lash! In England! Aye, there's the shame of it – not in Heatheness, but Christian England! They will be scourged; and I, whom they have comforted and kindly entreated, must look on and see the great wrong done; it is strange, so strange, that I, the very source of power in this broad realm, am helpless to protect them. But let these miscreants look well to themselves, for there is a day coming when I will require of them a heavy reckoning for this work. For every blow they strike now they shall feel a hundred then.'

A great gate swung open and a crowd of citizens poured in. They flocked around the two women and hid them from the king's view. A clergyman entered and passed through the crowd, and he also was hidden. The king now heard talking back and forth as if questions were being asked and answered, but he could not make out what was said. Next there was a deal of bustle and preparation, and much passing and repassing of officials through that part of the crowd that stood on the further side of the women; and whilst this proceeded a deep hush gradually fell upon the people.

Now, by command, the masses parted and fell aside, and the king saw a spectacle that froze the marrow in his bones. Fagots had been piled about the two women, and a kneeling man was lighting them!

The women bowed their heads and covered their faces with their hands; the yellow flames began to climb upward among the snapping and crackling fagots, and wreaths of blue smoke to stream away on the wind; the clergyman lifted his hands and began a prayer; just then two young girls came flying through the great gate uttering piercing screams and threw themselves upon the women at the stake. Instantly they were torn away by officers, and one of them was kept in a tight grip, but the other broke loose, saying she would die with her mother; and before she could be stopped she had flung her arms about her mother's neck again. She was torn away once more, and with her gown on fire. Two of three men held her, and the burning portion of her gown was snatched off and thrown flaming aside, she struggling all the while to free herself, and saying she would be alone in the world now, and begging to be allowed to die with her mother. Both the girls screamed continually and fought for freedom, but suddenly this tumult was drowned under a volley of heart-piercing shrieks of mortal agony; the king glanced from the frantic girls to the stake, then turned away and leaned his ashen face against the wall, and looked no more. He said, 'That which I have seen in that one little moment will never go out from my memory, but will abide there; and I shall see it all the days, and dream of it all the nights, till I die. Would God I had been blind!'

Hendon was watching the king. He said to himself with satisfaction, 'His disorder mendeth, he hath changed, and groweth gentler. If he had followed his wont, he would have stormed at these varlets, and said he was king, and commanded that the women be turned loose unscathed. Soon his delusion will pass away and be forgotten, and his poor mind will be whole again. God speed the day!'

That same day several prisoners were brought in to remain overnight, who were being conveyed under guard to various places in the kingdom to undergo punishment for crimes committed. The king conversed with these – he had made it a point from the beginning to instruct himself for the kingly office by questioning prisoners whenever the opportunity offered – and the tale of their woes wrung his heart. One of them was a poor half-witted woman who had stolen a yard or two of cloth from a weaver; she was to be hanged for it. Another was a man accused of stealing a horse; he said the proof had failed, and he had imagined that he was safe from the halter; but no, he was hardly free before he was arraigned for killing a deer in the king's park; this was proved against him, and now he was on his way to the gallows. There was a tradesman's apprentice whose case particularly distressed the king; this youth said he found a hawk one evening that had escaped from its owner, and he took it home with him, imagining himself entitled to it; but the court convicted him of stealing it and sentenced him to death.

The king was furious over these inhumanities and wanted Hendon to break jail and fly with him to Westminster so that he could mount his throne and hold out his sceptre in mercy over these unfortunate people and save their lives. 'Poor child,' sighed Hendon, 'these woeful tales have brought his malady upon him again; alack, but for this evil hap, he would have been well in a little time.'

Among these prisoners was an old lawyer – a man with a strong face and a dauntless mien. Three years past he had written a pamphlet against the Lord Chancellor, accusing him of injustice, and had been punished for it by the loss of his ears in the pillory and degradation from the bar, and in addition had been fined £3,000 and sentenced to imprisonment for life. Lately he had repeated his offence; and in consequence was now under sentence to lose *what remained of his ears*, pay a fine of £5,000, be branded on both cheeks, and remain in prison for life.

'These be honourable scars,' he said, and turned back his grey hair and showed the mutilated stubs of what had once been his ears.

The king's eye burned with passion. He said, 'None believe in me; neither wilt thou. But no matter; within the compass of a month thou shalt be free; and more, the laws that have dishonoured thee and shamed the English name shall be swept from the statute books. The world is made wrong; kings should go to school to their own laws at times, and so learn mercy.'[1]

1 See Notes to Chapter 27 at end of volume.

28 The Sacrifice

Meantime Miles was growing sufficiently tired of confinement and inaction. But now his trial came on, to his great gratification, and he thought he could welcome any sentence provided a further imprisonment should not be a part of it. But he was mistaken about that. He was in a fine fury when he found himself described as a 'sturdy vagabond' and sentenced to sit two hours in the pillory for bearing that character and for assaulting the master of Hendon Hall. His pretensions as to brothership with his prosecutor, and rightful heirship to the Hendon honours and estates, were left contemptuously unnoticed as being not even worth examination.

He raged and threatened on his way to punishment, but it did no good; he was snatched roughly along by the officers and got an occasional cuff besides for his unreverent conduct.

The king could not pierce through the rabble that swarmed behind, so he was obliged to follow in the rear, remote from his good friend and servant. The king had been nearly condemned to the stocks himself for being in such bad company, but had been let off with a lecture and a warning in consideration of his youth. When the crowd at last halted, he flitted feverishly from point to point around its outer rim hunting a place to get through, and at last, after a deal of difficulty and delay, succeeded. There sat his poor henchman in the degrading stocks, the sport and butt of a dirty mob – he the body servant of the king of England! Edward had heard the sentence pronounced, but he had not realized the half that it meant. His anger began to rise as the sense of this new indignity which had been put upon him sank home; it jumped to summer heat the next moment, when he saw an egg sail through the air and crush itself against Hendon's cheek, and he heard the crowd roar its enjoyment of the episode. He sprang across the open circle and confronted the officer in charge, crying, 'For shame! This is my servant; set him free! I am the——'

'Oh, peace!' exclaimed Hendon in a panic. 'Thou'lt destroy thyself. Mind him not, officer, he is mad.'

'Give thyself no trouble as to the matter of minding him, good man; I have small mind to mind him: but as to teaching him somewhat, to that I am well inclined.' He turned to a subordinate and said, 'Give the little fool a taste or two of the lash, to mend his manners.'

'Half a dozen will better serve his turn,' suggested Sir Hugh, who had ridden up a moment before to take a passing glance at the proceedings.

The king was seized. He did not even struggle, so paralysed was he with the mere thought of the monstrous outrage that was proposed to be inflicted upon his sacred person. History was already defiled with the record of the scourging of an English king with whips; it was an intolerable reflection that he must furnish a duplicate of that shameful page. He was in the toils; there was no help for him: he must either take this punishment or beg for its remission. Hard conditions; he would take the stripes – a king might do that, but a king could not beg.

But meantime Miles Hendon was resolving the difficulty. 'Let the child go,' said he; 'ye heartless dogs, do ye not see how young and frail he is? Let him go; I will take his lashes.'

'Marry, a good thought, and thanks for it,' said Sir Hugh, his face lighting with a sardonic satisfaction. 'Let the little beggar go, and give this fellow a dozen in his place – an honest dozen, well laid on.' The king was in the act of entering a fierce protest, but Sir Hugh silenced him with the potent remark, 'Yes, speak up, do, and free thy mind; only, mark ye, that for each word you utter he shall get six strokes the more.'

Hendon was removed from the stocks and his back laid bare, and whilst the lash was applied the poor little king turned away his face and allowed unroyal tears to channel his cheeks unchecked. 'Ah, brave good heart,' he said to himself, 'this loyal deed shall never perish out of my memory. I will not forget it; and neither shall *they*!' he added with passion. Whilst he mused, his appreciation of Hendon's magnanimous conduct grew to greater and still greater dimensions in his mind, and so also did his gratefulness for it. Presently he said to himself, 'Who saves his prince from wounds and possible death – and this he did for me – performs high service; but it is little – it is nothing, oh, less than nothing! – when 'tis weighed against the act of him who saves his prince from shame!'

Hendon made no outcry under the scourge, but bore the heavy blows with soldierly fortitude. This, together with his redeeming the boy by taking his stripes for him, compelled the respect of even that forlorn and degraded mob that was gathered there; and its gibes and hootings died away, and no sound remained but the sound of the falling blows. The stillness that pervaded the place when Hendon found himself once more in the stocks was in strong contrast with the insulting clamour which had prevailed there so little a while before. The king came softly to Hendon's side, and whispered in his ear, 'Kings cannot ennoble thee, thou good, great soul, for One who is higher than kings hath done that for thee; but a king can confirm thy nobility to men.' He picked up the scourge from the ground, touched Hendon's

'"Edward of England dubs thee Earl!"'

bleeding shoulders lightly with it, and whispered, 'Edward of England dubs thee earl!'

Hendon was touched. The water welled to his eyes, yet at the same time the grisly humour of the situation and circumstances so undermined his gravity that it was all he could do to keep some sight of his inward mirth from showing outside. To be suddenly hoisted, naked and gory, from the common stocks to the Alpine altitude and splendour of an earldom seemed to him the last possibility in the line of the grotesque. He said to himself, 'Now am I finely tinselled indeed! The spectre knight of the Kingdom of Dreams and Shadows is become a spectre earl! A dizzy flight for a callow wing! An' this go on, I shall presently be hung like a very maypole with fantastic gauds and make-believe honours. But I shall value them, all valueless as they are, for the love that doth bestow them. Better these poor mock dignities of mine, that come unasked from a clean hand and a right spirit, than real ones bought by servility from grudging and interested power.'

The dreaded Sir Hugh wheeled his horse about, and as he spurred away, the living wall divided silently to let him pass, and as silently closed together again. And so remained; nobody went so far as to venture a remark in favour of the prisoner or in compliment to him, but no matter, the absence of abuse was a sufficient homage in itself. A late comer who was not posted as to the present circumstances and who delivered a sneer at the 'impostor' and was in the act of following it with a dead cat was promptly knocked down and kicked out, without any words, and then the deep quiet resumed sway once more.

29 To London

When Hendon's term of service in the stocks was finished, he was released and ordered to quit the region and come back no more. His sword was restored to him, and also his mule and his donkey. He mounted and rode off, followed by the king, the crowd opening with quiet respectfulness to let them pass, and then dispersing when they were gone.

Hendon was soon absorbed in thought. There were questions of high import to be answered. What should he do? Whither should he go? Powerful help must be found somewhere or he must relinquish his inheritance and remain under the imputation of being an impostor besides. Where could he hope to find this powerful help? Where, indeed! It was a knotty question. By and by a thought occurred to him which pointed to a possibility – the slenderest of slender possibilities, certainly, but still worth considering, for lack of any other that promised anything at all. He remembered what old Andrews had said about the young king's goodness and his generous championship of the wronged and unfortunate. Why not go and try to get speech of him and beg for justice? Ah, yes, but could so fantastic a pauper get admission to the august presence of a monarch? Never mind; let that matter take care of itself; it was a bridge that would not need to be crossed till he should come to it. He was an old campaigner, and used to inventing shifts and expedients; no doubt he would be able to find a way. Yes, he would strike for the capital. Maybe his father's old friend Sir Humphrey Marlow would help him – 'good old Sir Humphrey, head lieutenant of the late king's kitchen, or stables, or something' – Miles could not remember just what or which. Now that he had something to turn his energies to, a distinctly defined object to accomplish, the fog of humiliation and depression which had settled down upon his spirits lifted and blew away, and he raised his head and looked about him. He was surprised to see how far he had come; the village was away behind him. The king was jogging along in his wake with his head bowed, for he too was deep in plans and thinkings. A sorrowful misgiving clouded Hendon's newborn cheerfulness: would the boy be willing to go again to a city where, during all his brief life, he had never known anything but ill usage and pinching want? But the question must be asked; it could not be avoided; so Hendon reined up and called out, 'I had forgotten to inquire whither we are bound. Thy commands, my liege!'

'To London!'

Hendon moved on again, mightily contented with the answer, but astounded at it too.

The whole journey was made without an adventure of importance. But it ended with one. About ten o'clock on the night of the nineteenth of February, they stepped upon London Bridge in the midst of a writhing, struggling jam of howling and hurrahing people whose beer-jolly faces stood out strongly in the glare from manifold torches; and at that instant the decaying head of some former duke or other grandee tumbled down between them, striking Hendon on the elbow and then bounding off among the hurrying confusion of feet. So evanescent and unstable are men's works in this world! The late good king is but three weeks dead and three days in his grave, and already the adornments which he took such pains to select from prominent people for his noble bridge are falling. A citizen stumbled over that head and drove his own head into the back of somebody in front of him, who turned and knocked down the first person that came handy, and was promptly laid out himself by that person's friend. It was the right ripe time for a free fight, for the festivities of the morrow – Coronation Day – were already beginning; everybody was full of strong drink and patriotism; within five minutes the free fight was occupying a good deal of ground; within ten or twelve it covered an acre or so and was become a riot. By this time Hendon and the king were hopelessly separated from each other and lost in the rush and turmoil of the roaring masses of humanity. And so we leave them.

30 Tom's Progress

Whilst the true king wandered about the land poorly clad, poorly fed, cuffed and derided by tramps one while, herding with thieves and murderers in a jail another, and called idiot and impostor by all impartially, the mock king, Tom Canty, enjoyed a quite different experience.

When we saw him last, royalty was just beginning to have a bright side for him. This bright side went on brightening more and more every day; in a very little while it was become almost all sunshine and delightfulness. He lost his fears; his misgivings faded out and died; his embarrassments departed and gave place to an easy and confident bearing. He worked the whipping boy mine to ever-increasing profit.

He ordered my lady Elizabeth and my lady Jane Grey into his presence when he wanted to play or talk, and dismissed them when he was done with them, with the air of one familiarly accustomed to such performances. It no longer confused him to have these lofty personages kiss his hand at parting.

He came to enjoy being conducted to bed in state at night and dressed with intricate and solemn ceremony in the morning. It came to be a proud pleasure to march to dinner attended by a glittering procession of officers of state and gentlemen-at-arms; insomuch, indeed, that he doubled his guard of gentlemen-at-arms and made them a hundred. He liked to hear the bugles sounding down the long corridors and the distant voices responding, 'Way for the king!'

He even learned to enjoy sitting in throned state in council and seeming to be something more than the Lord Protector's mouthpiece. He liked to receive great ambassadors and their gorgeous trains and listen to the affectionate messages they brought from illustrious monarchs who called him 'brother.' O happy Tom Canty, late of Offal Court!

He enjoyed the splendid clothes and ordered more; he found his four hundred servants too few for his proper grandeur and trebled them. The adulation of salaaming courtiers came to be sweet music to his ears. He remained kind and gentle and a sturdy and determined champion of all that were oppressed, and he made tireless war upon unjust laws; yet upon occasion, being offended, he could turn upon an earl, or even a duke, and give him a look that would make him tremble. Once, when his royal 'sister' the grimly holy lady Mary set herself to reason with him against the wisdom of his course in pardoning so many people who would otherwise be jailed, or hanged, or burned, and reminded him that their august late father's prisons had sometimes contained as high as sixty thousand convicts at one time and that during his admirable reign he had delivered seventy-two thousand thieves and robbers over to death by the executioner,[1] the boy was filled with generous indignation and commanded her to go to her closet, and beseech God to take away the stone that was in her breast and give her a human heart.

Did Tom Canty never feel troubled about the poor little rightful prince, who had treated him so kindly and flown out with such hot zeal to avenge him upon the insolent sentinel at the palace gate? Yes; his first royal days and nights were pretty well sprinkled with painful thoughts about the lost prince, and with sincere longings for his return, and happy restoration to his native rights and splendours. But as time wore on, and the prince did not come, Tom's mind became more and more occupied with his new and enchanting experiences, and by little and little the vanished monarch faded almost out of his thoughts; and finally, when he did intrude upon them at intervals, he was become an unwelcome spectre, for he made Tom feel guilty and ashamed.

Tom's poor mother and sisters travelled the same road out of his mind. At first he pined for them, sorrowed for them, longed to see them, but later the thought of their coming some day in their rags and dirt, and betraying him with their kisses, and pulling him down from his lofty place, and dragging him back to penury and degradation and the slums made him shudder. At last they ceased to trouble his thoughts almost wholly. And he was content, even glad; for whenever their mournful and accusing faces did rise before him now, they made him feel more despicable than the worms that crawl.

At midnight of the nineteenth of February Tom Canty was sinking to sleep in his rich bed in the palace, guarded by his loyal vassals and surrounded by the pomps of royalty, a happy boy, for tomorrow was the day appointed for his solemn crowning as king of England. At that same hour Edward, the true king, hungry and thirsty, soiled and draggled, worn with travel, and clothed in rags and shreds – his share of the results of the riot – was wedged in among a crowd of people who were watching with deep interest hurrying gangs of workmen who streamed in and out of Westminster Abbey, busy as ants: they were making the last preparation for the royal coronation.

1 Hume's *England*.

31 The Recognition Procession

When Tom Canty awoke the next morning, the air was heavy with a thunderous murmur; all the distances were charged with it. It was music to him, for it meant that the English world was out in its strength to give loyal welcome to the great day.

Presently Tom found himself once more the chief figure in a wonderful floating pageant on the Thames, for by ancient custom the 'recognition procession' through London must start from the Tower, and he was bound thither.

When he arrived there, the sides of the venerable fortress seemed suddenly rent in a thousand places, and from every rent leaped a red tongue of flame and a white gush of smoke; a deafening explosion followed, which drowned the shoutings of the multitude and made the ground tremble; the flame jets, the smoke, and the explosions were repeated over and over again with the marvellous celerity, so that in a few moments the old Tower disappeared in the vast fog of its own smoke, all but the very top of the tall pile called the White Tower: this, with its banners, stood out above the dense bank of vapour as a mountain peak projects above a cloud rack.

Tom Canty, splendidly arrayed, mounted a prancing war steed, whose rich trappings almost reached to the ground; his 'uncle' the Lord Protector Somerset, similarly mounted, took place in his rear; the king's guard formed in single ranks on either side, clad in burnished armour; after the Protector followed a seemingly interminable procession of resplendent nobles attended by their vassals; after these came the Lord Mayor and the aldermanic body, in crimson-velvet robes and with their gold chains across their breasts; and after these the officers and members of all the guilds of London, in rich raiment and bearing the showy banners of the several corporations. Also in the procession, as a special guard of honour through the city, was the Ancient and Honourable Artillery Company, an organization already three hundred years old at that time, and the only military body in England possessing the privilege (which it still possesses in our day) of holding itself independent of the commands of Parliament. It was a brilliant spectacle, and was hailed with acclamations all along the line as it took its stately way through the packed multitudes of citizens. The chronicler says, 'The king, as he entered the city, was received by the people with prayers, welcomings, cries, and tender words, and all signs which argue an earnest love of subjects toward their sovereign; and the king, by holding up his glad countenance to such as stood afar off, and most tender language to those that stood nigh his Grace, showed himself no less thankful to receive the people's goodwill than they to offer it. To all that wished him well, he gave thanks. To such as bade 'God save his Grace,' he said in return, 'God save you all!' and added that he thanked them with all his heart. Wonderfully transported were the people with the loving answers and gestures of their king.'

In Fenchurch Street a 'fair child, in costly apparel,' stood on a stage to welcome his Majesty to the city. The last verse of his greeting was in these words:

Welcome, O king, as much as hearts can think;
Welcome again, as much as tongue can tell;
Welcome to joyous tongues, and hearts that will not shrink:
God thee preserve, we pray, and wish thee ever well.

The people burst forth in a glad shout, repeating with one voice what the child had said. Tom Canty gazed abroad over the surging sea of eager faces, and his heart swelled with exultation and he felt that the one thing worth living for in this world was to be a king, and a nation's idol. Presently he caught sight, at a distance, of a couple of his ragged Offal Court comrades – one of them the Lord High Admiral in his late mimic court, the other the First Lord of the Bedchamber in the same pretentious fiction; and his pride swelled higher than ever. Oh, if they could only recognize him now! What unspeakable glory it would be if they could recognize him and realize that the derided mock king of the slums and back alleys was become a real king, with illustrious dukes and princes for his humble menials and the English world at his feet! But he had to deny himself and choke down his desire, for such a recognition might cost more than it would come to; so he turned away his head and left the two soiled lads to go on with their shoutings and glad adulations, unsuspicious of whom it was they were lavishing them upon.

Every now and then rose the cry, 'A largess! A largess!' and Tom responded by scattering a handful of bright new coins abroad for the multitude to scramble for.

The chronicler says, 'At the upper end of Gracechurch Street, before the sign of the Eagle, the city had erected a gorgeous arch, beneath which was a stage which stretched from one side of the street to the other. This was a historical pageant, representing the king's immediate progenitors. There sat Elizabeth of York in the midst of an immense white rose whose petals formed elaborate furbelows around her; by her side was Henry VII, issuing out of a vast red rose, disposed in the same manner; the hands of the royal pair were locked together, and the wedding ring ostentatiously displayed. From the red and white roses proceeded a stem which reached up to a second stage, occupied by Henry VIII, issuing from a red-and-white rose, with the effigy of the new king's mother, Jane Seymour, represented by his side. One branch sprang from this pair, which mounted to a third stage, where sat the effigy of Edward VI himself, enthroned in royal majesty; and the whole pageant was framed with wreaths of roses, red and white.'

This quaint and gaudy spectacle so wrought upon the rejoicing people that their acclamations utterly smothered the small voice of the child whose business it was to explain the thing in eulogistic rhymes. But Tom Canty was not sorry, for this loyal uproar was sweeter music to him than any poetry, no matter what its quality might be. Whithersoever Tom turned his happy young face, the people recognized the exactness of his effigy's likeness to himself, the flesh and blood counterpart, and new whirlwinds of applause burst forth.

The great pageant moved on, and still on, under one triumphal arch after another, and past a bewildering succession of spectacular and symbolical tableaux, each of which typified and exalted some virtue, or talent, or merit of the little king's. 'Throughout the whole of Cheapside, from every penthouse and window, hung banners and streamers; and the richest carpets, stuffs, and cloth of gold tapestried the streets – specimens of the great wealth of the stores within; and the splendour of this thoroughfare was equalled in the other streets, and in some even surpassed.'

'And all these wonders and these marvels are to welcome me – me!' murmured Tom Canty.

The mock king's cheeks were flushed with excitement, his eyes were flashing, his senses swam in a delirium of pleasure. At this point, just as he was raising his hand to fling another rich largess, he caught sight of a pale, astounded face which was strained forward out of the second rank of the crowd, its intense eyes riveted upon him. A sickening consternation struck through him; he recognized his mother! And up flew his hand, palm outward, before his eyes – that old involuntary gesture born of a forgotten episode and perpetuated by habit. In an instant more she had torn her way out of the press, and past the guards, and was at his side. She embraced his leg, she covered it with kisses, she cried, 'O my child, my darling!' lifting toward him a face that was transfigured with joy and love. The same instant an officer of the king's guard snatched her away with a curse and sent her reeling back whence she came with a vigorous impulse from his strong arm. The words 'I do not know you, woman!' were falling from Tom Canty's lips when this piteous thing occurred, but it smote him to the heart to see her treated so; and as she turned for a last glimpse of him, whilst the crowd was swallowing her from his sight, she seemed so wounded, so broken hearted, that a shame fell upon him which consumed his pride to ashes and withered his stolen royalty. His grandeurs were stricken valueless; they seemed to fall away from him like rotten rags.

The procession moved on, and still on, through ever-augmenting splendours and ever-augmenting tempests of welcome, but to Tom Canty they were as if they had not been. He neither saw nor heard. Royalty had lost its grace and sweetness; its pomps were become a reproach. Remorse was eating his heart out. He said, 'Would God I were free of my captivity!'

He had unconsciously dropped back into the phraseology of the first days of his compulsory greatness.

The shining pageant still went winding like a radiant and interminable serpent down the crooked lanes of the quaint old city, and through the huzzahing hosts; but still the king rode with bowed head and vacant eyes, seeing only his mother's face and that wounded look in it.

'Largess, largess!' The cry fell upon an unheeding ear.

'Long live Edward of England!' It seemed as if the earth shook with the explosion, but there was no response from the king. He heard it only as one hears the thunder of the surf when it is blown to the ear out of a great distance, for it was smothered under another sound which was still nearer, in his own breast, in his accusing conscience – a voice which kept repeating those shameful words, 'I do not know you, woman!'

The words smote upon the king's soul as the strokes of a funeral bell smite upon the soul of a surviving friend when they remind him of secret treacheries suffered at his hands by him that is gone.

New glories were unfolded at every turning; new wonders, new marvels, sprung into view; the pent clamours of waiting batteries were released; new raptures poured from the throats of the waiting multitudes; but the king gave no sign, and the accusing voice that went moaning through his comfortless breast was all the sound he heard.

By and by the gladness in the faces of the populace changed a little and became touched with a something like solicitude or anxiety; an abatement in the volume of applause was observable too. The Lord Protector was quick to notice these things; he was quick to detect the cause. He spurred to the king's side, bent low in his saddle, uncovered, and said, 'My liege, it is an ill time for dreaming. The people observe thy downcast head, thy clouded mien, and they take it for an omen. Be advised; unveil the sun of royalty and let it shine upon these boding vapours and disperse them. Lift up thy face and smile upon the people.'

So saying, the duke scattered a handful of coins to right and left, then retired to his place. The mock king did mechanically as he had been bidden. His smile had no heart in it, but few eyes were near enough or sharp enough to detect that. The noddings of his plumed head as he saluted his subjects were full of grace and graciousness; the largess which he delivered from his hand was royally liberal, so the people's anxiety vanished and the acclamations burst forth again in as mighty a volume as before.

Still once more, a little before the progress was ended, the duke was obliged to ride forward and make remonstrance. He whispered, 'O dread sovereign! Shake off these fatal humours; the eyes of the world are upon thee.' Then he added with sharp annoyance. 'Perdition catch that crazy pauper! 'Twas she that hath disturbed your Highness.'

The gorgeous figure turned a lustreless eye upon the duke and said in a dead voice, 'She was my mother!'

'My God!' groaned the Protector as he reigned his horse backward to his post. 'The omen was pregnant with prophecy. He is gone mad again!'

32 Coronation Day

Let us go backward a few hours and place ourselves in Westminster Abbey at four o'clock in the morning of this memorable Coronation Day. We are not without company, for although it is still night, we find the torchlighted galleries already filling up with people who are well content to sit still and wait seven or eight hours till the time shall come for them to see what they may not hope to see twice in their lives – the coronation of a king. Yes, London and Westminster have been astir ever since the warning guns boomed at three o'clock, and already crowds of untitled rich folk who have bought the privilege of trying to find sitting room in the galleries are flocking in at the entrances reserved for their sort.

The hours drag along tediously enough. All stir has ceased for some time, for every gallery has long ago been packed. We may sit now and look and think at our leisure. We have glimpses, here and there and yonder, through the dim cathedral twilight, of portions of many galleries and balconies wedged full with people, the other portions of these galleries and balconies being cut off from sight by intervening pillars and architectural projections. We have in view the whole of the great north transept – empty and waiting for England's privileged ones. We see also the ample area of platform, carpeted with rich stuffs, whereon the throne stands. The throne occupies the centre of the platform, and is raised above it upon an elevation of four steps. Within the seat of the throne is enclosed a rough, flat rock — the stone of Scone – which many generations of Scottish kings sat on to be crowned, and so it in time became holy enough to answer a like purpose for English monarchs. Both the throne and its footstool are covered with cloth of gold.

Stillness reigns, the torches blink dully, the time drags heavily. But at last the lagging daylight asserts itself, the torches are extinguished, and a mellow radiance suffuses the great spaces. All features of the noble building are distinct now, but soft and dreamy, for the sun is lightly veiled with clouds.

At seven o'clock the first break in the drowsy monotony occurs, for on the stroke of this hour the first peeress enters the transept, clothed like Solomon for splendour, and is conducted to her appointed place by an official clad in satins and velvets, whilst a duplicate of him gathers up the lady's long train, follows after, and when the lady is seated, arranged the train across her lap for her. He then places her footstool according to her desire, after which he puts her coronet where it will be convenient to her hand when the time for the simultaneous coroneting of the nobles shall arrive.

By this time the peeresses are flowing in in a glittering stream, and the satin-clad officials are flitting and glinting everywhere, seating them and making them comfortable. The scene is animated enough now. There is stir and life, and shifting colour everywhere. After a time, quiet reigns again, for the peeresses are all come and are all in their places – a solid acre, or such a matter, of human flowers, resplendent in variegated colours and frosted like a Milky Way with diamonds. There are all ages here: brown, wrinkled, white-haired dowagers who are able to go back, and still back, down the stream of time and recall the crowning of Richard III and the troublous days of that old forgotten age; and there are handsome middle-aged dames; and lovely and gracious young matrons; and gentle and beautiful young girls with beaming eyes and fresh complexions who may possibly put on their jewelled coronets awkwardly when the great time comes, for the matter will be new to them and their excitement will be a sore hindrance. Still, this may not happen, for the hair of all these ladies has been arranged with a special view to the swift and successful lodging of the crown in its place when the signal comes.

We have seen that this massed array of peeresses is sown thick with diamonds, and we also see that it is a marvellous spectacle, but now we are about to be astonished in earnest. About nine the clouds suddenly break away and a shaft of sunshine cleaves the mellow atmosphere and drifts slowly along the ranks of ladies, and every rank it touches flames into a dazzling splendour of many-coloured fires, and we tingle to our fingertips with the electric thrill that is shot through us by the surprise and the beauty of the spectacle! Presently a special envoy from some distant corner of the Orient, marching with the general body of foreign ambassadors, crosses this bar of sunshine, and we catch our breath, the glory that streams and flashes and palpitates about him is so overpowering, for he is crusted from head to heel with gems, and his slightest movement showers a dancing radiance all around him.

Let us change the tense for convenience. The time drifted along – one hour – two hours – two hours and a half; then the deep booming of artillery told that the king and his grand procession had arrived at last, so the waiting multitude rejoiced. All knew that a further delay must follow, for the king must be prepared and robed for the solemn ceremony; but this delay would be pleasantly occupied by the assembling of the peers of the realm in their stately robes. These were conducted ceremoniously to their seats and their coronets placed conveniently at hand; and meanwhile the multitude in the galleries were alive with interest, for most of them were beholding for the first time dukes, earls, and barons, whose names had been historical for five hundred years. When all were finally seated, the spectacle from the galleries and all coigns of vantage was complete – a gorgeous one to look upon and to remember.

Now the robed and mitred great heads of the church and their attendants filed in upon the platform and took their appointed places; these were followed by the Lord Protector and other great officials, and these again by a steel-clad detachment of the guard.

There was a waiting pause; then, at a signal, a triumphant peal of music burst forth, and Tom Canty, clothed in a long robe of cloth of gold, appeared at a door and stepped upon the platform. The entire multitude rose, and the ceremony of the Recognition ensued.

Then a noble anthem swept the Abbey with its rich waves of sound; and thus heralded and welcomed, Tom Canty was conducted to the throne. The ancient ceremonies went on with impressive solemnity, whilst the audience gazed; and as they drew nearer and nearer to completion, Tom Canty grew pale, and still paler and a deep and steadily deepening woe and despondency settled down upon his spirits and upon his remorseful heart.

At last the final act was at hand. The Archbishop of Canterbury lifted up the crown of England from its cushion and held it out over the trembling mock king's head. In the same instant a rainbow radiance flashed along the spacious transept, for with one impulse every individual in the great concourse of nobles lifted a coronet and poised it over his or her head – and paused in that attitude.

A deep hush pervaded the Abbey. At this impressive moment a startling apparition intruded upon the scene – an apparition observed by none in the absorbed multitude until it suddenly appeared, moving up the great central aisle. It was a boy, bareheaded, ill-shod, and clothed in coarse plebeian garments that were falling to rags. He raised his hand with a solemnity which ill comported with his soiled and sorry aspect and delivered this note of warning, 'I forbid you to set the crown of England upon that forfeited head. *I am the king!*'

In an instant several indignant hands were laid upon the boy; but in the same instant Tom Canty, in his regal vestments, made a swift step forward and cried out in a ringing voice, 'Loose him and forbear! He *is* the king!'

A sort of panic of astonishment swept the assemblage, and they partly rose in their places and stared in a bewildered way at one another and at the chief figures in this scene, like persons who wondered whether they were awake and in their senses or asleep and dreaming. The Lord Protector was as amazed as the rest, but quickly recovered himself and exclaimed in a voice of authority, 'Mind not his Majesty, his malady is upon him again; seize the vagabond!'

He would have been obeyed, but the mock king stamped his foot and cried out, 'On your peril! Touch him not; he is the king!'

'"*I forbid you to set the Crown of England upon that forfeited head. I am the King!*"'

The hands were withheld; a paralysis fell upon the house; no one moved, no one spoke; indeed no one knew how to act or what to say in so strange and surprising an emergency. While all minds were struggling to right themselves, the boy still moved steadily forward, with high port and confident mien; he had never halted from the beginning; and while the tangled minds still floundered helplessly, he stepped upon the platform, and the mock king ran with a glad face to meet him and fell on his knees before him and said, 'Oh, my lord the king, let poor Tom Canty be first to swear fealty to thee and say, "Put on thy crown and enter into thine own again!"'

The Lord Protector's eye fell sternly upon the newcomer's face, but straightway the sternness vanished away and gave place to an expression of wondering surprise. This thing happened also to the other great officers. They glanced at each other and retreated a step by a common and unconscious impulse. The thought in each mind was the same: 'What a strange resemblance!'

The Lord Protector reflected a moment or two in perplexity; then he said with grave respectfulness, 'By your favour, sir, I desire to ask certain questions which——'

'I will answer them, my lord.'

The duke asked him many questions about the court, the late king, the prince, the princesses; the boy answered them correctly and without hesitating. He described the rooms of state in the palace, the late king's apartments, and those of the Prince of Wales.

It was strange, it was wonderful; yes, it was unaccountable – so all said that heard it. The tide was beginning to turn, and Tom Canty's hopes to run high, when the Lord Protector shook his head and said, 'It is true it is most wonderful, but it is no more than our lord the king likewise can do.' This remark and this reference to himself as still the king saddened Tom Canty, and he felt his hopes crumbling from under him. 'These are not *proofs*,' added the Protector.

The tide was turning very fast now, very fast indeed, but in the wrong direction; it was leaving poor Tom Canty stranded on the throne and sweeping the other out to sea. The Lord Protector communed with himself – shook his head – the thought forced itself upon him, 'It is perilous to the state and to us all to entertain so fateful a riddle as this; it could divide the nation and undermine the throne.' He turned and said, 'Sir Thomas, arrest this—— No, hold!' His face lighted, and he confronted the ragged candidate with this question, 'Where lieth the Great Seal? Answer me this truly, and the riddle is unriddled, for only he that was Prince of Wales *can* so answer! On so trivial a thing hang a throne and a dynasty!'

It was a lucky thought, a happy thought. That it was so considered by the great officials was manifested by the silent applause that shot from eye to eye around their circle in the form of bright, approving glances. Yes, none but the true prince could dissolve the stubborn mystery of the vanished Great Seal; this forlorn little impostor had been taught his lesson well, but here his teachings must fail, for his teacher himself could not answer *that* question – ah, very good, very good indeed; now we shall be rid of this troublesome and perilous business in short order! And so they nodded invisibly, and smiled inwardly with satisfaction, and looked to see this foolish lad stricken with a palsy of guilty confusion. How surprised they were, then, to see nothing of the sort happen – how they marvelled to hear him answer up promptly, in a confident and untroubled voice, and say, 'There is nought in this riddle that is difficult.' Then, without so much as a by-your-leave to anybody, he turned and gave this command, with the easy manner of one accustomed to doing such things: 'My lord St John, go you to my private cabinet in the palace – for none knoweth the place better than you – and, close down to the floor, in the left corner remotest from the door that opens from the ante-chamber, you shall find in the wall a brazen nailhead; press upon it and a little jewel closet will fly open which not even you do know of – no, nor any soul else in all the world but me and the trusty artisan that did contrive it for me. The first thing that falleth under your eye will be the Great Seal; fetch it hither.'

All the company wondered at this speech, and wondered still more to see the little mendicant pick out this peer without hesitancy or apparent fear of mistake, and call him by name with such a placidly convincing air of having known him all his life. The peer was almost surprised into obeying. He even made a movement as if to go, but quickly recovered his tranquil attitude and confessed his blunder with a blush. Tom Canty turned upon him and said sharply, 'Why dost thou hesitate? Hast not heard the king's command? Go!'

The lord St John made a deep obeisance – and it was observed that it was a significantly cautious and non-committal one, it not being delivered at either of the kings, but at the neutral ground about halfway between the two – and took his leave.

Now began a movement of the gorgeous particles of that official group which was slow, scarcely perceptible, and yet steady and persistent – a movement such as it observed in a kaleidoscope that is turned slowly whereby the components of one splendid cluster fall away and join themselves to another; a movement which little by little, in the present case, dissolved the glittering crowd that stood about Tom Canty and clustered it together again in the neighbourhood of the newcomer. Tom Canty stood almost alone. Now ensued a brief season of deep suspense and waiting, during which even the few faint-hearts still remaining near Tom Canty gradually scraped together courage enough to glide, one by one, over to the majority. So at last Tom Canty, in his royal robes and jewels, stood wholly alone and isolated from the world, a conspicuous figure occupying an eloquent vacancy.

Now the lord St John was seen returning. As he advanced up the mid-aisle the interest was so intense that the low murmur of conversation in the great assemblage died out and was succeeded by a profound hush, a breathless stillness, through which his footfalls pulsed with a dull and distant sound. Every eye was fastened upon him as he moved along. He reached the platform, paused a moment, then moved toward Tom Canty with a deep obeisance and said, 'Sire, the Seal is not there!'

A mob does not melt away from the presence of a plague patient with more haste than the band of pallid and terrified courtiers melted away from the presence of the shabby little claimant of the crown. In a moment he stood all alone, without friend or supporter, a target upon which was concentrated a bitter fire of scornful and angry looks.

The Lord Protector called out fiercely, 'Cast the beggar into the street and scourge him through the town; the paltry knave is worth no more consideration!'

Officers of the guard sprang forward to obey, but Tom Canty waved them off and said, 'Back! Whoso touches him perils his life!'

The Lord Protector was perplexed to the last degree. He said to the lord St John, 'Searched you well? But it boots not to ask that. It doth seem passing strange. Little things, trifles, slip out of one's ken, and one does not think it matter for surprise; but how a so bulky thing as the Seal of England can vanish away and no man be able to get track of it again – a massy golden disk——'

Tom Canty, with beaming eyes, sprang forward and shouted, 'Hold, that is enough. Was it round? And thick? And had it letters and devices graved upon it? Yes? Oh, *now* I know what this Great Seal is that there's been such worry and bother about! An' ye had described it to me, ye could have had it three weeks ago. Right well I know where it lies, but it was not I that put it there – first.'

'Who, then, my liege?' asked the Lord Protector.

'He that stands there – the rightful king of England. And he shall tell you himself where it lies; then you will believe he knew it of his own knowledge. Bethink thee, my king – spur thy memory – it was the last, the very *last* thing thou didst that day before thou didst rush forth from the palace, clothed in my rags, to punish the soldier that insulted me.'

A silence ensued, undisturbed by a movement or a whisper, and all eyes were fixed upon the newcomer, who stood, with bent head and corrugated brow, groping in his memory among a thronging multitude of valueless recollections for one single little elusive fact, which, found, would seat him upon a throne – unfound, would leave him as he was, for good and all, a pauper and an outcast. Moment after moment passed – the moments built themselves into minutes – still the boy struggled silently on, and gave no sign. But at last he heaved a sigh, shook his head slowly, and said with a trembling lip and in a despondent voice, 'I call the scene back – all of it – but the Seal hath no place in it.' He paused, then looked up and said with gentle dignity, 'My lords and gentlemen, if ye will rob your rightful sovereign of his own for lack of this evidence which he is not able to furnish, I may not stay ye, being powerless. But——'

'Oh, folly, Oh, madness, my king!' cried Tom Canty in a panic. 'Wait! Think! Do not give up! The cause is not lost! Nor *shall* be, neither! List to what I say – follow every word; I am going to bring that morning back again, every hap just as it happened. We talked; I told you of my sisters, Nan and Bet – ah, yes, you remember that; and about mine old grandam, and the rough games of the lads of Offal Court – yes, you remember these things also; very well, follow me still; you shall recall everything. You gave me food and drink, and did with princely courtesy send away the servants so that my low breeding might not shame me before them – ah, yes, this also you remember.'

As Tom checked off his details, and the other boy nodded his head in recognition of them, the great audience and the officials stared in puzzled wonderment; the tale sounded like true history, yet how could this impossible conjunction between a prince and a beggar boy have come about? Never was a company of people so perplexed, so interested, and so stupefied before.

'For a jest, my prince, we did exchange garments. Then we stood before a mirror; and so alike were we that both said it seemed as if there had been no change made – yes, you remember that. Then you noticed that the soldier had hurt my hand. Look! Here it is; I cannot yet even write with it, the fingers are so stiff. At this your Highness sprang up, vowing vengeance upon that soldier, and ran toward the door; you passed a table; that thing you call the Seal lay on that table; you snatched it up and looked eagerly about, as if for a place to hide it; your eye caught sight of——'

'There, 'tis sufficient! And the dear God be thanked!' exclaimed the ragged claimant in a mighty excitement. 'Go, my good St John; in an armpiece of the Milanese armour that hangs on the wall thou'lt find the Seal!'

'Right, my king! Right!' cried Tom Canty. '*Now* the sceptre of England is thine own; and it were better for him that would dispute it that he had been born dumb! Go, my lord St John; give thy feet wings!'

The whole assemblage was on its feet now and well nigh out of its mind with uneasiness, apprehension, and consuming excitement. On the floor and on the platform a deafening buzz of frantic conversation burst forth, and for some time nobody knew anything or heard anything or was interested in anything but what his neighbour was shouting into his ear or he was shouting into his neighbour's ear. Time – nobody knew how much of it – swept by unheeded and unnoted. At last a sudden hush fell upon the house, and in the same moment St John appeared upon the platform and held the Great Seal aloft in his hand. Then such a shout went up!

'Long live the true king!'

For five minutes the air quaked with shouts and the crash of musical instruments, and was white with a storm of waving handkerchiefs; and through it all a ragged lad, the most conspicuous figure in England, stood flushed and happy and proud in the centre of the spacious platform with the great vassals of the kingdom kneeling around him.

Then all rose, and Tom Canty cried out, 'Now, O my king, take these regal garments back and give poor Tom, thy servant, his shreds and remnants again.'

The Lord Protector spoke up, 'Let the small varlet be stripped and flung into the Tower.'

But the new king, the true king, said, 'I will not have it so. But for him I had not got my crown again; none shall lay a hand upon him to harm him. And as for thee, my good uncle, my Lord Protector, this conduct of thine is not grateful toward this poor lad, for I hear he hath made thee a duke' – the Protector blushed – 'yet he was not a king; wherefore, what is thy fine title worth now? Tomorrow you shall sue to me, *through him*, for its confirmation, else no duke, but a simple earl, shalt thou remain.'

Under this rebuke his grace the Duke of Somerset retired a little from the front for the moment. The king turned to Tom and said kindly, 'My poor boy, how was it that you could remember where I hid the Seal when I could not remember it myself?'

'Ah, my king, that was easy, since I used it divers days.'

'Used it, yet could not explain where it was?'

'I did not know it was *that* they wanted. They did not describe it, your Majesty.'

'Then how used you it?'

The red blood began to steal up into Tom's cheeks, and he dropped his eyes and was silent.

'Speak up, good lad, and fear nothing,' said the king. 'How used you the Great Seal of England?'

Tom stammered a moment in a pathetic confusion, then got it out, 'To crack nuts with!'

Poor child, the avalanche of laughter that greeted this nearly swept him off his feet. But if a doubt remained in any mind that Tom Canty was not the king of England and familiar with the august appurtenances of royalty, this reply disposed of it utterly.

Meantime the sumptuous robe of state had been removed from Tom's shoulders to the king's, whose rags were effectually hidden from sight under it. Then the coronation ceremonies were resumed; the true king was anointed and the crown set upon his head, whilst cannon thundered the news to the city, and all London seemed to rock with applause.

33 Edward as King

Miles Hendon was picturesque enough before he got into the riot on London Bridge; he was more so when he got out of it. He had but little money when he got in, none at all when he got out. The pickpockets had stripped him of his last farthing.

But no matter, so he found his boy. Being a soldier, he did not go at his task in a random way, but set to work first of all to arrange his campaign.

What would the boy naturally do? Where would he naturally go? Well, argued Miles, he would naturally go to his former haunts, for that is the instinct of unsound minds when homeless and forsaken, as well as of sound ones. Whereabouts were his former haunts? His rags, taken together with the low villain who seemed to know him and who even claimed to be his father, indicated that his home was in one or another of the poorest and meanest districts of London. Would the search for him be difficult or long? No, it was likely to be easy and brief. He would not hunt for the boy, he would hunt for a crowd; in the centre of a big crowd or a little one, sooner or later, he should find his poor little friend, sure; and the mangy mob would be entertaining itself with pestering and aggravating the boy, who would be proclaiming himself king, as usual. Then Miles Hendon would cripple some of those people, and carry off his little ward, and comfort and cheer him with loving words, and the two would never be separated any more.

So Miles started on his quest. Hour after hour he tramped through back alleys and squalid streets seeking groups and crowds, and finding no end of them, but never any sign of the boy. This greatly surprised him but did not discourage him. To his notion there was nothing the matter with his plan of campaign; the only miscalculation about it was that the campaign was becoming a lengthy one, whereas he had expected it to be short.

When daylight arrived at last, he had made many a mile and canvassed many a crowd, but the only result was that he was tolerably tired, rather hungry, and very sleepy. He wanted some breakfast, but there was no way to get it. To beg for it did not occur to him; as to pawning his sword, he would as soon have thought of parting with his honour; he could spare some of his clothes – yes, but one could as easily find a customer for a disease as for such clothes.

At noon he was still tramping – among the rabble which followed after the royal procession now, for he argued that this regal display would attract his little lunatic powerfully. He followed the pageant through all its devious windings about London and all the way to Westminster and the Abbey. He drifted here and there amongst the multitudes that were massed in the vicinity for a weary long time, baffled and perplexed, and finally wandered off thinking and trying to contrive some way to better his plan of campaign. By and by, when he came to himself out of his musings, he discovered that the town was far behind him and that the day was growing old. He was near the river and in the country; it was a region of fine rural seats – not the sort of district to welcome clothes like his.

It was not at all cold, so he stretched himself on the ground in the lee of a hedge to rest and think. Drowsiness presently began to settle upon his senses; the faint and far-off boom of cannon was wafted to his ear, and he said to himself, 'The new king is crowned,' and straightway fell asleep. He had not slept or rested before for more than thirty hours. He did not wake again until near the middle of the next morning.

He got up lame, stiff, and half famished, washed himself in the river, stayed his stomach with a pint or two of water, and trudged off toward Westminster grumbling at himself for having wasted so much time. Hunger helped him to a new plan now; he would try to get speech with old Sir Humphrey Marlow and borrow a few marks, and—— but that was enough of a plan for the present; it would be time enough to enlarge it when this first stage should be accomplished.

Toward eleven o'clock he approached the palace; and although a host of showy people were about him, moving in the same direction, he was not inconspicuous – his costume took care of that. He watched these people's faces narrowly, hoping to find a charitable one whose possessor might be willing to carry his name to the old lieutenant; as to trying to get into the palace himself, that was simply out of the question.

Presently our whipping boy passed him, then wheeled about and scanned his figure well, saying to himself, 'An' that is not the very vagabond his Majesty is in such a worry about, then am I an ass – though belike I was that before. He answereth the description to a rag; that God should make two such would be to cheapen miracles by wasteful repetition. I would I could contrive an excuse to speak with him.'

Miles Hendon saved him the trouble, for he turned about then as a man generally will when somebody mesmerizes him by gazing hard at him from behind; and observing a strong interest in the boy's eyes, he stepped toward him and said, 'You have just come out from the palace; do you belong there?'

'Yes, your worship.'

'Know you Sir Humphrey Marlow?'

The boy started and said to himself, 'Lord! Mine old departed father!' Then he answered aloud, 'Right well, your worship.'

'Good; is he within?'

'Yes,' said the boy; and added to himself. 'Within his grave.'

'Might I crave your favour to carry my name to him and say I beg to say a word in his ear?'

'I will dispatch the business right willingly, fair sir.'

'Then say Miles Hendon, son of Sir Richard, is here without; I shall be greatly bounden to you, my good lad.'

The boy looked disappointed; 'The king did not name him so,' he said to himself, 'but it mattereth not; this is his twin brother and can give his Majesty news of t'other Sir-Odds-and-Ends, I warrant.' So he said to Miles, 'Step in there a moment, good sir, and wait till I bring you word.'

Hendon retired to the place indicated; it was a recess sunk in the palace wall, with a stone bench in it – a shelter for sentinels in bad weather. He had hardly seated himself when some halberdiers in charge of an officer passed by. The officer saw him, halted his men, and commanded Hendon to come forth. He obeyed, and was promptly arrested as a suspicious character prowling within the precincts of the palace. Things began to look ugly. Poor Miles was going to explain, but the officer roughly silenced him and ordered his men to disarm him and search him.

'God of his mercy grant that they find somewhat,' said poor Miles; 'I have searched enow and failed, yet is my need greater than theirs.'

Nothing was found but a document. The officer tore it open, and Hendon smiled when he recognized the 'pothooks' made by his lost little friend that black day at Hendon Hall. The officer's face grew dark as he read the English paragraph, and Miles blenched to the opposite colour as he listened.

'Another new claimant of the crown!' cried the officer. 'Verily they breed like rabbits today. Seize the rascal, men, and see ye keep him fast whilst I convey this precious paper within and send it to the king.'

He hurried away, leaving the prisoner in the grip of the halberdiers.

'Now is my evil luck ended at last,' muttered Hendon, 'for I shall dangle at a rope's end for a certainty, by reason of that bit of writing. And what will become of my poor lad! Ah, only the good God knoweth.'

By and by he saw the officer coming again in a great hurry, so he plucked his courage together, purposing to meet his trouble as become a man. The officer ordered the men to loose the prisoner and return his sword to him, then bowed respectfully and said, 'Please you sir, to follow me.'

Hendon followed, saying to himself, 'An' I were not travelling to death and judgment, and so must needs economize in sin, I would throttle this knave for his mock courtesy.'

The two traversed a populous court and arrived at the grand entrance of the palace, where the officer, with another bow, delivered Hendon into the hands of a gorgeous official, who received him with profound respect and led him forward through a great hall lined on both sides with rows of splendid flunkies (who made reverential obeisance as the two passed along, but fell into death throes of silent laughter at our stately scarecrow the moment his back was turned) and up a broad staircase, among flocks of fine folk, and finally conducted him into a vast room, clove a passage for him through the assembled nobility of England, then made a bow, reminded him to take his hat off, and left him standing in the middle of the room, a mark for all eyes, for plenty of indignant frowns, and for a sufficiency of amused and derisive smiles.

Miles Hendon was entirely bewildered. There sat the young king under a canopy of state five steps away, with his head bent down and aside, speaking with a sort of human bird of paradise – a duke, maybe; Hendon observed to himself that it was hard enough to be sentenced to death in the full vigour of life without having this peculiarly public humiliation added. He wished the king would hurry about it; some of the gaudy people nearby were becoming offensive. At this moment the king raised his head slightly and Hendon caught a good view of his face. The sight nearly took his breath away! He stood gazing at the fair young face like one transfixed, then presently ejaculated, 'Lo, the lord of the Kingdom of Dreams and Shadows on his throne!'

He muttered some broken sentences, still gazing and marvelling, then turned his eyes around and about, scanning the gorgeous throng and the splendid saloon, murmuring, 'But these are *real* – verily these are *real* – surely it is not a dream.'

He stared at the king again and thought, '*Is* it a dream? Or *is* he the veritable sovereign of England, and not the friendless poor Tom o' Bedlam I took him for? Who shall solve me this riddle?'

A sudden idea flashed in his eye, and he strode to the wall, gathered up a chair, brought it back, planted it on the floor, and sat down in it!

A buzz of indignation broke out, a rough hand was laid upon him, and a voice exclaimed, 'Up, thou mannerless clown! Wouldst sit in the presence of the king?'

The disturbance attracted his Majesty's attention, who stretched forth his hand and cried out, 'Touch him not; it is his right!'

The throng fell back, stupefied. The king went on, 'Learn ye all, ladies, lords and gentlemen, that this is my trusty and well-beloved servant Miles Hendon, who interposed his good sword and saved his prince from bodily harm and possible death; and for this he is a knight, by the king's voice. Also learn that for a higher service, in that he saved his sovereign stripes and shame, taking these upon himself, he is a peer of England, Earl of Kent, and shall have gold and lands meet for the dignity. More – the privilege which he hath just exercised is his by royal grant, for we have ordained that the chiefs of his line shall have and hold the right to sit in the presence of the Majesty of England henceforth, age after age, so long as the crown shall endure. Molest him not.'

Two persons who, through delay, had only arrived from the country during this morning and had now been in this room only five minutes stood listening to these words and looking at the king, then at the scarecrow, then at the king again, in a sort of torpid bewilderment. These were Sir Hugh and the lady Edith. But the new earl did not see them. He was still staring at the monarch in a dazed way and muttering, 'Oh, body o' me! *This* my pauper! This my lunatic! This is he whom *I* would show what grandeur was in my house of seventy rooms and seven and twenty servants! This is he who had never known aught but rags for raiment, kicks for comfort, and offal for diet! This is he whom *I* adopted and would make respectable! Would God I had a bag to hide my head in!'

Then his manners suddenly came back to him, and he dropped upon his knees, with his hands between the king's and swore allegiance and did homage for his lands and titles. Then he rose and stood respectfully aside, a mark still for all eyes – and much envy too.

Now the king discovered Sir Hugh and spoke out with wrathful voice and kindling eye, 'Strip this robber of his false show and stolen estates and put him under lock and key till I have need of him.'

The late Sir Hugh was led away.

There was a stir at the other end of the room now; the assemblage fell apart, and Tom Canty, quaintly but richly clothed, marched down between these living walls, preceded by an usher. He knelt before the king, who said, 'I have learned the story of these past few weeks and am well pleased with thee. Thou hast governed the realm with right royal gentleness and mercy. Thou hast found thy mother and thy sisters again? Good; they shall be cared for, and thy father shall hang if thou desire it and the law consent. Know, all ye that hear my voice, that from this day they that abide in the shelter of Christ's Hospital and share the king's bounty shall have their minds and hearts fed, as well as their baser parts; and this boy shall dwell there, and hold the chief place in its honourable body of governors during life. And for that he hath been a king, it is meet that other than common observance shall be his due; wherefore, note this his dress of state, for by it he shall be known, and none shall copy it; and wheresoever he shall come, it shall remind the people that he hath been royal in his time, and none shall deny him his due of reverence or fail to give him salutation. He hath the throne's protection, he hath the

Crown's support, he shall be known and called by the honourable title of the King's Ward.'

The proud and happy Tom Canty rose and kissed the king's hand, and was conducted from the presence. He did not waste any time, but flew to his mother to tell her and Nan and Bet all about it and get them to help him enjoy the great news.[1]

1. See Notes to Chapter 33 at end of volume.

Conclusion
Justice and Retribution

When the mysteries were all cleared up, it came out by confession of Hugh Hendon that his wife had repudiated Miles by his command that day at Hendon Hall – a command assisted and supported by the perfectly trustworthy promise that if she did not deny that he was Miles Hendon and stand firmly to it, he would have her life; whereupon she said take it, she did not value it – and she would not repudiate Miles; then her husband said he would spare her life but have Miles assassinated! This was a different matter, so she gave her word and kept it.

Hugh was not prosecuted for his threats or for stealing his brother's estates and title because the wife and brother would not testify against him, and the former would not have been allowed to do it even if she had wanted to. Hugh deserted his wife and went over to the Continent, where he presently died; and by and by the Earl of Kent married his relict. There were grand times and rejoicings at Hendon village when the couple paid their first visit to the Hall.

Tom Canty's father was never heard of again.

The king sought out the farmer who had been branded and sold as a slave, and reclaimed him from his evil life with the Ruffler's gang, and put him in the way of a comfortable livelihood.

He also took that old lawyer out of prison and remitted his fine. He provided good homes for the daughters of the two Baptist women whom he saw burned at the stake, and roundly punished the official who laid the undeserved stripes upon Miles Hendon's back.

He saved from the gallows the boy who had captured the stray falcon, and also the woman who had stolen a remnant of cloth from a weaver; but he was too late to save the man who had been convicted of killing a deer in the royal forest.

He showed favour to the justice who had pitied him when he was supposed to have stolen a pig, and he had the gratification of seeing him grow in the public esteem and become a great and honoured man.

As long as the king lived he was fond of telling the story of his adventures, all through, from the hour that the sentinel cuffed him away from the palace gate till the final midnight when he deftly mixed himself into a gang of hurrying workmen and so slipped into the Abbey and climbed up and hid himself in the Confessor's tomb, and then slept so long next day that he came within one of missing the coronation altogether. He said that the frequent rehearsing of the precious lesson kept him strong in his purpose to make its teachings yield benefits to his people; and so, whilst his life was spared he should continue to tell the story, and thus keep its sorrowful spectacles fresh in his memory and the springs of pity replenished in his heart.

Miles Hendon and Tom Canty were favourites of the king all through his brief reign, and his sincere mourners when he died. The good Earl of Kent had too much sense to abuse his peculiar privilege, but he exercised it twice after the instance we have seen of it before he was called from the world – once at the accession of Queen Mary, and once at the accession of Queen Elizabeth. A descendant of his exercised it at the accession of James I. Before this one's son chose to use the privilege, near a quarter of a century had elapsed, and the 'privilege of the Kents' had faded out of most people's memories; so when the Kent of that day appeared before Charles I and his court and sat down in the sovereign's presence to assert and perpetuate the right of his house, there was a fine stir indeed! But the matter was soon explained, and the right confirmed. The last earl of the line fell in the wars of the commonwealth fighting for the king, and the odd privilege ended with him.

Tom Canty lived to be a very old man, a handsome, white-haired old fellow of grave and benignant aspect. As long as he lasted he was honoured; and he was also reverenced, for his striking and peculiar costume kept the people reminded that 'in his time he had been royal.; so wherever he appeared the crowd fell apart, making way for him and whispering, one to another, 'Doff thy hat, it is the King's Ward!' And so they saluted and got his kindly smile in return, and they valued it too, for his was an honourable history.

Yes, King Edward VI lived only a few years, poor boy, but he lived them worthily. More than once when some great dignitary, some gilded vassal of the crown, made argument against his leniency and urged that some law which he was bent upon amending was gentle enough for its purpose and wrought no suffering or oppression which anyone need mightily mind, the young king turned the mournful eloquence of his great compassionate eyes upon him and answered, 'What dost *thou* know of suffering and oppression? I and my people know, but not thou.'

The reign of Edward VI was a singularly merciful one for those harsh times. Now that we are taking leave of him, let us try to keep this in our minds, to his credit.

NOTES

Note 1—Page 455

Christ's Hospital Costume

It is most reasonable to regard the dress as copied from the costume of the citizens of London of that period, when long blue coats were the common habit of apprentices and servingmen, and yellow stockings were generally worn; the coat fits closely to the body but has loose sleeves, and beneath is worn a sleeveless yellow undercoat; around the waist is a red leathern girdle; a clerical band around the neck; and a small flat black cap about the size of a saucer completes the costume. – Timbs's *Curiosities of London*

Note 2—Page 456

It appears that Christ's Hospital was not originally founded as a *school*; its object was to rescue children from the streets, to shelter, feed, clothe them, etc. – Timbs's *Curiosities of London*

Note 3—Page 462

The Duke of Norfolk's Condemnation Commanded

The king was now approaching fast towards his end, and fearing lest Norfolk should escape him, he sent a message to the Commons, by which he desired them to hasten the bill, on pretence that Norfolk enjoyed the dignity of earl marshal, and it was necessary to appoint another, who might officiate at the ensuing ceremony of installing his son, Prince of Wales. – Hume, vol. iii., p. 307

Note 4—Page 470

It was not till the end of this reign [Henry VIII] that any salads, carrots, turnips, or other edible roots were produced in England. The little of these vegetables that was used was formerly imported from Holland and Flanders. Queen Catherine, when she wanted a salad, was obliged to dispatch a messenger thither on purpose. – Hume's *History of England*, vol. iii, p. 314

Note 5—Page 474

Attainder of Norfolk

The house of peers, without examining the prisoner, without trial or evidence, passed a bill of attainder against him and sent it down to the Commons.... The obsequious Commons obeyed his [the king's] directions; and the king, having affixed the royal assent to the bill by commissioners, issued orders for the execution of Norfolk on the morning of the twenty-ninth of January [the next day]. – Hume's *England*, vol. iii, p. 306

Note 6—page 482

The Loving Cup

The loving cup, and the peculiar ceremonies observed in drinking from it, are older than English history. It is thought that both are Danish importations. As far back as knowledge goes, the loving cup has always been drunk at English banquets. Tradition explains the ceremonies in this way: in the rude ancient times it was deemed a wise precaution to have both hands of both drinkers employed, lest while the pledger pledged his love and fidelity to the pledgee, the pledgee take that opportunity to slip a dirk into him!

Note 7—page 486

The Duke of Norfolk's Narrow Escape

Had Henry VIII survived a few hours longer, his order for the duke's execution would have been carried into effect. 'But news being carried to the Tower that the king himself had expired that night, the lieutenant deferred obeying the warrant; and it was not thought advisable by the council to begin a new reign by the death of the greatest nobleman in the kingdom, who had been condemned by a sentence so unjust and tyrannical.' – Hume's *England*, vol. iii, p. 307

Note 8—page 505

The Whipping Boy

James I and Charles II had whipping boys, when they were little fellows, to take their punishment for them when they fell short in their lessons; so I have ventured to furnish my small prince with one, for my own purposes.

Notes to Chapter 15—Page 516

Character of Hertford

The young king discovered an extreme attachment to his uncle, who was, in the main, a man of moderation and probity. – Hume's *England*, vol. iii, p. 324

But if he [the Protector] gave offence by assuming too much state, he deserves great praise on account of the laws passed this session, by which the rigour of former statutes was much mitigated and some security given to the freedom of the constitution. All laws were repealed which extended the crime of treason beyond the statute of the twenty-fifth of Edward III; all laws enacted during the late reign extending the crime of felony; all the former laws against Lollardy, or heresy, together with the statute of the Six Articles. None were to be accused for words, but within a month after they were spoken. By these repeals several of the most rigorous laws that ever had passed in England were annulled; and some dawn, both of civil and religious liberty, began to appear to the people. A repeal also passed of that law, the destruction of all laws, by which the king's proclamation was made of equal force with a statute. – *Ibid.*, vol. iii, p. 339

Boiling to Death

In the reign of Henry VIII poisoners were by act of Parliament condemned to be boiled to death. This act was repealed in the following reign.

In Germany, even in the seventeenth century, this horrible punishment was inflicted on coiners and counterfeiters. Taylor, the Water Poet, describes an execution he witnessed in Hamburg in 1616. The judgment pronounced against a coiner of false money was that he should 'be boiled to death in oil; not thrown into the vessel at once, but with a pulley or rope to be hanged under the armpits and then let down into the oil by degrees; first the feet, and next the legs, and so to boil his flesh from his bones alive.' – Dr. J. Hammond Trumbull's *Blue Laws, True and False*, p. 13

The Famous Stocking Case

A woman and her daughter nine years old were hanged in Huntingdon for selling their souls to the devil and raising a storm by pulling off their stockings! – *Ibid*, p. 20

Note 10—Page 525

Enslaving

So young a king and so ignorant a peasant were likely to make mistakes, and this is an instance in point. This peasant was suffering from this law *by anticipation*; the king was venting his indignation against a law which was not yet in existence, for this hideous statute was to have birth in this little king's own reign. However, we know from the humanity of his character that it could never have been suggested by him.

Notes to Chapter 23—page 555

Death for Trifling Larcenies

When Connecticut and New Haven were framing their first codes, larceny above the value of twelvepence was a capital crime in England, as it had been since the time of Henry I. – Dr. J. Hammond Trumbull's *Blue Laws, True and False*, p. 17

The curious old book called *The English Rogue* makes the limit thirteen pence ha'penny, death being the portion of any who steal a thing 'above the value of thirteen pence ha'penny.'

Notes to Chapter 27—Page 573

From many descriptions of larceny, the law expressly took away the benefit of clergy; to steal a horse, or a hawk, or woollen cloth from the weaver was a hanging matter. So it was, to kill a deer from the king's forest or to export sheep from the kingdom. – Dr. J. Hammond Trumbull's *Blue Laws, True and False*, p. 13

William Prynne, a learned barrister, was sentenced [long after Edward the Sixth's time] to lose both his ears in the pillory, to degradation from the bar, a fine of £3,000, and imprisonment for life. Three years afterwards he gave new offence to Laud by publishing a pamphlet against the hierarchy. He was again prosecuted and was sentenced to lose what remained of his ears, to pay a fine of £5,000, to be branded on both his cheeks with the letters S. L. (for Seditious Libeller), and to remain in prison for life. The severity of this sentence was equalled by the savage rigour of its execution. – *Ibid.*, p. 12

Notes to Chapter 33—Page 601

Christ's Hospital, or Blue Coat School, 'the Noblest Institution in the World'

The ground on which the priory of the Grey Friars stood was conferred by Henry the Eighth on the Corporation of London [who caused the institution there of a home for poor boys and girls]. Subsequently Edward the Sixth caused the old priory to be properly repaired, and founded within it that noble establishment called the Blue Coat School, or Christ's Hospital, for the education and maintenance of orphans and the children of indigent persons. . . . Edward would not let him [Bishop Ridley] depart till the letter was written [to the Lord Mayor], and then charged him to deliver it himself, and sign his special request and commandment that no time might be lost in proposing what was convenient, and apprising him of the proceedings. The work was zealously undertaken, Ridley himself engaging in it; and the result was the founding of Christ's Hospital for the Education of Poor Children. [The king endowed several other charities at the same time.] 'Lord God,' said he, 'I yield thee most hearty thanks that thou hast given me life thus long to finish this work to the glory of thy name!' That innocent and most exemplary life was drawing rapidly to its close, and in a few days he rendered up his spirit to his Creator, praying God to defend the realm from papistry. – J. Heneage Jesse's *London, Its Celebrated Characters and Places*

In the Great Hall hangs a large picture of King Edward VI seated on his throne in a scarlet and ermined robe, holding the sceptre in his left hand and presenting with the other the charter to the kneeling Lord Mayor. By his side stands the Chancellor, holding the seals, and next to him are other officers of state. Bishop Ridley kneels before him with uplifted hands as if supplicating a blessing on the event; whilst the aldermen, etc.' with the Lord Mayor, kneel on both sides, occupying the middle ground of the picture; and lastly, in front are a double row of boys on one side and girls on the other, from the master and matron down to the boy and girl who have stepped forward from their respective rows and kneel with raised hands before the king. – Timbs's *Curiosities of London*, p. 98[1]

Christ's Hospital, by ancient custom, possesses the privilege of addressing the sovereign on the occasion of his or her coming into the city to partake of the hospitality of the Corporation of London. – *Ibid.*

The Dining Hall, with its lobby and organ gallery, occupies the entire story, which is 187 feet long, 51 feet wide, and 47 feet high; it is lit by nine large windows, filled with stained glass on the south side; and is, next to Westminster Hall, the noblest room in the metropolis. Here the boys, now about eight hundred in number, dine; and here are held the 'Suppings in Public,' to which visitors are admitted by tickets, issued by the treasurer and by the governors of Christ's Hospital. The tables are laid with cheese in wooden bowls; beer in wooden piggins, poured from leathern jacks; and bread brought in large baskets. The official company enter; the Lord Mayor, or President, takes his seat in a state chair, made of oak from St Catherine's Church, by the Tower; a hymn is sung, accompanied by the organ; a 'Grecian,' or head boy, reads the prayers from the pulpit, silence being enforced by three drops of a wooden hammer. After prayer the supper commences, and the visitors walk between the tables. At its close, the 'trade boys' take up the baskets, bowls, jacks, piggins, and candlesticks and pass in procession, the bowing to the governors being curiously formal. This spectacle was witnessed by Queen Victoria and Prince Albert in 1845.

Among the more eminent Blue Coat Boys are Joshua Barnes, editor of Anacreon and Euripides; Jeremiah Markland, the eminent critic, particularly in Greek literature; Camden, the antiquary; Bishop Stillingfleet; Samuel Richardson, the novelist; Thomas Mitchell, the translator of Aristophanes; Thomas Barnes, many years editor of the London *Times*; Coleridge, Charles Lamb, and Leigh Hunt.

No boy is admitted before he is seven years old or after he is nine; and no boy can remain in the school after he is fifteen, king's boys and 'Grecians' alone excepted. There are about five hundred governors, at the head of whom are the sovereign and the Prince of Wales. The qualification for a governor is payment of £500. – *Ibid.*

GENERAL NOTE

One hears much about the 'hideous blue laws of Connecticut,' and is accustomed to shudder piously when they are mentioned. There are people in America – and even in England! – who imagine that they were a very monument of malignity, pitilessness, and inhumanity, whereas in reality they were about the first *sweeping departure from judicial atrocity* which the 'civilized' world had seen. This humane and kindly Blue-Law code, of two hundred and forty years ago, stands all by itself, with ages of bloody law on the further side of it, and a century and three quarters of bloody English law on this side of it.

There has never been a time – under the blue laws or any other – when above *fourteen* crimes were punishable by death in Connecticut. But in England, within the memory of men who are still hale in body and mind, *two hundred and twenty-three* crimes were punishable by death![2] These facts are worth knowing – and worth thinking about, too.

1 This building was destroyed in 1902 and the school moved to Sussex. *Ed's note*
2 See Dr. J. Hammond Trumbull's *Blue Laws, True and False*, p. 11